The Vivisector

ALSO BY PATRICK WHITE

The Vivisector

PATRICK WHITE

NEW YORK · THE VIKING PRESS

First published in 1970 by The Viking Press, Inc.
625 Madison Avenue, New York, N.Y. 10022

Published simultaneously in Canada by
The Macmillan Company of Canada Limited

SBN 670-74739-4

Library of Congress catalog card number: 72-104137

Printed in U.S.A.

For Cynthia and Sidney Nolan

As I see it, painting and religious experience are the same thing, and what we are all searching for is the understanding and realisation of infinity.

BEN NICHOLSON

Cruelty has a Human Heart,
And Jealousy a Human Face;
Terror the Human Form Divine,
And Secrecy the Human Dress.

The Human Dress is forged in Iron,
The Human Form a fiery Forge,
The Human Face a Furnace seal'd,
The Human Heart its hungry Gorge.

WILLIAM BLAKE

They love truth when it reveals itself, and they hate it when it reveals themselves.

SAINT AUGUSTINE

He becomes beyond all others the great Invalid, the great Criminal, the great Accursed One—and the Supreme Knower. For he reaches the unknown.

RIMBAUD

The Vivisector

1

It was Sunday, and Mumma had gone next door with Lena and the little ones. Under the pepper tree in the yard Pa was sorting, counting, the empty bottles he would sell back: the bottles going clink clink as Pa stuck them on the stack. The fowls were fluffing in the dust and sun: that crook-neck white pullet Mumma said she would hit on the head if only she had the courage to; but she hadn't. (It was Mumma who killed the fowls when any of them got so old you could only eat them.) So the white crook-neck thing, white, too, about the wattles, stood around grabbing what and whenever it could, but sort of sideways.

"Why're the others pecking at it, Pa?"

"Because they don't like the look of it. Because it's different."

Oh, the long heavy Sunday with Pa's old empty bottles. There was an old stove beside the wash-house, he had bought, he said, as a speculation. The rust came off in flakes, which you tasted to see, because there was nothing else to do.

"How long you gunner be, Pa, before we have a look at the box?"

Pa didn't answer. He was too taken up with his business of the empty bottles. It was Mumma, anyway, who did the talking. Pa was a quiet man.

So you could only wait, and kick the rusty old hulking stove, and wait for Pa to take down the box, which he almost always did of a Sunday if Mumma and the others weren't there. When he had done his last sum of empty bottles, and carved the muck out of his pipe, and rammed in a few fresh crumbs of tobacco, and lit up, then, after a draw or two, he was ready to fetch down the box from where he kept it, out of reach, amongst the tins of soft soap, the bottles of liniment and turps, and the needles he mended the harness with.

Of course you knew all about all of what Pa kept in the box, but that made the things more important, and going over them one by one. Not that there wasn't a lot of uninteresting stuff as well: old family papers, particularly deeds.

"What are deeds, Pa?"

But Pa didn't want to explain, only that he had never been the better off for any blooming piece of paper.

So you didn't bother. They were less interesting than the hair of dead people. There was the locket with the hair of Pa's sister Clara, who died on the voyage out and was buried at sea. There were the photographs. There was the photograph of Grannie Duffield in a cap: her hands spread out against her skirt showed off the rings she was wearing. Her hollow eyes had never known you.

"When did she die?" As if you didn't know; but this was the Sunday game you played.

"Six months after landing at Sydney. She died of the consumption," Pa said, sucking on his pipe.

"And you were left with Granpa."

Pa didn't answer, but sucked on his pipe.

"Did you like her?"

"Course I liked 'er. Wasn't she me mother?"

"She looks funny."

"How funny?"

"Sort of different."

"Your grandmother was a lady. A clergyman's daughter," Pa added, sucking on his pipe: peugh, it smelled!

"Is Mumma a lady? And Mrs Burt?"

"Course they're ladies! What else would they be?" Pa sucked so hard his Adam's apple grew red and angry.

Granpa Duffield was a more, perhaps the most, interesting subject. He had a big nose, sharp along the edge, like a chopper. (Mumma used to say: "You can tell by yer grandfather's nose he was born a haristercrat.") And large, rather shiny eyes. His hair was beautifully arranged, at least for the photograph, in an old fashion. On the back of the photograph someone had written in brown ink: *Hertel Vivian Warboys Duffield.*

"That's my name"—dreamily—as though they both didn't know. "Why amn't I 'Vivian Warboys' as well?"

Pa puffed. Then he said: "One name's enough for a boy to carry around in Australia."

It was a good enough explanation. Of course everybody knew by now, everybody in Cox Street, but any stranger who didn't, laughed. "'Hurtle'? What sort of a name is that?" And it made you start what Mumma called sulking, because you couldn't go on forever explaining to every stranger that came: "'Hurtle' was the name of a foreign woman that married into my granpa's family. Only it was 'H-e-r-t-e-l,' not 'H-u-r-t-l-e.' When I was christened the parson got the spelling wrong."

All these mysteries were contained in the box. And the ring. The ring had a sort of bird on it, sticking out its tongue. The bird was cut off short, below the neck. What was left looked as though it was resting on a dish.

"That was your grandfather's ring. The police sergeant gave it to me when I went out to Ashfield to identify the body."

"After Granpa fell off the mule?"

"Yairs. He died of a seizure on the Parramatta Road."

"What's a seizure?"

Pa didn't answer at first. "Yer blood gets seized."

Granpa Duffield looked more awful than before, with his arranged hair and watery eyes. You couldn't look long enough.

"What was he doing on the mule?"

"Cor, Hurt, I told yer often enough! 'E *borrowed* the mule ter *ride* to the *center* of *Australia*. It was 'is dream." After that Pa's pipe didn't stop spitting.

"What happened to the mule?"

"I told yer! It *disappeared*. An' I never stopped payin' it off to the owner for a long time after."

They sat sharing the mysteries of their family. There wasn't much else to do of a Sunday. Except slip the ring with the tongued bird on and off of your biggest finger. Pa smoking, and pretending not to look.

But as soon as Mumma squeezed through the gap in the fence, with Lena, Edgar, Will, Winnie and Flo, Pa closed the box. Secrets weren't for everyone. Mumma started telling all she had heard next door, with the kids stuffing on Mrs Burt's cold puftaloons; Mumma used to say Mrs B. was a good soul who never ever would believe other people had enough to eat.

Although they told you you must love others, you couldn't always,

5

not when they were all smeary. Mumma was Mumma. And Will was different, who shared the bed; Will was hopeless.

Mumma said: "I could flop down, but have everything to do. Can't you kids make yourselves scarce?"

Pa had gone into the harness-room to replace the box. Bonnie was whinnying from her stall. All the fowls, the cats, had scattered on seeing the kids return.

Lena called: "Come on, Hurt, what do you say if we have a game of hoppy down at Abrams' entrance?" That was where the ground was level; there were no ruts like in the middle of the street.

He couldn't stand Lena in particular. She was four years older. There were the three miscarriages between, Mumma told Mrs Burt.

"I don't wanner play any hopscotch." He didn't either. "Not with you. You're not even lean. You're the scrag end."

Lena burst. She came up and donged him one with her skinny hand: Granma Duffield's without the rings; it had the sting of a leather strap.

He didn't care, though. He kicked her thin shins, and she went off pretending not to cry because she was an older girl.

Oh, the Sunday evenings.

Mumma said she ought to get the tea, but was going to sit for a few minutes at least. Which she did. In that old unravelled cane chair. On the veranda looking over Cox Street.

All the while the kids were screaming playing ball skipping Florrie had dropped the rest of her puftaloon in the dust the voice of their niminy-piminy Lena had united with Elsie Abrams's on the hopscotch court on the hard level ground at the livery-stables entrance.

He hung around Mumma, waiting for her to settle, and she didn't roust on him. In fact he could feel she liked it, in the heavy evening light, with the three or four big leaning sunflowers their petals gone floppy from the day's heat.

Several of the houses in Cox Street had neat pretty gardens, the houses themselves painted up. Not like our old place, he once complained to Mumma. With its once painted, now weatherbeaten weatherboard, and straggly self-sown sunflowers. But Mumma said they were lucky to find a place at that rental, and who would paint a rented home, even if they had the time, which she and Pa didn't, for the laundries she took in, and the empty bottles Pa went round collecting to sell. So that was that, and it didn't matter really, not with the two yellows of the sun and the sunflowers playing together, and the sticky green of the wilted leaves.

He began to smoodge around Mumma. "Oh, I'm exhausted, Hurt dear!" She sighed, but laughed, and took him on her lap in spite of the next baby inside. "You're too big." She wasn't complaining.

She liked him best, he hoped. But he wasn't a sook. He could run, shout, play, fight, had scabs on his knees, and twice split Billy Abrams's lip, who was two years older and a few months.

Now when he had arranged himself, and it was the time of dreamy, smoodging questions, he asked of Mumma: "What did Granpa Duffield do that was wrong?"

"I dunno as you could say he did anything *wrong*. 'E was too much a gentleman."

"Is Pa a gentleman?"

"Pa is different. Pa is a gentleman inside. Oh yes, Pa's a gentleman!"

"Then he can't be so different from Granpa Duffield."

"Well, Pa had no edgercation. Poor Pa was put to lumping bags of potatoes and onions for Cartwrights down in Sussex Street, to earn a crust for 'is own dad. Granpa liked to talk. He was so pleasant. He had a beautiful handwritin'. 'E could copy real lovely. And did earn a shillun here and there. But blew 'is cash as quick as 'e got it. And the remittance too."

The remittance was one of the mysteries you shared with Mumma. You would have liked to ask more about it, and how Granpa blew it, but you didn't dare.

Mumma was the one who dared, on a heavy Sunday evening. "Granpa loved 'is spirits. That was 'is downfall. That is why yer father never touched a drop."

She hung her head. Because of the laundries she was always doing, her skin stayed white and sort of steamy.

"Stop, Hurtle! Oh my neck! You're hurting, dear!" Then when they had rearranged themselves: "Your grandfather was a handsome man." She sighed.

"Was Pa handsome?"

After a pause, she said: "No."

"Were you pretty?"

He could feel Mumma and the next baby kicking together.

"Oh dear, I'm not the one to answer that!" When they had settled down she said: "No. I think yer father married me because of a pair of ear-rins. They was corneelun. Mrs Apps give them to me when I worked a dress for her little boy. The staff used to say: ' 'Ere comes that young feller. Better put on your ear-rins, Bessie.' I lost one after we married."

"Did Granpa Duffield like the ear-rins?"

"No. Oh I don't know. Granpa Duffield couldn't forgive 'is Jim for marryin' Bessie Tozer. At that time I was working at the *Locomotive*. Not in the *saloon*. Peugh! No, thank you! I was chambermaid. And help in the dinin'-room."

It was so beautiful on the grey splintery old veranda towards sunset.

"Will I be a gentleman?"

"That's up to you."

"And handsome?"

"I hope not," Mumma shouted. "You're bold enough. Anythun more would be too much."

After they had fought and kissed together, she sighed and said: "It's the edgercation that counts."

It sounded solemn, but he didn't altogether understand what it meant, nor want to. Not as the sun and the sunflowers were melting together, and he lay against Mumma's white, soapy neck.

There was so much of him that didn't belong to his family. He could see them watching him, wanting to ask him questions. Sometimes they did, and he answered, but the answers weren't the ones they wanted. They looked puzzled, even hurt.

He would play hard with the other kids in their street—Billy Abrams, Bill Cornish, William White, Terry O'Brien—then pull away and start mooning about by himself. Out of desperation he began to read. He read *Pears Cyclopædia*, the newspaper, Mrs Burt's "books," Eustace Burt had a dictionary (Eustace was a teacher), and Granma Duffield's Bible. The Bible was the hardest. He didn't understand not all of the words. It was the stories he went for: the blood and thunder. He drew too, in the dust of the yard, and on the walls. Perhaps he liked drawing best.

"You and yer scribbles, Hurtle! A big boy like you! I'll have Pa take the belt to yer if it ever happens again."

As if Pa would.

So while Mumma scrubbed the wall—she only made it worse grey—he sunk his head and concentrated.

"What's that you're up to now?"

Seeing as she had the suds made, she was spreading them on the floor boards, and had almost reached the island of his chair, pushing the suds ahead of her.

"Eh?" she asked. "Are you deaf then?"

"Reading," he said when he couldn't avoid it any longer, but he made it sound very low.

Though Mumma was on all fours he could tell the shock she got. "Readin? You haven't ever learned. You're still too young to read, love."

He didn't answer but ground his boots on the rail of the chair. She ought to have known he had been reading all this while, but Mumma was often too busy to notice.

As she went on scrubbing and puffing she asked in a tone of voice to please her little boy: "Whatever are you readin', Hurt?"

"The Bible," he had to admit.

Mumma, too, read the Bible, or liked to sit with it when she was tired.

"Well, well," she disbelieved, scratching at the board with the brush which was almost bald. "There's a lot of the Bible. I wonder what's taken your fancy."

He said, even lower than before: "I'm reading how she smote him with the tent peg."

"I never ever read *that!*" It made the handle of her pail clank. Her joints were what she called "set" as she clambered up.

" 'Ere," she said, "run along out inter the fresh air. Play with the others."

He looked up, and saw she was afraid of something.

"Eh?" she almost whimpered.

He put down the book and went outside, in case she started touching him with those wet, swollen hands, when he didn't want to be drawn into any grown-up person's whimpery mood.

Not long after that she came to an arrangement with Mr Olliphant. Mumma already cleaned the church. Now she agreed to scrub out the hall in return for the lessons Mr Olliphant would give her boy until it was time for him to go to school. Mrs Burt and other ladies in their street kept quiet, but breathed heavy.

It was certainly most unusual, not to say peculiar, the treatment young Hurtie Duffield was getting. "But don't you see, he's an unusual child?" Mumma called over the palings.

No one but Pa dared criticize to Mumma's face. "Let's hope 'unusual' don't mean 'useless.'" Because Pa had experienced Granpa Duffield.

Anyway, the visits to the rectory began, and if they didn't always result in lessons, Mr Olliphant offered books between attending to his parish duties. You could sit in the parson's study and read, without anyone suggesting you were unhealthy, or mad. The rector himself was a regular dry biscuit of a man, who seemed, for that matter, to live mostly on biscuits, him and Mrs Olliphant. They had had a baby, but it soon died.

Sometimes on dashing in, and before dashing out on further parish business, Mr Olliphant would mumble a biscuit over arithmetic. Arithmetic was too dry; you couldn't care much about that. *Amo, amas, amat*: that was better. It seemed to make Mr Olliphant laugh, the way you said it. And *Maître corbeau, sur un arbre perché*: that was from the *Fables*. The *Fables* were best, because of the pictures. He made a copy of the fox, with a tail like on a lady's fur. But Mr Olliphant came in and said he hoped you weren't going to develop a frivolous nature. You had to learn to be conscientious and not do things behind your master's back.

So you copied Mr Olliphant's voice instead, whether in multiplication or division, in French fables or Latin verbs, and became so successful at it, you could hear yourself like a book talking.

Of course you never turned the voice on at home; or not unless you wanted to pay somebody out.

Once he said in Mr Olliphant's voice: "Perhaps I shall soon be so well educated I shan't need to go to ordinary school."

"Edgercated! When you can't even learn to stop scribbling on the walls."

"That isn't scribble, it's a droring," he said in what was his own voice.

There were times when Mumma didn't exactly love him less. It was like as if he made her nervous, as if she had lost control of him, worst of all, control of his thoughts. She would look at him as though he was sick. Till he brushed up against her. He had learned that this worked with his mother, and with Lena and the girls. He had never tried it out on his father.

Pa didn't encourage you to touch him. You never ever saw him touch Mumma, unless when they had got into bed. Pa was at his gentlest, his most loving, when working with the things he seemed to like: their brown, wall-eyed mare, Bonnie; the spring-cart he brought the empty bottles home in; bits of old harness; tools and things. Perhaps he loved the shapes of those empty bottles. He was never tired of handling them.

When you were left alone with Pa he got the frightened look. The lines looked deeper that ran from his yellow nose almost to his blue chin, the eyebrows bristled worse, and the chocolate eyes began to flicker. You could tell that Pa was thinking of something to say. Not that, for most of the time, you could think of anything yourself, but it was up to a father to think of something.

So you waited, not exactly watching, while Pa's thoughts chased one another, and his Adam's apple wobbled.

"Well," he might sweat it out at last, "how many lessons'll the parson take to turn you into a gentleman?" And once he added, as a surprise: "The parson wouldn't like to admit, but you might get more of it from your dad. It's the blood, see?" He didn't usually become excited, but when he did the spit would fly.

Pa softened his voice in explaining his paraphernalia. "Watch this, sonny—how you apply the soap." He was standing in the yard, soft-soaping the mare's old black, mended harness, his thin mouth grown watery.

"Old harness is better than new."

"Why, Pa?"

He didn't want to answer that.

"It's been tried out," he said, flicking a strap as if to test it some more.

He hung the dismantled harness to dry on long, rusty-wire hooks attached to the boughs of the pepper tree. The softened leather had a soothing smell.

"Let me polish the brass. Eh, Pa? Can't I?"

Pa wouldn't say at first. Then he would give in, grumblingly. His hands trembled handling the things he respected.

You weren't all that interested in the old brass medals from off the harness, but liked to bring out the light in them. You got pretty good at it, and Pa began to drool, suspecting that his son might, after all, have been born with a skill.

"Apprentice yer to some good honest tradesman," on one occasion he said. "Learn a trade. It's all very well to read and write. But you can go too far."

Because you didn't know what to answer, you went away. You didn't love books all that much, but wouldn't have known how to tell Pa you neither loved an "honest trade." You loved—what? You wouldn't have known, not to be asked.

He loved the feel of a smooth stone, or to take a flower to pieces, to see what there was inside. He loved the pepper tree breaking into light, and the white hens rustling by moonlight in the black branches, and the sleepy sound of the henshit dropping. He could do nothing about it, though. Not yet. He could only carry all of it in his head. Not talk about it. Because Mumma and Pa would not have understood. They talked about what was "right" and "honest," and the price of things, but people looked down at their plates if you said something was "beautiful."

So Pa looked frightened when you met, unless there was some old tackle you could hold between you. It was easier for Mumma, who wasn't ashamed to chatter, and touch, and kiss.

All this while Mumma continued taking in washing for the well-off people in neighbouring suburbs. Their coachmen would drive up and leave the baskets of dirty linen. Almost always there were fancy things hanging on the lines in the back yard. He used to imagine the people, particularly the ladies, who belonged inside such flimsy clothes.

In the outer kitchen at night Mumma would be ironing while the kids played around.

"Leave it, Winnie!" she would say. "Mrs Ebsworth won't thank you for fingerprints on her good muslun."

There was always a steam, a smell of ironing filling the outer kitchen at night, and Mumma's exasperation, for some article she had scorched, or her hair uncoiling out of its bun.

"Arr dear," she said as she put up her hair, "it's plain enough we'll die poor!"

It was on such a night that Mumma told about an offer a Mrs Courtney had made her. He came in from the yard, and already some kind of strife had begun. Pa was sitting with his elbows on the table from which he had just eaten his tea. Pa was looking as black as the stove. While Mumma kept stamping with the iron on the ironing table in the outer kitchen.

"But the money's not to be sniffed at, Jim." She very seldom called him by his name. "Washing Mondays, ironing Tuesdays. Courtneys is one of the best families. Money to burn. Do you hear? And Mrs Courtney won't allow her things to be laundered outside her own home. Only Mondays and Tuesdays, Jim."

Pa sat, the corners of his mouth turned down, as if he felt it was him to blame.

"Jim? Mrs Burt 'as said she'll keep an eye on the little ones. Lena's at school." Silly Lena tried to look important. "Hurtle 'as Mr Olliphant."

So it was arranged, not then, but you knew it was as good as.

The mornings Mumma set out for Rushcutters where these Court-neys lived she seemed to walk different, as though she was trying to live up to the wealthy people she worked for. She stepped out with more style, even now that she was far gone, usually hum-ming or singing, as she avoided the ruts along Cox Street. She carried her belongings tied up in a clean towel: a comb, a piece of extra special soap, family likenesses, something for headaches and something for breath, and a purse for the wages Mrs Courtney paid.

"What's she like?"

"I never saw her yet. Mrs Courtney's a very important person. Always busy with ladies' luncheons, and balls, and committees. It's Edith the parlourmaid who brings me the money before I leave."

"What sort of house?"

"Ah—the *house!*" Mumma sighed and stamped with her iron.

"Hasn't she any kiddies?" Lena had put on the voice you use when you first catch sight of a little baby.

"One little girl. Her name is Rhoda."

"What? *Roader?*" The others all looked suspicious of a name no-body had ever heard.

"It's in the Bible," he said.

"Urrhh! *Hurtle!*" Lena probably hated him as much as he now hated Lena.

"Is she pretty, Mumma?"

"Rhoda's delicate," was all Mumma would say, as though they had taught her to be a lady down at Courtneys'.

But she was ready to talk about the "girls."

"What girls?"

"Why, the girls Mrs Courtney employs." Mumma seemed to think it wasn't fair to let on that anybody "worked"; *she* worked, certainly, she never stopped, and never stopped referring to it, but to accuse anybody else was a dirty trick.

The girls remained a mystery. He would have liked to imagine the grand mansion in which they lived, and Mrs Courtney in particular, but couldn't. A muslin veil hung between them.

He felt so helpless he began playing with himself. He was playing with himself in Mr Olliphant's study when Mrs Olliphant came in. She had the sniffles.

Mr Olliphant was sick. They prayed for him in church on Sundays. Mrs Burt said the poor soul's bones were crumbling away. He was replaced by that Mr Ruffles, who was enthusiastic, but not much more educated, it seemed, than everybody else.

For some while it wasn't known what to do with Hurt. "Better put 'im in the Infants'." Mumma wouldn't come at it yet.

One morning, it was a Monday, she began brushing at his hair, although he knew how to do it himself. She said: "Put on your cap, dear. I'm gunner take you down to Courtneys' with me. Provided you behave good. You know how to be good, don't you? Some of the girls are very refined, and wouldn't put up with a bold little boy."

He didn't say anything, but stuck his cap on. She gave him a wet kiss.

She took him by the hand, and they walked through the streets, quickly at first, then slower because of the baby inside her. Mumma was humming out of tune. He was able to withdraw his hand.

"This is my proudest day," she said. "They won't believe what I tell them. Or if you show them a likeness they won't no more than half look. They're so taken up with their own ideas, you've gotter show them the real thing."

"I don't want to be shown." There was a nail eating into his toe.

"Some of those maids," she said, "don't even listen to what you tell them about the weather." Then she began to advise: "You won't go round in front, will you? Or into the toolshed. Or bush house. Or spoil Mr Thompson's tuberous begonias? I dare say May, who's a good soul underneath, will dish you up something nice for dinner."

In spite of the baby inside, Mumma jumped a puddle. She was so excited at their outing.

He continued walking with his own thoughts, apart from Mumma, down through the streets where the better houses began. He touched the leaves of some of the glossy bushes to find out whether they felt as fleshy as they looked. Some of the flowers had a scent of ladies' powder. Birds rose and fell in the air like the notes of music out of the piano shops in Surry Hills.

When they reached the gate on which was painted

SUNNINGDALE
Tradesmen's Entrance

Mumma took his hand again. Going down the steps, she was not so much leading as leaning on him. He could hear her breathing.

"You won't do anything, Hurtle," she breathed, "to make me ashamed. You're what I've been trying to tell them about."

He could feel his face swelling with shame.

"You're what Pa and me knows we aren't," Mumma mumbled lower than before.

He would have liked to shake her off, but with all there was to look at, he forgot to try.

Everything at Courtneys' had a look of new. Even the banana tree. The dead leaves must have been picked off; the live ones might have been varnished. The rubbish bins shone like silver. The banana tree was swelling and fruiting, very purple. He was reminded of his own paler one. Then of Pa's wrinkled-looking, ugly old cock.

The girls, who were drinking their early tea, woke up quickly on seeing Mrs Duffield's surprise. One old tortoise and an upright person with no front exchanged glances of disapproval. A thick woman, who had shaved her chin, giggled and giggled.

The tortoise licked her lips and said: "Madam never allowed children."

The upright person crooked her finger in agreement.

"Is this the boy, Duffles? Well, I never! He's gorgeouser than the photo even!" This from a girl with a mole above her lips, who was all for kissing, but he didn't want it.

"I'm Lizzie," she crowed at him. She was wearing a stiff shiny collar. He could smell her, though not unclean, inside her starched lilac dress.

The girls' dining-hall was full of the glare of waxed linoleum: a yellow brown.

A woman heaved in her chair at the head of the table and looked back at the newspaper: it was yesterday's. She was what really mattered. And him. She was of a muddy brown colour, her eyelids thick, purple at the edges. The eyes were dull but interesting, with little specks of yellow in the whites.

Mrs Duffield said: "He'll be no trouble, May. Hurtle 'ull play in the yard. He's a quiet, sensible boy."

She was gasping, though, as she supped the hot tea Delia, the bristle-chinned "girl," had poured. Then she smiled, quirking up the corners of her mouth. He hadn't seen Mumma like this before.

"And what does his Lordship fancy?" Lizzie gave him a scone in which the melted butter had set again in lovely dobs.

Lizzie was their friend.

When May put away her paper, and heaved herself up from the head of the table. She buttered the corner of a loaf and spread it with thickest, purple jam. "This is what boys like." She gave it to him.

May seemed like a woman who wouldn't often speak: she was too important. Now as she went about her business, she was bulging out above her stays, under her brown dress, but no one would have drawn her attention to it.

"Cut some bread and butter for 'inside' and cut it thin, Delia," she ordered the bristly woman. "Can't be too thin. They like it to blow off their trays."

May herself had begun throwing kidneys about by the handful in the kitchen. The kidneys made a soft plopp. One or two she squinted at very close and chucked into a bin.

Mumma explained, though there wasn't any need: "That lady's the cook. If you speak to her, you'd better call her Mrs Noble."

After the rest of the girls had sat there a while longer, controlling their wind, and grumbling about conditions, they went to their work in other parts of the house, and Mumma took him with her to the laundry, where she lit the copper and filled the tubs. He didn't know how he would pass the morning. He looked inside the tool-shed, and stuck a horsehair from the shoulder of an old coat into a fly's arse. It was rather a large, striped fly, which flew bumbling up a windowpane. In the bush house he broke a tuberous begonia, and had to scuff it into the bark in which the fleshy plants were growing. Then he threw a stone at a thin tabby in a red collar.

But he couldn't think what to do.

On and off Mumma came out, and pegged wet clothes on the

line. On and off he went into the laundry, into the woodsmoke from the copper, and there was Mumma scrabbling at the clothes in the blue water, her skin shrivelled to a whiter white. Although Lizzie and Delia at early tea had spoken about slavery, Mumma looked happier at Courtneys' than he had ever seen her.

Some time after eleven o'clock tea, before what the girls referred to as "luncheon," Lizzie came to Mumma and said: "Come on, Duffles, I'm going to take you on a private tour of the millioneers' nest."

Mumma kept flicking the water off her wrists back into the tub, she had got so nervous. "Oh Lizzie, do you think we ought? She might catch us at it." You could see, though, Mumma wished for nothing so much as to see the inside of the grand house.

Lizzie said: "She'll be late back. I know. She's gone to Madame Deseeray to try on a new gown that's arrived." She took hold of Mumma by the wet wrist and began to pull.

Nobody had mentioned him, but he saw to it he wasn't left: the door covered with green felt, which shut out the noise of the kitchen from the rest of the house, puffed shut behind the three of them.

Mumma remained so nervous she could only hobble weakly in her old shoes in Lizzie's tracks. She was further embarrassed at sight of the upright person, whose name was Edith, cleaning silver in her pantry in a pair of gloves.

Lizzie the housemaid explained everything as they went. Mumma at first hardly dared raise her eyes from the patterned carpets through which they trod, but as he was only a child and supposed not hardly to be there, he was able to look around at what Lizzie was pointing out: at the "priceless porcelain," and naked ladies in gold frames.

"She's artistic," Lizzie explained.

"Oh dear!" Mumma sniffed, and would have liked to giggle.

"But if you ask me, He's more interested in the naked titties than any old art work."

Mumma made a clucking noise.

"He's a real man," their friend continued. "Alfreda knows it wouldn't do to twist his tail once too often. She dotes on 'er Harry."

"Isn't there a portrait of their little girl?" Mumma asked.

"Not when they've got the kid herself. A portrait would be harping on it."

Suddenly Lizzie changed her tone: "And does Hurtle Duffield fancy the naked ladies?"

"No," he said. They were curious, the big bubs, but dead.

"What's wrong with 'em?" Lizzie lashed back.

He hardly knew. "Old cold pudding . . ." was all he could mumble.

Lizzie nearly split herself, and Mumma had to laugh while blushing.

"What a caution of a boy!" Lizzie rattled.

They had come out by now into a round, domed room.

"Bet you never in yer life saw a chandelier," Lizzie proudly accused him.

He didn't answer. He hadn't, of course. But as he stood underneath, looking up through the glass fruit and flickering of broken rainbow, he knew all about a chandelier, from perhaps dreaming of it, and only now recognizing his dream.

They mounted the soft stairs: everywhere soft soft: it was so quiet and clean you wouldn't have known anyone lived at Sunningdale.

In the sewing-room the old tortoise from the maids' hall was going through a bagful of furs. Her superior eyelids obviously disapproved, but she wouldn't be one to criticize her fellow servants.

"Miss Keep, the lady's-maid," Lizzie told when they had gone past. "Herself the lady. Or so she would like to think. An old Tartar."

Lizzie dared to bounce on the Courtneys' great big bed, and lie with her hands behind her head, elbows pointing. "What's it like to be married, eh? I can only guess!"

Mumma could have told her for certain, but only got more embarrassed. "Ah Lizzie, somebody could come in and catch us!"

But Lizzie was growing dreamier. "I could take a tumble meself with Harry Courtney. He's a lovely man. The loveliest legs. But if I hung on by both 'is whiskers, 'e wouldn't notice. Maids don't exist."

Mumma was so upset. "Now, Lizzie, this isn't a nice kind of talk! Not in front of the boy." As if you didn't know all about it living at home. "It isn't moral talk at all."

Lizzie got up, snorting, and Mumma straightened the counterpane.

"Morals!" said Lizzie. "My crikey! I think they was invented by those who're too cold to need 'em."

When she had arranged her cap in the glass they drifted back down the stairs. Mumma's behaviour was becoming more practised: she followed her friend with long strides almost as dashing as Lizzie's own.

"I can imagine they go in for great entertainments," she said and hoped.

"They can't sit 'ere listenin' to each other's thoughts," Lizzie answered rather sharp.

As Mumma worked it out her eyes were shining: she had a reckless look.

Downstairs, Lizzie lighted a cigarette and puffed at it from stiff hand. "This"—she coughed—"is where Madam writes 'er letters, and where you'll get your dressing-down, if you've got it coming to you."

It was a smaller, mauve room, the furniture in black, with streaks of pearl in it. The room even had a kind of mauve scent, from a mass of violets, he recognized from the florists', in a silver bowl. Shelves of coloured books and photographs in posh frames gave the room a used, though at the same time a special, look. There was a hairpin on the carpet, and in a gold cage a white bird with red beak looking at them with cold eye.

He would have liked to muck around in the room but saw that Lizzie wouldn't have allowed it. She was becoming restless, and her fag was giving her trouble. Coughing and breathing smoke, she put it out in a little marble tray.

"And this"—she coughed, throwing open yet another door—"is Harry Courtney's study. They couldn't escape very far from each other even if they thought of trying."

Mumma moaned: there was such a glare of mahogany, a blaze of crimson leather, and enough stuffed birds in glass cases to frighten the live caged one in Mrs Courtney's room.

"All those books!" Mumma gasped. "Mr Courtney must be a highly edgercated gentleman."

"Oh, he doesn't *read* them! 'Sir' is a collector of *Australiana*. He has to do something with 'is money—and Alfreda sees he don't spend it on the ladies."

Suddenly Lizzie could have been sick of it all. Going back into Mrs Courtney's own room, deliberately savaging the soft, mauve-grey carpet with her heels, she could have been wondering why she had been wasting her time on the laundress and her boy.

She said: "In the first situation I was ever in—I was sixteen—

the old bloke—ugh!—'e was said to have a touch of the tarbrush—
'e tried to break into me room. I done a bunk from there."

She was so absorbed in her discontent, and Mumma by all she
had seen and was seeing, the sound of motion took them by surprise.

"Who are *you*?" the lady asked.

She didn't look, except quickly, at a child. She was staring at
Mumma, at her damp skirt, at her white wrists and red hands.

"I am Mrs Duffield," Mumma answered.

"Who? Oh—yes—the laundress," Mrs Courtney said. "We haven't
met, but I remember now."

Then she smiled a slow, sweetish sort of smile. "You are showing
the laundress the house. I'm so glad, Lizzie, you thought of being
kind to Mrs Duffield."

Under her freckles Lizzie became a dark red. "Yes, m'm," she
barely mumbled.

Mrs Courtney was wearing a veil. She began raising it: to take
a better look. The blue with white feathers of her hat slightly
stirred with the interest she expressed. "I didn't expect children."
She looked at Mrs Duffield's little boy, at Mrs Duffield's stomach.

With a sudden expert gesture she hitched back her veil on the
brim of her huge hat. "I congratulate you," she said. "He's nice,
isn't he?" She smiled. "A handsome child."

Mumma didn't know when she should answer, or what she should
answer, and the experienced Lizzie couldn't help her any longer.

It was Mrs Courtney herself who gave them the clue, moving
round her mauve room in the sound of her stiff blue dress, smoothing its wine-glass waist, rearranging papers on her desk, the bowl of
violets, a cuttlefish stuck between the bars of her bird's cage. She
said, lowering her chin, her voice: "I've had a very trying morning."

So her "girls" knew they should return to the part of the house to
which they belonged.

Although he expected her to speak to him she didn't, and he followed the others out.

At home Mumma let the iron stand while she tried to remember
a dream she had had.

"All this big house in which twenty other families could live. It
was like walking—wasn't it, Hurtie?—on mattresses. The china door-

knobs all beautiful and clean. And a chandelier. Does any of you know what's a chandelier?"

Lena answered: "No."

Then Mumma took a deep breath. Her face was shining. She was going to try to tell about the chandelier, and he could have run at her to stop her, because the chandelier had blazed up in him again, and he didn't want the others to share in anything so particularly his: not Mumma, not Lizzie, could have seen or experienced the half of it.

When Pa called from the table: " 'Ere, Mother, where's the pertater? You forgot the pertater."

"No, I didn't," she answered, "because here it is."

At once she grabbed the iron spoon. She served him out a dollop, and a dollop, from the old battered pot. Tonight the potato looked awful grey, till Pa messed it about with the gravy from the little bit of steak that was only for him. On a different occasion you might have felt hungry.

And Mumma returned to her dream, though she seemed to have forgotten the chandelier.

"And corned beef, and marmalade puddin' for dinner, only they call it 'luncheon.' "

"Did you meet the little girl when you was seeing over the house?"

"No, we didn't. I expect she was out for exercise with her nurse."

Then Mumma cleared her throat and began smoothing very dreamy with the iron. "We did meet Her, though—Mrs Courtney—by mistake."

"Was she pretty?"

"A real vision. A real lady. Everything about 'er floatin'—sort of."

"What was the colour of 'er eyes?"

"What was the colour of 'er dress?"

" 'Ow can I remember what was the colour of *anything*? I could'uv fainted."

"Her eyes were blue. Her dress was blue."

"There! Hurt remembers. Had 'is wits about 'im. But a child isn't responsible. Lizzie and me was the ones who'd get the blame. Now, Hurtle, a knife isn't for jabbing with. Not at the furniture. Ah dear, you kids won't leave us a stick to live with. Run out, all of yez, into the yard and let your father finish 'is tea in peace."

If you didn't obey along with everyone else it was because Pa had already finished. He sat belching and grunting for a bit: after a meal he used to say less than ever. He lit his spluttering pipe and went across the yard to the stable.

Mumma either didn't see you were there, or else she was admitting you to her thoughts: you were still so close to the outing you had been on together.

As she came round the table to take the plate Pa had been using she said, like to herself: "Fancy remembering the colour of 'er eyes!" Then, out louder: "I think you're right. They was blue eyes."

She was laughing, first to herself, then for him. "Like yours, Hurt! Blue." And instead of clearing the plate from the table she took his face in her hands and looked close into it.

"My eyes are grey. Sometimes they're on the greenish side." But he could hardly pronounce it: she was squeezing his cheeks so tight together she was giving him a fish's mouth.

"Blue! Blue like Mrs Courtney's!" She was so glad to have discovered what she wanted to be a likeness, she couldn't be persuaded it wasn't the truth.

So he became ashamed of his shabby, silly mother. He became ashamed of himself for loving, yet not loving her more. Because it was Mumma he loved, not Mrs Courtney. That was different: the vision made him shiver with joy; he wished he had been in a position to touch her.

He was soon sad and hopeless with all these feelings. He was afraid Mumma, trembling with excitement and pleasure, might begin to cotton on to how he really felt inside, so he dragged his face out of her hands and ran out to the others in the yard.

For next day's ironing, he didn't dare expect. But when the following Monday came he had on his cap. He was ready standing at the street gate.

Lugging her bundle, Mumma was looking thoughtful and anxious. She hadn't reckoned on him as well.

"How—" she said. "I didn't mean you to come, Hurtle. Not every time. That wouldn't be good for you."

Because he was determined to win he didn't ask in what way it wouldn't be good. He walked along. Here and there he skipped to lighten the silence.

"I mean it," she said.

But he saw she was weak this morning. The baby was too heavy in her. So he took her hand. And they walked along.

When they arrived at Courtneys' it was much the same as the first time, though they made less fuss of him because he was no longer a surprise. Perhaps Miss Keep looked more disgusted than before. Mrs Noble stared moodily through him and didn't offer him the thick spread of cherry jam.

"Watch out, Master Clumsy!" said Lizzie. "You just about murdered my favourite corn."

As he wore out the morning around the yard he began to feel he had been wrong to come. Mr Thompson the gardener wouldn't hardly speak. A grey wind was filling the empty clothes on the line.

He might have started a row with Mumma over a plug he didn't mean to pull out, if the door hadn't opened behind their backs and someone come into the laundry.

"I'm looking for my kitten." It was a small, though bossy, voice. You wouldn't have thought she hadn't seen him before.

"Well, Rhoda," said Mumma, "I haven't noticed your kitten. But don't expect he's lost. Cats are independent things." She had too many children to take much interest in pets.

Nor was Rhoda particularly interested, it seemed. She was looking at you, her head trembling on her thin neck. Her hair was pink rather than red. On one side of her neck she had a large birthmark the colour of milk chocolate.

"What is the kitten's name, love?"

But Rhoda wasn't interested in Mumma's polite interest. She had buttoned up her mouth tight. Her head no longer trembled but lolled on her frail neck. She probably hated him on sight. He could have hit Rhoda: except she might have died. She reminded him of the crook-neck pullet at home Mumma hadn't the heart to kill.

"This is my little boy. This is Hurtle, Rhoda," Mrs Duffield the laundress was only vaguely saying as she rubbed a garment back and forth over the ridges of the washboard. "How about taking him outside—have a game—the two of you? But gentle, Hurt."

Rhoda said: "No." All the pinkish curls shook.

She looked as though she mightn't have known how to play. She was so clean. None of the snot of Winnie and Flo. So frail, she might have broken. But her thin lips were firm, and probably spiteful.

Mumma laughed and said: "You're right, dear. Boys like rough games."

She bent to kiss the little thing, who ducked her head and avoided with the whole of her body. Mumma could only stroke with her hand the white dress she must have laundered recently. It could have been her nails you heard catching in the material.

"O—oohh!" Rhoda complained aloud.

She was going outside, not, you felt, in search of her cat, but away. The cat had probably only ever been an excuse.

As Rhoda left he saw she had more than a crooked neck: her back was humped. It gave him a queer turn to see the hump for the first time. He didn't mention it to Mumma. And Mumma didn't mention it. She kept on rubbing the sudsy clothes against the board, on her mouth a tight smile, which he knew had nothing to do with her thoughts.

The damp stone laundry, smelling of Lysol and yellow soap, began to horrify him. He had heard of prisons in which they tortured men in the old days. Mumma couldn't have escaped, she had the washing, she was used to it, but he who was cowardly and young, he was still also free. So he went quickly quietly out. It wasn't altogether cowardly, either, to leave Mumma with the washing and their nightmare thoughts. It was necessary for him to see the Courtneys' house again. The felted door went *pff* as he passed through.

And at once he was received by his other world: of silence and beauty. He touched the shiny porcelain shells. He stood looking up through the chandelier, holding his face almost flat, for the light to trickle and collect on it. The glass fruit tinkled slightly, the whole forest swaying, because of a draught from an open window.

He was himself again.

Now he could go on towards other private memories of the house. He could hear a pen scratching in the distance as his feet slid on the mossy carpet.

"Who is it?" the voice called. "Is it you, darling?" The pen was silent. "Rhoda?" the voice rose.

He reached the doorway. Mrs Courtney was seated at her desk with a tray beside her. While writing she must have been drinking what smelled of chocolate, out of an enormous gold-rimmed cup. She began to clutch her bosom, of which she was showing rather a lot. She wasn't properly dressed yet.

"Who—?" she began, angrily frowning. Then she calmed down. "Oh—you're the boy—the laundress's boy." Still frowning, but lazily, she asked: "What do they call you, dear?"

He told her his name, but he saw she didn't take it in. He was only a child: he didn't matter.

A mild sunlight made her hair look even looser than it was. Her gown had collected, loose and creamy, round her chair. The big blue velvet bows softly drooped. Above the cup, making up its mind, hung a bee attracted to the chocolate: it made you feel drowsy.

Mrs Courtney lowered her eyes. "One of my sleepless nights," she explained. "I'm not usually so late. I lead a very busy life."

If she had been caught out she wasn't going to apologize: this was a lady getting ready to enjoy a chat.

"Sit down," she ordered. "Or how can I feel comfortable?"

The eyes, when she raised them, were bluer than before. She cocked her head and smiled so sweetly at him, you wouldn't have thought she had the advantage: he might have been a man.

Then, when she felt she had looked too long, even at a child, she sank her mouth rather greedily in the cup of chocolate. She showed no signs of asking whether they could bring him some. But he didn't need it: he was full of the scent from Mrs Courtney's cup.

"Aren't you going to entertain me?" She laughed rather high.

It would have put him off if he hadn't fortunately noticed the photo of Rhoda on her desk. It was framed in gold, with golden branches wreathed round the picture, the branches flowering with blistered pearls.

He took the photo. "It's a good likeness," he said in his best voice.

"You haven't met her, have you?" Mrs Courtney didn't want her chat spoiled.

"Just now," he said, covering the frame with his hands so that he only saw the picture. "You did right to only take her head."

"Why?" Mrs Courtney gasped, but it could have been because she had jogged her cup of chocolate.

"Well, the back. You wouldn't want to see the back. The head is the best part of her."

"It's only a slight curvature," Rhoda's mother spluttered. "It can be corrected."

"You can see her skin is the kind of white that goes with red hair." He was still holding the photographed head framed in his two hands.

"Red? I wouldn't call it red." It was once more a laughing matter. "I like to think of it as 'strawberry.'"

He put the likeness back on the desk. Red or pink, Rhoda had the smell of red people.

"What a quaint fellow you are! What did you say your name was?"

"Hurtle Duffield."

"How did you learn to speak as you do?" Because all this while he had been speaking bookish.

"From Mr Olliphant."

"Oh, that's splendid!" She laughed. "And who is Mr Olliphant?"

"The rector. Only he's gone. He's sick."

She rearranged Rhoda's likeness. "You're lucky to have been taken up by a clergyman. Even if he's left you in the lurch."

She was becoming very serious, locking her hands together in front of her on the desk. As she leaned forward her lovely eyes began to bulge.

"The ethical side of life is so important," she told him. "Even when I am run off my feet—my husband says I undertake too much—I only have to remind myself of that. Nothing will make me neglect the charities I have taken up. Lonely seamen, for instance. And girls who—who have fallen by the wayside."

"Why have they fallen by the wayside?"

"Well," she said, "the city is full of vice, and human nature is weak. But we can't merely accept, Hurtle. We must help others help themselves."

He understood better now, but didn't know you could do anything about human nature: of the people he knew, one half called the other half hopeless.

Mrs Courtney was carrying on. "Then there's the question of cruelty to animals. It's *heart*-rending," she moaned and rubbed at a spot of chocolate she had spilled below her creamy bosom, "what I've seen with my own eyes. I'm at present organizing a ball to raise funds for the Society. Harry—my husband—tells me I'm mad to become involved with another committee. But how can one avoid it? When one's conscience becomes involved."

Her rings were shining fiercely in the sunlight, while the blue eyes had begun to blur.

"My husband is away in the country—at one of our properties," she went on. "He has to visit them regularly to see what the managers are up to. I decided early—on our honeymoon, in fact—I couldn't live in the country. I mean, I couldn't endure the idleness, when there is so much in life to tackle. Harry says I get nowhere for attempting too much." She looked at a little jewelled watch hanging from her by a gold chain. "But he's cynical. I adore him. I'm so nervous while he's away on these long visits."

She was looking older, for a lady anyway. Real ladies on the whole looked younger.

"How I've been running on! Tell me about your brothers and sisters," she ordered, to try to cheer herself up.

"They're just kids. Oh, one of them's a bit simple. That's Will. We sleep in the same bed." He suspected he had forgotten to use Mr Olliphant's voice.

"How delicious!" she said. "I mean, it's sad. But you're a most handsome fellow." She came up close and began ruffling his hair: he felt dizzy from the smell of her dress, and her too, underneath. "Harry will love you," she said. "He loves a manly, forthright boy."

But he didn't think he wanted to be loved by Mr Courtney. Pa didn't love: he only put up with you.

And Mrs Courtney had begun again to feel nervous. Her dress moved away with her. She began dabbing her lips with her handkerchief rolled into a ball. She went and pulled the bell.

When the parlourmaid came, she said in an altered, mistressy voice: "Find Miss Rhoda, Edith. She hasn't been near me this morning. I'm afraid she may be overexerting herself."

After Edith had gone Mrs Courtney explained to him, again as though he was a grown-up man, or just because she had to pull out the plug: "Nurse is a kind old thing, but not a good influence. She should bring me the child before I get up. Poor Rhoda! On top of everything else, she's highly strung. She has a *cat*. Which Nurse allows her to take to bed. It could give her asthma. Or something."

In her excitement she had taken his head and was holding it to her side. "How your mother must love you," she said.

He was so shocked he pulled away. She didn't seem to notice.

"Didn't you ever have another? Besides this Rhoda," he mumbled.

"Oh yes—*no*! Impossible!"

She stood knotting her rings against her flowing gown. She looked for the first time awkward: her mouth was pulled into an ugly shape; her hair was old. But he could remember what he had seen and felt.

Quite suddenly Rhoda had come in. She tended to move sideways. Of course the poor thing had her affliction to hide. He looked at her with disgust.

Rhoda turned her head away.

"Have you forgotten all about your mother, darling?" Mrs Courtney inquired with rash courage.

Rhoda didn't answer. She touched a flower in the carpet with her toe. Mrs Courtney held her breath watching Rhoda make the flower real.

The mother broke the spell. "Did you do your board exercises? Did you? I know it's unpleasant, but it's for your own good. Did Nurse see that you lay on the board?"

Rhoda made some watery sounds. Her head trembled on her frail neck.

"You see," Mrs Courtney told the air, "it's time we engaged the governess."

Again she pulled the bell. Edith came, quicker and thinner.

"Send Nurse," the mistress commanded.

Rhoda started a high crying, exposing through her stretched mouth her rather small, transparent teeth.

"I'm not the one to blame, darling," her mother explained. "We must only carry out what Dr Marshall ordered. Oh dear! *Darling*! Can you have got it into your head Mummy doesn't love you? My darling darling Rhoda!"

Mrs Courtney herself had begun to whimper like a little child, her lovely face crumpling into an old rag. She looked as though she was about to creep on all fours, to make herself long and thin like some animal children were tormenting.

It was then that Rhoda spat. It gummed itself to her mother's face. One end of the spit was swinging.

He would have liked to do something for both of them, but only his mind worked: his limbs were stuck, his heart was pumping.

Nurse came, a stout woman, with a white belt dividing her figure in two. She immediately began mewing for her little girl. The belt had a butterfly for buckle.

"Come away, Rhoda!" mewed the nurse. "A rest is what you need. I'll give you a licorice—all sorts—shall I?"

"The cat! How can you allow the cat?" Mrs Courtney howled.

"But she loves it!" The nurse purpled up.

When Rhoda and the nurse had gone, and Mrs. Courtney had wiped her face with her handkerchief, she said: "So distressing. What will you think of us? We're not at all like this, you know."

She went to her desk and started rummaging in a little bag made of gold chain. "Here!" she said. "I want you to take this, Hurtle, and share it with your brothers and sisters. And remember that nobody is good all the time, however hard they try to be."

He got such a surprise he almost dropped the sovereign he found she had put in his hand.

"As if I were an animal!" She had begun to whimper again. "But no animal suffers worse than a human being." She blew her nose on the now soggy handkerchief.

Because she was in such a state, sighing and rumpling the papers on her desk, and looking at her face in the glass, he didn't think Mrs Courtney would mind if he slipped away. Nor did she. She didn't seem to notice it.

He hurried back through the house, silent except for the Chinese vases rocking on their black stands, and a twittering in the chandelier.

Mumma was ropeable. Some wet sheets she was trying to peg to the line were cracking like whips. First they clung to each other, or Mumma, then they sailed open in the wind.

While she fought she complained: "Arr now, Hurtle, didn't I tell you to play around the yard? I been all around—round to the stables—and out in front." A wet sheet hit her in the face. "Where did you get to, you naughty boy?"

"I went exploring." To quieten her, he began helping her nicely with the sheets.

He didn't think he would mention the sovereign or anything of what had happened.

That night Pa asked, as he pushed the stew around his plate: "What sort of a day did you have at the famous Courtneys'?"

"The same," she answered.

She was in low spirits, it seemed. The stew looked grey because probably she had been too tired or too hurried to brown it; while you were still full of the jangle of crystal music and the warm-chocolate scent of Mrs Courtney's room.

When they decided he should go to school, and he was admitted to the Infants', all his hopes appeared to close.

"But I'm not an infant!"

"Poor kid! You can't help laughing," said Mrs Burt over the palings.

At least his parents were too upset to join in their neighbour's amusement, and Lena too important from several years' experience. Though it wasn't far, Pa was driving them to school in the cart, making an occasion of it. The lurching over ruts before they reached the metal threw the three of them against one another.

"Are you frightened?" Lena could have been hoping for it.

"No," he said, although he was.

A wind from the right quarter carried the smell of the nearby zoo. He remembered how the keeper had allowed him to ride on the elephant's head; he remembered the lion with the stream of yellow diarrhoea.

"I bet you are!" Lena harped.

He pinched a hold of her skinny arm, so that she squealed unaccountably loud.

"Hold yer tongue, Lene," said Pa, who was in his usual serious mood.

"But he's afraid and won't admit it! He's pinching me!"

"Hurtle ain't afraid. He's a man," said Pa.

It made Hurtle more afraid, not so much of a lot of schoolkids he didn't know, and anyway he was stronger than most: he was afraid of some shapelessness smelling of lions and elephants. Lena sat snivelling and blinking as if herself was going to be the target; whereas you knew that everything large enough, frightening enough, like death for instance, was being saved up for you.

"Like to hold the reins, son?"

"No."

His hands might have trembled. He wondered what would happen if he pissed his pants. And did let go one little spurt. At once his fear took on a shape: if he had had a pencil in his hand he would have drawn Death trumpeting.

He felt better after that. Sometimes he looked at people to see whether they had guessed his more secret thoughts. But Lena was just a thin thing, a girl, while Pa continued driving the cart as though Death had never appeared, trampling alongside of them.

Poor Pa, when he let them down at the school, he sat for a moment with the whip drooping from his hand. Pa never kissed in saying good-bye, but the lines grew deeper, blacker round his mouth. Today you would have liked to touch them. You could often burst with love, but had never found the proper occasion.

The moment they arrived at school Lena became ever so important. She began giggling with some girls of her own age, who looked at the brother distantly, and did not propose to make his acquaintance. Nor was Lena prepared to risk too much on her relationship with Hurtle. She said very bossily: "I'll take you to Miss Adams, then I must go with my own class." He had never heard her accent sound so thin and prim.

The Infants were taught in the basement of the school. The light, which was a yellow-green, floated down through barred windows just above ground level. The stone walls were cold to touch. Miss Adams was such a thin woman he began to wonder whether their Lena would become a teacher. He could see her in the same smocked blouse, with the same cold as Miss Adams had.

Now Lena simply handed over her brother, and shook her hair, and hurried away.

"Hurtle Duffield," Miss Adams said. "That's a comical name."

Of course. He was used to it by now. He even said: "It rhymes with turtle."

The kids who were standing near them laughed.

"I see you have a sense of humour," said Miss Adams. "I hope you will keep it till recess, please, and not make jokes in class."

She was too busy with her cold and commencement of school. She gave him and another boy copybooks to distribute: one where each child would sit.

All the while other kids kept trooping down. He saw a fair few from Cox Street, whom he knew because they had always been there. It made him sick looking at the other children, except a girl with fair, flossy fringe. There was a boy called Ossie Flood said he was going to bring one or two glassies for Hurt. You didn't want his old marbles, but Ossie seemed to want to hang on.

During break Tom Sullivan from Cox Street started making up to Ossie, whispering and laughing behind his hand. Ossie would have liked to laugh back if his long dopey face had dared.

"What was Tommo telling you?"

"Nothing," said Os.

"It was too long to be nothing. Go on, what was it?"

Ossie Flood's skin turned green.

"Tell, or I'll kick you in the guts."

This had always worked in Cox Street. And Ossie Flood began to tell. His biggest teeth were grooved and green. He told spitting excited frightened he said how Tommo Sullivan said Hurt Duffield was the son of a no-hope pommy bottle-o down their street, who carried around in an old cigar box a pedigree like he was a racehorse.

Going down the steps after break, Hurtle got up against Tommo Sullivan to tell him he was the biggest turd ever dropped from an Irish arse. He banged Tommo's head once or twice against the wall. Though Tommo was bigger, it came easy. Tommo actually began to cry. The stone walls made it sound worse, and you wondered whether you had caught the nits off Tommo's head, though they kept his hair shorn off close.

Miss Adams told her class she was going to start them on pothooks already that first day. Some of the kids could hardly hold the pencil: it wobbled in their hands. One girl's cheek was so full of tongue she looked as though she had a boil. Then Miss Adams encouraged them to join the pothooks by imagining they were making a little hooped fence. Hurtle was so shocked by her old pothooks he couldn't make anything at all.

He would have sunk pretty low if he hadn't suddenly remembered, and taken the pencil, and lost himself.

"What are you doing, Hurtle Duffield?" Miss Adams had smelled a rat.

Everyone looking.

"Droring," he confessed, though it pained him to do so.

It pained Miss Adams equally. He had to take it up to her. The girl with the flossy fringe giggled.

"What is it supposed to be?" Miss Adams squinted and asked through her cold.

"Death," he said and heard his own voice.

"Death?" Miss Adams was frowning. "Looks like a kind of elephant to me. An elephant with hair instead of hide."

"It is," he said. "An elephant in a lion's skin."

"But Death? An elephant is such a gentle creature. Large, but gentle."

"Not always it isn't," he corrected. "It can trample its keeper, without any warning, and rip with its tusks."

All the kids were interested. Some of them pretended to be afraid. Perhaps some of them were.

Miss Adams made a noise through her blocked nose. "You were supposed to be forming pothooks."

"Pothooks! I can write!"

"You sound like a vain boy. At your age. I don't like know-alls. Who was your teacher?"

"I learned myself, I suppose. At first. Then Mr Olliphant showed me some of the finer points."

Nobody else was making a sound.

"Mr Olliphant?" She was so ignorant she hadn't even heard of the rector.

"Seeing that you can write," Miss Adams said, "you will write me something, Hurtle. Something about yourself. Your home. Your life. A composition, in fact. If, as you claim, you are so advanced."

She made a sour, thin smile as she screwed up the drawing of Death and lobbed it into the basket.

He was glad to return to his bench. He would never write if he could draw, but he was so sick of school, it would be a relief to tell about himself.

He wrote and wrote to get through the time:

I am Hurtle Duffield age 6 though I often feel older than that. I don't think age has always to do with what you feel because my father and mother who are old never have the same feelings or thoughts as me. They do not understand what I tell them so I have just about had to give up telling. And I did not tell Mr Olliphant our parson (he has died) though he could read Latin and French, that is nothing to do with it. I get a lot of ideas sitting up the pepper tree in the yard. I like to watch the sky till the circles wirl, these are white, or shut my eyes and squeeze them till there are a lot of coloured spots. Mumma goes crook if I draw on the wall, only the wall in the shed where I sleep with Will at the end of the yard where Pa keeps keeps the harness that wall does not matter, I can draw there, and am droring a picture which will be a shandeleer with the wind through it when it is finished. I would like to draw everything I know. There is drawing. There is bread. I like if I can to get hold of a new loaf and tear the end of crust off of it and eat it. I love the smell of bread but the

bread at home is always stale because you get it cheap. Once
I drew a loaf of bread with all those little bubbles

School was over before he had shown much. Miss Adams told
them they could go. She looked as though she had a headache.

"Not you, Hurtle," she called down. "I'm waiting to see your
composition."

As she read it her head moved along the lines.

"You're a funny boy. What is a 'shandeleer'?"

But he couldn't go into that: it was his secret thing; and even if
he had tried to explain she wouldn't have understood.

So he puffed out his mouth as if he was sulking.

Miss Adams said: "You can go now. But remember that people
will dislike you if you pretend to know more than you do."

Nothing of further interest happened that first day, except that
the girl with the fringe let him smell her hankie. Because she was
starting school her mother had given her a sprinkle of scent, which
was why she kept on smelling the screwed-up ball of her handkerchief. Her name was Dolly Burgess, she said.

Lena and Hurtle Duffield continued going to school. They always started off together, because relationship made it unavoidable. Out of Cox Street, Lena usually broke away and joined up
with some of her friends, unless she was feeling down in the mouth.

One morning after she had broke the chamber Mumma sent her
to empty in the yard, they were still together walking past the
shops. Lena said, to get her own back on somebody: "I hope
you're behaving yourself in class. I hope you don't make a fool of
us with a lot of your old show-off."

"I don't behave any way at all. I act natural."

"Pigs act natural."

He kicked her shin. She gave him a push.

That was when he dropped it.

"Hey! Nao!"

It rolled down a grating, and he couldn't even see it for the muck
and darkness down below.

"Serve you right—whatever it was!" Lena screeched, rubbing her
shin on her other leg.

As they walked on he couldn't help blubbering. He kept it very
low, though Lena's presence made it sound louder.

"What was it?" she asked, now more interested than hurt.

"The sovrun Mrs Courtney gave me." He had never ought to carry it around take it to school his secret yet most solid belonging.

Lena was laughing her plaits off. "A sov-run! Why ever should Mrs Courtney give a boy like you a sov-run? I'll ask Mumma as soon as I get home."

"Mumma doesn't know."

"Course she doesn't! It's a fib! You're the biggest dirty fibber!"

Lena felt so superior she forgot her shin, she forgot the chamber she had broke. At least she marched on ahead.

Losing the sovereign reminded him he had lost Mrs Courtney as well. As term continued he asked Mumma: "Did you see Her?"

Mumma was off colour. "Why should I see Her? I'm the laundress —the washerwoman."

But on a brighter day she couldn't wait to tell: "What do you think? Mrs Courtney sent for all us girls because she's going to a masked ball. She thought we might like to see her fancy costume. Oh, it was a dream! And a black mask."

"What was her costume?"

"I don't know. Something French. Some lady who was friends with a king."

Mumma was in heaven, but it made him sulky.

"Why is she going to wear a mask?"

"Because no one will recognize her that way."

"I'd recognize Mrs Courtney."

"Ah, you're too clever!" Mumma laughed quite like Lena.

"Didn't she ask about me?" It rushed out in a stream of warm bubbles.

"Did she ask about you? For Heaven's sake! Why should a busy lady remember a little boy she never saw more than once?"

Twice, if Mumma knew, and the second time was the important one.

His hopes were low as he and Lena continued going to the rotten old school. He couldn't believe he was related to Lena any more than Lena could believe it. What made their relationship more embarrassing was that they moved him up, after a consultation between Miss Adams and Mr Boothroyd the head, into Lena's class. He was in many ways so advanced. In the higher class some of the boys were so big and backward you would have said they were men. Some of the girls were big already inside their blouses. He never tired of looking at the blouses of the older girls. It amazed him to think they would one day contain something as ugly and shapeless as Mumma's old tittybottles.

Sometimes the older girls would catch him staring at them. They would redden, and put their heads together, and snicker, and whisper. Then they would look straight ahead, as if he had never been there. It was all because of some trouble he got into. During his short stay in Miss Adams's class the girl with the fringe made up to him. He stole a licorice strap from Mrs Maloney's to give to Dolly Burgess because he was in love with the shape of her forehead below the flossy fringe. They shared the strap, chewing on it from opposite ends, and meeting at last in the middle. Through the blast of licorice, that soft, milky, girls' smell came in gentler gusts.

All this happened about the time Mumma had the new baby. There was such a pandemonium at home, he would climb the pepper tree to think about Dolly in absolute private; while everybody came and went: Mrs Burt lending a hand; Mumma wondering how soon she could carry on with the washing and ironing, they couldn't afford for her not to; and Lena burned the scrag end.

He got to like school: to wait for the break, to be with Dolly and watch the light tangle with her fringe. She had a dimple. She had rather pop eyes, but blue. She was an only child, the daughter of a watchmaker. For that reason she was always neatly and noticeably dressed. Her pants had points of lace on them. He asked Dolly to show him her girl's thing: it was still only a naked wrinkle. When he touched, she began at once to gobble and choke: eyes popping. She had been sucking aniseed balls. She ran bellowing away. Because he was afraid, he would have liked not to think about it, but the scent of aniseed kept coming back. He didn't know why he had asked Dolly to show, when he knew enough from Lena and their own girls, not to say Mumma. He put away his boy's one, which Dolly had been too frightened to touch in return.

Because Dolly told her mother, who went to Mumma, and Mr Burgess told Mr Boothroyd, the business caused him a lot of trouble. Pa got out a strap but was too worked up to use it. Old Beetle Boothroyd sent for Hurtle Duffield and gave him several cuts with a stick; only pride in his tingling hand prevented him crying. Not long after that he was moved up into Lena's class, where, said Mr Boothroyd, it would take him all his time to keep up.

If it had not been for his own thoughts, and reading his grandmother's Bible at home, life in the more advanced class would have been as intolerable as it was down amongst the pothooks. At high summer, the light lay brassy on the streets. On the way to school, the balls blazed over the pawnbrokers' in Taylor Square. Returning, there was sometimes a faint tinkling of tried-out music in the piano shops of Surry Hills if he parted company from Lena and wandered round that way. He did not understand music, but the idea of it refreshed him, as the coloured notes trickled from the darkened shops into the light of day. He would arrive home pacified.

Mumma had started taking in washing again while still weak from the lying-in. She had started going down to Courtneys'; along with her bundle of necessaries, she lugged the new baby. May very kindly let her lay him in a clothes' basket in the servants' hall while she was at her work. That way she could go in and feed him when he needed to be fed. Once she stood the basket in the sun beside the cannas in Courtneys' yard, but soon took fright, thinking how Miss Rhoda's cat might jump out and eat him. She had heard of such things. For the first time the baby began to seem real. You could imagine Mrs Courtney looking in the basket when she came out to give orders to the cook. The thought made you bite the inside of your cheek.

When it was at last holidays he decided he would go down to Courtneys' whatever Mumma might say. So he fetched his cap and hung around. He was determined.

She came out carrying the baby and the bundle. "What do you think you're up to?" She stuck out her chin.

"I can help you, can't I? I can carry your things."

Mumma looked less opposed.

"If we don't make a habit of it. You could get spoiled, my boy—very easy."

As they started out he took the cloth bundle. Mumma and he were both happy, he could feel. At this hour the streets were empty except for a few tradesmen and carters. The baby had become a thing again, in spite of being known already by name. They had decided to call him Septimus.

"Sep! Septo! Septer-mus!" The morning made you sing, bumping the bundle in time against your knee; while Mumma kept looking to see whether there was any of those early lazy flies on the baby's face.

"D'you think we'll have a Decimus?"

"What's that?" she asked, suspicious.

"That means 'the Tenth.'"

She turned her face away. "If God and your father is so unkind."

After that they walked rather flat slommacky down the hill, where maids had come out from the better houses to chat together shaking dusters, or sulk alone as they polished the brass.

At one point Mumma recovered and, looking at him, said: "Your hair, your complexion's a lovely colour, Hurtle." And smiled. "My colour, when I was a girl."

He couldn't believe Mumma's lumpy old damp hair had ever been any colour at all. He couldn't believe in his own hair. But in that case, how could Mrs Courtney believe in him?

Poor Mumma, he loved her. Because her hands were holding their new baby he hung on to her skirt for a while.

It was a long morning: he couldn't decide what to do. Lizzie told Mumma: "The old cat's out to luncheon with Mrs Hollingrake." Mumma wasn't interested.

At dinner he scoffed down a big dish of mutton and gravy. And sweet potato. There was lemon sago, but by then his pins and needles wouldn't allow him to enjoy it.

After dinner Mumma sat in a corner to feed the baby, while Edith and Miss Keep ran away quick so they wouldn't see. Certainly Sep knew what he was up to, his red fingers working on the veined tittybottle, like some sort of caterpillars trying for a hold on a pale fruit.

Mumma brought the basket into the yard, into the sun. "Seeing as you're here, you can make yerself useful. You can watch your little brother." She was still afraid of Rhoda's cat.

Even if the baby got eaten he would have to see the chandelier—and Mrs Courtney Mrs Courtney.

Oh the afternoon and the splotched cannas Mr Thompson came and went smelling of old man and manure.

But the sucking sound from the green, furry door immediately swallowed up any previous distress, and he was thrown forward into their cool silent house. He ran higgledy stupid for fear he might not find her, past the chandelier without even looking up, into the mauve room. There he pulled up short. A clock was ticking in the emptiness.

It must have been his lucky day, for he began to hear the gravel, the wheels, the door opening without Edith, the stillness of the house disturbed by certain stiff sounds. Of a skirt? A swishing through their house. A sort of singing.

Then she was standing in the doorway: her hat almost reached across it, prickling and sparkling with quills.

"Why," she called, "I know you!" She laughed. "You're Hurtle Duffield."

She came on. And stooped. And kissed him. She smelled of scent, and wine, and something more. She was staring at him.

She said, like Mumma: "Your hair, your complexion's a lovely colour." She added: "Enviable."

She laughed with pleasure looking at herself in the glass. "Do you like my hat?"

"Yes."

The hat floated as he had seen the boats on water when Pa took him down to the bay.

"You're not very talkative," she said. "You must learn to pay compliments."

She didn't seem in need of them, cocking her head at her own reflection in the glass. But she left off, and went up close, and bared her teeth at it.

"It was such a very boring luncheon," she said. "I'm glad you've come to distract me, Hurtle."

Every time she said his name it bonged on his eardrums.

She was taking the pins out of her hat, taking off the hat itself, rooting in her hair where it had got squashed, stirring it up with the points of the big-knobbed hatpins.

"What's those?" he asked, wanting to touch the knobs.

"Those are turquoise." She let him hold one of the pins and look at the gold, turquoise-studded shield. "Blue's my favourite colour. It's so flattering, don't you think?"

He'd never thought about it except as a colour.

"They were given me by my husband." She spoke the word as though sucking a lolly. "For an anniversary."

When she caught him looking at her she gave a little cough, and her face came down again to cover her thoughts. Some people, particularly those in trams, didn't like you looking at them.

So he said quickly: "This room's an octagon, isn't it?"

"Fancy! How did you know?"

"It's got eight sides, hasn't it?"

Although he was distracting her as she had commanded she

seemed only vaguely interested. There was that likeness of Rhoda on her desk. There was a second photo he hadn't noticed, in a silver frame, of a gentleman with thick whiskers beginning to turn grey. He had a large, rather beefy nose.

"Is that your husband?" He touched the nose.

"Yes. It is." She sounded very kind and satisfied.

"He looks strong for a gentleman."

She gave, not a bit like her usual laugh, more of a hoot. "I'll tell him that! He'll enjoy your opinion." She had put down the hat, and came at him, her dress sounding like a scythe through grass. "I could eat you up!"

And seemed to be going to try. Bending down, she drew him against her so close, so tight, he could feel the bones in her stays, and her own soft body above. He was looking right inside the little pocket, between, where the skin was shadowy, or yellower.

She went: "Mm! Mmmm! Mphh!"

But he wasn't in the mood for kissing. "Your jewellery's pricking me," he said, and got away.

There was a book lying open on the desk, and to distract her again he read out the title: "*The Sor—rows—of—Sat—an.* Is it any good?"

"Oh, light," she answered lightly. "Very light." She closed it up and put it in a drawer. "Did that clergyman teach you to read as well?"

"I read. But I'm at school now, where they learn you to forget what you know."

"Oh, but you must have books!"

She shot at the door of Mr Courtney's study, where you were supposed never to have been before.

"Look! Books! Some of them are almost too valuable to read. But my husband might break the rule for such a studious boy. If he takes a fancy to you. We'll have to see."

There could have been a pendulum swinging inside him. He could have been standing a foot above the crimson carpet as the scent of the leather worked on him.

"What are they about?" he asked and made it sound calm.

"Voyages. Explorations. By men whose appetite for suffering wasn't satisfied at home. They had to come in search of it in Australia."

By now he could have done without her. He would have liked to be alone with his thoughts. Through the window there was a small tree whose greenish-white papery flowers were crumbling worlds of light and bees.

There was a painting, too, in a space between the bookcases.

"What's that?"

"It's a painting by a Frenchman called Boudin," she explained. "We brought it back with us from Europe."

If she hadn't been there he could have climbed up to feel the smoothness of the paint.

"It's worth a lot of money," Mrs Courtney said rather dreamily; while he was advancing, dreamier, towards the group of dressy ladies huddled halfway between the flat sea and the bathing machines.

"Do you also know French?" Mrs Courtney, he heard, was using the teasing voice grown-up people sometimes put on for children.

"I can tell when I see it," he answered. "Mr Olliphant had the French *Fables*."

"*Je t'adore, enfant ravissant!*" She made her dress swish. "You won't know that. Which is all to the good. Men grow vain far too quickly."

"I'm not so stupid I can't understand the bits that sound like English."

If it was cheek, she had other things on her mind. Again she was looking at him as though he was something to eat. Or one of the little dogs ladies kept to pet. Then, not even that: something in the distance at which she had to narrow her eyes.

"Harry," she said, "would love to teach you to ride—a sturdy boy like you."

He didn't have time to work out what she was getting at, because she asked: "Is your mother well? They tell me she's had the baby." She didn't sound all that interested, but she had been brought up to pretend to be.

"Yes," he said. "Septimus. That means 'Seventh.'"

She drew her breath in. From the looks of her, she might have begun fondling him again, only Edith came and said: "Mrs Duffield is in a state, madam, wondering where he is."

The parlourmaid was ready to share this joke with her mistress. He hated Edith.

"Then he must go at once," Mrs Courtney ordered; she had finished her game and was perhaps annoyed her maid had found her wasting her time.

"There is so much to do," she complained to no one in particular as she led the way back into the mauve octagon. "I never seem to catch up."

She sat down at her desk, scuffling the papers, looking for something she must have mislaid. Whether she had found it or not, she took up a stone pen and began dabbling in a crystal well. She didn't even say good-bye.

Edith led him stiffly through the house. The rooms through which he had sailed breathless on the outward voyage looked darker and duller in the changed light. Two of the knobs in the parlourmaid's backbone stood out between her collar and where the roots of her hair began, below the cap: they were the only points of interest on the journey back, to where Mumma was creating in the laundry.

"Hurtle, I'll never bring you—never ever again! Running off and leaving the baby! There might have been an accident." Always at the end of a washing day she had that boiled look, of suet crust.

He hadn't any excuses to make; so he went and looked in the linen basket. "Doesn't he look good!" he said, paying a compliment as Mrs Courtney had advised.

Mumma only mumbled.

Presently Edith returned with the wages. "Madam would like to see the baby. But another time. She's too busy at the moment."

Mumma didn't answer. She put the money in her old purse, which she did up in the bundle with some slices of a pudding May had allowed for the kids.

Then they picked up their things and went.

That holidays he felt even farther from Lena and the little ones. Except Will, who would burrow into his back, in their sleep, in the bed they shared in the harness-room. Will was so soft and hopeless you couldn't help feel he was your brother. Not that you were *soft*. Mrs Sullivan came and complained: *That boy that Hurt has bashed our Tommy we didn't need the stitches but nearly did.* Pa got out the strap, but put it away after Mrs Sullivan left; he said she had an Irish grudge.

Poor Pa. Wish you could have felt closer to him.

Mumma kept her word about Courtneys'.

"Aren't I gunner go down there before the holidays end?" Mumma only made sounds and went on with what she was doing.

"But didn't they ask for me?" he always asked. "Didn't *Mr* Court-ney ask yet?"

Mumma looked down her cheekbones at the ironing or the stove. So he would climb up into the pepper tree where roosting fowls had whitened the branches. He would sit rubbing off the crust, thinking. Some way some something to show Courtneys what they had forgotten. If he could show what he knew and felt. Their bloody old French painting. Sometimes he looked at his pale thing to help pass the holidays he held up the skin and it shrivelled back he didn't know what he groaned as the morning stretched out blue as turquoise smelling of chaff and fowl shit.

The term was worse, though. He could never concentrate for look-ing out of the window. Beetle Boothroyd sent a note. But it was not that which put Mumma against him. She had already turned. She would kiss him, but her breath had tears in it, waiting to break out.

What had he done, then? She couldn't know he loved Mrs Court-ney. Because he didn't. He was in love with how she looked. Each of her dresses was more than a dress: a moment of light and beauty not yet to be explained. He loved her big, silent house, in which his thoughts might grow into the shapes they chose. Nobody, not his family, not Mrs Courtney, only faintly himself, knew he had inside him his own chandelier. That was what made you at times jangle and want to explode into smithereens.

It wasn't till next holidays, it was a Courtney Monday, Mumma began combing him.

"They've asked for you," she said, "so I've got to take you, or I wouldn't."

He made himself look stupid and unmoved.

"Remember," she said, "never draw on the walls. If you spoil the Courtneys' walls like you done the ones at home, I won't know how to take their money." Pa had said Mumma was too honest.

Now you didn't answer because your heart was being sucked in and out too fast. All this combing and smoothing: was it to do with what Pa and Mumma had been talking about?

That night he had gone across the yard after everyone was put to bed, after Pa had turned out the gas in the kitchen. He had gone across to snitch a slice of bread, a smear of dripping.

Pa and Mumma were in their room, where Septimus also slept.

This was where Pa accused her of being honest, and Mumma shouted back: "What are you, Jim, if not honest? That's what I married yer for. Nothun else that I can think of."

Then she raised her voice higher still, told him not to shove her. She was crying as they got into the jingling bed. You could imagine their rough skins together.

The house was full of sleeping children. Only the bed with Mumma and Pa continued creaking, sniffling, sighing.

The dripping was the lovely brown kind.

Mumma said: "There's rats again, Jim, I swear. I seen the droppings on the scullery shelf."

Pa coughed once above the jingle jingle of the loose brass. He let Mumma do the talking.

On she went. "Jim? DidnItellyer? There's rats? We oughter lay the baits. Eh? But nothun is ever. Without I do it. With me own hand."

It was always safer to cut and run before the bedstead quietened down, but now the voices in the next room wouldn't let you go.

The bed gave one last ring, like a bicycle almost on top of you. Pa sighing. He had had a hard day's work.

"Arr dear," Mumma complained, "when it comes to pleasure, you men are all the same—the decent ones, or the ones that knock yer teeth in."

Pa was coughing up some phlegm. "Never got nothing out of it yerself?" Unusual for Pa. "Did yer? Now did yer?"

"I got seven kiddies—that the father forgets when it suits 'im to."

You could hear the toenails scraping on the sheet.

"Pity the children—what they're born to if they're out of luck! That little girl of Mrs Courtney's with the funny back, at least she'll never suffer this part."

Pa was yawning. He farted once.

"You know, Jim, I pray—every night—for a better life—for ours."

There was a rancid bit in the dripping. What if it was true what Mumma said? She had seen the droppings on the shelf.

"All the children." Mumma sounded wide awake. "Hurtle in particular."

Pa grunted.

"Hurtle's beautiful," she said. " 'Is 'air's a lovely bright."

"The boy's a boy."

"A boy can be beautiful too. To anyone with eyes. Mrs Courtney's taken with Hurtle. Says 'e's adorable. And clever. Could be some sort of genius. I could'uv told 'er that if I 'adn't been the mother. Mr Courtney will want to see 'im. You should see Mr Courtney, Jim. Every one of 'is suits made to measure in London—so the girls was telling. Boots too. 'As 'is own last—in the shop—in London."

Pa snoring.

In the end it wasn't so interesting: you got what Mrs Courtney would have called 'bored,' and the dripping lying a bit bilious.

Then Mumma said, very distinct: "I would give away any of my children, provided the opportunities was there. Blood is all very well. Money counts. I would give—I would give Hurtle."

Pa's snore came roaring back up his throat. "Give away yer children?"

Mumma laughed a rattling sort of laugh. "Plenty more where they come from."

"That's all very well for the mother. It's the father they blame. What'ud they say? Can't support 'is own kids!"

"The father!"

"Wouldn't be ethical, anyway."

"Ethical's a parsons' word."

"What if the boy could 'ear 'is mum and dad entertainin' such an idea!"

Got out after that. Sand between your toes across the yard. The little sharp scratchy pebbles. Will was flopping around in the bed like a paralysed fowl. White eyelids. Glad of your brother to stop the shivers. Mothers and fathers, whoever they were, really didn't matter: it was between you and Death or something.

And now Mumma was combing out the dandruff because Courtneys had asked for him. Well, he would swallow down what he had overheard. His bumping heart would wait and accept whatever was offered or decided.

After they had passed Taylor Square, after they had got far enough on, Mumma walked with scarcely a word. Because of their important business they had left Sep with Mrs Burt, who had her new baby, and would give theirs a suck. Mumma's black old skirt was picking up the dust very easy: the hem had become unstitched. He tried to imagine her in Mrs Courtney's hat with the quills, but the tails of her hair hung down behind, where the comb couldn't hold them up. Her skin was yellow today.

She took his hand in her cracked hand. "Come on," she said. "What are you looking at?"

He began walking as he would, he felt, in a London suit, holding hands with Mrs Courtney, and it seemed as though the maid they passed polishing a doctor's plate was already looking different at him.

Mumma brightened, though one corner of her mouth was twitching. "Are you hungry, love? You'll feel better for a bite of something."

He ought to love poor Mumma for looking at him like that. He did, too: nothing else was real. There was nothing wrong in imagining a thing or two about himself and Courtneys.

Mumma saw he was having trouble with his boot. "If your sole's coming off, Hurtle, slide your foot along the carpet when you go inside, then nobody'll notice."

Her hand tightened as they began to clatter down the steep asphalt towards the "Tradesmen's Entrance." Once or twice his sole flapped.

Half the morning he spent in the yard, chucking stones at nothing.

"What are you—you haven't *done* anything?" she called, looking out from the laundry at the bush house where Mr Thompson grew the tuberous begonias.

"Edith will fetch you," she came again to the doorway to call, the drops falling from her hands which the water had pleated.

His throat swelled. It was the strong, steamy smell of pampered plants and tanbark.

But Edith didn't show up: it was Mr Courtney himself who came walking alongside the wall, smoking a square-looking cigar. He blew out the smoke firmly but gently. The rest of him fitted the head and shoulders you had already seen in the photograph. He was a large man.

They were looking at each other. Without giving anything away. The beard was as well kept as everything else in the garden and house. You wondered how it would have felt. All along the brick wall the geranium flowers were blazing up.

"Hurtle Duffield!" Mr Courtney said, and it was like you heard your own name for the first time: it sounded so important.

While Mr Courtney continued blowing smoke, and smiling, he was in search of more to say. His cuff-links, with their tangle of initials, didn't help him. His ears had large, cushiony lobes, from one of which he hadn't wiped the shaving soap.

"My wife tells me you're interested in books and things." He put the cigar back in his mouth as though he might have said too much.

You would have liked to show you weren't just a boy, and stupid. But the silence stretched and stretched. There was an insect brown as a stick clinging to a geranium leaf. You could only stare at the insect, and wish you had something to offer. If you could at least have come to life: climbed up by Mr Courtney's trouser leg, grappling his hairy suit, pummelling, punching, not exactly kissing, but plunging your face into the mass of frizzy beard.

Instead, you were slowly sweating, as still and mindless as the stick insect.

Again Mr Courtney took the cigar out of his mouth, and put his other hand, firm but fleshy, in the middle of your back. "Perhaps you could do with a piddle," he suggested, "before we go inside. You can pop round behind the bush house."

It was a relief to slip away for a minute or two, not that you had much to get rid of, but as you shook off the last drops on the heap of rotting grass clippings, the morning loosened.

When you went back Mr Courtney told: "Round about your age I remember going on a long drive. In the country. At night. With my father and Archdeacon Rutherford." He broke up his sentence with short puffs at the cigar, his lips glossy and contented.

It was strange, though comforting, to hear Mr Courtney's smoky voice mention his father's friend by name, as though taking it for granted that you too had known Archdeacon Rutherford.

"I would have given anything to stop the buggy. But didn't know how. In front of the archdeacon. He was a very thin old man. I used to picture his guts resting flat against his backbone."

The smoke from the cigar made the remembered scene look more dreamlike.

"I could have burst," Mr Courtney said, "I wanted so badly to pump ship."

You sniggered a bit to show you sympathized. But he didn't seem to care. He was looking inward at himself trying not to burst in the buggy at night. You had never seen an archdeacon but could imagine the old man's cold-looking hands.

As they came round the corner of the house, away from that part of it where maids' voices were clanging, the lawn stretched plunging in front of them, with the clump of tall palms, pigeons rising blue as cigar smoke, and Mrs Courtney coming towards them holding a sunshade over her head.

They seemed to have surprised her.

"What have you two been up to?" she asked, laughing.

"Having a talk," Mr Courtney said, then drew hard on his cigar.

The green lining of Mrs Courtney's sunshade flooded her skin with leafy light. You could have gone on staring up at her. From beneath the sunshade her blue eyes were less evident, although you felt they were poking around.

Suddenly she altered the angle of the sunshade and started addressing, not her husband, but her morning caller Hurtle Duffield. "I can only apologize for the roses," she said with some force. "The whole lot should be pulled out. They're miserable—*miserable*. If only I had time to see to everything. But I haven't."

As a visitor, you felt you ought to ask: "Doesn't Mr Thompson?"

"Oh *Thompson*! He has his own ideas."

Then Mrs Courtney, as though she had done her duty, and to do more would have been boring for everybody, took her husband by the arm, inclining towards him from out of the sunshade. The tips of her teeth showed transparent. Although there was someone else present, it didn't prevent her giving her husband a deep look. Her friend the boy was too young to need excluding.

At last it seemed perfectly natural to grab Mr Courtney's other sleeve, and he didn't try to prevent it. The sleeve you were hanging on by was very dry, coarse and shaggy, but new and rich, and as you walked, or occasionally hopped, or kicked out at the terra-cotta tiles edging a flower bed, till you remembered the loose sole, the Courtneys were strolling in step with each other, discussing some flat, unimportant matter. The three of them together were like a family.

So they went into the house, into the room with the books, which was referred to as "the Study." Edith, all lowered eyelids and knowing smiles, brought a silver tray with morning tea and extra-dainty, oozing scones.

As soon as you had licked the last of the butter off your fingers Mr Courtney got down to business.

"Let's see how he can read."

He was anxious to confirm what he had been told about the laundress's boy. His clean, rather hairy hands were grasping for a book. Sitting upright, waiting to perform, you might have been wearing the paper frill you had seen round the monkey's neck.

Mr Courtney dragged out the book he had been looking for; he opened it and said: "Now, Hurtle!"

The mottled pages of the damp old book made you feel something like religious. The Courtneys, waiting, looked religious, too: they could have been expecting to hear something they had never heard before, as you lowered your head and read from where your eyes picked up the print.

"This afternoon a little hawk came aboard and one of the men caught it, found it belonged to somebody on board the *Scarborough* who had let it fly away for its dirtyness, the man that caught it let it fly away again, and the poor little thing, in endeavouring to reach the *Alexander*, it fell in the water. I suppose it was drowned—"

There was an interruption from Mrs Courtney, who had begun to gasp and make sucking noises with her tongue. "Really, Harry," she said very loud, "what a piece to try him out on!"

"That's where the book opened, Birdie—by pure accident," Mr Courtney answered; the pet name seemed to make things worse.

She sat looking down at her locked hands, then up at the ceiling, the way Mumma did when trying not to cough in church.

Mr Courtney stirred up the pages of the book. "There! Try again. I'm surprised at the way you read." And again you felt the firm but fleshy hand encouraging the middle of your back.

Birdie said nothing. The mood of religiousness had passed. Although the Courtneys were so well dressed, you could imagine them, like Mumma and Pa, without their clothes, talking it over on the rattling bed.

They were waiting for you to read, though. Or at least Mr Courtney was. He wore a smile as he trimmed a fresh cigar.

So you read the words you found:

"Captain Walton has given me a puppy, have called it—Efford . . . ? after the dear sweet place where first I came acquainted with my Alicia, my virtuous wife. Captain Meredith ordered one of the corporals to flog with a rope Elizabeth Dudgeon for being impertinent to Captain Meredith, the corporal did not play with her, but laid it home, which I was very glad to see,

GARDNER WEBB COLLEGE LIBRARY

49

then ordered her to be tied to the pump, she had been long fishing for it, which she has at last got, until her heart's content—"

"Oh, this is too much!"

Though you realized Mrs Courtney was fidgeting all through this second bit, you didn't leave off till she called out. She had jumped up and was looking feverish and beautiful. Perhaps it was her anger which prevented the tears from spilling.

"Sorry, Alfreda," Mr Courtney apologized jokingly. "An accident again! We're magnets for the worst parts."

"Books don't open by accident," Mrs Courtney said. "They open where they've been read most. I'll never forgive myself," she continued very quickly, "if we've damaged this poor innocent—by accident."

At this moment you could have truthfully fallen in love with Alfreda Courtney, though you didn't need her pity. Grown-up people were more innocent than they thought themselves.

"Half of cruelty," she was telling herself, "is thoughtless."

He tingled wonderfully as she ruffled his hair, till he realized she might have been stroking air, her eyes vague with other thoughts.

Suddenly she compressed her lips and announced: "I must find Rhoda."

That made Mr Courtney angry. "Jove's sake, she isn't lost—or not yet! She's out with Nurse."

But Mrs Courtney was already fussing across the room, her clothes creating their particular sound and scent. You could only hate the hump-backed girl who was taking her mother away from you.

Mrs Courtney was breathing hard. "Nurse, indeed! Dorrie Fox has told me about a young person—a governess—of respectable family—who is most unhappy—lonely—with some horrid people at Muswellbrook. This Miss Gibbons could be the answer," Mrs Courtney decided as she floated out.

Mr Courtney was much angrier by now, but smiled at you through his beard. "The damn book," he said and shoved it back hard in its place on the shelf.

You remembered: "I was flogged once at school, but not as bad as that."

Mr Courtney was interested. "What did you do to earn it?"

Because you didn't want to tell you tried to look sort of frightened.

Mr Courtney put an arm around your shoulders. "I've got something to show you."

"What?"

If your voice didn't sound interested, it was because, on turning your cheek, partly to avoid the pricking of the hairy coat sleeve, you saw on Mr Courtney's little finger, a ring. It was of the same kind as the family ring Pa kept in the cigar box. So you had this in common. You couldn't have told Mr Courtney, because he wouldn't have believed. You rubbed your cheek instead, just a little, against the coat, because you had been brought that much closer. You could fall in love with both the Courtneys.

Mr Courtney was explaining: "Something that might interest you, Hurtle. See if I can find it."

Hurtle was now alone, and glad. He couldn't understand all that about loneliness and the governess at Muswellbrook. He had wanted to be alone more than anything so that he could explore the Frenchman's oil painting. So he got a chair, and stood on it. His heart was knocking, more than it had for Mrs Courtney. To touch the smooth, touchable paint.

By reaching up, his fingers slithered over the ladies' full, old-fashioned skirts, trembled on the bathing machines, and plunged towards the sea. He was sweating as his fingers arrived at the wet sand and pale water. He would have liked to lick the tempting paint, but the picture was hung beyond reach of his tongue. He could only stand on the leather-bottomed chair pulling his tongue in and out in an imitation of licking.

He heard a tittering behind his back. He turned round. He must certainly have looked a fool.

Her thin mouth was twitching and spitting as she laughed: her hair pink rather than red. She had that little, thin flower-stalk of a neck, its absolute whiteness becoming greenish where the shadow fell, and all over, a sprinkling of tiny moles, with the big birthmark the colour of milk chocolate on one side. He couldn't see the hump as he remembered: it was turned from him. She looked only a sickly girl, probably not much younger than himself. The worst part was: she had seen him giving himself away in front of the painting.

If she had been a girl at school he would have shown her a good smack in the face, but in the Courtneys' house, he sensed, you fought with words and moods. Because his instincts for this weren't yet strong enough, he was still at a serious disadvantage as Rhoda went *hee-hee-hee*, and rocked on the toes of her little thin-skinned pumps.

She stopped laughing. "I knew you were coming today."

"How?"

"They were getting ready for you."

"Why?"

"Because you're a boy. And Mummy thinks you're so delightful. You can read better for your age than most grown-up educated people. You're a prodigy. Mummy wants to discover a genius."

Rhoda tried to make all her accusations sting, and did. "Your mother is the laundress. That makes you all the more of a genius." She almost hiccupped with success.

She made him feel sick sad. Worse still, as he was putting back the chair in the place from which it had come, the loose sole of his boot doubled up between his foot and the carpet, and she noticed him stumble.

"Fancy letting you go out in a pair of boots that need mending!"

She made him remember that his clothes were darned, and that he had a patch on the seat of his pants. But he was stronger than Rhoda Humpback Courtney. He was the stronger by his mother's tubs of blued water and her mauve, white-crinkled hands.

"You're a little turd," he said.

She couldn't think of better than that: she could only come very close to him, her small face swelling with hate.

"Does your mother like you?" he asked as coldly as he was able.

"Of course she does!" she said with a grand conviction; but added in her own voice: "She whipped me with the riding crop. With the bone handle."

"What for?"

"Because I didn't lie on the board. Dr Marshall says it's going to improve my back. But I can't lie there all the time."

They were united for a moment by truth and silence. Outside the big windows the blue bay curved, the big soot-dark trees were pressing in on them. He would have liked to draw Rhoda. He knew how he would paint her, if only he had the paints. He could feel in his fingers the sticky pink which would convey her frizzed-out, girl's hair.

But Mr Courtney came back with a little gun. It was brand-new, you could see. A toy, or a boy's gun. Inside his beard and English suit, Mr Courtney—Harry—was acting as excited as a boy who had found it.

"Jove, Hurtle," he said, "isn't it a beauty?"

Rhoda turned away, prepared for them to ignore her. She didn't look at all put out, as though she wasn't interested in boys or guns, and knew she could get her own back any time she liked.

Because it was expected of him, Hurtle followed out to the edge of the lawn. He was still too close to the painting to share Harry's enthusiasm for a gun, neat and shining though it was.

As you watched, Harry loaded. There was a pigeon clattering out of a palm. Harry took aim, his shoulder muscle bulging out of proportion. He shot at the curving pigeon, and missed.

"Need to practise," he mumbled into his beard, working his shoulders as though to shrug out the rheumatism. Then remembering, he looked down: "You'll soon get the hang of it. In a paddock full of rabbits, you can't miss."

"There aren't any paddocks full of rabbits."

"Not here. At Mumbelong." Mr Courtney's voice had descended to a man's serious level; his eyes, too, were serious and moist.

Hurtle stood kicking with his sound boot at the springy mattress of lawn. He had blown his cheeks out to match Mr Courtney's seriousness. He wasn't going to destroy a vision by introducing anything real. He wouldn't say a word, because he knew from experience that impossibilities can be enjoyed in spite of their impossibility. So they were catching the night train, like the time Mumma left in a hurry to visit someone sick. Tunnels couldn't get blacker at night. He sat beside his friend, sharing his overcoat.

"Harry?"

Mrs Courtney's voice, trying to be natural, sounded coldly from the veranda; it sounded more educated than ever yet. Even Mr Courtney was startled. Rhoda had come out from the study to be with her mother because she expected something to happen.

Mrs Courtney was staring at the gun. Anger had enamelled her eyes. She could have been going to rush out, not at all ladylike, and grab the thing, and break it in half; when she changed her mind apparently. She started twiddling a little useless handkerchief. The blazing blue died out in her eyes: in their new misty thoughtfulness they looked almost grey. Although they were still fixed on the gun, she was thinking beyond: she seemed to have decided the gun didn't exist.

"Darling," she began, and lowered her eyelids a moment to show how seriously she ought to be taken, "we must remember he doesn't belong to us. Mrs Duffield will start worrying about him." She had such a soft pink smile.

"Mrs Duffield? Oh yes, the mother," Mr Courtney remembered in a hurried, grumpy voice.

They all bundled into the study, where only Mrs Courtney could have told what was in store for them.

She glanced once at the gun after Harry had stood it in a corner. Then she opened out in a high clear voice which reminded you of the voices of the older girls, its tone much more expert though, her clothes so much more complicated, and she chose to speak in a code he recognized by now as the French language.

"Il est intelligent, n'est-ce pas? Charmant! Il parle avec un accent atroce, mais on peut le corriger à la maison—lui tout seul avec cette gouvernante que je vais engager—et la petite, naturellement."

Possibly Mr Courtney was less good at French. He went: *Wee wee wee*; while Mrs Courtney laughed such glossy laughs, she was so pleased the way things were going. Because you had no difficulty in cracking some of the code your eardrums thundered to hear about your atrocious accent. It was no compensation to discover you were also intelligent and charming. In future he would talk extra book-ish at them, imitating Mr Olliphant, just as Mrs Courtney was imitating the French.

He heard Rhoda joining in. "It's always *la petite*! What about *la petite*?" The sprinkling of moles on her neck showed up like shot when rage or injustice made her pale, while the big leaf-shaped birthmark seemed to flutter.

"Take him, Rhoda, to the laundry," her mother ordered, trying to push them together.

But *la petite* had got the sulks. She wouldn't, and he was glad: it would have been humiliating to pretend you needed the sour ugly thing.

Finally it was Mrs Courtney herself who accompanied him, at least as far as the green door. There she stopped, and as she kissed him he seemed to be swallowed up in an envelope of scented flesh. He was only brought round by her jewellery pricking and hitting him.

"We shall meet again," she said.

"When?"

"Very soon, I hope. We must organize it!"

Then the green door puffed open, and he smelled the smells of ordinary life.

The following day, ironing day at Sunningdale, he was again ready to leave with Mumma although she had paid no attention to his hair.

"Oh no. Not on yer life. A treat is a treat," she said. "I don't know what the Courtneys would think."

"But they're interested in me. I know they'll be expecting me."

Mumma looked so ugly in her old braided shapeless black. She smelled of soap and beeswax. She said he was suffering from what was called delusions. He knew he would never make her see the truth.

When next Monday came round, it was his last chance before school began. So he grew cunning. He didn't take extra trouble with himself, not because he hadn't hope, it was because he might catch her off her guard, at the last moment slip past her opposition with rough haste and in his ordinary clothes. He was, in fact, full of hope. In his mind he revived the words and silences of Mumma's own hopes for him. His memory glittered with the moods of Courtneys' chandelier.

That morning, after the others had run off, he sat dawdling over the last grey slime of his porridge. She was preparing her bundle, with a few of those cachous, the headache powders, the old leather purse, odds and ends she would take with her and never use.

When he couldn't put it off any longer he said: "I bet they asked for me yesterday, and you didn't tell."

She laughed in an ugly way he didn't recognize. "Why should they ask?"

"Because they told me of things we was gunner do together." There was no use wasting grammar or accents on Mumma: you had to speak the way she understood.

"Oh," she said, "ladies and gentlemen *talk*! It's what they call 'being charming.' But what they say isn't what they mean. Otherwise they wouldn't get through all they've got to do—balls, and dinner parties, and all that. I *know*!"

"But Mr Courtney showed me a gun. We was going to the country."

"I believe 'e's gone—to one of the properties 'e owns. That's where 'is interests lie—where the money comes from. A little boy like you would only get in the way."

She picked the baby up, and began easing up the bundle with the help of her knee. When she was ready, she stooped and kissed you to show her love, but it was a level helping, like she doled out porridge or potato, to keep everybody quiet. If ladies and gentlemen didn't mean what they said, no more did Mumma.

"Oh, whoo-aahy?" he shouted after her when she had gone out the gate.

It sounded as feeble as it was, his voice whining back like that of a little blubbering kid. He couldn't have done better, though.

She went on, sometimes pausing to ease the baby's weight. Sep was growing too fast, too heavy, too greedy: the way he would grab hold of her by now she might have been a pudding he meant to guzzle whole.

Mumma didn't look back from the bottom of the street, only paused to hoist the baby higher.

Then the grey descended inside you.

He wished Mumma and the baby dead. Them all. *Courtneys!* Himself—himself most of all. The chandelier had gone out in him.

The day, beginning grey, spurted a drop or two, sprinkled at last, and settled into an afternoon of colourless rain. In all the time he had to spend there was nothing he could do, except remember the all-over grey street, with himself and Mumma a black stroke at either end: nothing between, unless he could have put a spitting bonfire. He imagined the yard at Sunningdale, with Mumma bringing in the wetter sheets, wet clothes lashing from the lines, looking naked. When she couldn't get the wash dried on the day when it ought to have been dried, Mumma would start crying and creating; she had to take the headache powders.

During the afternoon he snivelled a bit in sympathy, but broke off on remembering what he thought of her.

Something was blowing up: the big clouds were piling up like dirty washing. It was going to be a wicked evening, Mrs Burt called over the fence: a gentleman driving through Newtown had seen a roof carried away. Because Mumma was still at work, and Pa out with the cart, collecting, it made the kids feel important, if frightened. Only he didn't feel frightened: he wrote his name on the wall of the front room.

Pa came in at last, as the clouds, bulging worse, began to purple. There were green, bruised colours in the sky, then veins of white lightning. You pressed your mouth against the windows, first one, then another, drinking in the storm.

Some of them began to cry because Mumma was lost in it. And the house smelled cold. It smelled of cold ash. And dark. Somebody should have lit the gas. Pa wouldn't: he used to say it was the woman's job. Lena didn't, because she felt miserable: she had a cold and a gumboil. And you wouldn't, for watching the storm, from purple, to green, then the white veins like in yellow skin. Once or twice, in a white flash, the roofs of Cox Street seemed to billow up. Now he knew what Mumma felt with a red baby screwing its way out of her guts.

She came in through a burst of thunder, protecting Sep, whose head was bouncing against her shoulder. Mr Courtney—so he was there, he hadn't gone to the country—had ordered Rowley to harness the horses and drive her home. She was wet, even so.

"Has no one not even lit the bally gas?" Mumma shrieked.

The darkness was whirling with heavy shapes.

"Jim? Lena?"

Pa's hand let the gas flare blue, before it grew white and steady in the mantle.

They got the stove going. It roared too fierce, till Mumma damped it down.

"Well, I'd like to know!" she complained. "And where is Hurtle?"

Lena was sour because she had been told to change the nappy. "In the shed droring," she said.

"No, I'm not. I'm here."

"Well, if you're here," Mumma said, "you're the most unreliable of all."

She was that unjust, but had to make a quick stew: of a little scrag, and plenty of potato; the mildew had got into the carrot.

As she scuffled in the pan she began a dry snivelling, and this was worse than her anger.

Pa asked: "What's got inter yer, Bessie?"

"Lord knows how I'll dry the wash down there."

At one point she had a proper cry, but settled down after tea to Mrs Ebsworth's ironing. The storm had passed. It was a quiet night, except for claws of rain scratching from time to time at the roof. Although you went back to the kitchen after the light was out, to hear what Courtneys had really said, Mumma and Pa weren't talking tonight. There was only a short, wordless jingling of the bed.

The sky was a watery white by morning. It wasn't raining, but it hadn't stopped, and Mumma, mumbling as if she had a mouthful of pegs, said she wasn't going down there: nothing to iron, because nothing dry.

"Lucky school hasn't commenced." She used the word "commenced" instead of "begun" because of her respect for education. "Yer boots wouldn't stand the weather. Now stay inside, all of yez. I don't want any chesty children."

After the dishes were washed, and Florrie and Winnie helped on the dunny, Mumma herself went across the yard. Under the pepper tree Pa was harnessing the mare. He was wearing a bag across his shoulders, fastened in front with a new nail. The water was dripping from the brim of his hat. The pepper tree dripped.

For some reason, Mumma wanted Pa inside the harness-room.

"Where are you going, Hurt?" bossy Lena had to call.

"I forgot me pencil. I gotter get me pencil."

He ran across the yard. Hens didn't seem to mind rain once it got under their feathers. As he charged amongst them, two or three of their sodden bundles crouched low, combs flopping, prepared to be trod.

He got inside the dark stable. Hay and manure made it warm, safe, except the smell of ammonia shot up his nostrils; the shock of it started him shivering.

Through the door into the harness-room he could see Mumma already having something out with Pa.

"*What* about Hurtle?" Pa didn't want to know.

"What we discussed."

Mumma was making the bed he shared with Will, or at least she was pulling up the horse-rug they used as a cover.

Pa was making out he didn't understand.

"You know! Oh, you know all right!" Mumma was acting as rough as she could, drawing down her mouth and hawking up the words so that she was no longer Mumma, but one of the women outside a public house. "About Hurtle's future. Oh, you know all right!"

She left off shouting and began staring at the wall. It was the wall where you had drawn the chandelier. You had never been able to rub it out, to make room for other things; it was still there, though grubbier. You had drawn over it what Mumma called "the Mad

Eye." And now you were staring at each other, eye to eye, through the stable door, only Mumma couldn't see; she was looking frightened and again like Mumma.

Pa was walking up and down, a scrawny cock, in the wet old sack nailed to his chest. "I dunno, Bessie! I dunno what's got inter yer!" he stuttered back.

When Mumma fished inside her front and brought out a piece of paper. "Mr Courtney give me a cheque for five hundred pound."

Again she hawked the words up rough, so that the shock wouldn't be too much to bear. If it had been sovereigns she might have chucked them on the floor, and they could have scrambled for them, testing the coins with their teeth, feeling the splinters in their knees.

But here she had only the damp piece of paper to dangle under Pa's nose.

"You're a bloody cow! A bloody mother!" He might have been going to call her worse, because his usually hollow chest was filled, but he must have remembered he was the father.

"But what are they gunner say?" He couldn't stop trembling; he couldn't stop looking at the cheque: it might have been a forgery.

He hollered: "*No!*" once—before putting the cheque in his pocket, an inside pocket.

Pa said: "Some of you women never stop to think a man's responsible for his children."

Then Mumma let fly, enough to blast the harness-room walls: "Oh, the father! The father's right enough—to get on top—flick flick—then when 'e's ironed you out, off 'e gets, and there isn't no more to it, till the congratulations are 'anded out. The father! Does the father know what it is to be a walkin' pumpkin most of every year? Was 'e ever bloodied, except when 'e cuts 'imself with the razor? Not Dad! Who wipes their little bottoms? Who wipes away the snot? And bears with the bellyaches? I reckon it's the mother who has the right to decide what is right an' reasonable for 'er children. That is why I decided what is right for Hurt."

His name had never sounded so extraordinary as it glugged up through her loose shammy-leather throat.

"Jim?"

Because Pa had had enough, he was going out.

"Eh, Jim?"

Pa, who had always been a thin man, seemed to have grown

thinner; while Mumma stayed big and flabby even when there wasn't a baby in her.

"Only reasonable," she called to his back, rounding out the word. "Jim? I think I copped another one already." Then as Pa unchained the wheel of his cart: "I know I 'ave!"

Jim went off snivelling mumbling about his business, leading Bonnie; the rain had turned the brown mare practically black.

Mumma lowered her head against the rain, or the eyes of children burrowing in, as she went back across the yard.

Round about five the mare came dawdling down Cox Street. Unaccompanied, reins trailing, she was able to roam from side to side, pulling at the weeds and blades of pale grass which showed through the mud at the edges, or leaves over a garden fence. There was a fair few empties in the cart, though not what you would call a load, so that they slid and clashed, at times almost chimed. The mare knew her way, and was taking it easy, till a gatepost braked one of the wheels as she turned in at her home yard, and gave her a scare.

Some of the kids got windy seeing the pink insides of her nostrils as she threw her head up: to hear her whinge as though someone had jabbed her with a knee in her belly.

Mumma ran out. She didn't appear frightened. Perhaps she had already been through the worst. The rain had plastered her hair, and was showing up her body. It made her look younger. Serious, though. She had to remain active: too much depended on her. She grabbed Bonnie by the wet mane, then the headstall. At once the beast stopped prancing on her heavy legs, and tossing her head. She seemed relieved to find her freedom ended.

"'Ere! Youse! Hurtle! Lena!" Mrs Duffield strained her voice, trying to make it sound like a man's, because that way she would be obeyed.

They came scuttling. They were all three unbuckling. The familiar sound comforted: of cold chains swinging and clinking.

He was surprised to find how quick and skilful he was with the stiff buckles and rain-sodden leather. He would have loved to linger over jobs he usually avoided.

While Lena began a girl's thin moan: "What's happened to Pa?"

It was lucky Mrs Duffield didn't have to answer. Mrs Burt stuck

her head over the palings, wearing a bag and her husband's hat.
" 'E's up at the corner, Lene, dear—Mrs Duffield—with three or four
other gentlemen. I'd say 'e'll be back as soon as they put 'im out."
Mrs Burt might have been going to say "throw."

Usually the neighbour was on for a laugh at human nature. But
this evening her big face was solemn. She was heavy with rain and
sympathy. She knew too much.

"Leave the bottles for yer father," Mumma decided. "Pa 'ull un-
load the bottles."

Mrs Burt might have been tittering, only then, the other side of
the palings, or it could have been the sound of mild rain on iron.

Jim Duffield who never touched a drop came home after most of
them had put themselves to bed. She had kept his tea, if not hot,
not cold neither. He wasn't real shickered, she was glad to see.
Though bad enough. He was black-wet, and muddy up the legs,
soles squelching.

"Take yer boots off, Jim." She tried to make it sound like an order.

With no experience of drunkenness she didn't know what line to
take.

He sat down in his wet old boots and ate a little of the potato.
Very dainty. Looking at it along his nose.

Then she asked: "D'you think you've got enough, dear? There
wasn't that much meat, and it seems to 'uv melted on the bones."
She had never been good at soft voices, but tried.

He stopped eating. He felt his pockets, and began slowly dragging out the money he had shoved into them. He seemed full of
it: the Courtneys' money. It fell, or fluttered, onto the table. It lay
singly, buckled up, or in wads. Some of it landed in the plateful of
cold stew.

It was so quiet after the rain they might have dropped to you
looking at them from behind the lace in the outer kitchen.

Pa was picking one of the notes out of the gravy. He began
wiping the grease off. With one finger. Looking at the finger, at the
note. Like a person without their spectacles.

"Plenty of money!" He cocked his head at it. "Couldn't persuade
enough of 'em to drink it up. There was one or two paralytics, of
course. An' Josh Porter an' Horrie Jackson. You know about Josh
and Horrie?"

"Yes."

He knew she knew, but that was beside the point.

"Josh and Horrie are 'in' more often than they're 'out.'" He meant to draw it out slow. "Josh, they say, did in old Mrs McCarthy. But they'll never prove it—so they say."

She stood looking down at the money.

He stirred it up. "No money's too black to buy grog for lags."

He began hitting at the money, which made some of it fly up. She was forced to chase after it, clapping with her hands at the mould-coloured butterflies, herself sometimes drunkenly smiling, as she fell on her knees to grab at the money; when she should have stood, straight and solid, wife and mother.

"But we did it for the best!" She repeated a lesson they must have taught her in Mrs Courtney's pretty room.

"We sold 'im like a horse!" Although Pa included himself in the deal, she began to receive the blows with which he was punishing the money.

He was hitting out at her, not punching, didn't seem able to close his fists, but thwack thwack with straight arms. As she knelt on the floor they thumped against her neck, her head; while she raked in the fallen money, smiling with white lips, like a guilty girl who has to hide a lie, or a belly.

"We did it for love!" Her blubbering lips were having difficulty with the words.

"Or money!" He belted it out.

That finished them both: instead of the money, they began catching at each other, sobbing, rummaging in each other's clothes and hair, as if they were only now finding out about each other.

The bedstead might have disjointed itself, to which they had staggered out, but together.

When the brass had come to a standstill, Mumma was left drysighing. "Good job the children was asleep."

Pa didn't answer.

Mumma said: "Better shut yer mouth, Jim. Otherwise you might wake up and find a nasty taste."

She came out after that, back into the kitchen, herself and her other half: her belly. Her feet slopping. Her hair looked undone of itself. She was so tired she could scarcely have clapped her hands at a rat.

There was the money, though. The crumpled stuff she began smoothing out. Some of it had been damaged, but Mumma was a great one for mending things with glue.

All the money she put in a rusty tin she had kept for some future purpose. The hard wads of unseparated notes thudded into the old tin. Then she shoved it on a high shelf, where nothing could get at it, except only fire or a thunderbolt.

The room had never seemed so full of children, some of them still playing, others fallen in a heap of sleep. Somebody crunched across the pegs one of them had scattered. Pa half spoke the sum he was doing with a pencil, on a piece of crumpled paper, on his knee; while Mumma kept time with her head as she ironed other people's washed clothes, smoothing, sometimes stamping with the iron. The wedding ring was broad and brassy on Mumma's pudding-coloured finger. As she tried out a fresh iron, holding it some way off her cheek, she could have loved what she mistrusted.

This was his family. He should have loved them. He did of course: riding with Pa on the cartload of slippery bottles; Mumma's smell of warm ironing; the exasperating hands of younger, sticky children; in bed with Will; Lena giving him a suck of a bull's-eye, hot and wet from her own mouth. All this was family, a terrible muddle, which he loved, but should have loved better. Perhaps he was "too proud," as Beetle Boothroyd wrote in one of those notes. Didn't love *himself*, though. No. If he loved something he had inside him, that was different.

He wasn't going to cry, in spite of nearly pissing himself with fright at times. Courtneys were sending for him in the morning. He would show that Edith he hadn't been bought. But how would he wake up the morning after, looking at what sort of empty wall?

So he was frightened.

Mumma stamped with the iron. "Nuisances of frilly things! I'd never ever go in for frills, not if I was the nobbiest of nobs."

Then Lena, who looked as if she had a fever, she was so determined to appear awake—Lena asked: "Won't he ever come back to see us?"

It was such a loaded question, Mumma for once left Pa to answer.

"Not in the contract," he mumbled on his bit of pencil; since the evening he got shickered Pa was an even quieter man.

When somebody, it must have been Will, started a long, high moan. Several others joined in, like dogs.

" 'Ere! It's time you was in bed, all you kids!" Mumma had stamped with the iron on the stand, and at once she and Lena were pummelling, pushing, carrying out the younger children.

Because you weren't young, you hung around, but there wasn't anything to say to Pa.

When Mumma came back she took a fresh iron from the stove, and began to press with all her weight along a seam. Perhaps she hadn't noticed him. Or perhaps it was her way of making him hang around: soon she would say something which would explain all of everything forever.

Then she said: "Didn't you *hear*—Hurtle? Or does your ears want washin' out?" She stamped the iron extra hard.

Was she going to kiss him? She wasn't. He must have "bloodied" her worse than any of the others; or she could still smell the bottom she had wiped. She continued ironing, smoothing softer, afraid she might singe somebody's good clothes.

So he held it tight in his throat, and went.

It was a white night. All their hens were drooping white along the boughs, the boughs whitened by shit and light. Through the shit smells, musty of hen, moist-sweet of horse, he went inside the shed, Bonnie lifting a velvet lip, whinnying and shifting weight.

He burned his fingers lighting their candle. Sleep had flattened Will, white too, like uncooked dough, but the yellow light fell across the cracked plaster of the wall, from which you had never succeeded in rubbing the more private thoughts, or "drorings," or in making room for more. There would never be room enough for everything.

Now he stood for a while drawing on the patch of candlelight, himself only flickering at first, then more dreamily flowing, his head at the angle from which he saw and thought best. He was drawing Mumma's hollow body, with the new baby sprouting in it like one of the Chinese beans the Chow had given them at Christmas. Over all the chandelier. The Eye too: what Mumma called "the Mad Eye—it looks right through you." Aiming its arrows, the bow-shaped eye was at the same time the target, or bull's-eye.

There was so much, everything you knew, to include.

When Will began to stir to plop awake. "What you doing, Hurt?"

At least you didn't ever need to try explaining to Will: perhaps that was how Mumma had felt just now.

Well, there was drawing. He made a dash or two at Mrs Birdie Courtney's chandelier that wasn't between hollowing out Mumma's body he would have liked to creep inside to sleep tighter in warm wet love and white drool of hens if she would have opened to him she wouldn't.

2

The morning was a sparkling one. The varnished woodwork of the buggy in which he sat showed him how far from best his best clothes looked. Not that he was worried by it. Mr Courtney seemed far more worried.

Though they had announced in the beginning: "We shall send for the little boy on Friday," Mr Courtney himself had come, and alone. He was wearing a tweed cap, and a suit which looked new but probably wasn't.

As they drove away, down the rutted street, against the glare, Mr Courtney asked: "Would you like to take the reins, old man?"

Remembering another occasion when he had refused, Hurtle said he wouldn't.

His last sight of the faces at the gate had been so painful he decided to shut it out of his mind, to keep his own misery at the greatest possible distance. It was easier in the glittering present. The wheels of the varnished buggy were thrashing into the light, the horse's tail swished with light, while Mr Courtney's frizzy beard smelled as good as it shone.

They went a while in silence through the Surry Hills.

Hurtle pointed. "Those are the piano shops."

Mr Courtney replied: "Oh?"

There was no music at that hour.

When they got to Taylor Square there were the pawnbrokers'.

Hurtle said: "Once or twice my father had to take the ring to one of those shops. But he always got it back."

Mr Courtney was surprised, or shocked. "A ring, you say?" He tried not to sound inquisitive.

Then Hurtle took out the paper in which the ring was wrapped. "This is my family's ring. My father gave it to me when I left. He said I ought to have it."

Mr Courtney looked more than ever puzzled and shocked though he, too, was wearing a ring. After taking a look, he seemed to turn away slightly. He gave the horse a cut with the whip it didn't deserve, while the ring was being wrapped again.

Mr Courtney said, in what began as a mumble: "I hope you'll be happy with us—Hurtle—feel you're one of the family." He cleared his throat, and added for value: "We're a very happy family."

They were plunging down towards Rushcutters, into the richer streets. The horse's hoofs clopped faster on its own ground. Mr Courtney and Hurtle were bounced against each other, an experience each seemed to enjoy.

Mr Courtney was grinning as he put on the brake. "I hope you'll call me 'Father,'" he said.

The brake restored a certain stiffness.

"That's what your mother would like," Mr Courtney said, as if he felt in need of support.

Hurtle was not yet ready to commit himself: it was too funny and strange, and desirable, or sad.

They drove in through the stone gateway, over the raked gravel, past the clipped privets and a bunya-bunya the gardener had failed to tidy. It was his first experience of Courtneys' front entrance. Mr Thompson came round to carry the box Mumma had found for his few things. The box was a dusty green from lying under a bed at Cox Street, with straps so stiff they would hardly buckle. On seeing the box Mr Thompson looked surlier than ever.

Then Edith came, her thin neck dull and yellow inside the starched collar. She put on a look as though you and your things would probably need fumigating. He hated Edith. He must think of a way of showing her.

Inside the porch he might have started crying if it hadn't been for Mr Courtney's hand on his shoulder-blades. The hand made you want to giggle instead, because you could feel the guiding hand, strong and hairy as you remembered, gently trembling, as though Mr Courtney himself was frightened. If you didn't laugh, it was because you owed it to decent old Harry Courtney not to.

Mrs Courtney came and kissed. It was not as good a kiss as usual, less scented, too bumpy, nervous or apologetic like Mr Courtney's hand.

At once she suggested: "Come and we'll look at your room."

Mr Thompson had gone ahead carrying the box on his shoulder. The shirt, rucked up under his braces, looked rather dirty for so grand a house. Mr Courtney, your father who wasn't, slipped away as though he really was.

The room to which Mrs Courtney led, if not exactly large, was very large for one person. The walls, so solid, so white and untouched, had something suspicious-looking about them.

"What on earth are you doing?" she asked.

"Feeling the walls." If he had been free he would have liked to cover them with great curves of bird-flight.

"What an idea!"

She began to laugh as though she wouldn't get over it, staring at him in such a way he felt he must be looking very odd, in this foreign room which would never be his.

At home in Cox Street there was too much noise, too many children, for anyone to try guessing at your private thoughts. If he spoke to Mrs Courtney now, it was only to protect these thoughts. "Who is that?" he asked, though he wasn't particularly interested in knowing.

"That is the portrait of an officer who came here, I believe, with the First Fleet."

"Was he a relative?"

"Oh no," she said, and then more vaguely, sighingly: "No."

Almost at once she changed her tune and asked lightly, prettily: "I hope the room's masculine enough?"

She was moving a little jug full of flowers backwards and forwards on the chest of drawers. The reflection on the polished surface of the chest was a bright ball following the little silvery jug.

"What is it?" he asked, fascinated by the jug.

"Silver lustre. It's rather rare and valuable, so you mustn't be rough with it. I'm only leaving it here because I want you to like beautiful things."

The skin round her eyes was darker than he had noticed it before, her smile more wrinkled, because of course she was old, as well as rare and valuable.

"You're not very talkative today," she complained. She was looking at herself in the mirror, making a mouth like a pullet's arse the moment before it drops the egg.

If he was not talkative it was because she asked things he felt stupid in answering.

"Now I expect you'd like to unpack your belongings, while I have one or two duties to attend to." She rattled away very smoothly, and he wasn't convinced by any of it. "Then we must show you the nursery, and the schoolroom where Miss Gibbons will give you your lessons—you and Rhoda."

She patted him before she left, and he could tell that, now she had got him, she didn't know what to do with him, but hoped the nursery, the schoolroom, and Miss Gibbons would take care of him, or if all these failed, then Rhoda might solve the problem.

When she had gone he began, as she had suggested, to unpack his things, and found they no longer belonged to him. They were, in fact, taken away from him very soon. It would have been ridiculous, he saw, to mourn them, and in any case there remained what they could never take away, whether he would have liked it or not.

He discovered there were periods when the Courtneys who had bought him would not expect his company, when it was like living in a different house, almost in a different part of the town. At mealtimes, for instance. In the centre of the nursery, a large, white, light, but rather cold room in spite of a fire behind the high fender, a round mahogany table of massive legs had been laid with the cleanest cloth he had ever seen. An ammoniac sensation spread from his nose up to his eyes as he remembered that Mumma must have laundered the cloth. He had no time for more than this sensation, for seeing Rhoda standing the other side of the table, fiddling with the laid cutlery and wondering what else she might do. It was the first time they had met since his coming to the house to live. Mrs Courtney had been too busy explaining all the rules, which were so many he hadn't listened after a bit. Mr Courtney had shown him the lavatories he might use, and those were frightening: all that china and gurgling water; you hoped you wouldn't shit on the seat.

While remaining silent, Rhoda began jabbing the cloth with a fork as though to draw attention to herself.

"Guess what!" he said, because she made him sick.

"What?" She was unable to resist the moves of the game.

"You're my sister."

"Urchhh! I'm *not*!" She flung down the fork, which bounced and clattered against a plate.

"You must be," he said, "if they're my father and mother."

"I'm not! They're not!"

Her white skin had turned so red. Her pale blue eyes hated him. Then she said: "You're common."

He had never heard such a zinging in his ears. He went round the flaming table. He had meant to punch her in the teeth, but she frightened his fist into a hand, which landed rubbery, though hard rubber, about where that birthmark the colour of milk chocolate was plastered on her neck.

Rhoda opened her mouth to scream, but no sounds came out. She was pale with rage, pain, fright; it was impossible to tell which; but he knew that he was frightened. The sickly little mole-covered thing might have died of the blow: she was so delicate, they said.

When suddenly her teeth had got hold of one of his hands. He was too shocked pained to remember what to do.

"You mustn't bully me," she said, looking at him with those pale, swimming eyes. "I'm a sick girl."

What he might have said done next he only half imagined she might have stuck the fork into him he was weak at moments.

Fortunately the door opened and Lizzie came in with a tray.

He would have liked to pour out on Lizzie how he had left Cox Street, and everything that had happened since, but he saw she was going to ignore the part of him she already knew.

"Well, you children, I expect you're feeling rather peckish," she said, lowering her eyelids, looking down her nose, and speaking with Mrs Courtney's voice.

So he decided to play some of Lizzie's game. "What's those long green things?" he asked, because they looked no more like real food than Lizzie's voice was a real voice.

"Why, that's sparagus!" His ignorance made her even more superior. "Some of what the ladies didn't finish at Madam's luncheon yesterday."

Rhoda was showing no signs of their recent shemozzle. "I'm not the least bit hungry," she said. "But Hurtle," she said, giving him one of her mother's looks, "has been on a long drive."

"He'll be able to satisfy his appetite," said Lizzie, "with all these good things 'ere."

"But *She's* late! She's always late, except when you want her to be."

"Don't matter," Lizzie said. "That's what the hot-dish's for."

She had unloaded a leaden-coloured, heavy-looking dish with a very noticeable underneath.

"What is there?" Rhoda dragged the cover off the dish; she had to know. "Brains? *Brains!* I hate old boiled brains!"

"Miss Gibbons will decide about that," Lizzie said and left.

It was very still.

When Rhoda looked at him it was almost an invitation to be her brother: she so much disliked brains and Miss Gibbons.

"She came on Tuesday," she said. "She's silly." Then she remembered, tightened her lips on the laughter her thought had roused, and came hurrying, skipping, or however it was she moved; he didn't like to look too hard because Rhoda was a deformed person.

When she had arrived close to him she told: "She has a photo on the dressing table which makes her cry. I knocked it over."

"Did the glass break?"

"No. But it made her cry."

He was more interested in Rhoda: her face reminded him of the little quivering springs and things inside a clock he had once opened.

"He's a man," said Rhoda, "from somewhere—Cobar." She ducked her head and giggled. "She's so *silly!* She wears a big floppy bow on her blouse. A green *bow!*"

Suddenly she paused and put on a religious face. "My mother says she's terribly well educated. Her father's a clergyman. They sent her to one of the best schools and must have skimped to do it— or someone helped. Her name is Sybil. I saw it written in a book."

He was tired of the governess: he was too hungry, and at the same time the brains looked so unpromising. He kept on remembering their white, boiled look with the network of pinkish-brown veins when Rhoda tore the lid off the dish. Sinking your teeth in Rhoda might very well feel like biting into soft, white brains.

So although he continued looking at her, he was not particularly listening to what she had to tell.

Presently someone came in.

"You are Hurtle," the person said. "I hope you will be happy. Are you hungry?"

It could only be Miss Gibbons, because she was wearing the green bow. She had a smile which flickered on and off, thin and trembling.

"It's old brains!" Rhoda bawled.

"Very nourishing, too, Rhoda," Miss Gibbons said with a conviction that didn't convince.

In fact she was in such a twangle she started something in himself. Rhoda was at least boiling so hard she didn't notice.

The governess called for grace. ". . . for what we are about to receive . . ." She got through it quite professionally, no doubt because she was the daughter of a clergyman.

When they looked up there was a map in water spread across the tablecloth. Rhoda must have unscrewed the cap from the hotdish.

"Why do you do it?" Miss Gibbons was panting. "What have you got against me?"

Rhoda looked down at her place.

You could hear Miss Gibbons palpitating.

Hurtle loved her, and she wouldn't know. She couldn't know he was going to draw her sooner or later. He loved the hair at the nape of her neck: it was so faint it was only a dark smudge on her skin.

Rhoda said the brains would stick in her throat. "You've got to feed my animals first. Nursie always fed the animals."

Miss Gibbons hung her head over her clasped hands. Though grace was over she continued to behave as though she was praying.

"Go on! Like I told you!"

Then Miss Gibbons got up and offered a spoonful of brain to each of the toy animals arranged in the compartments of the nursery overmantel.

Rhoda watched to see whether any of her toys would be overlooked: in concentration her head drooped, her eyes looked drowsy.

"Go on!" she said. "The camel! You missed out the camel on the other side."

Hurtle thought Miss Gibbons was a fool to put up with any of it. On the whole he despised, he didn't love the tall young woman. Then again he pitied her. He pitied himself at the great white nursery table opposite the strawberry-coloured Rhoda. He remembered Mumma, pale as brains from the strain of laundering the nursery cloth. He bit into the inner tenderness of his lip.

"What is it, Hurtle?" Miss Gibbons roused herself to ask.

That evening at dusk a wind from the south threatened the suffocating warmth from the fire they kept stoked behind the nursery fender. The wind blowing through the grander rooms drove the cigar smoke ahead of it and thinned out Mrs Courtney's perfume. Edith and Lizzie, scuttling to fasten windows and doors, looked as though they only half believed they would prevent whatever they were expected to. As the long wads of ink-blotted cloud passed overhead, unravelled, then matted thicker than ever, the garden, though stationary, was slowly being poured into fresh, coldly boiling forms. It was not yet raining, but the wind in the leaves made them look a liquid black.

Rhoda said with the moist breathlessness he had begun to recognize as hers: "Let's go into the garden. I'm not supposed to. Because of the damp." In her feverish revolt she was almost jerking the doorknob off.

He followed her out. The wind hit them. He filled his lungs, excited by his own expanding body, his almost power over flying cloud.

Rhoda, on the other hand, he saw, was gasping. She was advancing sideways. Her hair was being lifted in little pink steamy streamers. The birthmark looked porous on her asparagus-coloured neck.

"This is *my* garden," she shouted.

She sounded so shrill and electric he realized she, too, had some important part in what was happening: in tortured trees and ink-stained cloud.

At the same time, what Pa called "common sense" made him shout back: "It isn't! It can't be yours! It's the Courtneys' garden, isn't it?"

It sounded as though Mr and Mrs Courtney were nothing to do with either of them.

"No." She grabbed his hand; the wind was almost blowing her away. "They don't know half of it. They're never here."

Rhoda led him deeper into the darkening garden. There were stone steps, the moss so thick in places his feet felt they were trampling flesh. It disgusted him, but she couldn't see it. She was interested only in what she had to show him. Each time she spoke he could feel her moist little fingers twitching on his hand.

"Those are guavas." She tried to make it sound like a secret.

He picked one from out of the sooty leaves, but it made his mouth shrivel up.

She was enjoying it all so much she didn't notice.

"And custard apples. They're too green to steal. The boys can't see them amongst the leaves."

"What boys?" he asked.

"Larrikins."

Was she trying to show him he had changed sides? He felt uncomfortably guilty, and tried to get rid of her hand; but again she didn't seem to notice, or didn't want to. She clung on. She was leading him. They were walking over fallen custard apples, through a scent of crushed insects, or sickly fruit.

"All these custard apples," his surprise moved him to remark, "you didn't pick them, and they fell off. They're rotting."

"We didn't pick them because we didn't want them."

"Then it wouldn't matter if somebody else took them, would it?"

"Don't be silly! They're ours!"

They were standing stirring a tub of liquid manure.

"Do you think you'll like me?" she asked.

"I dunno." He felt stupefied: his clothes hung in larrikin rags.

"I don't know either," she said, "whether I'm going to like you. 'Hurtle' is a name nobody else ever had."

The old broomstick fell back with a plop into the tub of liquid manure.

He mumbled: "I don't want to be like anybody else."

"I'd like to be like other people."

He couldn't see her so clearly now; she sounded like some old woman.

"They like you better," she added.

And suddenly something of the same fear got into him. He would have liked to find himself running with the mob of kids down Cox Street, away from everything to do with Courtneys. In the street where he belonged. If he belonged. He didn't belong anywhere: that was what frightened; although he had wanted it that way.

The big house looked by now like a ship of lights. Someone, a blur, was walking calling through the darkness in a would-be pleasant voice.

"That's Miss Gibbons. 'Lovesick Syb'—that's what Lizzie calls her."

"Oughtn't we to let her know we're here?" He could have rubbed up against the Lovesick Syb.

"No!" Rhoda despised him. "I know what to do without being told. We're supposed to go in and talk to Them while they finish dressing."

"Who?"

"Don't be silly!" She was dragging him along unknown paths. "Harry and Alfreda."

He wondered whether he would ever learn to play the Courtneys' game convincingly. Good thing people never really dropped to what was going on behind your face.

Rhoda was panting from the steep climb. "Have you ever been in love?"

He hesitated. "No. Not properly."

"I don't think I was either," she said.

Coming in out of the dark into the dazzling house, they were practically blinded. Rhoda walked prim and nice as she led him along the passages. They brushed past Edith, then Lizzie, but the girls didn't recognize them. He must learn when not to recognize. He could easily get the words and tone of a language; the difficult part was to know what you leave out.

Harry Courtney was in what Rhoda called his dressing-room. He was in his stiff shirt and braces, sitting pulling on black silk socks over his neat ankles and swelling calves.

"Hello," he said in a jolly voice, which didn't prevent you knowing he could have done without you. "I bet you've been in the garden."

"Not exactly," said Rhoda. "Anyway, not for long."

"I thought so," said Mr Courtney. "You smell like horses."

There was a long stain of liquid manure, they saw, on Rhoda's dress.

Harry Courtney had got up. First he began scuffing his hair with the tips of his fingers, to work in the pomade. Then he wiped the palms of his hands on his already glistening beard.

Rhoda tried sticking her head in his groin, but he pulled quickly away.

"Where are you dining?" she asked.

She was more interested in the box in which he kept his shirt studs and cuff-links. She took up a jewel and sucked it as though it had been a lolly.

"With the Egerton-Crawleys," her father told her.

Rhoda almost swallowed the ruby in showing her disgust.

Miss Keep the lady's-maid knocked at the door and asked with awful seriousness: "Madam is wondering whether the children are coming to talk to her. She can be seen now."

At once Rhoda became very tired. She slid into an armchair and began rubbing her cheek against the cover. She looked frail and pale. The moles on her skin stood out more than ever, and the manure stain looked longer, browner.

"Ladies don't cross their legs," Miss Keep advised.

Rhoda seemed to prefer her father, though he didn't encourage it; while Hurtle suddenly experienced a burst of agreeable powerlessness. He was drawn towards the form of the small, withered lady's-maid, or rather, beyond her. Silly-headed, he followed her out to where Mrs Courtney was expecting him.

She appeared fully dressed, but called: "I'm not quite ready, darling. Just putting the finishing touches."

Because she was so pleased, she spoke in her most accomplished voice. She was holding in her hand a looking-glass, which she cleverly slanted this way and that, so as everyone, herself included, could admire her hair from all angles. Bands of gold, coming together above her forehead in an enormous big blister of a pearl, prevented the hair from falling down. Her dress could have been ice if it had been standing on its own, but long cloudy trailers, fastened to the edges of her nakedness, melted the ice into moonlight instead. She was all in white, the big pearl lolling on her forehead, the diamonds jostling one another.

"Do you think I'll pass?"

He was too stupefied to answer her.

Even that made her laugh. "Nobody can call you a flirt!"

She was not in kissing form, he could see, because she was afraid of her clothes getting crushed, but she gave him a quick peck with pointed lips.

"Look," she said. "I'll show you. For a treat. Because you might be feeling—lonely."

She opened two big wardrobes in which her dresses were hanging. They looked surprisingly dead beside the live one she was wearing. But fascinating.

"Don't be afraid to touch, darling," she coaxed and cooed, "if it will give you pleasure."

She put out a soft hand, the wrist above it rippling with blue-white diamonds, and drew him towards one of the wardrobes. He let himself be guided, doubtingly.

In fact Mrs Courtney did something unexpected and very strange. She suddenly moved her hand to the nape of his neck and shoved his head in amongst the limp dresses. The sensation was at first one of blinding, then of a delicious suffocation as his face was swallowed by the scented silky darkness, through which Mrs Courtney's voice continued somewhere rustling.

He pulled out on becoming not exactly frightened, but because he might have overbalanced.

"Wasn't it nice?" She was so amused at what she had done. She kept on looking at him, to see whether she had succeeded in getting him drunk. Her teeth looked as though they were against him.

He felt ashamed, but it was some compensation to know you could see inside the faces of people who fail to get behind your own.

Mrs Courtney looked away.

"Have you noticed his eyes?" she asked Keep; and almost at once: "Darling, it's time! Where is Rhoda? Go and find her," she ordered, and it grated. "I know she doesn't love her mother. I shan't force her. But shall continue doing my duty."

She was twitching and quivering with an injustice in much the same way as Rhoda herself.

As he went out he heard Mrs Courtney—their mother—lower her voice for her maid and say: "Were you surprised at what I did? Children are like puppies, you know. And a new puppy can be attached to his owner by teaching him to recognize the owner's scent. Or so I'm told."

Miss Keep didn't reply, but made a kind of dry noise, or else she was still blowing powder into a pair of Madam's long white gloves.

He ought to have liked Miss Gibbons more, seeing as neither of them belonged to Courtneys, whatever Courtneys themselves might think. Miss Gibbons was so gently pleasant, especially in her grey Sunday dress. Grey, he supposed, was as close as she could get to colourless. He couldn't forgive her this feeble fear of drunkenness. Everything about Sybil Gibbons was feeble and gentle. She asked to be teased, or downright tortured, not by what you said but by what you didn't say, and most of all in the pleasant but colourless lessons she gave. She taught the subjects like History, Geography, and English—to him and Rhoda. Mr Shewcroft coached him alone in Latin and Mathematics, and Madame Parmentier came for French. On all these occasions he would refresh himself by staring out the window into the garden, or deeper, into himself.

He heard Miss Gibbons tell Mrs Courtney: "I should hate to accuse him of laziness. He is what I would call *indolent*. Or his mind is set on other things." Good old Sybil Gibbons: she wasn't such a bad stick.

Harry Courtney had explained in the beginning: "We've talked it over, old man—your mother and I—and we think you'd be happiest—at least for a while—doing your lessons at home." He sounded so serious and kind. "Until you settle down, learn our ways"—he cleared his throat—"and the language we speak. Then to some good boarding school. To toughen up," he ended with a rasping, bearded laugh.

Your mother and I: you would certainly have to learn the language. In the beginning, in fact, there were expressions which troubled everyone.

It was evening not long after he had come to live there. It was shortly before bedtime, and the three of them—Rhoda had a temperature—were seated in the little mauve octagonal room where Mrs Courtney answered letters and considered the serious problems of life.

"There's the question of what you should call us," she suddenly began.

It was making her excited, or embarrassed. She popped a chocolate into her mouth. He knew by the shape it must be the lovely liquid kind. If she didn't take care it would trickle out of the corner of her mouth. Or else it was this excitement she was having to control.

"Father," she said, "is satisfied you should call him 'Father.' 'Dad' I don't like at all. It can sound—not common—but *blunt*."

" 'Father' it is," Mr Courtney repeated uneasily.

Hurtle couldn't believe in it, but hoped they wouldn't read it on his face.

As for Mrs Courtney, she had almost finished her chocolate before coming to the difficult part. She looked at the box, but hesitated; perhaps she thought it would spoil her dinner.

"Now, in my case," she said, glancing at her front for a spot she might have made with the liqueur, "it's a more difficult matter"—she swallowed down—"because 'Mother' would sound far too severe, and 'Mummy,' I think, is not for boys. I have an idea, though. I hope you'll think it's a good one." She looked away, smiling like a girl. "I've been thinking you might call me 'Maman.' That's the French. It's so pretty. And will sound different."

Mr Courtney uncrossed his ankles and crossed them again. He pulled his waistcoat down over what wasn't yet a stomach.

Hurtle sat smiling at his own fingers in his state of not unpleasant disbelief.

"Well? You don't say anything." Mrs Courtney sounded vexed. "But we've got to decide. You'll be living with us. For always."

Though realizing how serious the situation was, he continued smiling. Perhaps it was the word "always." From what he had experienced already, he couldn't believe anything lasted.

"And we are your father and mother."

"As soon as we adopt you legally," 'Father' threw in, "you'll take the name 'Courtney.' "

"But my name is 'Duffield.' " He liked to visualize it written by a variety of means: in burnt cork, indelible pencil, invisible ink, carved out of stone, even tattooed: DUFFIELD.

"A man my father knew," he said, "went about with his name tattooed on his right arm. He could never ever get rid of it."

"But yours isn't tattooed on any part of you!" Mr Courtney burst out. "So you can't be compared with the cove your—Mr Duffield knew."

"No," agreed Hurtle dreamily.

When he was at last by document a Courtney, Rhoda said to him: " 'Hurtle Courtney.' I shan't call you by it, though." She was looking at him to see the effect.

"Don't ask you to," he said.

Suddenly he saw her as a white ant.

"What are you looking at?" she asked.

He had a dream in which the harness-room wall at home, covered with smudges and pencil drawings, was attacked by white ant, rustling as they trampled, shedding their wings as they crunched the timber under the plaster; it might have been biscuit.

"*What are you looking at?*" she insisted, digging into the palm of his hand with her nails.

"A dream," he said. "You had the head, the body, of the biggest ant. A white ant. The face was yours. Looking at me while it ate."

"I don't believe you!"

But she did. She flung away his hand, at the same time kicking him on the ankle.

He laughed. It wasn't entirely true. But could have been. She had.the pinkish glaze of the ants in his dream. So he wouldn't let on that it was half a lie.

She was closest to him of all his "family." Once he was moved to embrace her, but was just as suddenly repelled by the idea: he saved himself in time. You couldn't trust her anyway. Not that he could always trust himself. This, again, made them sort of related.

From now on he answered to "Hurtle Courtney" when addressed by those who visited the house: the loud-voiced rich, and quieter, poorer ones who paid him no end of fussy attentions while looking for recognition from Harry and Alfreda. The maids, who could neither gain nor lose by it, who didn't care, who had their own more pressing thoughts, called him automatically by his false name. Now that he was turned into this new and glossy person, it sometimes agitated him dreadfully to enter his real and secret life. Even at its most chaotic, he would have liked somebody, not to share it, but to know of its existence and importance. So he began to accept Father and Maman, not for what they were supposed to be, but because he needed them as witnesses.

"Look, Maman!" He couldn't stop himself running that evening into what Miss Keep always called the "boodwah." He was carrying the sheet of paper he might not have wanted to show if, on the spur of the moment, he hadn't felt the need for praise.

Maman was sitting slack in her stockings at the dressing-table with that same dreamy expression May wore in standing at the kitchen range. He was at first a little dazed by the glare of flesh; but Maman quickly grabbed something to bundle into. She was in such a hurry, the little smoke-tinted bottles with their lattices of silver irises rattled and jostled on the dressing-table, and threatened to topple over.

"What—Hurtle—you must always—knock!" She was gasping and frowning; her frowns looked black amongst the powder. "But what have you brought to show me, darling?" In no time she was again offering the part of her she wanted people to see.

He was still so dazed he hesitated to spring his surprise, which remained too private a part of himself, like Maman's nakedness. Very occasionally she would come into the bathroom and soap and sponge him, but his thing was less private than his drawing.

"What," she said, holding it away from her, "is this *me*?"

He began to feel ashamed, not so much of his own drawing.

"Oh darling, how clever of you! But I shouldn't have taken it for me, exactly. Do you see me like that? You've given me a melon chest."

He let her flow on; any possible answers were enclosed by the lines of his drawing.

"Have you shown it to Father?" she asked. "Father would be amused. He's so interested in everything you do."

He didn't want to show it to Mr Courtney—Father—he wanted to tear it up, turn the light out.

But Maman was inspired.

They swept along the passage. Father was in his dressing-gown. He smelled of soap. He hadn't yet begun to dress, though his stiff shirt was laid out with studs and links.

"Look, Harry, what he's done!"

The drawing made a wind as she thrust it at him.

Harry said: "By Jove, he's got a talent!"

The hot bath had left him lazy and indulgent. On his calves below the gown the hair was curling, and above, in the V which exposed his chest. He was wearing a pair of new shiny leather slippers. His feet were planted wide apart so that he might give a better opinion.

"Fancy if our son should turn out to be a genius," Alfreda Courtney said. She had put her arm through Harry's. She was leaning against his side as though only she had a right to, while they looked at the drawing, now slightly crumpled.

"But is it a likeness? I don't think so. Though it's most interesting," she said, "as a work of art."

She was still inspired. She would have to show it. Even if she was the victim, it was in a cause.

When Keep had got her into her dinner frock, and she was fully powdered, Alfreda Courtney descended to the servants' quarters, dragging her boy along with her.

She announced: "My son has done a portrait of me."

The girls all buzzed round, excepting May Noble. They went: "Mm-*mmm* isn't it look a telling likeness fancy little Hurtle."

They turned him into a real dwarf.

"Do you *really* think it's a likeness?" she dared them.

She had been basketed up, like the scent bottles, in a latticework of silver.

"Ooh *yairs*! Well, no. It depends."

"You, May," she asked the cook, "can't you spare us a moment?"

"The sauce might curdle." May went on stirring, like she was doing a drawing. She didn't look at his, but knew. They understood and respected each other.

But he began to hate the curdled drawing.

"What is the matter, darling?" Maman asked.

He couldn't tell her. She was such a long way off from him. She was left standing, her lips working the lip salve into each other, in the kitchen, in her blue-and-silver dinner frock; tonight there were only a few friends you didn't have to trouble about.

As an outcome Father engaged Mr Tyndall to give drawing lessons, and with this addition to the timetable, Mr Shewcroft was sometimes forced to wait in the hall with his Latin and Mathematics.

Mr Tyndall was slow and clean and dedicated to perspective. Nice families commissioned him to draw portrait heads. He was a silvery old man who wore his tie poked through a ring. Under the skin of his hands he showed up as blue as the legs of skinned chickens. He felt cold and remote if you touched him. If you got him to draw something, for the fun of it, to watch, his drawing was correct and silvery as himself.

"But that isn't the way I want to draw," said Hurtle.

"Which way, then?"

"I want to draw my own way."

"They'll laugh at you if you do. They'll think you're either ignorant or pulling their leg." Mr Tyndall spoke with conviction as he shaded his own silvery drawing of a hand. "Will you mind appearing ridiculous?"

"No." But he could feel himself going red, as he did whenever he told a lie.

He took his pencil, and might have made matters worse by working off his embarrassment on paper, only someone began thumping on the door. It was Mr Shewcroft upholding his rights.

Mr Tyndall looked at his watch. "Guilty again!" he said in his pleasant, old man's voice, which didn't sound guilty at all.

As for Mr Shewcroft, he never spoke unless he could not help it.

Leaving the room, Mr Tyndall seemed to lurch against him with a smile strictly for a colleague; or perhaps it was Mr Shewcroft who lurched against Mr Tyndall. It was almost a collision, with the result that Mr Shewcroft might have lost his balance if he hadn't found support by attaching himself with three tobacco-stained fingers to the edge of the table; while the guiltless Mr Tyndall cleanly left.

Though a younger man, Mr Shewcroft had retired from being a schoolmaster in favour of coaching private pupils. He was very thin. The skin on his face was large-pored, pockmarked: in some places it looked scarred. Hurtle often wondered whether old Shewcroft knew about the blackheads. He would have liked to give them a squeeze for him. There were mornings when the Latin tutor's breath smelled like a full ashtray, and worse. He can't have known and nobody dared tell him about it.

On one occasion Maman had said: "He hasn't *disgraced* himself. He hasn't exactly *fallen down*. But he does look so unsavoury, Harry."

"Poor devil!"

"Yes, we mustn't be uncharitable." Maman immediately altered her voice, because their boy had come into the room, and she was at her letter-writing.

Now this morning Mr Shewcroft looked his most unsavoury for Latin Unseen. His breath came in fiery gusts. Hurtle decided he might succeed better with the blackheads by digging them out with a little watch key; while Mr Shewcroft remained absorbed, not in the Latin Unseen, but in his own thoughts, some of them so painful they were visibly rising to the surface of his bilious eyes.

Hurtle wondered what would happen if his own mumbling voice, stumbling after Caesar, came to a stop. It did. There was the peaceful sound of doves murmuring or digesting.

"What is the use of Caesar, Mr Shewcroft?" he dared ask, though very low.

Mr Shewcroft was chewing on something, like a lump of gristle so big and unmanageable it couldn't be swallowed; nor could it be spat out, though it was only a boy who would see: so his eyes seemed to imply, as they bulged to bursting point, the veins in his neck swelling above the yellow rim of his collar.

When at last Mr Shewcroft spoke, his words were the gristle of words. He sort of groaned. "For that matter, what's the use of anything?"

He began to show his brown teeth, to clasp his always clammy fingers with their bitten nails, till you could hear the bones cracking, and the hands were drained white.

"You're a boy. You can't know. Not about injustice. Probably won't ever." He ground it out, while his terrible eyes looked the furniture over. "Always be too flush. You won't need to listen to what they're saying about you in the next room. They won't say it, anyway. They'll be too respectful of your cash. Well, good luck to you!"

He laughed, only his throat had grown too tight to let more than half of it out.

"If you're of no importance, even your bootlaces are against you!"

Hurtle looked down, and one of the twisted old bootlaces had been joined in an untidy knot on Mr Shewcroft's dusty instep.

You were so embarrassed you didn't know whether to show him the new penknife the present from Father or tell him something or tell him—what? Till you remembered the heart going *chuff chuff* how you behaved to those who were sick or broke or in any way bashed about you remembered at least how it began in Mumma's words.

"Don't you believe in God, Mr Shewcroft?"

"Good *God*!"

Mr Shewcroft laughed. His face turned green. Then he grew very quiet. He got up and, walking on a curve, his curved body left the room: probably gone to the lavatory.

Hurtle put in time drawing. It was a comfort to watch the drawing grow. Of the great eye. It wasn't Mr Shewcroft's eye; it wasn't his own: or perhaps it was his own, from looking at it so often in the glass. Anyway, there was the Eye. It might have started accusing him if he hadn't looked over his shoulder to find Lizzie had stuck her head in, looking very pretty in her crisp cap and freckles.

"Your teacher's gone," she said. "Left the front door open. Shickered worse than usual."

Lizzie's mouth showed such contempt in the way it formed the word, he could only share her attitude. He laughed back uglily, to let her see he was in the know.

But he kept remembering the knotted, twisted bootlace. He grew troubled, and finally afraid: because Mr Shewcroft didn't come again to give the lessons.

Maman said: "Oh yes, poor man, he won't come; he's sick."

"But what's he got?"

It was an afternoon of rain. The windows were plastered with skeins of rain; beyond them in the dark green garden, long wet bending wands were tangling with one another.

"He won't come," Maman repeated.

He noticed her hair had grey in it, though her face was young, her lips moist. She touched her hair.

"Shall we play a game?" she asked. "Where's Rhoda? Find Rhoda. Get out the cards and we'll play a game of grab. I don't know where that Miss Gibbons *hides* poor little Rhoda. I never set eyes on her."

When Rhoda was found they played, and the reds had never looked so brilliant as now, with rainlight touching them up. He was winning. Rhoda cheated. Nobody cared: it was too wet, and Maman soggy in the nose.

Herself a humpbacked queen, Rhoda shot out a card, and asked: "Does Mr Shewcroft have a wife?"

"He was a single man," Maman said, looking closely at the cards.

Hurtle almost always won. Cold behind the knees and feeble at the wrists since Maman put Mr Shewcroft in the past, he was full of shame. He dreaded something. Someone would notice his goose-flesh if he didn't distract their attention.

He laughed, his teeth chattering; he said: "Old Shewcroft was too ugly—all those pocks—blackheads. And breath! No one would want to be cuddled by Shewcroft."

Rhoda shrieked, and made the most of it to cheat.

"Don't be vulgar, Hurtle," said Maman, though on a sunlit day, and in a pretty dress, she might have enjoyed his funny remarks. "It isn't kind, darling." She sniffled at the cards; she said her cold made her look an awful sight.

"If I was to draw old Shewcroft I'd draw him as a sort of Jack of Clubs. A thin jack. Jumping off the roof."

Rhoda giggled very high. "Why jumping off the roof?"

"Because he was a bit *mad*!" He shouted it.

He was winning as usual. It was fortunate at this point, because Maman could pretend not to have heard. Probably only he had heard. Rhoda was grizzling because she had lost.

"Why does Hurtle always win?"

"There are more worthwhile ways of succeeding, Rhoda." Maman was trying to console her.

While he could only think of escaping from the room. He must.

"There was a man I knew," he began.

To be truthful, there was a man Pa had known, a coalheaver in Foveaux Street, who had cut his own throat for some forgotten reason. There was blood all amongst the coal dust.

"Where are you going, Hurtle?" Maman called.

But he wasn't prepared to answer, and nobody would prevent him going.

After collecting what he needed he went upstairs to his own room. It took him not much above an hour to do what he had to. Then he switched off the light and lay in the dark, shivering with exhaustion, excitement, fright.

She came, of course, as he expected, dreaded.

"What are you doing, darling? You're not unhappy, are you? Not thinking morbid thoughts, I hope? I don't want my boy to grow up morbid."

"I'm not your boy." He made it sound as cold as he could.

She was feeling round the darkness for him.

"Hurtle?"

He punched out and hit something soft.

"Then I shan't feel sorry for you! Not a bit," she said, very dry and angry. "You're a cold, cruel, nasty little boy at heart."

As though to illustrate her change of mind she went and wrenched at the switch beside the door. They were both wincing in the sudden light. Then he watched her get the horrors.

"You abominable child!" she almost screamed. "Where did you get the paint?"

"In the toolshed."

Still lying on the bed, he couldn't resist taking a look at what he had done.

"And *red* paint! If we had paint in the toolshed, I can't think why it was red. Black—yes, I can remember. But what use can we have had for red? I wonder if your father knew. Nobody," she said, "ever knows or cares. I am the one who has to think—to bear the brunt. We shall have to get the wall repapered."

She was so vexed she flung out her arm and knocked off the silver lustre jug. Against the carpet it looked like so many pieces of looking-glass. At least the jug had been empty: no flowers since the day of his arrival.

But he was too far off from Maman's rage. As he lay looking at the wall he almost wasn't listening to her. It was as though he lay at one end of a tunnel, looking at his painting-drawing at the other: its brilliance was increased by distance.

Until now, there hadn't been time to appreciate what his desire had driven him to do: his body, his thoughts, had been too much worked upon. Now he wondered why he had done it as he had, when he meant to show poor black "Jack" Shewcroft jumping off the roof, and here he was sprawling in the coal dust, like the coal-heaver from Foveaux Street, the blood running out of his cut throat, through his veins, and from his heart, which was like a little fountain squirting from his chest. That was the way the idea had worked out.

Maman must have calmed down. "You knew, then," she said, "all the time—that Mr Shewcroft had taken his life."

No, he only guessed—but because he knew. If she only knew, what he had painted on the wall was the least of what he knew.

"I could do another," he said, "in another few days—a better one."

He was still shivering with the horror of it. He hadn't had the courage to remember too closely "Jack" Shewcroft's face with the blackheads and scarred skin.

"I don't know what your father will say. He'll probably give you a sound beating."

He listened to her swishing, crying, but angrily, down the passage. He really didn't care whether Harry Courtney obeyed her orders and came to beat him. For the moment at least, he wasn't frightened. He was still too exhausted by what had turned out to be, not a game of his own imagination, but a wrestling match with some-one stronger; so he lay drowsily looking at the painting on the wall, particularly those places where he could see he had gone wrong. He had been led astray by the brilliance of the live red; whereas "Jack" Shewcroft's suicide should have been black black.

Presently he heard Harry Courtney let himself in. He heard her go quickly and talk to him fairly loudly, though not yet loud enough, in the hall.

Then he heard her raise her voice, practically shout: "Oh, but you must! As a discipline. For his own good."

When Harry, his father who wasn't, came into the room, he was looking stern but apologetic, and carrying that riding crop. Harry hardly dared look at the painting on the wall for remembering what she had sent him to do.

"They—your mother—" he began. "I can see for myself," he tried again, "how destructive you've been—Hurtle—and when boys are destructive, there's only one—one cure—they have to be punished pretty severely."

He was looking very big and bulgy. He no longer belonged to his English suit. The sleeve had rucked up along one of the arms, leaving a hairy wrist. Hurtle was fascinated by the twitching of the leather loop at the end of the bone-handled crop.

"Get up, Hurtle."

Hurtle didn't, couldn't. Legs wouldn't work. Of course he was afraid, too, while hypnotized by Harry Courtney's face.

For Harry had raised the crop. Like a big heavy old hairy woman, he slashed. Beard and all, his cheeks were flopping with fright. Hurtle felt the painful cuts, while Harry, you could tell from his eyes and mouth, was suffering them.

After he had slashed how many times he dropped the crop. He sat down trembling on the edge of the bed, looking at his large, clasped hands. What if you began to blubber? That might finish Harry. So you continued staring at him as hard as you could. Perhaps that was worse.

Outside, the rain had stopped. The swollen shapes of trees, hardly the same which could lash themselves to heights of spectacular fury, stood glooming in the half-light before moonrise.

In their own bright electric world he would have liked to crawl closer to his pretended father, at least to get the feel of his sleeve: or better, to be alone and cry, looking out at the darkness from which the moon would presently create a garden.

Harry said: "Next Thursday, Hurtle, I've got to go to Mumbelong. I promised to take you, I think. Well, it's time I kept my promise, isn't it?" Towards the end he raised his voice, and showed his teeth, which were very good; they never had anything wrong with them.

Hurtle made a few noises. Father was looking at him. Father made those little noises in his throat to signify that nothing unpleasant had happened, had it? There is a certain sensation of barely melted chocolate, and this was it.

That night Maman gave him a real chocolate before he went to bed, before she had her dinner. She was sitting in the mauve oc-

tagonal room where she wrote the letters: "to salve my conscience."
She was wearing what she called a simple dinner frock, with a
frosting of beads which rustled on her upper arms.

"Darling," she said, "you don't know how much you hurt me—in
doing what you did."

He was seriously interested. He saw there were real tears in her
eyes.

That was when she gave him the chocolate.

Maman said, because tonight she felt the need to explain away:
"I have been writing to a number of influential people asking them
to support the movement for prevention of cruelty to animals.
That is, in the wider sense. Because my particular interest is the
prevention of vivisection. I wonder if you can understand, darling.
Because hardly anyone in this country seems aware of what is
going on. I've heard the most hair-raising, heart-rending stories of
animals being sacrificed to science—living animals cut up—in experiments."

She was looking at him, or beyond him, or again, at him.

"Shrieking, tortured dogs. I've heard they punch them in the
vocal chords to silence them."

He was looking at Maman. She was so moved, he could smell the
scent of her emotion above the scent. He could hear the rustling
of the bead frosting on her sleeves.

"Darling," she said, "my children—you and Rhoda—will never
grow up cruel—if I can help it."

A lopsided moon, he saw, was balancing on the blurred and dripping trees. Father came in, dressed for dinner. They kissed good-
night. Then Maman leaned against Father. He saw how beautifully
they fitted together. He had never fitted together with anyone in
such a way. He wondered whether he ever would.

Father kept his promise about the visit to Mumbelong. He had
these three properties: Mumbelong, Yalladookdook, and Sevenoaks,
where managers were in charge, though as a young man Harry
Courtney himself had lived and worked on the land. When he was
particularly what Maman called "boring," he used to tell about the
blisters he had got digging holes for fence-posts, and dagging sheep.
Edith said Mr Courtney had made a fortune several times over
from sheep and cattle. At his best there wasn't any sign of it, like
when cleaning his teeth in his underclothes in the swaying train,

while the slimy water went slip slop inside the big, railways water-bottle. Hurtle lay on the other bunk, watching his father. In the dark, afterwards, he listened to his snoring. He had not felt happier since becoming his father's son.

They had to get up more than early so as not to miss the siding where the manager would meet them. Hurtle was so sleepy he couldn't find his boots: Father had to help him into them. Before they got down, Father put on an oilskin, not the overcoat of Hurtle's former imagining. To touch the oilskin made you shiver: it was so stiff and cold; but it made Father look real, more as though he worked. You were the one who was soft, in nambypamby new clothes, face ghostly green in the glass if you looked: only your thoughts were real.

When they got down at the siding, with their valises, and the rifle Father had told him to bring, there were lights in the darkness from what seemed to be a sulky. There was an old man's voice explaining to them the manager Mr Spargo had strained his back and was laid up. The old man's name was Sid Cupples.

"This is the boy," Father explained to Sid, making you sound more like a thing the Courtneys owned than their legally adopted son.

The old man made some noises from between his gums. "Fine little bloke," he gobbled. "A chip off the old block, eh?" As if he didn't know: perhaps he didn't.

They were entering a new world for which Father used a different voice. He seemed to be speaking the language old man Cupples would understand. Some way back Hurtle, too, had known how to speak it, or a version of it, but he no longer particularly wanted to remember. Driving in the sulky, with the lamps focused on the stones along the road and a few white thistles growing at the side, he remembered instead that other journey with the archdeacon and Harry's father, when Harry was a boy. He wondered what he would have said to the archdeacon in the new language he had learned, and which Father for the moment didn't want to use.

As they jogged, Sid began to grumble: "Wethers in the Five Mile aren't doin' all they could. I told 'im. I told 'im 'e oughter shift the wethers. Give it a spell."

Father was turning away from Sid, because he was the owner, who ought to be in league with the manager.

"I told 'im," said Sid, whose hands were scaly on the reins, "I told 'im 'e oughter bluestone the crick. There's worm in them wethers."

Father's oilskin was making a noise like sheets of metal. "Spargo's sick," he reminded Sid.

"I dunno if 'e's sick. Spargo 'imself ain't too sure. 'E oughter shift the wethers. I'm tellin' yer, Mr Courtney, now yer've come. Spargo says 'e ain't sick, or no more than a woman couldn't fix."

The two men were laughing together in the lamplit darkness for something they had both experienced. Although you were out of it, for once it didn't matter; there was too much else. Sometimes the thistles at the edges of the road looked like cut-out paper when the lamplight showed them up.

And then waking: because you must have fallen asleep, you were suddenly so lumpish and gummy; the darkness had turned into silver paddocks. The silver light was trickling down out of the trees, down the hillside; the rocks themselves were for a second liquid. There were rabbits humped in the white grass, then scuttering away.

Father and Sid were still talking their different language. They seemed to have forgotten you existed, though you joined them together, fitted tightly between Father's oilskin and Sid's smelly old overcoat.

Then Father remembered and said: "Fine sheep country, son. You wanter keep yer eyes open, and you'll pick up a wrinkle or two."

He was speaking as though Maman didn't exist, nor the painting by Boudin, nor the shelves of leatherbound books: when you knew all about them. Nor did he realize all the wrinkles you were picking up, not from the boring old sheep country, but from the world of light as the sun rose pale out of the hills, and the streams of liquid light were splashed across the white paddocks: from the sheep, too, the wrinkled sheep, huddling or trudging, coughing something that wouldn't come up; there were some so close to the road you could look right into their grey, clotted wool.

He almost put out his hands. "Shall I be able to touch one?"

"Touch what?" Father asked.

"A sheep. The wool. It looks sort of hard—tarry. I want to feel what it feels like."

Father grunted, not sure whether he ought to be pleased. "You'll be able to touch as many as you like."

"Make a wool classer of 'im!" Sid Cupples laughed.

But when they explained what it was, you were able to say with certainty: "No. I don't want to be anything like that."

"A squatter like yer dad is—or was," Mr Cupples corrected himself. "That's a real man's life."

Hurtle was silent because of what he knew they wouldn't believe.

The house was long, dust-coloured, wooden, amongst some dark trees, beside a river. While they were approaching, a dark chocolate dog ran out, followed by a yellow mangy one, each gnashing teeth and showing a long pink tongue. The dogs were followed by several men dressed in their work-clothes, one of them less rough than the others who brought Mr Spargo's apologies: he couldn't manage to get out of bed.

Hurtle was no longer introduced. There were too many people, and it would have been too much trouble. Father might even be finding him a nuisance now that there were all these men. It would make it easier to sneak off alone while they were at Mumbelong. He stood about, kicking some rusted tins on which the dew still showed, like sweat on skin.

At the same time he couldn't help being conscious of what was going on the other side of his eyelids. He knew that the rougher-looking men felt superior to Harry Courtney because he was rich and a gentleman, while the young bloke in a clean unironed shirt whose name was Col Forster was trying to please the owner for the same reason the men despised him. Col was a jackaroo, and very anxious about how he must behave as the manager's representative. Sid Cupples, who was leading the horse round to the stables, seemed to belong to neither side. He was too old. He knew better than everybody and was content with that.

Hurtle, too, knew better than everybody, than all these anyway, Sid Cupples included; not that he could have explained what he knew: because he saw rather than thought. He often wished he could think like people think in books, but he could only see or feel his way. Again he saw in his mind the rough-looking sheep. He itched to get his fingers in their wool, for the feel of it.

They spent several days at Mumbelong, in which time he did various things Father had planned he should do. He rode an old wide stubborn pony, which made his thighs stiff and rough. With that rifle Harry Courtney had offered in the beginning as a toy, he shot a rabbit through the back, and watched it kick its way to death. He watched a man called Eldred kill a sheep for them to eat.

Eldred hung it on a post, and skinned it, and dragged the guts out with his hands.

The whole of the visit to Mumbelong was more dream than real life, though Father took it so seriously. Somehow the light and colour were more important than what you were doing: that was the real importance of this dream-visit.

He also had an actual dream which remained with him very vividly. The sheep Eldred killed was hanging on the post, as in life, except that in the dream he hadn't killed, only skinned it. Maman was there, dressed for dinner. She was wearing the spray of diamonds in her hair. She was crying horribly, while busy, too. As she pulled the guts out of the sheep, the heart bleated through the open wound; the blood shot over the tails of her sables: it clotted amongst the sapphires. *Where is Rhoda*, she kept on calling, *I am looking for Rhoda she hurts me so.* Maman by now was the colour of the skinned sheep, its beautiful cave of green and blue, her bloody lips opening like the heart itself. *Help me Hurtle*, she called. While he could only stare at the strange beauty of the scene. *Crool crool cool and crool* she began to shriek *nasty little boy with eyes like knives.* By the time she started pulling at the big cushiony bowel her lips had turned the colour of liver. *I am your blood-mother I am only helping it to die to save it from the vivisector.* Her white neck all freckled with blood. *I know Hurturrl you would split my head open to see what there is inside.* Her hair had parted wider than the parting and the skull was beginning to split.

When he tore himself away and awake, Father was snoring on the other bedstead. From different parts of the wooden house came cries from other sleepers. He himself was so tied by the twisted sheet, and further hampered by his sweaty nightshirt, he could hardly escape. But did. By frantic effort. He ran stumbling stubbing on the way then out through some scattering of animals and furry splinters finally in the cabbage stalks he vomited up.

There was a thin moon in the sky, very beautifully carved. He began in the dim light to distinguish other things too: the patch of seeded cabbages, their stalks long, thin, ringed like stone; an iron windmill, motionless; and the solid mass of the house, with its sounds of life and dreamed-of death.

Next morning he went round the far side of the house while the others were preparing to leave for the paddocks. Father tried calling, but soon gave up. Hurtle thought he would look for stones in the river. Then he decided to explore the house, the several rooms he hadn't been into. One of these, which the wide veranda must have kept permanently dim, was Mr Spargo's room: he could hear somebody lying there. Since their arrival, Father had paid several visits to the sick manager. You couldn't feel Father liked him much, but some men seemed to find pleasure simply in being men together.

Mr Spargo was not altogether old, and very strong. He was lying on his back blinking at the ceiling. His eyelids were thick, white compared with the rest of his face, which was a burnt red. His coarse lashes were of the same light orange as the hair which covered all the visible parts of his body, and his thick, moist-looking lips stuck out rather as he breathed. Hurtle thought that if he were ever to draw Mr Spargo he would do him with a pair of horns.

When the manager caught sight, he heaved and said: "You're Courtney's boy, are yer?" Mr Spargo was one of those who would never attempt your name.

Then he tried to sound pitiful: "Reach me me terbaccer pouch, sonny. It fell down under the bed."

When you had done as asked, Mr Spargo remarked: "Chrise, me back's givin' me gyp!"

Close up, the smell of man was surprisingly strong, considering the look of bull.

"Waddayer doin' with yerself?" the manager gasped.

Because it was too complicated to tell, and wouldn't have sounded convincing, Hurtle said nothing. He knew that Mr Spargo was one of those people to whom he would never have anything to say. You were happier with furniture.

So he began to go silently away.

"Stuck-up little bastard!" Mr Spargo mumbled from his bed.

Like most accusations it was only half true.

Hurtle was glad to get away. During his stay at Mumbelong he was happiest with Sid Cupples, who seemed to suit himself on all occasions because of his age, and on this one, when the others left for mustering, had stayed back, either forgetting, or remembering something better.

Sid was sitting on the step of the hut where he slept with a horse-rug for covering. He immediately said: "Heard yer reachin' last night. It's the fat. The young fuller swamps the bloody tucker in fat. I tell 'im, but it don't do any good."

Because cooks said it was too lonely at Mumbelong, and they were temporarily without one, Col Forster the jackaroo had been made to take on the job. He seemed to like it, or anyway, he didn't complain.

Sid Cupples went on smoking. An advantage of Sid's company was that he didn't expect explanations, or even answers. Hurtle was content to hang around in the blue haze made by the old man's pipe.

Sid said: "Oughter move the wethers from the Five Mile. I tell 'im. I told the boss—Mr Courtney."

One of the old man's eyes was blueing over.

He said: "Too much dirty water. That's what's wrong with Spargo. 'E'd carry 'is bed any time a woman up an' showed 'im 'er monkey."

Mention of one animal seemed to remind him of another. He told about a possum they had caught on the place during a plague; the homestead roof had been full of possums. "Pissin' through the ceilin' onto yer plate. Till we tied a bell round the neck of this 'ere animal —see? Soon as 'e run after 'is mates, the mob of possums begun ter disappear. It was the blessed bell—see? It was like this possum 'ud gone off 'is nut. Put the wind up the 'sane' buggers."

Sid laughed and laughed at his memory of the bell-possum; but Hurtle was struck cold: by a vision of himself, the last possum on earth, tinkling feebly into a darkness lit by a single milky eye.

At night a shiver would start running through the poplars along the river. In the rooms of the homestead men were getting drunk together. Even the lips of the boss and the manager began to grow slobbery over their glasses of rum. Then they went out to piss off the edge of the dry-rotted veranda. Mr Spargo forgot his back when he had to let the water out.

On the last night Hurtle looked at Father, and Father didn't seem to recognize him.

There was a fuller moon, but not yet full. Everybody else seemed occupied, belching, and remembering for one another: dogs which had worked as dogs didn't work nowadays; stouter-hearted horses and nobler mates. There was nothing to do but pick your nose and wander through the disconnected rooms, in which lamps were burning uneven, and men's voices sagging beneath the weight of what they had to tell, particularly the weather, particularly the weather of long ago.

Out in the kitchen Col Forster was writing at something. There were pages of it amongst the grey-brown potato peelings. The lamp chimney had turned black.

"What are you writing?" Hurtle asked.

There was a breathing silence, while the insects batted round the glass chimney of the lamp, and Col held his hand to protect the paper.

Then he answered: "Is it any business of yours?"

Hardly fair, when you only wanted to know.

Then Col thought better. He had a broad face, and spongy, gentle fingers. "I'm writing a book. A novel," he said. "The trouble is, I haven't yet experienced enough."

"Can't you simply write it out of your head?"

"It wouldn't be real."

It was difficult to see the point, only that the jackaroo was troubled.

"You wouldn't understand," Col grunted, sucking at his bitten pen.

Hurtle said: "I'm going to be a painter." He was certain of it for the first time; or it had been decided for him.

Col Forster laughed: he had widely spaced, blunt teeth. "What sort?" he asked between gulps of laughter. "A house painter?"

"An artist. That paints paintings." Then you were tempted. "I'm going to be a great painter."

"Fancy yourself, don't you?" Col Forster couldn't laugh enough. "Well, good luck to you, kid! I'm going to write the Great Australian Novel."

Hurtle thought it couldn't be a very interesting book: poor Col had such a thick-looking skin, and those blunt teeth, and the kind fingers holding his chewed pen.

That night Hurtle Duffield didn't dream a dream. He got up early. He wanted to look at things he might never see again, not in their present shape: the moon, for instance; and the sun rising.

When they got home the wall had been repapered. Maman never mentioned it, but he was only half glad. He picked at a join in the new paper to see whether his painting still existed underneath. But he had to stop because just then Rhoda came in.

She told at once: "One of the men who papered the wall said a boy who painted a thing like that must have been born a shingle short. Or some kind of criminal."

"Bet he didn't."

"I swear!"

Since his visit to Mumbelong, Rhoda looked even sicklier. You could see the veins in her white skin. The thin straight line of her mouth was the same colour as the thin necklace of corals they had given her to wear. Her head always trembling. Perhaps she would die, and he wouldn't be sorry.

"What did you tell the man?" he asked as he brushed his hair.

"I told him to mind his own business, and you were my brother."

He saw in the glass she had tightened her mouth like she did after she had told a lie, her head trembling more than ever on its green stalk of a neck. Rhoda wouldn't die, though: her rages made her tough.

"I liked the painting, Hurtle," she said.

"You couldn't have understood it."

"Why couldn't I?" she shouted.

He didn't bother to answer.

"All right then," she said. "I didn't like it. I only said it to be nice."

She might have said or done worse if Miss Gibbons hadn't come and told them: "You're both having dinner in the dining-room as a treat."

"I know that," babbled Rhoda. "There's sweetbreads roastchicken freshstrawberries with icecream. I *know*!"

"You're hysterical," he said.

But instead of being angry she shrieked laughter, started spinning round and round, and rushed out of the room.

"Father's in the nude!" she shrieked. "He's under the shower!"

Miss Gibbons was so embarrassed she forgot to tell Rhoda off. She said in her tightest voice: "Did you enjoy your visit, Hurtle, to Mumbelong?"

He had forgotten all about Sybil Gibbons. She was a sort of forgettable person. Even living in the same house she mightn't have been there. Like junket. Suddenly he saw her as white against white, except for the dark skin round her blurry eyes, two targets, and her belt buckle.

He was so pleased by his discovery he said in the most bookish voice he could imitate: "It was quite enjoyable," but in case that wasn't enough, he got hold of her hand and rubbed it slightly against his cheek.

Sybil Gibbons took such a deep breath she might just have touched the stove. She bolted out to attend to something, perhaps at the same time have a cry. For very little reason her eyes would start watering. She was always mooning over that bloke instead of tearing the photograph up.

He went down, dawdling on the stairs, to feel each drop of crystal light trickle through him from the chandelier.

To welcome them, Maman had been wearing an apron over her dress as though she had come from cooking the dinner herself, which of course she hadn't.

"Oh Harry," she said, and when she came up for breath: "It's been so *lonely!*" In a house full of maids, and Rhoda, and Miss Gibbons.

She looked as if she could eat Father, who actually said: "Got something good for dinner, Freda?"

"And darling darling Hurtle!" she remembered.

She made him feel as shy as though they were kissing for the first time.

Rhoda had the sulks in the beginning. She didn't want to notice. Except Father. When he bent down to make it easy for her to kiss, she closed her eyes: you could see her lips reaching up like a blind pup searching for the tit.

Maman took off her apron. She twirled round, so that all the gauze of her skirt filled ballooning out. She told them: "All my family round me again—now at last I'm *deliriously* happy!"

Father smacked her on the bottom.

At dinner it was Rhoda who appeared, if not delirious, genuinely feverish, if you hadn't known: almost everything about Rhoda was put on.

She told them all, while looking at him: "I'm probably going to write a poem."

"That's interesting." Maman was only humouring her. "What will your poem be about?"

Rhoda at first pursed up her mouth; then she said: "About love."

It made you blow down your nose. Father couldn't laugh properly because his mouth was full of sweetbread; he usually stuffed it rather full. Miss Gibbons, on the other hand, was messing at her food very daintily. One of her shoulders used to droop as she ate. She could never afford to stuff her mouth because she was the governess. Now Rhoda's announcement had turned her as white as a plate.

Maman said: "Do you think you know enough about the subject, Rhoda darling, to be able to write about it?"

"Yes," Rhoda simply said.

It sounded so ridiculous. When suddenly you saw she was serious. She had a fuzzy, frightened look.

"You can imagine it," she said.

"Then perhaps you'll succeed," Maman said very coolly. "And we shall have another genius in the family."

He looked at Rhoda and dared her to be one.

"Who's the other?" she asked.

Maman looked mysterious. She was trying to turn it into a joke, but she badly wanted a genius.

"Who's the other?" Rhoda kept harping in a tinny voice, smacking her food with her fork.

Maman pretended the children weren't there and began asking Father a lot of boring questions about the management of Mumbelong, to show she was interested, though she wasn't.

"Eat up your sweetbread, dear," Miss Gibbons coaxed Rhoda, who wouldn't.

After the chicken had been served she kept on stabbing at one of the little pastry hearts May had sent in to decorate the dish.

There was fruit cup which made you feel sick, or perhaps it was the thyme and stuff in the stuffing.

Rhoda said: "I'm going to start a diary. I'm going to write in it everything I do. And thoughts and things." She was becoming feverish again. "And secret things."

Father said: "That's risky. You're too untidy. You'll leave your secrets lying about. Then other people'll read 'em."

"Secrets are more interesting if they're not all that secret," Rhoda said.

"I can see your point." Again Maman was humouring her: there was a point at which Maman was no longer amused by children.

A silence hung. Then the sound of Father licking his fingers after the bones. Everyone but Sybil Gibbons always enjoyed picking their bones.

"Miss Gibbons keeps a diary," Rhoda said at the height of the silence.

"Oh Rhoda!" Miss Gibbons protested.

Rhoda looked at Hurtle. He was pretty sure she had looked at Miss Gibbons's diary, but he wouldn't let her see he had looked at it too.

Poor Sybil Gibbons was trapped: she had blotches all up her white neck like red ink on blotting paper.

"If you're impertinent, Rhoda," Father warned, "you'll go to bed before the strawberries."

"What's impertinent? I only said!" Rhoda was crying; she could cry when she wanted.

"Jove, my calves are stiff!" Father groaned.

Maman advised him to rub some liniment in before bed, and she would massage them herself to show what a loving wife he had.

Love was never far distant that night in the dining-room. Only Edith didn't seem to know about it, as she changed the plates and handed the strawberries and ice cream.

Rhoda had recovered: she was licking her lips over more than strawberries. "May we work the board before we go to bed?" she was asking Maman while looking at Hurtle.

"What's this 'board'?" Something had happened while he was away.

"It's far too late tonight," said Maman.

Again Rhoda might have shown she was peeved if she hadn't shared this secret with Maman. They were both looking mysterious.

"Yes"—Rhoda sighed—"it's late."

"But what *board*?"

They wouldn't tell: nor would silly Sybil Gibbons when he asked her on the quiet; she was afraid of what they might do to her.

He dreamed a dream Maman was massaging Father's hairy calves Father began choking Maman she laughed because she loved when you tried to share their love they threw you off they wanted to make the bed squeak. He woke. He could have sworn he had heard it; but beds didn't squeak at Sunningdale.

It was not until the following evening when they were sent in to say good-night that he found out about the board. Rhoda had known all along it would be tonight. She was glittering with sweat where her hair began. She was jumping around inside her dress.

In the mauve-papered octagon Maman was waiting for them. She had arranged a card table in the center of the room, on it a kind of little polished board. It had two wheels and a pencil stuck through it. Maman was looking rather limp and far away. She was wearing velvet: it made him shiver when he brushed against it.

"Now, as I have explained to Rhoda already, there are foolish people who take the planchette too seriously. For us, it's only a game—an amusing pastime—which can't possibly cause any harm."

"But what's the planchette?" That he alone didn't know was terribly humiliating.

"Let me ask it the first question!" Rhoda's spit flew.

She spread her hand open like a claw, the tips of her fingers resting on the board.

"Something simple to begin with," Maman suggested. She, too, rested her fingertips on the board: particularly graceful Maman looked, and vague.

"Come on, Hurtle," she ordered. "But lightly, lightly! Don't *press*! The wheels won't run if anyone's heavy-handed. We must concentrate, but very, very delicately, through our fingertips."

Maman was sounding more serious than she had advised. She even closed her eyes.

Rhoda asked quickly, breathlessly, in an artificial voice: "Will it be fine tomorrow?"

It seemed a waste of a question; but, as they breathed, the little wheels, the board itself, began to quiver and sidle about. The pencil wrote on a sheet of paper Maman had spread on the table.

"There!" shrieked Rhoda.

"Quietly, quietly, dearest!" Maman shuddered and held her ears. "Planchette may refuse to work if she doesn't find a sympathetic atmosphere."

Planchette had certainly written, he saw, what could be read as a spidery *yes*.

"Now, Hurtle," said Maman, "what do you think you'd like to ask?"

He couldn't think: he felt so idiotic.

Then he asked: "What sort of day is it going to be?" Stupid.

His jaw felt as though shaped like a turnip. He had only mumbled his dull question, but the board was drawing his tingling fingers along with it.

Windy, it wrote.

"Oh, horrible! I can't bear wind." Already Maman could feel it disarranging her hair.

"Your turn," Rhoda told her.

"What can I possibly ask it?" Maman wondered.

He didn't believe that one.

She was settling herself, so as to become completely tranquil, so that she might compose her question. She was wearing yellow, yellow velvet. From closing her eyes, she opened them. She wasn't Maman: she was again Mrs Courtney, a fantastic stranger, as in the beginning. He thought of the halcyon, of which he had read, and fields of wheat he had seen as a painting in one of Father's books. She was so beautiful thinking of her question, sitting with her fingers poised extra lightly on the board.

"Tell me, Planchette," she said through rather a prim mouth, and as though no one was present, not even children, "tell me," she asked, "is there *anyone else*?"

"'Anyone *else*'?" Rhoda repeated; because the question didn't make sense.

It did to him; he couldn't have explained, but was on the verge of drawing back a curtain.

While the board moved—slowly at first—then violently: bucking and turning corners squealing; their wrists got twisted keeping up with it.

When it had stopped, Rhoda looked. "It's just a lot of scribble!"

Maman didn't laugh: she hissed. "That's because I was dishonest!"

"How—dishonest?" Rhoda sounded furious and scornful.

He knew Maman wouldn't tell: she was too relieved not to have been told what she no longer wanted to know.

Afterwards they asked a lot of silly but amusing questions. Seated round the table, their spread fingers touching on the board, they were a family laughing back at one another. Rhoda had a few gaps in her teeth. Maman's throat rippled under pearls.

Suddenly Hurtle knew that he would ask the question. He hoped the others wouldn't notice he was bursting trembling with it.

When he had shouted them down he very quietly asked: "What am I going to be, Planchette?" He added: "Please."

It was the most awful moment of his life, more awful than finding out what the Duffields and the Courtneys had arranged. They must all believe if they saw it written.

The board was wobbling hopelessly. Trundling heavily. It groaned. But wrote.

Though he was leaning forward to watch and read, Rhoda was so furiously concentrated she got there before him and shouted in his face: "*Painter*, it's written! What—a house painter?" exactly as the jackaroo at Mumbelong had said, to be funny; but in Rhoda's case she could only be jealous: he would have killed her, but was never able to think of words deadly enough.

Maman said in her calmest voice: "Well, then, let us ask, 'What *kind* of painter will Hurtle be?' "

The board joggled worse than ever.

Because greedy and jealous, Rhoda was always the first to read. "*An oil painter!*" she yelled. "Somebody must be guiding it."

"Why should they be guiding it?" He fairly blasted her.

"Because it's what you want to be."

"Children! *Children!*" Maman pretended she might almost faint. "If you insult the planchette, how can you expect another answer?"

That calmed Rhoda, or at least she acted calm. She said in a voice which sounded as though she had a cold: "I want to ask it what I'm going to be."

She did. For a long time the board remained motionless. Serve her right. He thought he might begin to laugh. At Rhoda. The name meant 'a rose,' too!

The board started some long sweeping runs. Rhoda had closed her eyes tight. She could have been praying, or anyway getting through her prayers.

The planchette was writing all right. Maman looked away, as though the answer might be too private for a second person to read. Nobody dared look yet. He wondered what would happen if they spelled out one of the words you could see written on street walls.

When the wheels stopped creaking, Rhoda leaned forward, her neck like a pale green bean-shoot, which he never liked to look at— it was so thin it made him sick with fright and worry: what if it should break off from the hump?

Rhoda was reading: "What—*wom*—?" It was such a spidery writing. "*Woman!*"

She might have been punched, like he had once punched a kid too low, in his former life.

"Someone is guiding it!" Rhoda shrieked.

"Darling! Darling!" Maman was trying to comfort her. "What

could be a nobler fate?" Even so, she couldn't help laughing, and that, too, had a tragic sound.

He remembered Mrs Burt next door: how her womb fell. Mumma had said she didn't know why wombs didn't fall more often, considering the punishment they took.

"But I want to *be* something!" Rhoda was mewing like a cat, protesting against her "noble fate."

Then Miss Gibbons came, because it was time for bed, and led away the sopping Rhoda. He was sorry for her after all.

He continued sitting a while with Maman, like one of the guests who stays on amongst the cigar ash when everyone is getting sleepy.

"How does it work?" he asked. "The board?"

Suddenly he knew what it felt like to be a serious-thinking man.

"Is it electricity?" he asked.

Maman shrugged, and lowered her eyelids, and smiled a sort of smile.

"Who knows?"

She didn't care. She was content to leave it as something mysteriously important they had experienced together.

Then she shuddered. She opened her eyes. She said: "It's time!"

She held out her arms from a great distance, and he was wrapped for an instant in the yellow velvet; he was smelling the dry scents of summer; there was a glint of the halcyon amongst the wheat.

After that, he returned into his clumsy body, and she was his mother again.

When he was in his pyjamas, and had brushed his boring old teeth, Miss Gibbons came to him and said: "Rhoda wants to say good-night. I think she has something to show you."

More than that he wasn't told. You couldn't get anything out of Sybil Gibbons unless you read her diary.

He went into Rhoda's room, where she was propped up on the pillows like Maman, but wearing a flannel nightie, and on each cheek a dry round patch of something pink. She must have rubbed on some dentifrice. He decided not to notice it.

"I want to show you something," she said, giving him a thin, dark-coral smile.

"What?" he asked, pretty sure it was nothing of interest.

She held out her clenched hand at the end of her stiffened arm. At least when she was in bed you didn't notice the hump, but her arm looked horribly thin.

"What is it?" you repeated, like some little kid, while coming closer.

She could have found something. A shell or something. Or a pebble.

She fanned her hand out wide. All the time it had been full of air.

But by now he was so close she threw her arms round him: to kiss.

There was a slight sigh or whimper in all her movements. She smelled of moist flannel, or rubber: the moisture after a bath. And baby powder. Inside it all the steamy scent of Rhoda herself.

When she released him from the kiss she took a deep breath and lay back on the pillows as though she had eaten a satisfying meal.

He was disgusted. In his own room, he had to remind himself Rhoda was his sister. And Mrs Courtney his mother.

Whatever the dreams he dreamed that night they kept on pecking at him, sticking their beaks into his mouth: he woke up next morning feeling shocked he had been so disgustingly disgusted with Rhoda Courtney his sister who had a slight curvature she was going to recover from. He used his fists to rub any remains of disgust out of his gummy eyes.

When he went in for breakfast Rhoda was already messing up her corn and kidneys. They didn't look at each other, which was more or less their usual habit. After breakfast, before lessons began, they went down the garden together, and that, too, was usual.

Rhoda said: "I had a dream, Hurtle. You were keeping a diary. You had written down what you think of me, and you tried to lock the diary up but couldn't find the key. You were furious, because you didn't want me to read it."

They were standing by the sooty little guava tree. He began to feel uneasy.

"But I don't keep a diary. I don't have to!"

"But in the dream. And I didn't have to look. Because I know without looking. That was what made you so angry."

He felt more than ever uneasy; even if she didn't always see, she was a pick-axe on some occasions.

So he changed the subject as hard as he could, and no dreams. "One night I couldn't sleep. I went into their room, and Father was on top of Maman. It was like fowls. Rhoda? You've seen fowls?"

His description wasn't strictly accurate, but out of a sense of—not delicacy, perhaps horror of her hump, he didn't say: "like men and women in real life."

"Fowls," he emphasized, "without their feathers," and laughed to make it sound cruder.

That ought to cure Rhoda. He was breathless from his own brainwave. But she didn't appear to have understood, or if she had, she wasn't going to admit. She went on picking at the soot on a guava leaf, and when she spoke she didn't answer his question.

"I'm tired," she said.

"But you've only got up."

Her legs seemed to drag.

"You're not sick, are you?"

Her hump looked enormous.

"I'm just tired."

After that, they didn't speak, but dragged back past the *Monstera deliciosa*, which Maman called the Delicious Monster, and the statues at the top of the steps. He was relieved that his thoughts, and Rhoda's, were again fully clothed.

By the time he had turned twelve he was growing so fast his knickerbockers soon wouldn't button at the knees.

Maman said: "Only since my children started growing have I realized how immoral it is to be rich: to be in a position to clothe them adequately at every moment of their growth is very immoral."

Rhoda didn't grow, or not enough to notice; it was Hurtle her son she saw when she made remarks like that. Sometimes, to help her conscience, she would postpone replacing his outgrown clothes.

"When am I going to get a new suit?" he had to ask at last.

"Think of the poor," Maman replied dreamily.

Certainly he had almost forgotten his Duffield existence, but to remember it now didn't seem particularly virtuous, not with his tight-fitting knickerbockers, and the ends of his coat-belt scarcely meeting.

"Oh, I know all about the poor!" He delivered it as cheeky as possible.

But Maman had her own thoughts. "You can't imagine what it's like washing the separator on frosty mornings. How blunt, red, hideous, fingers can become!"

"What separator? Where?"

It seemed she was late for some ladies' luncheon. She began rubbing the lip salve on, then rubbing it off again so that it shouldn't be noticed.

It was often suffocating at home. Once he shot a pebble at the chandelier, and the crystal chimed back at him. He drew a cock and balls at the back of the book during the old history lesson. If Sybil Gibbons found it, would she tell her diary? He would have to look. He was sick of the governess and the tutors.

When Mr Tyndall died of an angina pectoris they brought Miss Dora Finzi for the drawing lessons. Miss Finzi liked to arrange herself in positions, but her face had a cutting edge: it was more in the style of a serious man. "Whatever I teach you," she said, "you must reject one day, if you find you're not being true to yourself."

Her respect for him made him feel humble. He did a water colour one hot afternoon: of Miss Finzi, in position, in a many-coloured dress. They had bought him the water colours by then. They bought him the oils to humour him. His happiness should have been complete.

He said to Father: "When am I going to school—Dad?"

The children were still let in to say good-morning while the parents were lying in bed; it was perhaps their closest, their most agreeable hour together. In the smell of recent sleep, with the sound of doves around the palms on the lawn, Maman could believe that she loved Rhoda. Father, on his back, made the newspaper crackle, its print so fresh it came off on your hands as you lay beside him.

"Eh, Dad? When?"

"Don't say *eh*," said Maman. "It sounds common."

She had a greasy look by that butter-coloured light.

"My darling, darling Mummy," Rhoda smoodged, snuggling up, "let's play at my being your little baby."

Father was thrashing the paper about. Even nowadays he would turn aside from the *Herald* and throw off a kiss, or try to, as if you were still a kid. It was horrible. His beard pricked: the beard of a fusty old man you almost no longer knew.

"Well, then, when am I going to this school?" The lessons in Rhoda's schoolroom were so much rot.

Father said: "Next year." Sometimes he went as far as: "Next term." Or, on one occasion: "You're ready for it. We only didn't want to throw you to the lions before you'd learned the same roar."

Then Father laughed, or heaved, or wheezed, as he thrashed the paper about, the nightshirt open on his chest, on the grey-black hair. You couldn't be sure whether Maman ever noticed it; you could never be sure what older people saw. But a lot of blooming repulsive hair!

On one occasion Maman said: "You're not so big, Hurtle, that you can't get into bed with your poor old mother."

He couldn't say the idea made him sick. He wouldn't have done what she wanted if they hadn't been on their own: not let Rhoda watch him make a fool of himself.

Actually it wasn't so bad against Maman's silky side, and the hair, all around her on the pillow, smelling of washed hair. He closed his eyes and put his face in it.

"There!" she said. "You're still my treasure. You know you are."

In this darkness, of overflowing hair and pillows which softly gave, he had never been so close to what they probably meant by bliss.

When he opened his eyes, Maman, who resisted chocolates now on account of her figure, was scratching in a box on the bedside table. She soon heaved back into their former soft position; she stuck the chocolate in her own mouth, and warmed it up till she had it ready to offer: or so he understood, from the bird-noises she began to make. They were like two birds together, feeding on the same food, as they worked the chocolate, neither soft nor hard, neither his nor hers: the chocolate trickled blissfully.

Suddenly Maman went: "Mm—mm—*hmmm!*" rising to a high note.

She sucked in the chocolate so quickly his tongue almost followed it.

She sat up in bed. "Oh dear, what silly things we do! Childish things!" When she was the childish one: he wouldn't have thought of the silly trick with the chocolate.

Gathering up her hair by handfuls, she was smiling; but it was not for him: more for herself, it looked.

He got out of bed and began feeling for his slippers. He might have been treading on glass instead of the soft carpet. He straightened up, after spreading his hands to hide what he had to hide.

Hurtle Courtney liked to escape after lessons, shaking them off, together with Rhoda, go down alone through the dark-leaved garden, down the plunging, moss-cushioned steps, to the tree. It had a prickly trunk he learned to climb. He learned to lie along a prickly branch, over the street. Sometimes when people were passing he would make a funnel of his mouth, and let down the spit, sticky and silver, as of the tree itself, hanging, swinging in a string, and finally falling. Sometimes they looked up and threatened him, but more often the people hurried away pretending nothing had happened.

Once a mob of larries happened to pass underneath, and he spat from the branch in quick spurts. Through the tears in their clothes he could see their sunburnt nakedness; he could almost smell their gunpowder flesh. At once his former life began boiling up in him.

The others looked up and began pulling faces of hate. One of them had a catapult. Their voices went to work on him.

"Come on down, fuckun little silvertail! We'll put a frill around yer!" the hoarsest of them called up.

A stone numbed a place in his shoulder.

"Wait till I git down," he shouted back in a voice to match, "I'll drive the teeth into yer gob quicker than yer bargain for."

In fact he slithered out of the tree quicker than he himself had expected; the soles of his boots were thudding on the hot asphalt; to a sound of bone on bone he began rubbing out their faces, their hard flesh turning to ripe tomato as he let them have it. Blood was a taste he had forgotten: liquid pencils.

Then when they streaked off he ran after them in his burst Norfolk jacket and unbuttonable knickerbockers. "'Ere! Hey! Wait a mo! I got somethun ter tell yez," he called in the remembered language.

Unconvinced, the pack ran on, and as it became an increasing blur, there flickered through his mind the possum with the bell round its neck Sid Cupples had told about: the freak tinkling after them, driving the "sane buggers" always farther away.

So Hurtle Courtney Duffield gave up at last. He stood in the street, the two languages he knew fighting for possession of him. At the worst, though brief moment, when it seemed unlikely he would ever succeed in communicating through either tongue, he heard himself blubbering.

Not long after, he was due to start at a proper school. They had driven out to visit the Head, who spoke English, but wasn't. They walked through the old buildings, and the established boys in their uniforms looked at them with curiosity and disguised contempt, not only the long-legged, shaven men, but also the ink-stained bits of kids.

"You won't feel nervous, will you? You're too sensible." The Head's wife answered her own question.

She was a woman whose mouth couldn't contain all its teeth: some of them were permanently on view, with a fascinating tinge of grey-green; as if this wasn't enough, she kept wetting them with her lips to make them glisten more.

Of course Maman had to put in her word. "Oh, he's never *nervous*. Hurtle Courtney's a very cool customer indeed!"

He blushed for her, for borrowing an expression like "cool customer," which he had only heard men use. A group of older boys at the corner of one of the old stone buildings had obviously overheard: the boys were laughing at slang out of the wrong mouth. They were laughing at his own extraordinary name, and at Maman's hat, which was making her family look ridiculous. At least the boys could not have heard about Rhoda and her hump; Rhoda was stored up for the future.

His escape from the schoolroom at home might have turned out less a triumph of emancipation than an initiation into tribal horrors if there hadn't been a sudden change of plan. They were leaving for Europe—like that—because Maman couldn't bear to put it off any longer. Originally their party was to have consisted of themselves, Keep, and Sybil Gibbons. Then Maman decided she would do without her maid; besides being a grumpy old thing, Keep would never stand the foreign food. Then they lopped Miss Gibbons off. Travel was an education in itself, said Maman, and you could always engage people on the spot to teach any of the languages.

Miss Gibbons left a week before they were to sail. As they kissed good-bye, her hat got pushed to the back of her head and she looked as though she had been in some kind of accident. Her nose, gone red, sounded blocked as she spluttered: "I am so *grateful* . . ." It sounded silly in the circumstances, like a phrase out of a copybook, though certainly Father had handed her an envelope. Father believed you could make everything good with a cheque, but wasn't always let off lightly, as when Miss Gibbons spurted tears.

From the porch they watched Rowley drive her away. Poor old Sybil Gibbons would remain a pale thing: except in her diary. In one place in the diary he had found: "There are nights when I lie in bed and wonder whether I shall be able to prevent myself beating out my brains against the wall. I shall be thirty next January. . . ."

If he ever painted Sybil Gibbons he would show her pale green, vegetable flesh tortured by moonlight and hot sheets, her lips slightly open as he saw they would have to be.

Actually he soon forgot Miss Gibbons: there were the bony Frenchwomen, their tricolour faces, and wicked bums in spite of corsets. There was the French language, which hadn't come alive till now, in spite of Maman, and Madame Parmentier, and the books through which he had tediously ground. Most important of all were the paintings, which showed him a reality more intense than the life he had so far experienced. He was all the time drawing in secret, and destroying, and on several occasions he painted something. The inadequacy and necessity of his efforts drained him as despairingly as an orgasm in the bath.

Rhoda's life, too, seemed to become more secret the more they travelled, the longer they lived in foreign hotels. Though she wasn't growing all that much—Dr Mosbacher confirmed that in such cases the period of physical growth was brief—he could sense that she had grown away from him inside. All right, he didn't in any way depend on Rhoda; but there were times when he would have liked to be certain of what was going on.

At Wiesbaden, for instance, she announced without encouragement: "Hurtle, I'm going to show you something." Hadn't he heard it before? "I'm going to show you a poem I've written. Probably tomorrow. By then I shall have polished it enough."

He could hardly believe she had written the poem: she was looking too mysterious; and in fact she never showed it to him.

Rhoda was thriving on the mysteries she made in a succession of hotels, in the plush-upholstered nooks, to the tune of unexplained gusts of laughter, in the smells of dumpling and *Rehbraten*, and soil gone sour round potted palms; while something was happening inside her blouse, to what Maman continued calling "poor Rhoda's chest," and Rhoda herself had begun referring to her "strawberry" hair.

Because he might buy a sapphire in the morning, Father ordained that they were to economize over baths at night in the locked bathrooms of the foreign hotels. Behind the back of the *Kammermädchen* (or *femme de chambre*), the clean Australians replaced one another virtuously but secretly. In the steep baths of the steamed-up bathrooms of Belgium, Germany, and France, there were strands of strawberry mingling with the darker hairs. The rough bathrobes had grown heavy with damp by the time you inherited them. Even a dry robe must have flattened Rhoda, who had never taken a bath without a nurse or a governess at her elbow. But she loved to lie in hot baths. She lay so long, sometimes he would have to knock. (What if she had died?)

Always on taking over, he would feel guilty, lying in the bath where Rhoda had lain, surrounded by her watermark and a few strands of pinkish hair. He would jump out, skidding on the tiles, and rub himself down frantically. Once, for certain, she pieced together a torn-up drawing while he lay thinking in the bath.

They were all of them more or less obsessed by Rhoda.

In Brussels and Paris they bought her clothes to make her forget about herself. They bought her a hat which was like a Frenchwoman's hat on a little girl. Her head trembled in the old way while she walked, but there was a new swinging motion of the body, as though she had discovered importance in her hips, or might perhaps throw the load off her back. She looked at him and dared him to see, but knew that he did.

On coming out of the bedroom in Brussels, Maman told him: "Poor Rhoda isn't by any means well. We must ask them to send for a doctor."

"Oh, I'm well," Rhoda called from the room behind. "I'm always *well*. Only the doctors say I'm not. Behind my *back*!" She burst out laughing, or possibly crying, but Maman went in again and closed the door.

Again, Maman and Rhoda were arguing: it was the same bedroom above the glass wintergarden. "But the board, or the floor—it's the same. You *torture* me!" Rhoda screamed.

Maman was sobbing. "I was given my cross and shall bear it to the end."

Dr Marquet said, on coming out: "*Elle est quand même un petit peu hystérique.*"

Should you go in?

He couldn't resist it at last. Rhoda was alone in the darkening room. She demanded from her bed: "Where is my father?" But he couldn't tell her.

They could hear a thin violin at work under the roof of the wintergarden, which the management had netted with wire to stop people jumping through the glass. Rhoda tried to get hold of his hand. She did in the end, and he sat joined to her at the thumb, while the dirty light from the well closed down on them gradually.

And Rhoda said in the dark: "Don't think I'm going to die. I'll live longer than everyone."

Looking back over their travels, the memories clotted most thickly round St Yves de Trégor and London.

St Yves de Trégor was a small resort on the Breton coast, in the depths of a bay, on an estuary. It had a mournfulness of mud and gulls, of wind blowing across stony fields out of the Atlantic. All its colours were water colours. The most pretentious hotel was without even a locked bathroom, but the bedrooms were equipped with bidets on collapsible iron stands.

Why they stopped at St Yves de Trégor nobody could ever remember, except probably they were exhausted by diarrhoea. Nobody knew what had caused it, perhaps the shellfish, but every traveller in Brittany was suffering from the diarrhoea. It was the topic discussed most frequently in trains, that is, by tourists with other tourists, though Maman and Father refused to be classified as such.

On arrival at St Yves they were driven through the dusk, down narrow lanes between roughly piled stone walls. Their way was strewn with stones, from which the horses' hoofs struck sparks. One of the horses had a cough.

Some kind of embarrassment arose over the hotel rooms; the *patronne* considered the problem in her register through unusually thick glasses. In the end they were ushered to rooms which must have been occupied the night before: the beds were still unmade. Maman turned away from the sheets on the big wooden bed in the *chambre à deux personnes.*

Anger made Father's French more fluent. *"Mais c'est la nuit, et les lits ne sont pas encore faites."* It made no difference. The *patronne* and the *femme de chambre* couldn't disguise the sheets they were bundling up; and under one of the beds Rhoda discovered an unemptied chamber pot. Maman was too upset to correct Father's French grammar.

When the clean sheets were brought she began to whisper: "Are they damp? I'm sure they are. They feel like it." They weren't, though: only cold, sticky from salt air, and rough.

Rhoda was beginning to droop as she did when ready to fall asleep.

Maman said, taking out her hatpins: "We shall leave in the morning—by the first train."

But you hoped against it; everything you saw was of importance: a small ball of combed-out hair lying in a corner.

And in the dining-room, though Maman commanded soggy rice for Rhoda and herself, there was a big comforting soup, with lumps of bacon and chunks of potato and cabbage stalk, which the *patronne* herself ladled out from a huge cracked tureen.

The *patronne* said: "*Sont gentils, les p'tits, mais fatigués.*" She smiled at them, showing short teeth and pale gums, and you smiled back slightly sickly to match the situation.

The *patronne* was wearing a black crochet shawl with an uneven fringe.

Maman had reached the stage of laugh-crying: "In the morning—by the first train!" she reminded Father even before the *patronne* had removed herself.

Father's mouth was full of bacon and hot potato. "But it isn't so bad, Freda. Hurtle and I don't think it is."

Hurtle hoped all night that Father would prevail. All night he listened to the sea advancing over mud encroaching on his room a voice the voice of a woman rinsing crashing laughing the bidet must have. Somewhat early the diarrhoea came over him again. He had to get up. As he crouched and shivered on the raised footprints above the hole, a crying of gulls blew in at him. He looked out, and a liquid light had begun to sluice the estuary.

They spent three whole days at St Yves de Trégor. Maman never stopped pointing out how appalling everything was: the beds, the plumbing, the food, the *patronne* Madame Clémence, the doctor who arrived in bicycle clips and a celluloid collar to prescribe for her. Maman was exhausted by the diarrhoea: she had a deep grey line from each nostril to the corners of her mouth; and because her powers of resistance had temporarily left her, they stayed.

Father unbuttoned his clothes and sat about the beach, reading stale English newspapers and smoking cheroots. He had taken off his boots and socks, but it was too cold for paddling. Maman brooded over the postcards she hadn't the strength to write, even without her corsets. Because she wasn't allowed to go out, Rhoda hopped humming from room to room. She discovered a drift of dead flies, which rustled as she gathered them up from the windowsill.

Madame Clémence made a grand gesture with her arm, from under her short thick woollen shawl. *"Le paysage est magnifique, vous voyez. De grands peintres viennent de loin, de Paris même, pour en profiter."*

"Mon fils est peintre," Maman offered in a weak voice.

Madame Clémence said it wasn't possible. She said it was a charming occupation.

He did in fact paint a little picture, but secretly, the day before they left St Yves. He didn't show his painting because it was too unsuccessful, or too private. He painted the silver light sluicing the grey mud as he saw it from his window, and as focus point, the faintest sliver of pink shining in the fork of the estuary. His crude attempt made him whinge. In the end he hid his failure under the bed. He thought he wouldn't look at it again.

Probably he would never have started the botched thing if it hadn't been for an incident early that morning. He had decided to go into Rhoda's room, for no clear reason: he was drawn in that direction. As soon as he began to make the move he tried to stop himself, but couldn't. The loose knob on Rhoda's door was already rattling. Like his voice offering unconvincing excuses in advance. Before he positively burst in.

Rhoda was standing beside one of the spindly iron-legged bidets. She was naked down to the soles of her feet. She was trying to protect her privacy from this too sudden invasion of light. She was holding in front of her thighs a sponge which only half hid the shadow of pink hair.

Because he was so shocked he began to point, to grind his foot into the floor, to laugh his crudest and loudest. Before backing out. The rattling door slammed shut, but only thin, between them.

He ran into his room and squashed his face into a disgusting eiderdown, to try to blot out what had happened.

At midday they met in the dining-room. Rhoda sat staring from under sponged eyelids at the *gigot aux haricots.* Hurtle had plastered down his watered hair.

Maman looked at them embracingly and couldn't wait to tell: "Tomorrow we are leaving St Yves de Trégor!"

In the train he realized he had left his painting under the bed, amongst the fluff, against the slopping chamber pot. Rhoda was wearing a bonnet and a kind of long travelling cape, but would never again look fully clothed. As the train ran lurching through the fields, he saw her very vividly: the ribs of her pale body beside the iron framework of the collapsible bidet, her naked face, and the tuft of pink in the shadow of her thighs. Courage was taking hold of him again. He began to try her out in his mind in several different attitudes and lights. Invaded by his vision of flesh, he forgot the botched estuary.

"I do believe they intend to break every bone we possess!" Maman had discovered something fresh to protest against; it made her happy, even though her hat had been pushed over one ear when the lurching threw her into Father's lap.

While you let yourself gently flow with the motion of the train, soothed by the beauty of the forms disguised in Rhoda's deformed body, even in the old chamber pot under the bed at St Yves de Trégor.

Rhoda let herself be rocked, looking out of the window, and not. She probably hated him deeply for what he had seen, and would never let herself understand what else: the light he would show burning in the cage of her ribs; the belly sloping down from the winkle of a navel towards the flame she couldn't put out with her sponge. He would do all that he had to do. But not yet. It was too luxurious thinking about it.

London was very solid after France. Behaviour mattered an awful lot, with the result that you, too, behaved better, even alone in the hotel room. Though Maman and Father had visited London several times before, they were not as confident and experienced as you would have expected. They seemed to be apologizing to the serv-ants, which they never bothered to do at home. Everybody tried to pronounce better. Rhoda learned the language in no time and spoke it in a cold clear offensive little voice. It was more difficult for Maman and Father to keep up pretences, because they had always allowed themselves to say more or less what they wanted, and lose their tempers if they felt like it. For Hurtle the controlled tones of the English were no trouble at all, since he already had two other versions of English by heart.

Father took Hurtle to his tailor and ordered for his son a suit in the very latest fashion. When the scurfy old tailor knelt and stuck the measure hard up into the crutch of his pants, Hurtle realized from the glass how leggy he had become. He felt touchy, too. Before the tailor rammed the measure home—surely unnecessarily hard—he had never been touched, it seemed, by anyone other than himself. He hated it. He blushed at himself in the glass, and wondered whether Rhoda would have noticed.

On returning to their hotel ("not ostentatious, but highly approved") they found Rhoda seated alone downstairs, wearing that prim expression she put on whenever she decided to act the lady. She had crossed her ankles. She was looking at nothing in particular and enjoying her own attitude when Father and Hurtle walked in through the glass and mahogany doors. Immediately Rhoda looked at Hurtle. Still her face expressed nothing: not pleasure; not even recognition; but she made him feel a kid again, and he blushed a second time over that reflection in the tailor's glass as the old man held the tape-measure tightly rammed into the fork of his legs. Naturally Rhoda didn't know how he had resented being touched, but she might have known.

Then Rhoda herself blushed and turned her face away: Father had the tactlessness to try out a joke. "Do you suppose she's expecting a caller? I wonder who he is?"

Hurtle played up to it. "Will it be a real live lord, or only a tuppenny honourable?" He made his voice as raucous and vulgar as he could.

Quickly Rhoda uncrossed her ankles, then lashed them together again. She ducked her head when Father tried to stroke her hair in passing. "It was only a joke, girlie." But his apology and the attempt at endearment only made it worse.

Even Hurtle sympathized. She was no longer of an age to be teased, though strangers mightn't have believed. Where once she would have screamed back in her own defence, now it sometimes seemed as though she was trying to turn herself into marble to disguise even her visible thoughts; but Rhoda's marble remained afflicted.

There were occasions when they all visited the stately London art galleries, in the muted atmosphere of which, lords and ladies directed blue stares out of billowing shrubberies, or proudly reined in their horses before a perspective of park. Maman preferred the English to the French style in painting. Although she lectured the chambermaids on what Australians thought and felt, she dearly loved the lords and ladies she had never met. At least in the picture galleries there was no question of her meeting those of another age, so she was able to concentrate on art. Sometimes the paintings made her misty-wistful, or, particularly in front of sunsets, she behaved as though she was suffering from a stomachache.

Hurtle told himself: I mustn't feel like this about my mother, not even when I see and hear.

Father gave less trouble, because men weren't moved to carry on to the same extent.

Father said: "It would have been a solid investment, Freda, if we'd picked up a Gainsborough at the right moment."

Maman was too entranced to answer, in her pretty hat and Zouave jacket.

Rhoda was too bored. She followed, picking the skin at the corners of her nails: it was so boring in the galleries.

Father farted in front of a Sargent, the way old men never seemed to realize what is coming. And in an empty gallery.

Of course Maman didn't hear. It was Hurtle and Rhoda who did. Who started rocking. Then hiccupping, it sounded, the other side of a column.

"Shut up!" Hurtle hadn't meant to bellow.

"Stop hitting me!" Rhoda hissed.

It was like old times, in which they were brother and sister, down by the liquid manure at the bottom of the garden; till an elderly custodian restored them to their present ages, their formal relationship, by severely frowning at them.

Hurtle announced: "I'm off to my fitting. Where do you think they're going next?"

"Actually I've no idea," Rhoda answered. "I have letters to write."

She wrote endless letters to the maids at home, who replied only sometimes and illegibly. Rhoda waited for her mail as though her life depended on it.

Maman, too, had her fittings—it was so important to be dressed—but attended lectures, concerts, as well as matinées, with other Australian ladies. She coaxed Father to *thés dansants,* and to opera performances at which her shoulders shone. She adored Wagner and the elegant old Queen Alexandra.

Their stay in London might have remained insignificant and frivolous if its current hadn't quickened seriously on a certain wet afternoon. Father was away in Scotland, inspecting Aberdeen Angus bulls. Maman and Rhoda, both dressed against the cold, and with trimmings of damp fur, Hurtle in his velvet-collared overcoat, carrying the new silver-knobbed malacca cane, had set out shopping for the sake of shopping.

It was one of the greyest days, pierced by black monuments. Hurtle lost the others for a moment: they had all floated apart in the drizzle, the sound of wheels revolving in wet, the tramping of galoshes; when he found himself staring into a display window of horrible purpose. There was a little brown stuffed dog clamped to a kind of operating table. The dog's exposed teeth were gnashing in a permanent and most realistic agony. Its guts, exposed, too, and varnished pink to grey-green, were more realistic still.

The first wave of shock hadn't broken in him when Rhoda arrived at his elbow. "What is it?" she gasped from out of the drizzle. "Why—oh poor *dog!*" Normally she didn't care for dogs: they dirtied her clothes, and sometimes knocked her over; but from her anguish now, she herself might have been stretched on the operating table.

Maman came up. Rain had upset the texture of her furs. Her lips were parted in what had begun as a smile. She stopped in front of the plate-glass. Her teeth looked older than the rest of her.

"There!" Maman screeched, baring her teeth wider at the stuffed and varnished dog. "Ohhhh! That is what I should never forget! But did. The vivisectionists!"

A crowd was gathering to watch and listen.

"There's nothing so inhuman as a human being. We must never rest." Maman was calling an army into action. "Do you understand?"

The crowd couldn't very well. Maman couldn't either, except that she had been guilty of the sin of neglect.

"I wish Daddy were here," she whimpered.

Then she began to gather her fatherless children by the elbows, hustling them towards the kerb; she could rely on nobody; her musquash and velour had become most inadequate.

Heaped together at last in a cab, they might have enjoyed the comfort of warmth and closeness if Maman's conscience hadn't got to work again. "I believe that horrifying object was given us as a sign. It's time we left for home. I'm wasting my life—while so many defenceless creatures are being heartlessly destroyed."

It reminded him of the planchette: a drunken and accusing scribble; though Maman wasn't drunk, only frightened. Rhoda's face had clamped down white on the thoughts behind it. He, too, felt frightened, and wished they might be given a sign more consoling than the agonizing dog.

Maman missed dinner because the experience had brought on one of her migraines. Hurtle and Rhoda went down together, to the almost empty, unemotional grill room, where they ordered fried whitebait in little potato baskets, and drank lots of water while waiting. Hurtle could see themselves at a distance in one of the big gold mirrors, their reflections lit by the pink-shaded lamp on their small table. Inside the grotto made by the gilded curlicues of the mirror-frame, they sat looking rich, protected, and overdressed.

He was so shocked he felt his nerve-ends must be waving inside him like hair.

He looked away from the reflections, at the actual Rhoda, and deliberately said: "What are you supposed to be tonight—a Christmas tree? It doesn't suit anyone so stunted."

Rhoda pretended not to have heard, and went on rolling bread pellets, which came out grey, though her hands appeared clean.

His own behaviour on top of other things hurt and horrified him to such an extent he took up the pencil the waiter had forgotten and began drawing in the margin of the menu, as he always did when a situation became unbearable, practically as though playing with himself.

Then the whitebait were brought. They were delicious, and he gorged himself. Rhoda, too, had an appetite. When the fish was finished they started eating the potato baskets, though perhaps you weren't supposed to.

There was peach Melba after that, which they ordered because they recognized the name. Without the attraction of familiarity they would probably have followed each other in ordering: he and Rhoda, he realized, always did choose the same things. He might have gone into the matter if the syrupy sweet hadn't begun to make him feel sick. Or the gallons of water they had drunk. Or the memory of their panicky drive in a cab smelling of wet galoshes.

Rhoda could have been feeling the same: she was holding her handkerchief to her mouth; she was teetering, or tittering, or trying not to throw up across the table, over the big beautifully printed menu.

"You do it on purpose," she choked.

"Do what?"

It was his drawing, in the margin of the menu, of the little tortured dog clamped to the sort of operating table.

"I was trying to work something out," he mumbled.

"Oh yes, you're always trying to work something out—on somebody. I know *you*!"

He couldn't understand why she hated him so.

"Everybody says—all the girls: Edith, Lizzie, Keep—my parents were mad to attempt it. It could only fail—with you. From where you came. *You*!"

She took up a fruit-knife and jabbed it into his thigh. It didn't enter, but felt as though it nearly did.

"You're the one who's mad!" His voice sounded like that of a boy with the wind up. "Somebody 'ull see us."

He was shaken by the impression he seemed to make on others; it was so wrong: if he could have shown them.

But worse was happening: Rhoda had broken out crying, not the sniffly ladylike whimper Maman sometimes used on Father, but a big boohoo.

"All right," he said several times over.

The waiter came and asked, in the tone produced by English servants whatever the occasion: would they care for coffee? They wouldn't.

On the way up in the lift, a gold cage, carpeted like everywhere else, Rhoda had quietened down. An old man with a hook instead of a right hand stood hauling on a slack soft rope which bumped the lift from side to side.

Then, leaving the lift, Rhoda flashed the knife again. "The way you smarm your hair, Hurtle, reminds me of a Darlinghurst butcher boy." He might have been more conscious of the wound if he had felt less exhausted.

Maman called from the far end of their suite on hearing them blunder through the outer door: "Is that my children?" Her nose must have swelled. "Won't you come and kiss me?" Through the dark, carpeted, stuffy rooms and a strong smell of eau de Cologne, they went to do it, bumping against cabin trunks.

The following day Father arrived in response to a wire. He looked both happy and healthy after Scotland and the bulls. Something of a colder, less dangerous climate had freshened his skin. His eyes were clear.

But Maman wouldn't leave it at that, and Father's expression soon became involved with her uneasiness.

A few days later he came in and said: "Well, Alfreda, I've made the reservations, as that's what you want. We're leaving on the third. But it's most unreasonable," he added through thicker lips. "Before the Dublin Horseshow. Goodwood, too."

Maman revived for the first time since the afternoon they came across the martyred dog; when she had kissed everyone she said: "Oh, I know I'm right. I have my intuitions. I shan't feel happy till we're lying in our own beds." Again she made it a mystery: they might have been seated round the planchette; only then she had been smooth and golden, now her skin was grey and wrinkled as though the fog had got into it.

Rhoda began a little dance. Where anyone else would have galumphed, she made frail scratching sounds. He decided not to look, but couldn't help hearing.

Rhoda said: "I don't know why we ever went away. Wherever you go, you've still got to go on being yourself."

"Oh, but darling, you were getting so much out of it!" Maman was so put out; she liked to have things both ways.

Rhoda mumbled: "No." Then, raising her voice, she accused: "Only Hurtle has got something out of it. He's learned better ways of being nasty."

He turned round. Did she really believe this? Apparently she did. He started to defend himself, but his voice died in a croak. If that was what she believed. But did she? Then nobody would believe in his other, his real intentions.

3

They returned, though not to the old life. Something had happened in the meantime. The garden, the house had shrunk. The maids who had been kept on to ward off moth and rust were fatter than before and had lost some of their authority. Most noticeably, the chandelier had dwindled and dulled above the hall. The stone steps leading to the lower garden were, on the other hand, more than ever moss-upholstered, and the collapse of the latticed summerhouse during a storm presented a ruin round which the green lightning of childhood still occasionally played, orange fungus glared, and a smell of rot drifted, often sickening, sometimes thrilling.

Against this shimmer of sensation, practical arrangements were being made for the children's education. It was obvious Rhoda couldn't be exposed to the robust conventions of a school. Maman had visions of her knocked down and trampled on by a throng of normal, thoughtless girls bursting with blood and health after games. Hurtle didn't say he thought she might survive. Rhoda was so busy locking up her secret self she hadn't time to comment. She looked whiter than ever under the pink hair and lashes, and was perhaps secretly powdering. Her diary she kept locked too.

It was arranged that she should go to the Hollingrakes, who employed a governess, an Englishwoman, for their only daughter Boo and three or four other acceptable girls. The Hollingrakes had made their money out of sugar, and were quick to reject almost everybody in case they themselves shouldn't be accepted. Maman was almost abject in her gratitude for Mrs Hollingrake's acceptance.

Boo was a dark green, smooth girl, well developed for her age, otherwise refined, because her mother was determined sugar should be. The three or four companion girls were well chosen for attainments and prospects. And now there would be little Rhoda Courtney.

Hurtle was preparing to start his first term at the only possible school. As the separation from his family approached, he became moodily indifferent rather than sentimental, for Father was preoccupied restocking Sevenoaks with imported Aberdeen Angus, and Maman had her obsessions.

"What is wrong with my mother?" Hurtle asked. "Is she sick?"

Father frowned at first; then he cleared his throat and said: "No. She isn't what you'd call sick; it's her time of life." He would have liked to enjoy with his son the luxury of masculinity, but perhaps the boy wasn't old enough, in spite of long limbs and a voice beginning to shake off the gravel.

Whenever he came across it, his parents' vulnerability embarrassed Hurtle.

At school they despised him because he spoke English; so he had to relearn their language. Then they respected him for what he had experienced: those Paris prosses!

"Did your old man know about it?" the boys asked, gathering round.

"Did he *know*! He took me to the house. All the girls were lined up. We choose whichever we like the look of. I pick the one with the red hair. Don't know how much they stung him for. There was music while you wait. And a champagne supper afterwards."

Once he began laying it on he couldn't stop. Each girl, as he saw her, had a Toulouse-Lautrec throat. He could see where the stockings ended and the garters ate into the dollops of flesh.

It got round the school. A group of older boys sent for him. "What's all this about the French prostitutes?"

He had to tell it all over again. Some of the boys were lolling thoughtfully, chewing grass. Some of them had already tried a shave; others still glistened with silky down. Several were looking tight about the crutch.

There was a prefect Hubert Chanfield invited Courtney to walk with him of a Sunday along the creek. Where the yellow banks of dried clay became particularly steep, and the air was no longer circulating, Chanfield started smiling and showing. He asked Courtney to take down his pants. Courtney, when it came to the point, was humiliated by not yet knowing how he wanted to dispose of himself. He was ticking with excitement, though. He scrambled up the bank, clutching at handfuls of white grass, clay still clinging to the roots, and stalked off along the level ground, hands stiff in his trouser pockets.

School was tedious enough; the games he played to show he was able, the lessons at which he forgot what he had learned; but the holidays were, if anything, worse, in the diminished house with his parents and sister.

Maman had returned to a fury of letter-writing and committees, while continuing to harp on the theme of her wasted life. One of several dazzled spinsters usually present would assure her she was belittling herself.

"Oh no," she insisted, drawing down the corners of her mouth, "I'm frivolous, superficial, ignorant, thoughtless. I don't say I'm *altogether* without good qualities," she added, and the spinsters heard it gratefully, "but I have no illusions about myself."

Then she would dispatch her satellites on various little missions about the house, at which they were not quite servants, not quite equals; while she returned to her dashing correspondence: her nib could be heard gashing the parchment.

"Hurtle?" On one occasion she called him into the octagon, which had been repapered in primrose while they were away. "This is something I'd like you to take an interest in—now that you're coming of a responsible age." She clasped her hands as though starting a prayer, her rings shot by candlelight: black candles to match the japanned woodwork. "I want very seriously to found our own Australian Society for the Abolition of Vivisection."

His voice was preparing to crack a protest, not against his involvement in a cause—poor damn dogs—but against his involvement; he could not yet afford the intrusion on his privacy.

"I shall never forget," she said, "coming across the poor tortured—certainly only stuffed—little dog that cold wet afternoon." Her rising emotion almost flattened the candle flames.

All right. Hadn't he, too, understood and got the horrors?

"Heartlessness towards animals," she said, "could be the first sign of cruelty in human beings."

Actually Maman didn't care for animals. She had never kept them because she was afraid they might make demands on her time. But in her present emotional state they seemed to have touched her obsession with hurt.

"Where is Rhoda?" she suddenly asked.

He didn't know. If he had known, probably by now he wouldn't have told; the whole situation in the little stuffy familiar room had grown too murky.

To add to it, Maman had started crying. "Rhoda—" she sobbed—"we must all—*all of us*—fight against every *form* of cruelty—resist our passions."

She could have forgotten he was standing there.

"At least I shall pray for it," she gasped, and blew her nose.

The scene was over, it seemed.

Maman had always encouraged the habit of prayer. When they were young children she would sometimes remember to hear their prayers on her way to dinner, and the words would breathe a perfume, they would start to glitter with the fire of precious stones; while in her absence the same words remained colourless, disinfected, as in the church they visited before Sunday dinner when nobody had a cold.

Now Maman, in her crusade against cruelty and her own shortcomings, became more determined in her church-going. She had a visiting-card fixed in a slot at the end of the pew: her own personal card, because Father joined them only at Christmas and Easter. Rhoda went. Hurtle went in the holidays. Maman wore dresses certainly more sombre, but no less sumptuous, than in her frequently regretted frivolous past.

For church she mostly wore a veil, which she threw back over her hat before kneeling. Hurtle liked to look sideways at her face, at her splendidly proffered expression of remorse. In his preoccupation with the work of art he would forget she was his mother. She powdered thoughtlessly at times, which increaseed her headachy look. Her lips were extra pale for Sunday.

And Rhoda, her sharp chin propped on the woodwork, her eyes shut tight, what did Rhoda pray about? The removal of her hump? Or did she simply shut her eyes and hope that church would soon be over?

At thirteen he had prayed sincerely, persistently, at times with passion: he begged to be allowed to witness some kind of miracle. By fourteen he had lost the faith you were supposed to have in prayer, just as he had lost control of his voice. His face was a dreadful mess, not that other people looked at it except to remind him of his pimples: "Don't, dear, they might turn septic." He sat in church stroking his soft, silly shadow of moustache, not so much sulking at God as contemptuous of all the kidding going on around him; till a fragmentation of light, or the illumination of a phrase, or some simple irrelevant image, a table, for instance, cropping up in his own mind, started him tingling electrically, afraid he might never be able to pin down his own insights, let alone convey them to others.

The Sunday it occurred to him that if God didn't exist he was his own dynamo, his pride didn't come to his rescue. With nothing but the sound of his heart to fill the gap, he looked down at last at his flies, to see whether his anxiety might be visible to anyone else.

He was fourteen the year they returned from Europe: not long after, war broke out.

Maman was standing at the top of the stairs, nursing a hot-water bottle. "Thank God, neither of my darlings will be taken from me," she announced in a loud voice. "Harry is too old, and Hurtle still a baby." An outburst intended for her own relief, it must have been heard by everyone, for the house had the ears of maids and children.

"Not that I shan't suffer for the others." She clutched the rubber bottle tighter to her bosom. "As though they were my own." She did want to atone for something. "Ohhhh!" she moaned, holding up her throat to be cut.

Father, who wasn't all that old, dashed up the stairs like a doctor and took her by the wrists. "Come on now, Freda. Control yourself, or they'll hear you," he warned in a low, vibrating voice, which everybody did hear.

"Nobody understands," she complained. "You don't! Don't touch me, Harry! Not after those beastly women."

"Which women?"

"Your mistresses!"

"Name one."

Instead, she dropped the hot-water bottle, and Father picked it up and shoved it back in her arms as though it had been a doll. He was red in the face from stooping. Then they were mumbling kisses at each other before going their separate ways in the subsiding house.

Father was fifty-two by the passport, but grew older by encouragement. He sagged in the leather armchair after dinner, the snores trickling out of his mouth. He had shaved off his beard to meet the fashion. He had a thick neck, with a full vein in the side of it: their father of veins.

Something about him Rhoda must have found repulsive. When he slapped her on the behind as though she had been a little girl, she spat back at him: "Don't ever do that again!" Like the young ladies in church, she could have fainted and been carried out, but perhaps she wasn't old enough.

It was a half-world, in which they all saw the guns ejaculating blood.

Maman protested: "Why are you looking at me, Hurtle?"

He wasn't just then, and that was what she resented. She was also perhaps afraid he was no longer her little boy; for safety's sake, she would have liked to keep him permanently twelve.

Whenever she thought about it, Maman was frantically indisposed, nursing the hot-water bottle: the landings and hall smelled of rubber; but between whiles her energy wouldn't leave her alone. She rushed at the telephone and almost wound the handle off: to organize. She organized Mrs Hollingrake and her circle into making miles of wistaria out of crêpe paper in Mrs Hollingrake's own garage to decorate the Allied Ball. She sold buttons for Little Belgium from a little tray in Martin Place; she sold flags for Serbia; she represented La Belle France on an evening of *tableaux vivants* in the Town Hall, and none of those who applauded realized that Maman was so emotionally involved as she sat offering her throat to the knife.

When the performance was over, and everybody paying compliments, her still tricoloured face recognized him and anxiously asked: "Was I all right, Hurtle? Did I convince you, darling?" As if he were a grown man.

Though this was what he had wanted, he wanted it less now that it was happening. He was barely sixteen. He wanted to be accepted by the anonymous faces in a crowd; to be singled out was embarrassing, not to say shocking.

So he put on his surliest voice to answer. "*Mmm.* Nobody kept properly still. You could see them swaying. You were too made-up."

"That is the theatre." She couldn't bear to take her make-up off: it made her feel so professional. "The whole object is to heighten life—rouse the emotions. Actually," she lowered her voice impressively, "I believe the response has been enormous—financially, I mean."

During the war she fished out an old shawl from somewhere, comforting in texture, ugly in colour—brown; it made her skin look livery. She wore the shawl for quiet evenings at home. She was reading the *Pensées* of Pascal in English, in French, too, though more off than on: "to get the authentic flavour."

She preferred to huddle in the chair after putting her book aside, and remember aloud for herself and an intimate audience. "There were all those pines round the house. The deadening needles. They only couldn't deaden the wind sound. Always blowing. The lovely old pines. We used to collect the cones, and shake out the little kernels, and roast them, and eat them. We burned the cones on the hearth. Or in the bath-heater."

Her face would flush with happiness.

"We didn't have many luxuries. Louie used to brush my hair for me, as a treat. Nothing so agonizing as a wind from the south, on frosty mornings, as we washed the parts of the separator. The water was always too hot, and our hands too cold. Poor old Louie! She was a brick. She had to go, after the second mortgage."

Maman huddled in the brown shawl.

"I heard she died. Everyone at all close to me died."

In fact, she had no relatives but Uncle Fred, who visited Sunningdale once or twice, showing his collar-stud, of a glass ruby in a brass claw. At intervals he said: "You was always gone on the gingerbread, Freda." He drank his tea out of the saucer.

Maman never mentioned her uncle when she reminisced in the comfortable shawl. Perhaps he, too, had died by now.

She said: "Oh, I'm not afraid! Not of death!"

On that occasion she was nursing the hot-water bottle; she looked slightly feverish. "You can't prevent the slaughter," she said. "Men will always treat one another like animals."

He was so drowsy he wasn't prepared for a real claw; when she said, looking at him: "You, Hurtle—you were born with a knife in your hand. No," she corrected herself, "in your eye."

"What do you know about what I am?" If his voice had risen too raucous for the octagon, a sense of injustice prevented him caring.

"No," she suddenly almost soundlessly agreed, lowering her eyelids.

She lit herself a cigarette, which she did very awkwardly. She preferred the men to do it for her, and her boorish son wouldn't learn.

But the holidays were not all oracles and smoke.

"Rhoda must have a party."

Rhoda made a sharp face. "Why must I have a party?"

"Why? Because it brings people together. It would be selfish to live only for ourselves."

It was difficult to counteract the truth, but Rhoda sometimes attempted it. "Hermits don't live for themselves, although they live *by* themselves. I think perhaps I'm going to be a hermit."

Maman laughed at the quaintness of it. "But, darling, hermits aren't little girls!"

"I am not a little girl!"

She wasn't either; you could see.

"Not in my soul!" Rhoda was quivering white with her own daring.

Maman moistened her lips. Although in her serious, her more indisposed moments, she liked to talk about the soul, she seemed afraid when others did.

So she decided not to have heard. "But you *like* Boo—Nessie—Mary—Vi. They're your friends, aren't they?"

Rhoda couldn't say she didn't, or that they weren't.

These were the girls with whom she did her lessons, companions trained to ignore anything that might seem odd or repulsive; they wouldn't drop their cake and stare from the other side of the table. Boo, Nessie, Vi, Mary even performed acts of kindness: they offered Rhoda Courtney the expensive presents their mothers had bought for them to give; reaching down, as though they, too, had developed humps, they put their arms around her; sometimes they shared with her the secrets of their lives.

Hurtle suspected Rhoda didn't return the compliment.

"Well, then," said Maman, "there's nothing to be upset about. And Hurtle will join in."

"Go on! He *won't*!"

"Oh, go *on*!" She liked to think she could imitate a young man's voice. "When the girls are so pretty. And you so nice. I wish my hair was the colour of yours." She rumpled him.

His fury made him tremble. He dashed his hair back with his hand. Without her telling him, it didn't look all that bad, and had been some consolation during the pimples, which he noticed in the glass were gone, if not completely, then almost.

From her other level Rhoda was gravely looking at him. Maman had gone to make arrangements.

Rhoda said, and now they were neither brother and sister, young nor old, male nor female, they were not the dolls parents play with, or rats reared for experiment: "I didn't tell her, but there are some places where you can't let others come barging in."

Whatever their souls were, and he was inclined to see them as paper kites, they soared for a brief moment, twining and twangling together, in the pure joy of recognition.

"But the girls are your friends, aren't they?" he interrupted, in a flat imitation of their mother.

At once Rhoda helped him snap the string that had been joining them: she sounded only too pleased to do so. "Oh yes," she said, raising her chin, "Boo Hollingrake's my particular friend. She's got the most beautiful figure. Her hair reaches down below her waist. She wants to cut it off, though, and stuff a pillow with it, to send to a soldier at the front." Then, still speaking in her trance, still remembering, Rhoda pressed together the tips of the fingers of her left hand, planting them on her hollow chest, under what should have been her left breast: "Just here she has something like a crescent moon in moles."

Rhoda's own shotgun moles along her chaps looked sadly repulsive in the white skin.

"Have you seen it?" he asked hoarsely.

"She showed me when she was having a bath. She let me touch it, though there's nothing to exactly feel. Boo," she said, still remembering, still entranced, "is gold—a sort of golden colour."

So that he, too, was drawn into Rhoda's trance: he saw Boo Hollingrake floating golden in the porcelain bath, and as she floated, ferns stirred in the tepid water, minute bubbles drifted out of crevices; the tropic fruit he had never tasted lolled beneath the circling water, under one of them, just visible, the crescent moon in moles.

Rhoda's little, chalky, pointed face suddenly became frantic. "I shouldn't have told you," she gibbered. "Boo is my friend. It's like telling a secret. How do I know you won't tell Boo?"

She began tearing her handkerchief; a wheezing started in her hollow chest.

"Not likely," he said. "How am I going to tell? I'll never know her well enough."

But she wasn't convinced. She went off biting her thin lips. Later, when he passed her room, he saw her writing in her diary.

The day of the party the bell began to ring about three, when

Edith stalked towards the front door wearing her starchiest cap. The girls arrived, some in chauffeur-driven motorcars, the poorer ones by cab, with a whiff of chaff still about their clothes. All the girls were dressed in white with touches of differentiating colour. Boo Hollingrake, he saw from a distance, was wearing a sash in what was referred to as "old gold."

Rhoda came out to face her friends. Because of her size and shape her clothes were always made to measure, but today she was wearing a dress which looked as though it must have been adapted, and not very well, from something larger. There were so many tucks. It was gathered up in the wrong places. It was full of little holes, though carefully embroidered, which showed the ugly dress was intended for a party; and her white-kid, lace-up boots were obviously new, spotless, with a faint squeak.

The guests began at once to whinny and nuzzle and offer elaborately wrapped presents. There was a smell of young girl in the hall and what used to be the schoolroom. Although he had brushed his hair, and was wearing his best clothes, he kept far enough out of the way.

He heard, then saw, Maman descending on the girls: it took place under the palms, on the lawn. Maman also was wearing white, but more exquisitely gathered, crisp, with a pale blue sash: after all, it was a girls' occasion.

She was determined to jolly the children and see that everyone was happy. "Nessie, what a sweet dress! Isn't it sweet, Rhoda? One can see Nessie was born to wear clothes."

Maman moistened her lips. None of the girls seemed prepared to pay her a compliment. With downcast eyes they stood about, toying with battledore and shuttlecock. There was a dull thump as the feathered cock met the parchment.

"Rhoda, darling," Maman called, "don't forget there's ping-pong, too, if anyone feels like it. I must go and give Edith and Lizzie a hand."

Going towards the house, she called back as an afterthought: "Where's that Hurtle?"

He was keeping out of it. He went and had a look at his face. There was one gigantic last spot. He squeezed it: the core hit the glass. "Oh God!" he moaned, as if he hadn't discovered there wasn't one.

When he went down, Rhoda and her friends had disappeared, though their peculiar non-perfume lingered. They were nowhere.

The garden was choking with the scents of a humid afternoon. Moisture was gathered in crystal beads on Maman's Delicious Monster.

He sighted the girls finally in the ruins of the summerhouse. In some way they had all been liberated: perhaps it was the smell of rotting from the drifts of dead leaves which Thompson was by now too arthritic to rake up.

Vi was saying: "I'm writing to a soldier in Flanders."

"Does your mother know?" somebody asked.

"Oh yes. It's good for his morale."

They all snickered and giggled, though Vi herself would have liked to treat the matter seriously.

"There's a gorgeous *iceman*!" Nessie spluttered.

"*Where*?" they choked.

"Ours, of course!" Nessie was almost strangled by it.

They all began to talk, only Boo didn't, about Stewart Martin. Everybody had danced with Stewart. Well? They all almost fell on the undulating floor of the half-collapsed summerhouse.

The strange part was: Rhoda acted as though she understood about everything.

Suddenly Boo Hollingrake spoke. "I think Stewart Martin's a misery." Her voice sounded surprisingly mature.

Through the latticed light the other girls looked somewhat stunned. Rhoda was white with shock, or admiration.

Boo was gathering breath, everybody saw, to continue talking. The motions her dress was making seemed to imply experience.

"There's a chap," she said, "one of Daddy's managers"—she was QSC—"a Queenslander"—her breathing had slowed—"he's a crude sort of freckled brute, but a man."

Everyone else was so silent you couldn't help hearing a thud. The girls peered suspiciously through the lattice of light.

Rhoda said: "That was a custard apple falling."

Nessie Hargreaves giggled high. "Have you danced with the Queenslander?"

Boo smiled. "He isn't the sort of man you dance with."

Rhoda was giggling and jiggling as though she knew all about things. Boo Hollingrake was holding her mascot's hand.

"But I *have* danced with him," Boo confessed.

The others shrieked.

Hurtle tried to visualize through the jungle how far Boo had gone with this orang-utan. She remained coolly beautiful; all that was visible outside her dress confirmed what Rhoda had already told: she was of a golden colour. Her golden throat and summery arms were splotched with green where leaves withheld the light. Her nose was of such fragile workmanship it was a wonder the freckled manager hadn't broken it off as a souvenir.

"I think it would be awful to have a man messing you about," said Mary Challands. "I'd rather keep my clothes fresh."

"People take them off," Rhoda reminded.

The girls rocked, for here was their monkey, their mascot, standing naked for their entertainment while still dressed in her *broderie anglaise*.

Hurtle gushed sweat the other side of the hydrangea clumps. His tense knuckles were blanched as white as the big loose hydrangea blooms. For the monkey-mascot, to improve her performance, was pointing her toes and holding out her skirt in a little stepdance.

The girls might have gone on laughing forever if Boo hadn't raised her head.

". . . over there. Over in the bushes. Something moving."

The silence she got was so enormous her voice came out of it most beautifully: low but distinct.

"Amongst the hydrangeas," she insisted, and they followed the arrow of her finger with their eyes. "A man standing."

"A man?"

"Oo-ooh!"

"Mother! Murder!"

"There's a Chinaman jumping on girls out at Watson's Bay."

As they ran, shrieking and laughing, Rhoda led them along the paths. They forgot at first, and almost trampled on her. It made them giggle worse than ever, in their breathlessness, and flickering white.

Only Boo Hollingrake wasn't breathless, because she wasn't running away. She was walking instead in the direction of the hydrangeas, tearing up a leaf as she came.

"Declare yourself, you silly coot! Hurtle—Hurtle Courtney?"

They had scarcely spoken to each other. He couldn't remember her saying his name. He stepped out of the bushes, and a sharp cane, from which a flower must have been amputated, stabbed him in the flies, to make him look more ridiculous, it seemed.

"What were you doing in there?" Boo Hollingrake coldly asked; she might have been a governess.

"Waiting for a chance to jump out and rape one of you girls."

"That's not in very good taste." She looked down at the leaf she had been demolishing.

"Judging by the conversation, I thought you might have found it tasty."

She had turned, and was slowly, coolly, walking away. "Not in good taste at all—and coming from a spotty *boy*!" she called back.

It was the insolence of her hair, looped up loosely above the collar of her dress, which enraged him more than anything.

He had never run so purposefully. He got hold of one of her arms and pinned it hard behind her back. It must have hurt.

"You haven't forgotten all the good old larrikin tricks," Boo gasped, to hurt more than she herself could have been.

"What larrikin?"

"Don't pretend!"

When turned round, she was furiously beautiful. Above her upper lip the down glittered.

He kept on mumbling: "I'll show you 'larrikin'! I'll show you 'spotty boy'!"

Then she began laughing. It wasn't convincing: the muscles were too taut in her neck.

"Poor Hurtle, you're such a tyro!"

"That's a word you've only just learned. You're showing it off."

He let her go, though.

"Oh, I've quite a rich vocabulary," she said.

"A tyro among hetairai, eh? Bet that's one you haven't come across."

"Of course I have! Anyone can read the dictionary."

"A corker of a concubine!" he brayed.

She allowed herself to giggle slightly. "Don't be funny!"

She was moving away, but drawing him with her, it seemed, in the breeze she made; when he shouldn't have moved at all if left to himself: he was by now so rigid with excitement.

"Aren't the leaves cool," she murmured, pressing one against her face.

"Pretty cool yourself." He took her hand as though she had invited him.

135

"Oh, I'm not! I'm 'perspiring freely,' as they say. Feel!"

Now looking at him, she put his hand just below her throat, above where her dress began.

How it felt was not all that important, because almost immediately after, he was discovering so much more of Boo Hollingrake, on the leaf-mould, at the bottom of the stone steps, behind the *Monstera deliciosa*. She was drooling, sometimes in plain words: ". . . yumm not not mm such um beginnerm . . ." into his mouth. Above and below she was both mobile and contained, but if he closed his eyes he could float with her amongst the fern roots in the porcelain bath, guzzling the golden fruit right down to the crescent moon. He could have.

When Boo said: "Hurtle Courtney, you kill me!" She made her tongue as thin as a cigarette and stuck it between his lips.

It was so unexpected, he was throbbing and spilling inside his clothes, against her struggling thighs.

"Boo, dear? Boo? We're waiting for you. Tea-o!" The voice calling from the upper terrace only half expressed Maman's feelings; he could tell. He could imagine the smile as she tried to load her words with charm.

While the *Monstera deliciosa*, beginning to resist an afternoon breeze, was scattering gold coins through its perforations. The breeze tattered the banana leaves. Clashes of wind and light were occurring all the way up to the lawn, where Maman's skirt of girls' white was filling and spiralling. To keep her balance she had to plant her shoes in the mattress of buffalo grass.

"Boo!"

"Oh, drat!" She threw him off. "Old Freda's on the warpath. . . . Yes, Mrs Courtney," she called up, while darting at her hair, her dress. "I lost my slide. I've been looking for it. My hair-slide."

Her voice sounded true, whereas Maman's wasn't: too dry and monotonous.

"Oh, how ghastly for you, Boo! You'll never find it. The garden's turned into a wilderness. You must become resigned, dear."

Boo went shooting up a ladder of leaves and light. The soles of her shoes went *tsit tsit tsit* on the stone steps.

"But I've found it, Mrs Courtney."

She sounded so convincing.

Hurtle might have chosen to remain hidden in the cooling depths, but Maman was beginning to descend; he could hear her shoes grating on the steps. She would be watching her advance toe, her eyes narrowed anxiously, as though she half expected to fall.

At the bend she looked up and saw him. He must have been waist-deep in greenery.

"Hurtle," she said, "I hope you'll never do anything to make us feel ashamed of you."

"What?" He was completely defenceless except for his Adam's apple.

At least Maman wasn't prepared to let herself get carried out of the shallows. "Oh," she said, "you know—now that you're a young man."

As there was no avoiding it, he went up the steps, and she couldn't resist tidying his hair.

"You're such a comfort to me"—she linked an arm to one of his for the return—"now that all these dreadful things are happening, and Father away from home so much."

Since the outbreak of war Harry Courtney had felt it his duty to spend more time on his properties. He had stocked them up as part of the "war effort," and with the young men away in France, the most he could do was lend his managers a hand.

"Always remember you're a gentleman," Maman was saying; she might have learned it out of a book.

"But I'm not!" She, before anybody, must face that.

"You've had every opportunity. You've been *taught* everything. I don't know what else you could be."

"I'm an artist." He was, in fact, a thundering cart-horse.

"Oh yes, yes! We know," she said, "and it's wonderful to have a satisfying hobby."

Maman's faith in geniuses had failed since the wheels had broken off the planchette.

"The question of morality is what is important," she said, "*au fond*," sucking on it like a sweet, for her own comfort.

They ploughed over the endless lawn, up to what had been the schoolroom, where Edith and Lizzie had laid Rhoda's party feast. There were egg sandwiches, and banana ones, and yummiest of all, those which were filled with squashed chocolate creams. There were meringues, of course. There was rainbow cake, and a choice of iced coffee and fruit cup.

Maman recovered something of her girlishness. "Is everybody happy?" she asked in a jollying voice; her sash flew as she went the rounds.

The girls had turned into heavy, munching women, excepting Rhoda, picking like a bird. You couldn't say there was anything wrong with the food, only that Maman must have planned it under the impression that Rhoda was still her little girl, which, in fact, she had never been.

Nobody spoke. The guests were probably deciding what they would polish off next. A dimple opened on and off in Nessie Hargreaves' left cheek. From time to time Rhoda looked around disbelievingly: her dress had got crushed, and she kept tweaking at it; or she would look up at her friend Boo, whose dress also was somewhat crushed.

He wondered how he had ever been impressed by that munching cow. He thought he could see a spot beginning to surface on her chin.

"Rainbow cake! Nessie? Mary?" Maman bravely asked.

Without inviting her to take off her clothes, he could have painted Boo Hollingrake down to the last frond.

Rhoda was looking at Hurtle.

Something had risen up in Maman. She plumped down. She was not exactly crying, but gasping and frowning. She was working her handkerchief with the palms of her hands.

"Oh, what is it, Mrs Courtney?" Vi Learmonth ran: she was the kindest of the girls, and would have liked, if allowed, to join in a cry.

"It's nothing, Vi," Maman said. "No, that's untrue. It's bad news— some-somebody—a friend—killed at the war," she was able to gasp. "We heard this morning. Nowadays," she said, "news is nearly always bad."

Rhoda ran after Vi with little imitative steps; but she hadn't learned what else to do.

"This detestable war!" Boo sighed professionally and, looking down her front, brushed the crumbs off.

"Hurtle," said Maman, "bring me a glass of soda-water." She was still accusing him, not of something, but of everything.

The cars and cabs were sent for earlier than first arranged. Out of respect for Mrs Courtney's sorrow the girls remained subdued. Saying good-bye, they looked soft and juicy, like plump, white, folded moths.

As soon as they were gone Rhoda pounced. "Who was it?"

"Who was it what?"

"Got killed at the war."

"A boy called Andrew Macfarlane. Mrs Hollingrake discussed it with me on the telephone. We decided Boo shouldn't be told before the party. Boo was very fond of Andrew. They were childhood sweethearts: you might say they were half engaged."

Half an engagement so cruelly broken was too much for Maman. "Oh my darlings," she burst out, "how fortunate I am! There's still your lives to look forward to!" Carried away by her emotion, she clutched at whoever was nearest.

Rhoda looked comparatively dry, wedged under one of Maman's arms; or perhaps she had experienced worse than the death of Boo Hollingrake's Scot: all young men must have appeared rather hazy to Rhoda.

While Hurtle remembered the black knees, the square hands, the live hair of an older boy, in the bony cheeks signs of the blood which would run, which was still running, under the *Monstera deliciosa*. Boo laughing for the blood-bath. *Hurtle Courtney, you kill me!* They hadn't, but might have, killed Andrew Macfarlane between them. The sloshed blood looked glitteringly fresh on Boo's throat, on her lashing thighs.

Though it wasn't Maman he was looking at, she began again accusing him: "You never forgive—Hurtle—anybody else's weakness." And as she continued sobbing: "Everybody, in the end, is weak."

Himself the weakest, if he could have convinced her.

Rhoda cried a little to pacify her mother, then returned to her own dry grief of griefs, whether experienced already, or still to be.

So far distant from the killing, the war years weren't so very different from those which had gone before. Boys at school pummelled one another's bodies, muddled through algebra and Virgil, groaned, cheated, masturbated, waiting for an end to the prison term. Most of them took a ferocious interest in war. Some of those who left, immediately enlisted, looking like exalted novices entering a religious order. Those who remained yearned for the boredom of the holidays, which were only boring on the surface. During the war the secret ways had become more devious, behaviour more disguised, the coded messages more difficult to crack. The maids, even, seemed no longer to know what made sense. May said: "Dunno what I'm doin' 'ere; I'm gunner get out"; while there was no sign that she had the power to withdraw her face from above the pan which was steaming it open.

To have scalded her wrist and to be wearing a bandage soaked in oil was, in the circumstances, some kind of compensation. Her skin looked browner, more livery than before. She burped a lot, and didn't fancy anything above a biscuit. In the second year of the war she taught Hurtle the secret of spun sugar, and how to transform dull roundels of potato into the gold balloons of *pommes soufflées*.

"Now you know," she whispered as the little golden eggs bobbed swelling in the bubbling fat.

He was not only the neophyte, he might have been her lover.

"You've got good hands, love," she told him. "When I was a girl I worked in a surgeon's house. His was the same sort of hands."

She dared ask, only once, and very quickly: "Have you been paintin' any of those paintin's lately, dear?"

Her skin flooding with maroon, she lowered her eyelids and slip-slopped into the scullery. He was relieved she had decided not to expect an answer. Her sympathy moved him, and he respected her art.

He had taken to locking his door as soon as he got inside his room. He read a great deal, possibly to ignore the fact that he was still incapable of acting; he could only be acted upon. He read *Ziska: the Problem of a Wicked Soul, Lives of the Painters, Wilhelm Meister's Wanderyears, Pensées de Pascal, The Forest Lovers,* the Dictionary. He drew, too. He did a series of drawings of the war which was being fought in France, but tore them up on recognizing Goya. The thought that he might never be able to convey something that was his and nobody else's brought on such an intense despair he masturbated on the quilt, and was at once afraid they might find him out however hard he rubbed it with a towel. He wrote his name compulsively in margins, on the backs of drawing-blocks, once, guiltily, on a wall. Sometimes the name was *Hurtle Courtney*, sometimes more simply *Duffield*. He painted a painting in which the golden flesh of two bodies interlocked on a compost of leaves under a glittering rain of blood. The light—he couldn't manage the light: it remained as solid as human flesh. He would get up and walk round his room, which had been large enough till now. His sufferings, which had seemed intense, were as superficial as his painting. He destroyed the painting.

At night he lay rehearsing his entrace on a battlefield under coruscations of gunfire. A leader of men, he excelled at killing, endured unendurable hardships, and almost underwent an amputation. His wounds, of the most gangrenous kind, were deliciously healed by Boo Hollingrake's tongue.

In his continued absence, helping the war effort by occupying himself with his properties, Father wrote letters from which you suspected he, too, was living in his dreams:

Dear son,

Next holidays I mean to bring you up to Sevenoaks. Art and literature are all very well (civilization demands that we cultivate them) but I am inclined to think—in fact, I know at last that life as I am living it now is the "real thing." Every morning as I stand cleaning my teeth on the veranda, I catch sight of the distant hills heaped like . . . [*difficult to read*] . . . uncut sapphires . . . [*was it?*] . . . the dew shining like . . . [?] diamonds . . . [?] in the luxuriant grass, and I ask myself what painting could possibly equal this actual picture. The few hands left on the place are not less competent for being elderly. They are all good men and true. After a hard day's work we mess together, and if our feeding arrangements are on the primitive side, our own mutton and beef inexpertly cooked, with no elaborate sauces to titillate the palate, our appetites are fully satisfied—after which, complete, perfect rest!

Newspapers are stale by the time they reach us, but don't read any the better for it.

Give my love to your mother and sister. I have heard from an old acquaintance of a herbal treatment by which his invalid wife was considerably strengthened, and at once thought Rhoda might benefit from some such regimen. I shall write about this in detail to Maman.

I think often of my dear ones

yr affectionate
Father

P.S. The Black Polls are flourishing on the nearest thing to Scottish pasture.

P.P.S. Do you remember young Forster the jackaroo at Mumbe-long? He is killed. Have started negotiations with Shearing for sale of the Leichhardt manuscript letters and will donate the proceeds to the Red Cross. —Dad.

Harry Courtney, so far distant, so concerned for his dear ones, might have been at the front himself. He returned on leave from time to time, hands hardened, eyes clear. His English suits when he wore them again apologized for their elegance; his cigars must have turned against him.

His wife Alfreda said: "It's so gratifying to have reached the *comfortable* stage of life," all the while unpicking the socks she was knitting for unknown soldiers.

She had taken to wearing aprons to emphasize the seriousness of her intentions: she couldn't resist pretty aprons.

On his son's sixteenth birthday Harry Courtney bought him a set of ivory brushes inlaid with gold monograms; he bought him a set of cuff-links studded with chunks of sapphire; they stood together looking at the presents.

"Go on, *say* if you don't *like* them," Harry protested, while somewhere about him some of his bones clicked.

Hurtle was unable to express either his love or his misery. Harry shambled off, himself a slightly grizzled black-polled Angus.

The maids were flying with aired sheets which made a stiff, scraping sound.

"Darling? Harry?" Alfreda Courtney called. "They're making up the bed in the dressing-room. In my old age I'm such a terribly light sleeper."

She had unpacked his valise herself: the crumpled pyjamas smelling of dentifrice, and woodsmoke, and what was it? apples?

Listening to them call to each other from their separate rooms, Hurtle was surprised his parents could survive the daylight shallows, let alone the dangers of sleep.

He had gone into the William Street post office to buy stamps for Maman. "You don't mind, darling, do you? Say if you mind." She was clever enough to know he would be made to feel ridiculous by admitting it; but he did mind. He saw she was using him as her little boy—or her tame black-polled Angus bull. So he resented it. It was raining, too.

But on going into the post office, full of the smell of wet raincoats and galoshes, he realized at once that this was a significant occasion.

A young woman or girl was licking a stamp. You could see she didn't like the taste, but had to put up with it, her tongue flat and ugly in this commonplace employment. He wondered why somebody so obviously disdainful hadn't simply wet her finger, and minimized her disgust.

It was Boo Hollingrake, but changed, he saw, and of course older.

Since the party Maman had organized for Rhoda, Boo had gone out of their lives. Mrs Hollingrake had told Maman in confidence the poor child was desolated by the death of the splendid young man to whom she would have become engaged. Whatever Boo may have felt, she was packed off to visit relations in Tasmania. Her education was, pardonably, interrupted. When she returned, Mrs Hollingrake decided to send her daughter to boarding school: "to take her out of herself." In the emergency which arose, Mrs Challands, the mother of Mary, had engaged a governess and re-organized the depleted group. Maman was relieved to find that Rhoda, at least for the moment, wasn't becoming a greater problem.

"That Boo," Hurtle once inquired of Rhoda, "do you ever hear from her?"

"Oh yes, I told you—at the time I got the letter from her. She's staying near Launceston. She's making a collection of Tasmanian bush-flowers—pressed."

He couldn't imagine it.

And now, here was Boo in the William Street post office, licking a stamp for another letter. He would have liked to read the address on it.

Because it was a wet morning she was wearing a raincoat, which she had unbelted for greater ease. Under her coat she was dressed, you couldn't have said in mourning, because she was a young girl, but with a hint of it in her long black skirt and the big black bow flattened on the back of her hair. Her skin was whiter, as though in mourning, or it could have been from the weather. The skin of her eyelids looked thicker, heavier. The bridge of her nose seemed to have broadened, or coarsened, or she had a cold. But her white blouse was crisp, almost transparent, unostentatiously fashionable. She had that air of girls who don't look after their own clothes: they drop them on the floor and somebody else picks them up.

When she first noticed him she looked a bit put out: she might have been going to cut him.

Then she changed her mind, and said in the automatic voice of women of her class coming across one another in the shops: "Oh, hello, Hurtle. Isn't it a foul day?"

Though having nothing in particular to discuss, he spread himself to prevent her escaping before he was ready.

She told him about her stay in Tasmania. "They were very kind," she said in her mother's voice. "Actually they're related to Mummy. It's so cold the girls all wear woollen vests," she informed him—seriously, he realized.

He found himself looking through her blouse, at the just visible tones of her shoulders. He became conscious of the warmth of their bodies mingling spontaneously through their open raincoats.

But Boo Hollingrake remained mentally cool.

"How is Rhoda?" she asked, though probably she didn't want to hear. "I believe I owe her a letter. Or perhaps she's the one who owes." She giggled faintly. "Rhoda's so sweet. And Mr and Mrs Courtney—are they well?"

She hadn't said "your father and mother," because she was looking, now with interest, at an adopted son.

"They tell me," she said, "you're becoming an artist. Do you paint from the life?" It was a term she had picked up.

She didn't wait for an answer, but looked at her wristlet watch. "I'm late for my appointment. What a horrible, horrible day!"

And for a moment Boo Hollingrake shrank inside her clothes, as though the rain had got inside them, and the mud were creeping up on her: she might have been treading on dead, suppurating faces.

Then she remembered: "It's been so nice seeing you again—Hurtle. I must tell Mummy."

At once her brown, and temporarily shrivelled mouth swelled into a pale hibiscus delicately crinkled. She went down the steps into the street, where the car waited, together with an elderly, respectful, or overpaid chauffeur.

"Boo Hollingrake," said Maman, with the surprising directness she adopted when she wasn't the one threatened, "did you care for her, Hurtle?"

"I don't think I knew her."

"But of *course* you did! She was one of Rhoda's set. She was here at the house several times."

Maman "knew" those she had met only once, at bridge parties, or between the races. All her acquaintances were "friends": she remembered them by their pedigrees and hats.

"You *must* know her! The tall dark handsome girl. Rhoda shared her governess."

"I know the one you mean. But I didn't know her."

"If you must split hairs! What a funny old thing you're becoming. You're the one nobody knows. Not even his own mother," she added in a tone of satisfaction.

What had become of Mumma? he wondered. Though it wasn't in the contract to see her, her cracked hands would return, sometimes as a source of shame, sometimes of agonizing tenderness; but mostly he didn't think about her: a laundress was incredible.

"If there's no frankness between parents and children," Maman said, "I consider the parents have failed."

With Father away, it was the hour she enjoyed most: she enjoyed the failures and the accusations as they sat alone in the octagon; Rhoda grew exhausted early and would go to bed after dinner.

"Oh, I know I bore you, Hurtle," Maman used to say, "but may I enjoy your company?"

She would bribe him with a cigarette. "Your father would be furious. But just one—since you're a man."

He sat in her now suffocating room, smoking the one prescribed cigarette, feeling long-legged, large-knuckled, amateurish: he the professional chain-smoker behind the latrines at school.

Maman sewed—she was proud of her needlework—or talked, or wrote letters—talking—or read, again talking about it.

"Do you think Thomas Hardy shocking? I don't. I think the shock is overrated. He'd like to shock. But I shan't let him. What do you think?"

He didn't. He thought he must bore Maman, though in a way she appeared to enjoy his physical presence in the octagon, just as he enjoyed secretly the stuffy luxury of their hours together after dinner.

"Boo Hollingrake"—she returned to the attack—"there was an occasion when I thought, Hurtle, you were distinctly interested in her—at a party for Rhoda."

Maman bit off a thread, for she had taken up the sewing all her friends remembered to admire: Mrs Hollingrake considered it "exquisite work."

Hurtle was watching the smoke from his cigarette. "Mmm. Boo. I'm not all that interested in nice girls. They're too"—he coughed—"insipid."

Maman had discovered a brand of cigarette wrapped in brown paper—Russian—which made him feel so much older.

"That's your age," she said, striking him down. "Boys are often timid of young girls. It's quite natural."

She had been looking closely at her sewing: now she raised her head. "Won't you give me one—darling—Hurtle? A cigarette?"

She watched him strike the match. She held her hand to the cigarette as though they were lighting something as important as a bonfire. The match lit up her face. It was becoming almost transparent with light.

"Don't burn my eyelashes off!" She giggled smokily.

Then she settled down to devouring the cigarette. There wasn't anybody else in the room, least of all her son.

She began to talk, like people did when drunk or entranced: "Actually girls don't change, I think, from generation to generation. They're like moths blundering about in search of their fate. You know how moths hit you in the face—soft, velvety things—and are sometimes killed." She shuddered, drawing on her cigarette. "Nor do I think girls grow up into anything very different from what they were. They're still blundering about after they've promised to honour and obey. Oh, I don't mean they're dishonest—not all of them —but they're still quivering and preparing to discover something they haven't experienced yet."

She ground out her cigarette too soon. "Perhaps that's why women take French lessons." She still had that dimple he could remember seeing for the first time in the same room.

Maman continued sewing. "I remember when I was a girl I used to walk down the road—there were pines along the south side— walk, for something to do—in desperation. I had a muff. I used to clench my hands inside the muff. I wore serviceable boots, but dreaded meeting anybody in them. That was how I met your father."

It was incredibly dreamy: perhaps Maman *was* drunk; she wasn't, though.

"He sat his horse wonderfully. He looked wonderful. Men of that complexion do, in cold weather."

She threw up her head as though drinking down the image, the icy chill of which made her throat tauten: her breasts became as small as Boo Hollingrake's.

Then she laughed, and stuck her needle in the stuff she had been embroidering. "How did this begin? The Hollingrake girl. You must forgive me, darling. Isn't it time for bed?"

The house was so warm, so suffocating, smelling of dust in spite of a team of maids, he could have choked on the way to his room. The half-darkness through which he was climbing seemed to be developing an inescapable form: of a great padded dome, or quilted egg, or womb, such as he had seen in that da Vinci drawing. He continued dragging round the spiral, always without arriving, while outside the meticulous womb men were fighting, killing, to live to fuck to live.

He looked round, half expecting to see the womb had been split by his thought; but the darkness held.

In the most distant fuzz of light, the dining-room, he could see and hear Maman locking up the decanters; it wasn't fair, she used to say, "to tempt the girls."

Outside the room he had outgrown, the night was rocking back and forth. A wind sounded like rain in the glittering trees. On their way across the sky mounds of intestinal cloud began to uncoil, to knot again, to swallow one another up. A fistful of leaves flung in his face as he leaned out had the stench of men, of some men at least, who have overexerted themselves, of Pa Duffield, who was his actual father, in an old grey flannel vest, counting the empties as he piled them under the pepper tree.

He might have continued composing Pa for the unexpected pleasure it gave, if the room behind him hadn't begun to stir, the silence growing silky above the dry rain of streaming leaves.

She didn't wait for him to turn, but said in a congested voice: "Tell me what it is that makes you unhappy, Hurtle. I have a right to know." She tried to keep it low in pitch, but his eardrums whammed as though she had boxed them.

She had put on a gown she sometimes rested in, and to which she would refer as "that old frightful idiosyncrasy of mine": a field of fading rose, its seed-pearl flowerets unravelling from their tarnished stalks. She had done her hair sleeker than he had ever seen it, which made her head look smaller, almost schoolgirlish. Of course her eyes were older than any girl's. But not old. They seemed to have been refreshed: he saw them as unset jewels in shallows of clear water.

"Tell me what it is," she ordered him for the second time. "Try to forget I'm your mother."

She was obviously disturbed. Alfreda Courtney tended to avoid matters of importance, unless a "cause," like anti-vivisection or fallen girls, but somebody's personal distress could drag you out of your depth.

Till here she was: taking the plunge.

"But you're *not* my mother." He didn't know which of them he was rescuing.

"Oh, you needn't tell me! I didn't *make* you! I made Rhoda. I botched Rhoda. Like everything. Perhaps if I'd carried you inside me, a strong and beautiful child, Harry wouldn't blame me now. Harry can never forgive me Rhoda." It sounded as though she had somehow to dismiss poor old decent Harry Courtney.

"I never noticed him blame you."

"No," she said. "How could you? It's something only I could notice."

In spite of its expression of bitterness her mouth was more brilliant than he remembered: the lips half open like those of a person half asleep.

She closed her eyes to prevent him looking into them.

"You're right," she said, frowning, or twitching. "You're not my son. If you had been, I wonder whether you would have loved me more—or less."

Whiffs of perfume reached him out of his childhood, from dressing-tables, and the clothes in wardrobes: if only he could have smothered in it; but the perfume was drawing him back to the present.

Her fingers, "still quivering and preparing to discover," were playing on the skin of his arm.

"Give me—" she said, "let me hold your head."

She didn't wait for a reply but took it in her hands, as though it were a fruit, or goblet. She began gulping at his mouth: they were devouring with their two mouths a swelling, overripened, suddenly sickening—pulp.

He spat her out. "You're drunk, aren't you?" He sounded horrible even to himself: himself too recently drunk on the same short sharp slugs from the decanter which might have "tempted the girls."

She turned round, hunching up her back, and went out coughing, crying, almost vomiting, it seemed, leaving him with the guilt of half-remembered dreams: of being received.

He began quickly to undress his hatefully immaculate body, and should afterwards have strapped himself down on his novice's bed. Instead, propping himself on an elbow, he began to draw with a detached voluptuousness the mouth, the eyes. The lips were hatched with little lines, or slashed with wounds, the brilliantly cut eyeballs sometimes glaring sometimes fainting in their display of light. He only couldn't convey the perfume of bruised mignonette and brandy: these remained confused in his hand.

He tore all of it quickly up. She was knocking at the door.

"Hurtle?" She was so tired, or ill.

She had put on an old flannel nightgown she liked to wear in winter whenever she was feeling indisposed; though now it wasn't winter.

She explained: "I have a neuralgia." The water in the half-filled rubber bottle, which she planted on herself for warmth, mumbled to and fro, her hair hanging loose: she had brushed it out for the night.

"Hurtle," she said, "your father will be coming home at the end of the month. I want nothing to distress him—in these times."

The hot-water bottle made a slucking sound as she shifted it from the angle of her neck. Her breasts looked baggy inside the flannel. She was old and yellow, his mother, her face seamed.

"Darling," she said, pushing back the quiff of hair from her boy's forehead, "I know you'll understand and help me." Her voice died away because of her sickness, her veined hand imploring him to recognize her helplessness.

Now it was he who could have vomited: he could have gone down retching howling holding on to the set folds of her old flannel disguise which didn't; but at least if he was going to destroy her, it wouldn't be in the way she expected.

"All right," he said, "all right," like the mug he was, "I won't say anything. I won't be here."

"You—won't—be?"

"I joined up."

"Joined what?"

"Enlisted."

It was a lie he would have to live up to.

"I'm leaving for camp. Perhaps this week. I'll know tomorrow."

"I can't believe it!" She flung away the hot-water bottle, which cannoned off a corner of the chest of drawers. "After all we've done for you! All the thought! The love!"

The expense, too, went hurtling through his mind.

"But something must—I'll telephone"—she never lost her faith in the telephone—"somebody with influence. Because your father would never forgive me. At your age! You're only a boy!"

"I'm sixteen. Lots of them have gone at sixteen." He only couldn't believe in himself.

"You're doing it to kill me."

"If you're not killed in one way, you are in another."

"Ohhhh!" Her voice mounted as she went out warming up her slack arms.

Well, he had broken the caul: it lay all sticky gelatinous around him; he was panting from the effort.

Rhoda who was sleeping—what would she say?

The days which remained were out of season: they belonged to a state of timeless suspension, very still, very clear. Phrases of speech launched from a distance floated towards him like sound-bubbles. Doves' plumage had the look of armour. When fright wasn't tunnelling its way through his guts, he rose buoyantly on the thought that all his shortcomings would lie behind him in a few days: the derivative drawings, his share in Maman's dishonesty, the goose-flesh which came when Rhoda touched him.

He said: "Thank God, I'll soon be doing something."

Rhoda and he were standing in the angle of the stone steps, looking down through the muzzy green of hydrangea scrub and custard-apple trees.

Rhoda mumped her doubts; then she said: "I wonder if you'll be tough enough."

"You can be anything if you've got the will."

His own daring made him shiver. He saw more clearly than ever how small Rhoda had remained, how downright deformed she was beside his swaying tower.

"I would have been tough enough," she said. "They could saw both my legs off."

"It's all very well to skite. They haven't sawn off any part of you. You don't *know*!" Because she might possibly have experienced something far more intense than he could guess, he tried to drag her with him to the surface.

But she began to cry quite openly. She took his hand, and seemed to be trying to work the skin off with her fingers.

"Will you write to me, Hurt?" she was asking and crying. "Will you? From the front?"

"Oh *yairs*!" he said to pacify her.

The word "front" sounded so real he was scared stiff.

4

The young man beside the sea-wall stuffed into his mouth handfuls of the limp chips and encrusted fish he had bundled up in newspaper behind the management's back. In the mild, light-smeared night, eating this greasy food became a delicious orgy: himself drifting; rubbing up against the stone wall; staring. The slow sea and the long tongues of oily light made half the feast: the silence, too, after the clatter and yammer of the place where he worked. Languages you can't understand give you a headache finally, and the chitter of knives and forks in grey water, in a greasy sink. At the caff-eye.

The young man continued to drift, forgetting and remembering. The sound of the grass reminded him it had always looked dead and white. He passed a bench in which one of his feet had caught, between the slats, when he was a little boy.

There were prawns, too, in his parcel. He tore off the shells and flipped these off his fingertips. The prawnflesh was beginning to turn, but he ate it.

The park was quieter than he could have believed. Since war ended, he often felt his life might last forever, provided he didn't die of starvation.

Hitting the waters of the bay, the prawnshells made a hollow sound. His mouth was hanging open, he realized; but he wasn't crying: it was the sweat round his eyes from washing up the knives and forks, or some of the grease had rubbed off his fingers from the batter blanketing the cold fish.

He spat out a few fragments of shell. He ran his tongue round his mouth to get the most out of everything.

During the war his mother had written:

Dearest,

I still can't believe you have done this to us. To run off and enlist when there wasn't any *real* need! I had always imagined you to be more thoughtful, Hurtle. Your father and Rhoda felt the blow most keenly. For their own good I have refused to let them talk about it. As for myself, I am blessed with a resilience which helps me bear the disappointments in life.

We are otherwise in good health at home, your father seldom here, of course, for keeping an eye on the properties. Although I am *physically* exhausted, I expect I shall continue to hold the fort; too many others are dependent on me.

Rhoda has taken a snapshot with the Kodak we gave her for her birthday, and I am enclosing the picture—to show you, darling, I have not *entirely* gone to pieces!

Edith, whom you never liked, is knitting you a balaclava, though that is supposed to be a surprise. Keep has become practically senile: she can no longer distinguish between a simple mid-afternoon frock and a *grande toilette*. What to do with her? I rack my brains. We can't get rid of the old creature—I mean, of course, *pension her off*. She has been so long a member of the family she would only fret if separated from us, and not know how to occupy her time.

Ah, Time—if only I had as much again! I scarcely ever read, and fall asleep whenever I do. I run from one committee to the next. On Tuesday night there is a ball (costume), the proceeds to go to the Red Cross. Mrs Hollingrake is arranging a set. I don't intend to tell you what I shall be going as, because I know you would tease me if I did.

I should mention that I have also started working for the Church. We have a new rector at St Michael's. Mr Plumpton is a tower of strength—a Charterhouse man—such a beautiful delivery. He has lent me several books on which I must concentrate more deeply when I can find more time. I often wonder what they really *mean* by "meditation," and if those who practise it, honestly do. Must ask Mr Plumpton for his opinion.

Darling, we must all *sustain one another* in these terrible days. Do you still pray, Hurtle? Of course I have no idea what you believe: I have no idea what anyone believes, and wouldn't be so tasteless as to inquire. Everybody has his private needs, or possibly, *strength*, which is above need. I know that God will love me when I am old and uninteresting, and, I only pray, not hideous.

We are seeing something of a young man called Julian Boileau who is very sweet, very kind to poor little Rhoda. He would be in every way acceptable if it weren't for our unfortunate "condition." I think Rhoda understands, which makes the situation more tragic.

When I cannot sleep I try to explain to myself why you almost never write, or when you do, why you tell me next to nothing. Have I done anything to make you hate me, Hurtle? Or is it simply that I am your mother who . . .

In Rhoda's snapshot Maman was putting on her gloves, getting ready for church perhaps. She was wearing a smart little biplane hat, with a strap beneath the chin to safeguard against age and the ruder elements. Her smile hoped to be interpreted as proof of her indestructibility.

Destroyed automatically rather than wilfully, Maman's letter and Rhoda's snap were trodden beyond retrieving into the prevailing mud. He would write to her of course, to them all, when he was less tired; that was the subtlest reason for his silence: he was weighed down by an excess of hardware, leather, webbing, drenched khaki, and a wristlet watch.

He tried to believe in himself, even in that part of him his family believed to exist. His failure to do so could explain why he had stopped writing to them.

At the height of the bombardment he felt he only believed in life. At its most flickery, with the smell of death around it, life alone was knowable. His ghostliness yearned after its great tawny sprawling body. He found himself praying for survival: that he might reveal through the forms his spirit understood this physical life which now appeared only by glimpses, under gunfire, or in visionary bursts, by grace of melting Verey lights.

Once after the shit had been frightened out of him, he tried to visualize God, but saw instead a patient black-polled bull giving at the knees, blood gushing from spongy muzzle as he went down under the axe.

"Your father" had written:

. . . the difficulty of finding reliable hands now that we are involved in this infernal war. For this reason (and if I can make something on the deal) I have more or less decided to sell Mumbelong and Yalladookdook, to concentrate my strength at Sevenoaks. I have improved the pastures, the place is generously watered, and in a good season can become an earthly paradise. What possessed me, I wonder, never to have brought you here while you were still a boy? I could kick myself. You would have had grand sport with that rifle. The house is certainly a rambling folly, but could be brought up to date and made very comfortable and attractive if your mother would only contemplate it. (She says nothing will induce her to retire to my *Valhalla*: the draughts would kill her if boredom didn't.) But you, my dear boy, will understand, I hope and believe.

I am writing to you in the office after breakfast: it is cold but dry, winter weather. I went down at sunrise and forked out their ensilage to a paddockful of sturdy young Angus bulls I am proud to think I bred. Life on the land continually offers a sense of creation, power—I hesitate to say: omnipotence. Standing on the dray under the winter sun this morning, I found myself longing for the time when you will inherit Sevenoaks and experience this for yourself.

The turn the war is taking has made everyone I meet doubtful of the outcome, but I refuse to let myself become depressed. I flatter myself I can see farther than the others. You will be back with us, my dear fellow. Those we wish to, do more often than not "miraculously" survive. . . .

He must write to his Father of the Bland Bulls, but was mostly too exhausted to attempt even the stilted expressions of love parents gratefully accept. He himself was grateful for the truth of some of what Our Father said. He remained miraculously unscathed, at least his physical envelope did, while all those around him were dying. He listened to their sighs of relief as they gave up the ghost. He, the unrelieved ghost, must in some way give thanks for the paternal love protecting him; when Our Father wrote:

. . . wondering whether to tell you about something which happened last Wednesday morning, and have finally decided to. I had ridden down to inspect a stand of lucerne at the bend in the river below the house. I had just got down from my horse, when I fell in what I can only describe as a kind of "dizzy fit." I don't know how long I lay there, not very long I imagine, as the horse hadn't strayed away from me. The poor beast was still trembling. I, too, was shaken by my experience, suffering from pins and needles, and wondering what else might be in store for me. (So much for "omnipotence"!) However, I am glad to report I have more or less returned to normal, although as a precaution I am taking things very slowly. (I wouldn't breathe a word of this to anyone else, least of all your mother. But you are my son.)

How, I wonder, can we reach that Merciful Power who alone can prevent the destruction of our world?

He must write to Our Father and tell him he loved and understood him, better even than before his fall from omnipotence. All that was needed now, in order to communicate, was a moment of total silence and light.

. . . you don't write, Hurtle. This is a black winter even at a bonfire. I get them to bring in logs and stoke up these great stone fireplaces. Then I light my lamp and I'm well enough off: progress can't improve on lamplight. But the few men left on the place are senile or imbecile, the cook a misshapen, toothless hag. Those we gather round us usually change shape: I don't know why I should expect more. I don't, for the most part, since my fall. Even when you are finally free, you won't come, and I don't blame you. Your life is your own, regardless of parents. This stone mausoleum is fairly cracking with frost tonight. Don't think for a moment I want to accuse you of not having faith enough in your father. . . .

In their dream Our Father put his black arms around him, which he shrugged off, while longing for the confirmation of grace. They stood looking at each other across the trampled sorghum, the smoke from which, rising into the frosty air, smelled of molasses. It was only this brief moment before he returned into his rain- and sweat-sodden clothes, the puttees cutting him off at the knees.

In spite of his not writing, it was Rhoda who wrote more than any of them:

. . . at last finished with governesses. The other girls I seldom see nowadays, though we have promised one another to meet. Some of them have become engaged, I hear. Mary Challands told me in confidence she is receiving instruction from a Roman Catholic priest. Although life at home is not so very different from what it was before, I am for the first time, you wouldn't call it "free," but other people have forgotten about me. Even Mummy doesn't remember to tell me what I must do, because she is always either too tired or too busy. If I were a man I would enlist in the Flying Corps. At great heights, in perfect isolation, I think I might at last become truly free, and would have no fear of crashing.

I don't know why I have suddenly turned what Mummy calls "morbid," when I set out to cheer you up.

On Friday we went on a small picnic with a friend you haven't met. Julian Boileau drove us down the coast in his motorcar. It was what they describe as a "perfect afternoon," but I kept wondering what you would have thought of it. I couldn't help feeling you and Julian wouldn't hit it off. He is so attentive to ladies they are all charmed. (He brought a bottle of champagne specially for Mummy, who is never at her best sitting on the ground.) He has rather pointed teeth and a fascinating moustache. There's something wrong with his eyes, which is why he hasn't joined up. Poor Julian is very kind, but treats me as though I were a little girl, whereas he is only twenty-eight himself. I think being on the short side gives me an unfair advantage over other people. When they look down at me, I am forced to look up through them. This is something I have never felt with you. I know we are not related by blood, but that isn't necessary; blood relationship can often be a disadvantage. As I see it, we have been brought closer together by suffering from something incurable. . . .

What? he almost shouted against the gunfire. He must write to Rhoda in the first lull, or during his next leave, after giving longer thought to her preposterous remark. The most he could remember their sharing was an occasional laugh at somebody else's expense. He would never have allowed Rhoda to intrude on the important, the true part of himself, because the truth might have warped or shrivelled up; so her odd assumption could only be accepted at the level of a joke.

Again she wrote:

. . . unnecessary for you to write, Hurtle. I know you think of me on and off, because a relationship like ours is at a deeper level— like a conscience.

Yesterday was my eighteenth birthday. I woke early, and was moved to tear up and burn all the diaries I have ever kept, all the easy half-truths. When I was younger I wanted badly to be some kind of artist, in imitation of my brother: I think I was hoping to offer people something more acceptable than myself.

Now I realize I shall never be anything but that, and must try to make it a truthful work.

Father came down for my birthday. He has given me a choker of seed-pearls, very pretty, and an ermine muff; Mummy's presents were a cage of Java sparrows—and a *diary*. Fortunately she can't have known I had burned all my diaries that morning; it was too early for her, and she no longer goes behind the scenes. Mummy's present is bound in ivory, with a gold clasp and key. In any case, it's only an ornament.

There wasn't a party in the evening, thank God, because of the war, but a few people looked in: Vi and Boo, Julian Boileau, two young officers returned with wounds, a sailor. You wouldn't know any of the men. Vi played for them, and there was dancing. It was all very jolly and intimate. Mummy revived. She danced, but couldn't persuade Father. Mummy danced on the landings and along the passages. She invited the maids to come in because, in 1917, we've got to be democratic. Everybody but May came. They drank my health in port after the music had stopped. The sailor disappeared—to be sick, we discovered afterwards.

Although she is still my friend, Boo Hollingrake has grown away from me. I think she is hiding something—perhaps an engagement. Even if things had been different, I would probably have remained a spinster, just as you are what they call a "virgin soul." . . .

A *what?* He had always hated Rhoda; even if she had been normal, she would have grown up gimlet-eyed, unnatural.

. . . Julian is always very sweet to me. He brought me a Persian kitten on my birthday, which Mummy is afraid will claw the furniture and mess the carpets, but I am determined to keep Pushkin. In addition to being Julian's present, he is so appealing, and already attached, when I had always heard cats were cold and selfish things. I am only afraid of his being crushed: he is so small. I smuggle him into my bed, and nobody knows.

On the night of my birthday "gathering," after everybody had gone, Mummy developed a headache, and I sat up with Father while he finished his cigar. We talked, and didn't talk. He would have liked to reminisce—*about you*; but I can never help him. Because I am small and a girl, he talks literally above my head, spitting out the words as though he had become in·some way afflicted. I would love to show him that I love him, but he doesn't care for me to touch, and nothing I ever say alters the expression of his eyes. . . .

There were moments when Rhoda became so recognizably himself, together they blotted out the twin nightmares of war and misunderstanding.

Rhoda wrote:

My dear Hurtle,
Our Father is dead. He died on Tuesday of a stroke. I found him lying on the floor of Mummy's little sitting-room: he was already gone. Mummy is inconsolable, as though she were responsible. But everybody is responsible. He could never forgive me because he made me. I loved him, and couldn't have shown him even if I had been allowed. I think it is never possible to show those we love—only to try to pick them up after they have fallen.

You wouldn't believe, but on the same day my Pushkin was hit and killed while crossing the street. Do you know that a cat looks like a human being as he waits to hurl himself under the wheels? Of course he must have been sick and distracted, too. I picked up his poor little body, so limp—the fur and other mangled remains. . . .

He *must* write to Rhoda. During several days' leave he carried around a sheet of paper which grew grubby at the edges in his pocket. His stylo wouldn't work. He was carrying a pencil, too, the lead of which he drove into the ball of his thumb, through grasping it. In the end he didn't write: he did a drawing of some moss roses, which he stuck in the envelope, and sent.

Rhoda didn't reply, perhaps because the last shot had been fired; for the guns were suddenly still: there was an armistice. Those who had survived were presumably saved. The knowledge floated, palpitating, on the waves of silence, flooding the travesty of fields, and on into the streets of cities, where people had begun to rejoice for the privilege of dying in other ways.

During the year in Paris when he washed dishes by night to justify himself by day, he was Duffield again. A fresh start, but at the same time a squalid one, seemed to call for the old name. In any case, how could he ever be a Courtney? However intense the nostalgia, he was no longer a member of his "family" as he looked back: at decent Harry, the Edwardian torso now disintegrated; at Maman, no doubt still dancing "on the landings and along the passages" in girls' white; at little pink-eyed Rhoda, nibbling at the edges of what she would never be allowed to consume.

He had gratified at least some of the desires of all three. If he had left them bearing him a grudge, it was because total love must be resisted: it is overwhelming, like religion. He certainly wasn't religious: he was an artist. But didn't this reduce him to the status of little pink-eyed Rhoda nibbling round the edges? The association made him focus his mind on other, immediate realities.

When not washing dishes at *Le Rat à l'Oeil ouvert*, he was hanging round l'Huissier's studio, with two American ladies of doubtful age, a youngish Englishman of taste, and sundry Scandinavians, all of whom were making the "new" approach to art. Painting was going to be pure at last. It should have been very new and exciting, but he found it wasn't what he wanted to do.

If he continued paying for l'Huissier's formula in hard francs, it was because he hadn't yet thought how he might extricate himself. In the same way, his physical attitudes were uncertain. He was either hunching himself at his drawing-board, hoping to contain the smell of dishwater and poverty, or alternately, on more extrovert occasions, he flaunted his condition, from unwashed hair to piss-stained crutch.

Although the kindlier of the American ladies bought him a meal and wished to discuss "organic integrity," and the youngish Englishman arranged himself tastefully on a divan after coffee, he remained virtually friendless because he had nothing to offer in return.

He was bankrupt by the war, he would sometimes explain, though only to himself. There were also the occasions when, sitting in his cupboard of a room, holding his thunderous head, in the smell of grey water he had brought in with him at four a.m., he knew that this wasn't true: what he needed was to go home, to renew himself, if there had been somewhere specific, some person left with whom he might establish contact. It wouldn't have occurred to him to write to Maman or Rhoda: these links were broken, together with others less obvious in the emotional chain by which he had always secretly imagined he might haul himself to safety. So he sat in his cupboard-room, rocking, cherishing the dregs of a sour red wine, and listening for the bursts of gunfire, the scattering shrapnel, which no longer came.

In one of these fits he remembered May Noble his fellow artist. He would write to May. Detached, and as he remembered, honest, the cook might be expected to illuminate the situation—if she replied.

May did reply:

Dear Mr Hurtle,

I got the palpitations when I read the Name at the bottom of your note, had begun to wonder if you hadn't died behind our backs ha-ha!

Thank you for your kind news which reached me just in time at "the old address." It is disposed of as they say by agents since your Mommong left. You will of been told about it all. It isn't for me to remark on, but a person wouldn't be human. It was a very nice weding it appears, I didn't go. St James's, all the nobs! Edith went, she was always more cool and calm, she could always dress the part, while I have my bunion which mean I can't get a shoe on without its hell.

Well it was a white weding in spite of her a widow. Your Mummy we know liked a display specially if it was her own self. There was no bridesmaid. With all the other frills Edith says it made it funny, no maids. Little Rhoda wouldn't of looked right poor thing though she and me we never hit it off. Then who else for the maid? Not old Mrs Hollingrake ha-ha! Any way they are now all gone Miss Rhoda too to live in England your Mummy always said Australia was common. I hope our Mr Julian Boilew will treat her kind. A lot of these marriages with young husbands are over after the first few kicks. And Rhoda always on their hands.

Hurtle dear I oughtn't to say but have invented a dish which is the real mackay of lobster and creamcheese and double *fresh* cream with a scent of brandy and extra chunks of lobster flesh you mould it and it looks and tastes a dream.

Well dear, I wonder if we will ever meet. I am going to a lady on the North Shore (never thought I would end up there) she likes it nice and plain, but the money's tidy. Edith is well placed, practically only cleaning the silver, with a newspaper man up Bellevue Hill.

Well dear Hurtle love, I hope to see you turn up before I am wearing a nappy with the Little Sisters of the Poor.

Your ever afectionate
May Noble

P.S. Edith read about the funny will you will of heard of how Mummy gets it all. Of course she will see about her kids but it is odd that Father who was so fond of you and Rhoda should have left it that way, as if he didn't care. Keep is passed on did you know at Maroullan. She piled it up, but nobody to leave it to except a neece she was always fighting with. Well, that is the way it goes.

Edging along the sea-wall, flicking prawnshells into the water, his old army overcoat rubbing and catching on the pockmarked stone, the young man had every opportunity for night thoughts, except that the night itself, with its smears of oily light and sounds of lolling, tepid sea, was so accommodating.

Then, too, his early dislocation, when Duffields sold and Mr and Mrs Courtney bought him, helped him accept May's information as final. He hadn't bothered to keep up a correspondence with someone he remembered with affectionate respect: she had fulfilled her purpose. In any case, he hadn't the cook's new address. He had even less clues to the whereabouts of Mrs Julian Boileau and her entourage. Returning home by cargo, he had sometimes wondered whether the glittering liner they were passing carried the Julian Boileaus in it. He visualized them stretched on deck-chairs, sipping a frosted nightcap and making languid conversation. Rhoda he imagined, head between the rails, watching their long turbulent wake, just as he was standing watching his.

Of course he could have exerted himself, through agents, solicitors, lapsed acquaintances, to trace his ex-"family," but lacked the ultimate belief in the efficacy of family ties. He was dependent on himself for anything he might become, and when he was too tired, too poor, too hungry, too discouraged, self-opinion was his consolation: to sign himself *Duffield*, not on the half-realized paintings he almost immediately painted out, but on those he was still only capable of painting in his head.

In the deserted park at that hour the sounds of Sydney were solider than the shapes of night: opaque florescence of a foghorn somewhere in the harbour; drawn-out squeal of a leaping train; empty bottle slapping fat water; a smoker's cough. In the not-so-deserted park he realized somebody was approaching, following the curve of the sea-wall, stubbing and rubbing. At moments it sounded as though a thigh was cannoning off the stone upholstery; while he continued leaning, elbows riveted to the wall: he should have been able to avert the collision, but didn't seem to have the power to move.

"Holy *Moses!*"

A woman's rather large, soft, furry form spattered against and around him: not all soft; her forehead on his was hard as a billiard ball.

"Thought I hit an iron post!" she yelled. "A bloody lamp-post without the lamp!"

Because she had got a fright she sounded angry at first, then began to laugh, her laughter smelling of scent and brandy. "You haven't got much to say," she said, as she continued standing against him, as he continued standing or leaning where he had been put.

"I don't feel like it." He heard his own awkwardness.

"Feel like what? Wait till you're asked!"

"Thought it was the man who asks—and the woman decides."

"Not always she don't! By crikey, no! More often than not, she takes what comes. Arr dear!"

She leaned over the wall beside him; the tail of her fur hung down black, pointing at the water.

"I've always been hopin' ter find something of value in the sea." The brandy was making her dreamier. "A pearl, or somethun. And never found nothun—but a used Frenchie!"

Again she went off into shrieks, not particularly for him, for some larger audience of abstract night faces, and as she laughed a finger of light picked at the gold in her open mouth.

She must have felt his recoil, for she began revising her performance at once; she stuck her arm through his and said: "What about goin' for a little walk? Up to my place. Eh? What do they call you, dear? Eh?"

"Hurtle." He let her have the naked truth.

She sounded melancholy. "Some of them think from the start you're gunner come at blackmail. They think of funny names."

"My name isn't funny," he rasped. "Or if it is, it's the only one I've got."

"Is it?" She disbelieved. "They call me Nance," she told him in an ever so slightly formal voice.

He hung back: suffocated by fur and brandy, he'd had enough of Nance.

"Aren't you comin' up to my place?" she asked and tugged, hopeful still.

"I got a hole in me pocket."

She started shrieking again. "You have, eh? Then you can walk behind and do it for nothun!"

The silence shut her up at last.

"If that's what you meant."

"No," he said. "It wasn't what I meant. I meant I'm stone-broke."

He began to slip away over the trampled grass. If he had dared, he would have started running; but the woman might have started, too, her fur flopping, her breath trumpeting after him.

"What makes you think it's a luxury?" Not only her voice, the sound of her feet was following him over the dead grass. " 'Oo never asks, never finds out."

He imagined too strong a jaw raised against the night to deliver its oracle.

He didn't answer, but went on slithering across the park, his army overcoat by now as heavy as an inescapable dream.

On the edge of an oval, faint dandelion lamps were flowering.

"Hey, dig?" she called. "Wait a mo, digger." She was thundering over the iron ground. " 'Ow d'you know we wouldn't *like* each other?"

"How do *you* know?" he answered feebly back.

Light from the lamps had turned his coat a sour greenish-yellow. His skin must have gone that colour of old pennies, with burnt-out sockets instead of eyes.

"Eh?"

Her brandy breath alone told him they were almost level again.

"People do like each other," she said. "It isn't all business, is it?" She added at once: "You gotter find out, though."

She was a fairly large woman, in a large black hat, of lace or net, at the back the largest wired bow, which had failed to keep its symmetry. Not unnaturally, the artificial light had turned her lips and cheeks to puce: her lips, her eyes, were the moister for exertion, or booze.

"Bit obsessed, aren't you?"

"Obsessed? I'm not educated," she grumbled, lowering her eyes.

Shame made him simplify his accusation; he said almost gently: "You've got only one thing on your mind."

"They won't let yer forget about it."

Walking side by side, they could have been quarrelling home from the tram-stop after an evening with relatives. His arches, he felt, were falling before their time, while her shoes accompanied her voice in a gritty patter.

"Can suit meself," she was saying. "Now and agen. If I like. I'm not a bolster."

"Aren't you drunk?"

"I'm not sober," she said. "Or I wouldn't be trottin' like a donkey after you."

It didn't destroy their intimacy: it seemed, rather, to solder it. Their feet sounded leaden on the hill. Of course he could break away at any point, if he chose, as he had done already in his life. Or had he? Had the breaks, perhaps, been chosen for him?

He tried to concentrate on a Poussin he had seen in the Louvre: solid enough evidence of the painter's own infallible will.

"Anyhow, we got here," she said.

Standing for an instant in an archway which draped the shadows on her in better imitation than the old black fur, she was looking at him out of the depths of another woman, offering him experience itself rather than the shabby details of it.

Then she was dragging him under what appeared a half-raised curtain of iron lace and cobwebs, into what must have been the carriage yard of a once considerable house. He was walking on the balls of his feet, bumping rubbing against her shoulder as if he, too, were suddenly drunk.

"I oughter tell you"—she had taken his arm and, holding it to her, begun to milk it from the biceps down—"to tell you there are people in this house who are jealous of others. But I mind my own business. Strickly."

He didn't expect they would encounter jealousy at that hour, when a door opened on one of the landings. Almost at once it closed, on a glimpse of blue light and a jaw sprouting orange stubble.

"Who was that?" he whispered too loud.

"The landlady. She was in the trade herself once. But developed varicose veins."

"Is she decent?" he chattered as they went on bumping their way up the once graceful stairs.

"As a matter of fact," said Nance, "a cow's arse is decenter." She nearly burst herself, and because he was joined on to her he reacted equally to their Siamese joke.

The light she switched on brought immediate sobriety. It was not a large room, and almost all unmade bed. Such furniture as he caught sight of had most of the drawers and doors open. There was a door open, too, on a balcony converted into a kitchen, from which drifted a slight, and probably permanent, smell of gas.

"Well," she said, looking, her nose swivelling at him, "you're a bit different to what I expected. Aren't you?" Her sighs and snorts sounded partly reconciled, however.

"Nothing's ever what I expect. Not exactly," he answered, because he had to say something.

It was true, though, particularly as he watched the woman take the squashed lace hat off the head of hair to which it had been pinned. She wasn't the bobbed sort. Her thick black tail of hair was kept wound round behind with the help of a tortoiseshell and paste buckle. It was the kind of hair, he could see, which would always be coming down: too much of it, and too heavy.

" 'Ere," she said, kicking off her shoes, "aren't you gunner take yer duds off? A busman's holiday don't last forever. I sometimes get a client as early as the milk."

In her enthusiasm and hurry a roselight had begun to pour out of the straining camisole; her natural, moist mouth had worked off the cheap veneer; the whites of her eyes, rolling and struggling in her fight for freedom from her clothes, were brilliantly enamelled with naked light.

"Don't know why I'm wastun me time! What are you staring at?" she shouted.

He was staring at the streaming golden paddocks on which the sun was rising through his boyhood as he sat between Sid Cupples and Father. The ridges were perhaps more silver than gold, the gullies more shadowy in which the strings of ewes heaved into a rolling scamper.

"I love you, I *don't* think!" she muttered. "You're bloody stoopid!" Coming and nipping him on the cheek. "Or perhaps yer dad told yer not to forget the pox."

Nothing seemed less likely as she began to strip resistance from him, layer by unnecessary layer. (Father would only have thrown a fit to see the suit crumple round his ankles—if it hadn't been so nasty cheap.) She was peeling, paring; he might have been something else: some exotic fruit.

While his own fingers began itching out after homelier pears, bruised in parts; the gash in a dripping watermelon: the marbled, sometimes scented, sometimes acrid flesh of all fruit ever.

He let down her hair. It fell around them.

He experienced a shock when Rhoda was projected for a moment in amongst the other slides: the pink shadow in her little legs. It might have ruined everything if Nance hadn't been in control.

"Not too bad," she kept muttering between her teeth. "'Tisn't—bad." Might have been Boo Hollingrake, except that Nance was holding the Delicious Monster against her periwinkle of a navel.

Or again, after they had plunged, struggling through the grey waves of the unmade bed, she mumbled on between their mouthfuls: "Wonderful—the way—they—worked—out—the joinery!"

Ahhhh they were flooding together in cataracts of light and darkest deepest velvet.

Sometime that night, or morning, for the oyster tones were taking over, he got up from the sticky sheet to rummage through his pockets for a cigarette. When he had found one he sat on the edge of the bed. She dragged once or twice on the fag, then returned it, and began tracing his backbone with her finger.

"Was it the first time you did it?"

His vertebrae might have crushed her finger: she withdrew it at once, sucking the breath back through her teeth.

"What makes you think that?" He couldn't sound surly enough.

"You was shivering like a dog they threw in the water."

He decided not to answer; and she began as if trying to level out his back with the broad warm palm of her hand; but it was too much for her: she threw herself on him in the end, for her own purposes.

"Oh God," she kept gobbling and crying. "Love me—what's yer bloody—love me—Hurtle!" gnashing and biting and sobbing, until he took possession.

She was only really mollified when finally he sat up astride her, looking down at the mess of flesh and wet hair. All this time of after-love she kept an arm over her eyes.

Somebody came knocking at the door and she got up as she was, to open. He caught sight of an old biddy in felt slippers holding a pudding basin to her apron.

"What is it, dear?" asked Nance, protecting herself against the draught.

"I thought ter make a puddun, Mrs Lightfoot, but am fucked for fat," the old woman said. "Could you loan me a penny or two for suet?"

"A puddun at five in the mornun? You muster wet yer bed, dear." But she scratched around on the dressing-table and gave the old thing half-a-crown.

"I won't forget. A nice slice of puddun for Mrs Lightfoot."

"You could light 'er breath with a match any hour of the twenty-four," Nance said when her neighbour had gone.

She was shivering now. It was so grey. Her shivery, suetty flesh was grey, and the desert range of the sheets. Two or three blades of clean steel had struck between the slats of a blind.

"You're like the others," she observed, sandpapering her arms with her hands.

For he was buttoning up his underpants, perhaps too fast for etiquette.

"Silly, bloody-lookun men! Silly-lookun *plucked* men! You all look plucked once you've had what you come for."

It made him laugh; but she'd lost her sense of humour.

"I didn't want to tangle with the milkman." He laughed.

"Why the milkman?"

"Or whatever the early client is."

She couldn't cotton on to the reference, and started sniffing, sniffling, got down on all fours beside the grate, poking at the black gobbets and grey flakes of dead fire.

He had to leave off what he was doing: the complicated problem of buttons in a room from which he was trying to escape. He was fascinated by her again. Where there had been golden-pear tones, a matt charcoal had taken over, with the long black shadows of her hair flowing into the deeper shadow of hearth and grate. He was fascinated by the burnt-out cleft of her formal arse.

Nance was holding a match to a ball of grubby paper and a couple of pale splinters of kindling.

"I'm gunner sleep," she announced. "If I'm in luck, I'll sleep all day."

Her drooping cheek, chalky at the edges, was gilded afresh by the little flame.

"Shall I be able to get in?"

"When?" she asked, listening.

There was the sound of paper catching fire.

"I dunno," he said. "When I come."

"Course," she said. "Course you can. It's me business, isn't it?"

Her thigh thumped the carpet as she reeled over onto the pivot of an elbow. "You had it free for once: that doesn't mean for every time. I've always been practical," she said. "Greasy little dish-washer!"

As she lolled looking at him from out of her tent of hair, her chalk-and-charcoal skin, her black lips, began yet another transformation. Shavings of golden light were crumbled on her breasts and thigh through the slats of the decrepit blind; little rosy flames began to live around the contours of her mouth, so that he was forced to get down on his knees beside her in his half-dressed, goose-pimpled state, to identify himself with what was at last a vision of his power: he didn't doubt he would translate the world into terms of his own.

Whether she realized or not, she allowed his mouth a moment's entry into the warm, but now directionless current of hers, then bit him, with affection rather than passion.

"Oh Christ," she bellowed, "I gotter get some sleep, you little bastard!" and flopped back on the gritty carpet.

He was by no means a "little bastard." In spite of the wretched, rucked-up suit and cheap, bulbous-toed shoes, he was a man of some distinction. He would have invented it for himself if the eyes of others hadn't told him, particularly those of women and girls: respectable ladies, old enough to enjoy detachment, smiled happily at his looks; disgruntled, shapeless housewives devoured him greedily, bitterly; neat young colourless women, of erect carriage and fragile jawbones, blushed for their own timid thoughts and averted their faces; schoolgirls nursed their lapful of Globite and yearned after the abstractions of love as the tram rocked their slommacky bodies.

It was always worst, or more open, in trams. He remembered how, in his boyhood, his thoughts had often fallen victim to the eyes of strangers. It was a moment of delicious shame, sometimes even consummation. No chance of that since experience had given him a key of his own. He was so quick to lock the intruder out, he might have felt lonely if it hadn't been for his thoughts: not the consecutive, reasoned grey of intellectual thought, but the bursts of kaleidoscopic imagery, both flowering in his mind and filtered sensuously through his blood.

On the surface he was employed at Cafe Akropolis, Railway Square. He got there around five p.m. and did whatever was asked of him: gutting and scaling fish, peeling and slicing potatoes, with spells of the greyer washing up. Sometimes his thoughts would flare up marvellously even then. He knocked off anywhere between midnight and two.

Nick asked: "You painting the home out?"

"I'm painting," he answered.

"You no take care, Jack, you spoil your good clothes." The Greek offered his piece of advice with indifference: he respected material virtues and wasn't responsible for his employees' habits.

About one-thirty that morning Duffield left with the standard parcel of left-over fish. It was only twenty-four hours since his meeting with Nance beside the bay. On and off during his daylight freedom he had considered returning to her room after he knocked off at the Greek's; but now he hurried back towards his own, as though to a meeting with a lover. From this distance he couldn't believe in himself as ponce, in the prostitute as mistress: he could only believe in his vision of her, which already that day he had translated into concrete forms. Hence all those dribbles and flecks Nick the Greek had noticed on his "good clothes," the hardened scales of paint he hadn't had time to scrape off his skin.

Though in a different locality, the house where he lodged was not unlike the one in which Nance Lightfoot lived. In spite of the hour a quarrel was still in progress the other side of a closed door; on the landings lingered smells of gas, and of food recently grilled and fried; the cold was beginning to encroach. He caught the sole of his shoe on a stair, and wrenched himself free for the last lap, the sole applauding or deriding.

He couldn't break quick enough into his room, and on yanking at the cord which provided light, there stood the three studies of Nance propped on a converted balcony after the style of Nance's own. Two of the versions had gone so cold he dropped the parcel of fish scraps. He rushed, mumbling moaning for his own shortcomings, and kicked the boards into a corner. Then he got down and tried to help the abortive paint with his fingers, but already it had hardened. Only the black-and-white drawing of the spreadeagle female form coaxing fire out of a grate led him to hope; though he kicked that, too, more gently, up the arse. He threw himself on the floor and lay there functionless, till the abrasive carpet began to grow meaningful, under his cheek, and in his mind.

It seemed to him that he loved this woman he hardly knew as a person: at least he loved and needed her form. Whether he desired her sexually was a matter of how far art is dependent on sexuality. He remembered with repulsion, if also recurring fascination, the stormy tones of a large bruise on one of her thighs. He had kissed, but could he have loved the bruise? Could this coarse, not exactly old, but lust-worn prostitute love her new ponce after one drunken encounter? He couldn't believe it. She needed him, though, for some reason she kept hidden behind the forearm shielding her eyes after the throaty confessions of love.

He fell asleep on the floor, realizing how he could convey the shadow from one of her sprawled breasts.

That morning he worked austerely and perhaps got somewhere with the spreadeagle Nance; but it was only one aspect of him in her. He would have liked to splash amongst the gasping, sucking, tropical colours which had flooded them both in their struggle towards a climax. He tried to concentrate, but couldn't. He began fiddling, rubbing, masturbating in nervous paint on a narrow board.

Although it was four o'clock and he knew he was expected at the Greek's, he had to see her.

He almost ran along the streets, until in the one where Nance lived, he started looking for a sign.

Several women had come out of their houses and were moving casually towards their beat. An old derelict bag was standing in the entrance to Nance's place: from looking glum, she brightened up.

"Mrs Lightfoot is expecting you, mister," the old girl called, relieved to rediscover a mission in life. "She's on the third—third floor up—green door—on the third"; she was the same biddy who had been "fucked for fat" in the small hours.

He went up after merely mumbling back at his informant. She didn't expect to be acknowledged, though.

Nance was arranging her hair above her eyes, in heavy loops, or drooping nests, in the dressing-table glass.

She said: "Hello. Thought you'd come. I thought you might'uv come last night."

She began hacking angrily at the looped-back hair with the axes of her hands, then gave up.

"I was busy, though," she admitted: certainly her eyelids looked thick.

She sounded both prosperous and brutal. Her cigarette, hanging heavy from her mouth, scented the room, which smelled also of cut leeks, or armpits.

As she sat in the yellow glare from her dressing-table, with its rattling handles, warped brushes, scattering of beige powder, and a souvenir kewpie, he pressed against her from behind, and she turned round, fastening her teeth in his skin through the V of his open shirt, dragging her fingernails down along the flitch of ribs.

"Ohhhhh!" she moaned in an ascending scale, then said very primly: "I got business to attend to."

"What sort of business?"

"Well," she said, reshaping her mouth, "there's a bloke I know wants me to put some money into a sandwich shop. Might be something in it, don't you think? All-night snacks along American lines."

"Didn't know you were the financier, too." To some extent he felt resentful: to find her less dependent on him.

"You gotter put it somewhere when you make it. I was never shook on the loose board. Some bloody cutthroat might rip it up one night, and you with it."

He laughed slightly.

"Eh?" She laughed back. "Aren't I right?"

But he was remembering his version of her cleft, spreadeagle arse.

"Besides"—she transposed her voice to a patently virtuous key— "this is a returned man—see? The bloke who wants to start the business—only one lung—got gassed or something in France."

"You go for the diggers," he couldn't resist remarking.

"Jesus and Mary, are you the only pebble on the beach?"

Little did she know it, but he was.

Or perhaps some suspicion of it did cross her mind: her mouth softened as she stood up, and her eyes darkened under the brim of the hat she had just put on. Reaching for her handbag, she knocked it off the dressing-table.

"Come with me—Hurtle—if you like," she said quietly. "It oughtn'ter take long."

After stooping for the bag she appeared to him in yet another light, dominated by her serious eyes under a garish royal-blue velvet. She had spoken his difficult name as though she wanted him to compliment her.

"I might come along," he said. "Some of the way, anyway."

She had made him shy. He avoided her. He stood playing with

the coins in his pocket, looking at the Alma-Tadema print hanging from a nail above the bed.

"Interested in art work?" She would have been pleased for her refinement to be recognized. "That was given me as part payment by an old boy who ran an art shop in William Street. Just before they took him over. Poor old bugger was short in more ways than one: he had only one ball."

"Looks as if you fancy the ones!"

"Don't it!" She rattled, laughing. "I never ever thought of that!"

They went downstairs, watching their step on the discoloured marble. Laughter and precaution brought them closer together. He looked up, and saw them in the blotchy mirror on a lower landing: a woman leaning on her lover.

And it was the same in the streets: the women he saw she knew turned away out of delicacy on catching sight of Nance Lightfoot with the genuine article. It made her walk more self-consciously, looking at her insteps, or sideways into shop windows. In one or two instances, girls they passed put on a syrupy expression and asked: "How are we, Nance?" and she smiled a smile he hadn't noticed on her till then. "Good, thanks," she answered, "how's yerself, dear?" as they parted.

It wasn't all that far to the solicitor's office where Nance was to meet the one-lunged digger.

"We can't be there too long," she coaxed as they approached. "It's late already, and the solicitor bloke'll wanter be makun tracks."

In the doorway they ran across a frail green-tinged individual with pinched nostrils who was apparently Nance's partner-to-be in the sandwich shop.

"Oh Mick—Mick Rafferty—this is my friend, Mister—er . . ." Her voice trailed away: she looked flushed, probably too ashamed to reveal his first name, while realizing she hadn't learned his second. To help her would have made it look worse.

The one-lunged digger suggested her friend should wait inside, but Hurtle said he would hang around. Nance left him with smiles of the purest banality.

Yet he was haunted by the harsh gloss of the royal-blue hat, by the changing architecture of the face, and the unconscious poetry of the eyes.

She didn't know herself. For that matter practically nobody in the street had woken up to themselves. A few glanced at him angrily in passing, and at least mentally edged away, holding him responsible for their moment of unwilling consciousness.

It was not very much later when Nance came hurtling back down the stairs and out of the rundown offices. "There! I wasn't gunner let them palaver. But it's late, love. What's the dago gunner say?"

Down the sleek asphalt hill the evening traffic was spurting through the purple shallows.

"Praps I'm going to give the dago the go-by—tonight and any other night."

"What—give up yer job?" Nance was shocked: at once she began working on his arm. "Of course I wouldn't let you *want*. I'm only thinkun of yer self-respect."

They walked on rather aimlessly. He hoped she wouldn't notice he was touched, because he wouldn't have known how to explain why. Here lay the great discrepancy between aesthetic truth and sleazy reality.

"I'll find something. Clean windows," he said to keep her quiet, "or floors."

"Haven't you any ambition?" she asked with such a humourless earnestness, again he couldn't help feeling moved.

He sniggered to hide it. "What about yourself?"

"Why should I be ambitious? I got a steady, remunerative job. But a man's different." Then, as they walked on, she said: "And you're not just a man."

"Are you in love with me?" He gave it a metallic edge.

"I'd like to be," she said, and again, bitterly: "Oh yes, I'd like to be!"

Still walking, she started stirring up her handbag, looking for something to blow her nose on. He would have liked to help her, but he couldn't.

At the bottom of the hill she recovered her cheerfulness. She said very brightly: "You never told me where you live, Hurtle. You never even told me yer other name—like we was still on blackmail terms."

He told her his name was "Duffield," and then, for good measure, that he also answered to "Courtney."

"You're not wanted by the johns, are yer?" Probably she believed that: she threw off a shiver and plastered herself closer to him.

"Anyway," she said, "they're both of them aristercratic names. Or so I'd say." She was too trusting: her big ripe purple mouth.

They mounted the hill and soon entered the city proper.

"If I'd thought we was coming as far as this I'd have dressed different," Nance said, with glances at the plate-glass.

Passing a cooked-food shop, he grew reckless. "What d'you say if we pick up a chicken and take it back to my place?" He dreaded the inevitable reply: she was so very trusting.

"That would be lovely, dear. Then I'll know where you live. You don't know a person before you've seen their home."

He avoided more by ducking inside the shop and choosing one of the imitation-looking roast chickens. He was sixpence short and had to come outside to confess it.

"Sixpence won't put you in debt," she said, looking inside the sloppy old handbag.

The chicken, still warm inside the paper, seemed to lubricate their progress, though they continued only slowly strolling.

Nance might have liked to hurry it. "Is it much farther, dear?" she asked at last.

"No," he answered, thinking of the drawings on the balcony.

They were passing one of the pubs towards the Quay when she stopped and said: "We'll make it a little celebration, Hurtle. But the booze's gunner be on me."

While she was in the bottle department the uneasy ponce nursed the parcel of chicken outside: he had to tell himself he was an artist.

She came out smiling, as though life begins all over again with a sealed bottle.

"One day," she said as they strolled on towards what she didn't know was coming, "I'll have to tell you the story of my life. You wouldn't believe it, but I was a nurse for a whole twelve month. I got so sleepy I didn't know in the end if I wasn't standing on me hands. They tell yer you mustn't become involved with the patients. As if you could. Even sponging round a bloke's dick. You're too dead tired. I don't say some of them didn't proposition me, but I never became involved. I don't think anybody who's at all professionally inclined becomes involved except with their profession— except now and agen."

Nance stepped across what a sailor had just vomited on the pavement.

"At the end of a year I got out. How could I ever 'uv become a starched-up nursing sister? The grammar alone. Mother was set on it, and it probably broke 'er heart. Though I married Snow Lightfoot. He was a postie. The kind that turns scraggy later. Poor Snow—always hurryin' ter reach the next box."

He told Nance it was the house in which he lived.

"Oh dear, you didn't oughter let me go on about meself!" She giggled; but she looked fulfilled.

On the way up she changed again: on one of the landings she stood listening. "I don't take to that door," she said in a haggard voice. "Have you got an instinct, Hurtle? Or are you just another male?"

All his instincts were concentrated on what he was about to, and dreaded to, reveal—but had to.

He unlocked his door and threw it open.

"They say I'm psychic." Nance was gasping less from her confessions than the stiff climb.

At once she was smelling around the room, like a bitch where a dog has lifted its leg.

"Well," she said, "it's a real man's turnout."

Again she had changed, and a sonorous melancholy, which was also approval, filled the room. It did look naked, felt cold, and he didn't know how to answer for it.

In the circumstances, he got down on his knees and began to light the gas-fire: that way he could also keep his back turned.

"What are those?" Nance was asking.

"Those," he said, without turning to look, "are studies—drawings —for paintings I'm going to do."

He could hear the gasping of the gas-fire. He had never been aware before of the composition of its flame.

"What," she said, "you're an artist, then?"

He didn't contradict, while listening to her heels roaming around.

"They'll run you in," she said. "For doing a woman like that. With 'er bum cut in half. And tits hangun. What's she doin'?"

"Lighting a fire."

The worst was over: he sat back on his heels.

Nance was yanking the cork out of a bottle of the cheapest brandy. She had torn a leg off the varnished chicken.

"Fancy you an artist!" She spoke through a mouthful of chicken, wondering, it seemed, whether to feel resentful or to devour the artist along with the flesh she was gnawing off the bone.

He was reminded of Goya's "Saturn."

"I don't think I ever met an artist before—but may 'uv—when I was in bed with one and didn't know it. There's a lot a person'll never probably know. You could know a murderer all yer life and only find out when it's too late."

He let her go on. He swilled a good third of a tumbler of brandy. With his mind's eye, he saw how he would take his drawing "Nance Spreadeagle" a stage further, into the architecture of the body. The abstracted form offered itself almost too easily, which was not surprising: the brandy all but ate flesh, while the shrill heat of the gas-stove raised perception to fever-pitch.

Sitting on the edge of the bed, Nance was licking her fingers, making a dainty job of it. "Some artists, I read in a magazine, leave fortunes when they pass on. Fancy if they make you a 'Sir'! Course you need a business head behind yer." She looked sideways at the balcony. "What d'you say if I let you paint me in the nude, Hurtle? It 'ud all be experience. And if you give me half-a-dozen tits, they'll be less likely to recognize me."

He began undoing her dress, to shut her up.

"Stopput!" she said. "I'm serious."

She was, too. It was Nance Lightfoot's practical night. They lay together on the narrow bed, but he couldn't have made love to her, because her mind was rushing with a different kind of abandon into other labyrinths.

"Suppose I don't go in with poor bloody One-lung Rafferty, into the sandwich business? That's too bad, but you've sometimes gotter think about yerself." Her fingers were totting up his flies, but absently. "Supposing I concentrate on you, eh? Hurtle, love? D'you think anybody's gunner buy this sort of art work? 'Tisn't exactly pretty, is it?"

"Not supposed to be."

"What is it, then? Explain to me. All this about modern art."

"If you could put it in words, I wouldn't want to paint."

Brandy, and gas-heat, and Nance Lightfoot, too, were making him doze. When he woke there was less sound of traffic in the street. Nance must have finished the brandy: he heard the bottle thump across the carpet and reach the lino.

She had turned nasty, it seemed. ". . . got a crick in me bloody neck lyin' on this narrer bed talkun to a corpse. When I only wanter help yer. You're just not realistic, Hurtle. Or perhaps it's me. To get stuck with an intellectual no-hope artist . . ."

While trying to soothe her navel, he longed to explore every silence he had ever let slip through lack of appreciation. The gas-fire continued hissing at him in blue.

Suddenly she had got her mouth, or muzzle, into his ear: the words were propelled like bullets. "What your sort don't realize," she wasn't saying, she was firing into his brain, "is that other people exist. While you're all gummed up in the great art mystery, they're alive, and breakun their necks for love."

"You attend to that, don't you?"

"What?"

"Love."

"That? There's more love between the iron and the board!" She kicked out, but as her shoes were off, she hurt herself. "Oh God," she moaned in a kind of mental revulsion, "when I think of men! The stockbrokers that are gunner miss their trains, the waterside bulls, the ones that apologize for their trusses, and those that are afraid they'll carry home a load of syph! Oh God!" She continued heaving and protesting.

He wanted to console her great curveting body. "Why do you do it, then?"

"Because I do ut good," she shouted. "It's my *art*—ha-ha!" She got, or fell, off the bed. "And brings the gravy in."

The fire had given up, the gas withdrawn to the wrong side of the meter. There was an inky silence in the room before she began feeling her way round the wall. Then she pulled the light on: it was so sudden it wrinkled them both disastrously.

She was mumbling, looking for her shoes: ". . . knock off a coupler shickered sailors. Pay for the ART-work! By this timer night, the Navy's pretty free."

Hobbling and excoriating.

"Don't say it's dishonest. It isn't dishonest if they're so damn stoopid. Oh God!" She joined her mouth to his. "I couldn't 'uv made love to you tonight. It would 'uv been sinful. You didn't know I was religious, eh?"

He listened to Nance Lightfoot tumbling down the stairs.

Next morning he began to work, but felt too dry, too corrugated. He got the wind up, too. He was less an artist than the night before: throwing up his job with the Greek to impress a prostitute.

Soon after, he stopped work altogether. He went through the advertisements and decided to apply for the job of cleaner in one of the big department stores. He was taken on, and agreed to start the same night. It had quite an antiseptic effect after Nance Bloody Lightfoot.

Most of that afternoon he mooned around. There was a soft, lyrical breeze; there were pale, lettuce-coloured streamers of light above the indolent harbour. The mood he was in, and the prospect of a new job, prompted him to extravagance: he took the little ferry to Kirribilli. The voyage was so gently soothing he almost fell in love with poor bloody Nance. He would have liked to feel her thigh against his as the ferry rocked them. He could even have put up with some of her marshmallowy ideas.

On the way back a wind sprang up. The sea grew metal scales, and over the charred city an angry light reminded him of what he was. All his fellow passengers looked so soft and vulnerable. Nance, if present, would have suffered worst of all.

That evening he ate a cardboard-and-gristle pie near the Quay before going back to his room to change. He would do so quickly, he decided, without looking at the drawings.

On the way up, the landlady called to him that a letter had been delivered by hand: a kiddy had brought it; which endowed the letter with greater virtue. He carried it up, examining it, trying to recognize the semi-literate writing.

The envelope contained a five-pound note and a scribbled sheet:

Dear Love,

This is to show I will keep to the contract I think we made, didn't we, last night. Sorry contracts was all we made. Sometimes I get mean with myself. It must be the only quirk I inherited from poor Mum.

Not seen Rafferty again, but will have to inform the solicitor all-night snacks are off. It sounds cruel without I also tell the other half of it, which I can't very well—that I am "in love." Anyways, on thinking things over, the sandwich dodge wouldn't work, one look at Mick's mug and they would start to quote the Pure Food Act. That is how I see it, don't you?

This evening the indications are I will be employed all night. There is a football team been given the address. I will think of you between the scrums.

I kiss you every where,
Nance

I don't understand those bloody paintings or drawings or whatever they are but they may be something. If I could draw I
would do you more realistic than life. How I would love it.

That night, pushing the mop draped with a waxed flannel round
the floors of the deserted store, he had never had less faith in art.
He blamed Nance rather than his menial employment. Art as he
had known it, as Maman's little sissy boy, as a priggish, pimply
youth, or l'Huissier's know-all pupil, had appeared more desirable,
not to say more convincing, than life; when Nance Lightfoot, in her
drunkenness, had started raising doubts. As he polished the scarred
floors, a vision of Nance's solid limbs seemed to prove her argument.
He began to erect against his overall. He could have thrown the
mop away, marched up to Darlinghurst, jumped the queue, and
rooted the pross like any self-respecting ponce; till he remembered
the arm protecting her eyes from him, the glad shudders of fulfill-
ment, that most innocent place where the hair springs out of the
naked temple, a drop of semen lost in stubble. So the ponce was
donged. He was her lover again: he was the lover of his perjured
art, by which he would celebrate the permanence of her rolling
belly.

The following day, in his cramped room, a sense of freedom
started him whistling and singing, until he realized the wrestling
match was on: to re-create the body as he saw it without losing the
feel of flesh. He knew, or thought he knew, how to fix the formal
outline; perhaps he had already done so. Now he was faced with
laying on the colour: the lettuce tones; kohlrabi purple; crimson
radish; old boiled swede for the shabbier pockets of skin. What he
conceived that day was vegetable in form and essence: limbs spongy
in substance, though still crisp enough for breaking off; the necklaces around the fibrous throat carved deeper by love-throes. Like
all human vegetables, she was offering herself to the knife she only
half suspected.

At the end of several hours he stood it face to the wall. He
couldn't look at it any more. He fell on the bed, and the rusty frame
pinged and wheezed back at him. He was swallowed by a clutter
of eiderdown—or paddocks of sleep.

For it was in fact the same journey as they jolted through the
early light the same gullies in spite of the dazzlement of rock and
dew the hills offering the same outline he tended to lose sight of

since climbing down since hearing the future crunch away out of reach with those he had depended on.

Instead, it was herself standing at the bedside feeling his forehead.

"What is it?" she asked. "What were you dreaming?" Herself dreamy by contagion.

"Nothing." He drew in his breath too sharply between his teeth.

"Whatever it was, it looked good," said Nance.

Honestly he couldn't have told her his dream: it was too formless.

"There must have been some woman you never told me about," she insisted.

He would have to get away from Nance: the smell of her powder, the spearmint she was chewing. The thought of her peering again at his work made him want to lock the balcony door.

When Nance was, in fact, his work; and he had only begun creating her.

"You don't look half sour," she mumbled through the gobbet she was chewing.

Then she stuck out her tongue, exposing the strings of warm, chewed, putty-coloured gum.

"Here"—she came and sat on the edge of the bed, tearing the paper off a strip of fresh spearmint—"stuff in some of this. There's nothun like gum for puttin' the juice back inter life."

With his tongue he warded it off, still scented, still brittle. "Pffeugh!"

"It's what they all do now."

"I'm not 'they,'" he announced too prissily.

"No," she said, "you're the real aristercratic prick—in yer grandad's ring."

For safety's sake he had taken to wearing the ring, and she had asked him to tell her what it was.

"I could shit on you," he told her now.

"Go on," she said, "if it'll do you any good—through yer grandad's bloody old ring!"

"Oh Christ!" He rolled over so that he would have his back to her.

"I was never taught to be blasphemous," she said.

. . .

"Hurtle?"

. . .

"What were you dreaming about when I come in?"

181

. . .

"Hurt?"

Because there was something in her voice, something which added to what he was trying to convey in paint, he turned again towards her and said: "I don't know, I tell you—truly. But once I went on a journey with my old man—my foster father—we got down very early from the train, and drove and drove in a buggy. There were paddocks on either side. I was half asleep. Perhaps I'd dropped right off. Then suddenly the sun came up."

"Oh yes, I know!" Her voice was moaning and grappling him to her. "Your limbs are still numb, but your thoughts aren't!" Her eyes were country eyes.

Everybody, it seemed, even Maman, he remembered, had experienced the original thaw; so he fitted his mouth into Nance's similar one, and they were throbbing together in the painfully bright light of memory.

When they had finished she showed him what she had brought: a pork pie looking as edible as a castle; a cream horn the raspberry blood had begun to stain; and a polished apple. The little girl couldn't have exposed herself more completely under the pepper tree in the yard.

He should have thanked her, but as he was hungry he broke into the crenellation of the pork pie.

"How is it?" she asked humbly.

"All right," he answered or munched. "How were the footballers?"

"Oh, strong!" She pulled up a sleeve to show; then she pulled it down again, and said in short sharp tones: "I don't wanter talk about men. Or sex. I just do it as a business, like anything else."

"What about us?"

"Isn't that love?"

It made him feel guilty scoffing down her pork pie.

"I want you to tell me about yer paintuns," she said.

"Aren't you trying to turn them into a business, too?"

"Well, it is in a way," she said, frowning it out, "isn't it? But if it keeps you happy. And if I finance yer—to keep you happy—I oughter get my dollop back from the investment."

"Where does the love come into this?" He looked at his watch.

She said: "It just does. I love you. You've gotter love somebody, haven't yer?" She was sitting on the edge of the bed, jiggling one of her heels.

"I suppose you have. In the end," he said. "But I've got to think about my job."

"What job?"

He told her.

"Don't you trust me?" She sounded genuinely dispirited.

Actually he trusted nobody, not even himself, or only that part of him which, by some special grace, might illuminate a moment of truth; but he hugged her and said: "Yes, I trust you, Nance. Of course."

She should have been consoled.

They went downstairs, and up George Street, towards Martin Place. The first lights of the evening were still looking too electric.

"If you love me," he said, "would you be prepared to marry me?"

Perhaps it was subjecting her to a test more brutal than she deserved. She did harp on realism, though.

When she had thought a bit, she said: "No." It sounded final. "If I married you," she said, "I might become your prostitute."

As they walked, swinging hands like any pair of lovers, he realized he was the prostitute: he was seducing Nance Lightfoot into giving him, not money, not her actual body so much as its formal vessel, from which to pour his visions of life.

On reaching the corner where they would have to part, Nance began, very heavily matter-of-fact: "I'm going away, Hurtle, for a day or two—professionally. The old sod gives me the gripes, but why pass up the good hay?" She stuck her nose into her handbag and continued more spasmodically: "Case you—run—short, love—better take these." She produced a couple of screwed-up notes.

"What d'you think I took a job for?"

She looked puzzled.

"The job? Of course. But this will buy any little luxuries." She turned it over on thick, bemused lips.

While flickering on this private situation of whore and ponce, which he found so repulsive, her eyelids began to exert a fascination: the slightly scored, greasy skin had escaped the ritual powder, not that the loaded mouth looked more protected; but he remembered kissing the eyelids when it was not expected of him, and how she had fallen back, not crying but gasping, whinging, as though he had struck too deep.

"Well," she said gloomily, "you're gunner be late, aren't you? For the job."

"I'm late already."

They didn't have any more to say to each other in words, or even deeds, though she floundered an instant in his direction before making up the hill towards her known pastures. He didn't waste more time himself; the night had grown too purple and tactile: it smelled of pittosporum, and fried food, and petrol, and quenched asphalt, and women's powdered bodies as he went quickly up the lane, and in at the staff entrance.

He would write to Nance, he decided, while she was away. It would be waiting for her on her return: to tell her what?

In fact, he didn't write; he was too busy. By night he worked in Picaninny Wax and Scrubbs' Ammonia; but by day he painted. It left very little time for eating, washing, defecating, let alone practical thoughts of Nance.

He put her out of his mind while his drawn-out orgasm lasted: he had already decided to call this painting "Electric City." The few hours he slept were dreamless, he believed; the lumps in the kapok had become a luxury; in one sleep he may have dreamed, for he woke working out of his mouth the rather rubbery texture of nipples.

Sunday he put his painting away (if Nance could only be put away) and took the train up the line to a random destination. The fact that people did refer to it as "up the line" added to its desirability, as of some lost world, or Mumbelong. He got out and walked beyond houses into the scrub, where he lay down, and rediscovered the smell of ants; but his hands, exploring stone, recovered flesh. He wondered whether he could retreat from, let alone escape, Nance.

But did he want to? The smell of crushed ants and the glare of mica convinced him finally of something they had experienced together. He would never try to tell her, however; he mightn't be able to, and the attempt would cheapen it.

Instead he began to create a radiance of mica round the jagged rock forms. He only got up when the shade started turning cold. While Maman's voice reminded him, he dusted himself with a handkerchief: it was about as close as Maman and Nance would ever come to meeting. Maman was probably dead, though. She *must* be dead. Rhoda, on the other hand, was his age: she could live forever.

Nance was away longer than she had expected. He decided not to comment on it as he was only employed by her.

"Were you lonely?" she asked.

"No. I was painting most of the daytime."

"But that's alone, isn't it?"

"Yes. Only I'm not lonely if I can paint—and am allowed to think my own thoughts."

"Funny," she said.

She had bought a bag of jelly-beans; she offered him a handful of them.

"What do you think about?" she asked.

"How I can convey in paint what I see—I suppose—and feel."

"Then I won't ever understand what you think about—not going by those things you paint," she said, looking at him sadly.

They were walking hand in hand, and the light of warm late-afternoon added poignance to her remark. All the walls looked old and crumbling, except where held together by the billstickers' collages.

"Isn't it possible for two human beings to inspire and comfort each other simply by being together?" He wanted that: otherwise the outlook was hopeless.

"I dunno what you mean," she said. "If you don't know what the other person thinks, it's like a couple of animals." She walked looking down. "For that matter," she added somewhat gloomily, "it's still like animals when you know what the other person thinks."

She had left off her make-up for the afternoon, and was wearing a cotton frock, inside which her easygoing figure was given full play. She had, for the moment, something of the unconscious nobility of some animals, moving intently on felted pads.

"What do *you* think about?" he asked, still very kind: this afternoon he loved the woman in the animal.

"I dunno. Money. A big dark cool house, full of furniture and clothes. And a big American limousine. I'd have to have a chauffeur to drive me about—with a good body—just for show, though. I wouldn't mind if the chauffeur was a wonk."

He was cannily relieved to find he hadn't yet featured in her thoughts. "What else?" he dared to ask.

"I'd have one of those big whatyoumecallem dogs—that film actresses have."

Her fantasies were making her breathless. "I'd have *you*, Hurtle"—

she turned on him her big eyes and great beige, unpainted lips—
"because I love you, love."

It was his night off, and they were, in actuality, on their way to
the pictures. They were, it seemed, already in key. The jelly-beans
she showered on him were of the same colours as her confetti of
imagination.

"D'you think we'll make ourselves sick," he asked, "guzzling all
these lollies?"

But Nance had removed to another plane. "Those old buggers you
go away with—I wonder whether they're worth it. You have to
work pretty hard, and don't dare pick up another job on the side.
Not with them paying the hotel. Though you're still paying the rent
at home. This old George Collins, for instance, is very generous up
to a point. We did the posh down in Melbourne. He let me choose
an evening gown. Took me to a dinner dance. But there's always a
battle for the hard cash. He's got a wife who's been an invalid
since soon after they married. He says she won't allow 'im to touch
'er. She knows what goes on but acts blind, provided she's got what
she wants in the home. George—he's a building contractor—rup-
tured 'imself some years ago. Now he's afraid 'e's got a prostate
coming on, and wants to make the most of 'is time—if it wasn't for
the hernia. Oh God," she suddenly moaned, "these old men turn
me up—when you wake, and there's the truss hangun off of a chair!"

She had taken off her hat, so that her head was now completely
hers.

"They got the dough, though," she sighed, "if you can dig it out
of 'em."

Not even her spoken thoughts detracted from her head this evening. Treading through the shallows of light, she looked remote
and classical. He would have to use her in another context: the
head with its heavy-hanging coil of hair.

Just then they arrived at the flea-box, and burrowed into its flaking
façade.

When they were seated Nance hissed: "I'm happy," looking
round glitteringly at the grubby grey interior.

She got him to fetch her peanuts and another bag of lollies. He
bought them with his own money. She looked at him reproach-
fully, only the absence of make-up took the weight out of it.

In any case, the first picture had begun, and because it was a
comic one, nothing could be taken too seriously. Their bodies ac-

companied the sharp runs of the piano. As the custard pie flattened itself on the cross-eyed comedian's face, Nance recoiled; then she hooted: "That's somethun I'm gunner try out on Billie Lovejoy!" her teeth gleaming through her laughter and the zinc-filtered light. Again, she shrieked: "They're not gunner bust up all that good furniture?" They were, it seemed, specially for Nance. By the end she was coughing with peanuts and fulfilment.

During the slides in the interval she got him to buy a couple of Eskimoes.

While they were cracking the chocolate shells and their narrowed tongues began to appreciate the shock of cold, Nance leaned towards him and whispered: "I could get down, Hurtle, with you, between the rows. Don't you know I love you?"

He did, of course. They couldn't have been anything but lovers. The tremulous music would not have let him escape; for the big feature picture had begun, and though its direction was not yet altogether clear, it seemed to promise the agreeable agonies of other people's frustrated love.

Nance took his hand and put it between her thighs, but flung it away on seeing how serious the picture was becoming. She was soon sobbing for the two aristocratic sisters parted and lost in the Revolution.

"That one can take care of 'erself. Tereese is strong—she's got 'er health. But the blind girl—Helenore—gee, she's frail! I bet someone'll give 'er a baby. That's what's gunner happen. Wait and see. Helenore's the sort that gets landed." Nance wiped her face with the back of her hand.

From time to time she said: "I'm not gunner look at this bit. It's too sad." Instead she put her head on his shoulder, and huddled, or rocked to the piano music; once she fiddled with his flies; she bit the lobe of his ear and said: "We know better, don't we?" and giggled.

He could have rooted her there and then.

Again the long sad picture had got possession of her. That was what she wanted: to be slowly and sadly possessed by a lost marquise in crushed organdie. And what he wanted was not the common possessive pross he loved by needful spasms, but to shoot at an enormous naked canvas a whole radiant chandelier waiting in his mind and balls.

He eased away from Nance after that, and felt for what she might have done to his flies. They were intact, and he grew detached from the boring picture.

The lost marquise had the baby, but by what turned out to be the right man: a disguised duke. You wondered how the child would grow up. Into a Rhoda Courtney? Or, for that matter, Hurtle Duffield? All children, he suspected, start out as yourself. Finally his egotism made him feel ashamed.

When the lights went up Nance's face looked large-pored and countrified from the absence of paint and steam of emotion. "It's lovely to have a cry," she said, "at the pictures." She looked around, parading her virtue for anyone who might appreciate it.

They got up and shambled out, the piano still racketing away: it was playing "Smiles," he recognized. The grey walls of the theatre were so agreeably negative.

Down the steps the night air hit them. Nance's face immediately tightened. Under the commonplace but pretty confetti of light, she bowed her head, noble in a sense that he looked for and needed. She didn't attempt to paint herself out. He suspected this would be their wedding night.

Her whole room confirmed it. Though arranged so differently, the furniture, with drawers open as usual, looked of a colour and size in keeping with a ceremony. Inside the cocoon of her yellow room, of her splendid golden body, the occasion remained proportionate, and after she had put out the light, the night continued showering pink and green confetti through the black window.

When they had come, Nance said: "I will never ever let you go, Hurtle. We could die now."

Then suddenly he wanted to leave. He didn't want her to comment on what she imagined he had experienced or seen. However clumsy, slippery, he had to escape quickly from the whore's increasingly stuffy room: to protect what she had given.

"What?" she shouted. "You're not gunner leave me? I bought a few savs I thought we'd do for supper."

He gave her a kiss. It tried to be tender, but he himself felt it to be dry: all the moisture in him had gone into their marriage of light; while her body continued arching against his, the bristles which had begun shooting again from a neglected mount of Venus prickling on his hand.

"The savs!" she moaned and slobbered into his mouth.

As he ran downstairs with his loot a door opened on a landing. He recognized the orange chin of the landlady and retired whore. There were whimpers and other apparitions on the way, not least the shaggy rat he kicked off where the yard opened: then rags of wet washing clinging to him as he burst through.

He fell on his own bed and dreamed in his clothes about the Boudin above the fireplace in Harry Courtney's study, in which ladies walked over stretches of firm sand tilting their parasols. There were no quicksands, it appeared, to swallow them down.

Suddenly he had begun to live the life for which he had been preparing, or for which he might even have been prepared. At the end of the years of watching, of blundering around inside an inept body, of thinking, or rather, endlessly changing coloured slides in his magic-lantern of a mind, the body had become an instrument, the crude, blurred slides were focusing into what might be called a vision. Most of the day he now spent steadily painting, still destroying, but sometimes amazed by a detail which mightn't have been his, yet didn't seem to be anybody else's. There were one or two canvases he had dared keep, in which dreams and facts had locked in an architecture which did not appear alterable. When his fingers weren't behaving as the instruments of his power, they returned to being the trembling reeds he had grown up with. If he had not been dependent on Nance Lightfoot for "any little luxuries," he might have taken to drink or smoke, and trembled more violently than he did. His nightly journeys through the deserted store, through the smells of virgin drapery, floor-wax, ammonia, and his own sweat, exhausted and prepared him for the next ordeal.

Because next morning remained an ordeal: he was so flabby, frightened that his only convincing self might not take over from him at the easel.

Nance sometimes left him alone for days, either from diffidence or a kind of tact. He thought she was afraid of the paintings on the whole.

When she was most afraid she became her most brutish: she would begin to strut. "Once I promised to take off me clothes, and let yer paint me in the naked. Well," she said, kicking at something he had just finished, "I muster been pinko at the time. I'd probably come out wearun a prick and balls for luck." She laughed right back to the uvula: probably pinko now, too.

Sometimes he chucked her out, but often his own animal responded to hers, and they would fall down clawing at each other, curving and writhing in uncontrolled but logical convulsions; till only the grit on the carpet was left.

On one occasion she sent back a note soon after she had left:

Dear love Hurtle,

I am no good to you I know, dragging you into the gutter where you don't belong. I won't love you any less if you tell me it is over and I must get, but know that without you inside of me I am not whole, I am not

Your
Nancy Lightfoot

He couldn't have told her, because he needed her: not the humiliating fivers, not her "love," necessarily; but because on one level he was resuscitated by the breath he breathed, the saliva he drank, out of her mouth, and because on a purer plane they solved together equations which might have defeated his tentative mind, and which probably never entered Nance's consciousness.

Poor Nance, there were other material developments he would have to explain. As an introduction, he bought her a little ring, of two gilt serpents intertwined. He found it in a junk shop on Church Hill; apart from the prettiness of the conceit it was of little value.

"What is it?" she asked dubiously: "Is it gold?"

"No. Silver-gilt."

"Eh? Looks pretty tinny to me. But it must have cost money, antique jewellery like that."

They had sat down on the grass in the Domain, and her face was darkened with shade from the figleaves.

"Why did you spend all that dough on me? Eh? Even if it was me own."

The way she drew down her mouth, loaded at one corner with a cigarette, she appeared to be trying to make herself look particularly coarse.

"Or wasn't it my money, cock? Where else did yer strike oil?"

He might have felt insulted if he hadn't been holding the knife to Nance. "I made some," he said. "I sold a couple of paintings."

"Oh, you did, did yer?" She had almost eaten off her lipstick. "Who in hell would buy a couple of *your* bloody paintuns?"

He must be very patiently gentle with Nance. "A woman," he said.

"What sort of woman?" she hawked, spitting out a shred of tobacco. "A lady?"

"I don't know. I was told a woman."

"What sort of woman or lady would buy one of those nutty paintuns?" Then she considered: "How d'you mean you was 'told'?"

"By the dealer."

"What—does anybody deal in rat shit?"

She was panting by now, unsticking the hair above her forehead, freeing the grass- and fig-stained frock her haunches had pinned too tightly to the ground.

"Which of the pictures did the person buy?" Her ears were pricked.

"The one I call 'Electric City.' "

"Oh, *that!*" She sniggered and tossed away her cigarette. "What else, Hurt?"

"I don't think you saw it. One called"—he hesitated because he was about to expose himself—" 'Marriage of Light.' "

They sat staring out from under the Moreton Bay fig at the dazzlingly iridescent water.

Nance was holding her head at an angle which made her neck look brittle. "That was my painting," she said, or gasped.

"You never looked at it." He could have flattened her. "Or once, I think, you kicked at it."

"I saw it," she insisted. "I know I'm supposed to be too big a dope to see. I'm only good for stretchun out on the kapok. But I seen *you*, didn't I? In the fuckun dark!"

She took a handkerchief out of her bag and rubbed her mouth very vigorously; then she spat; and sat with her hands palm upward in her lap.

He lay chewing grass, hoping the blood wouldn't burst out of his veins, the breath explode in his chest: it would be terrible if Nance enjoyed glimmers of sensibility.

"I liked it," she said in a dead, even voice, "it had sort of sparks in it. It was my paintun." Suddenly she was shedding the last rags of her aggressiveness. "I practically painted it with me own bloody tail"—her voice rising before dropping.

Seated beneath the giant fig, she was the first original work of sculpture seen in a Sydney park.

Around them was a sound of what could have been pure silence, out of which she dredged up her voice to ask: "What did they fetch?"

"One of them twenty-five. The other thirty: it was a bigger painting."

"Good Christ, you're not much of an investment! Or else somebody's a shyster."

He couldn't answer her.

"But whichever it is, I gotter have my whack. That was in the agreement."

"Not yet you can't, Nance. I'm buying a piece of land." He swallowed a gusher of green spittle before rejecting the empty grass. "Up the line," he added desperately.

He couldn't explain that the suburban bush, probably Africa to her, was in a sense his Mumbelong.

"And wotcher gunner do—'up the line'? *Paint?*"

"Yes, Nance. Paint."

"And live by the ladies that take yer down?"

He couldn't answer that either.

"Or Poncess Nance!"

Her coil of hair was halfway down; her eyelids might have been walnut shells.

"Am I ever gunner see yer?" she asked.

"Whenever you feel like it."

So it was settled beneath the spreading fig, on the uncomfortable fruit, some of it still sticky, some already petrified. From big blubbering orphaned baby who needed comforting, Nance became the insatiable goddess, who only didn't think of tearing bits off her victim and throwing them into the blue waters of the cove.

It was a wonder they were able to recover their identities merely by his stuffing in a shirt, and her harnessing a torrent of hair; but they did: they bared their teeth at each other, lowered their eyes once, and resumed their actual lives.

Caldicott advanced him money against three more paintings; so it was possible to buy the strip of scrub on which, he had begun to feel, his creative life depended. The dealer, a mild creature of indeterminate age and sex, ran a little gallery at the top of some stairs not far from where Duffield lived. The gallery itself was almost always empty, except on occasions when ladies in twos and threes tried out their taste on the several paintings exposed for that purpose. The muted ladies appeared almost paralysed by their own daring.

Duffield couldn't arrive quick enough at the office or cupboard across the gallery where Caldicott the dealer usually sat, wearing a leather eye-shade the colour of milk chocolate above his hairless, milky face. Caldicott was in such practised taste he practically couldn't give an opinion on any subject, but would sigh and giggle his kind regrets as he sidestepped.

"I can't say there's any actual rush, Duffield, for your work." Caldicott tried to adjust the eye-shade so that it would give him greater protection. "But there's a more *general—growing* interest in painting amongst people of the better class—and where *one* has rushed in"—he sniggered, and stroked his hairless jaw—"there may be others preparing."

The risk he had just taken encouraged the dealer to remove the eye-shade for a short spell. It had left a crude red mark across the milky forehead, at which Caldicott began to dab with a beautifully initialled handkerchief. His eyes, in contrast to the shade, were bitter chocolate, and in spite of the delicately discoloured lids, not as weak as you would have expected.

"It takes time and you are ahead of it." He lowered his eyelids on his own epigram.

"In the meantime, I've got to live," the painter suggested.

"Oh yes, by all means—to live." The dealer showed his teeth in amusement. "You have employment, haven't you?"

"Yes, I'm a cleaner—at Morgan's."

At this contact with life Caldicott bowed his head over the blotter: though he had never laboured, he had been reared in a country where labour is theoretically a sacred rite.

"Then you will always be able to eat. Nobody need starve in Australia."

"But when I withdraw to the scrub, how am I to paint and eat, Mr Caldicott? Unless, of course, I live off the immoral earnings of a woman."

Caldicott almost fell apart. He enormously enjoyed someone else's joke in doubtful taste. Though his latest painter was so unknown, so unfashionable, he might begin to cultivate him in a tentative way: ask him to dinner with a broad-minded few; bad taste in a protégé could be a social asset.

The hushed ladies in their striped voiles and black-and-white polka-dot crêpe de Chine adored Mr Caldicott. Instinctively they recognized *Maurice* as one of themselves by the way he tweaked at his non-existent string of pearls; while on a grander, terrifying plane they accepted him as guardian of a world of art they could never hope to enter, married as they were to barristers, bankers, physicians, graziers even. So the ladies no more than hovered round his cupboard door, entrance to a desirable, though forbidden Hades, murmuring felicities such as: "Thank you, Mr Caldicott—so stimulating—so gratifying to see we are coming of age in the arts."

Once, a lady more perspicacious, more informed than the others, stuck her head inside the cupboard and announced in a whisper made to carry: "I'm glad we're not going as far as *Picasso!*"

She stood there flickering her eyelids, waiting for her measure of praise: and the dealer laughed the conniving laugh his client expected, and rearranged his invisible pearls.

"Oh, Mrs Farquharson," he suddenly remembered, "this is one of our artists you're going to hear more of—Mr Hurtle Duffield."

The lady flickered appreciatively, and recoiled. It was difficult enough to introduce to her barrister, her banker, or her grazier, a water colour of grazing sheep, without the artist who had painted it.

On one occasion when a fair gaggle of ladies was appreciating an exhibition, the painter asked the dealer: "Is she any of these?"

"Is she—who? Oh, Mrs Lopez! No. She's young, and"—he averted his face—"some consider, dashing. She was here recently; but went away again. She lives away. She was widowed soon after her marriage. In Ecuador. Or was it Peru? Very tragic—though I can't say anyone ever met Mr Lopez. (She intends to remarry, I believe, and live in Berkshire.) But don't let that discourage you. The word carries when a lady buys a painter—if the lady has means—and Mrs Lopez has very substantial means of her own. All these"—Caldicott's bitter-chocolate eyes darted out at the tasteful ladies—"are chicken-feed." Vulgar for Maurice: it must have been the humidity.

His only patron removed, Duffield plunged downstairs. He could feel the sweat running down his ribs, probably rotting the seams of his shirt. To take courage, he tried to visualize his strip of scrub, and the house he had begun to build—it wouldn't be much more than a shed—in which he proposed living. His blood-blisters and scabs were positive reminders; but the house, founded on an Australian instinct he hoped he possessed, rose only groggily in George Street.

Nance hadn't seen the house. He hadn't been seeing much of her: they had started on the phase in which each considers the next move.

Along the street the asphalt was heaving and undulating, a flickering of deck-chair stripes on colourless ladies, one of them half-emerged from the chrysalis of widowhood; heat on summer oceans was the colour of jade; in Sydney, brutally blistered brown. What could an Australian lady of means have married in Ecuador—or Peru? Berkshire was the more likely place.

The careering trams didn't prevent him becoming involved with his "Marriage of Light," which the faceless Mrs Lopez had carried off. Nance Lightfoot took him by the hand. There was no mistaking the heat they generated together, as he re-enacted the details of his painting; but neither Nance, its source, nor Mrs Lopez, its buyer, nor any future owner, could lay claim to what was sprinkled with drops of his blood. The taste of it on his tongue made him draw back his lips, out of repulsion, or exhilaration. Suddenly, in plate-glass, there he was: more than real. He might do a self-portrait with warts. He had never contemplated it before. The prospective orgy of knowing himself encouraged him to run up the stairs, to the room he was soon going to leave.

However crude and basic the house or shack on the edge of the gorge, it was the artifact he had made. Helped by its primitive nature, it soon settled into the ironstone and eucalypt landscape. The rocks might have been fired on a primordial occasion before it was decided to disguise the cleft of the gorge with its austere fringes of vegetation. It remained an oven in summer. Not surprisingly, trees sown in rocky crevices had taken the colour of smoke, of ash, their leaves narrow and listless, but tough. Even now, smoke would unravel without warning, its pungent strands threading through the bush. The whole of one night he stood by his unfinished house and watched the gorge snap and gnash at its own flames, as the trees went up in a clatter of fiery blinds. In the first light he himself felt ashen, not to say emotionally charred, while he still waited with a hacked-off branch to protect, if necessary, his timber skeleton of a house. It continued standing. The half-empty water-tank glittered as the morning clapped its eye on the un-painted iron corrugations.

The bush never died, it seemed, though regular torture by fire and drought might bring it to the verge of death. Its limbs were soon putting on ghostly flesh: of hopeful green, as opposed to the ash tones of a disillusioned maturity: the most deformed and havocked shrubs were sharpening lance and spike against the future.

He liked to scramble down the face of the gorge through the evening light, chocking his boots against rock, clinging to the hairy trunks of trees, his fingers slithering over the slippery, fleshier ones. Once he caught his mouth trying out the response of one of the pinker, smoother torsos. He was never so happy as in the com-municative silence of the evening light. Sometimes he remembered he had been a painter before growing physically exhausted: muscle-bound, wooden-headed, contented.

He hadn't seen Nance Lightfoot for months when he was handed her letter at the post-office-store.

Dear Cock,
What are you up to "up the line"! I bet the art ladies are bring-ing you picnics of champers and chicken mayernaise. Well good luck to them and art, but not all the mayernaise on Darling Pt is going to paint my painting back the marriage one.

I am wondering about you dear Hurt, whether you have got enough to eat—and bush fires on top. I will come up to see you one of these days, so dust the art ladies away, I am a bull where ladies is concerned.

I am hungry I don't mind telling you after a diet of commer-cial travellers and railway porters. I lie there. I let them look at my armpits.

There was a bloody Irish merchant seaman bilked me out of the money and pinched half a bottle of gin. You could of stood his socks up on their smell.

Dear love and Cock, I will die of you if I don't soon see you, just the shape of it. Course I don't mean that, I mean more than that. I could eat you up raw.

Nance

She had done a drawing on the bottom of the page which the postmistress would have liked to get a look at, only he went outside.

No suggested date for the visit, but the threat had thrown him into an uproar: he heard that squelching sound in his ears; as he turned off into the scrub he could feel the blood padding through his veins. Nance had unnerved and nerved him at the same time; when he got inside the shack he began to unpack and lay out his neglected paints.

All those months at Ironstone his physical energies had been too thoroughly drained off by the building of his house and the difficulties of day-to-day existence. He decided to eat less, to avoid further calls on Caldicott and Nance. He lived off damper, dried beans, rice, lentils, and the woody swedes he grew himself in the thin soil of the ironstone escarpment. At one point he joined a road gang, and worked with it for a few weeks; with the pay, he debauched himself on butter, tea, and sugar. Occasionally he made drawings, little more than notes, which couldn't relieve his cynicism, nor his rage for physical exertion. He belched sour, and often wondered what had ever persuaded him he might become a painter.

Later on he realized he had been expressing himself in his tentative house: a wood-carving of necessity.

Caldicott had paid him a visit. The dealer walked with a slight limp, the origin of which the painter didn't discover. Caldicott arrived mopping himself. He had on a tussore suit, the coat of which he was carrying over a shoulder: abandoned, for Caldicott. His hat was a new Panama through which the sweat was spreading. He looked not so much amused at his protégé's eccentricity as amazed at his own foolishness. The veins were bursting out of his flushed, hairless skin as he stumbled limping down towards the ledge on which Duffield had perched his misguided shack.

Caldicott peered into the gorge, and must have found the gulf between art and life at its most repulsive. "Do you really think you can live in this place, Duffield, and work?"

"That's what I've been doing. I've almost learned to knock a nail in straight." Duffield refused to indulge in the nuances on which Caldicott throve.

The latter expectedly winced. Secretly he hoped his own life might appear a work of art to others, and with this in view he collected paintings, rare objects, limited editions, and kept the gallery in George Street to encourage interesting boors like Duffield whose bad taste might eventually be excused as genius.

"In any case," he said, swallowing down an astringency, "you look aggressively healthy—don't you?"

Duffield felt all scabs and blisters as he fetched a couple of bottles of beer standing in a bucket of lukewarm water in the shadow of the iron tank.

They drank the warm beer out of cups, while the shade of Edith the parlourmaid hovered round them: for a moment the white sun caught the rim of her salver, and Hurtle swallowed his beer in knots.

With Caldicott, distaste was now becoming business. "I am planning a mixed show for February. Will you be ready for it? Oh, conventional on the whole; but you, Duffield, will provide the controversial salt." Flatter just a little.

Duffield had become a mumbling groaning lump of man, or rock. "I don't know. I don't know when I shall be ready." He kept shifting his position on the very uncomfortable chair.

"What—aren't you painting?" Caldicott looked at him with a kind of disapproving admiration: as though his protégé had turned out to be a disguised labourer.

He took a snapshot or two with a camera he produced jokingly.

Presently Duffield led the way, and they ate some rubbery cold salt beef on a table in the long half-built room; or Caldicott messed the beef about, carefully, rejecting the gristle with the tips of his lips.

When the meal was over, Duffield brought out a bottle of brandy. After the first sip, Caldicott had to look at the label: he shuddered to find his suspicions confirmed, but went on with it, out of camaraderie—or was it mateship?

The sun, at its heaviest, was bulging over their heads. Heat was scratching the corrugated iron.

"Well, dear boy"—Caldicott smiled his milk-white smile—"provided you're happily involved in the experiment!"

Then he put his hand on Duffield's thigh, in a gesture halfway between unconscious affection and conscious appraisal. Almost at once he removed the hand: he could have burnt it; his smile was trembling painfully.

"Keep February in mind," he fluctuated. "I should like to hang *three* Duffields. Three should allow them—some of them, at least— to grasp that your intentions are serious."

Towards the end he had raised his voice, hoping to hear it ring out in impersonation of a forceful man; but what they both continued hearing was Caldicott's echo accusing him of a slight indiscretion. Or wasn't it so slight? He looked at Duffield: one could never tell.

Duffield warmed towards Caldicott limping away through the scrub in his escape back to civilization. If it had been in his power, he would genuinely have liked to help the man out of his cabinet by smashing the panes; but he had never felt so impotent.

When his visitor was long enough gone to be out of earshot, he took the brandy bottle and chucked it into the gorge, where it hit a rock and exploded into a galaxy. He hoped Caldicott hadn't heard after all. With guilt on his heels, how much more noticeably he would have limped. He wasn't accusing his friend of his frightened little attempt: he was demonstrating against an emotional state of his own, which had unexpectedly given birth to this plume of transcendental glass.

And now, what most disturbed and disgusted: Nance was coming; though she still hadn't given a date. In preparation he took to shaving every morning; he shook out the rumpled bags he used as a mattress between himself and the floor.

As self-protection he had started painting again: his visual abstractions soothed, if they didn't completely satisfy him; but his thought was growing, out of rock and a shower of glassy light.

Nance didn't come, and he grew dirtier, more sullen, afraid his material resources might give out before he had arrived at what he was vaguely hoping to achieve: when Caldicott sent him a cheque, without comment, let alone explanation.

The same day he walked into Hornsby to cash the cheque. On his way home, the postmistress at Ironstone was refurbishing her staghorn ferns by pulling off the dead outer skins. The great heads from which the antlers rose were looking aggressively frontal and glossy, bulging from the trunks of the camphor laurels. The postmistress was a pale widow, who told him through pale lips that staghorns derive their nourishment from the air. She was proud of her ferns: she didn't know what she would have done without them after her husband passed on.

It seemed to him that many of them were nourished by air: Caldicott (or so one hoped); the postmistress at Ironstone; himself even. Only Nance smacked her chops over a life-giving diet of glutinous, smoking meat.

He decided to get up early the following morning; in fact, he was seldom seduced into lingering on the ridge of potato sacks on which he had woken. An intensifying golden light was dusting the pelt of that lean animal his body. Stroking, scratching it, he was so detached, it owed him nothing but its captivity under a roof. His tactile mind was the part of him he cosseted: encouraging it to reach out, to cut through the webs of dew, to find moisture in the slippery leaves, the swords of grass, before the sun had sucked it up.

He got into his pants, incidentally rather smelly, and stiff with recent wipings of paint. He strutted up and down, digging his hardened heels into the splintery boards, tearing at a loaf he had bought the afternoon before, guzzling, and thinking, and loving; while the moisture tinkled; feathers shook free of dust and dew; the morning shrieked, called, whipped, and tolled out of the gorge. In between, silence made the loudest affirmation of all.

Glutted finally with bread, light, sound, he returned to the attack on those giant rocks with which he was obsessed: to dissect on his drawing-board down to the core, the nerves of matter; but pure truth, the crystal eye, avoided him. He the ruthless operator was in the end operated on, and he flung off, groaning and dry-mouthed from the austerities of black and white. There were several versions of the same theme, some of them more advanced because less ambitious, and he healed himself by adding to their flesh, by disguising their scars, with touches and retouches of paint.

"What's it this time, I'd like to know?"

The shock made him blunten what should have been the razor-edge of a mica sun.

"Rocks," he mumbled, resentful, nauseated: under it all, frightened.

"Looks more like cauliflower ears. Bloody boxers' ears mucked up forever by the glove."

He couldn't avoid looking round at her.

He saw that Nance and he were strangers to each other, only that Nance, who believed strangers didn't exist for more than a second or two, had dumped all the stuff she had been lugging, was wetting her mouth, from which exertion had worn off most of the lipstick, and opening her eyes wider and wider, to swallow him up.

He was stifling in the sweet, steamy smell of city nights.

200

"You're good!" she munched when her appetite allowed. "You're harder, Hurtle, than you used to be."

"What have you done to yourself?" he complained.

"What?" She blenched as she went through the possibilities.

"Your hair."

"Oh," she said, "that's the fashion. Don't you like it?"

She took off what, no doubt, she hoped was a dossy little hat. They had cut off the great dusty tumbling mare's-tail of her hair. In place of it she showed a strong, pale-as-a-candle, shaven nape.

"*I* like it," she said complacently, "though it's gunner cost a lot in the long run. Have to get used to it—like payin' the gas and electricity."

Her calves bulged more than he remembered, but he had never seen them so exposed, unless in the entirety of physical passion.

"Look," she said, beginning to unpack her largesse from the carriers. "That's potted pig's-cheek." She smelled it. "Could 'uv gone off on the way. Didn't oughter 'uv brought pork."

Much had gone off, he suspected, since her cornucopia was emptied into his cell. Now that he had her, he didn't in any way want her, or the grey marble of the pig's-cheek, or pickles, or the rope of saveloys, or oranges—oranges everywhere: big open-pored navels rolling off the table. The dossy little hat was drifting gauzily over the floorboards. She was so absorbed in her activity she didn't seem to notice that the pendulum pearls weighing down her lobes were bashing her savagely on the cheeks. She was looking for a tumbler, she said, to freshen up her "corsage," but settled for an empty bottle when told there wasn't such a thing as a glass. She filled the bottle with water from the tank, and after taking off their silver paper stuck her wilted orchids in the neck.

"A bloke give them to me Friday night—a business noise from Brissy."

Nance was so unconscious of her own vulnerability he couldn't continue feeling resentful over what he no longer found in her, if that had ever existed: perhaps he had created it as something he needed at the time. He had to begin loving her again for what she was in the concrete present: her chipped-lacquer look; the restless activity of those fake pearls chained to her ears; the forms of her timeless body at the mercy of a travesty in salmon sateen.

But he couldn't have freed her. Didn't want to touch her even.

Nor did she want to be touched, it seemed: not after their first, and formally passionate, embrace. She was determined to appear hard, bright, self-contained, proficient in any of the domestic rites he mightn't have thought she knew about; or possibly she was intimidated by unfamiliar surroundings.

She kept turning round to look.

"You're sort of pigging it—and like it!" She looked at him with the bright indulgence of a big sister, haunches overflowing the hard chair.

Again staring around, rubbing her biceps as though to warm them, she said: "Golly, it's quiet!" and laughed.

"It isn't. You can hear something happening all the time."

"I know *that*," she said through her flaked lips, still rubbing at her own gooseflesh. "This is what I come out of. There was always the sound of heat, and hens, or a dog's bark, or a sheep's cough. Oh yes—the ache of it! If I heard a sheep cough now, I'd jump out of me bloody shoes."

She was wearing gold ones, kid, which the stones must have martyred as she came down the track. When she saw him looking at them, she hid her feet under the chair.

She said: "There's an economical puddun I learned from Mum I'll have to make for yer while I'm here if I can remember what you put in."

On and off she picked at the food she had brought, which no longer looked as though it were there to be eaten. Nance seemed to prefer gum: perhaps the motion of her jaws made her feel she was doing something.

She looked into the gorge. "What do you think you're gunner get out of paintun an ugly old rock?"

"That's what I'm trying to find out. Could be the answer."

"Eh?" Her frown was an excruciated one. "I may not be what you'd call educated," she was beginning.

"Oh God, Nance, I'm not *educated*!"

"But you know enough not to make sense."

She sat training a piece of hair to curl around one of her cheekbones: the swinging pearl might have left a scar.

"But rocks, I mean—who's gunner ever even pay a tenner for a rock—without there's someone sittun on it."

She crossed her legs, and bunched her knees, and drew up her skirt, but dropped it again in helplessness.

"Nature's all right," she said, "but it's too big for most people.

Last Sunday, Billie Lovejoy—the old cow with the orange bristles on 'er chin—my landlady—Billie said: 'Why don't we take the ferry, Nance, and go on a little spree to Manly?' Why I agreed I couldn't say. I wouldn't value Billie Lovejoy not above a potful of piss, only that she's 'uman—'uman, see? And a woman. Well, we took the ferry. There was a bloke tried to contact, but I wasn't operatun that day. And I sorter got the gripes. All that water! And me an' Billie sittun on the Steyne—the rollers they was too *big*—and glassy—beltun up the beach. Gee," she moaned, living it again, "I would 'uv trotted straight back for the return ride if it hadn't been for the fellers lyin' on the beach. 'Uman, see? The 'uman touch."

Her experience slowly released her limbs: they unlocked, and she turned her face towards him. Her lips, he saw, were almost as pale as those of the postmistress at Ironstone.

"That's the trouble, Hurtle," she slowly said. "That's what you aren't. You aren't a 'uman being."

"I'm an artist." It sounded a shifty claim.

"You're a kind of perv—perving on people—even on bloody rocks!"

After erecting what appeared to be this impassable barrier, she asked where was the dunny, and he showed her.

When she returned she said: "Pe-ooh! It pongs! You ought 'uv dug it deeper."

"Couldn't. Too much rock."

So they were up against it immediately. He no longer knew whether he was an artist, an ascetic, or a prig, as Nance Lightfoot's conversation lurched like iron trams through the afternoon. But occasionally, as she allowed what she would have condemned as silence to creep up out of the gorge, he detected a changed key: birds sat longer on branches, their eyes brilliant in stuffed bodies, while little liquid tremors exerted the hitherto listless leaves.

Till Nance jumped up. "Better get you yer tea, hadn't I? Like I was your girl—not the Woolcott Street pross that ponced you." Throwing the rope of saveloys around her throat, as though it were a fur, or feather boa, she cackled at such a pitch every arrested bird was at once transformed into a shadow in motion.

He let her do what she had to do. She boiled some of the saveloys, and they sat down and ate them after they had picked the skins off. The thick, rubbery skin toned in with the dress Nance was wearing for the country.

Afterwards they continued sitting amongst the crumbs. At least he had his thoughts, and she presumably hers, as she tried to force a lump of gristle from between her teeth, first with her tongue, then with a peeled twig. What if he and Nance stuck forever in the enamel of daylight and their own separate entities? He didn't like to imagine. Didn't have to, anyway; for the ashes of light had begun to fill the gorge, and as the red-hot ironstone cooled off along the ridges, and the heaped branches of the uppermost trees blazed in the last of the bonfire, a wind rushed in to douse: there was a hissing, and spitting, and clapping, and lapping, as the stream poured over live rocks and reviving leaves, the engulfed trees swaying, and tugging at their roots like submerged weeds, the gorge moaning its fulfilment.

When the flood burst in through the windows and down their throats, Nance held the helmet of hair to her head; he was afraid she might be going to say: "Gee, it was a hot day, but now the change has come, and it was worth waiting."

She didn't.

Though they recognized each other's bodies with delighted shivers and confirming touches, and though they staggered outside, holding hands, towards some intention unnamed by either of them, the cold floods of air and whirlpools of darkness divested them of their clothes of flesh. They couldn't have entwined so closely if they hadn't been so disintegrated, as part of the formless lunging and heaving, bitter-tasting lashed leaves, scabbards of flying bark, sand giving to the fingers, and stones which bruised, but barely bruised, the consciousness: they rushed into each other as the gusts of wind had entered the skeleton of the house.

He woke as usual on the rucked layers of bags he still used as a bed. Nance was sitting up, in that very early light he took for granted: she was sagging horribly; her short, half-trained hair was hanging down around her grey face. Though they were dead sober in that there hadn't been anything to drink, she looked like someone willing herself not to vomit.

She was swaying and saying: "I've gotter get out of here—Hurtle."

"Why, Nance?" He tried to soothe her with the palm of his hand; she didn't respond. "I thought you were here for a holiday." He could hear something inside himself padding and squelching at thought of her departure, as it had for her threatened arrival. He said: "I want you to stay, Nancy." It was a form of her name he hadn't used at any point in their relationship.

He fastened his mouth on the target of a breast while listening for an answer.

She flipped him off.

One of the oranges which had rolled off the table the afternoon before was lying almost at the edge of their "bed." She took it up and threw it, not exactly vindictively, at a canvas the other end of the room.

"You an' yer old rocks! There's too much I don't understand." Then she turned to him and said: "You've got as much out of me as you want for the present."

He heard himself try to contradict, but it sounded mumbled, disconnected: to make it more convincing, he returned to stroking her arm.

"Go on!" she said, pulling it away. "You're such a one for lookin' for the truth in everything, you oughter recognize it now."

"What's true of one of us can be true of the other. You mightn't have hit on it otherwise, Nance."

"Oh golly, yes!" Her throat tautened as she tossed back her hair, holding up her face, not for his pleasure, but in a purely self-centred gesture, snorting down her suddenly finer nose, laughing through her blunt, wide-spaced teeth. "I'll smell the pavement to-night! I'll hear the bloody trams! None of that prick prick of insects, or leaves, or whatever it is."

Now she allowed him to stroke her arm, which was bent back, almost double-jointed, in support of her arched body.

"It's funny," she said, "you go on the job and know more or less what you'll get. It's what you never find that keeps you at it."

Then, realizing the extent of her confession, she collapsed whimpering: "I dunno what made me say that."

They fell upon each other, on the bags, in the tenderest demonstrations either of them could make: their mouths had become the softest, the most accommodating funnels of love.

"You're my real steady bloody permanent lover that I need and can't do without," she cried, and rubbed against him, and cried.

He was reminded of an old face-washer, often grubby, one of the maids had crocheted for him, in wide mesh, comforting in warm, soapy water: the opalescent shallows of childhood.

He could feel that Nance, too, had been comforted: their eye-lashes were scratching the same message.

While she pulled her stockings on, snapping the elastic a couple of times to make certain, she said: "Now you'll be able to get back to yer rocks—because I know that's what you want. But next time I come up"—he was genuinely happy to know there would be a next time—"you'll have ter paint me sittun on a rock showun me Louisa and everything. Praps I'll wear a string of pearls. I know a girl that might give me the loan of an ostrich fan. I bet it'll make your name, Hurt."

After she had run her finger round what had been the potted pig's-cheek, she went. He watched her salmon buttocks swinging through the scrub. Once or twice the sateen caught on spikes, and for a moment opened into a pink parasol.

He was both exhausted and rejuvenated by what she had drained out of him. In the slippery light and pricking silence, the pink rocks were still drowsing and exhaling: they hadn't been fired yet.

For several weeks he remained shut up in himself, that is to say: in his painting, while living off Caldicott's gratuitous cheque, or guilt money, and the energy generated by Nance's visit. If it oc-curred to him that Nance was prostituting herself to his art, or that Caldicott was his own blackmailer, he guessed each was perverse enough to enjoy the voluptuousness of any suffering involved.

Whatever the moral climate, the painter continued perving on and painting Nance's hated rocks. He stood each new version where he could catch sight of it the moment he woke. He saw most clearly by that light, and would jump up and sharpen a cutting edge, or intensify the reflections of his thinking sun.

Until a morning when his glittering cerebrations bred in him such a hopelessness he trod flat-footed across the boards, alone in his aching, powerless body, and began a version practically unre-lated to those he had done already. The big, pink, cushiony forms suggested sleeping animals rather than the rocks of his mind: they neither crushed nor cut, but offered themselves trustfully to the one-eyed sun scattering down on them a shower of milky seed or light. Done without forethought, unless he had planned it in his sleep, it was over so quickly, compulsively, he didn't want to look at it for fear of finding the disaster he suspected. He sat instead on the edge of the creaking veranda, dangling his empty hands between his thighs, while the gorge gave up its long, writhing viscera of mist.

Caldicott wrote:

Dear Duffield,

Since February is approaching this is to remind you of your promise of three paintings for my mixed show. The others, so far, are a pretty staid lot. Dare I say: we depend on you to set the Harbour on fire!

I enclose for your amusement the two snapshots we took the day of my visit.

Kind regards

M.C.

In one of the snaps Caldicott was shyly attempting to look amused at the unlikely situation in which he had landed himself. His suit, his shirt, his forearms, all looked wrong for the occasion, but he stood propped against the edge of the veranda, hoping from under his wilting Panama to smile the unlikeliness off. In one corner of the picture the unpainted iron tank glared in ferocious competition.

Caldicott had added a postscript to his letter:

I don't doubt these pictorial records will eventually increase my importance in the eyes of Australia, not to say the world.

Hurtle grimaced to read it, and to look. He didn't care to recognize the more substantial figure in the second photograph. He loathed what he saw. His only reason for wearing clothes could have been to appear clothed. He remembered deciding to receive his guest barefooted, to offend his sensibility. Now he was appalled by his own dirty, horny feet. In the snapshot they looked deformed. Or was it distorted? Just as you distort appearances to arrive at truth.

Caldicott had come off better. After setting the camera for the picture, he had hurried round to add to the composition, in which he was shown as little more than a tremulous, adoring ghost.

Duffield tore the two snapshots into little pieces, and began stumping with quick, febrile steps on flat, calloused feet through his jerry-built house. Not even his work offered a refuge: he had emptied himself of the obsessive rocks which had occupied him for so many weeks.

February became a swelter. He sweated into Sydney on several occasions, blaming either Caldicott or Nance. The three promised paintings he delivered to the gallery on time, while suggesting he had only looked in by chance. A length of hairy, ungracious cord lashing the canvases together made his cargo look uncommonly crude.

Caldicott pushed back his chocolate eye-shade and advanced on the corded bundle, the spit glistening out from between his exquisitely oval teeth. "Needless to say, my—my expectations, Hurtle, are enormous."

Only recently Caldicott had pointed out that his friend might call him "Maurice," but Hurtle had continued to resist: he was clumsy with first names, unless addressing dogs, or Nance.

He stood mopping himself with a handkerchief he had washed for the visit and dried on a bush: it was a blinding white, and still smelled of the sun.

"I don't expect anything to come of it," he kept repeating. "And you'll be the loser!" He laughed. "But I take it you know what you're up to."

Caldicott, as often, could have been wanting to communicate something of great, though difficult importance, but Duffield was already making his getaway down the stairs, in unaccustomed boots.

He ate a sandwich in a tea-room, sprinkling the ham with some of the dry mustard provided by the management. He wondered whether to wait, or go at once to Nance's place. To wait would have been a formality; so he started off through the afternoon steam, foolishly carrying a bunch of uniform rosebuds disguised in a hood of tissue paper.

Nance was lying lumped on the bed grunting in her sleep. The stained upper sheet, which eventually she would give for laundering to old Mrs Gorman the midnight pudding-maker, had scuffled up around her armpits. She rubbed her head against the pillow, and groaned, her eyelids too heavy to open, her throat too dry to utter.

So he got in beside her without even taking off his clothes, only removing his boots after some trouble with the knotted laces.

It was a relief, though, finally. When he had come, and the acid was no longer eating him, he lay caressing her hair with a hand which seemed to be recovering its normal function after a long period of feverish stress, such as an illness, or some creative activity. To remain in his present normal employment he would have given anything—except the gift he was cursed with.

After her first half-awakened grimace of recognition, Nance continued lying with her eyes ostentatiously closed. Her sleep-sallowed face looked content, smiling slightly, perhaps for her own formal pretence, or his importunity. He regretted his rough approach, though probably her vocation had denied her the luxury of a man who wasn't clumsy. If only he could have afforded something more beautiful and valuable than the bunch of drooping roses, but even if he had been able, he could think of nothing which would have impressed her by its value, and pleased him equally by its beauty.

Presently she opened her eyes and said: "You're a prickly old sod, aren't yer? And yer buttons are eatun into me flesh."

As she swept him off, she was all flesh, his appetite for which was satisfied: his only remaining pleasure lay in the sallow tones of her skin, and the texture of her breasts, like those bland cheeses which reward the eye rather than the tongue.

"What have you brought me?" she asked, although it was too obvious.

Her indolent buttocks had grown tense as she approached the dressing-table and caught sight of the tissue cornet wrapping the flowers.

"They're not flowers, are they?" She was performing an instinctive ritual. "Arr dear, what a lovely bokay! All flowers are lovely."

The rosebuds drooping from her hand had the heads of strangled birds.

"They've died." He forced his hoarse voice. "Too much sun. They couldn't stand the heat." His failure to offer a suitable apology made the situation more oppressive, or so he felt, in Nance's cluttered, whore's bedroom.

She, on the other hand, resounded with a tenderness he hadn't heard in her before. "They'll revive," she said gently, stroking the dead heads with her fingers.

She fetched a cut-glass jug, and stuck the roses in it, and stood it on a greyish lace doiley. Splayed against the dressing-table mirror, the bunch looked more lifeless than before.

"Red's best," she said. "I hope I'm buried with red roses. Why should you always have white at funerals?"

He would have liked to get down and kiss her in the shaven crutch, only he wouldn't have known how to explain his impulse, and in her present state of reverence she might have been shocked.

She made them a pot of bitter tea, wearing her continued nakedness like a favourite old comfortable dress.

"Now that you've delivered the pictures to Mr Thingummy, and are free and easy—we hope—I'm gunner come up again to pay you a visit at that place of yours."

She had cut some slices of a stale pound cake, and was easing out a date stone carefully from her mouth so as not to endanger a dicky tooth, while talking, and looking at her toenails from a thoughtful distance, and dusting the crumbs from between her breasts.

"This time it'll be a real visit—now that I know what the conditions are. I'm not a fool, you know, though I dare say you won't admit it. Anyway, this time I'll come, and you can paint me—as I am, I mean."

She looked very serious, religious. He could have begun to paint her then and there, linking the necklaces of Venus round her throat to the bluish, shaven mount.

"Well," she asked, "for fuck's sake, what's the matter? What are you starun at?"

That recurring question desolated, as the bottle on the dressing-table suddenly riveted him. "The bottle"—his tongue managed, though thickly—"what is it?" The half-swallowed cake was choking him.

She followed the direction of his glance. "Oh, it's an old-fashioned scent bottle. Some old thing I picked up cheap from a junk dealer who began to have tickets on me."

The air was so languid she was fanning herself with a hand on which the crumbs trembled; while he continued staring at the scent bottle on the dressing-table. Shaded from mauve to smoky grey, and sheathed in silver irises, the bottle was a version of those which used to stand on Alfreda Courtney's high altar.

"I suppose I'm sentimental," said Nance. "I love the *old* things."

She might have learned it from Maman herself, who rose like a genie of the scent bottle, accusing him of faithlessness: to a class which had adopted him; to the education invested in him; to a love not so very different, which smelled of melting chocolate and illicit brandy, instead of musty pound cake and a whore's powder. Maman was sniffing, though.

Soon after that he got up, buttoning his coat, saying he ought to catch his train.

It hadn't occurred to Nance till now that she was naked. She looked down and discovered her breasts were apparitions, her navel almost an operation.

"You do love me?" she whimpered, holding herself in her arms.

His lips tried to reassure her through a flavour of moist dates.

He left her at the crack of the door, just as on the first occasion, her landlady Mrs Lovejoy had stood at the crack, showing the orange bristles on her chin.

Those first days after his visit to Nance in Sydney he did several little studies of her, which he would elaborate later on when the inclination took him. The ideas in his head were still too hectic and fragmented. He either saw in colours, and the architecture eluded him, or else he was obsessed by forms: Nance's yellow cheeses; suddenly out of the past Rhoda's Cranach figure standing beside the iron-legged bidet. In desperation he almost settled for the self-portrait he had been for some time considering. But did he, any more than the others, see himself as he truly was? His doubts drove him to scramble down to the bottom of the gorge, slashed by swords, whipped by wires, trampling on the board-walk of fallen wood, sinking in the mattresses of rotting leaves. Reaching his nadir, he lay full length and buried his face in brown water, gulping at it, watching it lap round the picture of his distorted features.

Obviously he didn't know himself.

Caldicott sent him the review from the *Herald*:

. . . that this country has been evolving an art of its own immediately recognizable for its honesty and truth, which Hurtle Duffield attempts to explode. In his three canvases here on view he reveals a pretentious predilection for sensuous exercises in egotism. He doesn't convince us in either of his two manners: the meticulous dissection and abstraction of nature, or the sloppy, self-indulgent, anthropomorphic forms executed in bestial colour. Is he trying to pull somebody's leg? If so, he doesn't succeed. Let us at least hope that Duffield is rewarded by the sight of himself in display . . .

Caldicott added palliative words, hardly more than a blur after what had gone before:

. . . know you are not one to be rattled by tastelessness of this kind. . . . It is important to remember there are others who understand and value. . . .

About the same time a note came from Nance:

How did the show go, Hurt? Didn't see a thing about it. But I almost never get down to a read of the papers. I am too busy.

That night Duffield stood on the edge of the gorge and let out his anguish. It came up out of his chest, his throat, in increasing waves. He was fortunate to enjoy such an immense privacy, for the waves of rage and anguish broke loud enough to reach the indifferent public and the poisonous press. Then he shut up. If his roar had suggested a wounded lion, its echo returned in little protesting driblets of sound, as if from a soul still haunted by the self-pity of which its earthliness had died.

He went into the house, stubbing his toe for good measure.

He had practically decided on a portrait of the self he had not yet explored to its bestial depths when he received a letter from Caldicott:

My dear Hurtle,
    I am happy to be able to report that Mrs Lopez, or Mrs Davenport as she is now, has bought your "Animal Rock Forms"; so you see, her interest in your work has not only continued, it has increased. As she is at present living overseas (at Kingston Bagpuize, Berkshire) Mrs Davenport had commissioned a competent representative to choose a painting from the present exhibition. Needless to say, I am delighted for you . . .

Duffield got drunk on a bottle of crème de menthe, which he bought partly because it nauseated most. Afterwards he slept with the faceless Mrs Davenport on an iron bed he had found at a dump.

The following morning he remembered to finish Caldicott's letter: poor Maurice never deserved the treatment he got.

    . . . on the 3rd of next month I am planning a small dinner party—intimate friends only—at which I shall hope to see you. Everybody is *interested*. You will only help yourself by responding to their interest—if you can forgive the vulgarism.

He didn't reply to Caldicott: his clothes alone would have prevented him going to the dinner party. The shade of Harry Courtney goggled at the dreadful suit, not to mention his unscrubbed body; his armpits stank, and he almost didn't care.

In fact he cared enough to drag the easel into relationship with the glass, and prepare for the portrait: the self-portrait.

If he saw others too clearly, if he smote them, not with the tent-peg but the paintbrush, it was only fair that he, too, should come in for it. His larrikin self might have ducked, but decent Harry Court-ney's son had been doled out a sense of honour on speech days. He might have inherited from Harry and Maman one or two of the vir-tues to which they had vaguely addressed themselves; their influ-ence was otherwise in no more evidence than the collar-boxes and English tweed, the right accent and the right names they had urged him to put his faith in. Atavistically he was at the mercy of a laundress and a clergyman, an aristocratic, no-hope drunk who had died of a stroke on the Parramatta Road, and poor scrawny, nor-mally T-T Pa, counting other people's empties under the pepper tree, before going in to get kids with Mumma on the squeaky bed. All of these he had in his fingertips. The razors were probably his own, not inherited, nor consciously acquired.

As he worked at what was becoming the portrait, the razors took over: they couldn't resist the quick nick. He remembered the two cutthroats in the long black monogrammed box, with which Harry Courtney improved the sculpture of his beard, or in later years exposed his face. *See, Hurtle, they're too dangerous even to touch, never to touch Father's razors.* He couldn't resist just a flick: a fly with the razor. His down shivered to feel the steel. How simply awfully the blade carved through the leather strop easy as warm chocolate. *What did I tell you it isn't the damage it's the dishonesty of doing things behind my back the risk of cutting yourself or some-one—Rhoda—injure somebody for life.* Decent Harry grew so steamy with imagination you watched the blood not running it was too fascinated to run arrested on severed fingers. Father had not made you promise never to do it again, which was honest of Father. You hadn't done it again in fact because it was frightening the ease with which the blade had carved through the strop.

He had never been altogether dishonest: nor yet entirely honest; because that isn't possible. Even saints kid themselves a bit. God or whatever couldn't have been entirely honest in creating the world.

While working, he had to recognize the almost voluptuous love with which he carved his own cheek out of the paint, down to the board: his not convincingly ascetic cheek. The nick to the corner of his not quite honest but human—he hoped—watchful left eye produced the authentic shudder of love. Even the practice of mere skill, those weightless wet dreams of art, rejoiced his mind and refreshed his body.

From withdrawing into his private world he was forgetting about his body. He had seen it as cruder. He had encouraged it to coarsen, to resist values he might still find himself longing for. Maman had done a better job than either of them realized in forcing his head in amongst the scents of the wardrobe. Then the stoppered, clotted, *fin de siècle* scent bottle on Nance's dressing-table. He hadn't screwed the Maman in Nance, but might just once, for the experience.

He took a rest after that, or rather, his no longer clottish body roamed around the scrub. He stopped to stroke leaves he didn't see, but apprehended. His mind was floating in pure contentment the crushed-out scents the pricking silence of heat and scrub.

Presently he felt the need to go back: to find out how much of the truth reflected by the mirror had united with how much his mind might have confessed. He was at once wearily dejected and daringly fleetingly pleased. He went so far as to smile at his alter ego of the board: when his conscience in the mirror caught him at it. At least teeth were a permissible vanity in any man—but his didn't appear in the portrait, only in the glass.

So he frowned back at the flat, glum, half-truthful reflection of himself, and began to slog drudgingly. Half of life was drudgery, he had discovered, and by now had begun to suspect ninety per cent of painting was uncreative, at most a laying on of paint, building up to destroy.

So he gouged out his turgid features, reassembled his failed colours, wiped off the smears: it was a long way from razor-play.

Once during the afternoon, at its most monotonous, against the buzz of blowflies and the stench from a lump of corned brisket, he made a mark that became a positive signpost: his no longer adolescent figure could still have been leaning in desperate ennui beside a window which prevented his closer approach to the outer world. He caught the curve of the body with one slash of the razor, and wasn't ashamed at confessing to survived elegance.

Of course he really loved it. He loved the elegance. He loved himself. Himself gathered into the corn-coloured folds of Maman's dress. However much of a coarse, thickset, moral scavenger the present showed, a lyrical onanist of the past hadn't been altogether suppressed. Here he had caught the two of them in flagrant delight, in his own unlikely body, in paint.

He threw down his brush after that. He could have shouted, but it would have been for what he knew might look otherwise in the morning; so he walked away through his rickety, amateurish barrack of a house. It would begin to darken. Soon there would be nothing left but the prospect of a next day.

During those weeks he went several times to the city, for no reason he could have given. If he had wanted to escape from the portrait he couldn't have done so: he carried its photograph in his head. At the height of his passion for it, he would look around him at the faces in the street, and some of them, misinterpreting his expression, would frown a warning. If he had lived up a flight of stairs round the corner, he might have found a pretext to accost a stranger, for no more perverse reason than to force an anonymous, preferably innocent face into a relationship with the unfinished portrait. Whether the unknown responded with rapture or disgust would have been immaterial: proof that he existed for others was what he guiltily hankered after.

He would go along finally to Nance. On the first occasion she pulled the door open a crack and asked in a rusty-sounding voice: "Wadderyerwant there?" though she must have known by now what everybody wanted.

When she saw him, she dragged the door wider open. "Arr— come on in, then—if it's you." Even so, she begrudged him the welcome; she was looking fat and overpowdered; she narrowed her eyes at something that might be in store for her.

How to convey to Nance what she wouldn't have believed? He could only flounder in her: she might have been a field of heavy-pollened, white daisies.

"What's got inter yer?" she said at last. "Am I someone else?"

If she suspected it, she didn't sound put out, nor did she expect explanations, preferring to supply her own.

"All you men are in love with yerselves. That's what it amounts to. When a man feels real good about 'imself, he has to have a woman, and it's called love. At least the poofs are honest. They look around for another poof." What she visualized gave her the giggles. "To be on the right track, you oughter be, all of you, one big set of poofs!"

She was so equable she might have been persuaded to collaborate, if the air of afternoon detachment hadn't been snatched away from her soon after: she developed that expression of swim or sink, it didn't matter, as they were swept together into the blowhole, themselves boiling and lashing. Her isolated gull's cry died away under the grinding of the iron trams.

On the stairs as he went down there was a sailor on his way up. What the sailor and the whore might do together couldn't make Duffield jealous: his own collusion with the woman who passed for Nance Lightfoot was too complete.

On the next occasion, however, there she was, dressed to go out: formal after her fashion.

She yanked the door wider open. "This is a funny time to come!" It was more or less the same time as before. "I gotter go out," she threatened. "An appointment. If you'd like ter know, it's a bloke who's on 'is last leg."

Although she had painted her lips into a big patent-leather rosette, they were thin and straight under the grease.

"If you gotter," she said, "you gotter be quick."

She didn't expect conversation, but began dragging off her clothes, those over her head with such determination some of her hair remained standing on end after it had been pulled through.

His belt-buckle nicked at something passive, wall or flesh, as he whipped it through the loops of his pants. The formal room was all sounds. His body had never sounded so lean as when the superfluous clothes slithered and coiled.

As for Nance, lying straight, almost rigid, she looked positively thin: he thought he could see her exasperated ribs milky-blue under the skin.

That afternoon they made the geometry of love, its sparest bones.

"I'm gunner be late," she accused as she got up and forced herself back into her clothes, "when I guaranteed to be on the dot." She was professionally committed: in spite of her haste and distraction, she found time to repair the damaged parts of her face.

Nor could he resent her obligations on this second occasion, for he was beginning to feel his way to the end of a labyrinth in which he had been lost several days. The suburban train couldn't carry him fast enough, his unemployed hands locked between his thighs. All along the street becoming country road, along the track he followed through the scrub, he leaned into the wind, to arrive quicker, to walk inside his no-more-than-necessary shack.

There his *Doppelgänger* was leering at him out of a distorting mirror. He took a brush and extenuated the rather too desirable mouth into a straight line. He was right. The eyes agreed. The shoulders sank into place. For the rest of daylight he hung about, dabbing and wiping, tidying his paint, unexpectedly meticulous in attending to unimportant details. He realized his physical mouth was hanging open, his breath snoring in a solid stream from between his lips, as though he had just woken from a demanding sleep.

In the morning the clear light had already begun to destroy his achievement.

That afternoon he walked into Ironstone, for relief, and found Caldicott's letter:

Dear Hurtle,

I had been hoping for a visit, or for some indication of plans for the future. I don't want to impose on you; but an artist needs to talk, surely? Or is he nourished solely by self-expression and self? Obviously he is! I am not accusing you, I hope, only suggesting you may not be aware of the effect you have on other people.

You mustn't think I am trying to possess you: or perhaps I am. I believe that any human being of more than average sensibility is an artist in his life, and particularly in his relationships with other human beings. There the least creative of us cannot resist the impulse to create.

So I am, after all, the guilty one! I should like to hear from you. I should like to see you, at the gallery, or better still at my flat, where I should have an opportunity of showing you the few beautiful objects I have gathered round me, and which make my life excusable.

Several weeks of arthritic aches and neuralgic pains have left me depressed and dull. I made the horrid discovery that white ant has got into my *À Rebours* and eaten all but the boards. However, I mustn't burden you with my megrims.

Are you in need of anything, I wonder? I enclose a small cheque as a sign that I am interested in your future work. I respect your attitude while selfishly wishing to alter it.

Your contrite
Maurice C.

P.S. A lady with artistic daughter is nibbling bravely at one of your rocks. Alas, a husband and father must first be enticed.

He tore up Caldicott's letter as soon as he had read it. To treat letters in this way had become a habit: he felt less obliged to answer them. Never so important to be free as now; for he had painted out the self-portrait, and was working on a fresh version: more austere, essential, more honest, he hoped, than the over-painted, self-indulgent, by now only nauseating, rejected naturalistic trash.

The line of the mouth decided him: the mouth changed on his return from visiting Nance. The straight line which at first appeared to have solved the problems of the whole had in the end destroyed; its honesty bred dishonesty in the parts.

Re-creating his own body, he worked quickly, for him, almost as though he knew in detail what he was about. He should have enjoyed a sense of revived assurance. He would have, if it hadn't been for Caldicott's love-letter. That was what it amounted to: poor spinsterly Maurice C., his intellect inviting a rape which discretion would not have allowed his body; he was even paying in advance.

The skeleton portrait had already become such a glass the painter turned his back on it. He was too agitated for the moment, too furtive in his glances from one mirror to the other, to put his faith in glass. He hadn't torn up Caldicott's cheque. He had kept, and would have to cash, the cheque. He was shamefully in his friend's debt, for the reason which remained beyond his control: he would never control his desire to paint.

So he returned at last to wrestling with the honest version of his dishonest self.

He had worked all that week, in exhilaration, exhaustion, hunger, black hate; then an orgy of messy uncooked food fished up out of the jagged tins Caldicott's cheque had bought. If you could prostitute yourself in one way, perhaps you could in another. But he visualized Maurice C.'s blue-white limbs, like those of a plucked and drawn chicken, shot with the tones of invisible giblets. (Sudden, even more awful thought: was Caldicott by any chance Mrs Lopez-Davenport?)

At that point he received the next note from Nance:

Hurtle Duffield you selfish male bastard do you think I am nothing more than a prostitute? If I could paint I could paint a picture of what it is like to be alone at the time when you used to come. My brain my guts would be laid open like at the abatore. That old quilt of mine gives my body prickly heat as I lie and wait. Well, the roses you remember you brought I kept them till they turned brown and even then didn't throw them out. Oh dear the smell of men and rotting roses, it gives me the heebie jeebies at five o'clock of an afternoon. I wish the tram would go over me.

I wonder whether you will come this arvo? Bet you won't. So I will go down and knock back a brandy at the old Castle with my friend Iris if she is still around. These is lean times. Val Costello got pinched lifting from one of the fancy counters at Foy's, Reen Hislop frisked an alderman's pockets while he was giving her the quick lunchtime screws. Both Reen and Val are out at the Bay.

I was never so "blue" darl, but will not feel my bluest till I get home and find you have been and gone.

Your sweetheart
Nance Lightfoot

While he worked they were encroaching on him from all quarters: Nance Lightfoot and Maurice C., Mumma and Pa, Father and Maman, Rhoda and her Hump: all resentful, all demanding. In another calling he might have risked destruction by the polypous love they were heaping on him. In the given circumstances, he had to resist them with his mind when his instincts letched after them.

He painted at times with a grimness which was flashed back and forth between glass and board. This skeleton *Doppelgänger*, with his armature in greys and blacks, would no doubt have survived outside pressures if it hadn't been for a conspiracy taking place between the necessary and the unknown: reckless purples began to stain the premeditated; pools of virulent green brooded.

He suddenly suspected something else might have been planned; as, indeed, it was.

Nance arrived. It was late on an afternoon. He saw her coming down the track, the stones trying her shoes as usual. This time she was dressed in black. The black dress and the late light gave her a coppery tinge.

"What," he said, "are you on your way to a funeral?" He could have hit her if there had been something suitable to do it with.

"Could be a funeral," she hawked. "Don't know why ever else I come to this place. Funerals—or wedduns!"

She made the doorway.

"I got somethun in me eye, from lookun outer the fuckun train, thinkun I might 'uv been carried on."

She went straight up to the glass which had served for weeks as his conscience, and began pulling her eye about as though it were set in elastic. The whites were inflamed, and the light made them look worse: hunted out of the gorge, it clung burning along the ironstone ridges, infusing human blemishes with all the ominous tones. Nance looked thinner than usual, leathery, too: her arms were in seamy, oiled leather, as she stood pulling at her eye. A dented gold armlet she was wearing round the left biceps drew attention to the sag.

"You've lost weight." He had to exert himself to make conversation with the visitor; but she didn't appear to hear.

"It's best to forget about it," she was saying, "and you'll find it's gone when you wake up."

She was drunk for the occasion: he could tell by the shape of her mouth.

"I got somethun for yer," she said.

This time it wasn't food. She untied an old draw-neck leather bag embossed with worn waratahs. Age and light had rubbed the leather a metallic green, dull beside the bright heads of foil on the bottles, one of which had already been cracked.

"You can't come to the country," said Nance, "without you fortify yerself."

She fussed and swaggered over her supplies, at one point thrusting her pelvis dangerously far out from the rest of her. He had never seen her so lit, and possibly, vengeful.

"Don't think I *don't*—love—the *country*."

She was walking about, collecting breath for declamation; so he went out for a little.

It was soothing to hear the sound of himself making water, or the black note of a stick breaking under foot as he stumbled around in the grey dusk. A satin-sounding bird in abrupt flight might have burst from out of his eardrums. He couldn't have pinpointed where he was in the kindly formlessness which took his presence for granted. The house was no longer visible; he wished it had been swallowed up, together with Nance and the self-portrait, both no doubt prepared to accuse him on his return.

When here he was, almost barking his shins on the house. A plan, divine or not, seemed to reveal itself always when least desirable.

He went in and began striking matches. Surrounded by the dazzle of his own light, he couldn't see Nance at first, though he could hear her snuffling. She coughed once or twice.

"Caught a cold," he suggested coldly, slipping the chimney off the lamp.

"Not that I know of. It's me occupational bronchial tubes."

The room always looked stranger just after he had lit the lamp. It was the worst time to see it: he could never believe it belonged to him, perhaps because other people had recently owned the few bits of furniture; and now, here was Nance, not belonging either, squeezed by choice into an outer corner of the otherwise empty, derelict bed. She had plaited her arm into the ironwork at the foot as though to stabilize herself.

She looked even yellower by lamplight, her face, particularly the mouth, swollen with brandy and resentment as she sucked on a tumbler she had found and filled.

"What are we going to quarrel about?" he asked.

He came and sat down beside her because they were the official lovers.

She tossed back her hair, and sat, or hung by the ironwork of the bed, her chin raised, her throat haggard. "I don't care about anythun enough tonight—not you or me or anythun—not enough to quarrel about."

The strained physical attitude to which she was clinging made her words and her laugh sound colder, clearer, more truthful than they might have sounded if she had remained lumped in a heap of normal drunken disgust. He had never heard Nance sound so detached from a situation.

But she was involved, it began to appear; she was only nervous of the recitative she had to force out of her:

"When I was a kid we was never so hard up we didn't manage most years to get away from the place that killed my dad in the end—the bad seasons and the mortgages—we used to head for the coast and camp there for a couple of weeks it wasn't much more than a hut that belonged to a Mrs Peabody I forget who she was who charged somethun but only a little. It was a small place not a town just a few matchboxes littered around off the road beside the sea the grass left off gradual where it was stitched on to the sand."

She was speaking with her eyes shut, and the hairs at the nape of her neck glistened with the strain of narration and hanging on to the iron of the bed.

". . . the air so soft it used to get inside of yer clothes and make yer feel downright naked. I never felt such water as the sea milky early round yer ankles. Dadda would catch fish. We used to live off fish—and scones. And sweet pertaters. I was skinny then. I was frightened of most things. A crab comin' at me sideways with its claws raised. Blood. I got me first blood at Brinkwater. It scared me out of me knickers, and Mother too ladylike to tell. Then I got used to being scared or you couldn't keep it up or it felt too good lyun in the sun on the sand where it began to get firm watchun yer bubs grow you could sometimes you could see they'd grown since the night before. After the hair begun and I got over it I was proud it was so black it was shiny like most of the sea things seemed to be."

Her voice had grown monotonous. She choked at times: the words must have tasted glutinous.

"I would 'uv liked somethun ter happen I didn't know what. I had some idea of some man I'd never met not young perhaps as old as Dadda but bigger I could see the dark hairs on his wrists wearun a big old green rather hairy overcoat come walkun up the sand with that sound yer feet makes in sand. It was most often cold early. I'd be shiverun with cold or praps it was from waitun. Till we lay together inside of 'is coat. I never had much idea of what happened with this strange man. I think we put our mouths together and it was like we was drinkun each other the sound of the sea pourun over and into us. The rough sand and hairy coat. I can't remember if we ever spoke. I remember the whites of 'is eyes were unusually white, and the white sky at the back of 'is head."

She opened her eyes, and the words came clicking hiccupping out from between her bare lips.

"This man I never met I hoped could 'uv taught me somethun I mightn't 'uv otherwise understood. Not about sex. Well, about sex as well. I used to stick me fist in me mouth and bite it and rub me arms on the dry seaweed till they looked like they had a rash. Sometimes the birds flew so low I could feel the noise of their wings and got the idea my head might be split open and would swallow up one of those white birds then when the wound had closed I would see things as they're supposed to be. Eh? D'you think I'm a nut? I'm not. There was a girl I knew her name was Eileen Gilchrist Sister Scolastica they called her after she'd been shaved. I often wonder if she found what she was lookun for when she went whoorun after all those bally saints."

Nance's arm was so eaten by the iron flowers he tried to free it from its discipline of memory and the brutal bed; but she wouldn't let him.

"I learned about it but it was Dadda who taught me. It was the hooks he taught me with at first. As he dragged 'em out of their pink gills. 'They don't feel nothun,' he said, 'not if you're quick, fish is made for us to eat.' Course I loved fish. I was always hungry. I loved that fresh fish tastun of the sea after the rancid salt mutton at home. But the hook frightened me," she said, "all ways. Dadda said: 'All you gotter do is not to think about it. If you start blubberun it's no good you're lost I'll give yer a bloody good beltun.' I hated it. I hated the look of 'is dirty-lookun old man's john. He wasn't old I suppose or not any older than the man in the green overcoat."

She had begun to shiver: all the old ironwork was rattling.

" 'E had a scraggy neck. I used to watch 'im pickun the last bit of flesh from the fish's backbones in the shack we rented from Mrs Peabody at Brinkwater. I thought you bloody old bastard you dirty bastard I'll never ever like you any more but oh God I waited for 'um to do it to me again but 'e didn't 'e might never 'uv done it 'e seemed to 'uv taken a great dislike to me. Mother was always lovun, but disappointed. She had a hare-lip they'd sewed up badly. She'd been a teacher and because the kids had tormented her she used to say: 'I thank God Nancy you was born whole and will lead a happy life.' "

Nance suddenly got up and went racketing towards the table to fill her glass. She took a good swig of brandy. The silence made it as though she hadn't told anything of what she had been telling. Then she seemed to remember.

"For Chrissake!" She tore the foil off a fresh bottle, and found an old cracked cup. Holding the cup waist high, she came to him where he had been left stranded on the bed.

"Here," she said, not ungently. "Take it. You need a drink. It's my life, but you had a share in it."

So he accepted the cup, and drank, not with the sacramental reverence her voice of a moment before had seemed to invite, but by burning gulps. He sat guzzling the bad brandy. He wanted to participate in Nance's life as he hadn't before, although he had been her lover. He knew every possible movement of her ribs, every reflection of her skin. He had torn the hook out of her gills; he had disembowelled her while still alive; he had watched her no less cruel dissection by the knives of light. You couldn't call an experience an experiment, but he had profited by whatever it was. His centrifugal rocks suggested something of her numb throbbing; but he hadn't till now entered into her life as he had into her body. Now she had given him the last bubble the sea trails along the firm sand: he lay with the stranger, or Nance, or the stranger, inside the hairy overcoat; her old man's dribbling dick threatened to club him.

In fact it was Nance who clubbed him. "That night in Rushcutters bloody Park when I got caught up with Duffield it was that old digger's coat you was wearun I got a sight of it it had the green look of old pennies as I'd always imagined and nothun you did or said would 'uv thrown me off though it wasn't hairy like I'd always imagined the overcoat would be."

He began to belch. "God, this brandy—it's filth, Nance!" he heard the educated part of him bleat. "It's going to rot us."

"Yes," she said, "it's crook. But that isn't what rots a person."

She remembered and went back to the table, and resumed guzzling and slopping the brandy till she was sucked under again.

"Not what I imagined," she said. "Nothun is ever what you expect. Some big thug who comes upstairs lookun for a stretch you wait for 'im to knock the wind out of yer or rip you up when 'e starts tellun you about 'is bloody pigeons you can't coo enough to please the pigeon-fancier it's more often the little ones some little mingy watchmaker or bookkeeper who snaps at yer nipples with 'is wobbly dentures or tries to hamstring yer with a penknife."

"You're obsessed," he maintained, because by now he had got up and helped himself again, and his head was rolling, and recovering, and leaping, at the length of his neck. *"Obsessed!"* The word looked magnificent.

"Yes," she grumbled. "I'm obsessed. Like you're obsessed—by what you like to think is the truth."

She let out a long, uncontrollable burp.

"Nothun is ever what you expect. I never thought I would 'uv taken up with a so-called artist I was lookun for somethun else I would 'uv done better to 'uv got fixed up with some bloke who expects 'is chop at five-thirty 'is regular root Saturday because you're married to 'im anyway he thinks you are you aren't inside you are free but with an artist you're never free he's makun use of yer in the name of the Holy Mother of Truth. He thinks. The Truth!"

She spat it out on the floor.

"When the only brand of truth 'e recognizes is 'is own it is inside 'im 'e reckons and as 'e digs inter poor fucker *You* 'e hopes you'll help 'im let it out."

No less metallic than the brandy he was drinking, the lamp's narrow dagger of light had found its mark.

"By turnun yer into a shambles," she trumpeted.

"A shambles all right!" he lunged back.

"Out of the shambles 'e paints what 'e calls 'is bloody work of art!"

Suddenly she grabbed the lamp, and the light, from being restricted and austere, blazed at the self-portrait which he was hoping she wouldn't notice, or intended to ignore. She had only been saving it up, it appeared. She made it look devilish: furtive, ingrown, all that he had persuaded himself it wasn't, and worse than anything else—bad, not morally, but aesthetically.

"There," she said, holding her torch. "That's Duffield. Not bad. *True.* Lovun 'imself."

She returned the lamp comparatively soberly to the table; while he continued flickering and fluctuating inside. The brandy threatened to choke him, uncoiling down his throat like a rope of burning light. All his past was splintering; he had never been able to catch it in its true prismatic colours: the colours of truth—as he saw it. His only true achievement was his failure. The self-portrait, though toned down by the shadow to which it had withdrawn, was sprouting jagged diagonal teeth, womanly gyrating breasts, the holes for titivation by lipstick and tongue and prick.

Of course this isn't real; soon we shall soothe each other back into our actual bodies.

He heard himself, like the worst of captions at the flicks: "We still have each other, Nance."

"Like shit we have!"

She made it spatter brown across his forehead. And now he did begin to resent to accuse if not appreciate the situation. Anyway, took the tip. He was beginning running out along the short instinctive track over the same fallen leaves. A rock almost shocked him back but not. He ran. Or shambled on.

Flies die in the dunny at night on yellow squares of the *Truth* you wipe your arse on.

When he lumbered splurging back it was the sandshoes he was wearing she shouted: "What have you got!" not a question: a proclamation.

"What you told me."

"I told yer you should 'uv dug it deeper," she shrieked. "It wouldn't 'uv stank. Not so many blowies. An' no one would 'uv been tempted."

"You can't dig through rock. Not humanly possible."

He began very patiently and seriously to smear all that he repudiated in himself. He had thought he knew every inch of that painted board, till working over it now. With enlightened fingertips. As he worked, he bubbled at the mouth, wondering wondering what would be left.

Nance watched for a bit. Then she turned away. She got down, inside her dress, on the rusty bed. She was shrivelling. The lamp pointed at her old shammy-leather breasts.

"Leave it!" she moaned in the end. "For Chrissake, leave ut!"

"But I stink!"

He knew he smelled loathsome. By now they had both reached the depths.

In between, bursts of exquisite purity, of rubbed leaves, of sprinkled dew, made them writhe.

He comforted her rags of flesh, but it was no more than comfort. He kissed her hare-lip, her disgusting john. Once she rose above him, and he thought she said: "My darling darling you are what I have lost."

Again, she was ticking off an inventory: the eyelids she suspected; the hair between his breasts; his slack, his slender, his humbled balls.

Then stopped.

"That ring," she was mumbling and fumbling.

"What about it?"

"What's it *for*?"

He couldn't have explained to Nance it was for poor bloody Pa Duffield. "It's just a ring. A family ring." She couldn't have understood it was connected with the Adam's apple of your incredible, but true, father.

"But a *ring!*"

"All right," he shouted back, "we know it's a *ring*"; there was nothing he didn't know without her harping on it.

It was his worst perversion: to have hung on to a ring, long after the money was spent, the five hundred they sold him for. Or pretention: worse than anything Harry and Alfreda Courtney had tried to put across, blazing with brilliantine and diamonds under the chandelier.

"You're right!" He supposed it was one of his selves still shouting at this whore beside him. "What's in a ring?"

He could tell Nance was frightened: he could hear, he could feel her, gibbering, blubbering, her fingers dithering; when all he wanted was to get up off the shuddering bed not to harm anybody but reach the door to fling the ring.

"There!" he croaked, after his moment of triumph.

"Wadderyerdone?" Seemed to need confirmation of what she had been watching.

"Nothing to hurt anyone living." It was a lie of course: he could feel the wound deepening in himself. "I just wanted"—he sighed it—"what I should've done long—ago—get rid of the ring."

He could hear the shock in Nance: it hissed between her teeth. "Throwun away a valuable ring yer grandad solid gold!"

As he fell down beside her but apart she began moaning for all the abominations ever committed by man or woman: sometimes she blamed herself, sometimes him.

Presently he fell asleep. When he woke he seemed to be alone in a dark room. A light, not of the sun, was moving faintly amongst the trees. At one stage he got as far as the door. Holding her smoking torch, Nance was stirring the fallen leaves with her foot. It looked feebly done, but if she had acted more forcefully she might have overbalanced. Then she got down, very methodically, on all fours, the better to look, but the lamp gave only the feeblest light: black smoke was pouring out of the slanted chimney.

He found his way back to the bed and slept several ages in hell. Or was it awake in life? In which Nance was slucking at some brandy. She was standing at a narrow, untrue table. But he couldn't properly see Nance: the hair was hanging over her face. Of all those who came and went, none was more terrible than Maman. *Surely you don't mean you can't you didn't forget to insure?* Her sapphires were incredulous. *After all we've paid for your education!* He was insured against none of the calamities. At least they had taught him not to cry, or only in deepest privacy.

The sun delivered him by waking him. Stupid bloody Nance must be at it still, by raw sunlight. She had brought back the lamp: it was standing on the table, blacked out. She had been at the brandy again, he noticed.

He swallowed her dregs for company, and went out shivering into the raw red morning. The glitter, and all the brandy he had swilled, made his eyes ache, his mind function only furtively. He was glad he could see no sign of Nance: it gave him the chance to get down, bitterly, achingly, on his knees, and have a look for the lost ring. He worked very quickly, full of irony and disgust, turning over dead leaves, scuffling sand and pebbles, but quickly, and quicker, in case Nance showed up. In more assured privacy, in less harried circumstances, he might have settled down to enjoy a spate of self-pity.

Now there was no time. He stank. He hated himself. He hated Nance; who didn't show up, however, to receive his hate in person.

Supposing she had left him? He raised his head, listening to the possibility of that.

He called: "Nance? *Nance!*"

Perhaps it was the early morning air, but his call was returned to him, clear and youthful, out of the mouths of rocks normally heavy and sullen with heat. He continued calling, not yet begging; in fact he darkened his voice with anger: and it kept floating lightly back. He who was a man had been reduced, it seemed.

"Naa—aance!" his voice nancied back to him.

He more or less, no, he wasn't running, but got back as quickly as he could, to the house, to find some reason for assurance.

The old draw-neck leather bag with metallic sheen and choker of embossed waratahs was lying where it had been left, and the hand-bag, stuffed with credentials and the tools of her trade. Nance hadn't left him—or had she? The shoes. She hadn't. Nance's soul, such as it was, might have drifted loose, but her professional body couldn't have walked off without the shoes.

He would have liked to celebrate his relief in some of the awful brandy, but the three bottles were stone-dry.

There had been a fourth, he remembered. He went out very quickly. He no longer called, but looked, with an intensity which cured his aching eyes and head. A curtain of cold sweat gathered on his eyelids waiting to fall.

In the meantime the sunlight had sharpened. Its glass teeth met with glass. Along the ironstone ledge directly below the house an explosion had taken place, he realized: of glass, and less spectacularly, flesh. The splintered glass almost rose from the rock to slash his conscience, but the flesh made no move to accuse. Nance in her black dress was lying like an old bashed umbrella on a dump. There was nothing of the curious sinewiness of nervous inquiry and recall which had distinguished her body the night before. The fall had rucked her skirt high up her big white legs, now heaped like leftover trimmings of dough or marzipan. One big white breast had squeezed its way to freedom. If it still suggested life, it was of the very passive kind: of some variety of great polyp plastered to a rock. He couldn't look at her face: the sun had gilded it with too savage a brilliance.

He began climbing slithering crashing grazing sideways down his ribs snapping the wire of plants his nails tearing at finally torn.

On arrival, he stalked round her, hoping something he had experienced before this encounter with the full stop of suffering might help him deal with it; but nothing in his life or art did. He got down at last beside her, on his knees, and laid his forehead on a rock, the corrugations of which didn't fit with his; as he hung there, sweating and trembling, groaning aloud for the inspiration withheld from him.

All through the nightmare of police and ambulance which Nance's death brought on, there was something real pricking at his mind, something he had forgotten to do, until, finding the axe in his hand, he began to hack. But the board on which the self-portrait was painted turned the blade. The axe too blunt? Or was he too weak in his present condition? He scraped a while ineffectually at the board, its surface still encrusted with his own faeces as well as paint. Then he took the scarred monster, eyeing him to the end, and threw it out as far as he could over the gorge, his muscles, his lungs straining. It clapped and clattered at first, before bowling rather tamely down, only occasionally whamming against the side of a tree, then drowning in total silence.

At least in this instance nobody would inquire whether it was murder or suicide or accidental death.

✳ 5 ✳

Most evenings towards sunset, the bench the Council had fastened to the pavement was fully occupied by neighbourhood acquaintances. Although they would sit staring out over the wasteland, with its deep swell of lantana and sudden chasms of ash-coloured rock, the landscape meant less to the ratepayers than their glimpses into one another's lives. Even a total stranger could be persuaded to ignore landscape while exchanging the snapshots of experience, particularly as the sun was going down. But on this occasion, as the blind sockets of the white-faced houses squeezed together on the opposite cliff, reflected their evening illusion of gold, a solitary figure had possession of the bench.

It was too good to last, however: a second form was bellying towards it, down the street which sloped along the vacant land. The man on the bench averted his face, and from sitting somewhere about the middle, immediately moved to the far end.

The new arrival looked only fairly expectant: what he hoped for was a yarn, and so many people nowadays were surly. A large man, he advanced at a deliberate pace, breaking every now and again into a somewhat less calculated toddle; but his confidence appeared immense in planting his broad buttocks on the bench for nothing short of a long stay.

"Well," he began almost at once, "nobody can complain about the weather, can they? I'd say it's set good." He laughed slightly as encouragement.

Then he looked towards the one he hoped he might persuade to become his temporary companion; but the other shifted where he sat, and made what was neither an answer nor a groan.

The large man waited. The other was younger than he had estimated from a distance; he took a quick look around to see if there was anyone who might suspect him of wrong intentions. Then he laughed again, louder than before, his fat-chinned laugh. Of course this stranger wasn't all that young: not young at all, in fact.

"I like to take a constitutional," the large man confessed, "after I've shut up shop. Got to think of your health, eh? Business isn't everything."

Again the other didn't come good with an answer, but made a noise which he seemed to hope might pass for one, while settling deeper in his overcoat.

The fat man would have liked to stare at what he had found. He did glance deeper than at first, but quickly away, and grunting it off.

"Never seen you around before. Get to know the local faces from running a grocery business. I lead a very normal life. It's the right way, isn't it? Plain food, regular evacuation, and fresh air. So I come down 'ere every night while the wife's preparing somethun for tea." He coughed, and his teeth made a pebbled sound. "Don't live in these parts, do yer?"

"Near enough," the other said, shifting again, and reorganizing himself inside his rather shaggy overcoat.

The grocer would have liked to assess the stranger's status, but it wasn't easy. Too many contradictions: good clothes, not old either, probably very good before sloppiness set in; good hat, too, of an excellent felt, the band of which had been allowed to get sweaty; made-to-order brogues, with white scars in the tan, and laces tied anyhow.

"That's a fine overcoat you got"—the grocer couldn't leave alone. "I like to see a good cloth. I'd say, at a guess, that was imported. Bet it's English."

"Oh? It could be. Yes. I think it was." The stranger sounded unhappy.

"There's nothing like English cloth. Of course we was all English in the beginning, unless you count the Irish. My old man used to say—'e come out from the West Country—'Nobody need be ashamed if 'e brushes 'is clothes, shines 'is shoes, and 'as a decent *hair*cut.' "

The stranger's hair was decent cut, even fashionable: those side pieces like the Prince of Wales's. He had let it go, though: needed trimming.

Suddenly the grocer overflowed. He leaned along the back-rest of the bench on which they were sitting, and stuck out his pulpy hand, and said: "My name's Cutbush—Cecil Cutbush. It's a funny sort of name, isn't it? But you get used to it."

There was a marbled moon coming up behind them almost before the sun had gone. Cutbush sighed. He didn't understand why the stranger hadn't completed the exchange of names like any other decent friendly bloke. He didn't hold it against him, though. Perhaps the man had his reasons: could have been a released prisoner or something like that.

The grocer sighed again. "It does me good to come down 'ere. If it wasn't for the dew I'd be tempted to sit on indefinitely. And the wife. She'd create if I didn't come in. Says she's afraid of murderers." He paused to look over his shoulder. "It isn't that at all," he resumed. "Can't satisfy 'er nowadays. Doesn't want to leave me alone. Even during trading hours. 'You'll 'ear the bell, Cec,' she says, 'and as often as not it's only a kiddy come for a pennorth of lollies.' There's no puttin' 'er off. And at our age." He realized, and added: "You're younger, of course. It'll still come natural to yer."

For a moment he suspected his new, desirable, but peculiarly unresponsive friend hadn't been listening to him. Then again he could tell that he had. He was the kind that can listen and think at the same time: deep.

"She's a bloody awful cook." Mr Cutbush changed the subject, or almost. "But I didn't marry 'er for 'er cookun." He laughed his rather throaty laugh. "And got what I asked for. I shouldn't complain." He remembered to inquire: "Does yer missus do yer well? At the table, I mean."

"I'm not married."

"Go on! You don't say! There's time, though." The grocer glanced towards the other's crutch.

Here and there on the shore of the lantana sea there was a glint from tins not yet completely rusted.

"Perhaps you're better off, mister. Knock up a grill at yer own convenience."

The stranger apparently didn't hear. He sat staring out over the lantana-filled ravine: a potential suicide perhaps?

There was a sudden outbreak of what might have been taken for murder by anyone not in the know: the grocer was; he knew it as the laughter of lovers locked together in the lantana depths.

As an antidote to possible embarrassment, he turned and said to his difficult friend: "Not much of a view, but a touch of nature in the middle of the city. I can see that you're a nature lover."

The man laughed for the first time. "Yes and no! I was watching the skyline. There's a very brief phase when the houses opposite remind me of unlit gas-fires."

Obviously a nut. But an educated one. To humour him, the grocer asked: "D'you think the phase is on its way?"

"I'm afraid we must have missed it—while you were talking."

"Well, if I made yer miss something, I can only apologize." The grocer flounced on their common seat.

They sat in silence for a little, while the sunken sun tightened its vice on the last of the horizon.

"No." The stranger had sunk his chin: you could almost see down the rims of his eyes. "I don't think I missed it after all." It came so long afterwards, Mr Cutbush couldn't at first understand what it referred to. "Or if I did, I must have wanted to."

He turned his first smile on the grocer, who appeared captivated by it: fatter, complacent, broody; but suddenly again, tentative and uneasy.

"I had a peculiar experience tonight." Cutbush wet his lips, and decided to share it. "I looked in at a window, and saw a person—a gentleman—standing without a stitch. Had everything to hide, too."

Though he threw open his hairy coat, the stranger evidently wasn't prepared to reveal more than his naked thoughts. He leaned forward, hands locked between his knees, chin thrust at the growing darkness.

"I came here this evening," he said, "because I particularly wanted to be on my own. I don't know why: most of the time I am alone; though I have more friends than I can cope with—or acquaintances, at least. I am not in need—of any thing, or any one."

He challenged the darkness so aggressively, the grocer recoiled. "Okay, okay, mister! Good for you!"

"When I saw this house I bought—several years ago—I said to myself: 'This is the house I shall work in, and die in.' It's not in any way an exceptional house. You can walk about in it, though. And it's on a corner. It has entrances on two different streets—so that you can easily escape from a fire—or a visitor. Oh, it's *pleasing!*" He unlocked his hands, and immediately locked them again.

The grocer sat looking at as much as he could see of the hands. "If you have a house, that's something," he suggested listlessly. "Not everybody can afford to buy their own home. Not everybody's that successful."

"I can't say I'm not successful—*now*—not that it means anything." The grocer spat. "I dunno." The conversation was becoming too clever. "This house"—he yawned—"is it in this neighbourhood?"

The stranger continued leaning forward in the dark the sun had left and the moon hadn't yet demolished. "I had another house. It was burnt down. Fortunately. Yes, I think—fortunately—in the bush-fires which came soon afterwards. You see, I had a friend who died."

"A friend, did you?" Revived interest made the grocer shuffle his behind around on the bench. "And 'ow did 'e die, sir—your friend?"

"I don't know, and shall never know. They couldn't decide—whether it was suicide or accidental death. Or murder. Well, of course it wasn't murder—because I'm here. She could only have fallen over. She was drunk—and maniacal. That's what they decided. It was too obvious."

"Was your friend a lady, then?"

"I've been accused of loving myself. How could I? When I've always known too much about myself." He stopped so abruptly his breath made a sound like a snore. "I wonder why I'm telling you this?"

The grocer, too, was amazed. "Some people," he began very slowly, diffidently, "are driven to loving themselves—as a sort of consolation."

"But I've never been in need of consolation! I have what I know and what I can see. I have my work."

"Ah?"

"Not that it's as simple as that. Not always. Not when it's dragged out of you, in torment and anguish, by a pair of forceps."

The grocer couldn't remember a telephone booth nearer than the one in Laggan Street, and the larries had stripped that.

"Do you believe in God, Mr Cutbush?"

"Eh? That's what we were taught, wasn't it? I'm not going back on that. That is, I wouldn't be prepared to say I don't exactly not believe."

"In the Divine Vivisector!"

"The—what did you say, sir?" Though he hadn't understood, it chilled the grocer: he could feel it trickling down his back.

The moon was by now showering its light on a world which

looked as plain and consistent as your hand—but wasn't, it seemed. In the distance a tram was screaming like no normal public conveyance, and although the waves of lantana were set as solid as the marble in a tombstone, you looked again and saw them twitch like sleeping flesh.

It was his eyesight: never been the same since the ammonia exploded in the back shop.

"I believe in Him—I think," his companion was saying.

The stranger's eyes weren't exactly glittering with tears, because a man wouldn't cry—or would he after all?—in front of another man. The grocer was tingling with a sympathy it mightn't have been proper to offer.

"Yes, I believe in Him," the stranger repeated. "Otherwise, how would men come by their cruelty—and their brilliance?"

The grocer didn't know how to rise to the occasion; but something mild and reconciled in his companion's tone reminded him of an incident, interesting, if irrelevant.

"There was a bloke I knew—a caterer, name of Davy Price—decent, decent all the way—got into a spot of trouble when an entire weddin' party died of food poisonin'. 'Our mistakes are what we make, Cec,' Davy says to me, 'and it's only us can live them down.' The following night 'e blew 'is brains out."

The anecdote now seemed very irrelevant indeed, but even so the grocer was put out when his friend made no attempt to respond.

"Not only that"—he cheered up a little to remember—" 'e did it on this very same piece of vacant land. They call it The Gash—did you know?"

The connection between past and present worked, the grocer was relieved to see. The stranger was enjoying a change of mood. Still sitting, he began to slap his thighs with the flats of his hands. The sound it made was hard and brisk.

"I can't tell you how much it's done for me—our talk. I didn't expect anything like this. I'll go home now and work."

"What—you work at night, do you?" Distant footsteps on the asphalt made the question sound even darker.

"Sometimes. It depends. Things look different by artificial light. Some paintings seem to crave for it the moment you conceive them. I think of others in terms of daylight."

Ah, this was it. "You're an artist, then?"

"Yes. I paint."

"Go on! I never met a real professional artist!" The grocer wasn't quite sure how to take it. "Can you make a livin' at it? Looks as if you can," he answered himself, because the good, if neglected suit and imported overcoat were there as evidence.

"I'm not interested in business," the painter said, "but can make enough for my purpose—which is painting. I can even cut a dash if I want to. And I sometimes want to."

It looked strangely frivolous as he shrugged at his own desire, like women the grocer had seen through windows shrugging off their own reflections in the glass: not that this man appeared to have anything of a woman in him.

"Yes," he was saying, "they're buying me—almost as if I was groceries." He glanced at the grocer, who didn't know whether to defend his trade or accept a compliment. "A couple of years ago London and New York began to take notice. So poor Maurice Caldicott was vindicated. He was my agent—and friend—a dealer who took me up, and stuck to me—for the wrong reason, I found out."

"What reason?" asked the grocer, though facts interested him more than motives.

"He was in love with me."

"What—a man?"

"Why not? He was a human being, and human beings aren't allowed to choose what they shall love: woman, man, cat—or God."

The grocer might never have listened to a more seductive argument. "That's an idea I never thought of, and now you put it like that I don't believe I chose my wife. I thought I did. Oh, I wonder 'oo I would 'uv loved if I'd been allowed to choose!" His mind scarcely dared clothe the abstraction with flesh.

"My friend Caldicott died a couple of years ago, after what they call 'a long illness'—in agony. In the last days of his vivisection he told me he had never held my unkindness against me, because he considered anybody in any way creative needs a source of irritation. He was happy to think he had provided me with just that."

"What did he die of?" The grocer felt guilty asking a question he could answer himself, but he would have been ashamed to have caught the other's attention.

The artist bloke didn't notice. "I wish I could remember Maurice more distinctly. He was too pale. I used to find him insipid. He might have been a saint. But it's easier to visualize the devils than the saints."

Mr Cutbush would have had difficulty in visualizing either, and feared his companion might descend again into some confused private hell.

At least the artist had got up from the bench; his figure in the moonlight overawed the grocer, who became squat, pursy, apologetic: not that he wasn't as good as anyone else.

"Bet you have a good time when you paint a picture." He smiled up, showing ingratiating teeth. "Bet you'll go 'ome and paint a picture of all this—all this *moon*light. I'd like to see what you make of it."

"A great white arse shitting on a pair of lovers—as they swim through a sea of lantana—dislocating themselves."

It was the sort of joke an educated person could afford to make. The grocer laughed, of course, but wondered whether he wasn't being made to laugh at himself.

"Pleased to have met you," he said, holding out his hand as in the beginning, to round the meeting off. "You won't have lived long enough in the neighbourhood to know I used to be a councillor. But resigned. Yairs. Business and family obligations." He bent forward to pick up the pencil he had been playing with, and dropped: it was of the blunt kind worn behind the ear.

When he looked up the artist was already moving off: sloppy-elegant walk: not unlike a normal person if you hadn't heard him throwing off like a Roman candle: all *talk*.

There was another outburst of strangled laughter from the wasteland.

The unusual encounter, the feel of dew along the bench, his own blind thoughts still nosing after his new friend's electric suggestions —didn't remember to get his name out of him to tell the wife—had left the grocer with the shakes. He began recklessly, in spite of the lamp-post in the near distance, to expose himself, then to masturbate at the lantana. Yairs. All this talk of creation. He sat hypnotized, watching the seed he was scattering in vain by moonlight on barren ground.

The painter looked back once, but only very briefly, at what he already knew; it was already working in him.

6

Caldicott had said in the beginning: "You can't possibly live in it as it is, dear boy. I couldn't, anyway. The furniture's too ugly: too many knobs. There's too much stained glass. I couldn't live with someone else's furniture: that's what it remains when you take it over holus-bolus with a house."

He had already developed the yellow tinge which intensified towards his death. "That's what *I* think. But you, Duffield, are different." Caldicott laughed; his behaviour apologized to others for the effort he was making.

It still surprised Duffield to hear anyone address him by name, but he showed no sign of this in his considered answer. "The furniture doesn't put me off. I've always lived with other people's furniture, except for a table I made myself at Ironstone. I think I'll learn something from living with this lot." He kicked out at random and struck a finicking rosewood leg.

The table at Ironstone, solid in appearance, but unstable on acquaintance, was too painful to think about. He had kept the curtain of hair tightly drawn in front of her face, for fear he might catch sight of one of the transformation scenes.

The house in Flint Street he had bought cheap from a distant cousin of the deceased owner anxious to be rid of an embarrassment. The deceased had lived on in it many years after her father, a retired produce merchant, died. The house was at least spacious, and in the days of the produce merchant, who built it, must have had pretensions. Urns still stood on the parapet, and iron lace luxuriated. Gutters, on the other hand, had melted into festoons, and the split and rusty down-pipes gushed whenever there was a deluge.

A lot would have to be done about the electric wiring; he

239

would see to it in time. Some of the rooms were without wiring at all. On the upper floor, where the daylight poured in for painting, there was a single electric bulb on the end of a long flex, to be carried after dark from room to room. He would have to improve on that, too.

But from the beginning, in spite of its imperfection and disrepair, he had a secret passion for his house. Nobody would invade this one, on the corner of Flint and Brecon Streets. In that quarter many of the street names were Welsh: Rhoose, Lavernock, Dolgelly, Jones. The masked houses had a secretive air, which didn't displease him: he wasn't one of those who resented lowered eyelids, for he had usually known what lay behind them.

The back entrance to his house opened on Chubb's Lane. Here the clothes-lines and corrugated iron took over; ladies called to one another over collapsing paling fences; the go-carts were parked and serviced, and dragged out on shrieking wheels. In the evening the young girls hung around in clusters, sucking oranges, sharing fashion mags, and criticizing one another's hair as though they had been artists. There was a mingled smell of poor washing, sump oil, rotting vegetables, goatish male bodies, soggy female armpits, in Chubb's Lane.

The two faces of his house complemented each other; one taken away might have upset the balance: together they made what was necessary for his fulfilment and happiness. Though what was happiness? Painting—even taking into account its agonies and failures. And who could define balance? Probably all the inhabitants of Chubb's Lane and nine-tenths of Flint Street considered him a crank, but had been prepared for crankiness by the former owner of Number 17. After a couple of years, when it was realized he would pay his bills like anybody respectable, and had neither seduced young girls nor buggered little boys, he was accepted by the neighbours with smiles which, if not exactly warm, were the politest any of them could muster. They got used to him standing, afternoons, at his upper-back sun-drenched window over the lane, or on the sagging balcony of the upper front, where an increasing araucaria shaded his familiar face with menacing black and flesh-green. None of them would have known they were his daily bread, and that when he retreated suddenly into the rooms where they had never been, it was because he could postpone the moment no longer: he had submitted their blander substance to the acid of his own experience, and must now begin, often resentfully, always compulsively, to paint.

To the neighbourhood he was, sort of, the Artist. As they didn't understand what it amounted to, some of them generated spasms of hate; but they couldn't direct it, or not for long: he had become part of the landscape, like the iron railings and the gas meters. Because he was what you might have called handsome, there were girls who would have liked to develop a crush, if there hadn't been something which prevented them. In one light he was their admitted possession, their almost pride, in another as shameful as some of their submerged thoughts. He was referred to as Old Hurtle the Turtle before he had begun noticeably to shrivel. Few of them would have cared to run the risk of his company walking from the tram-stop. The flintiest granny of the neighbourhood might have been reduced to silence and little-girlhood by one who was not, as they admitted, old of limb or feature, but who must have been born older than any of them could aspire to be. So they preferred to avoid situations in which they might be reminded of their inability to solve his queer conundrum.

Nor did it occur to him to help them in a relationship which was above words.

The evening of his meeting with Cutbush, years after his purchase of the house Maurice Caldicott had found for him and his distant patroness Mrs Davenport had helped him indirectly to buy, he was walking with unusual briskness through the streets, here and there slapping an iron lamp-post, for company, or because for the moment he didn't have the means of expressing himself in any other way. He laughed once or twice on remembering his conversation with the rather cagey grocer. He glanced up at the marbled moon. If he had exposed himself to someone he was only faintly disturbed: it was doubtful he would ever see that person again; and hadn't the grocer exposed himself? Striding across the suburb which conveniently separated their lives, his own footsteps sounded solider than the whole architecture of moonlight.

On arriving home he let himself in through the front door. Under the influence of the overgrown araucaria the night looked even whiter. The roots of the tree had broken the pavement and lifted it up. Although he knew, he often forgot abcut it, and tripped, and had to steady himself on the trunk where it pressed against the railings. The bark oozed a resin which might have felt sticky and unpleasant if it hadn't been for the other irremovable encrustations collected on his hard palm, almost that of a labourer.

Tonight as he clanged through the iron gate he gratefully smelled the scent from the weeping trunk. Dew was already gathering in the rusty gutters, spilling down the burst pipes. He still intended to have something done about the pipes and gutters, but always enjoyed hearing the dew trickle as far as the excrescent moss with which the foundations of his house were cushioned.

Not that the house was his by more than title; it belonged to those who had originally lived there: the late Miss Gilderthorp and her produce-merchant father, with whose possessions the rooms were furnished. Possibly this was the most an artist of any kind was spiritually entitled to. He had come across few other painters, and then only sniffed around them. He wouldn't have pried into their beliefs; but he had seen that investments were a great comfort and a source of increasing corruption to one fashionable painter he had met. So he was unhappy with his own money when it came: while prudently investing it. He allowed himself one or two luxuries, such as the patronage of a good tailor, made-to-measure shirts, jars of imported *pâté de foie*, a bottle of Napoleon brandy. He also dabbled in luxurious fantasies: he might invest in an expensively scented mistress and lie with her on the late Miss Gilderthorp's bed, on the sheets he boiled himself—when he remembered—pushing them round the copper with a stick, in a lean-to at the back; or he could imagine buying an exotic car, an Isotta or a Bugatti, which he had heard about but never seen. He had never learned to drive; he would arrange to have his car driven, in the small hours, into the shed which opened on Chubb's Lane: where he could watch it when he felt inclined. He saw himself sitting on the supple upholstery, which would never lose the perfume of its youth, or opening the bonnet to examine what would never become a smelly machine; it would remain a system of philosophy, which, in its visual aspect, he would paint. He would paint.

As there was so much he had to paint, the fantasies he was amused to indulge in came no closer to actuality than masturbation to fulfilled love. While the houses the other side of Chubb's Lane spawned their bawling little sun-tinted, photographic children, he poured out his paintings. Nobody in the neighbourhood had seen them, but they read about him. The *Herald*, after mentioning "two

Duffield canvases recently acquired by the Tate Gallery, London, and one by the Museum of Modern Art, New York," warned against the evils of success. He was hardly affected by the warning, and only superficially by the sales. He went on living, and spawning, protected by the house and furniture which were never his own.

This evening after he had let himself in, "his" house took on a festive air. He soon had electric pears hanging in different branches of it. For company more than anything else, he liked to turn on all the lights, finishing up with the powerful bulb, still lolling on a long flex, which he would carry from room to room on the upper floor, and finally aim at their focus point: his easel.

Then, after running down, on this evening of some significance, he first fried himself eggs and bacon in the kitchenette Miss Gilderthorp had partitioned off from her father's original stone kitchen. The little room, with its asbestos walls and unshaded bulb, smelled of congealed fat, and something not unlike urine, the source of which he had never been able to trace.

He loved his eggs and bacon. He liked to fry the eggs till the ruffs stood out, brown-edged and stiff, around the yolks. He never cut the rinds off the rashers: after he had finished eating, he enjoyed sucking the rinds while considering what the night contained.

The world of moonlight and lantana was dragging at him tonight: the big-arsed moon aiming at the dislocated lovers; the crypto-queer grocer-councillor machine-gunning them from the Council bench. He could see how his composition would be divided.

But what had he *said*? He tried to remember, but couldn't hear all the inflections of his voice, or what exactly the grocer might have heard.

Drifting in this vaguely unhappy cloud which had risen on his mental horizon, he neglected the bacon rinds, even the lantana lovers. What he visualized instead was the big tureen: chunks of pork floating in it; the coarse *tranches* of bubbly bread. Our Father Decent Harry had tucked a corner of his napkin into his collar; it was allowed "in foreign parts."

It was Courtney, not Duffield, who mooned his way back to the upper rooms. The stair rail, polished by hands, was also roughened by resin, wrinkles of paint, smears of the honey which he loved to eat comb-and-all: Alfreda Courtney would have thrown a fit on the stairs.

He wandered for a while around the upper floor, carrying the blinding pear on its flex, before adjusting it to meet his easel's needs.

But diffidently.

He was afraid on almost all nights: more on this propitious one; so much so, he began thinning out the scumble of objects on the chest of drawers, searching for, fumbling at the envelope received the same afternoon, one of the few letters in recent months he had been tempted to open. Was it the texture of the paper? Or scent? Or the handwriting? It could have been the hand of a woman or a man.

For this third reading he held the letter at a distance in the full glare of the naked bulb. In certain circumstances, he knew, his normally hard dry palms became damp spongy ones.

Dear Hurtle Duffield,

If you haven't yet heard I am again settled in Sydney, it is because I am only now venturing back into circulation. I returned here a year ago, after the death of my husband; since then I have been almost entirely occupied in overcoming the obstinacy of an architect and builders: after all, it is I who must live in the house and my friends who will criticize it.

I hesitate to attempt a relationship in the flesh with any artist whose work I have admired; but surely after years of being on intimate terms with six—no, seven of your paintings, I should throw off my diffidence?

Would you be free to come here at 6 p.m. on the 7th of this month? By then I hope the last traces of sawdust and smells of paint will have vanished, and we shall be free to talk without unpleasant distractions.

I am most excited, I assure you, to make your acquaintance, or perhaps I should say: confirm a friendship which already exists.

Sincerely
Olivia Davenport

Olivia. He wrinkled up his nose somewhat, and remembered the bacon rinds he had forgotten. Understandably, Caldicott hadn't thought it necessary to warn him against ladies of means who collect paintings. He had learned about them by experience, some of it congenial. He had nibbled at Turkish delight while listening to problems of the soul, not to say the marriage bed. More than one husband would have been proud to admit Duffield's relationship with his wife's soul.

But *Olivia*: and twice widowed.

While he had suspected Caldicott of playing a drag role, poor old Maurice had been cleverly forming a client's taste. Six—or no, seven paintings over the years. What distracted now was the thought of those paintings exposed to the eyes of somebody unknown, even if the messages had remained necessarily obscure.

Olivia Davenport: her name alone had dynamited the solid marble night and his intention of developing the big-arsed moon, the lantana sea, and the gunner-grocer shooting sperm at marked lovers. So when he had dragged at Miss Gilderthorp's collapsed and almost intractable venetian blind to shut out the exploded ruins, he sat down at the desk in the corner, and allowed an impulse to take possession.

It was a curiously weightless relief: to draw his sister Rhoda Courtney standing beside the bidet on its iron tripod in the hotel bedroom at St Yves de Trégor. If he had betrayed a timid, wizened tenderness by raucously breaking open the door protecting her nakedness, the drawings were at last a kind of formal expiation: Rhoda's hump sat for moments on his own shoulders. As his resistance of years collapsed, he knew how he should convey the iron in crippled bones; he saw the mesh of light, the drops of moisture in the Thermogene tuft. With few pauses, he made several drawings, each of which contributed something to what he wanted.

He might have waited till morning, but was so convinced every iron line had set, he fetched a board he had prepared that afternoon, and began his "Pythoness at Tripod." He was seething with it. He would hardly need to accept Mrs Thingummy—Davenport's invitation for the 7th.

In each of the two rooms on the upper floor was a bed: he would sleep on either, according to his mood and the demands of his work. There was in addition a rusty stretcher where he had dossed down once or twice, in the little junk-room, or cupboard, which opened on the upper landing: dreams influenced his choice or rejection of a bed. Now that he was working at this painting, his sleep was always brief and broken. He would wake frowzy, battered, tormented by guilt for something left undone. He could have lain longer, combing out his armpits with fingers sticky from his night of paint, but wasn't allowed; he had to jump up at once: what if he ever died in his sleep, leaving a skeleton pythoness hung with a rag or two of imperfect flesh? If he thought about death it was usually in terms of work unfinished, and for this reason he found death terrifying.

While working he ate very little: eggs—sometimes swallowed raw; bacon, because it soothed him to suck the rinds. He drank quantities of coffee, with milk or without. Often he was infuriated to find his mouth full of dregs: he was forced to spit them into the sink, and continue spitting; he couldn't get rid of the last of the bloody horrible dregs.

But his painting was coming along, together with two new versions of it. As the meeting with his patroness approached, the act of painting became a duel between Mrs Davenport and Rhoda Courtney. Rhoda's pointed mask wore at times an expression of malicious cunning; while at her obdurate worst, he would bring on her rival, at least her swashbuckling figure, for he hadn't solved the problem of Mrs Davenport's face.

Early on the day of his social engagement he thought he wouldn't go. Rhoda was parading such an air of tenderly rapt dedication to her oracles, she could have won; in fact at that instant he was so well pleased with what he had done, he caught himself standing back, his mouth furled in a juicy funnel as though to suck up the milky tones of Rhoda Courtney's sickly flesh. He left off as he began to dribble.

Shortly after, he decided after all to appear at Mrs Davenport's. Opposed to Rhoda's iron will was his own desire to preen. (During lunch he had gone so far as to make an idealized drawing of himself on the back of an unopened letter.) So now he nipped along to the bathroom and put a match to the geyser. The brown stain on the bottom of the bath didn't encourage total immersion: instead he washed his neck, his feet, his armpits, and his crutch.

Unlike his face, his body was still unravaged, and he would dress it well, in a suit by Benson (late of Holly & Edwards, New Bond Street). The back, he realized from the glass, was a masterpiece of cutting.

A dash of Cologne on a handkerchief, in which he sank his face: he should have heard his spurs jingle; but he was at once depressed by the weight of everything imaginable.

He went down down, the depth and length of his house, it was never far enough in a crisis, out to the wreck of what had been Miss Gilderthorp's conservatory. It was in almost every event the least effective antidote to melancholy. This afternoon a jaundiced light had blundered in through the vaulting of deathless aspidistra, the tracery of asparagus fern, to splinter into fragments of many-coloured glass and rustling, empty chrysalides on the tessellated floor. From outside there was a scent of runt apples rotting in the arrow-grass at the roots of the privets.

He backed out of the conservatory, carefully shutting the door on what he must preserve for some use still to be decided.

A survivor-parlourmaid, tough as an aspidistra, heavy with powder instead of dust, opened the door of Mrs Davenport's large house. Of a period no longer fashionable, the house had been made desirable by wealth. There were glimpses of tame sea through clumps of bamboo and strelitzia, but a bed of salvia burning too fiercely spoiled to some extent the jade-and-tussore effects of the bamboo.

"Mr—Duffield? Oh yes, Mr Duffield!" The parlourmaid gave him her whiskery smile. "Madam will be so pleased."

She led him over floors of long, dull red, beautifully waxed timber, explaining that her mistress was upstairs changing. The size of the house, and the clatter of their feet alternating with a stealthy padding as they trekked across islands of Bokharan rugs, seemed to force the maid into collusion with the guest.

In the smaller room into which she introduced him, three ladies were unexpectedly seated, two of them discussing their friends while the third listened, brightly erect.

When the maid presented the new arrival, murmuring something which approximated to a name, the two chatterers were silenced. Out of the embarrassment caused by the surprise entrance, the prettiest lady inquired in the jolly voice you put on for your friends' servants, especially if the friends are rich: "How are your feet treating you, Emily?"

Emily replied: "No better, Mrs Halliday. My feet will be the death of me," and hobbled out.

The silence was not lightened by the commingled perfumes of synthetic flowers, not even by the more aseptic scent of gin. He sat down in what had become a waiting-room. Each of the ladies, in her way, appeared to be estimating his possibilities. There was a Miró on one wall, a Léger? yes, but a bad one, on another. Very white and austere, the walls.

"Don't you drink?" Mrs Halliday suddenly ear-splittingly asked, making great play with a decanter and her bracelets. "So good for you!"

"Yes," he agreed, "but not now," his voice sounding hoarse. He might have to use his wits.

The third and hitherto silent lady braced herself to make a contribution. "Mr Trotter—my husband—never touches alcohol before sundown. It's a matter of principle."

"Good for him!" said the military-looking one in her peaked cap and studded belt. "But not for me, Mrs Trotter," she added, and took up a copy of *Vogue*. It returned them all to the waiting-room.

A wave had begun to rise in Mrs Trotter, from out of her bust, flooding her neck, and reaching the roots of her naturally carroty hair, till her face and throat looked completely covered with a claret birthmark.

Mrs Halliday averted her eyes. "What's that wretched Olivia up to?" She parted her jewellery in search of a watch.

"Changing, we were told," the military lady reminded them. "If you ask me, she bloody well forgot she was expecting us."

"Mrs Davenport's so terribly busy." Mrs Trotter might have been defending herself. "She's promised to help me with the crèche. She's promised me a cheque. Only she's almost run off her feet."

The military one guffawed.

"Truly, Mrs Horsfall!" Mrs Trotter protested. "Don't be unfair!"

But Mrs Horsfall continued guffawing into the pages she was looking at. "Here's Maggie Purser going as Emma Hamilton!"

"Don't slay me!" Mrs Halliday was wearing a hat with a latticed brim through which she liked to use her eyes. "At least it'll come natural." She was turning this way and that, and frowning through her pastrywork. "Why does Olivia allow her gardener to plant salvia of all things? It's so ghastly—I mean—so municipal—and hidjus."

The salvia beyond the window did appear an unchivalrous mistake beside the cooler flowers of Mrs Halliday's person, to say nothing of the austere room, with its few dispersed but perfect objects.

"I'm mad about Mrs Davenport," Mrs Trotter clumsily confessed.

Mrs Horsfall sat turning the pages. "I'm going through a sort of depressive phase."

"Oh *neoh*, Jo darling!" Mrs Halliday tried to assist. "All you need is a change of something."

Mrs Horsfall closed the glossy pages and let the magazine fall plunk on the pearl-shell table. "Charitable, Moira, this afternoon." She sat back, grinning and basking.

By moments they became aware of the man sitting amongst them. Mrs Trotter almost apologized once, but didn't dare in the circumstances.

Instead she asked, and again she was plastered with the claret birthmark: "Do you think Mrs Davenport's unhappy—all alone—since Mr Davenport died?"

Mrs Horsfall said: "Guy's death was an immense relief. Guy Davenport would have made any woman's life hell."

"I understand"—Mrs Trotter had difficulty bringing it out—"he died very tragically."

Mrs Horsfall took aim at Mrs Trotter. "He was walking on the roof of a train. He was decapitated," she said, "by a tunnel."

Mrs Trotter made a sincere though wrong sound, while opening her handbag to look for help.

"I wonder Olivia didn't sue the L.M.S.," Mrs Horsfall continued. "Anyone else would have."

"Oh, but surely, darling—walking on the roof of *their* train?" Mrs Halliday pointed out.

"Why not? Olivia would have looked divine in court. She could get away with anything. But she didn't need to."

"The money's all there." Mrs Halliday spoke as one who had seen the bank statements. "She wisely kept her hand on the purse."

Mrs. Horsfall laughed approvingly, and sank her chin.

"They say there was another husband—a Mr Lopez," Mrs Trotter almost whispered.

"Oh, that!" Mrs Halliday threw Lopez away. "That was something brief and mysterious. In Peru, wasn't it, Jo? Nobody knows, and nobody asks."

"She must be awfully unhappy," Mrs Trotter said, and her claret eyelids thickened.

"I'm sure not," said Jo Horsfall.

Mrs Trotter opened her handbag and shut it. "They say she's a nymphomaniac—and a nymphomaniac can only be unhappy."

"What? Olivia?" Mrs Horsfall roared, Mrs Halliday shrieked, and a pair of bulbuls bathing in a giant clamshell on the lawn flitted into a pomegranate tree, where they sat shaking their shocked topknots.

When Mrs Halliday had subsided she said on the level: "One very good authority claims that Olivia's a Lesbian."

"A what?" Mrs Trotter asked.

"Rot, Moira!" Mrs Horsfall drew down the corners of her mouth. "A girl I know put the acid on her, and it didn't work."

All three suddenly icily remembered the man.

"Is Olivia an old friend?" Mrs Halliday appealed, looking at him through her lattice.

"I've never met her."

Was it believable? they considered in silence.

"I didn't catch your name," Mrs Halliday twittered amusingly. "Emily does mumble so."

"Duffield."

"Oh. Ohhh? *Neoh!* Not the artist—the painter? *Duf*-field!"

Thus bombarded he could only hang his head while the room reverberated.

"I adore paintings," Mrs Trotter said as she had been taught. "I'm going to get one—when we've properly settled in."

Mrs Halliday and Mrs Horsfall were left fishing for their compacts.

Beyond the garden the sea was dying. There was no indication how the silence might have ended if the door hadn't opened. Someone, their hostess apparently, came in.

"I'm so terribly sorry—*every*body!" She held out her long hands so that the palms were helplessly exposed at the ends of her arms.

In her apology she included the man who happened, incidentally, to be there. She kissed all the ladies, reviving Mrs Trotter's claret birthmark; the man she embraced with her most candid smile.

Mrs Davenport was wearing a suit of white pyjamas, *tout simple* —or not so *simple*: it was too elaborately subtle; whereas the natural white streak in her brilliantly black hair looked shamelessly artificial. While the three visiting ladies chattered against one another in the same high social key—of their regrets for their hostess's neglect, of the races and the cricket, of Maggie Purser—Mrs Davenport came close up to him and said in a very confidential tone: "Aren't you drinking, Hurtle Duffield?"

He said: "No, thank you," prim for him.

Then, because she remained so cool, particularly her eyes, which were of a clear, unperturbed grey, he blurted quickly, clumsily: "On the other hand, give me a gin and water. A long gin—with not much water," anticipating the first draught, the sweet, fumigating fumes.

He intended to stay where he was, but found himself collaborating with his hostess amongst the ice and crystal. He dropped several cubes of ice, and would have begun grovelling after them.

"Leave it!" she ordered, kicking out with a gold sandal.

The ice shot under the table.

Her technique was so assured she must have acquired it at an early age. She took it all for granted, with a touch of contempt for what her guest must inwardly despise; while the ladies continued intoning in the background:

"Oh, darling . . ."

"No, darling . . ."

". . . all the helpers would be enchanted, and the babies, too, if you would visit, Mrs Davenport, any afternoon . . ."

The nymphomaniac, or Lesbian, remained superbly cold: probably frigid enough to have killed off her brace of husbands.

"I must apologize particularly," she confessed to her male visitor.

"It isn't what I expected!" But he laughed as the sweet gust of gin explored his skull and eased him out.

"Nor did *I* expect." She added one of her brilliant smiles. "You didn't answer my letter."

Downing the rest of the gin, he couldn't see the point.

"Mus go mus go darling!" Mrs Halliday was shrieking, blinking through her latticed brim.

"Mus go mus go you beastly old Oliviur!" Mrs Horsfall was tightening her silver-studded belt.

Mrs Trotter said: "Mr Trotter—my husband—and I—would be most honoured, Mrs Davenport, if we could entertain you one evening—to *dinner*," she managed to remember.

Olivia Davenport, with her long crimson fingernails and one rope of knotted pearls, was so amused by it all as she handed them over to Emily. " 'Bye, darlings!" she screeched according to convention.

Almost before the maid had whisked them off the scene Mrs Davenport returned very gravely into her other self. She was certainly a work of art, but not his, or not at the moment: he saw her as a too facile van Dongen.

While swilling her gin, his memory kept trying to unravel something about her. From the expression of her eyes she might have wanted to assist.

She was sucking on her knot of pearls, when suddenly she leaned forward and said: "Boo Hollingrake."

"But your eyes were brown."

251

"Grey. One thing you can't change is eyes."

Yet he distinctly remembered a brown, smudged, steamy beauty in the perforated shade of the *Monstera deliciosa* at the bottom of the stone steps.

"I can see you most clearly," he said, because the other was too private a vision, "in the William Street post office, on a rainy morning. There's no reason why I should remember you so vividly on that occasion. You'd come there to post a letter. You were looking sad—and mysterious. Your eyes must have been grey, if you say they were. I was buying stamps for my—for Freda Courtney."

Boo Hollingrake rejected her pearls finally; she shook her head. "I'm sorry, I've forgotten all about it—if it was of any importance to you. Girls of a certain age are inclined to look sad and mysterious, especially on wet mornings. I think they feel they must make amends in some way for their own dullness." Her delivery was crisp, her glance ironic.

He wondered whether she had also forgotten their more spontaneous encounter. There was no sign that she remembered how frenziedly her thighs had worked; of course she could never have been aware, not even at the moment itself, of the stickiness in his underpants.

Olivia Boo Hollingrake Lopez Davenport got up, feeling her way back into the sandals she had slipped off. "I expect you'll want me to show you the paintings."

She said it so casually the paintings were probably her greatest interest. She introduced him to the Braque, the Picasso, the Max Ernst, several Klees, and others, and others. He was becoming a little sour, and was glad he could disguise it under gin.

"How is it," he asked, "I never heard your real, your *baptismal* name?"

She made a deliberately stylized grimace. "I loathed it, till I realized it was something I was stuck with, and that I'd better make the most of it."

Leading him from one painting to the next, Olivia Davenport reminded him of certain women introducing men you suspect of having been their lovers. She was so cool and practised: he could feel his jealousy increasing. He wondered about his own miserable works: whether she had shoved them in the laundry, or even whether she still owned them. Rich women who had bought cheap sometimes couldn't resist showing they knew how to sell better.

"As you're a painter," Mrs Davenport said at the critical moment in his bitterness, "you're probably dying to worship at your own shrine."

He tried to hide his shame by making indeterminate noises into his dwindling gin.

"If only you'd replied to my letter, and told me you were coming," she said severely, "I could have had the gardeners bring them down."

"A little exercise won't hurt us." He hoped he wasn't too blatant in helping himself to another drink.

"It isn't that. I'll have to take you into my bedroom," she said without a trace of coyness.

In the circumstances, his own attempt at humour sounded disgracefully arch. He heard his: "Don't expect we'll find it untidy!" before an attempt to drown the escaping remark in a cackle of ice.

She seemed determined to ignore what she didn't want to hear. She began leading him upstairs. Like her possessions, whether the white silk she was dressed in, or the stone head of a Buddha in a niche, her movements were of a true perfection. She had the most beautifully straight back. Of course Boo Sugar Hollingrake could bloody well afford to be straight-backed and simple.

On a half-landing there was a strip-lit painting: a Boudin.

"What's this?" He couldn't believe it.

"Can't you tell?"

"Yes, I know. But where did it come from?"

"I bought it at the sale, after Mrs Courtney—Mrs Boileau—had left."

Whether the Boudin was a good one he couldn't have judged at that moment. It was something he had grown up with and out of; its reappearance made him weak at the knees.

"I'm glad you bought it," he said. "I expect you remembered it from when we were children. It used to hang in Harry's study."

He would have liked to explain to her how the Boudin had become a reality of his own at St Yves de Trégor, where he had noticed, for the first time, flat, firm sand lying like flesh under a white muslin of sea.

But even if he had been able to explain in words, she mightn't have allowed it. "Oh no. I don't think I ever noticed the Boudin at

Sunningdale. I can't remember. Nothing like that interested me as a child. Paintings were only furniture. No, I bought this one later on simply because it appealed to me as painting."

She was so sure of herself; till arriving at the landing Mrs Davenport flawed her performance: she tripped against the top stair. For a moment her behind stuck out like that of an awkward, angular girl. He felt he wanted to embrace this loss of perfection. He did put out his hand, but she had already recovered herself without his help.

"You're far more sentimental than they say!" she gasped back at him over her shoulder in a voice which surprised him: it had the same timbre as Rhoda's.

Immediately after, she turned; they were facing each other on the landing. "Where is Rhoda?" she asked.

Olivia was pale, probably only as the result of nearly falling on her face, whereas he could imagine himself looking pale from the shock of her mind cutting into his.

"I don't know. She went away with Maman," he stammered, "after the remarriage. During the war I lost touch. She isn't my sister, you know," he offered as an unconvincing excuse.

In any case Olivia must have known that. She had sensed the larrikin in him after the rout of girls had stampeded through the hydrangeas in the lower garden at Sunningdale.

Now, standing at the top of the stairs, she said with a sincerity he couldn't doubt—in fact she barely avoided turning it into a whimper: "My poor darling monkey—Rhoda!" Then she led him into what became her bedroom.

He couldn't at first look at anything but his own paintings: they were too crude, disproportionate: and those clotted, painful textures. He kept spinning on his heels, as though to avoid renewing acquaintance, except superficially. But he couldn't have avoided. They were hanging on every wall: his imperfections and his agonies. He went up very close to his "Marriage of Light"; in that way, involved with the technique, he was less conscious of the body of an actual woman fragmented in the cause of art. Not Nance Lightfoot lying broken on a rocky ledge. That was another picture of course, unpainted, and in every way too *black*: black dress, wounds stitched with the jet of flies, already the long caravans of ants. Not least, his own black horror kneeling beside his murder. By comparison, the "Marriage of Light" was a declaration of love, and if he concentrated on the more objective aspects, he could throw modesty away and congratulate himself, on having achieved his intention as a whole, and for the brilliant sensuousness of many details.

But while gyrating drunkenly, breathing colour through his strained nostrils, brazenly putting out his hand to stroke the paint, the origins of his present joy kept blowing back at him in black gusts. Even the most abrasive of his "Rock" series, the best of which Mrs Davenport had taken pains to collect, resolved themselves in his mind's eye into a configuration of large, soft, passive breasts.

"Not the sort of thing to hang in a bedroom," he grumbled in self-defence.

"Which?"

"All these paintings of rocks. I did them as a kind of endurance test." She wouldn't have the eye to see through his dishonesty.

"Why shouldn't I, too, pass the test?" she asked very coldly.

Perhaps she had passed it. So much obsessed by his own paintings, by the love, disgust, and at times fear, which they roused in him, he had hardly noticed the bedroom. Apart from the paintings there was very little in it: an unexpectedly virginal dressing-table, and a bed narrow enough to appear ostentatious.

"In any case," she said, "I find the paintings far less cerebral than you want to suggest; and as I'm the one who owns them I see them as I like to see them. Look at these"—she touched the sleeping-animal rocks which had upset a critic's sensibility when they were first exhibited—"actually sentimental. I almost said 'feminine,' " she added, "but perhaps it wouldn't convey what I mean. On the whole I find women less feminine than they're supposed to be, and certainly more realistic than men."

Her grey eyes were picking holes in him, though her breasts, pointed at him through the white silk, accused him less than he would have expected, far less, in fact, than Nance's big clanging doorbells: those had accused him most of the time.

Suddenly the outer Mrs Davenport seemed to soften, as though she had become engrossed in a private vision. "This is the painting which appeals to me, I sometimes think, more than any I own."

She liked to stress ownership: or she chose her words carelessly: or they interpreted meanings differently. In any case she had dismissed him as she advanced on her "Marriage of Light."

She was mouthing: ". . . all that I understand as beauty . . ."

If she had known poor bloody Nance.

". . . in the morning when they open the curtains—that's its best moment."

In her conventual room.

". . . after they've left me I lie looking at it. At my 'Marriage of Light.'"

In that narrow bed: even now grinding her neck against the pillow.

She was exposing herself completely. Here was another one, he saw, offering her throat to be cut, but by a more tortuous, a more jagged knife. Well, he wouldn't' accept the invitation to a second murder.

Rising from her vision, Mrs Davenport turned to him, smiling a smile of deliberate sweetness. "I wonder whether I don't understand your paintings better than you do yourself."

If he wasn't visibly rocking on his heels, she must have smelled his rage, but pretended she hadn't; the social graces were so well developed in her.

"Actually, Hurtle—I'm going to call you 'Hurtle'—I sometimes feel artists are so preoccupied with technical problems they lose sight of what they're trying to achieve. That's why so many paintings, poems, remain technical exercises. Only the great artist"—she was observing him closely—"*senses* where he is going, though he may not understand."

She was so clearly convinced, he felt confused in his reactions to what she had been expounding. She had turned him into a clumsy plumber: or Pa Duffield's boy.

"I'd like to discuss that with you," he collected himself enough to say, from inside his imitation of a Bond Street suit, "because I think you may be right."

But Mrs Davenport had finished dispensing her patronage. She was reminded by the chiming of a little crystal clock, perfect also in its way.

She said: "I'm sorry. I must turn you out," still smiling with an exquisite clarity and reasonableness.

For the moment there was no point at which he might pierce her composure. She was too well encased in the shining armour of the fashionable-rich. The most he could do was cultivate his own ungraciousness while remaining in her power, for she had got possession of that only important part of him: his paintings.

As he began lumbering unwillingly away from them, he forced out what he intended as an accusation, but which could have sounded like a reproach: "One of the eternal dinner parties! I can imagine the sort of thing: barristers, stockbrokers, perhaps a scoured grazier or two—and the successful wives!"

She gave what no doubt her satellites would have considered a "delicious chuckle," pressed a bell, and came and linked her arm with his.

"As a matter of fact," she told him, "I'm planning to eat a poached egg—off a tray—in bed. I've had a rather trying afternoon."

Walking towards the stairs, they shared the intimacy of her revelation, and he allowed himself to enjoy not only her poached egg, but the casual motion of their conspiring bodies.

"May I pay you a visit? May I telephone you?" she asked when they had reached the half-landing and were standing underneath the Courtneys' Boudin.

"There isn't a telephone." He couldn't help feeling proud of his wisdom.

She didn't appear to notice it, however. She answered with the same grey-eyed seriousness which was one of the more attractive aspects of her strength: "There are other ways of getting in touch."

He was looking into her cleavage. The scent of that elaborate cleanliness on which she had endless leisure and money to spend might have turned him into frustrated sculpture if the parlourmaid hadn't been stationed at the foot of the stairs. He realized how expertly his departure had been organized.

"Thanks, Boo!" She might even have planned that he should sound adolescent in his leave-taking.

But as he started down the last flight, trying out the carpet with suspicious feet, she leaned forward and caught him by the sleeve, and kissed him coolly on the mouth.

"It was so good—" she breathed, "so good to find you again—after all this time."

Emily's presence and their returned youth made it look so chaste.

He stumbled on, to the foot of the stairs, where the maid waited approvingly, repowdered in the meantime to the roots of her moustache.

He didn't look back because he was afraid he might have caught Olivia Davenport frowning, or wiping her mouth, and in any case the front doorbell was ringing: it was rung a brassy twice.

"Oh dear, I can't stand bells!" Emily was giggling and jittering. "Never get used to 'em! It's me nerves: bells give them a start."

At the door a young man from a florist's van handed in a sheaf of roses: the tissue of white paper made the perfect white buds look frostily remote.

"Lovely roses! But they don't last." Emily laughed, a few grains of powder trembling on the hairs of a mole. "Good thing they don't— the house 'ud be chock-a-block."

He would have liked to read the card inside the semi-transparent paper; no doubt the maid didn't need to.

She was still nursing the veiled roses as he got away up the slope. He walked, and walked. He walked through Rose Bay, Double Bay, and was halfway past Rushcutters, when his intention had been to hail a taxi in the beginning. At least physical exertion restored him to himself: he began to see how he would convey Rhoda Courtney's skeletal pelvis. He would always have his painting.

The house shook as he slammed the door: then the dust the silence settling.

He was working at four versions of "Pythoness," eagerly and angrily. So as not to interrupt, he was living on hard-boiled eggs, and had grown costive. He found himself straining and groaning on the seat. In the end it worried him more than Rhoda's transparent, milky flesh. There was a smell of sour milk in Miss Gilderthorp's scullery, subtler than the smell of the dunny at the back; he preferred the dunny to the French-smelling water-closet in the house.

The day the front doorbell rang he had a fit of Emily Davenport's nerves, but his constipation allowed him to button at once, and quickly reach the door.

In the porch the telegraph lad was lounging and picking.

He said: "It's a reply-paid," without appearing impressed by anything about old Mr nutty Duffield.

Mr Duffield read: "Must repeat must see you Friday pm whatever time convenient wire love Olivia."

The contorting boy asked: "Want me to take the reply?" He was scratching himself through his flies.

"Yes."

Old Duffield was scooting down the hall and back. Worked up. Couldn't keep his mouth shut.

He said: "Yes, thank you, Andy. I shan't be a minute writing it out."

He was an awful sight: an old, nutty man, covered in paint.

Old Duffield held the form against a tree-trunk so you couldn't hardly read what he was writing: "Yes Friday any time provided visit short working Hurtle."

Hurtle?

The telegraph boy lifted his long leg and settled his serge crutch in the saddle.

Olivia Davenport was due on Friday afternoon. In a two-day panic which preceded her visit, he had tried to introduce some order into his house. He had never attempted it before, and hardly knew where to begin, wandering from room to room trailing an old shirt for duster. The shadow of his prospective visitor, standing between him and his work, made him hate her. He flung aside one of the finnicky chairs, and a leg flew off willingly. So he gave up. Why should this woman, whose detachment was a mask for a meddle-some nature, want to interrupt a life she couldn't possibly under-stand? Everything about it was foreign to her: the dust pockets, the brooding plush, the ruined conservatory with its leathery plants and its chrysalides—all necessary to him by now, as on another level, his work. But even more disagreeable than the lack of understand-ing she must bring to his house, to his manner of living, was his suspicion—no, the certainty—it was downright shocking—that Olivia Davenport understood his painting.

She arrived at three-thirty on the Friday afternoon.

As he opened the door the car which had brought her was driven away so discreetly it became noticeable to the whole street, in much the same way as Mrs Davenport's simple black drew attention to her elegance. She was very plainly dressed indeed, excepting for the rope of knotted pearls, each so large anyone would have taken them for false, and on her hat a little wreath of intermingled amethysts and diamonds. The hat was in the shape of a helmet, with a glint of metal from the cocks' feathers curved in a sickle under her chin. Her face was longer, the line of the jaw more em-phatic than he remembered; it could have made a less wealthy woman look plain.

"I feel *horribly* guilty taking up *any* of your precious time." It might have been sincerely meant, but she had forgotten to change her voice: this was the one she used in the other world.

She seemed to realize her oversight at once, for he detected an irritated preoccupation.

He said: "It won't be wasted. Nothing is. If I'd felt it was going to be a waste of time, I needn't have let you in, need I?"

"That's true," she agreed: a little dry, but without abandoning the politeness she had been taught.

She came in, and he thought he might not have been able to stop her if he had wanted to; entry was her birthright. She smelled very fresh: of bunched, sweet, cottage flowers—a scent which didn't go with her appearance any more than with the smell of gas from the meter under the araucaria. (One day get it seen to.)

"You won't find it very comfortable here," he felt he had to explain. "I bought all this junk with the house. I haven't done anything about it yet."

"It looks fascinating. Lovely old things!" But her sigh cancelled her formal approval.

Helpfully, she seated herself on a tightly buttoned sofa in the living-room. She kept her gloves on.

Seeing her out of her water made him warm towards her again. He wanted to sit beside her, and did.

"I was afraid you mightn't like the place," he said. "Maman would have disapproved," and remembering the ritual words: "Don't you want to take your hat off?"

She expressed a kind of wry surprise. "No. My hair's awful," though from what you could see it must be perfect: as helmeted as her helmet of a hat.

She did begin to take her gloves off. He watched her hands emerge, whiter for the black skirt, finally the crimson talons.

The hands thus exposed, the simple dress could no longer pretend to disguise.

She lowered her eyelids and said: "Hurtle, I hope you're going to show me what you're working on."

"Yes. Presently. There's time."

He looked for rings. Not even a wedding ring. Two husbands, and her hands still chaste.

"I'd be curious to know about the husbands."

"I wonder you need ask. Everybody knows more about them than I know myself."

"And still more curious about the lovers."

"There aren't any!"

He plaited a hand with one of hers.

"Oh no! Definitely none! Not again!" She was passionately against it.

"Am I condemned—in particular?"

"Not you in particular." Then she added in a quieter tone: "Yes—*you!*"

They were left looking at each other's hands. Though she hadn't attempted to withdraw, her fingers remained cool and unresponsive in the knot of his blunter, harder ones, grubby with half-removed paint and ingrained dirt.

She appeared fascinated by the veins in the back of his hand, but threw off her trance, and said in her more worldly voice: "I've lost my appetite for suffering!" while looking at him with an expression of bright greed.

He remembered the cakes he had bought, and went to make tea. Of course the gas-burners were clogged. Where would he take her if she wanted to use the lavatory? Out to the dunny? What had she got up to after he left her alone? Most women would have come barging into the kitchen with ironic or unhelpful suggestions.

He looked in once, on the quiet, and watched her bending over a water colour he had done as a youth: of Alfreda Courtney in a yellow dress. It became obvious that Mrs Davenport was the most insidious kind of deceiver.

"Those pearls—aren't you afraid of burglars?" he asked in a deliberately blatant voice on bringing in the tea.

"I'm not interested in jewellery," she said, to make him look as vulgar as he deserved.

Actually she was looking at the cakes.

They were the little frosted apathetic cakes in paper frills from a shop in a poorer suburb such as his. The thick white cups, the only ones he had, were rattling against the tin tray. The brown teapot stood firm: it was solider.

"Well, the paintings, then—thugs could break in and—probably not steal—slash them."

"That," she said, tearing her glance away from the cakes and giving him her most brilliant smile, "that would be an act of God!"

Coming from Olivia Davenport, it made him snigger. She was rich enough to dispense with God: as for himself, not exactly rich, but pretty well endowed.

"Of course you're heavily insured." He was letting her see him at his worst.

"Oh yes—*insurance*! But what does it cover?"

Was it possible that Olivia Davenport couldn't be got at?

They sat drinking the strong red kitchen tea: the same he liked to drink before starting work, because it woke him up and steadied the nerves. Olivia refused the cakes, but at one stage in their conversation she fingered a paper frill with one of her long red nails, holding her head on one side as though the cakes were a work of art she was making up her mind about. Instead of waking her, the tea seemed to have made her dreamy. He watched her eyes through the rising steam. There was a faint sheen of perspiration on her powdered nose. Again a flaw, or sign of defencelessness, made him feel more tender towards her.

"When I was living in Peru—with my first husband," she began to explain tentatively, "I experimented a little with coca. The Indians chew it, to make their lives more endurable."

"And was it rewarding?"

"To me, slightly nauseating at first, then—nothing. I only did it to please my husband, who'd already formed the habit. He had an idea something was eluding him. He was convinced I had some secret I was keeping from him—perhaps *the* secret. As he became more degraded and desperate, he began to feel that if I joined him in taking the drug, I might share the enlightenment he suspected me of having. So to pacify him I took to coca. And couldn't share my 'secret.' I couldn't even share his degradation. I failed him in this, too! Oh, he died most horribly, in every way unsatisfied! I don't want to think about it."

"Did you love your husband?"

"Why—yes! Of course I loved him." She put down the thick-lipped tea-cup as though she wanted to be rid of it. "There are different ways of loving, aren't there? Poor Pepe! I felt sorry for him."

She got up, dusting from her black skirt the crumbs from the cakes she hadn't eaten.

She adopted a slightly swashbuckling stance. "What about the paintings you're going to show me?"

Those husbands.

"Has nothing ever eluded you?" he asked.

"That isn't to the point," she said in her high, clear, worldly voice; she frowned, too, though not enough to suggest her equanimity had been disturbed.

"These are all works of mine." He jerked his head at the surrounding walls.

There were, in fact, several drawings, water colours, and small careful oils of an early period, which had become part of the sentimental furniture of life. He no longer regarded them as pictures. He didn't want to show Boo Davenport his paintings.

"I don't think you take me seriously," she said.

While crouched forward on the edge of the sofa, halfway between staying and rising, he had put his hands over his face, and found himself agreeably situated: he could look at his unwelcome visitor through the bars of his fingers, if he wished, or withdraw into the darkness of his hands. It occurred to him how uncomfortable the tightly buttoned sofa had always been, but he knew in his heart he would never change it. The uncomfortable sofa, the physical discomfort of most of a lifetime, was of minor importance to the irritation caused by Olivia Davenport's presence. In the darkness of his hands the problems of Rhoda's flesh flickered tantalizingly. Sometimes he was closer to, sometimes farther from solving them. Her skin had the transparency of thinned-out watery milk, the shrill smell of milk on the turn; while under the skin the flesh should have the tones, rose to yellow, of skinned chickens. From behind his fingers he could recall the pliability of chickens' breastbones. He had never touched Rhoda's breastbone, but it must have had the same sickening pliability as those of the dead chickens.

He shivered for his discovery: when through his fingers here was this Boo this Olivia Davenport wasting his time.

"I can't think why you sent me that telegram," he said irritably, "why you had to see me—to tell me about Peru and your husband's vice."

Now that his face was hidden from her, she would probably reveal the real reason.

"Don't be childish! I wanted to see the paintings!" She sounded positively passionate; there were knots, he saw, in her long throat.

"It wasn't me, then." He laughed, sniffing through his agreeably protective hands. "You wanted to dig up the paintings—your acquisitive instinct at work again—perhaps get hold of something good that isn't for sale."

Mrs Davenport looked at her watch. In her extreme politeness she spoke in the most cultivated accent she knew: nothing refaned-

Australian about it, very cold and incisive; she had had the best elocution teachers. "If you'd rather, I can walk in the street and admire the scenery till my car calls for me in half an hour." At the same time she picked up her bag, opened it, shut it, without discovering what, if anything, she had been looking for.

He was particularly pleased with those passionate knots in her throat, the long legs, the useless hands. He could have fucked Olivia Davenport, and risen from their crunching bed still in a splather to give the last touch to Rhoda Courtney's salt-cellars.

Suddenly he removed his hands from his face: he felt so cheerful. "You're not angry with me, are you? for asking a few questions?"

"Why should I be angry?" She obviously was: those who have money are always angry to realize it isn't of value.

"Silly old Boo Hollingrake!" He smacked her on the bottom as vulgarly as he knew how.

Then he led the way upstairs. Accepting the role he had given her, she followed.

"Go in there," he ordered when they reached the landing, "into the front bedroom."

She went in as he began to open up the little junk-room.

In front, at that hour, the light would be all wrong: the dark green reflections of the araucaria. He would try out a few old experiments or failures, and get rid of her. She would go down devotedly satisfied to her long black sugar-fed limousine.

She sat at one end of the bed, on the rusty wire, leaning slightly against the roll of lumpy kapok, the stained ticking. While he was bringing out a few failed canvases and botched boards she looked as detached as she had seemed telling about Peru.

Give her a shot of something.

"What's that?" she asked, her expression returning from a distance.

"That's a drawing—oh, a sort of night-piece—oh, something I knocked off recently, and may come back to, when I've finished what I'm working on."

"Isn't it horrible! I don't mean aesthetically," she corrected herself. "Aesthetically I think it could be wonderful." She knew all the moves. "What's this figure?"

"That's a grocer. His name was Cutbush. He's machine-gunning the lovers."

"I realized that."

He began to put the drawing away. Shouldn't have shown it.

"What's the significance of the moon?" she asked.

"Ah," he said guardedly, "the moon!"

"It isn't the grocer who predominates, or the unfortunate lovers. It's really a painting of the moon, isn't it? Why have you made it so vindictive, when it should be gentle and reconciling?"

"Oh God!"

He must get the drawing away. He had declared himself in front of Cutbush, whom he probably wouldn't see again: he couldn't admit to any weakness in front of Olivia Davenport.

"It's too early to discuss a drawing I may develop as a painting." He was conscious of the pedantry in his excuse.

While returning the drawing to the stack he was appalled by the silence he had left behind in the front room.

"But what are you working on now?" she called, her voice too rich, too vibrant.

He felt too tired, too awkward, stacking his paintings and drawings in the suffocating junk-cupboard. There was a child's potty-chair he often wondered how Miss Gilderthorp had acquired. Or was it her own? Her old shrivelled buttocks had once been little rosy ones.

Olivia had come out on the landing. ". . . to mistrust me when I could be your friend—when I probably understand you better than anyone has ever—when I make absolutely no demands . . ."

Because he was afraid, he didn't want to leave this small airless room, with its scurf of dead blowflies and the unexplained potty-chair, for the hazards of the landing.

"What's in there?" she suddenly asked, in a pure but imperious girl's voice. "In the back room?"

He shot out. "That's my bedroom." He sounded as pure as she, but strangled.

As she was going in, he caught her by the rope of pearls, which held, surprisingly: he was lugged in, united to her by the pearls.

They pulled up together in front of Rhoda Courtney.

When she had looked, Boo closed her eyes; she began to sway her head; she began to moan convulsively, and with an uncharacteristic lack of restraint. He was reminded of Nance on the occasions when she had reached a true orgasm. So, now, Boo Hollingrake sounded both appeased and shattered by her experience.

In self-defence she cried out: "How could you be so cruel to poor little Rhoda?"

It was his turn to become emotional; in an attempt to disguise these emotions he heard himself shouting: "How can you say it's cruel? It's the truth!" He heard his strained boy's voice protesting against unjust accusations; while the glass showed him as a handsome, dissipated, middle-aged man making excuses for his weaknesses.

Olivia-Boo was distractedly moving about the room as though stunned by a whole family of Rhoda Courtneys. He had already painted several versions in various stages of abstraction, and would probably need several more.

"How is it," she gasped jerkily, "why, I wonder, have you made no effort to find her, when she seems to have meant so much to you?"

"You know the way it is," he answered, in a subsided, bluntened voice, "the life you lead—you don't lead it—it gets thrust on you, and carries you in a direction it's difficult to alter."

She kept returning to the original, comparatively naturalistic portrait of Rhoda, which didn't satisfy him as it was.

She began to whimper: ". . . why *I* made no effort to get in touch?"

She was drawing him into a union of tearful complicity; whereas the only relationship he could envisage with Olivia Davenport was one that displayed panache.

He was relieved when the doorbell rang.

Olivia immediately dried her eyes. "That must be my man," she said in an attempt at her normal tone of voice.

It was an opportunity to start easing her out of the room.

But she had become completely, and considering the speed of the transformation, surprisingly self-possessed. "You'll probably hate me," she said, "but would you consider selling me the one on the easel? And I don't expect a studio deal."

"Not for all the sugar in the world!" He was pushing, shouting, laughing at her; with none of it did he appear to have upset her equanimity, so he couldn't resist trying out an even cruder insult: "Those husbands you killed off—I expect they discovered too late they were diabetic!"

She decided to ignore that one too. "It's not only as a painting that it haunts me, it's part of my life—yours too—that we've lost, Hurtle."

The importance she apparently attached to the painting began to make him feel humbler; and perhaps because the chauffeur had been stationed in the street, just as Emily the parlourmaid had been stood on guard at the foot of the stairs, he would have liked to offer Olivia a genuine tenderness which hadn't yet been asked for, and which certain conventions and their own natures might always prevent them expressing.

"Perhaps I'll *give* you the painting—when I've finished with it; and after we know all about each other." A kind of love token.

As they stood on the landing his hands were outspread to test whether she was prepared to accept his advance.

But she laughed and said: "The thought of knowing everything about anybody gives me the horrors!"

He could only see her back as she was walking ahead of him down the stairs. She went buoyantly enough, considering the depths to which he had proposed they should plunge together.

"Twice I've found out all there is to know about a person," she said in an almost jaunty voice. "I haven't the courage to face it again. I thought I'd made that clear in the beginning."

She had taken such precautions to protect herself against the future, he was tempted to push her down those steep stairs; but Olivia Davenport might have survived.

In the stuffy living-room below, with its islands of bourgeois furniture, the climate was more temperate.

"Oh dear," she twittered, "you've made me keep my hairdresser waiting. You don't realize, darling, what you've let me in for."

Since she had returned to the surface, recovered her handbag, and could repair the damage to herself, she was full of the affectations and inflections of the class to which he had been given the opportunity of belonging.

She was mumbling both her lipstick and her words: ". . . must keep in touch . . . to meet my friends . . . some of them could be useful to you, Hurtle darling . . . mm-mm . . . though I don't want to coerce you, you know."

The point of the crimson lipstick withdrew—*click*—into its gold sheath. She smiled at him out of her slick mouth. Her grey eyes had never looked so gravely brilliant and detached.

"There are two people in particular I'd like you to meet: two of my dearest closest friends."

He couldn't have felt less interested. "Are they from the old days?" he asked apathetically. "Anybody I used to know? Or might have heard of?"

"No. They're comparatively recent—quite recent, in fact. They're visiting Australia."

He was reminded of Maman, who had never been able to distinguish between acquaintances and friends, or whose friends were all acquaintances.

"Which sex?" he asked with increasing disinterest.

"One of each." Olivia Davenport composed a dimple in the right corner of her mouth: it made her long face look slightly depraved.

Moving towards the door, she launched forth on what could have been a rehearsed leave-taking. "At the risk of embarrassing, I shall thank you for an *illuminating* experience. Disturbing, too—horribly." She turned in the hall for not longer than an instant. "Are you embarrassed?" she rattled on, showing him the enamelled whites of her eyes. "I don't believe you are: you're too vain, and enjoy what you do to people."

An old bamboo hatstand threatened to topple as she brushed past it with a little less than her usual grace.

Was he vain? He was tired. He was glad he would soon be alone with his paintings. He had never thought of himself as vain.

Whether it was true or not, he'd better put on a smile while dragging the door open for her; but he could feel the smile thinning into a simper as he gurgled and glugged inanely in the idiom used by the Davenport world: "Bye bye Boo bye dear see you next time watch where you're going Boo that's where the dogs do it," his mouth stretched like a piece of elastic about to perish: when he wasn't old, any more than vain.

The chauffeur, a youngish man with the servile good looks not uncommon to his occupation, shut her in. Mrs Davenport arranged herself in a curved position. As she was driven away from the slum in which she had been visiting, she made a sign with her bag from the other side of the glass. She wore the expression of having accomplished something, but nonetheless she felt relieved now that it was over: she was probably dying for the attentions of the hairdresser's plump white pansy hands.

Duffield slammed the door after realizing he had been standing there longer than was necessary.

From now on Olivia invited him, and he went to her house on several occasions, partly out of curiosity, and partly to exorcise staleness when it threatened his relationship with his work. He soon realized that to accept her invitations was to experience the refinements of boredom, though Olivia herself never failed to give a technically accomplished performance. She was expert at springing little surprises: like a new jewel, specially designed by Cartier or Bulgari; or a visiting professor of Chinese. She had the reputation of being educated, and certainly she had amassed an exotic litter of knowledge. He had overheard her remark to a distinguished Orientalist: "I can't say I *know* Chinese, but confess to four hundred characters," while allowing the scholar to take her in to dinner. Perhaps her four hundred characters got her by, with the help of Schiaparelli and a cabochon ruby or two.

Mrs Davenport's friends could be divided roughly into three categories. There were the hectic, iridescent, frittering fly-by-nights. Olivia had a weakness for the rag bag, and these were her collection of gay snippets: gin would never drown them, nor Benzedrine overcome their colds, only make them more endemic. The fritterers held their drinks rather high and downed them quickly. They appeared to know everybody, but everybody: their conversation was a perpetual tip-and-run.

Then there was the old, slow, swollen-veined, heavily tactical train of tortoises, moving their arthritic necks in the direction of the conversation they were making: some of them relatives—revered, theoretically loved—old barristers, doctors, heaviest of all, the graziers, and old lipstuck ladies who forgot what they had begun to tell, but continued bravely throwing in Galsworthy, Asprey, and Our Pioneer Families. All of them tortoises, when not elephants, sometimes a stiff flamingo, but old: some of them on sticks, some with signet rings eating into skin-cancered hands. All had known her so long, they enjoyed the privilege of referring to their hostess as "Boo": she might have been hundreds-and-thousands, the way they sprinkled their anecdotes with her name.

Finally, there were the foreigners. Olivia adored consuls, and the English she had met on board ship or in hotels at Cannes or St Moritz. She was most nearly taken down, but never quite, by an English accent. She loved to speak French with the Italians, and Chinese with the Japanese, and they seemed to understand one another.

How had she got Chinese? He must remember to ask her on some private occasion, though Olivia wouldn't always tell.

At one of her parties she came up to him, linked arms, trickling diamonds over his sleeve, and casually mentioned: "I thought I had something of interest for you, but they couldn't stay. *He* isn't at all *well*. He suffers from a *gall*-bladder, or something."

"Who?"

"But darling," she said, in the amusing-peevish voice she sometimes affected at parties, "my Greeks—the Pavloussis. I never stop telling you. He owns ships. Disgustingly rich. He's thinking of starting a passenger-cargo line between here and Europe."

She pronounced "Europe" as though tasting her own party for a flavour she feared it might lack. She narrowed her eyes, and dared him to reject a mystique of worldliness she wanted him to believe in. He even suspected that if he hadn't been present and her guests demanded appeasement, she would have denied her faith in the paintings: such was her appetite for superficiality and approval. His was nil; though he took them from time to time in homeopathic doses, not altogether hopefully, as a cure for accidie.

Because he hadn't expressed regret for her vanished Greeks, Boo Davenport said: "I'm afraid we bore you, Hurtle. We're not *clever* enough." She deliberately used the word "clever," which he had discovered was charged with mock-innocent chic for members of her clan. Annoyance wouldn't allow her to lay claim to one grain of intellect; she let it be understood she shared the native idiocy of her childhood companions and approving elders, who otherwise might have criticized her relationship with the painter as "perverse": which, no doubt, it was.

He couldn't help laughing, and she couldn't help asking: "What are you laughing at?" Her irritation increased when he began silently stroking her back as they stood facing the roomful of guests.

In his gyrations, he had noticed the naked back decorated with a number of little rosy bows, or lovers'-knots, or no—bite marks.

"Have you a maid who dislikes you too much to protect you?" he whispered as he accepted one of the ritual kisses she was moved to dispense.

"Why?" she asked, swallowing her breath abruptly.

She began touching her thighs, feeling her wrists, glancing down her cleavage.

"There's Gladswood," she admitted. "She's given notice, just when I was on the point of asking her to leave."

Shortly after, she found an excuse for withdrawing from her guests, and returned draped in a lace shawl, so ostentatiously modest it went with nothing about her.

"It belonged to a great-aunt," she told him. "I believe she was married in it." The present wearer's attempt at pious serenity still didn't make the shawl hers.

"I know you're accusing me," she said in a moment they had to themselves, "and one day I'll explain."

While recognizing in Olivia Davenport a core he desired to possess, and which she was apparently determined he shouldn't, he escaped from her parties with a sense of relief: at least the purpose of his going there. In the white hours of morning, sticky with dew and Moreton Bay fig, his head was clear as he followed the silver tram-line on foot, round the scalloped bays, then up the hill to his own darkness, with its clutter of partly developed ideas and smells of dust and cold fat. Upstairs, he would start walking from room to room, dragging the long flex behind him, hanging the electric pear above half-finished paintings, which only now revealed themselves.

On one occasion, however, the electric moment occurred in Mrs Davenport's "salon." It was one of the flatter evenings, after supper: collars were wilting on male necks; ladies were gazing out across the water with a nostalgia born of night and perspiration; when a young girl, white as lard, of turnip forms, some protégé or relative the hostess hadn't considered important enough to introduce, fell into an armchair, turned up her eyes, opened her mouth, and began to moan, then laugh, sob, thump, and heave, rolling her white eyeballs, thrashing the upholstery with the calves hockey had given her.

There was considerable commotion. Some of the guests, determined that nothing was happening, walked stiffly away, engaged in what looked like a conversation too grave to be interrupted. Others, younger, drunker, dragged one another into neighbouring rooms, from which their partly suppressed giggles burst in polyphonic spurts round the convulsive solo of the anonymous virtuoso.

"Won't somebody *do* something?" hissed one of the aged tortoise-ladies out of her cuirass of lamé and sapphires, though an energetic barrister had dashed to the telephone and rung almost every doctor in town: all of whom were socially engaged.

Actually the old lady was looking, as she spoke, at the painter who happened to be standing beside her. Her sparkling claws might at any moment fasten themselves in his arm.

"It's frightful!" she rasped. "Do look! She's having a kind of fit. So dreadful for the parents: an epileptic on their hands!"

It was frightful; so much so, he couldn't stop looking at it: the girl tossing and lowing, sometimes the colour of her own cerise taffeta, sometimes washed white, or drenched with a sickly plant-green.

Her mother in black, her jet trembling in a vertigo of anguish or resentment, was kneeling beside her. "Tell me, darling," she commanded, "what is it? Baby? What is it you want? Or what do I do to you? Only tell me—my only interest is your happiness. Oh! Oh *Muriel!*"

The mother's words acted like a blow: the girl gulped; then she threw back her head and stuck out her cerise tongue, before lolling forward again, rolling her china eyeballs.

For an instant the possessed one glanced at the only other of her kind, and they were swept up, and united by sheet lightning, as they could never have been on the accepted plane.

She looked at him, and he saw past her green-sickness and menstrual torments into the hazy future of a bungled marriage and hushed-up attempt at suicide. If his had been the right knife, she might have planted it there and then in her turnip flesh, in front of an audience, and risen laughing from the death which obsessed her.

Instead she lolled and dry-retched.

Fortunately at that moment the hostess returned from supervising a detail of her party somewhere else in the house. She saw at once, and went, her flanks rippling with scales of light, and took a crystal jug, and dashed its contents of iced water into the girl's face. (The chunks of ice were, probably, not the least of the cure.)

"There—you see—hysteria!" She spoke with authority, and everybody knew Mrs Davenport was always right.

Under the shock of the iced water, and blows from the ice cubes, the girl's face certainly returned to its natural shape. Her neck looked so ashamed. The cerise dress had turned almost purple where the water had soaked in. She sat staring in horror at what were her own nipples exposed by the clinging disaster of a dress;

till a cluster of kindly ladies led the mother and daughter out: to try to restore their self-possession.

Mrs Davenport rang and asked for Emily to be sent. While less noticeable on state occasions, the parlourmaid's rank wasn't diminished: she was older and had been there longer than the more athletic, operative servants. Now she advanced, in blancoed shoes, over the dark mirrors of floors; tonight her self-importance had obviously increased.

"Tell Turner, Emily"—Mrs Davenport pretended to order, when she was in fact conferring—"tell him to run them home in the car."

Emily appeared discreetly shocked. "*Which* car, Miss Boo?"

Mrs Davenport frowned at the implication that she was ignorant of protocol; but Emily had been with them so long: as far back as a grandmother.

"Well, not the Rolls—naturally," said the mistress. "Mrs Devereux wouldn't want to be made conspicuous. Something—something *homely*: the Austin, say."

Emily looked appeased; while Mrs Davenport tore the head off a tiger lily which was going brown.

The muted guests, who had been listening, began making their excuses; though it was not the end of the party, some had suffered a genuine shock; and the most brazen of the gigglers felt they wanted to remove themselves, to be able to pull out all the stops. There was a constant sound of doors, cars, feet, lavatory cisterns. Two or three promising young men, who lived in boarding houses, slipped into the dining-room to fill with lobster salad the strong manila envelopes they had brought for that purpose.

"You're not leaving, Hurtle?" Mrs Davenport complained.

Even if she had been offering herself, he wouldn't have wanted her tonight: he was too engrossed in his vision of sheet lightning.

She followed him into the hall. "You don't think I was brutal, do you?"

"No!" he laughed. "Accomplished!"

"It was the only pratical thing to do: young girls must be saved from themselves."

When they had exchanged the conventional kiss, a heated one on her part, and he had refused several lifts, he began the walk home. There was actual lightning over the sea: silent puffs, in which he again saw the girl's eyeballs populated with the ant-forms of anxiety.

On arriving home he noted them down on a block he came across on the shelf of the bamboo hatstand. He tore off the leaves and put them away, almost at once forgetting where: Rhoda in all her aspects was his continued obsession.

He worked most of the remaining night, and began again in the afternoon, drifting from one version to the next. He slashed brutally at one Rhoda Courtney, but got what he wanted: sheet lightning invaded the eyeballs.

Olivia Davenport came to him soon after three, the hour when she must have finished lunch. She came without messengers of any kind, and no sign of a car, not even a humble Austin. Her mouth must have been done in a hurry: one arc of the bow was drawn higher than the other.

He was furious. "Why do you want to come here wasting my time?"

"Didn't you say nothing is ever wasted?"

As he was unable to contradict she pushed past him into the hall, the obscurity and airlessness of which was pervaded by her scent of flowers. Again on this occasion she was dressed in black, brief and unerring.

She made him feel older, grumbling, mumbling, unsavoury, flat-footed.

Looking at herself in the glass glued into the jungle of Miss Gilderthorp's bamboo hatstand, she said: "I know you think I'm brutal by inclination."

He laughed through the phlegm which had gathered in his chest during the concentration she had destroyed. "You wouldn't know what brutal is—to break in on somebody's work! You wouldn't know what work is, beyond composing menus, and rubbing out your armpits." He laughed through grosser phlegm than before.

She was arranging her already perfect hair. "I mean that girl," she said, "Muriel Devereux. Madge Devereux, the mother, is Mummy's second cousin."

For a moment Boo Hollingrake looked as though she had forgotten why she had come. Her nostrils narrowed in judgement on the smells of the house. Then she remembered.

She took his hands and began working on them as though they were dough, while insisting: "Let me be with you! Show me the paintings! Let me look at Rhoda!"

In her anxiety her splendid teeth had become those of a little

274

girl, with minute bubbles between them, while he was older, surlier, frowsy in his work clothes. His crutch was probably smelling of piss; but he wouldn't worry; and she would pretend not to be aware.

They were going slowly up.

He had been working in the back room, where he had slept the night before. The mattress-ticking was exposed by a ruck of grey blanket he had pushed back on waking. It was several weeks since he had stuffed the last of the sheets into the copper in the shed at the back. (Must remember to boil the sheets.)

Olivia stood at first too obviously respectful, then began prowling round with what sounded like insolent familiarity; but any attitude she adopted would have been distasteful to him. He must see that she remained behind his back.

In this way he kept his world reasonably well divided, as Olivia Davenport kept hers divided, perpetually, and expertly. He worked, at first jumpily, then with a sombre, bitter-tasting resignation through which he saw what he wanted to achieve but small chance of getting there, finally with a voluptuous directness in which his brush could do no wrong: it was continually turning blind corners to arrive at a fresh aspect of truth.

He even forgave Boo, who was so quiet he began to wonder whether she might be up to something. According to the glass, she was lying on the unmade bed, only vaguely looking at the paintings she had asked to see, perhaps already sated with them. As he continued gently stroking paint to life under the eyes of this *voyeuse*, he and Olivia could have reached one of the peaks of their relationship.

The conceit amused him, though not as much as catching sight of Mrs Davenport's reflection reaching up through its abandon to pick its nose with one long crimson fingernail.

Presently she said in a smooth, convinced voice: "You're losing her. You're giving her something Rhoda never had."

"*What?*" The shock made him tremble; he threw away the brush.

He had been working on the least figurative and probably final version of the "Pythoness at Tripod."

"Perhaps it isn't—was never intended to be Rhoda," he lied.

"That's how it began," she answered drowsily, "but became too hysterical in feeling."

He could have been struck by lightning: he was, in fact, still involved with the incident of the night before.

"Well, we know Rhoda was hysterical," Olivia went on. "But she was always conscious of the reasons for hysteria. That was her great virtue—and why you hated her. She was never a human cow driven by something she couldn't see or understand."

Olivia opened her eyes and dared him to contradict.

"What do you mean—hysterical—a human cow?" Of course he understood, but that didn't prevent him trying to laugh it off; he resented her intuition.

"You know perfectly well"—she wouldn't leave it alone—"that poor dumb lump of a girl: Muriel Devereux. You're bringing the two of them together—Rhoda and Muriel—to suit your own purposes. Is it honest?"

"Only the painting can answer that—when it's finished."

He could have strangled Olivia. As he approached her he could have shouted: I am what matters; without me the painting couldn't happen, and you and your kind would have that much less to babble about.

Instead he said humbly: "You're right, Boo; but the painter's only human after all, and uses human means to disguise his shortcomings."

Yes, he could have killed her, but bent over her and touched her hair with this rather admirable humility he had found.

Suddenly she drew down his face and thrust her tongue into his mouth; when she wasn't lashing at his tongue with hers, she was gouging his eyes with her cheekbones.

"I could show you," she kept gasping, "a trick or two."

A bracelet of heavy gold-and-cornelian seals kept bludgeoning, and ringing in his left ear. It looked as though she meant to stun him into subjection: till he put his hand.

Then it was she who began to tremble. "Oh no! No!" She arched her back, sawing against the pillow, trying to get round the knee which was pinning her.

"Lie still!" he was begging her at one stage, because he might, quite sincerely, have taught her something she didn't know about.

But Olivia Davenport seemed determined to demonstrate that rape is not inevitable.

When she was mistress of the situation, they lay looking at each other from the slipless pillow, and Olivia started explaining, using her most candidly grey-eyed expression: "Actually, I came here this afternoon for a reason you wouldn't guess." She hesitated, then announced with a touch of what was coyness for her, though in the key to which Olivia Davenport climbed for social commerce: "I've had a little windfall." After another hesitation she asked: "Hurtle, I wonder whether it would make you happy if I bought you a nice car?"

He couldn't believe in her innocence; he sat up shouting: "With gold spittoons? And a gold pisspot for emergencies?"

She said meekly, but again unconvincingly: "I was only thinking of your happiness."

While he crawled about the floor searching for the brush—his special one, which he had so rashly thrown down—she was arranging her hair in front of the original and most naturalistic version of Rhoda Courtney. Although he couldn't have admitted it, he was proud of the painting: it was so translucent.

"We must find Rhoda," Boo had decided dreamily. "I feel she'd do both of us good."

On his hands and knees amongst the fluff and splinters as he searched for the evasive brush, he couldn't make sense of any such sentiments.

"How—do us *good*? Rhoda was never a saint."

"She's your sister."

"Not even that. She's a malicious hunchback, if we have to admit the truth."

"We both loved her."

"Oh balls!"

Boo Hollingrake didn't hear, but Olivia Davenport launched herself in the higher key she favoured for social intercourse: "I *must* produce my friends the Pavloussis. I shall give a *formal* party—a dinner—so that the gall-bladder can't escape: provided he accepts in the first place; but *she*'ll make him." Olivia laughed for her strategy. "Cosma, poor darling, is a bit of a bore. I adore him. And Hero is doing him an honour by being his wife. I love her."

"Who?"

"Hero. They pronounce it differently."

He had found his brush. "Why do I have to meet these Greeks?"

"Because I'd like to think I've contributed something, if not to your happiness, to your work."

After that he let her out. They seemed agreed nothing further could be accomplished for the moment.

It was some time before Mrs Davenport was able to compose her dinner party, because the Pavloussis were in Tahiti, and at one point it looked as though they might return to Athens from there, through Panama. Pavloussis was not only hypochondriac, he was so enormously rich he could afford to change his mind without warning and for no very convincing reason: except that now he had more or less concluded his business in Australia; his representatives could dispose of the rented house and their two cars, and arrange for the dog, cats, and aviaries to follow them to Greece. (All these animal and bird possessions, together with a little part-aboriginal girl, had been acquired by the Pavloussis since their arrival in Sydney.)

Mrs Davenport sent Duffield written messages every other day to keep him in touch with the Pavloussis situation. The notes were delivered by the chauffeur in one or other of the Davenport limousines, together with jars of *marrons glacés*, tins of grouse, and, more appropriately, Hymettus honey. Often he didn't read the letters; but it would have been foolish to waste the food. Particularly he enjoyed the honey: in one tin there was the corpse of an imprisoned bee, which he ate as an experiment, but forgot to notice whether the bee itself tasted any different from the honey which had both nourished and killed; he was too engrossed in a drawing he was making, in which twin eyeballs opened into avenues of experience.

He did read Olivia's crucial note, because he was forced to make use of it; he had run out of paper in the dunny at the back.

. . . if you write down 28th April, Hurtle: the Pavloussis will dine with me that night, and are already looking forward to their meeting with you.

Cosma has been *soi-disant* ill, on a diet of toast and Vichy at Papeete. Rather than attempt the long journey through the Canal, he will return to Sydney to consult a Jewish doctor who knows his peculiarities. (Cosma insists that doctors must have a dash of Jewish.) I do hope you will like Cosma. He is, I must admit, a funny old koala with black eyelids, which must have grown blacker from Vichy, and hypochondria, and toast.

I think it is my darling Hero who has forced him to listen to reason. I long to see her. She has fallen in love with Australia. However, she too has her problems: her Maltese dog is sick; then there is this little aborigine—Soso they call her, though her name is Alice, whom Cosma insisted on more or less adopting for humane reasons. You will *adore* Hero.

I have not yet decided whom to ask on the night: I want it to be intimate and *sympathique*. I want us to remember it.

I have sold the Léger, unashamedly, to somebody who doesn't know it's a bad one. Why not, if he's happy? Really that Léger was *the* great mistake of my life; that is what comes of relying on agents and dealers instead of giving the matter *the benefit of one's own judgement*.

Dearest Hurtle, you should pat me on the head for not disturbing you at your work.

In haste,
I love you!
Boo

Shall engage the Italian woman for prawn cutlets 28th as you so adore the ones she does.

When he had read the letter he wiped himself with it, not from malice, but because there was no other way out.

The dunny at the back, though pretty thoroughly trussed with bignonia, enticed the morning sun through its open door. In this shrine to light it pleased him to sit and discover fresh forms amongst the flaking whitewash, to externalize his thoughts in pencilled images, some of these as blatant as a deliberate fart, some so tentative and personal he wouldn't have trusted them to other eyes. Once he had recorded:

God the Vivisector
God the Artist
God

surrounding with thoughtful piecrust the statement he had never succeeded in completing. On the whole it didn't disturb him not to know what he believed in—beyond his own powers, the unalterable landscape of childhood, and the revelations of light.

It surprised him to find he had scribbled on a patch of whitewash after reading Olivia Davenport's informative letter: *My Maltese dog is sick . . .*

Out of respect for Olivia's sense of ritual he had taken his dinner jacket to the cleaner, and would smell of it. Not that it mattered. It was more serious when the cleaner's tag caught in the zipper, and he wasted half an hour freeing himself. So he was late reaching the house, when he had planned to arrive in good time, even before the hostess had come down, while the canvas was still, so to speak, virgin. On such occasions he liked to help himself to a couple of stiff ones, after which his body and mind became supple enough to cope with the hazards of composition; for experience had taught him that all parties are partly your responsibility, the horrors more so than the triumphs.

On the occasion of Mrs Davenport's intimate dinner for her Greek friends her house was splendidly floodlit. No crevice of it was exposed to the dangers of mystery. Its extra-solid, white-drenched mass and the increased formality of the balustrades, shaven lawns, and stereoscopic trees seemed to proclaim that the material world is the one and only. If doubts entered in, they were encouraged by the less than solid wall of bamboos to the west. Nothing could be done about the bamboos: they looked and sounded tattered; nor the sea beyond, which slithered shapelessly, in deep blue to downright black coils.

It would have been a chilly night, at least for the time of year, without that slight friction of excitement, of cars arriving and driven away, and activity in the kitchen wing: a sound of flung pans, almost of clashing cymbals, as the voice of an impeccable servant, dropping the accent she had caught from the mistress, accused somebody else of buggering up the charlotte russe.

A manservant he hadn't seen before, but who claimed to recognize him, received Mr Duffield at the front door with the virtuoso flourishes of the professionally obsequious.

The man asked: "Will you be requiring anything, Mr Duffield, from the pockets?" as he peeled the overcoat off its owner's back.

In the hall, as though she had been waiting for her favourite guest, old Emily, half member of the family, half honorary nuisance, came creaking forward in her fresh starch.

"Thought you was letting us down," she hissed, her fingers pinching at his sleeve. "The Greek gentleman is sick. And She won't come without. Poor Miss Boo! Fourteen guests on 'er hands! I tell 'er a bricklayer sees more for 'is pains than a fashionable lady."

The manservant, his professional soul disapproving of unorthodox, not to say senile, confidences, hurried the guest towards the long drawing-room, Emily calling after them in a low, penetrating voice: "See you later, dear. They say not only the husband's sick, but the Maltese dog is worse."

Any further remarks were drowned in the orchestration of lights, crystal, ice, jewellery, and confident voices. As he was led in, the expressions of some of his fellow guests showed they were prepared to carry on as though he hadn't arrived. One or two, whom he met on and off, looked at him with the eyes of amateur blackmailers. Some he didn't know pretended that they did, and a lady of Presbyterian cast and an inherited pendant locked up her long cupboard of a face and turned her back.

He stood in the arena, his chin sunken, like a bull watching for the first signs of treachery.

Mrs Davenport, whether intentionally or not, must have been the last to take notice, but whipped round when she decided to, and was fully prepared. She was even wearing a crimson dress, a deep crimson, devoted to the lines of her flanks, her thighs, until the knees, where it began to flounce and froth and lead a life of its own: a bit obvious perhaps, in its effect, if it hadn't been of such a rich, courtly stuff, reminiscent of carnations with a glint of frost on their rough heads. She came forward, aiming her most stunning smile, trailing invisible streamers of carnation perfume. But the cleverest details of her informally formal *toilette* were the sleeves: these were pushed back to the elbows, in heavy rucks, and although they must have been worn permanently so, she gave the impression of having that moment deserted the sink, her wrists dripping pearls and diamonds instead of suds.

"Darling," she said, with a distraction she might have been finding delicious, "I'm simply at my wits' *end!*"

She bathed her cheek in his, so that all those gathered in the room hushed their mouths for a second in their half-emptied glasses as they meditated on an ambiguous relationship.

"They haven't, and probably won't—*come!*" She performed the passage in a series of little perfumed trills, her mouth melting within a few inches of his own.

"All the more scoff," he said, "for those who did." Forced by the angle to look down his nose at the convention of her lips, he was afraid he might develop a twitch.

"Oh, but I was so *counting* on them!" Tonight her *mèche* of natural silver had divided, and was standing erect like a pair of horns above her frown. "For *your* sake," she added.

He realized their relationship had subtly altered: Olivia Davenport was hanging distractedly, practically limply, on his arm, looking imploringly up. She could have been imploring him to take over a responsibility, or accept a sacrifice. He wished he had arrived early, as planned, for the couple of stiff whiskies he had been counting on.

Just then the hushed voices of the guests began mounting; there was a pronounced collision of ice cubes, and all the confusion of announced and important arrival in Mrs Davenport's off-white drawing-room.

She hurried forward, ululating: "Darlings, I'm so *relieved*! We didn't realize—that is, we understood Cosma was indisposed."

A small woman was laughing big. "Why should you misunderstand—darling? Cosma is always indisposed. It doesn't mean he won't come just because he has a pain in his pinny."

This echo of an Edwardian nanny cast up on the shores of the Levant started the guests frantically laughing, with the exception of one, at whom the speaker happened to be looking. He was, in fact, too interested to respond.

And immediately she looked away, at her husband, to discover how he had reacted to her frivolous betrayal.

Pavloussis the shipowner was advancing at her heels, an undirected smile guarding his rather fleshy face; his eyelids looked particularly black behind his thick spectacles; his shirt front was studded with black pearls. From behind the smile he started hoisting himself to the tedious level of communication. "It is not I," he said, correctly, and coughed, "it is our little dog which is sick."

Because her head was turned in his direction, you couldn't estimate the degree of his wife's approval, except that she kept repeating in something like a ventriloquist's projected voice: "Yes, yes! Our little dog. Poor little Flora!"

Her husband continued smiling. He seemed to be holding the smile between himself and the demands of a foreign language; while her attitude suggested she was ready to translate his silences into pronouncements: Cosma Pavloussis, when put to it, would make pronouncements.

Finally she offered her face instead to the assembled guests, and everyone was charmed. It was foreign, but so sweet, several of the ladies were audibly agreed. If they didn't praise her more highly, it was because they had run through practically the gamut of their vocabulary. Instead they put on their heartiest grins, and might have been preparing to rush in and start fingering the object of their admiration once the formalities were disposed of.

"Quite a work of art, Duffield. I hope they won't break her." It was Shuard the music critic, whom he knew slightly, and disliked. "She's far too dainty."

Shuard's judgement might have done Madame Pavloussi more harm if he didn't regularly reduce Mozart to "daintiness" in reviewing for the evening press.

The lady of the amethyst pendant and Presbyterian ancestors found the little Greek far too "burnt." What would her skin be like in a few years' time? A rag, she suggested, moistening her sallow teeth at the prospect.

A mutually appreciative exchange of opinions between Shuard and the Amethyst Pendant gave their neighbour the opportunity to withdraw to the point of isolation he most enjoyed in crowds, and from which he could glut himself on Madame Pavloussi.

She was certainly small: a figurine burnt to an orange-brown, or terracotta. What saved her from exquisiteness, or the excessively sweet, were the modelling and carriage of her head: the head sat rather oddly on the body, as though by some special act of grace, and she wouldn't be surprised to have it fall. The eyelids intensified her expression of fatality, and the disbelieving smile with which she rewarded those she found herself amongst.

As she was led, her dress moved with the liquid action of purest, subtlest silk, its infinitesimal bronze flutings very slightly opening on tones of turquoise and verdigris. Again, her miraculous dress was worn with an odd air, not of humility—fatality. It was surprising that, in shaking hands, she appeared to be grasping a tennis racket. Such an incongruous show of strength could have been part of a game she had specially learned for Anglo-Saxons. Her other, passive hand she carried mostly palm upward, which made you wonder if Madame Pavloussi wasn't in some way deformed; till in a spontaneous gesture she put the hand to her hair, and for the moment was unable to hide an enormous pearl in a nest of diamonds. At once she returned her hand, her arm, to their original cramped position, as though the ring was too heavy, possibly also something she didn't care for, and she would rather lay down what fate was making her carry.

While Mrs Davenport was showing off her jewel of a friend, the husband was walking up and down on an independent trajectory. Sometimes he paused to look at a painting, or take up an object of virtu, or glance at a human face, without ever really emerging from the legend of his wealth. Those who were forced to pass him lowered their heads and walked softer, for fear of impinging on a cultivated unreality; while his smile of sickly, almost doddering benevolence was aimed at no one in particular. Though older than his wife he was not yet old, nor even elderly, but seemed already to be rehearsing the role of an old man with a beautiful character.

In brushing against one whose eyes invoked the particular of which the generality is composed, Pavloussis shied away. "Wonderful people! Beautiful house! My wife is enjoying herself," he pronounced, still smiling, not for his particular examiner, but for a whole abstract cosmos.

Duffield was interested in the little sacs of dark skin at the corners of the shipowner's eyelids: they provided something ugly, excrescent, in the otherwise excessively bland.

This non-meeting occurred very quickly and, it seemed, irrelevantly. He returned to his increasing grudge against their hostess for not introducing Madame Pavloussi after insisting that they must be forced together. Her friend's presence had drugged Olivia: she looked haggard, vulgar even, as she stuck her nose in a glass of gin; while Madame Pavloussi nursed her glass with both hands, as though it had been a handleless cup of innocent spring water.

Passing and repassing at the end of the room, his calves aching with tension, he heard a woman remark: "But I adore his paintings." A second replied: "I adore *him*! He's always been one of my heartthrobs." He should have treated his adorers kindly, but allowed them to peter out in the abashed smiles of schoolgirl crushes.

The major-domo confessed to the hostess in velvety tones that dinner was served.

Mrs Davenport's voice sounded comparatively raucous: "Oh, thank you, Spurgeon; I hope everyone's as ravenous as I."

The Amethyst Pendant folded her disapproving lips over her moist, greenish teeth. As a headmistress and an O.B.E., she couldn't allow herself to approve of any kind of eccentricity.

The hostess's example released something: what should have been a leisurely and graceful progress to the dining-room became a bit of a rout; the burr and bray of male laughter jostled with the thin reeds of girlish giggles; a banker just missed knocking a Tang horse off its stand; while the guests of honour smiled indulgently, seeming to find nothing, or perhaps everything, unusual.

It was at this point that Olivia Davenport remembered what she had forgotten, or was forced to face an anxiety she had been disguising. Her head held high, as though to keep her hair out of the water, she started an awkward swimming movement against the swell made by her mismanaged guests, dragging her friend after her. Jerked out of her Tanagra graces into a state of uncertainty, Madame Pavloussi's attitudes became Cycladic; she followed bravely where she was drawn, her shoulders slightly hunched, her bronze dress opening and closing on its depths of turquoise and verdigris. Her arms appeared stumpy from closer, as her legs would be, too, he guessed, under the play of liquid silk.

On reaching their objective Olivia Davenport shook the invisible drops off her immaculate coiffure, and announced with awful distinctness, if only for themselves: "Hero—this is my great friend Hurtle Duffield. My two dear friends! It's rather like bringing together the two halves of friendship—into a whole." Then, as though she might have said something too "clever" for a social occasion, she explained more practically: "I'm giving you Hurtle, Hero, for dinner."

There was no sign that a plan had been discussed beforehand by the two women. In fact, Madame Pavloussi, standing in front of him, continued looking dazed, if not frightened, by the possibility that she was intended as a sacrifice; while there flickered briefly through his mind an image of himself trussed on a gold plate, threatened by a knife and fork in her small, rather blunt hands.

Olivia was barely allowed to enjoy a sense of achievement: Emily's creaking shoes were approaching through the shallows. When she had paddled close enough to clutch her mistress by the arm, she advanced her lips, which tonight were powdered as pale as her cheeks, and began a piece of muted recitative:

"This Italian lady has locked herself in the convenience, dear, and won't come out to do the prawn cutlets, because she says Ethel was unkind to her, and she couldn't help bumping the charlotte russe. Now Ethel is wondering what ought to be done, Miss Boo?"

"Oh God, who am *I*?" Mrs Davenport stamped, and frowned black.

Emily appeared shaken to discover that the one who should have known the answer didn't.

"Can't Spurgeon fetch her out?"

"Mr Spurgeon washes 'is 'ands of it, dear."

Olivia remembered to smile at her two favourites before repeating: "Oh God! Nothing I undertake fails to turn into a shambles. The simplest little occasion! Come with me, Emily!"

She marched off through her shambles. Objects in jade trembled on their pedestals as she managed her explosive dress. Emily followed, slower, on account of her rheumatism and her status.

"Shouldn't we find the others?" Madame Pavloussi anxiously asked, because the laughter sounded several doors away.

"Yes," he agreed, but casually. "There'll be no prawn cutlets, but an otherwise excellent dinner."

Madame Pavloussi was already striding on her short legs across empty rooms. "I am wondering what will become of my poor husband. He will feel unhappy, left to so many strangers."

"I shouldn't have thought he needed protection."

"I suppose not." She sighed.

They turned a corner, and the thunder told them they were almost there. Madame Pavloussi appeared less anxious to arrive.

"Look at this painting!" she whispered, and nudged him conspiratorially. "Is she a girl? Or an octopus?"

"Probably an octopus." He laughed at a good joke.

It was the original version of Rhoda Courtney which Olivia had winkled out of him. In other circumstances he might have resented the reaction of this charming, but probably ignorant woman. Now he forgave, because she herself was a work of art, and he would have liked to fall in love with her.

"You agree?" She laughed back; her teeth looked short, and strong, and real.

"I'd never thought of the octopus. You're right, though." She had given the painting a new life, in which suckers grew from the thin arms, the tones less milky-pink than grey.

If left to himself he would have continued thinking about it; but Madame Pavloussi's nostrils had taken up a scent.

"You don't know the girl?" she asked.

"She was my sister."

"Oh, I am so, so sorry!" His companion was gasping, and twisting her enormous pearl.

He was less conscious of her as he flirted with his slowly developing vision: the octopus-Rhoda, sponge attached to one sucker, beside the more or less unalterable bidet on its iron stand.

"You say she *was* your sister. Your sister is dead?"

"I don't know," he had to confess.

Madame Pavloussi's eyes had begun to water: they were magnificent in their horror—or was it pity? He could not yet have told with any certainty.

"But you must admit," she cried in self-protection, "the painter is cruel. Why do painters have to deform everything they see? I do not understand what is modern painting about. Perhaps you will explain to me—one day—I mean, after dinner."

"Of course—if there's time." Lucky he hadn't signed his painting.

She appeared so distraught he would have liked to take her hand, but here they were on the threshold of the dining-room.

The marooned guests were standing around, wondering, though not yet seriously. While waiting, they admired the table. Their first thoughts had naturally been for the place cards, and some of them were still preoccupied with these; through bad eyesight or discretion they had not yet discovered what they were in for.

"Aren't the little stands exquisite! She really has exceptional taste," one lady was remarking.

Shuard, who was ready to set up as an authority on almost anything, assured her that the little jewelled claws which held the place cards were "genuine Faubourg."

The two late arrivals couldn't take an interest in the cards as their fate was already known to them.

Madame Pavloussi gestured at her husband in a far corner. He was still wearing the abstracted smile, which might or might not have acknowledged his wife's sign. It was more likely directed at the whole and nothing of the room, while Monaghan the banker talked on at him. After tempting the shipowner to express his views on the recent rise to power of the German National Socialists, the banker gave up and switched to yachts. Pavloussis seemed to remain untouched.

"You see, your husband was in no need of your protection."

"No," she agreed vaguely.

Either she was disappointed, or else her gaffe over the subject of the painting had made her shy; if it hadn't been for their hostess's decree she might have moved away.

The shipowner had an enormous nose, like a ridge of grey pumice, or lava; and brilliantine failed to remove a texture of coral hummocks from his hair. As the banker's yachts began foundering, Pavloussis spoke through his smile, in a voice unperturbed by its own foreignness or irrelevance. "My pressing problem at present is cats. I have four of them. I no longer love my cats, which are selfish and unlovable. I must only find how far I am morally obliged to them. Can you advise me, please, Mr. Monragan?"

The banker turned a congested red and laughed too loud at the foreign joke; while Madame Pavloussi murmured to herself: "Yes, yes, the poor cats."

Although several of the others had joined in the laughter the situation was becoming too strange; on the whole the guests were beginning to look uneasy and unshepherded.

"It would be far more sensible if everyone sat down." The headmistress was coming into her own. "Boo has been called away for a little to attend to some domestic matter."

The company did as told: most of them appeared relieved to have returned temporarily to school.

"Isn't it a pretty table?" continued the headmistress, whose name was Miss Anderson. "Boo was always original; but the bird, I remember—the bird belonged to Constance—Mrs Hollingrake."

Association with an important family and knowledge of its history made Miss Anderson proud. The bird was dutifully admired, except by the banker, who scowled at it: who ever heard of a glass bird, standing amongst a litter of rock, in a dish of water, in the middle of a dining-table!

The headmistress couldn't resist glancing in a certain direction. "I'm sure Mr Duffield must appreciate the arrangement: it's so artistic." Then she burned, all along her downy lower jaw.

No doubt she detested his paintings, and probably this was as close as her uprightness would ever let her come to malice.

But the crystal bird in the centre of the table, to which she would have drawn his attention, if it hadn't already been drawn, seemed to him one of the happiest surprises Olivia had ever sprung. Perched on a crag of rose quartz, its wings outspread above the crackled basin of shallow water, in which glimmered slivers of amethyst and a cluster of moss agates, the crystal bird could have been contemplating flight in the direction of Hero Pavloussi seated immediately opposite.

"Right, Miss Anderson," he called back to the headmistress. "We can go some of the way together."

Nervousness, or a wish to interpret subtleties, made them laugh at his flat and fatuous repartee. Miss Anderson looked mollified.

Under cover of their approval he glanced at Madame Pavloussi to see what impression Olivia's conceit had made. He caught what might have been the last refractions of a childlike pleasure in the pretty-coloured stones before she lowered her eyes. She sat rather glumly looking at her own hands, her chin drawn in as though suffering from indigestion, or a surfeit of English.

At that moment Spurgeon threw the door open, and Mrs Davenport returned to her party, as from a recent triumph. A slight glitter in the whites of her eyes, perhaps from a snifter of gin en route to the dining-room, increased her dash and rakishness. Sitting down at the table, she destroyed the castle in lace and linen waiting in her place. The rucked-up sleeves of the carnation dress had grown positively businesslike.

"I've discovered tonight that I'm both a locksmith and a plumber." Then she added, looking at him across the table: "But there won't be any prawn cutlets." Her face was so expressive of radiant fulfilment it must have confirmed for some of those present that the painter was her lover.

He would have liked to watch Hero Pavloussi for her reactions to Olivia's return, but his right-hand neighbour began to break down the barrier which, till now, he had kept between them.

She worked with skill and confidence. "Since we first met, Mr Duffield, in this house, I've bought two of your paintings."

He couldn't remember the woman and failed to read her name on the card.

"Which?" he asked: when his paintings became merchandise he could only practise resignation if he wasn't stung to ribaldry.

She mentioned an early work—he could only just visualize it—and one sold more recently to pay a heavy bill at the tailor's.

The woman's appearance gave no clue to a former meeting. She was wearing an elaborate headdress of rigidly set toffee curls. Her face was square-cut, not exactly coarse: it had been too carefully worked on; the throat thick and rather muscular; her jewels, though unremarkable, represented a solid investment.

"Who sold you the paintings?" he asked, because it was his turn.

She mentioned a Syro-Maltese who passed for French, flickering her silver-green eyelids, composing her orange mouth without disguising her satisfaction.

"Diacono? Then he must have stung you!"

"Oh, don't say that!" the woman protested in mock despair. "I was so anxious to own a Duffield; and you make it too difficult for us to collect you." Even when admitting her weaknesses, she gargled her words so effortlessly she must have been to a very good teacher.

He grunted. "I don't remember your name," he admitted.

"Elise Trotter." She dipped her smeared eyelids.

Of course—Mrs Trotter! The claret "birthmark" no longer rose up the muscular throat to plaster itself on the square-cut face. He laughed with genuine pleasure, almost affection, but could see she suspected his laughter. She grew opaque as she made a pass at the kind of soup which satisfies nobody, except possibly the cook who has sweated to clarify a convention rather than a soup.

"Wasn't there a crèche?" he asked.

"Fancy your remembering!" Elise failed to restrain Mrs Trotter's gush of pleasure, and only now the claret birthmark began clothing the heavy face.

Almost at once she recovered her self-possession and confided very earnestly: "I love to do something for the children. It's so rewarding." She turned her social conscience towards him. "As a matter of fact," she continued, "I want to persuade Olivia—she's so generous of her time—to visit the crèche on Mothers' Afternoon."

"Mightn't it start a revolution?"

"Oh no! Definitely no!" Mrs Trotter bit into her theme with conviction. "Poor people only hate the rich politically—in the abstract, as it were." Here she lowered her artistic eyelids. "They adore to see them in their clothes and cars."

He felt guilty for his own ambiguous allegiances, and would have liked to look towards the one who had been given him, if not as his mistress, his spiritual bride. Wasn't the crystal bird poised in flight towards the chosen couple?

But Hero Pavloussi had been appropriated by the companion on her left: an intellectually aggressive young man from Adelaide, a lecturer in Greek, with a reputation for sodomy. The jealous groom resented his bride's sodomite.

Boo Davenport was saying: "You refuse soup. Fair enough; soup isn't to everybody's taste. You turn up your nose at this rather *exceptional* mousse. How do you exist, darling? On air? Tell me—do—for my figure's sake!"

Pavloussis shifted position and sulkily churned out: "Noh! I eat. I eat bread. I drink water." They had, in fact, brought him what he had asked for: a basket of bread and a jug of water. "I eat and drink thus, because I suffer with the intestines."

His wife looked at him in pain, though he didn't notice; while the young man from Adelaide was explaining the *Oresteia*, which to his certain knowledge only he was capable of understanding.

Pavloussis sulkily consented: "I will try a small spoonful of your mousse."

"But it's *my* mousse!" Mrs Davenport made an amusing pretence of protecting her plate with her arm. "Let them give you some of your own."

Not only his face, his whole body refused it. "Mmm! It is good—your mousse."

It pleased him to lean over her as he ate, an arm extended along the back of her chair. Apart from anything else, the hostess was put out because the cutlery was being disorganized.

Madame Pavloussi wrenched herself away from the *Oresteia*. "You see—Cosmas is so *bon enfant* he can't bear to offend her, although he suffers, and will pay for it." She laughed in melancholy sympathy.

"I'm glad you consent to address me. I thought you'd cast me off."

"I—had—*cast*?" Though she was feeling her way, it sounded like a whipcrack; she ground her short teeth together. "You are too successful." She took a great draught of wine. "I am afraid." She dried her lips methodically. "I am not successful at anything—except that I catch a—a *good* husband. And then it is not I. It is Cosmas. Who begs me till I have to accept." Her laughter became reckless.

The lecturer had begun again to whisper from the other side.

"Yes, yes!" Madame Pavloussi shrieked back. "Athens is dusty. It is so dusty, Cosmas has the servants dust his shoes each house he enters." She glanced at her husband. "They love him for it. Yes," she shrieked, because the lecturer was bombarding her, "modern Athens is primitive. You do not have to imply. There is poor sewerage. Every summer we go to an island, and there is even less sewerage on the island." She laughed and nodded her sculptured head.

"Ken—my husband—has bought a Bentley. He's terribly thrilled with this new relationship." Easing one of her earrings, Elise Trotter looked across at Olivia Davenport.

All the while the stately maids were weaving in and out, thin and middle-aged, bearing dishes. The black Spurgeon drew corks and wrapped the napkin, sometimes ever so slightly bloodied. The maids were so fragile, they suggested white fans, open at some precise degree of mathematical formality.

"Success in all these young countries is something so concrete." Madame Pavloussi dared the painter to contradict.

"In any country." He had to watch the shipowner, seated the other side of the table, forking up his hostess's saddle of lamb.

"Yes?" Madame Pavloussi, for the first time, seemed prepared to give her right-hand neighbour her full attention.

"It is too fat, and too pink," Pavloussis complained as he gorged himself.

"You are a bear, Cosma!" Mrs Davenport laughed; the Greek was certainly very shaggy. "I love you!" Whenever he paused, she fed shreds of lamb into the receptive mouth.

Suddenly Boo remembered and looked across. She was smiling in a leisurely way at Hurtle Duffield.

He was about to tell her friend Hero Pavloussi: "I am particularly interested in the shape of your earlobes"; when he changed it into: "Clever of you not to wear jewellery like these other overloaded women."

"I wear this ring which Cosmas has given and wishes me to wear. Otherwise, too many jewels are too heavy—and one may always be forced to part with them too suddenly." She ended in a fit of coughing, which brought the tears into her eyes. "Oh dear!" she said weakly, smiling, at last.

Nobody had noticed because everybody was engaged: it was what would be referred to as a marvelous party.

When they reached the end of the meal, and the strands of blue smoke were woven into those of light, phrases falling thicker and more broken from out of the general amorphousness of conversation, onto the shimmer of underwater jewels and the bird floating on motionless wings, he realized he had never been in love, except with painting. He had been in love, he recognized it, with his own "Pythoness" standing permanently beside the tripod-bidet. This was what made his encounter with Madame Pavloussi—Hero: still a myth rather than a name—of particular significance. He was falling in love with her, not in the usual sense of wanting to sleep with her, to pay court to her with his body, which, after all, wasn't love. Physical love, as he saw it now, was an exhilarating steeplechase in which almost every rider ended up disqualified for some dishonesty or another. In his aesthetic desires and their consummation he believed himself to be honest; and in his desire to worship and be renewed by someone else's simplicity of spirit, he was not forsaking the pursuit of truth. So he was falling in love with Hero Pavloussi. It had begun, he thought, as they stood in front of the "Pythoness" Olivia Davenport owned; when Hero had innocently planted in his mind the seed of an idea: the octopus thing.

Remembering the exact moment was to experience something not unlike the orgasm of sensual love. Then, was he again no more than in love with an endlessly sensuous prospect of paint, to which, in her innocence, she had given him access? And how absolute is simplicity of spirit? He looked at the shipowner's hairy wrists, one of which lay heavily along the back of their hostess's chair, while the other was held erect and exposed, as Pavloussis smoked, with almost spinsterly precision, one of his own Greek cigarettes.

In the drawing-room afterwards Miss Anderson spilled cherry brandy down her front. "Don't worry!" she kept assuring those who wanted to lead her out and mop up more thoroughly; "*I am not worrying: Mr Duffield was so kind as to lend me his handkerchief.*" She laughed, and her buck teeth showed, transparent and reckless. She arched her back, as though a man's arm were pressed in the small of it, herself revolving. He looked at Miss Anderson with different eyes.

The party was sagging under the weight of food and drink. Monaghan the banker had become too congested to keep up the pretence of waking. Mr Trotter—Ken—had cornered the lecturer in Greek and was explaining to him the virtues of his new Bentley; while ladies in groups were inclined to remember girls they had known, now unidentifiably swallowed up in marriage.

"What is this?" asked Pavloussis, touching something with a hairy finger.

"That is a solitaire board," Mrs Davenport explained. "A game —so called. Ladies must have played it only to exercise their wrists."

"Will you teach me this game?" The shipowner appeared fascinated by the whorled marbles, which he kept turning in their mahogany sockets.

"Oh darling, must we? How trying!" Olivia protested yawnfully.

At the same time she made him carry chairs to a table on a little

dais at the farther end of the room, where she proceeded to instruct
with exaggerated conscientiousness. They were soon so unnaturally
absorbed, their absorption could only have been imposed on them.

Madame Pavloussi said: "My husband is so good. He is a simple
man—a peasant. I hope you will learn to know him, Mr Duffield."

Mrs Davenport refused to have the curtains drawn in any of the
waterside rooms. Some of the guests had walked out, in spite of the
chill, into the garden, where the artificial moonlight had been turned
discreetly off. The actual moon was not quite perfect, but perhaps
more precious for it, in the thick, velvety texture of night, above the
electric outline of the bays.

Hero said: "I have never lived for any long time out of sight of the
sea. I would not find it natural to live without it."

It was almost too natural their walking out of the house together,
not by mutual consent, but as the game of solitaire had been imposed on other players. Hero had covered her head as protection
against the cold. In the beginning all her remarks were chattery
and banal. She tended to stride: to try to disguise the fact that her
legs were rather short; while he felt shivery and dull: even miserable in his dullness, for he had expected something different. Was
it possible his love for Madame Pavloussi would culminate on the
operating table on a prearranged afternoon?

Looking back, the rising wind filling her hood, the classic light exposing her face, she gave the impression of being in flight.

"I have seen Cosma for the first time on the quay after we escape," she needed to explain. "After the Catastrophe—at Smyrna—
we escaped to Chios. It is his island. He is from a village in the
interior, where his mother still lives, and he still goes to visit her. I
have been there once, but she doesn't respect me: I have nothing
of my own—not a penny—all of it was lost in the Catastrophe—and
I cannot talk to her about jam. She has two daughters and a niece
who live at the port where I have met Cosma the first time. They
are the kind who spend months to think of the handbags they will
order from Athens. You know? All the girls are married to confec-
tioners."

They had reached the water, where a balustrade had been built
to prevent people falling in. In front of them the sea was both dark
and restless, as opposed to the solid, illuminated house, with guests
strolling on the terrace, some lacing themselves with their arms to
brace their bodies against the cold.

"After we reach the mainland, we have stayed in this house on the outskirts of Athens belonging to a cousin of my father. He is very mean. He has locked up the furniture. So my parents sit on packing cases while the servants bring them cups of coffee. All the servants are here from the *tsiphliki*—oh dear, I am too tired to remember English—the *estate* we have had in Asia Minor. They would like to do something for us, but we have nothing. They can only bring coffee, and cold water from the well."

She stood looking out over the bay, speaking in a dry, high, starved voice. Perhaps she realized, because she coughed slightly, and lowered it, to make it sound more natural. There was a gramophone playing something he had forgotten, and people laughing, at a house along the point.

"In Athens they organized the refugees," she continued in a more controlled, convalescent voice. "My sister went to teach at a school. She is the learned one, and had some slight experience among poor Greek children in Smyrna. I was given work at a bank, because I have a head for figures. Oh yes, I have always been practical!" She snorted in apology. "But I was not for the bank in Athens. I work work, and am sick in the end." Her voice was drying out again. "One evening I have fallen in the snow walking from the train. I haven't the strength or the will to get up, only to lie and sleep in the snow. Late that night some people passing took me to a house. I didn't care. I was too happy lying in the snow, which has become in the end beautiful and warm, and—yes, sanctifying."

She spent a year in a sanatorium on the side of a mountain.

"When my strength came back I should have felt more grateful. That is the terrible thing: not to feel grateful enough. A woman I got to know brought me a pretty summer frock, out of kindness; she is not at all an affluent woman. I cried, and she thought it was from gratitude, and because I was cured—it was such a day, smelling of warm pine needles—but I was crying because I didn't care. She never got to know the real reason. I have tried to make it up to her since, but have never adequately succeeded; it is now too easy for me to give presents."

He stood against the balustrade bracing his calves, not so much because the night was chilly, as because, in this present rise in a fluctuating faith, she must be the pure soul he was longing for. He couldn't remember having met another, unless May Noble the Courtneys' cook, though May had been in a sense an artist, and he wanted to admire somebody who was a human being.

"What about your husband?" he asked, testing her in a thickened voice. "Where is Cosma all this time? When does he reappear in the story?"

"I shall tell you. It was with this same woman, my friend Arta, I was sitting one day during the visiting hour, not long before I was to be discharged. A man passed Arta thought she recognized as an acquaintance. She called him in. He and I also recognized each other from Chios. He was a man who had helped us bring from the destroyer the belongings we had rescued from Smyrna: our few relics! I found him most sympathetic on the quay at night, but almost anyone who was not a Turk would have appeared acceptable. Now when he had gone Arta told me: 'This is Cosmas Pavloussis, who has already made a fortune out of shipping—a peasant from Chios—a millionaire!' Arta was more impressed than I. I became furious with myself. I did not look down on him for being a peasant. I blamed myself for being deceived by his simplicity: anybody so rich could not be entirely honest. So I said: 'What an ugly man— and hairy!' Arta I remember laughing and replying: 'Hairy men are said to be the kindest, and I should think, the warmest!' But I found her remark repulsive," Hero broke off primly.

"I thought you were the practical one."

"Oh, but I am! Wait! After I left the sanitorium and the bank was persuaded to take me back, Cosmas informed himself through Arta. He asked to see me. I did not want him. He send me presents. I do not want them. At this time I did not know what I wanted or what I was like. I was like some empty thing—some jug waiting to be filled up—with purpose. Then he sent a representative to my parents asking them to give me to him. He offered to pay them a lot of money, when in normal circumstances it is the father of the bride who pays the groom to take her. My father was ironical at first, because the *tsiphliki* of my grandfather was so great it took a man a month to ride around it on a horse. Then they change their tune: 'Why not, Hero? He is a good man, isn't he? He was most courteous and considerate the night in Chios when nobody knew a thing about anyone. You praised him then.' Because the circumstances were not comparable I did not bother to argue. I sulked. Till one morning, I remember, I break my nail opening the drawer of a steel filing cabinet. I suddenly think: 'Why do I not marry this peasant-millionaire and lie all morning in good sheets without opening my eyes?' My parents were delighted. They ask: 'What has changed your mind, *koroula*?' I said: 'Nothing'—just like that—'nothing!' I said: 'The night is dark enough to hide any marriage, provided there is money.' They pretended not to hear."

She began whimpering and squirming, her nose thick with catarrh, her voice with distaste. "You see? Isn't that practical?" she asked.

He could only agree.

"So I married Cosma for the wrong reasons. From the wedding I have the *bonbonnière*—too ornate, because he wanted to show how far he had come." She blew her nose. "But I got to love him. He is such a good man. He respected my feelings from the beginning. Some Greeks are like goats, you know: the heat of the day is the same to them."

She broke off to look over her shoulder. "I am happy," she said.

"Then why are you disturbed, Hero?"

"I? Why I am *disturbed*—Mr Duffield? Oh, *well*! Anyone who breathes, anyone who exists, is disturbed. But I am not *disturbed*. Actually—I will tell you something: I was not healed, not completely, till Cosmas took me to Perialos. That is an island off the Asia Minor coast. It is an island of saints and miracles. Are you religious?"

"No."

"I am not. But you don't have to scratch a Greek very deep to find that he is. Even my sister Elly, who is a practising humanist, who married a schoolteacher—another peasant—and lives in a village—to demonstrate her faith in mankind, Elly will go so far as admitting she is a Byzantine. Because, you see, the faces of the people —you only have to look at the icons—are still so close to the saints. I, on the other hand, cannot admit to faith if God allows the Turks to put out a man's eyes and crucify him on his church door."

He might have questioned her logic but asked instead: "What happened at Perialos?"

She was so interrupted they found themselves listening to the sea.

"Nothing," she said at last. "Or nothing I can tell you. It was in the air."

He heard his own frustrated breathing on being forced to withdraw from the experience she was unwilling to share.

"What time is it?" she asked, looking at a watch she wasn't wearing. "Shouldn't we be going back inside the house? It is so cold. Feel my arm," she chattered and laughed.

He did as he was invited, and felt the rather chill goose-pimples on what had been assured pottery; her grainy flesh made him regretful for the pure soul of his invention.

She linked her arm to his, and turned him round, and said in simple anticipation: "Cosmas will bring you to Greece. We must take you to Perialos. I have not dared visit it again till now." Her pure joy reinstated her in his opinion.

They walked towards the terrace, the wind off the sea bashing at them; and the shipowner came out of the house and called: "I have learned the game!"

When they met, he kissed his wife gingerly. "You are cold—darling." (From time to time the words either of them used in the foreign language came out tentatively, as though they suspected they might be borrowing something which didn't suit their personal vocabulary.)

"No, darling," she answered, encouraging him. "I am not cold."

"But you feel cold."

"Truly I'm not." Then she added: "Women can bear more than men." She looked towards her fellow guest. "Mr Duffield must have suffered many pains tonight listening to my life history."

"Oh!" The shipowner cleared the phlegm from his throat, but remembered not to spit. "You've been trying that out on him, have you?"

Arm in arm, the Greeks laughed together, perhaps collusively.

When they went in, the party had almost collapsed. Some of the guests had already left; others were standing about in their coats listening to an endless anecdote one of them had started, their eyes grateful for anything which might delay their departure. Elderly faces admitted their age; younger ones no longer attempted to disguise their youth; even the splendid house looked more human for an evening's litter. Emily's blancoed shoes crunched over broken glass as she went punching the cushions and complaining about cigars. Her face was the colour of old age, and wore the superior, peevish expression of aged servants who have chosen to stay up longer than they are expected to.

While he was clumsily but comfortably getting into his coat without assistance, for the major-domo had disappeared, Miss Anderson approached and said: "Mr Duffield!"

In the pause which followed, the down along her lower jaw appeared to rise in prickly hackles; at no time that evening had she looked so plain, so frumpish, her tight mouth so disapproving; yet her eyes were curiously luminous and large from some embarrassment or fright she was in.

"I would like," she said, "to say"—she almost hiccupped—"how much your paintings have meant to me. Fulsomeness is disagreeable, isn't it? But you will forgive me." She closed her jaws, and bowed her head, and went quickly through the front door.

Such an unlikely confession on the part of the headmistress filled him with a hope that some of his other judgements were mistaken, and that any doubts he may have had for the innocence of Hero Pavloussi's motives had been bred from a flaw in himself.

The chrysanthemums Mrs Davenport had massed at the more dramatic points of her house to emphasize the splendour of her party were looking in some cases draggled and shrunk, when Olivia came up to him carrying a few broken flowers which smelled of brown water and autumn.

"Are you tired?" she inquired pointlessly. "I must remember to ring the masseuse in the morning. I can't bear chrysanthemums. But what else is there?" She thrust in his face a couple of enormous crushed mops, and a smaller bloom, lithe as a buttoned foil.

As the remainder of the guests had already thanked, and only needed to trickle away, she stuck her nose in his neck. "Tell me, darling—what did you think of the Greeks? Isn't she interesting?" Then she blew giggling down her nose. "Gorgeous!"

Boo was slightly drunk, of course: rolling her head against his neck. Suddenly her tone altered. "I can guarantee her!" she said. "I mean her exceptional qualities."

She could have been a friend defending a friend with the steely loyalty friendship demands; while at the same time her voice was that of the professional procuress: harsh and collected.

Perhaps it was an ambiguous hour, for she softened after that, and kissed him on the mouth, complaining: "I am not drunk, as you think, only exhausted. My trouble is: I love you all—whether you believe it or not—and would like to believe you love one another." She kissed him again. "Will you tell me?" she pleaded. "After you've experienced it?"

Lolling against him as they lingered on the chess board of the empty hall, she gave the impression that she had; whereas social occasions, and assignations planned for her friends, could have been as close as Olivia came to sexual pleasure.

"Good-night, Boo." He kissed the mouth she would have liked to appear fulfilled. "I'll leave you to your beauty sleep."

She flung off, condemning or camping with her right hand, knowing that Emily would pick up the jaded flowers she had dropped.

He went out. All the cars had driven off, except one: an illuminated glass capsule in which the Pavloussis were seated, bending over the instrument panel, arguing in full voice about something which was also making them laugh.

They left off, however, as though by prearrangement, and she wound a window down.

"May we give you a lift?" she called in Olivia Davenport's clearest tones.

Her husband was peering over her shoulder. The skin round his eyes made him look like an owl: it was so thick and encrusted, the eyes not all that blind.

"Yes," Pavloussis insisted, in a silky tenor instead of the bass which would have suited him. "It is no trouble, Mr Duffield."

"Thank you. At this time of night I like to walk."

Madame Pavloussi stuck out her hooded head. "I would like to visit you, Mr Duffield, and see your paintings."

"Any time," he invited, "and Mr Pavloussis."

"Cosmas is so busy." She pronounced it "beesy," which made it sound more emphatic. "I will rather bring Olivia." The husband's imbecile smile appeared to approve. "Although Cosmas is the one who really understands."

The millionaire was preparing something ponderous. "In the island of Chios"—he doled it out—"in the village of Mesta—where my old mother still lives—there are Picasso murals in the square painted long before Picasso."

The car began to bound forward; thrown together in deeper conjugal conspiracy, the occupants laughed and called: "Good-night, Mr Duffield!"

He was relieved to find himself alone with the indeterminate images time would form.

It was nearly three weeks after her party when he received a note from Olivia asking if she might bring her friend Hero to look at the paintings. Three weeks meant a busy life, extreme discretion

—or indifference. He was surprised at himself, too, for giving so little thought to the Greeks since their meeting, but matters of greater importance, germinated on the same occasion, had occupied his mind. He scarcely left the house for working. He would run out, usually at dusk, and walk hard round a block or two, when the faces he passed, if they didn't ignore him, appeared to take fright. He would hurry back with food, anything that could be quickly and easily eaten, and after stuffing his mouth with handfuls of torn-out bread, salmon straight from the tin, or chunks of marbled bully, he continued working. Sometimes he cut his hands on the tins and the blood worked in with the paint.

The day of the visit he felt neither inclined nor prepared for ladies of sensibility. Somewhere, he tried to remember, he had an opened tin of chocolate biscuits. He looked and found he had a couple of spoonfuls of tea-dust; to save time he had been drinking water, sometimes a swig of alcohol to cut the knots.

Finally, he put the visitors out of his head: till the sound of the doorbell and knocker in collaboration brought them back.

After she had drawn a short breath Olivia said: "I hope we haven't disturbed you."

"Why? Isn't this what we arranged?" Though his coldness was natural, his surprise must have sounded exaggerated.

"Oh yes," she hissed, "but other, more important things crop up."

She was out to show she had understanding, but the attempt was too obvious. He continued looking coldly at them. They lowered their eyes.

Each had studied her appearance, no doubt in consultation, to make it look unstudied. Olivia was wearing an old, though well-cut, coat and skirt, her hair, without a hat, slightly dishevelled. Hero was dressed, surprisingly and unfortunately, in brown, though fashion might have called it "cinnamon": it made her look dowdy, livery, black. Her one affectation was a bunch of violets, which she stood holding like a little girl, and raised to her nose in moments of doubt or embarrassment. In the beginning her embarrassment was almost unbroken. He couldn't leave off looking at the violets, which she kept permanently raised. He noticed the violet tones in her brown, livery skin.

Because there was nothing else he could do he led them upstairs. Once the front door was shut, their scents closed in on him, and his senses began to respond.

He laughed at one point on the stairs.

"What is it?" Olivia asked severely.

"I remembered there was a Greek I met. In Paris. After the war. Her name was Calvacoressi, I think—Hélène Calvacoressi."

He heard the toes of their shoes stabbing at the uncarpeted stairs.

"Was she a cocotte?" Hero asked in a prim tone he had detected at times on their first meeting.

"I think she was only a woman," he answered mildly.

He couldn't understand why he had allowed them to come, or why he had been prepared to expose himself by letting them look at his paintings. But they had reached the top: the loose boards on the landing were creaking; he could hear a sound of friction on one of the women, from subterranean silk, or hot rubber. He could hear one in particular, breathing as though submitting to fate; free will was an illusion formerly encouraged by free limbs.

Olivia coughed and said: "Hurtle—I've been telling Hero how I used to come to your parents' house—to play—in the old days."

He grunted. Which version, he wondered, had she painted?

They went into the front room, which was larger than the back studio-bedroom, thus more formal in a way; but it was cold, too: the cold light of a cold day splintered through the araucaria.

"If you'll sit down I'll show you some paintings."

He hadn't meant his voice to sound ironical, but it did: he had noticed some rat pellets on the floor boards. There were no chairs, only the grey waste of the bed he hadn't had time to make. He had slept there the night before: the room still had the smell of sleep.

They sat down, Hero Pavloussi and Olivia Davenport, uneasily contiguous. Hero held the violets over her mouth and chin. Her eyes appeared luminously tragic, though possibly this was what Greek convention demanded.

He began, only dutifully, to turn some of the stacked canvases and boards. None of the paintings interested him now; in fact he wondered why he had painted some of them, and the presence of his two visitors drained them of any significance they had ever had. Yet each of the two subdued women seated on the bed had worked in him at moments in their relationship as compellingly as his original compulsion to paint the dead paintings he was showing.

Hero was mostly silent, relying on her bunch of violets to express subtleties of which she would have been incapable. When she was not brooding behind it, she sat forward, one arm resting on her crossed knees, wrist rather limp, the ball of violets gently moving back and forth. He followed it with his eyes: it might be a turning point.

Whereas Hero was careful to confine herself to monosyllables, Olivia made several practised remarks. She was a professional at the game of looking at paintings, and liked to exercise her skill even on her off-days. This was one of the off-days, just how far off she was only beginning to realize. She was bored. She was haggard. She was probably menstruating.

One canvas, he noticed, was so appallingly muddy he couldn't believe it was his.

"I'm afraid I have nothing to offer you but some stale chocolate biscuits," he heard himself announce.

Hero was innocent enough to play. "Why should you offer us anything else when you're showing us the beautiful paintings?"

Olivia displayed her long white throat and a contrived smile. She began to hum. She was so at home she turned her back on the paintings; she started strolling about, looking at dust, at the corpses of flies, out the window, or, more specifically, inward at her own thoughts. This left him in greater intimacy with Hero, which, after all, had been the real purpose in Olivia's bringing her.

Finding herself unprotected, Hero looked for mercy. Instead of a congestion of uncertain, borrowed opinions, signs of a personal life again began to flicker in her.

"I'm sorry if I appear so ignorant—which I am—Mr Duffield—but interested."

Her awkward apology restored her beauty. Her heavy eyelids were particularly noticeable. Moreover, they looked sincere. A kind of tenderness was established between them, so innocent he wouldn't have felt ashamed of it in the most cynical company.

"Nothing I've shown you so far is very important," he clumsily mumbled. "Not today, at least. Perhaps it's the light. Or one of the metabolic days." Hero's presence made him feel ashamed of his pretentious word the moment he had used it.

Looking out of the window, Olivia was saying: "You'll have to cut down that tree, Hurtle: it's too depressing. It soaks up the light, and will probably fall on the house if you get a gale from the right quarter."

Her friend shivered, and looked more livery than before; but whatever influence Olivia had, she couldn't quench Hero's eyes: they had the curious fixed intensity of the eyes of saints painted on wood.

"What's that?" She suddenly sounded passionate. "This painting you're putting away? Why don't you show it to me?"

It was something he had begun to bring out, and returned automatically to the wall. "I didn't expect you'd take to it. No other reason I can think of."

"But why not? How do you know? You know nothing about me. From what I have seen, this is something I will understand."

Was she determined to atone for her gaffe over the "Pythoness"?

For the first time since their arrival Olivia's interest appeared aroused. "Which is it?" she asked, disbelieving and possessive.

She left the window and came round.

"Oh, that! That's repulsive! It's obscene! I remember it as a drawing only." She held it against the painting for springing up behind her back.

"Why shouldn't it appeal to me, though? That is what I am questioning," Hero insisted. "In some senses I am myself obscene and repulsive. Why must I not recognize it?"

Because he didn't know enough to be able to contradict her, and Olivia, who probably did, appeared to have no wish to, they continued all three staring at the painting: which lived as never before.

"What is it called?" Hero asked.

He hesitated. "I haven't decided on a title, but at the moment I think of it as 'Lantana Lovers under Moonfire.'"

"Oh yes, I know it! Lantana—it is from the most detestable things! And look at these houses along the ridge"—she indicated with the bunch of violets—"they remind me of the houses of Athens—at a time of evening—just after the sun has gone. I tell Cosma they are like gas-fires from which the heat has been turned off: so grey, and —burnt-out."

She might have shot him. He began laughing uncontrollably, teeth almost chattering: to find that, in spite of the distance between them, there was a point above the lantana from which they were able to communicate.

Even more uncontrolled, he asked: "And what does Cosma think?"

"Oh, Cosmas agrees. He is most innately perceptive."

Olivia was furious to find herself left out. "The whole thing's disgusting. Not as *painting*—morally. It's Duffield the exhibitionist at his most abominable!"

A grain of truth in what she said didn't prevent him enjoying it, anyway for that moment.

"So—so unnatural!" It was thrown in for good measure, but had a girlish sound.

"You're not exactly a child of nature yourself, Boo." He squeezed her under her left breast.

Probably she would never forgive him his blatancy, and in front of her friend Hero Pavloussi; while Hero might have remained unaware: she seemed genuinely to be concentrating on the painting.

"Tell me what it means," she asked, looking at him seriously.

"But darling," Olivia shrieked, "*you*'re supposed to *know*!" Having mastered several hundred characters of Chinese, she couldn't bear to think she hadn't learned the language her friend was talking with her friend.

Hero calmly said: "No. I don't know. That is, I know in my insides what it conveys to me. But I do not know the painter's intention. It is probably something quite different. All right. I accept that. But the painting also has something for me personally."

In defending her convictions she had abandoned the ball of violets, which lay on the muddle of grey blanket.

Guarded in the presence of Olivia, who already knew, he began to explain the meaning of the painting: the lovers in their vegetable bliss unconscious of a vindictive moon; then, on the earthly plane, the gunner-grocer aiming at them out of frustration and envy from the street bench. There were so many gaps in his explanation he could feel himself sweating.

"Yes, I see," Hero was saying earnestly—she was probably quite humourless—"the moon is in one of its destructive phases—like anybody. That, I understand. The innocent lovers are under attack."

"But they're not innocent. Nobody is—not even a baby." To take her revenge, and make everything as clear as crystal, Olivia let fall her words in an accent not unlike Hero's own. "And they're under no ordinary attack. Can't you see? The moon is *shitting* on them!"

If Hero understood the word she didn't show it; perhaps it was one she hadn't learned.

"Like an enormous seagull!" Olivia shrieked.

Hero wavered somewhat in her interrogation. "And this figure? Why is he a grocer," she asked.

Again it was Olivia who answered. "He was a grocer in fact. I can remember his name was Cutbush. Even the best painters owe something to reality."

"That's right. I met the bloke one evening on this bench. He had something rotten about him, but only slightly, humanly rotten in the light of the Divine Destroyer. I mean the grocer's attempts at evil are childlike beside the waves of enlightened evil proliferating from above; and he usually ends by destroying himself." He was unwilling to go any farther.

But Olivia was determined to add a last humiliating touch. "Hurtle sees him, I think, as a damned soul in the body of a solitary masturbator." Her crimson nail accused the trajectory of milky sperm dribbled across the canvas.

Now that she had perverted herself, and possibly someone else, she was ready to return to normal. She took hold of the points of her elbows. She looked excruciated, and peculiarly solitary.

Hero, on the other hand, appeared to have gained in stature; she had lost less dignity than any of them; presently she raised her head and said: "This painting may be everything that is claimed for it. But I recognize something of what I have experienced—something of what I am." She held her head higher. "I would like to buy it, Mr Duffield, if you will accept me as its owner."

She could only be atoning for her gaffe over the "Pythoness"; but whatever the source of her radiance, he was dazzled by it.

Regardless of Olivia Davenport, he said: "I'd like you to take the thing, forgetting about money for once."

"Oh no!" She showed her blunt little teeth in a smile. "Cosmas would never accept. He is too respectful of business obligations."

Olivia, too. She had undertaken to bring about a transaction. However different in its kind, and painful the emotional approach, she seemed appeased by what promised to be a round conclusion.

Hero insisted. "Please, sir. You must tell me your figure."

What the hell, then: hadn't his value increased since Mumma and Pa sold him in the beginning? He named a pretty steep sum.

At mention of real money, Olivia recovered her delicacy: she began going slowly down; the sound of her feet on the uncarpeted stairs, and of her shoulders thumping the plaster of the narrow stairway as she swayed from side to side, made the silences in between stream out far more audibly.

Hero sat scribbling a cheque with a casualness he had never been able to master, and a fountain pen of a kind only to be found in rich women's crocodile handbags. With still greater casualness she tossed the cheque onto the littered chest, as though she felt they had both been contaminated enough by such a sordid contract. His offering the painting in the first place as a gift was evidently a feeble, if spontaneous burst of idealism. Or had Olivia told her he was the product of a dirty deal between Cox Street and Sunningdale? And had Hero forgotten the circumstances in which she had taken up the offer of her hairy millionaire?

Still in business, he asked where he should send the painting; she replied without second thought: "Surely you will bring it? My husband will like to see you. He is so busy. But I will let you know."

She was so practically, so earnestly devoted to her man of affairs, it was pretty certain the event Olivia had been so anxious, then so unwilling, to procure, would not take place.

"Is that agreed?" Hero asked; then changing her tone, she said: "We must have exhausted your patience." And again, her voice blurring with emotion: "The Divine Destroyer—is that what you truly believe?" She took his hand, and for a brief moment seemed to be looking in it for an explanation of some division in herself. "No, you needn't tell me," she hastened. "It is true. There is that side as well. I know it."

At once she turned her odd behaviour into conventional thanks: she had taken his hand for no other reason than to shake it, which she did with candour, grinning at him with the shy pleasure of a little girl.

"Thank you—Hurtle—so very much."

The burnt and brooding terracotta had gone from her cheeks: they glowed with a suffusion of rose: he would have expected the juice to run out if he had bitten into them.

"Time's up!" Olivia called from below in a stop-watch voice. "The car, Hero!"

Nothing of what had taken place prevented their glances from shuttling in and out of each other in the room above; there was no need for answers where vibrations existed.

To avoid giving way to these, he had to betray a third person: "Olivia is the victim of her chauffeur. We'd better go down."

Madame Pavloussi laughed her scented laugh: it was the scent of cloves, or pinks. "Not the chauffeur," she said, negotiating the stairs. "Only herself dominates Olivia."

Mrs Davenport stood watching her friends as they came downstairs.

Madame Pavloussi remarked in her accent of languid cloves: "We have been discussing you, darling. I have said only now you are what is known as Pure Will."

Olivia Davenport looked at Duffield, giving him a slow, shuttered stare, before exploding into a rackety laughter. "Naturally I respect time. Don't you? Where should we be? Where would Hurtle be?" She composed her lips in a private smile intended for him; it implied: I shall write you a letter and invite you to discuss in detail everything that has happened.

"Oh, I agree," Madame Pavloussi said with exaggerated conviction. "You are so right." Now that she had returned to earth she seemed determined to sound flat. "Where should we be? There is this mercantile thing this afternoon to which Cosmas has asked me to come. Wives will be worn!"

"Oh, but darling, how perfectly ghastly! And you can't go like that—in brown. Wouldn't it be more *sympathique*—Hero—if you came home with me—and rested?"

"I am not tired," Madame Pavloussi assured her.

They were fitting themselves into the car as the chauffeur stood holding the door. Obstacles imposed on them by their formal lives and rubber disguises made them crawl and wriggle.

As they were easing the rubber and the expressions on their faces, he realized the train of events hadn't allowed him to show them the Octopus-Oracle, his main obsession since Hero Pavloussi had sown it in him the night of the party. Now he was glad he hadn't exposed Rhoda's gelatinous body to their gibbered judgements: Olivia inspired by her passionate love for someone she only imagined she had known; Hero ready to lament by heart deformity and the lost little sister, if she didn't turn her back on a reminder of her gaffe. Rhoda was subtler than either of them could have grasped. If he hadn't been able to love Rhoda, he couldn't love his own parti-coloured soul, which at best he took for granted; at worst, it frightened him.

While the two women were driven away, showering recognition on him each with royal flutterings of a hand, he wasn't certain, but fancied he could see Olivia holding Hero's other hand.

He waved. He couldn't care. He was still too obsessed by the grey suckers of the Octopus.

He received two letters on almost identical paper by the same afternoon delivery.

Dear Hurtle,
    Although I have in my head a letter explaining my behaviour the day of our visit, I hesitate to write it down for fear that my argument will not convince you.
    Because, for certain reasons, I always fail in love, I was hoping to experience a kind of voluptuous fulfilment through those I love, but suddenly felt in myself the old excruciating disgust, as though I were helping destroy something which might never be recovered, by letting the enemy into the last stronghold of purity.
    If I appear to have behaved deceitfully in the beginning towards Cosma Pavloussis in spite of my affection for him, it is because most men have minds and interests which prevent them understanding their wives' actual needs, whether sensual or psychic. I still believe this, and with anyone but Hero might have been prepared to finish the game. Now it is you who are the loser, Hurtle. I am not—I have to admit if I am honest—because I shall still enjoy in Hero the delicacy which at the last moment I resisted handing over, and which only another woman is capable of appreciating.
Affectionately yours,
Olivia D.

"Delicacy" did not prevent him letting out the fart he had been preparing. He began to crumple Olivia D.'s literary letter, but the stiff, expensive paper resisted.
    The letter from Hero Pavloussi, which he expected to be even more stylistic, wasn't at all: it came straight to the point.

Dear Mr Duffield,
    I have discussed the matter with my husband, who will be delighted to receive you and the painting on Friday 26th of this month at 11 a.m., if a morning call doesn't too much inconvenience you. It is only difficult in the case of my husband to arrange another appointment because he is always too busy.
    I will explain to you how to find the house. You will take the main road till past the convent, after which you will turn left in a kind of loop. Shortly on, there is an afterthought from this loop, aimed directly towards the sea. Do not miss it. The house is a medium Sydney house in the Tudor style. There are tamarisks at

the gate, and inside, a bed in the shape of a starfish planted with what I think the gardener has called violas (blue and yellow).

Although we are leaving probably fairly precipitately for Greece, my husband and I are anxious to start the experience of living with the painting, rather than crate it up with everything else and only see it when we arrive.

We look forward, both of us.

Sincerely
Hero Pavloussi

If you should miss the turn, we rent the house from a Mrs Cargill, whose name is known.

He ordered a van to take him with the painting: when a second letter forced a change of plan.

My dear Mr Duffield,
You will forgive us I hope, but my husband asks for a meeting same time only the *day following* the one we agreed.
So sorry!

Yours in haste
H. Pavloussi

On the agreed morning the van put him down with his veiled painting at the door of what might have been described as a medium house, though in "Sydney-prosperous" rather than the Tudor style. The tamarisk canes were still naked for winter, and the violas (blue and yellow) had been removed from the starfish bed since Madame Pavloussi wrote her instructions; the bed itself, not yet replanted, was built up high with rich-looking soil from somewhere else. He might have felt depressed by these signs of impermanence if the native sea hadn't been sparkling and prancing round the promontory on which the amorphous house was pitched.

After the van had gone, while he was standing juggling with his awkward painting, trying to control the wrapping the wind was tearing at, a man who looked like a gardener came round the side of the house carrying a heavily loaded sack. The man crossed the gravel, making for that part of the garden where the lawn sloped down towards the water. As he walked, the sack became convulsed by a struggle inside it. The sinews tautened in the gardener's neck. He looked a bilious yellow under his weatherbeaten skin.

"It's a pretty crook go when they ask yer to drown a bagful of flamun cats!" he spat at the stranger.

In his state of controlled agitation the man didn't wait for an answer, but crunched across the last of the gravel and reached the more soothing stretch of lawn.

"Wait on, Mr South!" a child called, before her dark legs slid down, then the seat of her pants, and her inverted dress, out of the branches of a tree. "I wanter watch an' see what happens."

When her dress had subsided it showed her to be a little part-aboriginal girl.

"Not on yer life!" the gardener shouted back. "An' you're bloody lucky you're not in the bag along with the cats."

The girl might have started sulking if she hadn't had the stranger to look forward to; now that she could see him properly she began to eye and sidle while pretending not to.

"Why are they drowning the cats?" he asked.

"Because everyone's goin' away."

"Isn't that a bit sudden?" In spite of the warning in the letter, he hadn't been prepared for such a ruthless departure; his discovery left him feeling breathless, purposeless, stunned, bracing the wind-raked canvas against his thigh.

The child didn't answer, but took a bull's-eye out of her cheek and began to examine the run stripes.

"You're Soso, are you?" he asked. "The adopted daughter."

She looked at him in shocked surprise, if not actual animosity. "I'm Alice," she said rather rudely; then thinking it over, she began to dimple and simper. "Yes. They call me Soso."

"Will you enjoy going to Europe with your parents?" he asked like the kind of visitor he had most despised when a child; still under the influence of recent developments he was only capable of imitating others.

The girl shook her head. "I'm not goin' anywhere but La Perouse."

It was too involved for him to continue its unravelling. Besides, he had to deliver what had been reduced to a parcel of merchandise. He realized his hands were trembling on the string.

"Where is your mother?" he asked.

"Why, at La Per—" But again Soso took over; her burnished skin lent an additional silky slyness to her smiles as she minced her words: "She's havin' a read—in her little *salong*—waitin' for Mr Duffield the painter."

To be treated so objectively seemed only natural in such an unlikely situation.

"I'll take you to her," Soso announced importantly, opening the front door.

At the same time, from inside the house, a maid advanced on them, her hands outspread as though to ward them off. "You know you was to stay outside in the sun because of what happened with your hair," she warned the child.

"All right, all right, bossy old cow!" Soso told the maid what she could go and do to herself.

In the circumstances the visitor was ignored; the maid, growing stringier than before, gasped and hissed back: "You'll catch it, my girl, if Madam hears words! You're not out at the Reserve, you know."

The child turned and said: "Come with me, please, Mr Duffield," in the voice of a composed, educated woman.

She marched him through the house and into a small morning-room in which Madame Pavloussi was seated upright, reading, or at least holding, a leather-bound book. He must have been expected, but his suddenly appearing, and in the child's company, gave the mistress of the house a shock: her face opened too quickly, and she almost mismanaged her stage book.

"Oh dear! It is kind—darling—to bring—but why did Gertrude not announce?"

Her formal duty done, Soso marched across the room and out.

Though there was no practical reason why the caller should have been announced, Madame Pavloussi seemed put out by the fact that a convention hadn't been observed. The smile kept fluttering on her mouth, and as on a previous occasion, her cheeks lost their look of sculpture: he half expected the scent of warm apples.

She said in an uncertain voice: "It is not possible, in these days of upheaval, to give attention to every detail—particularly with a rented maid."

"Why 'upheaval'?" he asked as gently as he could; her collapsed English seemed to call for it.

She was examining him more openly than he had felt before. On their previous meetings her eyes had appeared concentrated on, almost glazed by, some conflict of her inner life. Now her attention was directed outward, or was struggling out, along with her pretty, fluttering smile.

"My husband," she started to apologize, "must return to Greece by flying boat yesterday night. I will leave as soon as the arrangements are made to dispose of our belongings in Sydney. There are the cars. There is the lease of this house." She drew her eyebrows together. "Then we also have our obligations to animals and humans," she added with a moist pathos.

He remembered the sackful of cats, and she lowered her eyes, perhaps on catching a reflection in his.

"My husband is so upset not to have been able to receive you with the painting."

The painting had been left in the hall, but it did not occur to her to ask about it: she was too upset by her husband's being upset. Slight emotional upheaval, the slight melancholy of temporary separation, suited her best, he saw. She was on too small a scale to cope with passion or disgust. On a previous occasion, too much fire had shown up her features as ugly, and her limbs too stumpy for her body. Now, comparatively passive, she was almost perfect.

"Poor Cosmas! He talked about this painting at the last instant, before boarding the flying boat. He asked me to give you his own personal apologies." She handed her caller a letter.

The envelope had not been sealed: its contents were flowery and repetitive; the shipowner finally commended his wife: ". . . in whose taste and judgement I have every faith."

You couldn't help wondering whether Hero Pavloussi had read the letter her husband left unsealed: nothing more natural: except there was the law that nice people must behave unnaturally.

"Well, there it is!" She became automatically brisk. "Will you take a coffee, Mr Duffield? Or should I offer you a drink? I am hardly acquainted with your habits." Her smile was bright and brittle to match.

"You needn't worry." He hoped he said it pleasantly. "I only came to deliver the painting, and to talk to your husband about it—if that was what he wanted." By now he was sick of the thought of his own painting.

"One thing," she said vaguely, "you must tell me where I can get it packed."

She was moved on an erratic wave of agitation, caused no doubt by a sense of the upheaval to which she had referred. The room was an intimate one, and might have appeared sympathetic if it hadn't been for the actual owners' department-store taste. In it all, there were a few leather-bound books, of the same tooling as the one Hero had been pretending to read. (He realized she was coming into focus, physically at least, and that he was thinking of her again as "Hero.") The book was printed in Greek, and again he was reminded of the mental and moral labyrinths which might prevent them ever meeting.

"There is so much," she protested, taking a cigarette from a box she couldn't have rented. "There is the little girl, for instance, whom you met—Alice—or Soso, Cosmas likes to call her."

She lit the cigarette with an enormous lighter, and though he had never seen her smoke, she showed that she was technically adept.

"Oh yes," he returned to one of the points at which she seemed lost, "the adopted daughter."

"What? Adopted?" She blew two streams of smoke most professionally out of her nostrils. "That was an idea. Cosmas is always full of ideas: he has his moral responsibilities; then he forgets." She laughed affectionately, afterwards drawing on her cigarette with an unexpected hungriness. "Oh yes, we *intended* to adopt. But I couldn't feel it was practical. The mother is an aboriginal woman from—this Reserve—wherever it is. She was allowed to come here recently to visit her child, and the little girl was left with what I think you would call 'nits.'" Hero Pavloussi was so comically distressed. "She was infested!"

Her cheeks grew hollow from drawing on her cigarette.

"Fortunately our laundress . . ."

He felt sick with apprehension for his innermost core, for one of his most precious secrets, and for Alice-Soso's fate, which to some extent matched his own.

"I adore our laundress," Madame Pavloussi said, "a charming young Irishwoman called Bridget O'Something." Again she laughed for the comicality of it.

The possibility of his enjoying an innocent relationship with Hero was slipping from him as miserably as a miscarried child. At least he now understood about this from having personally experienced it: he felt wet about the legs.

"Bridget knew," Madame Pavloussi brightly explained, "that you rub the hair with—kerosene? Oh dear, the smell was appalling!" She wrinkled up her smoke-infested nostrils before exhaling. "I can tell you!" she breathed. "And poor Cosmas is so easily disillusioned. I think it was this finally which decided him not to adopt."

"Alice won't go with you to Greece?"

"Oh no! No question of it. It would be impossible." She sighed.

"She will go back to her mother—at this Reserve—at wherever it is. Of course Cosmas will give money," she added, "and probably in the long run the child will be a lot better off." She had sat down and was smoothing her skirt.

"How did the cats also disillusion him—that he should have them tied up in the sack?"

She drew down her mouth, in that peculiarly Greek manner, and with it her whole face: its cast was of an ugliness to rouse the imagination.

Then she looked at him piercingly. "You are testing me, aren't you, Mr. Duffield—Hurtle?" She closed her eyes, and actual tears began to come. "Oh, you don't know! He is so good! You can't understand!"

She got up and strode about the room, arms crossed on her breast, hands gripping her own shoulders. She might have looked overdramatic, even ridiculous, if her drama hadn't made her suffer. "*Everybody*," she cried out, and repeated more softly, "everybody has their faults."

He saw many progressions from a drawing he had done the night of their first meeting: the stone head lying in the dust beside the formal, stone body; only, in the drawing, the eyes were open.

He said: "You'll feel differently when you've wound up your affairs and returned to Greece. How will you go?"

"By sea?" It was a question, not an answer. "Oh yes," she said. "Cosmas only went by air because time was involved—and business. I have time to spare."

She was standing in the centre of the room, on a carpet so aggressively hideous it was surprising she wasn't sucked down into its maroon and brown roses; but the lines of her skirt, of her torso, again those of an archaic sculpture, were indestructible: to remember her as an aesthetic experience should be enough.

"When you've tidied everything up—I mean, the packing, and the cars, and the little aborigine—shall I come to see you?"

She said: "Oh, it will take time. Yes. You see, apart from everything else, my Maltese dog—poor little Flora—whom you haven't seen—is sick." He could, in fact, see her, smell her, pink-eyed and shivering in the nest of flannel. "She has—I don't like to think—only the vet more or less promised—I can hardly say—a cancer. This is what, more than anything, upset Cosma, because he is tenderhearted. I am the practical one."

The stiff, sculptured folds of her skirt did not prevent her advancing, till she was standing quite close to the chair in which he was sitting.

"I will rather come and visit you," she said, "because it is inconvenient for you to travel all the way to here."

She was examining him, and he could see the veins of her eyeballs with all their tributaries.

"Is Sunday objectionable?" she asked. "On that day I can arrange for our little girl to go to her mother at La Perouse."

He only hesitated because he could see the grain in her naked lips as they hovered above him, and the hair so very distinct where it had been strained back from the temples.

Just when he was preparing to give the logical answer, the stringy maid appeared and, looking out to sea, announced: "The vet has come, madam, about the dog."

"Oh," she said hoarsely, "yes," her stone lips barely moving.

An almost summer sunlight slatted the floor of the room over Chubb's Lane. He had half-latched the shutters through which the sounds of the neighbourhood entered, only slightly muffled by Sunday. Now that he was free to observe, he hoped the striped and spangled light would divert anyone else's attention from what could otherwise have appeared huggermugger and drab. For him, the light created something festive in his familiar but probably frowzy surroundings. To remember that a flight of motes was of the same substance as passive grey domestic dust had always delighted him.

"If you're hungry, I can open a tin of herrings," he suggested, "and there's a loaf of fairly fresh bread."

She made a mumbled sound, at the same time rejecting his offer with a movement of her head against his shoulder. She was behaving like somebody stupefied by a heavy meal in the middle of the day and the sleep which comes after it; though probably she hadn't touched food since breakfast, if she had eaten then.

"Herrings in tomato sauce: not an attractive proposition; but easy, and quickly over." It might have sounded like talking to himself in an empty room if she hadn't again uttered that animal, mumbled sound.

He couldn't tempt her: whereas she had been so hungry on arrival he had hardly closed the door on the street before she fell on him ravenously, propelling him with her greed somewhere that remained unlocated till he thumped against the padded shoulder of an old dusty sofa and cannoned off the corner of a crashing whatnot.

At some point he was infected with her appetite, and took over. If he had been left with breath, he would have liked to explain: yes, you are here, and now there is no reason why morning afternoon evening should be in any way distinguishable if that is what we decide we need. But he had grown ravenous himself. From nibbling to biting to attempting to swallow her burning earlobes. On the cracking stairs. It would have been neither surprising nor resistible if their gluttony had thrust them through the splintering banisters and they had landed below in the hall. Instead they gyrated or slipped crouching bruised against the stair-boards. Once he almost gouged out the eye of her suspender. While her corkscrew-tongue kept trying to drag from his throat an imagined resistance to her thirst. Feet stumbled, crass and blunt, always mounting, it seemed, raising a dust which started them both coughing.

"Hero?" He coughed it up pointlessly; for she had lost her normal identity, and the one she had acquired was nameless.

As they were climbing the stairs her fingers, or claws, used his ribs as rungs. Then, as though she had reached the summit, she seemed to hang from him, suspended by no more than her pelvis and adhesive mouth. Though just when they made the precipice of the landing, and might have toppled right back to the start of their ascent, they were held together by their hearts' chuffing, not in unison, that might have been fatal, but one valve taking over where the other failed.

On the landing: their knees trembling and knocking. He felt cold behind the knees, kneecaps thin and breakable. Now he was thirsty rather than hungry, now that the last of his saliva had run down outside their mouths, evading their attempts to drink each other up. So, on the landing, he began to tear her breasts apart, to get at the flesh inside the skin: the scented, running juices; in a drought even the bitter seeds could be sucked and spat out.

He hadn't tasted more than the small rubbery nipples when she cried out: "You are hurting me! We are animals!"

"Yes, Hero. Come in here."

He hadn't intended to take her into that one, but nothing develops as conceived: the pure soul, for example; the innocent child, already deformed, or putrefying, in the womb.

They got their clothes off in the back room he hadn't intended. The cold mattress-ticking rustled through their swollen veins; the leather asterisks stamped themselves on their half-melted skins.

At moments they were laughing together over something, and he wondered whether he knew what it was. Certainly their love-making sounded pneumatic at times; their lust took on grotesque shapes. Yes, love had its puddingy moments. LOVE: that was what they were laughing at; but immediately stopped shocked short grinding their teeth into each other's teeth. The portcullis wouldn't allow them asylum. They looked into each other's eyes and there were no depths to reach: there were the positions of love.

After demanding the ultimate in depravity, she ran out flat-footed looking for the bathroom, nor did he direct or advise her, because she would arrive at that, too, by instinct: the bath with the brown stain on the bottom; the French-smelling lavatory bowl; the droppings of verdigris under the geyser; her daemon would cope with all of it. Holding his arm over his eyes, a hand over his dribbled crutch, he waited for her return.

They might have lain all their lives sleeping side by side on the thawed mattress-ticking.

When he woke he noticed that his own body, although more muscular, looked more defenceless than hers because whiter, nakeder: in fact, flesh. You forget about vaccination marks. Here were his, their white, sweating scars waiting to drop off in the end as the scabs had in the beginning; whereas hers were baked into a terracotta arm they might dig up a thousand years hence and produce as evidence of "civilization."

She turned over, and her breasts were two extinct volcanoes he wouldn't approach; they could erupt all over again: himself drowning in lava.

This was where he said: "If you're hungry, I can open a tin of herrings."

They lay a long time barely fondling the parts they had appropriated from each other.

Somewhere in the late afternoon, judging by the resentment with which the inhabitants of Chubb's Lane were throwing the crockery around in their sinks, she sat up yawning her mouth off, stretching her arms to release, but in fact knotting them. Then she stomped over the boards, on squelching feet, her naked body forced by a recall of prudery into constricting angles, and started floundering about through her handbag. The bag, which he hadn't noticed, sounded an old shapeless valise stuffed with superfluous necessities, the search a sordid one, at least for anybody as perfectly achieved as Hero Pavloussi. In the end she came across the cigarettes.

Scratching an armpit, he said: "You're quite a bit different from what I expected." He continued scratching voluptuously to celebrate his relief; prolonged perfection would have made intolerable demands.

"I was no different from what I am." On lighting a cigarette, she came clumping back to the bed, for modesty's sake more than ever in the shape of a half-open jackknife. "It is you who want always to create something—even people. Because you see them mostly at their worst, you have wanted somebody at her best." Seated again on the bed, strengthened by a comfortable attitude, she was able to behave most objectively. She gathered him into her hand. She was examining him as though these wilted flowers, or bruised fruits, or catch of squid, had never known her creative touch; they were her specimens.

"Cosmas my husband"—she sat frowning at the penis in her hand—" is one of these men who must build a monument. I am to represent perfection for him. In the first place, I am of a class he never had access to, except through his money. Of course I married him for his money. My mind told me: however else could you marry such an unpolished man, except for the advantages; so don't deceive yourself. At least I could be honest about it. But however crude my motive for marrying a millionaire, it was not as crude as what I discover as the real reason. I find I marry Pavloussis for his body. I am soon distracted by this in many ways gross peasant, and he is shocked to find that his monument will become a monument to lust. Because where he is not sensual and lustful with paid women, Cosmas is pure pure. He is soon quite impotent from disappointment in his wife. I remember him telling me: 'Not even a prostitute would behave like this. It would offend against her conventions.' I said: 'But you are my husband, whom I married for his money, and now I find you give me joy. Am I not to express this?' It was even more shocking for him that I try to rationalize my behaviour. He could understand and accept my marrying him for his money, but not the other. About this time he cancelled a visit to his island—to his mother—because I believe he could not dare to produce his wife."

"How did he dare dispose of his 'daughter,' and drown the bagful of cats?"

"That is not to the point!" She rejected her lover with a forcefulness that made him whinge.

Anger drove her into a less comfortable position. She sat on the edge of the bed, rounding her shoulders to shut him out, with stiffened fingers manipulating her cigarette. She was making a business of smoking; but it did not ease her feelings, as her mouth showed whenever the glow gave it away.

"Very much to the point," he persisted, "if you talk about rationalizing behaviour."

Her silence sounded a sulky one.

"Or are Greeks perhaps cruel by nature?" he couldn't help suggesting.

"*Who* is cruel? Greeks? Turks? Man is cruel!" she shouted back. "God—God is cruel! We are his bagful of cats, aren't we? When God is no longer cruel many questions will be answered." She was so furious she accompanied her accusations by striking the mattress with her stiffened hand. "You drive me to blaspheme!" she shouted louder still.

"But you've told me you're not a believer."

"No. I do not believe. But blaspheme every day!"

She burst into such a torrent of grief it was now his turn to be shocked. He tried to comfort her by caressing her racked body; but this was not what she wanted: she shook him off in a flurry of wet hair.

"What I do believe in," she cried, "is my husband's goodness, because I have experienced it. You will not believe in it because of the bagful of cats. He loved the cats—which he killed. Yes, he killed them. Why do we kill what we love? Perhaps it is because it becomes too much for us—simply for that reason."

"You could have saved the cats."

She grew quiet at once. "Why—yes—I could have saved the cats by giving an order after he had left. But I am myself also condemned, as I sit waiting in the house, and the drowning do not care about the other drowning." She reached out. "Do you see?" She laughed hoarsely as she dragged him down with her into her watery inferno.

Their indecently resigned struggles inside the bag must have been observed and judged from a distance by the shaggy god from under his black, heavy eyelids.

She said as they were drawn apart at last through the apathetic depths: "Will you turn on the light, please, Hurtle? I will be going now."

He touched the dry mattress-ticking to which he had been returned. What fascinated him still was the texture of the wet bag, or condemned cell, in relation to the matted, elastic bodies of the prisoners.

"The light?" she repeated. "Were you sleeping—darling?" she remembered to add.

"No," he said, reaching for the flex, "not sleeping."

Neither sleeping nor waking: it had been one of those moments when you half-consciously watch the slides experience is fitting into the frame of a dissolving mind; such a slide, perhaps, would best convey his conception of the drowning lover-cats.

"How many were there?" he asked and smiled.

"How many what?"

"Cats."

"For God's sake! I don't remember!"

He didn't worry; two lovers could add up to an infinity of cats.

Faced with the problems of disguise, Hero was only momentarily irritated. It was most important that she should cover her strongly made, stumpy legs. She bumped around in search of tumbled clothes, her webbed hands outstretched. Soon she was snapped back into her formal identity: hooked and smooth.

As for himself, he got very easily into a minimum of garments, with that slight feeling of grit or sand which comes between the contented skin and its covering after making love.

Hero was suddenly upset. "Oh darling, did I do this to you? How bestial! I am disgusted!"

He hadn't felt them, but she made her mouth into a tender shape to apply to the scratches, almost gashes, in the crook of his arm, and to the little bows, or lovers'-knots, or bite marks the glass showed him in the angle of his neck and shoulder.

She only left off kissing or sucking when he asked: "Are you also Olivia Davenport's lover?"

"Poor Olivia! I don't think anyone—and I include her husbands—was ever her lover."

It didn't quite answer his question, but he had no intention of insisting.

"Will you believe me when I say it is possible to love two people at once?" she asked very gently.

"No." He tried to answer gently: it sounded brutal.

They embraced for the illusion she had hoped to nourish, and for his own stillborn idea of the pure soul, and in this way came perhaps closest to loving. Their clothes were a comfort, and their undemanding skins.

When she left he went with her, and they wandered the peacefully dead streets in search of a taxi.

"But you haven't any shoes!" she saw and protested, but not enough; his bare feet were no longer so incongruous as her clothed body.

"I will telephone you, darling," she said, and he didn't bother to remind her that she couldn't.

The pavement felt cool and agreeably abrasive to his bare soles now that his commitment was slighter; yet this, too, was an illusion: he would go to her in the Tudor-style mansion, from which only the cats had been exorcised.

As she leaned out of the taxi, looking back, not necessarily at him, the street lighting and her appeased lust had ringed her eyes: they had never appeared more luminously suppliant.

Though he didn't see her in the days which followed, he didn't escape for long at a time; the sack wouldn't let him. Smells of sea lettuce of sea of putrefying bait of motorboats haunted his nostrils. Pa Duffield returned, not to protect, but to assist at his destruction. *Don't go near the water son you never learned to swim.* I can learn can't I not to drown. *Better not trust the water.* The flannel vest with discoloured buttons made Pa look scraggier, more distrustful. *Nobody likes to rear a kid an' all for nothun.* Or five hundred quid. Pa himself, veins blue in his knotty hands, was helping tie the neck of the sack. *This is for love Hurt so lie quiet damn yez all of you lovecats.* While he was tying the string Pa was crying the way they do. The neck choking the daylight out you had only a moment left to recognize God by his black eyelids. You might have shouted balls if Hero hadn't been so devout. Many cats with parti-coloured skins were fighting their sentence inside the bag ever more heavily clinging its smell of sugar soon drowned.

Rising from his dreams, he started working wildly. He worked Monday Tuesday Wednesday Thursday. In addition to the preliminary notes and several drawings, he had painted two versions by Friday. He would have liked to sleep with Hero on the Thursday, but tore once again into the wet sacking.

On the Saturday—shades of Pa—he took an all-in bath, and put on his second-best, the tobacco-coloured suit, because he was planning to go and see his mistress the Greek woman. He had to come running back though, several times, to look at his "Infinity of Cats." Most of the condemned animals were still noticeably furred, but their writhing despair and the action of the water made some of them look skinned, or human. By the time he left to find a taxi he realized the bath had been a wasted move: he was in such a sweat he smelled as rank as a tom. He didn't care.

At the gates of the Tudor-style house the tamarisk canes were almost visibly sprouting flesh-coloured plumage as the sultriness increased, while all over the star-shaped bed small green anonymous plants were flopping in the overfortified soil. He should have felt like celebrating the sub-tropical spring, but noticed in the porch the figure of Alice-Soso, the aboriginal "daughter," seated on a dented Globite case.

When he had paid off the taxi he asked: "Are you going away?" as though there had ever been any doubt.

Soso pursed up her face into the shape of a doughnut.

Perhaps to make amends for his pretended ignorance, of which he was now ashamed, he said: "You'll feel happier out at the Reserve. Your mother loves you, doesn't she?"

Soso snort-laughed. "She got paid to take me back." She sat twisting her hands together. "Mumma loves anything that comes her way. And it pays to love." She glanced up with a glint which comes from experience.

He looked away on catching sight of her expression. Was he, as she seemed to imply, prostituting himself like anybody else? She was most disturbing, sitting on her case, with her louse-free hair beautifully arranged for her return to the Reserve.

Then the rented maid came out, and Madame Pavloussi the temporary owner of the house, who was also his mistress.

Hero, on seeing him, gasped as though plunging into cold water, but immediately concentrated on the child.

"Did you look through all your drawers, darling, and cupboards?

If I must go quickly away, it will make it difficult for me to forward the things you forget. Did you remember your *toothbrush*?"

The thin maid kept darting out on little sorties, shading her eyes, challenging the car to show itself. He realized he had seen her before, at the mercy of other contingencies, in *Pop-eye the Sailor*; the discovery made him laugh.

At which Hero began a kind of Greek lament: "You have my address, Aliki? And will write me a few little words from time to time? Because Mother will always take an interest in your welfare. And dear Daddy."

Alice whispered: "Yeeehs," disposing of the moment with a rapturous smile; she didn't look at Mr Duffield, but he sensed they were in league: they might have suffered the same fracture.

Just then the car crawled round the side of the house, which appeased the maid, and threw Hero up against her departing "daughter."

"My poor kitten!" she blurted with complete and genuine abandon. "Daddy is going to see to it you will never want." The child allowed herself to be embraced. "It is nobody's fault, Aliki. It is only Fate who arranges it."

Alice couldn't have believed in Fate. She was opening the car door and arranging herself on the back seat.

Hero frowned, because she had visualized it otherwise. "Won't you sit by Sotiri?"

"Nah. They're gunner see me drive up like a lady." Alice didn't look back or wave, though the maid was prepared for such emergencies.

Madame Pavloussi was left too abruptly with her lover, who decided to let her down lightly by making conversation. "The chauffeur's a Greek?"

"Yes," she said, smiling. "We found him—Sotiri. Isn't it a nice name? It means 'Saviour.' "

Then they went in, and he noticed the painting still propped against the hall wall, packaged as he had brought it.

Madame Pavloussi said: "You don't know how all that is happening recently is tearing me in pieces. I never thought I will become so attached to Australia."

After they had gone inside what Soso-Alice had referred to on the first occasion as the "little *salong*," Hero turned on him with that same brown, Byzantine hunger, and when she had locked the door,

324

he rooted her—that afternoon you couldn't have called it anything else—on Mrs Cargill's Axminster carpet.

Their obscenities over, she had to face him, because the geography of the house and the presence of servants didn't allow her an escape to the bathroom. She knelt shivering in front of him, and said after crossing her arms on her breasts: "I have written to Cosma and told him I cannot join him because you are my lover."

He noticed in her skin the verdigris tints from some play of fortuitous light. He even felt jealous: that he should have made his discovery pragmatically rather than intuitively.

"I can't deny I'm your lover," he agreed, glancing at one of Mrs Cargill's *Town Cries*.

"Also," she said, "I cannot bring myself to kill my little dog Flora —who is suffering from this cancer. You see, I believe in miraculous recoveries."

Hero was shivering worse than ever: so much so, it was transferred to her detached lover.

When he had drawn her down, they lay together, no longer sexually, gooseflesh rasping against gooseflesh. They were holding in their arms mild dyspepsia, incurable disease, old age, death, worst of all—scepticism. He couldn't suggest to Hero Pavloussi that his paintings alone might survive the debacle, because it wouldn't have been of comfort to her; it was no more than a slight satisfaction to him while his body continued a source of pride.

But he bowed to it. His bones almost clicked with the speed at which he rejected the flesh in favour of the one substance: paint. He got up, removing his skeleton from her arms.

Soon after, they escaped from the horrible room, and she asked, manoeuvering it skilfully over her teeth: "When shall I see you again?"

He didn't see her as often as he expected, because officially and socially she was sticking to the story of her departure. He might have felt aggravated if it hadn't been for the series of drowning cats on which he was at present working, and which more than filled any possible void.

On an occasion when the need for him brought her to Flint Street, Hero said: "I believe you are so egoist, Hurtle, you have already forgotten what I have given up for your sake. I cannot see you loving anybody—*ever*."

Even so, she spoke with a pronounced satisfaction, accepting her punishment along with the pleasure she had chosen. If he appeared to her more bitterly mysterious than seemed natural, it was because she deliberately turned her back on his paintings.

She did once remark: "You are so wrong, so *perverse*, to pick on this one deed of my darling Cosma, and pump it up into a big moral issue and theme of art."

It trickled round him while he worked, half-listening. Since her physical presence had come to mean less, he was less disturbed by having her there. At one point he hooted his approval.

"What is it?" she asked. "Is it again my English?"

"'Pump it up into a big moral issue'!"

"What is wrong with this?"

"Nothing. It's—very—nice. Only you're not—vulgar enough to see."

He stood back to examine this most fiendishly obdurate corner, which still refused to collaborate.

Sometimes she sat listlessly, but respectfully enough, because her lover was inescapably a painter. She could accept the condition; the actual symptoms were what revolted her: they could have been dropsical or pustular.

Anyway, she wasn't going to look—while he continued stroking his doomed cats.

Returning from the heights and depths of his trampoline act with Hero Pavloussi, he was thrown hot and spattering into his paintings of the drowning. In all but one of these versions, the victims' fate was ordained by implication and a presence of light. But in one painting he couldn't resist introducing the Satrap Himself: he was almost completely covered with black hair, the face livid, except for the eyelids, which were black, too. The painter couldn't touch the eyelids tenderly enough: the doomed god became as tragic as the cats he had condemned.

"If I give you nothing but what is ugly and ludicrous, then I have failed," Hero said gloomily.

"How do you know if you haven't looked?"

"Oh no, I haven't looked at what I *know* would be ugly!"

"If it's ugly as you say, it hasn't had time to grow beautiful. It will, though. It's true enough, anyway, and I'm truly, humbly grateful, Hero, for what you have given me—you and Cosma."

As far as he could fathom, his fault lay in loving her more in her drowned condition. He even loved her cheated husband. Now that he was filled with this love, and could have poured into her some of the tenderness he had spent on the paintings, for there was still an abundance of it, she pushed him away and got up.

"You are all dirty with paint," she complained. "Shall we go and eat somewhere, if there is anywhere that will have you?"

The banality to which she had deliberately reduced them both by her condemnations did not detract from her beauty. He had forgotten about it during his preoccupation with her tortured, dripping, shivering soul. Now her actual head began to engross him equally, though differently. Since he had transformed the drowning Hero into a work of art, he desired her physical beauty less. He might covet it from time to time, as on the spur of the moment he might have coveted the rose quartz or the crystal bird on Olivia Davenport's dining-table; but his desire for material possessions was not a deep one.

She must have grown conscious of his admiration, if not its kind or degree, because she began moistening her lips, nervously smiling, glancing obliquely at the glass.

"If you do love me, as I think you are perhaps too sensitive to admit," she said, putting out an encouraging hand, "why can't we make together, out of our love, something beautiful and lasting instead of morbid, drowned cats?"

He put on his coat. He was afraid she might see herself as a kind of Boucher: a vision of pink tits and dimpled cheeks.

The next time she came to him he had a surprise for her.

"What is it?" she asked quickly, breathlessly, so that he was particularly conscious of her short teeth, and on one side, towards the back, a gap he hadn't noticed before; in spite of the rapacious expression of the open lips, with which he was familiar from the moments when she was about to satisfy her lust, her head had never looked more perfectly cast: a masterpiece.

His hesitation, and preoccupation with something about her appearance, made her repeat nervously: "What—is it?" Immediately after, she changed her tune; she put on a knowing look, and thrust herself against him, as though joining in the joke: it was the usual surprise. "Won't you show me?"

They were standing by the doorway of the increasingly cluttered junk- and store-room on the upper landing.

"Well," he hesitated still, "you may be disappointed. It's only another painting."

"Is it *the* painting?" She forced him right into the room. "The one I know you can make if you want to? *Our* painting!"

She made it sound like jazzed-up Tchaikovsky.

"It's our painting all right." She had driven him up against the board he couldn't bring himself to turn. "Whether it's one you'd approve of, I can't tell without your looking at it."

He realized his heart was beating as it used to sometimes while he found the courage to speak the truth in front of Maman. His repeated downfall was his longing to share truth with somebody specific who didn't want to receive it. Was it why he had failed so far in love?

"Go on!" Hero Pavloussi was by now positively shouting. "I know by your expression it is something horrible and degrading. I don't want to see it, but show!"

At the same time her fingers began struggling with his in her determination to turn the board and share in his depravity.

He was probably grimacing back as desperately as she, when the board fell flat on its back: the dust shop up from the floor.

Hero Pavloussi began to cry and cough. "You see? It is worse! It is a pornography! Are you trying to kill me?"

If, as the tone of her accusation suggested, she meant him to join her in rejecting his painting, it was not because he was persecuting her, but because—he could see more clearly now that he was looking at the painting again—this showed an act of self-destruction: the figure of the woman was deliberately aiming the blow at her own heart.

"Ohhhh!" She was moaning like a whole Greek chorus in the airless junk-room.

"Don't you at least find it *formally* acceptable?" He was stuttering like a breathless youth out of the few phrases he had learned.

She had hidden her face in her hands and was perhaps still looking from between her fingers.

"Tonally, then," the youth in him shouted; or was it: "*Totally!*" while in a cold flash he stood at the end of his life listening to rats scampering through an otherwise deserted house.

Then he realized Hero Pavloussi was running down the actual

stairs, faster, faster, hurtling, practically throwing herself, it sounded, from the last flight. Her footsteps on the pavement were less tragic, in fact a dwindling stampede, in which she went over on a heel, once, almost throwing, then righting herself. It was this pathetic rather than tragic sound, of some swollen-footed, human beast of burden hurrying with bursting carrier-bags to catch the tram, which almost made him love the "pure soul" *manquée* of Hero Pavloussi.

That he couldn't love her entirely, or call out through the window, or run after her offering the small change of the flirtatious male, was due to the fact that he was left with his painting in the darkening cubby-hole of a room, and in the painting they each existed on another level, neither pathetic nor tragic, neither moral nor, as she continued erupting in his eardrums, "pornographic." They were, rather, an expression of truth, on that borderline where the hideous and depraved can become aesthetically acceptable. So, in the hot little dusk-bound room, the man's phallus glowed and spilled, while the woman, her eyes closed, her mouth screaming silent words, fluctuated between her peacock-coloured desires and the longed-for death-blow.

He felt too weak for more. Taking his painting with him, he went into the front bedroom, already cooler and darker for the encroaching araucaria. Lying beneath its fringed pagoda, on the unmade bed, he saw how he might illuminate the woman's face still further. But in the morning. For the moment he could only lie and add up the sum of his working life, the details of which remained with him indelibly, unlike his age: he could never remember that; your age is something forced on you by other people.

He must have been sleeping. His consciousness throbbed back into him too suddenly and too hot, like the final episode of a second-class film ending in a flash of transparency: he heard the clatter. Night had fallen in the meantime, but by no means opaque. His dry tongue, flickering, tasted a lemonade of light filtered through the araucaria.

He was frightened: no, not frightened; nothing is frightening this side of exhausted creativity. He was even interested in the sounds of somebody moving about in his house—still far down—climbing upward.

He reached for the flex and switched the light on. The footsteps sounded less tentative. From more determined, they became downright aggressive as they reached the landing.

"Why, Boo," he said when she stood beside the bed, "what sort of party have you come from?"

For Olivia Davenport was dressed in a man's black suit, its austerity barely holding out against the luxury of her figure. Over her travesty she was wearing a long bottle-green cloak kept together at the throat by a silver chain. A shaving brush stood erect at the back of her Borsalino.

She began hectoring at once: "This is no laughing matter, Hurtle." Certainly she was dead pale, but a pallor which might have been assisted. "Hero has almost killed herself. She didn't want you to be told, but I felt you ought to be—as you drove her to it."

"Where is she?" On all fours, he had begun the search for his lost shoes.

"At her house. She telephoned. Fortunately I was free to go."

As he was groping amongst the fluff and splinters, Olivia told how Hero had tried to open her veins.

"If she had succeeded you would have been responsible. Wouldn't you?" It was her pleasure to rub it in.

"If she had wanted to succeed she would have," he said rather wearily, putting on his shoes. "Only then she wouldn't have been able to indulge herself on the telephone."

Olivia didn't gush tears, but wilted somewhat inside her drag; what she said sounded soggy-nosed: "Always the people one loves most end up the most unlovable."

"Has Hero let you down?"

"Oh—*Hero!* Don't be ridiculous—irrelevant!" But Olivia herself had faltered into irrelevance: she couldn't resist, at least with her eyes, foraging around for paintings.

"What's this?" she gasped, though she might have known, and he didn't bother to tell her she was bending over the reason for Hero's false suicide.

"Ohhhh!" She began moaning in crescendo, and here he was reminded of Hero, only Olivia's was a contralto voice. "I wonder if you know how good you are? But of course you do! You're too detached, too hateful, not to."

He had a strong desire to eat something before facing further hysterics.

But Olivia turned on him. "You've made me drunk!" She did actually appear to reel inside the swirling cloak. "May I kiss you for it, Duffield?" She didn't wait to be allowed. "If Hero had more taste, she might respect you as an artist though she can't love you as a man."

Going downstairs, he tried to remember what, if anything, he had in the fridge; while Olivia talked on about—love? art?—he couldn't be bothered to work out which, according to Olivia, was which.

"Don't you agree?" she called out.

He called back: "Yes. Oh *yes*!"

"I don't believe you were listening. What were you thinking about?" she asked.

"Cold sausage!" he remembered in triumph.

Olivia also remembered. "Poor little Hero!" She began to suck her teeth and whimper. "Only a woman could understand her behaviour."

"Why," he asked, "did you go to her dressed up as a man?"

Olivia slightly hesitated. "I look well in it," she said in an honest voice; then she added with a hard, dry laugh: "And because women cling to their illusions—even after they've tried to kill themselves."

He had found the plateful of sausages. Under their film of fat the cold cooked sausages were glowing: a milky, opalescent blue. He remembered from Mumbelong a dented baking-tin left out for cats, its dregs of milk transformed by the frost into a skin of bluish ice; human skins turning blue with cold, or gin; old men in particular, their veins, and foreskins from which the former brazen stream had dwindled to an anxious trickle.

"How repulsive! Revolting!" Olivia screamed, looking at the plateful of sausages and shuddering into her travesty cloak.

He could only shake his head. He was tucking into the sausages, and in any case he could not have told her about, he could only show her, the bloom on blue. So he thrust the plate at her, and she did actually finger a sausage; after scraping off some of the fat on the edge of the chipped plate, she began to mumble on what might have been a giant lipstick she had made the mistake of buying.

But this wasn't the reason for her thoughtfulness, which finally she let out. "That painting, Hurtle—would you consider selling? I'd treat it with more respect than anybody else, and of course it would go, in the end, with the others, 'to the public.'"

Then, suspecting herself of tastelessness, she bit enormously into the sausage, and her face which that evening had shed its van Dongen chic for the gas-lit concavities of a Greco Christ, was further transformed, by strain, into a large, costive, powdered arse.

So they stood: smiling, chewing, swallowing, half communicating over the empty plate, in the grubby asbestos limbo which had served Miss Gilderthorp as a kitchen.

All the way to Hero Pavloussi's they remained in that state of half-cocked reality, neither life nor art, which is perhaps the no-man's land of human failure. Olivia was driving a long, low-slung, bottle-green car, to match her cloak. She had taken off her man's hat, and her woman's hair blew at times darkly softly around her head, particularly when they took the corners. The silver *mèche* stood up like horns above her forehead.

All the dark, Welsh-named side-streets of the neighborhood in which he seemed to live were failed. Speed and the street-lamps left them looking the colour of brooding moss.

His "success" flared up at him only in the main thoroughfare, particularly in the garish windows of fruit-and-vegetable shops. If he had also experienced the daytime wilt, by night as the trams clanged and sang, swinging and lurching, the vegetable senses revived vertiginously.

Olivia was forcing the dark-green car. At an intersection a confusion of traffic held them up. "Oh *God*!" she protested, banging her rings on the wheel.

By night he almost believed in invocation.

They were easing past a jacked-up tram. The new blood was fermenting on the warm asphalt. Blood in the street made it impossible to envisage, at least for that moment, a murder, let alone a suicide, in a house.

He and Boo were jerking jolting in the smooth car past the scene of the accident. It was close enough to become their own. They could see the sweat on her forehead below the line of frizzy hair— as the head lolled—in the real situation. Was it what somebody wanted? Or hadn't wanted enough? but succeeded in bringing off.

As they were pressing on, into a less congealed air, Olivia's voice started a high flacker above the competing traffic. "My mother thought all suicides were immoral. She herself suffered a horribly prolonged old age. Her jewel-case and the deed-box were always within reach. The sheets she died in had been hemmed for her by her mother, to set her up when she married. It's wonderful how material things used to last. I think it was that, more than anything, which helped the owners believe in God."

"They believed in themselves. That's why," he shouted above the sound of speed.

"The—why? Oh bugger, I've taken the wrong road!"

She began hauling on her mistake, hand over hand, down the choppy side-streets, past the moored houses in which middling incomes were snoring and protesting. As for the occupants of the car, sheer intricate activity gave them a status and importance which made God unnecessary. Speed, after reducing your flesh, leaves you on equal terms with the natural forces which have replaced Him. It was exhilarating at least.

Olivia Davenport steered them down the moonlit streets and finally out along the promontory where the Tudor mansion stood. The moon and a still night made the sea look more solid than the land.

"There! I've done my duty!" she said.

The drive, their conversation, perhaps also their share in the past, had left Olivia with an expression both haggard and childlike.

"Aren't you coming in?" he asked without wishing to encourage a witness of his reunion with Hero.

"No," she gnashed. "I've said all I have to say to her; and don't want to spoil things for you—darling." Looking along her nose at the dashboard of her car, slightly smiling, she sounded complacent rather than vindictive.

Dew was falling around them: on the enamelled surfaces of car and camellia bushes; on the sheet of sweating zinc which represented the sea. Boo seemed to expect him to kiss her. It was one of the bumping kisses of childhood, if cooler from the cool, metallic-tasting dew.

She drove off, stamping on it.

A long time after he had rung, the thin maid came to open, in a blue flannel dressing-gown, and hair he had only guessed at on previous occasions.

"I'm sorry to trouble you," he said.

She winced at him, and made it obvious she was doing a supreme favour—but might have enjoyed doing it.

He decided to support the fiction of Madame Pavloussi's departure for Greece. "I was afraid you might all have gone by now."

"Gone? I go with the house. And if anyone else is going, they haven't spoke about it."

So the fiction wasn't supportable.

"Is she better?" he asked more tentatively still.

"Wasn't ever sick. Not that I know."

They stood looking at each other a moment before her cartoon face began frowning for the sleep she had been torn out of.

"She's up there," she said, wincing and frowning and indicating with her head. "You'll see the light on." Whatever else might rouse the hackles of her scepticism, she firmly believed in his adultery with the foreign woman.

Left alone in the dark hall, he went up towards Hero's light.

She was lying stretched out in an attitude which looked studied but probably wasn't. As sooner or later she would have had to produce her bandaged wrists, there was no reason why she shouldn't expose them in the beginning; so her arms were arranged along her body, outside the sheet. For the same reason, there was no point in keeping her eyes closed. She had probably closed them instinctively on hearing his approach up the stairs, but decided against defence as he pushed the door wider open: the lids were raised to a degree where interest can still pass as apathy.

Whether she knew it or not, she already had him at a disadvantage. In her moments of ignorance, lust, childishness, or recovering from the hysteria of a half-intended suicide, Hero's eyes remained noble works of art. They couldn't be connected with failures of the human mind or body; they were too lustrous, and dark.

Because she could hardly explain the situation away, she used a convalescent tone of voice. "I am so sorry. I am all the time trying to remember whether I have shut the street-door on leaving your house, Hurtle. It has worried me so much. If I did not close it, thieves could have broken in—to steal—the paintings."

"Don't worry: I'm not yet in the stolen class; and if you hadn't left the door open, I mightn't have let in the visitor: I mean your emissary—Olivia."

"Did Olivia? I didn't send her." She became more invalid, moving her head against the pillow, her lips paler. "Olivia is so devoted she cannot believe her friends might survive without her help."

Certainly Hero sounded helpless, but the white-bandaged wrists, in collaboration with her terracotta skin, reminded him that his delicate acrobat was only temporarily inert. As soon as he went to her the butterflies of tension were fluttering again under his fingers, the worm in him was raising its head. He wondered whether her conscience suffered as little as his on hearing the clash of teeth on teeth as they bit into the same fruit.

When they had finished their tender meal, and she was crying, and wiping her eyes with her hair, and moaning: "Oh God! Oh God!" he whispered into her ear: "Not when you've had your cake."

Since they were all invoking God tonight, he remembered Effie a kitchenmaid, in her big pink going-out hat, mopping and crying: *God can strike me dead if I ever do ut again I'd never ever 'uv done ut in the first place if I'd ever known what I was gunner let meself in for so there it's the truth May Lizzie.* What have you let yourself in for, Effie? *Nothun cheeky boy or not what everyone thinks though Lord you can never be that sure.* So, as Hero cried, presumably on account of her botched attempt at suicide, his head was filled with the old hurdy-gurdy tunes, and crushed pink sateen and a tattered moon, and the mound of crystal-sprinkled rock-cakes none of the girls would have dreamed of touching, out of respect for Effie's fate; only he dared to finger, to pinch up, to suck the least of the crystals, on the quiet.

As soon as Hero had finished crying, she seemed to grow more practical. She opened her eyes, while continuing to flutter the lids at something remote she hadn't been able to focus on, or face. Washed clean of the immediate past, the eyes themselves shone with an unusually noble candour.

"I know you only respect the truth, so I will be perfectly honest with you, Hurtle." He admired the sculpture of her jaw. "I do not understand why I have told you—except that I was emotionally upset—that Olivia went of her own accord. No," she said, "I have sent Olivia to bring you to me, because it is necessary to tell you I receive a letter from my poor husband."

Giving Cosma his official title made him sound more ominous.

"I have read this letter many times. It is in my handkerchief drawer"; she half rose on the bed as though prepared to prove the letter's existence. "But it is useless to show you"—she fell back on realizing—"it is written in Greek, of course. My husband, who had no formal education, writes other languages only through secretaries."

Though physically languid, Hero continued clambering over mountains, while he chafed her skin, and considered the significance of Cosma's reappearance.

"He writes very kindly—because," she said, "my husband was always a gentle man. But he is far kinder than I would have expected—in this letter I now receive. He says"—she breathed tenderly—"he realizes how he has failed me—'conjunctively,' I think, is the translation. I have told you about his scruples—which I believe are a curse from his old mother. My husband," she continued in her translating and translated voice, "respects you as an artist and a man, and can understand my taking you as a lover."

"When he doesn't know me?"

"Doesn't *know* you? He has met you at the party of Olivia! How my husband doesn't know you?"

Hero was so incredulous, her lover was left hanging by her beauty, which offered such a hold he could only continue gratified: the glistening mesh of her eyebrows alone.

Dreamier, or practical, she announced from her pillow turned to swansdown: "My husband writes that, *nevertheless*"—she translated it so meticulously—"he will always be prepared to take me back because of his great love for me." Hero closed her eyes. "Isn't that touching, Hurtle, and nice?"

Oh God! Her lover was touched more than he could have expressed, and suddenly tired. So far he had conceived in paint no more than fragments of a whole. If he were only free of women who wished to hold somebody else responsible for their self-destruction; more difficult still: if he could ignore the tremors of his own balls, then he might reach his resisted objective, whether through mottled sausage skins, or golden chrysalides and splinters of multi-coloured glass perhaps purposefully strewn on a tessellated floor, or the human face drained to its dregs, or the many mirrors in which his sister Rhoda was reflected, or all all of these and more fused in one—not to be avoided—vision of GOD.

To escape from its immensity, and the shocking literalness of his forced admission, he sank his head between the unconscious breasts of his ex-mistress Hero Pavloussi.

When the words began reverberating from her diaphragm: "My darling—Hurtle—you know what my answer will be—the only possible answer: that my lover needs my love—that I cannot leave him—even if his object is to destroy me."

He could feel her stumpy, webbed hands ostensibly caressing his ribs, as though to create something out of wood. There had been a kitchen table at Cox Street, which had borne with knives, and

336

children's boots, and hot irons. Mightn't the Whole have been formally contained from the beginning in this square-legged, scrubbed-down, honest-to-God, but lacerated table?

He let her caress him: he was too well occupied to answer.

He was painting, but had not yet found the direction he must take; he forced himself, as in making love with Hero whenever she demanded it: in each case it was an exercise.

Once when she came to him she showed him cuts in the palms of her hands, and a deeper wound in one knee; drawing down her mouth into its ugliest shape, her chin weighted with contempt, she described with such anatomic detail and idiomatic fluency a certain sexual act, she made him ask: "But where can you have learned such things?"

"Oh!" she blared. "Where did I? How am I to know? Gutters are too much alike." Her face looked bloated; her cracked laugh sounded as though she were drunk, or hallucinated: or real.

Then again, her aggressiveness would dissolve, and she would cry into him for protection: "I can no longer expect to reason with myself. Pray for me, won't you, Hurtle? I have neither learned the language of love nor prayer."

On returning into what passed for her right mind, she sleeked her hair down and said: "No more than anybody else, Hurtle, you are not what you are supposed to be."

The truth in what she said didn't help. He could help neither of them, and must resist anyone else's entry into that void in himself which would blaze eventually with light, if he was to be favoured again.

She left him alone for so long he had to go and investigate. It was late afternoon as he approached the house. Around the headland the happiest conjunction of light and water, of gentle ripples and rosy swaths of tender cloud, promised a climate of equanimity and affection. Going down the gravel towards the star-shaped flower bed, it occurred to him how he might make use of those particular cloud forms, when he was jolted out of himself at sight of a strange car stretched along the drive in front of the porch.

Almost at the same moment a large, powdered woman came out of the house, wearing a hat studded with what looked like macaroons.

"It'll be like old times, Gertie," she said as though talking to her sister, but it was only the maid who went with the house.

The maid lowered her chin and simpered. "Oh yes, m'm. Yes, Mrs Cargill. Won't it?" She could hardly wait to become re-enslaved, but decently.

The lady stood, and the light glanced off her teeth and her thick glasses. Once or twice she licked her lips to make sure the enamel was intact. The chauffeur started going through the motions, but unlike the maid, he had so worked it out he was on neither one side nor the other.

Both Mrs Cargill and Gertie stared in the direction of the caller. The maid looked stern, while her rightful mistress might have been suspecting the approach of a disease: a not unpleasant one, which her friends would turn into a tactful joke, perhaps even congratulate her on catching.

"Oh dear!" She suddenly laughed, and whispered loud: "The inventory, Gertie! We forgot the inventory!"

The maid scurried into the hall and returned at once with a clipful of fluttering documents.

"Inventories make me feel guilty," Mrs Cargill still whispered out loud. "But tenants with the best credentials can give you a surprise. I wonder why we let? For the money, I expect!"

"Oh yes!" the maid giggled. "We need the money, don't we?"

In sisterly fashion she began pushing her mistress inside the highly polished car. Her cuffs twittered as she waved. She was so relieved to feel herself again loaded with reliable chains.

Only when Mrs Cargill had been driven away, temporarily, from her own house was the maid prepared to acknowledge the caller.

"Is Madame Pavloussi expecting you?" she asked with a polite insolence he returned.

"No. She isn't. It's more of a surprise like."

She hated that. She couldn't be sure whether he was quizzing her profession, or whether Mr Duffield was of a class she despised.

"Madame Pavloussi's in the little *salong*." The maid flung a magic word which must preserve her from any possible humiliation.

"What!" he said. "Isn't the drawing-room ever used?"

It wouldn't be today: all the dust-covers were on.

He went unaccompanied into the room where Hero had always received him, perhaps on account of their intimate relationship.

"The lease is up, I gather." He would save her the trouble.

"No," she said, and dabbed at an imaginary cold. "Mrs Cargill has returned sooner than she expected—for family reasons—from her trip to England, and it will suit us both if I hand over."

Again she dabbed at her non-existent cold, turning her face so that it was touched with the glow which had delighted him as he came down the drive. He kissed her as tenderly as the rosy hour demanded.

She didn't return his affection, but said tight and dry: "I have had to make an important decision. My poor little Flora—I have had to destroy her."

"Your *who*?"

"My little dog who is suffering all this time—so much—of a cancer. It is selfish of me to prolong it."

"Oh yes—Flora." He realized he had never seen the dog which had been the reason they almost hadn't met.

"So it is over," Hero concluded; she didn't cry, perhaps because she had cried too much on less tragic occasions; she blew her nose, and looked at the backs of some books of the unread kind belonging to the landlady.

"Why did you never let me see your dog?"

"Oh, but darling, I did not want to involve you in unpleasantness."

To insulate them more securely from any unpleasantness arising from the disease and death of her pet, she switched to the driest possible subject: ". . . Mrs Cargill's solicitor, with whom I have spent—yesterday—almost the entire morning. It was deadly!" she remembered, and frowned. "Why this man must he repeat everything six times? Am I stupid? Or am I merely a foreigner? And Mrs Cargill accusing me—not of *stealing* a silver ladle—which is not in the inventory. I think she is probably a very common woman. Her old silver ladle, which I have never seen, must be of the same ugliness and commonness as everything else in her possession."

"Where will you go, now that you're leaving the house?"

The false atmosphere she had encouraged should have made separation a painless matter for them both; but the sea had begun to darken and lift, impinging on the organized room; an invasion of night scents and moisture started them both gasping for breath, their minds' furniture palpitating, and in some cases, bleeding.

"Where I will go?" Hero was locking and unlocking her naked hands: he hadn't noticed the heavy pearl since the shipping magnate left; while she smiled in advance over something which might sound impossible or idiotic. "I will tell you," she said, and it relieved her shoulders to take him physically by the hand, and drag him down to the level of practical planning. "I will go back to Greece. Oh no, not to my husband. My husband is too generous; I would not impose myself on him. In any case, I will take my lover with me."

"What if he won't be taken from his work?"

"Oh, his work! I am his work, too, aren't I? You are not so little egoist, Hurtle, that you won't admit you haven't finished creating me."

Though he could feel himself bridle under pressure from Hero's persuasive hand, it was not a matter of vanity. He realized, on the contrary, he had been feeding on her formally all these weeks, and that the least related corners of his vision borrowed her tones of mind, the most putrescent of which were often the subtlest.

Hero seemed as unaware of the cynicism of her remark as she was of her lover's attitude. "It is now so long since I have seen the island I have been telling you about—Perialos. You will remember how my husband took me? It is this island I wish—I *must* visit again." She kept dragging at his hand in search of the encouragement she wasn't receiving. "I feel the devils may be cast out in the holy places of Perialos."

"I wonder whether grace is given as freely as we're asked to believe."

"Why will this not be given," she shouted, "if I am determined?" She was positively yanking at his hand as though somewhere at the top of his arm a bell existed.

By now they were standing in almost darkness; there were a few last flames licking the leaden masses of the city in the distance; Hero's face was brown and sweaty.

"And what about *my* devils?" he asked. "What if I want to hang on to them?"

"Then you do not love me! If you did you would want us to be one—one being—through every possible experience."

"Like a husband. I'm not your husband—not even an exorcised one."

"Oh, you are so brutal!"

"I'm an artist," he had to say, though it sounded like a vulgar betrayal. "I can't afford exorcism. Is that what you've sensed? Is that why you want it?"

"Oh, but you misinterpret! Deliberately! You do not want to understand!"

She couldn't spit it contemptuously enough at the darkness surrounding them: while he was tempted by his half-conceived landscape of Perialos, in which the wooden saints were threatened by their own tongues of fire.

None of their journey in the flying boat particularly impressed him. The changes of temperature alone made him feel sick and disgruntled. In the air he huddled in his overcoat and longed for his abandoned house; nobody would coax him out of it again. In any case, after childhood, or at most youth, experience breeds more fruitfully in a room. None of the forms which rose up to meet him as they glided down, none of the colours which should have drenched his senses, was as subtly convincing as those created out of himself. At any point he might have demanded to break away, if he hadn't been obsessed by his preconception of Perialos: something Hero would never make him admit.

"Are you ill, Hurtle?" she used to ask. "Have you a fever, darling?"

She had taken to feeling his forehead for the fever she couldn't find. She was so solicitous their fellow passengers began to guess at something peculiar. They watched for clues, particularly on touching down, but were irritatingly frustrated: what their X-ray eyes might have detected through a bedroom door didn't take place in dormitories; the sexes were segregated at their ports of call. Though on land a torn-off branch, stuck in the tropic silt, would shoot overnight—they had seen that for themselves—in the air the fingers of crypto-lovers remained dry, brittle, unproductive, even when grafted into one another. So you had only the expression of their eyes to go by: their eyes would glow at times with that suggestion of phosphorescence which emanates from swamp water at night.

To add to the irritation, and downright mystification, this Madame Pavloussi, obviously a woman of means, was wearing an old fur coat, certainly Persian lamb with probably a sable collar, but all so shabby you wouldn't have been seen dead in it. Her breath reeked like a full ashtray. She was such a hell-bent smoker it was a wonder she didn't eat the cigarettes, which she took from a shagreen case, when she remembered to fill it, paper packs otherwise, lumped together with passports and tickets in an old crocodile handbag. There was a notecase to match the bag, with a gold monogram, elegantly done. Once the notecase tumbled out: you could see it was stuffed with notes; it was Madame Pavloussi, not the man, who had the dough. The man didn't bear too much looking at: too seedy, and sort of morbid. You would have liked to understand what they saw in each other: her in her shabby old Persian lamb, teeth browned by nicotine; him in his food-spotted English tweed, and funny eyes. The eyes gave you the gooseflesh, because he wasn't exactly looking at you: he was only looking.

Over Rangoon suddenly the lovers kissed, or it was Madame Pavloussi the Greek woman loving up to her paid man. He'd probably carve her up in the end, in some hotel bedroom, and pack her in suitcases, before the staff dropped to it. It would be her who'd drive him to murder by talking at him nonstop: pity you couldn't have heard what it was about.

It was about Perialos. "We mustn't waste any time in Athens. The more I think about it, the more I am convinced Perialos is our great hope." Unconscious of the island gestating inside him, she was willing him to keep her company in being saved.

They spent three, four days in the hot white dust of Athens, where they put up at a modest hotel frequented by European families and English governesses on their way to or from a job. By day he scarcely saw Hero, who had business to attend to, family to visit. She had become foreign and remote: for which he was grateful; but she began to feel she ought to console him.

She said on the third morning: "Did you hear that woman coughing the other side of the wall? It had the sound of an English governess. Poor things, their gentility means everything, and at the same time they are hungry for love. They end by losing all their sport."

The same night a sense of compassion reminded Hero to ask him to sleep with her. It was the eve of their departure; she was naturally preoccupied: the outcome was conjugal at best; at worst, prophylactic.

"How fearful," she said, "if we left the tickets for the *vaporaki* under the mattress! I dread all this confusion of departures. The broken-down taxis!" She sighed, and heaved, remembering her duty towards him, or the English governesses. He could almost feel her listening for the governess with a cough the other side of the wall.

On coming out of the bathroom she said: "These island steamers are very primitive, you know." She was trying to brush her hair sleeker than it had ever been. "They put the used lavatory paper in baskets in case it blocks up the hole. Fancy! My Aunt Phrosso had a basketful blow in her face on the way to Corfu. She never travel again by Greek." Hero laughed with a kind of coarse delight. "This is my poor country! Ah Perialos—how I dread and long for it!" she ended in a voice of doves.

As she cosseted, and finally plaited together, the live snakes of her hair, the raised arms suggested sun-warmed pottery. The woman who had been in bed with him, amiably submitting to a sexual routine, was in no way related to her. Perhaps the fault was his: he felt numb; his hands ached with possibly arthritic pains. Only when they were lying in their separate beds, and he was opening the door of his house in Flint Street, his fingers began again to flow: the pain was squeezed out. He practised cupping his hands to control the evasive paint, with which he must convey the grey-to-violet dove-tones and glistening, plaited snakes.

When he woke from this spasmodic nap he felt more refreshed than he had been by the bleak orgasm he had pretended to enjoy with the woman in the other bed. She was now crying and moaning through her sleep; while the English governess had started coughing again, perhaps out of sympathy, the other side of the wall.

He was powerless to do anything about anything except fall asleep for the second time: from which he was woken by Hero Pavloussi shouting at him in a grey, hostile light; it was so early.

"Wake up, my God!" she shouted. "You don't realize: this day of days, the taxi may break down on the way to Piraeus!" Her vehemence made the handles on the dressing-table rattle.

Then she started bashing at the fragile, antique telephone, to make sure their coffee would be sent up. She had thickened, coarsened overnight, or so it appeared as she bent to test her suspenders. Her skin looked greasy, livery. He downright disliked her as she stood dipping one horn of a croissant into her coffee.

"Did you see Cosma?" he asked.

It was the first time since their arrival either of them had used the name; if it hadn't been for the sight of her dunking the croissant, he probably wouldn't have brought it up now.

At once she resumed her true proportions. "No." Her head had recovered its nobility. "I am cheapened enough, but would not cheapen myself any further by doing such a thing to my husband."

"I saw him—I think—the afternoon before last."

"How?" She was listening like a frozen cat.

"In an arcade."

"Which arcade?"

"How do I know? I can't read the Greek lettering."

He had been pretty sure it was Cosma Pavloussis, in dark glasses. They had almost collided. Then the persistent smile, there for anybody who cared to receive and interpret it the evening of Olivia's dinner, reappeared on the face of the shipping magnate, or his double, as he sheered off and stood looking at a millinery display in a shop window. If he hadn't been wearing the dark glasses, it would have been possible to identify him by the little sacs of sallow skin at the corners of the eyelids.

"What was he doing?" Hero asked.

She was standing with the remaining horn of a soggy croissant pinched in trembling fingers; there were crumbs floating on the surface of her coffee.

"He was looking at some rather tawdry hats in a shop window." Then he added, because her face seemed to be expecting it: "He's probably doing some little dancer or actress on the cheap."

"I will not love you any more or less, Hurtle, if you draw for me jealous pictures of my husband. Nor will you lower him for me by anything you say."

"But didn't you tell me he could only sleep with paid women after you'd upset his moral values?"

She answered gently: "Yes," and stuffed into her mouth the remains of the croissant.

Again, as she was bending over a suitcase, smoothing the contents before fastening it, she said very gravely, softly: "I pray that God will bless us at Perialos."

He thought it extremely unlikely that God would show them acts of mercy even on that island of saints; but in his role of stand-in groom he took the bride's hand, and she appeared shyly grateful for it.

The steamer making the voyage to Perialos was appropriately primitive. On the gangways the tightly knotted strings of passengers shuffled with short, bemused steps dictated less by the loads they were carrying than by a ritual in which they were taking part. Hero hadn't painted on her mouth. Jostled by these bearers of sacrificial kids and hens, or heady offerings of stocks and roses, he felt more innocent, stilted, wooden, already in a sense half-shriven.

They lay all night in their narrow bunks. He slept only an hour or two. There were the distant sounds of vomiting, moaning, invocations, kids bleating. Once for an instant, in a sloping corridor, on groggy legs, he was the only living thing. In the lavatories there stood the baskets of used paper, as Hero had predicted.

That night she didn't speak. He suspected her of praying, and because he had begun to love her again he would have liked to add his petitions to hers; as this wasn't possible, he filled the darkened cabin of his mind with an involved white calligraphy, which he saw as a correspondence of sorts.

Very early the swell subsided, and they entered a blue morning in which veiled islands were swimming, or in some cases, hedgehogs of brown rock. The steamer functioned at two speeds: one for the immediate foreground; the other for the passive distance on which they might never make an impression. Kerchiefed women continued calling to their Lady for protection, and a theological student spouted like a whale over a consignment of peasant cheeses spread on a covered hold for the passage between islands.

Later in the morning the two foreigners were standing on the sheltered side of the wheelhouse. Since her association and her fur coat had removed Hero Pavloussi to a plane from which Christian voices and glances fell away incredulously, she had been clinging desperately to her companion's arm for support. They didn't stop looking ahead: both, he felt, weak at the knees, like discharged hospital cases, or a not yet consummated couple.

Hero finally managed to free her voice from her throat; it allowed her a gummy whisper: *"Perialos!"* Then the wind had fallen: they had slid the right side of the stone arm of a protective mole.

As soon as it was possible, all the initiates began pouring down on the paving, pushing and shrieking; there was a bleating from some quarters, from others a flapping of wings: an inverted cock raised his head, gasping, glaring, wattles quivering. Those who had been waiting for them seized the asperged cheeses and carried them away. A white glare embraced the whole cosmos, excepting those for whom the ceremony had been arranged. It made their arrival more alarmingly significant; they moistened their lips, and looked at each other lovingly, appealing for sympathy in what they were about to undergo.

He said: "We were stupid not to have booked a room. Or do you think everyone else belongs?"

"I do not know where is there to book." Hero was struggling with the stones of words.

A great personage of the Church made his exit from the little steamer: his staff of office, his veils, proclaimed him. Several monks ran forward. Like hens expecting to be trodden, they hunched over the hand they kissed, before the single bucking taxi drove him up the mountain to the monastery.

"It is not necessary to book. There is always somewhere." Hero smiled, but looked as though she had never been on an island before.

Her coat, which she had taken off when the wind died, was trailing from the crook of her arm. Coming down the gangway, she had torn a hole in the fur, but it seemed of no importance to her. The landscape had begun falling into place: which he divided automatically, for the moment feeling more informed than exalted.

Alongside the water a short distance from the mole stood an ochre stucco cube which passed for an inn. Hero came to an agreement with the pirate-landlord for two narrow rooms, each with an iron bedstead and crocheted cotton quilt.

"Isn't there a double room in the place?"

"It is better like this," she whispered quickly, though it was doubtful whether the innkeeper would have understood.

So they had reached Perialos. At the now deserted quay two lambs were being dragged from a dinghy, tails flumping, cries rasping and reverberating; a horn from one of them broke off in somebody's hand.

Their landlord suddenly excused himself.

Hero explained: "There is a funeral today, which he has to go to. He is better than he looks."

They exchanged the smell of damp sheets in the rooms for that of urine in the corridor. They went down to look for food, which they found farther along the quay.

They ate a few sea-scented prawns and lengths of naked cucumber: then a dish of something.

Hero smiled across at him as she masticated. "It is good, isn't it?

Primitive, but good. The *soodzookakia*!" The tepid brown "sausages" aroused all the reverence in her.

Because he wanted to love her particularly on this day of their union through atonement, he smiled back, while hoping to disguise the gristle collected between his teeth: as in hers, he noticed.

"I don't want to waste any time, Hurtle. I will tell you what I am planning." Hero looked down at her plate, into the tomato dregs with their outer edge of oil. "We will go first to the Convent of the Assumption—which we—my husband and I—have visited once before. Then to Theodosios. This is a hermit who is living not so very far away from the convent, beside the chapel of St John of the Apocalypse."

"But was this the island?"

"No. That is Patmos, which is given to the Italians. John only passed through Perialos; but he performed miracles here," she added with grave authority.

Pushing back the cutlery through the oily dregs, he felt deeply in love with Hero his hushed bride and fellow neophyte.

They started as soon as she had changed into a very simple, expensively cut cotton frock, and headed in what she remembered as the direction of the convent. They had only gone a short distance through the village when a procession burst on them out of a narrow side-street. What must have been practically the whole population of the port chattered and jostled like the steamer passengers at the beginning and ending of the voyage. Greeks, the peasants at least, all seemed to understand whatever there is to know in their sphere of life, as well as in the greater sphere described with geometrical precision behind it. Only the rich and the foreigners didn't know: so the peasants were sorry for them, the confident black glances and glistening smiles seemed to imply.

The procession parted slightly, and he realized this was not only a matter of life.

"It is the funeral we were warned about!" Hero stood clutching the upper part of his arm, like a woman furtively estimating a prospective lover's strength.

The procession flowed towards them. They were caught up in the forked stream of kerchiefed women, and men walking on a curve which criticized the two foreigners. Then came the Church, bearing banners and emblems in gilded wood. The tattered priests and their tallow-faced acolytes obviously intended the two lost souls to participate in the mystery of which they were the guardians. The object from which this emanated was even halted for an instant: when the strangers caught sight of a very old woman on a bier, head lolling on a lace pillow. Though still convincingly a partner to life, she was at the same time removed from the living herd trampling around her, for the corpse, with the yellow, pleated mouth, and hair dressed in a kerchief identical with those of the live women, was wearing those geometrically described arcs of eyelids which everybody revered, and some looked as though they aspired to.

A middle-aged woman with a beard spoke to the foreign lady, whose mouth couldn't cope with the reply. Soon afterwards the procession wobbled on, with laughter and prayers.

"What did she say?"

"When we have come for such other reasons, she wanted me to kiss the corpse!" Hero could have been spitting out the sensation.

They continued through the now empty streets, and came out at the foot of a mountain which she said they must climb. He recognized the blocks of marble melting as they ought in the direction of miracles and martyrdom. On the summit stood the great monastery, manned against assault. An old man came down from drinking on a terrace, and began pissing in the wrong quarter; the wind blew it back at him. Troglodytes, variously bearded, scampered out of their caves and off amongst the olives, scattering dung.

Hero chose a narrow track through caper vines and renegade artichokes. "This is a short way," she explained, her back rounding under the effort of the climb.

She couldn't get there quickly enough; but as her memory had misled her, and the way turned out to be far from short, she was forced to rest from time to time. At such moments his spirit was free to roam the landscape which was becoming his. He made notes, mental ones: then, as he grew more at home in it, marks, and sometimes fairly elaborate drawings, on a pad he had been carrying in his pocket. Occasionally his directions were worded: ". . . here angels fold their wings—very wooden . . . goat-hermits (devils?) . . . tongues of fire announcing the miracle—or simply a progression of light . . ."

Once Hero inquired sulkily: "What are you doing, Hurtle?"

"Putting down one or two things as a reminder."

Fortunately she was too much occupied with her own thoughts

to ask further questions; for in her present state she would not have tolerated varieties of exaltation. So they went their separate ways, whether straying to one side or other of the actual path, or each forging deeper into a private labyrinth.

Burnt by the sun, and glazed by their respective missions, they reached and crossed the ridge.

"There!" she breathed, pointing. "This is the Convent of the Assumption."

The buildings, partly hidden by cypresses, olives, and the conventual wall, were of a pale earthen colour, and suggested human rather than ascetic pursuits. He was more impressed by the wandering coastline and beyond it the blaze of sea. On a peak—no, you couldn't call it that, but the apex of the eastern slope of the island—stood a white chapel, thin as a needle.

"There is the Church of St John—the house of Theodosios beside it. After the convent we shall visit them." She spoke sternly, as though daring him to object. "Down there"—she nodded vaguely in the direction of a sandy inlet—"is where the saint landed. They say a spring gushed out, and is still running."

"Shan't we go there as well—to find out whether it is?"

"Why should we? We have more important things to do."

He was reminded momentarily of a prim teacher determined to hang on to her half-sceptical beliefs.

While they were approaching the convent a couple of girls in grey frocks, or lay habits, ran out of the gate and sprang sideways on noticing them.

"They are some of the orphans these good nuns are taking care of." Hero spoke with a sentimental sententiousness; but to him the disappearing girls had the look of sturdy, hairy animals bounding amongst the rocks and thyme.

"You will love the abbess: she is so sweet," Hero whispered à la Olivia Davenport as they stood at the studded gate the girls had slammed shut.

The bell tinkled away, then subsided as they listened to it.

"Do I look a scarecrow?" Hero whispered very loud, hoping for praise; her bare lips, revealing no more than the transparent tips of her teeth, were trembling.

He didn't have to answer, because a small, spry, ageless nun dragged the gate open.

Hero began to speak to her in the tongue peculiar to Greeks and saints, which naturally he couldn't understand. In the circumstances he was glad Hero was deaf to the language in which he communed with devils.

The small nun smiled, laughed, looking, not at the suppliant, but in complete innocence at the man. She led them along a path edged with round, whitewashed stones and equally rounded basils of a clamorous green. At one point he trod over the edge and the scent shot up and around.

Hero and the nun seemed to have a lot to tell each other.

"What is she saying?"

"Nothing. I am telling her that Greek light illuminates. I can breathe Greek air. I am renewed."

They passed a dormitory where snivelling girls were lying on narrow beds.

Hero hurried him on. "She says the abbess has a cold but will be delighted to receive us. Everybody is with cold. There is an epidemic."

They had been swept into a chaste slit of a room overlooking the luminous sea. There were several upright chairs, signed photographs of royalty and politicians in clothes of another age, three or four indifferent icons, and a daybed covered with an embroidered rug, or blanket. It could only have been the daybed which suggested the seraglio. He had to look out at the sea to remind himself they had been brought there by urgent matters of the spirit.

The abbess appeared with a suddenness and elasticity which made him wonder if she was wearing anything under her habit. She was of medium height, neither young nor old, neither plain nor pretty, but so agile, so supple. He saw her on the daybed rather than the upright chair she chose.

She was chattering away at what seemed a worldly, superficial level, which obviously irritated Hero as her veneer of sentimental piety wore thin. Hero wanted to get down to business with the abbess: to talk about herself, the richly putrid state of her soul, and how her conscience had made her reject her dear Lord and Husband.

Just when she had begun to get a word in, the little portress-nun returned, carrying a tin tray with a bottle of ouzo and glasses on it. The nun was so jolly about it all, she mightn't have known what the bottle contained. She poured out a couple of liberal tots.

Hero angrily refused hers, but the innocent nun appeared as unconscious of anger as she was of the danger in men. He thought he could detect a scent of the basil against which her skirt had brushed.

When the nun had retired, Hero aimed again at the abbess, who sat with her hands folded, her eyelids lowered, smiling at something, probably not of a spiritual nature, but a concrete object in the world she had left. Hero's explosive monologue must have been boring her: she looked so much the picture of a lady in a drawing-room; once or twice she seemed to remember her cold and coughed genteelly behind her hand.

Without the ouzo he, too, might have been bored by the situation, He poured himself another in case the abbess forgot to suggest it: while becoming occupied with a series of slides, which his mind accepted, rejected, improved on, without yet finding the perfect slide, or fusion of near misses. Sometimes it was Hero on the day-bed, sometimes the abbess; at times it was Hero in the abbess's habit, at others the abbess exposing her supple, odalisque contours. In each case, hands were plaited behind the head, elbows cocked at the viewer.

It was this which drove him to take out his fountain pen and make a little drawing on the palm of his hand. He was delighted with his discovery of flesh against the unevenly distempered tomato-coloured walls of the parlour, even more with the narrow windowful of luminous sea.

It was probably sight of the fountain pen which caused Hero's ripened rage to burst. "She is impossible, this woman, this *abbess*: she is so stupid, and so vulgar! Somebody once told me she is the daughter of a Salonica baker. She looks like it, doesn't she? She herself is made out of unrisen dough! It is from sitting here with the Turks just across the water which makes these women so oriental. I shall not be surprised if lovers come up from the village at night and the nuns are too passive to send them away." Her final conjecture made her part her lips in triumph.

He put away his pen. "Are you sure she can't understand you?"

"Not a word," Hero had decided. "She is too stupid."

The abbess had been dreamily looking smiling at his hands during the conversation in which she couldn't take part.

"What has she done or said," he asked, "to annoy you so much?"

"What? She asks why you have become so silent. When you are here before you have talked with her. She thinks"—Hero was becoming raucous—"you are my *husband.*"

"But didn't you tell her I'm your lover, and that you want your conscience tidied up?"

Hero ignored him.

He felt so lazy after the ouzo, and the abbess was smiling more than ever in her dumb language.

Fortunately the door opened and the jolly little portress reappeared, dragging behind her two of the orphans. From the arms of the hulking girls dangled embroidered mats and runners and fringed bookmarks.

The abbess smiled and murmured.

"These are the girls' works," Hero interpreted unwillingly, "which will help her maintain her orphanage."

He chose several pieces of the embroidery, though it didn't really interest him. On feeling in his pockets he found his wallet wasn't there; he must have left it behind at the inn.

Hero paid, somewhat contemptuously: while the abbess extended her upper lip, without having drunk any of the ouzo, still dreamily murmuring, staring at the full crocodile notecase.

Hero said: "All these girls are whores. They have all had bastards, or are in process of having them."

The girls sniggered and blushed over what they couldn't understand. Embroidered on their glowing skins, pimples shone with a virulence of chickenpox.

It was time for the visitors to leave, whether their mission was completed or not. As they passed alongside the dormitory windows, the girls lay snivelling and sniggering on their beds, one of them too obviously hugging a bellyful of sin under her blanket.

The abbess turned to the sympathetic husband and said in English of a kind: "Girls, seeck, seeck. *Grippe.*" She mimed it by clutching her small, animated breasts.

"You see? She understands."

"Hardly a word." Hero laughed; she had modified her opinion, though.

Strands of purple were by now visible in the sea or sky along the coast. A conventional piety had reappeared in Hero's face: she was possibly hoping for a blessing on taking leave of the condemned abbess. He felt drunk and sick from the ouzo, but exalted by the light and colour of the sea-sky.

Soon after they had left the two nuns (perhaps there weren't any more) and two attendant orphan-whores at the convent gate, Hero turned on him as though he were to blame. "You see? Why did we expect more? Even Cosmas was sceptical of this woman."

She walked down the track, her head grown disproportionate. A phalanx of goats, or orphans, dashed out and away from a tangle of evergreens.

"It was I who was foolish enough to believe in the possibility of regeneration." Even so, it was her lover and her absent husband she accused.

"Can God be sceptical of us?" he suggested.

"I am beginning to think so." She sighed at the purple evening. "But wait"—she suddenly remembered and took heart—"wait till we talk with this hermit—Theodosios. This is a saint who will plead for us." In her conviction, and the blaze of hieratic gold, she turned her face towards him, her sins as good as forgiven.

His unregenerate soul could feel no more than sympathetic towards her state of mind, while worshipping the aesthetic variations of its incarnation. It was the same with the landscape. He was conscious of God as a formal necessity on which depended every figure in the afternoon's iconography: goat-troglodytes; the old man pissing against the wind; orphan-whores; the procession of mourners; a martyred Hero. The ouzo in him, which should have helped dissolve, made him cling, on the contrary, to outward and visible signs. There were moments when his fingers were forced actually to cling: to jags of marble, or lichen-spotted olive branch, to steady himself on the ascent.

"If we're mad enough to climb up to this chapel," he reasoned aloud, "probably the most you can expect is half-an-hour's rambling conversation with a crazy monk, and we'll break our legs coming down in the dark. Who'll carry us, I'd like to know?"

"God will," she answered from ahead.

It didn't sound incongruous in the world of light through which they were climbing.

Actually Hero was in pretty bad physical condition. As they mounted the last earthwork separating them from this soaring arrow

353

of a white chapel, she was breathing like a broken-winded horse. The heel was coming off one of her shoes.

"Even the clothes we wear are degenerate," she gasped and ranted. "If I had been truly sincere—single-minded—I would have walked here on my bare feet."

For a moment he was afraid she might be preparing to throw away the offending shoes.

So he returned to the subject of her recent disgust. "Is the abbess in touch with Theodosios?"

"This abbess! Why should such a holy man interrupt his spiritual life for the babble of a silly, worldly woman?"

"In sickness, for instance: she could send him food and help. Didn't you at least inquire after him?"

"I will not be bullied, Hurtle"—she stumbled—"with what I have failed to do. In any case, how could I get a word in with this woman? She is all the time complaining about the price of oil—the tear and wear of girls' drawers. She is hinting at me that I should maintain her convent. Like all greedy people, she thinks she is the only one who has a right to be the bloodsucker."

At this point, if she had been wearing her fur coat, Hero would have settled deeper in it; but she wasn't: and they had reached the narrow plateau in front of the chapel.

"I myself no longer know which way to approach. I am afraid," she said, jittering after his hand.

He led her, or was led, round the side of the chapel to a white-washed cube, probably the hermit's cell. They trod regardless through one or two rows of sprawling, droughty tomatoes and artichokes run to seed. Hero began calling reverently in Greek. On entering the silence, they found nothing except an iron pot upside down on the uneven dirt floor.

"Of course, at this hour"—she became all tremulous smiles—"he will be at his prayers. I do not want to interrupt. But time is so precious."

They led each other back, trampling through the artichokes and tomatoes. They were caught between the purple east, which would never open to them, and the burning west, the blaze of which they mightn't be strong enough to endure.

Hero was calling tinnily in imitation of the convent bell. Blundering up the chapel steps, he could sense they were wasting their time: there was a smell of cold candle droppings, and rotten woodwork, and general mustiness. All but one of the icons had been prised away from the crude iconostasis, and the eyes of the survivor gouged out: by Turks from across the channel? or the devils of Perialos? The sound of birds' wings might have soothed; light might have furnished the abandoned chapel with a panoply against corruption, if one remorseless spear hadn't struck at a subsiding mound of human excrement beside the altar.

Hero was raging: her tongue looked like an ugly instrument in blunt rubber. "Are we lost? Do we come all this way for—*nothing*? Yes, of course we do; it is not so very extraordinary. Cosmas would have warned you: this hermit—who is dead, or gone—was a filthy old man, covered with oil-spots and candle wax. He wore his hair in a pigtail because he was too lazy to screw it into place, in its bun. He smelled sour—of urine, and cold beans. Cosmas said he had lice: he had seen them moving around, he said, on the *croûte* at the nape of his neck; but I would not accept that, much as I respect my husband."

"If you knew all this, what was the point in coming back?"

"For the words he spoke—which I have never been able to remember—not their meaning—I hear only the sound of them."

They were feeling their way back with their feet down the outside steps of the chapel; when she began to blubber hopelessly. "I think we have lost our faith in God because we cannot respect men. They are so disgusting. And cannot address one another—except mumbling."

It was Hero who might have drunk the ouzo. She was drunk, but with her disillusion and helplessness. He tried to support her. Hadn't she been his mistress, more than that, his creative source? He would have liked to point out the scaly sea, like a huge, live fish, rejoicing in its evening play, but he might have mumbled like the vanished saint. Perhaps if he could have done a drawing: but Hero only understood the visions of her own inferno.

They slithered hobbled down over rocks scratched by thorns whipped by avenging trees down past the convent everywhere silence except for dew dripping through dust onto dust down into the village which might have died in their absence if a dynamo hadn't given it a pulse a lit doorway bursting into laughter a tree swelling and ejaculating.

They slept in their separate cells; or he lay on his iron bed, under a damp-smelling sheet, his eyelids flickering then rigidly open be-

355

neath what had been the ceiling: he could visualize Hero doing the same.

Next morning, while they were sitting below, over little cups of muddy coffee at a marble table, Hero asked: "When we will return to Athens, Hurtle, what are your plans? Will you continue your tour into Europe?" She sneezed once or twice, because by now the convent cold had broken out in her, too.

He should have felt ashamed chewing so ravenously at the crust of bread; but the bread was good; and the act allowed him time to appreciate his release. Fortunately Hero's expectations weren't excessive: round the café table there was an air of camping out. She looked listless, bloodshot, nicotine-stained. While she scratched her parting with unvarnished nails, he could afford to swallow down the last knot of half-masticated bread with complete naturalness. The last of the yellow crumbs fell from his lips and scattered down his chest. He knew he hadn't bothered to wash the sleep out of his eyes: altogether, he must have looked this woman's awful counterpart.

"No," he said, shaking his head, half choking on the swallowed bread, "I shall go back to Flint Street."

"So soon?" She yawned. "It is not practical to come such a distance and waste the fare."

He might have told her that, in his case, the only life he could recognize as practical was the one lived inside his skull, and though he could carry this with him throughout what is called the world, it already contained seeds created by a process of self-fertilization which germinated more freely in their natural conditions of flaking plaster, rust deposits, balding plush, and pockets of dust enriched with cobweb. If he didn't try to tell her any of this, it was partly because she wouldn't have been interested, and because of certain apocalyptic moments on their journey to the other side of the island: though these, too, might have been experienced in time amongst the broken glass and tarnished light, the empty chrysalides and dark, indestructible plants of the conservatory at Flint Street.

Hero had drunk her medicinal coffee down to the dregs. "I do not understand the mind of an artist. He is too egoist, too enclosed," she said without any apparent resentment. "I am glad I am, in the end, dependent on nobody or nothing but myself."

Because her final statement didn't bear looking at, she avoided his eyes, his hand which continued to offer the conventional gestures of affection. After all, hadn't they been flung together in the more humiliating figures of the trampoline? They had learned the secrets of each other's underclothes.

Hero pushed back her coffee cup, and raised her voice in self-defence. "Dependent not even on God. Not even on my husband. If I tell you I intend to remain in Athens, you will immediately think: 'Ah, she is crawling back to Cosma!' I know he will take me if I wish. I have it in writing." She made a move towards her bag but changed her mind. "I do not wish it. Nobody is responsible for me: least of all those I love—or worship."

Forgetting she had finished it, she took a mouthful of her coffee, and now had to spit out the muddy dregs; however he remembered Hero, and there was still the return voyage to Piraeus, this might remain the key version: the black lips spluttering and gasping; the terrible tunnel of her black mouth.

"*Dreck! Dreck!* The Germans express it best. Well, I will learn to live with such *Dreck* as I am: to find a reason and purpose in this *Dreck*."

All this time a little golden hen had been stalking and clucking round the iron base of the café table, pecking at the crumbs which had fallen from their mouths. The warm scallops of her golden feathers were of that same inspiration as the scales of the great silver-blue sea creature they—or he, at least—had watched from John of the Apocalypse, ritually coiling and uncoiling, before dissolving in the last light.

"See—Hero?" he began to croak, while pointing with his ineffectual finger. "This hen!" he croaked.

Hero half directed her attention at the hen; but what he could visualize and apprehend, he could really convey only in paint, and then not for Hero. The distressing part was: they were barking up the same tree.

Their lack of empathy was not put to more severe tests because the proprietor came to the table. As he wiped the marble surface he made some confidential remark in the language the ex-lover found he still resented.

"*Alitheia?*" Hero replied, craning. "He says," she explained, "the *vaporaki* has been sighted from the mole. Oh dear, I detest these departures, particularly from islands: there is little hope of recovering what one has left behind."

The iron claws of the marble table vibrated on the ground as they pushed back their wobbly chairs.

"Have you got the tickets?" Hero gasped. "The keys—I must make sure—the keys!"

The golden hen flashed her wings: not in flight; she remained consecrated to this earth even while scurrying through illuminated dust.

✻ 7 ✻

At the smallgoods where he always bought his milk the girl said: "Thought you'd knocked off the milk. Thought you'd gone on a diet or something."

"I could have gone away, too. Or died."

The girl didn't understand it was meant to be a joke. She looked pleasantly serious, with her fresh face, and moustache of perspiration beads. It was going to be a hot day.

"No," he said, guilty on account of his attempted joke. "There are times when I just don't bother."

"You could have it delivered. Why don't you have it delivered?"

The healthy, humourless girl obviously had his interests at heart: she looked at him so earnestly.

"I don't want to. There are days on end when I don't want to think about, I don't want to be bothered with the stuff."

The girl found it difficult to believe. "But an elderly gentleman like you ought to take care of himself."

He laughed a rather metallic laugh and looked to see whether there was a glass handy.

"I'm fifty-five."

"That's about what I'd have reckoned."

He felt almost bound to take his revenge by seducing the smallgoods girl, only she might have been the kind who is hiding a crush on her grandfather.

"And you can't tell me you're not a gentleman," she said in triumph, "because I know one when I see one."

He knocked over the empty milk bottle he was returning, and the girl, realizing she was paid to conduct a business, began concentrating on the till.

"After living the fifty-five years you so correctly dropped to," he told her, "I've reached the conclusion the only truth is what one overhears."

The girl registered the sale. "Eh?" She laughed, and the perspiration shot off her and landed on the clanging till. "You've got something there! I bet we'd hear a lot of dirty cracks!"

The early heat made him feel he wasn't up to more, so he took his bottle of milk and went.

All through the streets there was already a hard, yellow glare. Old men, older than himself, were putting out garbage bins, rank with fat-trimmings, cabbage spines, and prawnshells. The singlets the old men were wearing exposed their veined arms, dark as stringybark from the elbows down, skinny-white about the biceps. Women of all ages were going sleeveless on such a morning: their skins had the soapy, large-pored look; their hair was set too tight, either with brilliantine or perspiration. What had started as an adventure, to move around freely inside your dress, almost nothing else on, was becoming a martyrdom as the blazing yellow lid was screwed tighter, and the women dragged from one station to the next.

In spite of what he saw around him, he felt at large. His clothes were still easy on him. His bare feet followed paths of unconsumed shade, enjoying the texture of the pavement. They were elegant for naked feet: long, fine-boned, unscathed by a lifetime of shoes. He found himself looking at them with such pleasure they should have been someone else's; he might have grown cynical of his own complacence if he hadn't caught sight of his hand.

Swinging a milk bottle by the neck in the green light from the pollarded planes, it became noticeable. His hands were beginning to give him away. They had started shrivelling, certainly only slightly, and only with a freckle or two, but which might become cancerous.

The freckled, in some cases, scabby hands of the old men putting out garbage trembled from their exertions. They immediately fumbled after tobacco: the cigarette paper, stuck to a lip or held between papery fingers, stirred tinkling in the vestige of a breeze.

His disgust made him walk faster, no longer choosing the shady paths, stalking with white hatred across the burning asphalt. He had never been so relieved to reach 17 Flint Street. He bundled in, most inelegant, past the iron gate which dragged, under the araucaria: an elderly gentleman of fifty-five.

And how dead the house since he had gone out unsuspecting for milk: the interior smelled of age and dirt, no longer of cool, but of a sour, creeping damp. Worst of all, he had grown hostile to all these paintings since the chopper, in the innocent hands of the smallgoods girl, had descended on his own innocence. The paintings, the earlier ones you end by accepting like inherited moral traits, had withdrawn apathetically into the walls on which they were hanging. They were less humiliating, however, than the bravura of technique, the unsolved problems of space, the passages of turgid paint, which glared at him from the later ones standing around the skirting-boards. Most disturbing of all was the painting on the easel in his top-back studio-bedroom. Before his going out it had struck him as having a lucidity, an almost perfect simplicity: the essence of table and chair-ness of chair, which he had been trying to convey in the previous versions of his "Furniture," all lost with his going out; the smallgoods girl, by performing a simple operation on his mind, had done away with the membrane separating truth from illusion.

In this throbbingly illusionless state he realized the bottle of milk was growing hot in his tenacious hands. He left the appalling window which opened out of the easel onto his interior emptiness. He went downstairs so quickly the house shook; his bones were jarred. On arriving in the kitchen he found he must have left the milk in the bedroom, but would have had no taste for milky coffee; he drank a mouthful of cold black, pouring the rest of the poisonous stuff down the sink.

It was the heat. He was constipated, too: when a smooth, velvety stool might have been the great rectifier; much more depended on the bowels than the intellect was prepared to admit.

Inside the vine-hooded dunny with its back to Chubb's Lane, heat became a positive virtue, an assistance to the stiff pelvis. While he sat straining in the heat which was half smell, he noticed the aphorism he had started to scribble on the whitewash—must have been twenty-five years ago—and never finished:

> *God the Vivisector*
> *God the Artist*
> *God*

Permanently costive, he never would find the answer: it was anyway pointless, not to say childish.

As the sounds of life flowed along the lane behind him, breaking and rejoining, his only desire was to mingle with them. He did,
for an instant or two, and was rewarded with a gentle content, behind closed eyelids, in his secret shrine: till the woman's voice
began.

"See in there, Ida? That's where the artist lives—wotchermecal-
lum—*Duffield*."

"Go on! The one that makes all the money?"

"That's what they say. Never seen a sign of it meself. Look, Ida!
Look at this fence!"

He was wide-eyed for what they were going to see.

"Ooh dear! Don't, Jean! Don't!" Ida was giggly. "You'll have the
rotten old thing come down."

"Don't you worry. The vines 'ull always hold it up. Look at the
bloody cracks in the walls. Look at the *down*-pipes! No one 'ud
think Mr Duffield was 'is own landlord."

"Arr dear!" Ida giggled.

"They say there's cockroaches flying around inside as big as bloody
rats."

"Oh, peugh!" Ida shrieked. "I don't believe yer, Jean. You're layun
it on!" Then she said with conventional reverence: "Must be old,
isn't 'e?"

"Yes, 'e's old all right—and crazy as a cut snake. That's what art
does for yer."

He was so fascinated by what he was overhearing it scarcely referred to himself.

"'E's old," continued Jean, and seemed to be spitting something
out. "But not so old, mind you. I was walkun down Flint Street the
other mornun—that's the front side of the residence, see?—and old
Duffield come runnun down the steps laughun and talkun at everyone and nothun."

"Might 'uv been for you, Jean."

"Nah. Duffield's a nut. But this is the point, madam. 'Is bloody
flies was all open. Greasy old flies!"

"Ooh dear! What did I tell yer? Might 'uv dragged yer in! Might
'uv raped yer!"

"It 'ud take a better man than nutty old Duffield. I didn't tell my
hubby, though."

"Don't blame yer. I was never raped—except nearly—once."

"They say it's the most terrible thing can happen to a woman. Takes away 'er self-respect."

"Yairs."

They were moving off.

"Look, Ida, I lay in bed all night wonderun what I could do for 'im. Take 'im a knuckle of veal perhaps. I didn't, though. Poor bugger, what does 'e get up to? All alone. In there. 'E's gunner die. Amongst the cockroaches and oil paintuns. And nobody know."

"Nothun ter do with you, Jean. We've got our own."

As soon as he was alone he pulled his pants up. Thanks to his constipation, he wasn't delayed by wiping: one advantage in being an octogenarian nut.

He went upstairs and dressed a little: that is, he put on a pair of elderly sandshoes. He came down and pulled the door shut on Number 17. The impact might have started him off feeling younger if he hadn't noticed the veins in the back of his hand.

But it was in some compelled sense a festive occasion: the articulated trams his still athletic body mounted; green prawns and pink in the Quay windows; the ferry sidling under him. Already the jaundiced torpor of the morning was dissolved in blue water. The light cut like diamonds. A breeze was flirting inside his shirt.

He sat down on one of the benches towards the ferry's bows. He was prepared for any kind of encounter: what he got was a man, probably as old as himself.

The man remarked that it was hot, but they would cool off when they sailed. The companion he had chosen for the voyage grunted and withdrew inside himself, erecting awnings over his eyes against what he might be about to endure. At the same time he was impatient for it: the hand supporting the long face was trembling; the sinews of the arm were tense all the way down to the blanched point of the elbow.

The new arrival dusted the bench with his newspaper. "Pretty smutty the seats get." He was smoking a well-matured, fuming pipe which erupted when he coughed. "Can't be helped, I suppose." The man laughed good-humouredly and proceeded to sit on his own half-charred tobacco crumbs.

His new companion was vaguely, disbelievingly soothed. It was the light, of course, and the smooth, glassy water as the ferry swam free of the wharf.

"Just the morning for playing truant." Everything the smoker said was launched with a courtliness older than his years.

You couldn't help looking at him: in his decent black suit and carefully dented hat, he was the kind that made you feel younger, and at the same time older, much older.

The man was unfolding his paper. "I'm a printer by trade," he explained, looking and not looking at the print he was holding. "A business of my own. But I'm lucky in employing a team of men I can trust under any circumstances." He straightened out the paper, to help him, it seemed, past a chokage possibly caused by emotion. "I won't say it's all truancy," he continued. "Duty, too. I make a point, every now and then, on a nice day, of visiting my young sister. She's a polio victim—living at Manly—the air's bracing. We're very close, my sister and me"—again he straightened the straight paper— "so it's pleasure as well as duty, isn't it?" The man's vulnerable, not quite educated voice broke abruptly off, and he turned to his companion as though appealing for approval.

You longed to give it, but didn't know how to. If it had been possible to draw the printer's attention to the elaborately careless design of gulls lashing and flashing in the ferry's wake: but the man would have thought you crazy, or callous.

To bridge the unorthodox silence the printer asked: "Don't you find at our age—I'd guess we're roughly the same—a man grows closer to his family? Only natural. Provided there is a family, of course."

"A sister." Must have sounded too pinched, unnatural; then suddenly he wanted to add, and did: "My sister's a cripple, too." He was almost panting.

"Well, now," said the delighted printer, "isn't that a coincidence? But not so bad she can't get something out of life, I hope?"

"I don't know. I haven't seen her—not since before the war—the first one, that is. She'd left before I got back. Families can drift apart."

His own contribution to banality made him feel elated, but the printer was obviously disturbed by an enormity in what he had been told. He had taken off his well-conditioned hat. He sat staring at the moving water.

"War is a terrible thing," he said, paying his respects. "I was in it myself."

He began to speak of Gallipoli, the blood and bowels of which were soon shimmering with the gentle radiance of a landscape for a rustic picnic; bodies cannoned off bodies in bursts of manly horseplay; the air vibrated with the strong tones of masculine friendship.

"No, I wasn't at Gallipoli," his companion had to admit.

France was mentioned, Flanders. The printer was entranced to exchange a few of the place names which had crystallized in his memory. A single pearl of saliva had formed in one corner of his mouth.

"I would like," he said, fumbling in his pocket, "to take the liberty—yes—of offering my card. Name's Mothersole," he half apologized. "Used to be ashamed of it as a boy."

The recipient of the card stared at the name, and at the sound though unfashionable address. He stared longer than he might have, because he hadn't a card to offer in exchange.

Mothersole, he could feel, was looking at him rather pointedly. "Because I'm inquisitive by nature," the printer laughed and admitted, "may I ask your name and line of business?"

Duffield said: "Duffield." His heart was beating like a drum; the voluptuousness of his forced confession was intensified by the flow of water around the ferry; he was almost intolerably happy to receive the trust and friendship of this rather boring, decent man.

" 'Duffield,' " Mothersole repeated over sunken chin, "a good, solid, English name."

At risk of ruining it all, Duffield confessed: "I'm a painter—an artist."

The printer heaved round, shining with enthusiasm and his morning shave. "Well, now, if you're an artist, I must try to interest you in a project I've had in mind. The idea"—he lowered his voice for modesty's sake—"is to print some little books for children—of unusual format—in the shape of animals, say—written by myself, and illustrated by some artist I haven't discovered—till perhaps now!"

Duffield was glad of the printer's card: he could continue staring at it.

"Of course I don't know—are you a successful artist?" Mothersole asked.

"I'm said to be."

"Then you won't be interested. Forget about it." He turned to resettle himself, and at the same time half changed the subject. "Any children? Are you married?"

"No. No."

Incredulity prevented the printer speaking for some time; then he said: "I'm a widower. My wife died at the end of the war—this second one. It was too much for her." He might have consoled himself watching the flow of water, but thought to ask: "Were you in the Second War as well?"

Duffield laughed. "I wasn't caught a second time; or rather, I took on some camouflage work. It didn't last long. Because we didn't see eye to eye, they decided I was mentally defective. Fortunately my lungs gave out. I developed pneumonia—twice in one year. You can imagine how thankful I was for those lungs—and my mental defects. The war years are too remote from art—from life, you might say—for any kind of artist. You have to get through them—intellectually, at least—the quickest way possible."

He realized the effect his irreverence was having on his new friend Mothersole. As for himself, he was hurt because his words were not his own: they were forced out of him by some devilish ventriloquist, to help destroy what he should, in any case, never aspire to. Almost the only thing he and Mothersole could hope to share was the morning of radiant light and water.

"I was in the Second War," the printer murmured piously. "Not very actively, I must admit. I spent nearly three years sedentary, administering transit camps in the Middle East. I had to be in it—because of my boy."

What if you had got a son, and the copy showed the same flaws as the original? Or worse still: if the copy had shown a flawless mediocrity? Mothersole at least was of a nature to forgive faults in the source of his fulfilment.

"I lost my boy," he was telling. "But I have my grandson. That's a consolation. It wasn't enough for my wife, though. You might say she was another of the casualties of war."

Now that they were crossing the Heads, the swell from the ocean was jostling the sturdy ferry: it had started rolling. Some of the passengers silently turned a greenish yellow; others tried to laugh their sickness off. Only the two incongruous friends or associates seated on a bench near the bows appeared unaware of any change in climate or course: except that the more disreputable figure leaned forward as the ocean gale struck them, and was baring his teeth, still in a strangely unconscious way, as he spoke.

"I wonder whether that's really the reason she died. It's difficult to know what people die of. For instance, I had a mistress. I took it for granted I'd killed her, because her husband wrote me a letter telling me straight out that I had."

The printer looked startled at sound of a word he wouldn't have dared, he had no need to, use. He might have relit his pipe, but continued clutching it by the bowl after a glance in the direction of the wind.

"For a time I accepted my guilt: even though I kept telling myself she had used me as an instrument of self-torture. She was a very beautiful woman when she was least unhinged; but depravity could make her coarse, brutal. She was the most depraved woman I've ever met. It seemed she had to degrade herself for being unworthy of her husband-God—a rich old satrap, who drowned cats by the sackful—like other gods when they tire of them."

Shrunk inside his clothes, the printer might have liked to shrink even farther: into his private cosmos if it had still been attainable.

"Well, he succeeded in making me believe I was the cause of his wife's death. I couldn't paint for several weeks." Better keep it at that level. "Then, at the end of the war, I had a letter from a woman friend of Hero's telling me what really happened."

"Of who?" The printer had wet his lips; he was inclining on his near buttock.

"Hero. My mistress was a Greek."

Mothersole could only shake his head, as though depravity had invaded the beaches, the mateship at Gallipoli.

"This woman told me Hero had spent several of the war years in an asylum. She suffered a lot from malnutrition, like most of the Greeks during the German occupation. She used to talk about me in connection with what she called her 'unsuccessful exorcism': this woman Arta Baïla told me. Shortly before the end of the war they moved Hero to a hospital, where she died of a cancer. The shortage of drugs made her death a particularly agonizing one."

"Mr Duffield, if this story is too painful—there is no need—" the printer kindly suggested, his own face drawn with discovery.

"So I didn't kill her, as her husband said. She died of cancer."

The gulls still wheeling in beautiful balance were diving for something, possibly sewage, in the ferry's wake.

"Or does one really know what sows the seed? Is cancer entirely a physical disease? Did I help kill by failing her? You see, we were never lovers. Oh yes, we fucked like animals; and I was fond, very fond of her; but I didn't love her, I can see now."

The more sheltered waters of the harbour could have been taking over, though there wasn't any visible evidence yet. One particularly smooth gull flew so close Mothersole ducked.

"Have you ever been in love?"

"Who? I?" It was too incredible a question for the printer to understand at first. "For years of my life, Mr Duffield, I was a married man."

"Yes, I know. But you make it sound like a well-sprung bed. Isn't love—more, shall we say—a matter of suffering and sacrifice?"

Mothersole's face might have looked pained if it had looked less bewildered. "I've had my fair share of that," he mumbled in rather a surly voice.

"Yes, I suppose so. And I have my work."

They were both pretty haggard, if not seasick like several of the others, after an unusually rough crossing of the Heads.

As they slid into smoother, sunlit waters, Mothersole took out a handkerchief to wipe the salt off his suit. "What sort of things do you paint?" he asked.

"Well! For some time now, tables and chairs."

"A funny sort of subject, if you don't mind my saying so."

"Why? What could be more honest? I'm not talking about the gimcrack: there's dishonest furniture, just as there are dishonest human beings. But take an honest-to-God kitchen table, a kitchen chair. What could be more real? I've had immense difficulty reaching the core of that reality, in I don't know how many attempts, but think I may have done it at last—or thought so until this morning: when everything died on me."

"How do you mean 'died'?"

"Exactly that. It no longer—in fact, none of the paintings of a lifetime—had any life."

"But once a picture is painted, how can it alter?" Mothersole was not concerned about paintings: he might never have noticed one; he was distressed by a state of the human mind.

"Paintings die like anything else, a great many with their creators, and this morning I realized, I think, that I'm already dead."

They were slipping through a sea grown oily and passive, through broad bands of a yellow sunlight, towards the solidly constructed wooden wharf. He would have liked to reach out and touch his temporary friend before the latter finally escaped: for Mothersole shared with the kitchen table that same commodious banality, the simple reality of which was so enviable, and at the same time elusive.

The printer was getting up. "Aren't you coming?" he asked, because it was polite to do so. "The gangway's down."

"No. There's no longer any reason why I should. I'd only waste an afternoon on the beach: drying up." He paused, because he scarcely dared. "And I may have got what I wanted."

The printer's rubber soles were beginning to withdraw him with matter-of-fact sounds of suction. "I shall remember our talk," he said. "You have my card, haven't you?" He might have liked to get it back.

The two men looked at each other, and smiled as each realized he would probably never meet the other again except in nightmares or moments of sentimental weakness.

For the return journey the ferry filled with the same kind of nondescript faces, if none was of the quintessential Mothersole. Their glances no more than flickered over an undesirable element: on the other hand, the sun in their spectacles could have accounted for their expression of distaste verging on apprehension.

As for the outsider, he no longer needed his Mothersole. His teeth grated as he regurgitated the nonsense he had talked while in the throes of rebirth: Hero's death; his own; that of his paintings. (In his right mind, he never let himself be drawn into talk about his painting, just as he shied away from those who wished to discuss variations on the sexual act.) He remembered another occasion when he had risen from the dead, by seminal dew and the threats of moonlight, in conversation, repulsive, painful, but necessary, with the grocer Cutbush: and now was born again by grace of Mothersole's warm, middle-class womb.

Presently he went and stood at the stern. He took out the printer's card. When he had torn it, he scattered the pieces on the water as Mothersole himself would have wished, if his ethos had allowed. Gulls fell rapaciously, swerved deceived, curving away. He continued watching the seed he had sown in the white furrow; some of it began at once to germinate, to reach such proportions his mind was already grappling with their sometimes exquisite, sometimes bitter fruit: particularly the apricot-coloured child-faces with their dark, crippled *Doppelgänger.*

Apart from Rhoda, who was ageless, why had he never painted a child? He had never desired to get one, but a work of art could be less of a botch. Sitting with his hands locked, he was fidgeting to create this child. Or more than one. Or many in the one. For after all there is only the one child: the one you still carry inside you.

So the light was exploding around him as they reached the Quay.

He walked home against an afternoon gale, climbing hills with a speed made possible by the impetus of his thoughts. When he let himself into the darkening house he began at once to drag at the switches. He ran, almost thundering, from room to room, bringing them to life. His despairs of that morning were vibrating on the walls, even the one he hadn't faced for several months: the cancer glowed inside the monstrance of Hero's womb as the wooden saints of Perialos raised her up, the sea coiling and uncoiling round the foreshore in its ritual celebration of renewal.

How could his unborn child fail to stir amongst these miracles of the risen dead?

8

It left him. He would sit whole mornings in the Sulka dressing-gown, a present from Olivia before the war. (For lack of ideas, he might have used the vision of his own tarnished splendour, but remembered another self-portrait.) He stood by open windows looking out, and faces looking up were immediately averted as though they had been hailed on: people never understood that desire is a kind of invisible hail. He continued looking, not so much out, as into himself. As the weather cooled off he exchanged the Sulka robe for an old matted woollen gown with droppings of porridge and condensed milk down the lapels. The gown had become an extension of himself; it wouldn't be discarded. Sometimes he added to the patina dribbles of fresh milk, for he had taken to drinking it regularly; he told himself he liked it.

"Why don't you have it delivered, sir?" asked the smallgoods girl, whose name was Maree.

He smiled. "It wouldn't be worth it."

"Save you the trouble of having to remember," she complained, pouting for his shiftlessness, and his smile: the smile was too mysterious.

He used to drink the milk from the bottle at the open window. Then he began forgetting, and would find the milk had turned to curds. There was a sour smell in the scullery, of more than milk: of his own memory. He would pour the curds, plopping hatefully out of the bottle, into the sink, and mash them down the hole. The stench shot up his nostrils.

He had prepared boards and a canvas or two, and made a number of drawings, but of faceless abstractions. They didn't convey the joy he knew he was capable of expressing if desire and idea came together in him. On one occasion he drew a stiffly wired bouquet of flowers, to which he almost succeeded in adding the face flowering at its heart. As it was, the stiff bunch remained too precise, rather sterile. Once he drew the head and shoulders of a boy, of silver outline, swimming in a sea of light or fleeces, but found to his disgust it was himself he had drawn from memory, the sulky still swaying through the dew-sodden sheep on the expedition to Mumbelong with Father. He destroyed the drawing. Whatever the accusations, he was not, he never had been, in love with himself: with his art, yes; and that was a projection of life, with the ugliness and cruelties, for which some of his critics held him personally responsible. He must have waited till now to create his late child because love is subtler, more elusive, more delicate.

Occasionally he woke in such physical pain he was afraid his body might give up before he was ready. It was about this time, too, that he read in the paper the account of a Japanese youth of twenty or so, in whom an actual child was found growing: the slow-developing seed of his own unborn twin. On sleepless nights a thought began tormenting the elderly, "successful" painter: had he been deluded into mistaking a monstrous pregnancy of the ego for this child of joy he was preparing to bring forth?

He would lie sweating in the dark, from time to time groaning aloud. Why not? There was nobody to hear; till one night he became conscious of a presence. He felt for the switch of the electric bulb hanging over his bed. Near his feet a rat was sitting on the blanket. Neither he nor the rat stirred for several light-years: they could have been a comfort to each other. Then the rat turned, thumped the boards as he landed on them, not in fear, and slowly moved away, dragging his long tail into outer darkness.

That morning began earlier than most. He slid out of bed, hunched, but slowly purposefully moving, in no way fretted by any of the worries of the night before. The light was silver, still only in tentative possession amongst the ink splashes and deeper pools of dark. He thought he saw something he must do to the archetype of a table he had painted several weeks back, but would wait till sunrise. Through the fringes of the araucaria, above the roofs of houses, the sea was stirring and glinting as though sharpening itself against itself. He, too, felt keen. There was a sound of billiards—no, milk bottles. Farting once or twice, he went down barefoot to drink some of the milk he had fetched from the smallgoods. (Ought to have it delivered, of course, as she said.)

The earlier part of the morning he lingered over the opening of shutters, to enjoy the clear light which swilled out the rooms; he could even feel it; he could feel the light trickling down inside the gown, over his not unpleasantly frowzy skin. In this state he could have enjoyed most things. The sounds of morning were still thin, but precise. The voices of women calling to their children hadn't yet been roughed up; the men hadn't begun throwing their weight around.

There was one room in his house for which he had never found a use: a small surplus parlour, with pieces of Miss Gilderthorp's frailest palisander upholstered by this time in dust tones. The parlour led to the conservatory. Now when he opened the shutters, the light which entered, cold and pure, filtered through laurustinus and privet, increased the room's spinsterish air.

On the other hand, the derelict conservatory was already buzzing, murmuring, drowsing in a tousle of tranquil gold: it was a light reflected out of childhood, in which he should have been gorging on handfuls of stolen crystallized cherries instead of aimlessly trampling around, dragging the dust off aspidistras with the skirt of his old frowsty gown.

It was while he was in the conservatory that the front doorbell started ringing. It rang too long, too hectically, for normal circumstances: it made him spin round once or twice on his heels before going to investigate. He wondered if it mattered that his feet were bare; he was, in any case, naked inside his dressing-gown.

She asked: "Is this Mrs Angove's place?" looking angrily ashamed.

She was carrying a white-enamelled billy, with a chip out of the lid about the size of a thumbnail. The lid grated slightly as she waited for his answer. It was the billy, he felt, which was making her angry.

"No," he replied, from a long way back in his gummed-up throat.

She was wearing a long thick golden perfect glistening plait: the reason why his voice had taken so long to rise to the surface.

"No. She doesn't live here. I can tell you where you'll find her, though." It was fortunate he could.

All the while the rather leggy child was frowning and twitching. Her impatience made the billy rattle.

"You see that house down there—the beige one on the opposite side—about six away—fairly narrow?"

The girl only made a breathing sound.

"But you must," he insisted. "It's unmistakable: the one with the mock-Romanesque windows." Showing off to a child.

She seemed disgusted rather than impressed. She certainly wasn't frightened. She had that clear skin which mottles: it had mottled up the arms as far as the short, crisp sleeves, and up her long stalk of a neck; only at the nape, where the plait began, the skin remained mysteriously opaque.

"That is where Mrs Angove lives," he said, he hoped, benevolently, while suspecting it sounded pompous. "Lucky I know Mrs Angove, isn't it? and was able to help."

Mrs Angove was rather a cranky old woman (perhaps not so old) with a hip.

"Is she sick?" he asked, coming down the steps as the child descended.

"I don't know. She's a friend of my mother's."

"Anyway, you're taking her something good. Soup—is it?"

Just then the child caught her toe in a crack in the path, and some of the soup slopped out of the billy and splashed her skirt.

"Oo-er!" she shouted in a different voice: she probably had several. "I've made a mess of me dress!"

Very little of a mess.

"Would you like to clean it up?" he murmured without confidence.

The child didn't answer, but slid through the half-open gate and marched towards Mrs Angove's, her walk deliberately wooden, holding the billy well away. The heavy plait hanging down her back barely swung.

He went upstairs and began to draw the head of a girl: of about twelve? thirteen? fourteen? He was no good at guessing the ages of the young, perhaps because age wasn't the straitjacket the well-intentioned would have liked it to be. In any case, the drawings he was making, one after the other, were not necessarily of the child who had come to the door, except for the plait; that was identifiable. Sometimes the drawings petered out in line: arabesques, not entirely frustrated, nor yet voluptuous. In one instance he wound the plait into a formal coronet with which he invested the head, and at once saw his mistake; he had made her a woman too soon: the eyes which he had left sightless on purpose began to stare with an expression he found offensively knowing. It was the mystery of pure being, of unrealized possibilities which fascinated him in children's eyes.

Come to think of it, there were few children with whom he had been intimately acquainted: only himself—and Rhoda—each of whom was born old. Still, you didn't have to know them: not if you knew.

That evening he decided to put on one of his suits from an earlier period to go to the party of a Mrs Mortimer he had met at an exhibition of paintings and vowed at the time not to meet again. Now, to escape a state of mind balanced between elation and dread, he found himself craving for a world he had hardly entered since before the war, and even then hadn't cared for.

Mrs Mortimer lived in a ground-floor flat overlooking a private beach. He saw, to his disgust, he was the first arrival. From Mrs Mortimer's point of view, it couldn't have turned out better if she had arranged it that way herself.

"Fancy, Hurtle," she said, though they had spoken for no more than ten minutes at the exhibition, "I didn't imagine for a moment that I'd tempt you—with my boring old party, I mean!"

"Nothing better to do," he mumbled, because he had been caught, and there seemed no alternate answer.

"Oh dear, you do live up to your reputation!" Mrs Mortimer was so delighted she came and rubbed her cheek against his.

She was a stocky woman with a thyroid throat. During her husband's life, she had suffered from his good looks and roving eye. He had also left her hard up, she told her new acquaintance at the exhibition. Perhaps this was why she was now blushing all the way up her goitrous throat: her flat cried her poverty in accents of discreet luxury.

Mrs Mortimer was one of those who collected paintings. "Not a single one of yours, darling!" It made her arch. "But that's understandable: I'm a poor woman." By this time she was not so much referring to fact as taking it for granted he had been educated in the right conventions.

"What do you think of this Pascoe?" she asked, manoeuvring him past a Modigliani she must have forgotten. "I can't judge him objectively, of course. Nobody who's fallen into the bastard's hands should even try to."

She was not looking at Pascoe's painting, but at the centre button of Duffield's shirt, while scratching herself, slowly and thoughtfully, with an index finger, between her breasts. At the exhibition he had suspected Mrs Mortimer of wanting to have an affair with him to confound her handsome, late husband. He was conscious of vibrations now: if they were weaker on this occasion, certainly he felt pretty sexless after the early morning start and those sheets of still directionless drawings.

"Someone's arriving," Mrs Mortimer said, taking his hand and squeezing it, "and I haven't had time to tell you about them. Don't you find a dossier is a comfort?" Was she going to be magnanimous and serve him up to someone else? "I do hope you won't be bored by all these silly people," was as much as she could whisper; nor was he able to explain he aspired to be a *tabula rasa*, not a stud.

Mrs Mortimer's party was so much the same in different clothes he wondered at what date the archetypal party had been held. The ladies screamed, or cooed, from stylized positions which suggested they were somehow out of joint, eyes straying, anointed eyelids fluttering as they wore the few cultivable topics, either marvellous or ghastly, to further shreds. The men were in general solider, not to say heavier: patches of light were reflected in their well-groomed shoulders and flanks, and you half expected a jingle of brass when their hostess, an adept at flicking the social whip, drove them straining from their last objective to the next.

One of the husbands, a mature grey with a hint of the investor in his walleye, came up as though he would like to conspire. "Painting anything lately, Hurtle?" He mentioned that his own name was "Ian."

What could you reply? am I breathing? am I shitting? You mumbled instead: "No. Not for the moment. Nothing to mention"; before turning your back.

It was difficult to remember why he had come. In his dated clothes, and corroded mask, he had reached a stage where he was at home only with objects; so he began to wander deliberately about the room: a pursuit they were content to leave him at. (It was enough to have him amongst them, to be able to tell afterwards how he had failed to control his language, his wind: *Really rather horrid, my dear, when I'd always understood he was a charmer.*) So he wandered through the congested room. There was a daguerrotype, with the features of Mrs Mortimer herself, of an old lady brutally lined, managing her best dress against a potted palm and painted clouds. On a full-dimensional table nearby stood a bowl of faintly pink, faintly scented single roses, into which he stuck his nose, clumsily, unashamedly.

"Hurtle, darling, here is something which may interest!" Mrs Mortimer came over to announce in a muted blast of gin. "There are two young women across there, both attractive, both intelligent, and all of them married. What more could you ask for?"

As she spoke, she was coaxing the palm of his hand with a finger expertly bent; while the two young women on the opposite side of the room, perhaps sensing they were on the market, smiled coldly at their drinks. Mrs Mortimer was not deterred by coldness from any direction: her role of procuress was more important than her un-filled sexual desires.

"Somebody told me Olivia Davenport's in town," said a plain and shiny American girl he had been avoiding.

"Darling old Boo! Yes. Isn't she adorable? She's begun to feel the weather, but I'm expecting her to totter thisaway." Mrs Mortimer tossed her mane like a skittish filly.

"Well now, won't that be a pleasure—a pleasure renewed! We met last winter in Nassau. She's the sweetest, loveliest person. Age hardly matters—I mean, you can be as old as *stone* if you've got that special *radiance* Mrs Davenport has."

The American girl had grown that much shinier for recollecting her experience in Nassau. Her orange canvas, college-style hat played up to the shininess: so dowdy and confident her connections must have been of the best.

He couldn't wait to see the Little Old Lady the American girl thought she had met; while Mrs Mortimer, always patting her party along, started muttering cynically: "Don't you realize you're stand-ing beside Hurtle Duffield the famous painter?"

"Oh *no*! Not Duffield!" squealed the American girl. "Whoever it was can't have felt more excited to come all this way and discover Australia! The man on board who gave the talks told us about you, sir—oh, about Dobell, and Drysdale, and I dunno who—but *Duf-field!*" From squealing, she changed her tune and her expression to suit a few drawn-out cello-notes: "Mr Duffield, I'd like you to know it's the most important moment of my life—intellectually, and spir-itually."

He could hear his own breath expiring, feel the flesh shrivelling on his bones, before sticking his nose into the bowl of roses he had more or less appropriated; they had the rare scent of tea roses; all the hairs were distinct, like the hairs on young golden skin.

It was most opportune that Mrs Davenport should arrive, though with so little thunder her entrance might have gone unnoticed; in fact her whole attitude implied she was only "looking in." Though somewhat blanched, she was not all that altered. Her face, perhaps, had been remodelled in white kid, to which had been added a pair of wattles, now quivering with motion or emotion, as she advanced, still erect, into the room, eyes apparently amazed inside their circlets of blue, steps short and tentative: Olivia could afford to play the timid cassowary.

Mrs Mortimer hurried to rub against her darling Boo. Then, in the hush, she began to trumpet, holding her glass of gin as though a torch to show off her prize: "Boo, this is Sharman. You know Sharman. She's here from Texas."

"Oh yes—Sharman." Mrs Davenport's white-kid cheek twitched into a dimple; she tweaked her rope of legendary pearls; she was wearing a little hat: a humble, ugly, smart hat.

"And Hurtle Duffield," Mrs Mortimer followed up.

Mrs Davenport offered her fingers, but he couldn't arrive at their natural shape for the gloves she was wearing: of a coarse suede, of a blinding, virgin white; nor did she expend any words on him, though everybody was waiting for them. Instead, she pursed up her bloody mouth, and narrowed her eyes, so that all those little milky wrinkles appeared at the corners. Then she lowered her chin, as though she had the wind, and raised it again, after quickly conquering that same wind. She barely whispered: "Hurtle—" before petrifying; and everybody watching the two stone figures knew for certain they had been lovers.

At this point Mrs Mortimer skilfully separated her star guests, and began to fling "Boo darling" round the room. Something clicked into place, and Mrs Davenport remembered her first, her childhood language. She was gargling down amongst her pearls: her teeth showed, and like the pearls the teeth were real, if tiny. It occurred to him on catching sight of the teeth that Boo Hollingrake still contained the kernels of reality, and that she must be made to admit it, if only once, since she dared expose her fragile, discoloured, old-childish teeth.

But there wasn't an opportunity, and he continued straying

amongst the objects in the impoverished Mrs Mortimer's room. He thought: never have I gone farther in the wrong direction, when that chipped billy, the lid, did it have a blue circumference, which might be why the chip suggested an act of fortuitous brutality, like a thumbnail hit by a hammer. In his distraction, he always ended up at the bowl of single roses, each with its tuft of slender golden hairs.

At least nobody else would want to intrude on his peculiar, immoral, not to say frightening colloquy with a bowl of roses, unless it was somebody equally peculiar and out according to the code of Mrs Mortimer's set.

"Duffield? You don't, or won't, know me."

It was—not at once, but by degrees—Shuard the music critic, whom he hadn't seen for years, and never more than briefly. Shuard's hair, the most noticeable thing about him, grew in waves of steel wool in which the Gumption was visible; the unctuous pores round his nose were still pricked out in black; his hips and buttocks had perhaps increased in suavity. Otherwise he was a nondescript man who lived by journalism and a sprinkling of knowledge, and dining out: he could tell a dirty story better than most.

"I'm not accusing you," Shuard said. "I've been on what I call my sabbatical from the *Evening Star*. But have now returned to the fray," he added, looking the room over.

Duffield answered in the same vein. "Peggy Mortimer has a bargain or two: intelligent, charming, and safely married." He clamped his jaws: an alliance with Shuard, even against cabbage stalks, was something of a betrayal.

Shuard laughed his brown-gravy laugh. "All a bit long in the tooth, I'd say. I spent a delightful winter in Berlin: every night a little girl on either side. Every night two *different* little girls, mind you—only to warm the bed, of course."

Have to laugh. If you could have shaken Shuard off: but he clung like cobwebs, in grubby festoons; so you began to match grubbiness with grubbiness. "One advantage of old age: the hot-water bottles put on flesh, and begin to breathe."

Shuard laughed so appreciatively he had to use his handkerchief; as soon as he was disengaged he started off on a different, though only a slightly different tack: "I can remember—years ago—dining with the old girl over there."

"The which?"

"The Sugar Fairy—the Davenport. Oh, it was a slap-up affair: a Greek tycoon, with a wife. I don't remember anything about it, except that you took the wife down to the water while the old boy was learning a game of marbles. I've sometimes wondered what happened."

"Oh?"

He did manage to shed Shuard, by practically rubbing him off on the corner of a table, and there on the other side Olivia Davenport was standing, holding up her throat, in conversation with a Santa Gertrudis bull.

It didn't prevent her turning at once and asking most anxiously: "Yes, Hurtle?" An extra white-kid chin appeared: she was obviously frightened, as though she might have to face a topic they had skirted before.

"Do you know about Hero?" he asked.

"About whom?" She flickered her eyelids: she had made a point of stressing the grammar.

"Hero Pavloussi."

"Oh—Hero! She was so sweet." Mrs Davenport visibly dragged up around her the idiom which was safest, the smile which was blandest.

"Did you know that she died?" he insisted.

"Hero *died*!"

"Yes," he said, "of cancer."

At first Boo Davenport didn't appear to understand; then she began crinkling her eyebrows against the tastelessness to which she was being subjected.

"Of cancer!" he repeated, or shouted.

She lowered her eyes. "I didn't know. How dreadful!"

At the same moment Mrs Mortimer led forward a young man who was designing for the theatre, and Mrs Davenport drew a deep breath: her smile invited the designer to protect her against further violation.

"I've never known her in better form," Peggy Mortimer burbled half into her gin. "Isn't she a very old friend?" As she waited, looking for clues, her mouth remained plastered to the glass, like an active sea-anemone.

He got away. He went out, and down, over the private beach. First there were the trampled succulents, the creeping couch-grass,

380

then the sand. There was a bar of blood across the sky, almost parallel with a cramped, grey-skinned sea.

"Hurtle?"

It was Olivia. She came running out; it looked strange, because of her height, and her reputation, and her now wobbly ankles; besides, she was at the mercy of the rebounding mattress of soft sand. She lumbered on, however, till they both reached where moisture made for firmness.

There she began: "Of course I knew. It was the shock, I think—of your dragging me out in public—that forced me to deny it. I knew. I knew! Cosma wrote me a letter with all the more harrowing details of Hero's life after she left him. He said he held me responsible for most of what had happened—that knowing me and my friends had made her unbalanced."

"Did you believe him?" Because she seemed prepared to.

Olivia could have been counting the ridges in the wet sand. "Certainly she loved me."

"Certainly?"

"Oh yes. There was a time when she couldn't move without me. I wasn't prepared to be possessed to that extent. I couldn't breathe."

"But you know Hero was my mistress."

"I gave her to you—for that purpose—not to kill!"

He took her by the wrists. "How many murders, Boo, are ever proved?"

"Exactly. Very seldom the ones we know anything about: that other case, for instance."

"Which other case?" He could hear his voice progressively rising on the slack, evening air.

"The prostitute"—Olivia's voice had grown equally discordant—"who fell or threw herself off a cliff—I forget where it happened."

He was too tired, or too old, to defend himself against false accusations. "But Hero died of cancer, didn't she?" He had found the strength to shout that.

It was surprising none of the elaborate figures in Mrs Mortimer's illuminated living-room broke. Olivia Davenport recovered enough of her social conscience to hold her breath, to turn her head, to find out; but the guests were too involved in spinning "charm" and reflecting "brilliance" to notice or hear the regrettable maniacs on the beach.

"Cancer"—Olivia had become so blatant she, too, was now positively shouting the forbidden word—"is sometimes only the *coup de grâce*; and suicide, more often than not, is another kind of murder."

In more objective circumstances he might have agreed with her. At the present moment, with the livid landscape pressing too close, and the limp air an extra skin, he could only hate Olivia.

She said, without great concern it seemed: "Do you want to break my wrists?"

He immediately dropped what he had forgotten he was holding, but couldn't divest himself of his accuser.

"Of course I didn't know the prostitute," she was saying, "only what I've been told. But you—*we*—might have saved Hero if we'd been a little less technically accomplished, slightly more experienced in living."

His breath whistled. "I believe—or I think I believed at the back of my mind—that a condemned soul might help save another." What had he ever believed, when he wasn't painting? If he knew, he might have finished the inscription on the dunny wall. "Anyway, we tried—didn't you know? dragging all the way to that island of infallible saints; but the saints had left, and God was a millionaire her spiritual pride wouldn't allow her to make use of."

"Oh, husbands," Olivia mumbled, "no gods ever died so quickly or so easily."

She was looking at her feet, and now he, too, noticed that the tide had come in and was washing over the tops of their shoes, stirring a scum of weed and straw, lifting an empty sardine tin and a used condom. They should have moved, but couldn't: their feet mightn't have belonged to them.

"Always at my most desperate, or cynical," Olivia said, watching as the sea continued sucking round their ankles, "when I've most hated men for their lies and presumptuousness, and their attempts to reduce love to a grotesque sexual act, I've felt that somewhere there must be some *creature*, not quite man, not quite god, who will heal the wounds." She raised her head and drew down the corners of her formal mouth. "Perhaps that's why we look to artists of any kind, why we lose our heads over them."

"Possibly!" He took her lightly by the hand. "But better wait till they're dead. What they have to tell or show improves with decontamination—if it doesn't go up in hot air, or sink into a wall."

When they reached the drier sand Olivia Davenport began moaning like an elderly woman. "How wet! I wonder whether I'll catch a cold? At least they won't notice in there: everyone will be too drunk by now." She prepared to return to the rout he no longer felt in any way committed to.

He walked along the beach looking for a way back to the road, his shoes squelching under him. There was still a smear of crimson staining the membrane of sky: it made his blood quicken. He was not yet destroyed, or not the artist in him: the flat monochrome of a world beneath the crimson sky-mark was his to re-create in its true form, visible, it seemed, only to himself.

On the third evening after his harrowing but necessary encounter with Olivia he was cleaning some brushes in the bedroom-studio overlooking Chubb's Lane. A placid golden light and the practical rather humdrum nature of his job encouraged a belief in compatibility. He tried to imagine how it must feel to inspire respect, as opposed to adoration, mistrust, or hate: if you were a joiner, say, or locksmith, or watchmaker, even a grocer. Not a grocer. Grocers, he remembered, could have an affinity with evil and with artists, which threatened the harmonies the bland evening was pouring out.

Along the lane there was not a discord: certainly the sounds of life, but broken bottles were temporarily debarred; or had the minutest splinters of glassy conflict already begun to fray the curtain of moted light?

"If we're gunner play, why don't we play?"

"Come on! We're playing, aren't we? What's wrong?"

He could see the first speaker: her sweaty concern; the brown-ringed brown eyes; big floppy cerise bow crowning the black frizz of hair against the opposite palings of the lane. Her companion of cooler voice remained invisible, closer to his side. At one point he caught sight of what must have been the cause of contention: a ball rising high above the hooded dunny.

The voice of the concerned girl pursued the soaring ball: "O-ohhh!" in the long arc of a moan.

"You wanted to play silly old ball, didn't you? Well, I'm playing! See?"

"We mighter lost it."

"I caught it, didn't I?"

"Wasn't your turn."

"You're not mature, Angela, wanting to play at silly ball. I wanter go home and study." The cool voice narrowed, and he recognized the code of priggishness.

"Go on then! I'll play by meself. Who wants to study? I'm gunner get married soon as I can leave school."

"My mother says I mustn't think of getting married too soon."

"Mmmm. Who's gunner pay for yer if you don't?"

Three or four driblets of the tossed ball punctuated the silence that had formed.

"Not yer father!" Angela tried out.

At once the ball rose so high the sun turned it into a burning replica.

"What're you up to, Kathy? I'm gunner lose me ball—me new ball!"

"Your father'll buy you another one."

Voices hesitated after that: time paused; till the molten ball, cooled by its descent, began to re-form, thumped solid, rebounded, and thumped again in somebody's back yard.

"You've lost me ball!" Angela moaned, her ripe-banana skin sweating worse than ever.

"We can go in and get it, can't we?"

"Not in there! I'm not gunner go in there. He's funny."

"He's only an old man."

"Some old men—I'm not goin' in there!" Angela's cerise bow flackered past the metal-bound palings as she moved up Chubb's Lane. "You only done it—lost me ball—because you wanter go home and study."

"You're *obsessed*, Angela!"

"I'm what?"

For an instant a glistening plait raised itself above his dilapidated fence, as though to strike.

He watched the ball settle by shallow bounces at the roots of the *Bignonia venusta* which crowned the dunny. Then he began to go downstairs, very quickly, youthfully, breathing deeply. He could move with ease because he was still wearing the dressing-gown he had put on that morning and which one thing and another throughout the day had prevented him from improving on. At the same time he knew that improvement wasn't necessary: his returning the ball had been prearranged; nor would he appear as the bogy which troubled the stupid Angela's imagination: for Kathy he was only an old man. The fact that she could already perceive some, if not all of the truth, made her his spiritual child of infinite possibilities.

Reaching the yard, he picked up the now motionless ball out of the dregs of yellow light. The felt was still warm. As he explored its form with his hand he was relieved to be able to tell himself the ball belonged to Angela, not to Kathy, and that anything he might say, probably of an uninteresting and mundane nature, would be directed at the owner of the ball. Any exchanges between himself and Kathy would be conveyed by implication and silences.

But nobody came. He waited, holding the tingling ball: till he could no longer bear the felted chugging in his side.

The situation was going flat when a hand appeared, tackling the latch through the cut-out in the gate. Then she was standing in the gateway as she had stood at the door the other morning when she came with the billyful of soup, looking for Mrs Angove. She was wearing that slightly cold, expressionless expression some children can put on, and which is the most complete of all disguises.

"The ball landed in the yard," he said. "I'm glad you've come to fetch it, because I shouldn't have known where to find you, to return it."

"It doesn't belong to me," she replied, accepting it with mysterious concentration. "It belongs to Angela Agostino, who I play with sometimes."

She continued looking strangely at the ball in her hands: it could have been a homed pigeon. At any moment she might start stroking what was neither a pigeon nor hers.

"To Angela," he repeated. "What is *your* name?" Although he knew, he wanted to make her say it.

"Kathy."

"Yes." He was burning to know more, if not everything. "But your other—your family name."

She didn't want to tell, it seemed; then she said or mumbled: "Volkov."

"Kathy Volkov. Are you Russian?"

"No. Australian."

"But your father? Where is he from?"

"I don't know."

"Are there many of you?"

"There's my mother. I must go now," she said, still looking at the strange ball in her hands. "Mother will be wondering where I am."

"Is your mother Russian, too?"

"No." She began to sound sulky. "She's Scotch—*Scottish!*"

"And Australian."

"No. Mother will never be anything but Scottish."

Along the lane the light was wilting like the marrow flowers on dusty beds in back yards.

Kathy Volkov said: "I must go. I've got to practise."

"At what?"

"The piano."

"Ah! So you're a pianist—an artist!" He spoke gently: he didn't want to mock, but to test her. "Are you going to be a good one?"

She looked at him. "Mr Khrapovitsky says I will be."

"Yes. But you're the one it depends on in the end. You're the artist."

Her face appeared to grow more opaque. She had blue, but by no means passive eyes.

"Have you the will?" he asked.

She was pouting, and wouldn't answer; so he saw he had gone too far; he said: "I hope, Kathy, you'll come and see me again. It'll do us good to exchange ideas."

She could have been glad she had the ball to hold.

"You don't agree?"

"My mother mightn't let me."

"What about this father of yours? Doesn't he make any decisions?"

"He went away."

"Then I hope your mother will let you come."

To encourage everyone concerned he put his hand as kindly as he could on her back: he was conscious of the shoulder-blades, and above them, the modest beads of her vertebrae; but she rid herself of the hand by a few quick shrugs.

How could he appease her? In desperation he began looking around: in his yard not even a dusty flower.

"Aren't you the painter?" She spoke with abrupt formality.

"Yes. I do paint."

A little smile was creeping on her face. "My mother says she would never let a painter paint her, because then you are at their mercy, worse than the mercy of a husband. A husband goes away. But the painter has painted the painting."

"Yes, the painting. And you are your father's child. Hasn't that occurred to your mother?"

Instead of answering, she was preparing to manage the ramshackle gate.

"You must feel close to your mother."

"I have to help her: she needs me, and then—she's my mother."

"It's very fortunate if you can feel close to your parents. So often one isn't really theirs."

"What do you mean?" She was frowning, nostrils twitching: she was clutching the ball so tight she had deformed it.

"I mean one can be so remote in spirit from one's actual father— or mother—it's as though one doesn't belong to them. Spiritually," he dared, "one can be someone else's child."

It probably sounded too highflown and muddled for her to understand; though certainly she seemed more tranquil, even drowsily acquiescent.

His own bliss caused him to make a regrettable slip. "To be truthful, I don't believe the artist can belong to anyone."

She glanced at him quickly as though he had reminded her of something, but looked away again at once. "I never felt for long that I belonged properly to anybody—excepting my own room."

She started blushing: a radiance the last of the light helped fix on a space waiting for it in his visual mind.

"How old are you?" he asked irrelevantly.

"I was thirteen last Friday." With equal irrelevance she gave a short snicker.

They parted gravely, politely: the latch continued tinkling in his head.

That night he started work on the flowering rosebush. Each of the big scalloped saucers of single roses was given its tuft of glistening human hairs. It was natural that the face should flower at the centre of the bush, humanly radiant amongst the not dissimilar roses, and not all that unnatural for the bush to be growing at the sea's edge, under a livid sky.

When morning came he felt surprisingly fresh, standing in front of his finished painting: only his eyelids, dry and fragile, might have been segments of ping-pong balls.

After he had rested a little he began to draw what became during the days which followed a more abstract version of the "Flowering Rosebush": the face at the heart of the bush reduced to an eye, its remote candour undazzled by its setting of rose-jewels; the original seascape dissolved in space by fluctuations of gelatinous light, in which a threat of crimson was still suspended.

At intervals he made other drawings: one of a cool, naked, fairly naturalistic, though sexless girl, which satisfied him to the extent that he propped it up against the easel in the back room. The drawing was taking possession of him, he felt, as he walked up and down through the house, alternately dazzled and distressed by details of a painting it might become. He lay down finally, nursing a kind of anxiety along with his restless excitement, and fell into a sleep full of opposing influences.

He woke hissing, shuddering, though unable to remember anything of a dream which might have fed the anxiety already latent in him. On another level he was conscious of a delicious sense of voluptuousness.

Then the rattling began: or was, more probably, repeated. He recognized the sound of the loose knob on the back door. From upstairs he couldn't identify the voice calling on and off.

He looked along his body at the state of erection in which they had as good as discovered him; but his shame was quickly disguised by slopping into a shirt and pants. He went down through the awakened house towards the feverishly rattled doorknob.

Kathy Volkov was standing on the step. He felt genuinely surprised, because sleep had loosened the ties between them, or at least the superficial ones.

He probably looked disagreeable; he certainly sounded that. "Good Lord, Kathy, what on earth are you doing here?" He was even on the verge of adding: "again!" But that mightn't have convinced either of them: she was too unfamiliar an experience.

He knew his hand was trembling on the door.

"I brought this," she said. "My mother won't let me keep it. Isn't it nice?"

She was holding in her arms a skinny, growling, tabby kitten, or half-grown cat, which flattened itself still flatter as he looked it over.

"I'm not a cat lover," he said.

"Arrh!" The extra effort to restrain the elastic cat with her arms made her protest vibrate, like a groan. "Did you ever have one?"

"No."

"How do you know, then, that you aren't a cat lover?"

"No! No!" He thought he no longer cared for Kathy Volkov.

In his determination to resist he was trying to look his crankiest, exaggeratedly shaking his uncombed head; the door he was holding swung and creaked as his whole body rejected the unwanted cat.

Kathy's mouth had taken on a shape of ugly, rubbery desperation. Her nose had grown hot-looking and shiny: she might have been preparing to cry; when the cat, at its flattest, its most tigerish, sprang out of her arms and through the doorway into the house.

Kathy seemed less surprised and startled than he. "There!" she said. "That's an omen! Isn't it?"

He began to feel furious. "An *ill* omen, if you like! What am I going to do with a cat?"

"Feed it—and it'll keep you company."

"But I don't want it! I've got my work. I've got the wireless."

"Anyway, we'd better find the thing." The cat had aged her and made her suddenly practical.

She walked very straight, straight past him into the house. Her plait, he noticed, had become two. The two pigtails, although comparatively thin, looked rather guileful, lying limp on the shoulder-blades he had touched on another occasion.

"Where's your friend?" he asked as he followed. "The little Italian. Why didn't you bring her?"

"Oh, Angela. She's not all that much of a friend. There's nothing much in Angela. You wouldn't find her interesting."

Not only practical, Kathy was assured today. Now that she had got inside the house she was walking with the short, confident steps of a woman of the prissier kind. He could imagine the mother.

"As soon as we find this damn cat you'll have to take it home." His bare feet made the decision sound more emphatic.

"Mother says it'll eat too much."

"Somewhere, then. There are plenty of people for cats."

"I do know one other person, but she's got too many."

The house was hardly his any longer as Kathy stalked through it on her long, loosely articulated legs.

"Fancy living in it!" She stared at the furniture with her borrowed, older woman's eyes. "It's good, though. I like it. It's not nearly as bad as they say."

"Who says?" They were standing in the little, suddenly far more precious, derelict conservatory.

"People."

"Who haven't seen it!"

"Ooh, I love *this*!" She began turning in the conservatory, not exactly in a waltz, but swinging her thin pigtails. "Isn't it dreamy!"

"It hasn't been kept up. It's nothing—a ruin."

"Oh, but I could use this!"

As she continued turning within the conservatory's narrow limits, she began also to hum. A golden tinsel of light hung around her lithe, mackerel body; while out of the dislodged tiles and shambles of broken glass her shuffling feet produced discordancies, but appropriate ones: Kathy Volkov would probably never teeter over into sweetness. There was a smell of trapped warmth and inward-pressing privet. Once or twice she slapped down the leathery tongue of an aspidistra.

"Yes," she sighed, subsiding.

They found the cat crouching amongst a hoard of cardboard boxes at the far end of the scullery. This was at least convenient. He filled an empty herring tin with milk he had brought from the smallgoods the evening before. Some of the milk, and a smear of tomato sauce, slopped over on the flagging.

"There!" said Kathy Volkov. "You must shut it in for a few days— and feed it—and talk to it—then it'll know it belongs." She closed the door behind them as they left the kitchen.

"It's all very well giving advice when you won't have to live with it."

"No. But I could."

She plumped down with such force in one of the chairs in the living-room the dust shot out visibly: the motes were suspended in her radiance.

"I could live here all right!" She spoke so vehemently, passionately, she was no longer the pretended older woman, but again the little girl who was his ever-present spiritual child. "I could live here, and practise somewhere at the centre of the house, and nobody would turn nasty."

"I might."

But she didn't seem to take that seriously. She was sitting with her legs stretched out in front, dreamily looking at the toes of her dusty shoes. After all, she had more or less won the battle for the cat's adoption.

"What kind of music do you play?" he asked very carefully.

"Do you know about music? I don't believe you're interested in it."

"Well, of course I am! I listen to it regularly on the wireless."

In the kitchen there was, in fact, a primitive radio in a worm-eaten, dulled mahogany case, with a moon of tarnished brocade through which the sound filtered: music edged with tin; foggy oracles of voices. Years ago he had bought it second-hand. There it stood, looking as though it belonged to a wind-raked seaside cottage to which a sea captain had retired. It was corroded; sometimes the knobs would stick; but it continued to give service, and he would tune in from force of habit. You couldn't say he didn't understand music: though its meanings were probably those his unconscious desired at the moment of listening.

"Yes," said Kathy, sticking her tongue deep down inside one corner of her mouth: she might have had a gumboil; he had forgotten all about them till now. "You may *listen* to music. A lot of people do. But you wouldn't die without it."

"Well, no. I wouldn't die without it. That's a bit extravagant, isn't it? even if I were a musician." At once he heard how insensitive he was to his own youth as well as hers. "That is, I'm a painter," he added more humbly. "I suppose I'd have died—at your age—if I'd been prevented from painting and drawing."

They were united for a moment in his submerged living-room: never more than a waiting-room of the spirit, in which he had restlessly lounged, or sat rigid on the edge of a chair, grinding his jaws together; till release came with the force of an afternoon southerly, and he would run upstairs, the problems of his real, his creative life, dissolving inside him.

Now it was Kathy Volkov sitting on the edge of the chair. Suddenly he saw how little of the child there was in her: her eyes were terrible as she tortured one of the thin pigtails, untying and retying a crumpled pink bow.

"You couldn't understand how I must! I *must*! How I'll die! Nobody could ever understand!"

"But I do! I was young, wasn't I? Aren't I an artist?"

She was already so much the egotist her eyes were blind to anyone or anything but herself. He wanted to protect her from that situation. At this instant he was prepared to give himself up wholly to the salvation of Kathy Volkov: so he began walking towards her, on his knees, like the beggars he could remember outside European cathedrals; while her eyes continued blazing in a blind fury of desperation.

All at once, just before reaching the island or chair on which she was stranded, his excitement over Kathy, his admiration, his own need for her, melted into an agonizing and helpless love. He almost failed to prevent himself blubbering at her, dragging her down to such a wretched level of reality, he probably would have disgusted her forever.

Instead, when he reached her, in this wholly ridiculous kneeling position, he managed to get possession of her head. "I'm the one who could help you—if only you could see!" He was holding her head against his, making a virtue of the awkwardness. "I haven't had a child—I know—but know what it is to have been one—in much the same situation. Can't that be a consolation, Kathy? To both of us? To me, it almost makes you my child."

Still holding her head, he could see her eyeballs beginning to grind around in their sockets.

She wrenched herself away from him. "But I'm *not* a child!"

How it echoed!

She had got up and was standing over him, menacingly, it appeared for the moment.

Then she altered her voice and said very quietly: "Can't we see the rest of the house?" She slid her fingers along the backs of his fingers; she said: "It's interesting."

His bones started to creak and click: only now he realized how rheumaticky he was becoming; but she had taken him by the hand and was helping him up as a matter of course. He looked along her long, skinny arm and saw the potential strength already exerting itself, partly muscular, partly as reflections of sinewy light.

He heard his feeble dust-coloured voice trying to disguise the sounds of age: "I've read about copper bracelets and rings to draw it off—arthritis, I mean—in some way, apparently, they absorb the inflammation."

Because none of it had any connection with herself, she only made a grunting sound, and he was ashamed of having told her something so uninteresting and irrelevant.

She was looking vaguely here and there. "Did you paint all these paintings?" She still didn't sound interested, though.

"Yes." He was content to let his "child" lead him through his own house by the hand.

"They're so different from one another," she commented languidly. "Not all by the same person." With her far hand she had got hold of one of the pigtails and was sucking the end.

"Well, of course! These down here are mostly early paintings. I hadn't yet found my style. But I like to think there are already signs of it."

She made a sucking sound, in no way committed, through a mouthful of wet hair. He felt repelled and had to remind himself that sucking a pigtail was a childish habit.

"Isn't it the same with composers? Aren't they derivative at first? And what about interpretative musicians? I bet your tastes and style as a musician won't remain fixed—not if you're any good."

The narrow stairs were forcing them gravely together as they mounted. Here, too, there were paintings on the wall, and he could tell by the twitching of her fingers, the angle of her head, that she was glad they were there: you can escape from arguments by looking absently out of windows, he knew from his own experience.

As they continued their precise ascent he tried again to winkle her out. "Who is your favourite composer?" He would have frowned on any such question put to him as a boy.

She sighed, then mumbled quickly: "Tchaikovsky, Rachmaninov, Liszt. Liszt's my favourite. He's so difficult. And brilliant."

"Good Lord!" It was dishonest, because none of them, till now, had been of great importance to him. "What about Bach, Mozart, Beethoven?"

"Oh yes! They're wonderful, aren't they?" she murmured sententiously, like a lady at a reception.

They had reached the top landing. In the front room they stood looking out through the araucaria-coloured light, over the roofs, at a slow sea.

"But you can't understand about Liszt!" She was smiling convinced out of the window. "Mr Khrapovitsky says I must start studying the First Concerto now. It doesn't matter how many years I take." She was swaying slightly: at the end of the unspecified period, the chandeliers would crash about her shoulders, and her shining head rise untouched.

"What's that?" She dropped his hand to point.

It was one of the later, almost completely abstracted versions of his "Pythoness at Tripod": something he mightn't have shown Kathy if he had given the matter consideration in advance.

"It's an abstract painting." He tried to make it sound discouraging.

Why had he never grown a moustache? An uneven fringe of hair above the mouth might have been a great help in not explaining things.

Kathy was saying: "I know a hunchback, a friend of my mother's. I thought it was horrible at first. Now I no longer think about it." Her eyes suddenly took aim at him. "Why did you paint the hunchback?" She was prepared to wait for his answer; then she couldn't. "Because it was more difficult! Do you see? Like Liszt!"

"No," he said, trying to remember. "I had my purely painterly reasons: those come first, of course. Then I think I wanted to make amends—in the only way I've ever known how—for some of my own enormities."

She brooded over the painted board; or perhaps she was looking inward at the difficulties of Liszt.

"Don't you pity your mother's friend?"

"Mmm."

She hadn't suffered enough: because pity was not yet one of her personal needs, she hadn't bothered to understand, let alone confer it.

She was again leading him, no longer by the hand, but stalking ahead on her cool, proppy legs.

She glanced inside the junk-room. "There's a smell of rats in there," she said.

"You can't escape from rats in any of these old houses."

"There's none in ours. My mother's too afraid of rats breathing on the food: that's what gives you hepatitis. Every month she takes the lino up and scrubs the boards underneath."

"Perhaps that's why your father ran away." It may have been a dirty one, but it made her smile. "Was he an artist of some kind?"

"He was a seaman—but left his ship. He married my mother while he was in hiding. He did marry her, whatever they tell you."

"I've heard nothing."

The story of her father, which had halted them between the upper rooms, had also emphasized the shape and intensified the colour of her eyes: they were mercilessly blue and clear-cut.

"Do you remember him?" he asked.

"Not much. I can remember—once. It was very early. The light was a funny, damp grey. He had a smell I'd never smelled before. I remember that because it was so different from what I was used to—the smell of my mother."

Her eyes had faded. The old floorboards were audibly ticking.

"And after he left—was that the last you heard of him?"

"We heard from somebody that he'd been seen on the opalfields."

"From sea to opalfields! He could have had something of the artist in him, even if he didn't know it."

"Yes!" She was so pleased she bared her teeth; her hand began burning crushing his; her eyes would have stared wider open if their shape had allowed.

She began trembling violently. "That's what I see in this concerto I've begun studying with old Khrap: the colours of opals! That's what I want to try to give it when I know how."

But at once she grew embarrassed. "What else?" she mumbled. "Isn't there anything else to look at?"

They dragged on automatically, again bound together at the hands, and stumbled into the back room, from which he hadn't thought of moving the drawing of the nude girl, simply because it hadn't occurred to him Kathy Volkov might worm her way so deep into his house and life.

Now he was horrified at this climax.

"Is that supposed to be me?"

"Not consciously. It's the figure of a girl."

She ignored his reply. "But you haven't seen me. My navel isn't that shape." Her hand fell apart from his, only too easily now. "And I'm different there." She went and touched the dark smudge at the meeting of the thighs. "Otherwise it's not a bad likeness." Her use of a word peculiar to unexceptionable women paying morning calls long ago made her judgement sound uncannier.

He would have liked to take the drawing-board down, or at least turn its blank back to them; but his ingenuity had dwindled, like his strength. He flopped down on the old plangent bed, where the state of its rucked-up grey blankets and grubby sheets were immediately emphasized by his presence.

Fortunately an inner distraction seemed to prevent Kathy's noticing as much as she might have noticed, or else the objects which attracted her attention were closer to her own interests. After taking up and reorganizing one or two things on the chest—chunks of quartz and agate, a dried-up pomander which she sniffed at briefly, a pewter mug full of buttons, pins, and the melted ends of sealing wax—she began to talk to him in disconnected snatches, while showing no sign of expecting answers.

"D'you really use sealing wax? I've always wanted to. I use coloured inks according to how I feel. Shall we write to each other, Mr Duffield?"

The formal address destroyed the enormous headway he felt they had made in their relationship.

He answered bleakly tentative: "There won't be much point in writing, will there? if we continue to see each other?"

She became more nervously excited, twitching as she talked and moved. She looked out of the window, eyes unflinching, at the now blindingly yellow light.

"Of course there'll be a point!" She was forced to close her blinded eyes; she was smiling slightly: she had a rather thin mouth. "Don't you think we'll put in the letters the things we don't say to each other? I mean—you couldn't *say* the things you paint, could you?"

She was swaying in the blaze of evening. His head felt as though it were reduced to skull, with the thoughts feverishly rattling in it.

"My dear child"—it sounded unbearably gauche—"will you let me hold your head—as we did—before? I want to remember the shape of it."

He did long—yes, to drink it down—swallow it whole—its beauty.

She opened her eyes and grinned rather heartily, like a girl in a newspaper photograph. "What a funny thing! I've got to go and practise. This is the time." If she had been older, she might have been warding him off with appointments at her dressmaker's or hairdresser's.

But she did, in fact, come towards him, over the endless, intervening floor.

Now that he had what he wanted, love and terror were flapping inside him in opposition. He must smell terrible, too: an old, unsavoury man. That, certainly, and their uncomfortable attitude, not to say his silliness as he laid her head against his, must ensure purity.

He closed his eyes, feeling he had achieved a definite stage in relationship with his spiritual child.

But she began to resist. "It makes me nervous if I'm late for practice." She breathed close to his ear. "I've got to sit down always at the same time." Her cheek, fidgeting to escape, must have been grated by his more abrasive one; but she didn't shed her kindness. "Here's a surprise for you!"

She popped into his mouth what began as a smooth jewel, but which melted abruptly into all that was soft and sweet-succulent. At the same time she seemed to crest over on him, breathing or crying, enveloping him like a wave.

"What is it—Kathy—darling?" he rattled as he was sucked under.

"It's like he smelled when he kissed me! My father! That only time I can remember."

He despaired more and more for the delicate relationship he had conceived: because her own innocent natural scent and distress over her lost father were cancelled out by the skill with which she had planted kisses in his mouth. That, too, could be innocent, of course: pure innocence, or ignorance. If he had not begun to suspect the innocence of his own desires he could have better accepted such an interpretation of Kathy Volkov's behaviour.

Then, when they were growing together like two insidious vines, she tore herself away with a force which should have reassured him.

"Good-bye for now!" she said and giggled.

If he didn't wince, it was because his normal reactions had been sent too far astray. "Can you let yourself out?" he feebly asked. "I don't want to come down," he added, even feebler, and something about work.

"Sure!"

He might have hated her for that, but was prevented by some of the silent expressions she had used, and for the shape of her unconsciously noble head.

She began leaping down the stairs, practically tearing the banisters down: so it sounded. "I'll come tomorrow," she called back. "No—not tomorrow—but soon—to see how the kitten's doing."

He had forgotten the wretched growling cat.

"If I don't come," she shouted up, "I'll write you a letter like we arranged."

He was almost composing his.

After some other semi-intelligible and not particularly relevant information, she shrieked: "Gee, I almost broke me neck!"

She went out banging and clattering. The silence continued vibrating some time afterwards; while he huddled in a corner of the bed, already sensing the agonies of an empty letter-box, or worse still, her clear voice as it rocketed up the stairs on arrival, accurately aimed at his vulnerable core.

About dusk he got up and went out. There was laughter in the darkening streets; a window opened and shut; a breeze was blowing through dusty lace. Up at the thoroughfare a spawn of artificial light had begun to hatch and pulsate. The drunks were spewing. On a corner a big patent-leather mouth, boiling bust, and acquisitive eyes might have been for hire if he had brought the cash with him: but he hadn't: no conventional defences could now protect him from the attacks to which he was being subjected.

He walked around, past the wide bright shops, down the stale side-streets, over hacked-off vegetable stalks and slivers of dogshit. Up a lane, where the last of an apocalyptic sky was burning the top of a paling fence, a figure had bent over a little go-cart, dispensing meat to cats. The cats lurked, mewed; some of them advanced when coaxed; in the shadows others growled and coughed over the charitable offal with which they were being fed. There was little love lost: the cats were gorging themselves on what was their due. Perhaps the voluntary martyr was rewarded by not being accepted; as the food was doled out, claws occasionally reached up to slash, and once a pair of growling jaws seemed to fasten in the charitable hand. The cat person continued bending over the improvised cart. The stench had become predominantly horseflesh; while the cat lover's sex remained indeterminate: a small person, however. (For God's sake, not another child!)

The voice offered no immediate clues while ringing clearly enough in the narrow, deserted lane. "Prrh! Prrh! Puss? PUSS! You big devil, I know *you*! You *cat*! Claw me! Well, *claw* me! What good did it ever do *any*body?"

As she withdrew her clawed hand, the cat person became a woman.

"Big Swollen Cheeks!" she spat at the mangy, chewed cat: while throwing him another gobbet of dark flesh.

She straightened up, or would have done so: coming level with her in the wasted light, the intruder saw that she was a hunchback. And more. He had hardly recovered from the other attack when here was this fresh one.

"Not—Rhoda?"

"Yes, Hurtle." Raising her face on its thin little neck, she bared her teeth: in the half-dark, they appeared fine and curved, spaced like a cat's.

The smell of horseflesh was overpoweringly rich.

"Yes!" She confirmed her identity in what sounded like a long hiss; while he began to crush, not her cat's paws, her bird's claws, the once delicate made coarse and stiff and knobbed.

He no longer minded the smell of horse.

"Rhoda!" He was spouting, gasping. "Rhoda? Rhoda! Rhoda!"

She didn't join in, though once he thought he caught sight of her uvula waving up at him out of the cavern of her throat.

If he hadn't sensed the child buried in this old, shabby woman—she looked much older than he, no doubt ageing more quickly as the result of her physical affliction—he would have said she was quite unmoved by their finding each other: whatever the life she had led, it had taught her to control the expression of her face and the behaviour of her deformed body. It was only through his intuition that he could feel her spirit reaching out, in spite of her, to embrace his; while he, as always, fluctuated: half exhilarated to identify the sister of his conscience, half disgusted to know he would always have to overcome a repulsion; he had only ever been able to love Rhoda at moments of leave-taking, or unusual stress, as now, in their grotesque and strained reunion.

He heard himself saying: "You haven't changed, Rhoda. D'you think you've changed?" which was only half of what he meant to ask, and did: "D'you think *I've* changed?"

She wiped her hands on the sides of her dress. "I couldn't very well give an opinion. Not yet." She laughed her same cold little laugh. "Physically, yes. Who hasn't?" Her hump hadn't, and it was for that reason, he could see, she had paused an instant. "You were so good-looking as a boy: dashing and dreamy at the same time. But nobody would expect you—by our age—not to look dilapidated."

While she was speaking she tugged several times at the cord she used for pulling the go-cart; the wheels made a painful squealing sound, and the few remaining cats made off.

"The light," he pleaded reasonably, "you mustn't pass judgement by—not even a street lamp—a glimmer down a lane!" But although his argument was sound enough he knew it was wasted. "Why don't we go back to where I live, so that we can talk, and get to know about each other? Rhoda?"

He even took her by the hand, and forgot he was repelled by the stickiness of drying horseflesh. She disengaged herself, not, he felt, on account of any dislike for him—in fact, she appeared completely indifferent—but perhaps because Maman might have considered it a breach of the conventions.

It was not that either. "I've done my duty by *these* cats, but the others may be missing me."

"Which others?"

"The cats I have living with me—fourteen of them—no, fifteen since yesterday."

"If you'd rather, let's go to your place." She had made him pitch his voice too high: it bounced with a boyish insistence.

"No."

This should have been final, but he couldn't believe it was; although she was walking away, the go-cart sometimes grating, sometimes squealing behind her, the pace suggested indecision.

He ran after her.

"But Rhoda—after discovering each other! Isn't it human?" As he coaxed he watched obliquely for signs of her giving in: he might have been her young brother; the stone manners of this old woman made him feel gauche.

Then he had a brainwave. "I've got a cat! Come along to my place. Won't you? Somebody—a friend—dumped it on me. You can advise me what to do." He knew nothing about anything: even by this stage in his experience he was incapable of dealing with the contingencies of life.

"Oh," she snorted, "cats! There are too many of them."

But because he needed her—he suddenly realized how desperately—he must use every means to trap her.

He was forced to grow cunning. "I'll make us something good to eat. What about a Welsh rabbit?"

Rhoda was as unimpressed as he would have been in a similar situation. Trudging along, they might have been returning from the lower garden of their childhood, if he hadn't noticed her shoes: the dated strap-shoes of an elderly, dowdy woman, but designed for Rhoda's dwarf existence; he wondered where she got them.

She had neither accepted nor refused his latest proposition when they reached the thoroughfare. All the lights were focused on them; traffic whizzed towards them and whammed past; here and there, shopkeepers looked up from their evening transactions to take in a pantomime.

Something extraordinary was happening: a man of distinguished head, of fairly youthful, even athletic body, clothed, it seemed, only in the name of decency, in shirt and pants and a pair of old sand-shoes, had started to blubber shamefully. Of course he was old, really; he couldn't have disguised it. As he walked along blubber-ing, the bugger kept blowing out his lips and sucking them in and hiccupping—well, it could have been from emotion—while leading a freak of a woman by the hand. It was the cat woman! A sour little puss herself. But what could you expect: her hump and all? As they shuffled and staggered, pulling the blood-stained cart be-hind them, tears had boiled up in the cat woman's cold eyes and were running over the pink rims. So the couple advanced: past the wilting spinach and flabby turnips, the trays of squid and dull-eyed mullet. It was no wonder decent people left the two derelicts plenty room to pass; drunks, or more probably, metho artists, didn't enter into their substantial, working lives.

It was the bunch of keys in his pocket which helped him take hold of himself: the keys to the house in Flint Street.

"I've lived here," he calculated roughly, "thirty years! Didn't you know about it? You must have known."

"I'd heard, of course. I'd read. I've even seen you once or twice. But what good would it have done either of us if I'd come thrusting myself?"

The more clearly he saw, the more cunning he grew. "We could be a help to each other, couldn't we?"

Again he tried taking her hand. It was cold. She withdrew it to back the stinking cart under the araucaria.

"It's a comparatively large house," he began to explain before remembering: "Oh, not compared with Sunningdale!" He heard their double silence and was glad those hiccups had ended. "I want to show you over it."

As he opened it, the house seemed to stagger under his determination.

"Wait here," he ordered in the hall.

He ran ahead to switch on the lights of all the rooms in his once proud, now suppliant house. In the scullery he kicked the herring tin Kathy had made him put for the cat; he heard the milk scattering: probably some of it on his pants. By the time he returned, reducing his run to a strut, Rhoda had left the hall and advanced into the living-room, so he could see this grimy old woman, his sister, in clear detail. She was standing with her head, her small triangular white face, poked forward: looking. She was more like an animal than a woman, perhaps as the result of her association with cats.

She spoke, though. "I don't like to imagine what *they* would think of it all."

"If you judge it by Courtney standards!" He tried to ease his irritation by pulling up his slack trousers. "But people live differently, on the whole more honestly, now. What were we but a bunch of new-rich vulgarians gorging ourselves and complaining?"

Rhoda's expression became so fixed and wooden he had a vision of her perched like a ventriloquist's doll on Boo Davenport's knee; the mouth moved: "Oh yes," she tinkled, "but I'm glad to have lived some of my life under a chandelier!"

Again he had to pull up his pants, which had only started slipping since he met her: she irritated him so. "I can do without chandeliers—or think up one of my own."

"Oh, I agree. There's very little that is necessary, beyond a crust of bread and a hole to curl up in."

He must try not to feel so irritated: when she was his sister, whom he loved. Of course the real reason for his irritation, he had to admit, was not her failure to appreciate his home, which he had stopped seeing as an actual house, but her continued unawareness of its *raison d'être*—the paintings: all of which, even the most tentative youthful ones, were shimmering tonight, for Rhoda, in their true colours.

Rhoda only nosed past them: not even a cat, more of a rat, a small white one, its pinker charms dulled by age and grime. The pink, moist hair had become a dirty grey-white fuzz. The seams of the little sharp white face were almost pricked out in black.

She did pause once, beside, not in front of, his water colour of

Maman. "The yellow dress! Pretty dress—" Her voice trailed as she moved on.

He would have to remember she had probably grown into someone quite different from what he had decided she was. Even if he couldn't love this, or perhaps any, version of his sister, he was still full of affection for her: just as you can be fond of an old worm-eaten, ugly piece of furniture for its age and associations; the emotion of affection is not less genuine than love.

And he needed Rhoda, he mustn't forget.

He returned to the cat. "I forgot the cat."

"Oh, cats! What's this?" She was pointing from where they were standing in Miss Gilderthorp's dust-coloured morning-room, or lesser parlour.

"That's the conservatory." For the first time since bringing Rhoda home he was ready to make excuses. "It's nothing much. There isn't a light in there, anyway. And it's a bloody wreck—always has been."

"Looks interesting," she persisted, peering through the glass door.

"Only a ruin."

"Can't you shine a light through the door? Oh, go on, Hurtle, do! Don't be a meanie!" Her assumed girlishness, with its edge of sarcasm, brought them closer than they had been that night.

So he got up on an unwilling chair and shone the parlour light-bulb through the conservatory door.

"Oh, I like that! It has something. It has a poetry," Rhoda calmly said.

Was she daring to appropriate some idea which hadn't yet suggested itself? He had never seen the conservatory by artificial light. Certainly the blacker shadows and the far more brilliant refractions from broken glass made him share her reaction; but he didn't want to share: the conservatory was too private. Strange it should appeal to all three of them.

He got down off the creaking chair and the light resettled in its rightful room.

Rhoda sighed. "I'm liking your house better; but oh dear, I no longer care for old houses. I'm too old. You're old, too—older, as far as I can remember—but not my kind of old."

She began shuffling, and he thought he could detect, for the first time, a wheezing.

He remembered: "The cat! It's in the kitchen—the scullery. The kitchen's pretty grim, but you'd better see everything, Rhoda—where I live."

Following, she became increasingly fretful. "All kitchens are awful," she complained. "I practically live on bread and cheese. Couldn't touch meat after cutting up the horse every evening."

"The old girl who lived here before put in this hideous asbestos box of a kitchenette to make things easier, you see."

Rhoda's head followed his explanations. Something had released the catch which had been holding it: now it could function freely on its spring.

"This is the scullery. I believe it's called a 'walk-in pantry' nowadays." They enjoyed a slight giggle together. "This, incidentally, is where my friend left the cat. Puss? Puss?" he called.

Rhoda seemed definitely to have tired of cats.

"Out here," he continued revealing, "is the main part of the big, former kitchen—which is never used now. Isn't it grim?"

"Ghastly!"

"Cool, though, in summer."

"I wonder what became of May?" Her interest in their old cook made Rhoda look as though she were following a scent; she found, almost at once. "Why, of course, she must be dead!" she shrieked.

He hated that damn cat. "Puss? Puss?" he called in an affected, amateurish voice.

"Might as well save yourself the breath. Cat must have gone," Rhoda said. "You left the back door open."

She was right: startled by the apparition of Kathy, he must have forgotten to close the door between the main kitchen and the yard.

"I've had no experience of cats," he said. "I was relying on my friend."

"And the friend's had none either."

"There's still the whole of the upstairs to show."

"Oh," she said. "Is there?"

She began shuffling more noticeably: worse still, wheezing on the stairs. He tried not to feel guilty by remembering that Rhoda was to be employed as a moral force, or booster of his conscience. If only she could have realized how necessary she was; but she mustn't know about Kathy, or what Kathy could grow into if the powers over which human nature has no control established a dictatorship.

He was doing the honours of the upstairs in a kind of estate-agent voice: ". . . bath's a bit stained. The old-fashioned geyser never lets you down once you've learned its tricks . . . junk mostly in here—got to have somewhere to store paintings—and I sometimes sleep on the stretcher if I feel like it . . . the two bedrooms are also studios—move about from one to the other—they're so different—different in character—the light's different."

He was glad the board with the drawing of the nude girl was no longer standing on the easel in the back room, though Rhoda, from her behaviour to date, mightn't have noticed even that. Circumstances she had experienced had forced her in on herself, and any part left over for active living was probably concentrated on the cats.

So he would have to tread with cat-like delicacy in introducing his proposition.

"This back room is rather hot and boistèrous at times. One doesn't always feel strong enough for it. Children's voices can begin to batter down one's self-defences—and the voices of women defending their rights. I'm afraid Chubb's Lane is on the slummy side."

"I no longer question the conditions of life."

"I think, on the whole, you'd probably feel more at home in the seclusion of Flint Street. The room's larger, too—more comfortable."

They had gone in. The advanced abstraction of the "Pythoness" was still standing against the wall. She glanced at it with indifference: while her animal nose continued sniffing out the real prospects of the situation.

"Don't you think a room like this would suit you, Rhoda?" he carefully asked. "Naturally, a lot would have to be rearranged. I expect you have things of your own."

"Of course I have my personal belongings. I have a little room of my own—in the house of a friend. She's most kind, considering she's such a meticulous person, to put up with my peculiarities. It's what I can only describe as Christian charity. She must have suffered herself, but hasn't been damaged by it. She couldn't begin to understand your and my compulsion to plumb the depths." Rhoda laughed nervously.

"Then you don't think you'd like it here?"

"I didn't for a moment believe there'd be any question of my liking it here. Isn't this where you live, Hurtle? Lives are too private."

"Yes—but dying. Do you feel you want to die, perhaps undiscovered, in a rented room?" Now that he had invented such a persuasive argument he almost reached out to clutch at some part of her.

"I've picked too many dead cats out of the gutter: death's nothing to be afraid of." She moistened her pale lips.

It seemed incredible that Rhoda should resist such a practical solution.

She seemed to have read his thoughts, for she murmured: "In any case, I couldn't manage the stairs—in my condition."

She was certainly looking very pinched and chalky. She sounded as though she was sucking on a comb and paper: while smiling at him.

"And all these paintings," she dared only mumble.

"What about the paintings?" he dared her back.

They were possibly coming to it now.

"Well"—Rhoda coughed and smiled—"I might be vivisected afresh, in the name of truth—or art."

"How? How?" He was so shocked.

"Don't you remember that dog we saw with Maman somewhere in London? I shall never forget its varnished tongue."

How could he forget the smell of their own wet frightened fur as they huddled together escaping in the cab?

"But what has that to do with art?" As if he didn't know the answer.

She was looking at a painting which seemed to illustrate her argument, and which, he realized, with cold resignation, might break down his defence. When and why had he brought the painting out? Could it have been there during Kathy's visit? Sometimes, he knew, he would get out of bed, still half asleep, and rummage after an old work to prove a point he had been trying to make in his late dream, then return to continued sleep. Afterwards he would find this visible evidence of his dream-life standing against the wall, and often fail to remember the circumstances which had called for it.

The painting at which Rhoda was now staring so painfully was an early "Pythoness": judging by the naturalistic treatment, probably one of the first. His own horror at their finding themselves in the present situation couldn't prevent him from experiencing a twinge of appreciation for his forgotten achievement: the thin, transparent arm; the sponge as organic as the human claw clutching it; the delicate but indestructible architecture of the tripod-bidet, beside which the rosy figure was stood up for eternity.

This aesthetic orgasm lasted what seemed only a long second before the moral sponge was squeezed: its icy judgement was trickling in actual sweat down his petrified ribs.

He heard Rhoda's voice. "I was born vivisected. I couldn't bear to be strapped to the table again."

"I can't help it," he apologized, "if I turned out to be an artist." There was little else he could say.

"Shall I fry you some eggs?" he asked as he led the way downstairs. "There's some bacon, but it may be rancid."

Rhoda laughed her high little laugh; breathlessness seemed relieved by a descent. "Eggs and bacon were always scrumptious at night! Oh yes, do, Hurtle, do! The bacon might be of the kind which tastes rancid from the beginning. I adore bacon when somebody else cooks it for me."

It was delicious to discover that, on this level, they were still brother and sister: it was the triumph of their education by Maman in superficial intercourse, and they were probably both grateful to have had it.

"Maman used to cook eggs for us in the bedroom when the money was almost blown. She loved to put on a pretty apron. We'd moved to Battersea by then. Mr Boileau was very bored. He was trying to meet somebody richer."

As he got out the pan he asked: "How did Maman die, Rhoda?"

"I think she died because she felt it wasn't worth living without the inessentials."

"Poor thing!"

"Yes." Rhoda sighed. "Poor thing!"

Their affection and regret were of the superficial, nostalgic kind Maman herself would have approved, although, enclosed by the asbestos box which passed for a kitchen, it seemed incredible ever to have been children, or that Maman had been any kind of mother.

As the fat began to spit and the eggs to shrivel, Rhoda was telling him about her life: ". . . various rich, elderly women. I was officially a companion. But it never really worked. They only felt they had a duty towards me—because of my curvature. At least that worked well enough on the conscience of one of them. She left me a nice little pittance."

He knew by the tone of voice, she would have liked to draw him into a conspiracy of confidences; but he was concentrated on the eggs.

"Something to live on modestly," Rhoda said; then she raised her voice and giggled. "And I've got a pension—an invalid pension! Doesn't it kill you? I'd never have had the nerve, but a friend said I should apply. She herself was born poor. I think poor people have more nerve when it comes to self-humiliation."

He was fascinated by the freckled eggs. The ruff of one was ballooning to such proportions he hoped he wouldn't ruin it. He knew exactly how he would have painted the lacy, freckled egg.

"Are you rich, Hurtle? They say you've made a packet. I suppose one can't help it once one begins. I read about a sale of paintings to the United States."

It made him squint more closely at the eggs. "I can't say I'm poor," he mumbled.

There was a soft spatter of rain on the window. He was feeling depressed again. He had ruined his best egg while practising self-indulgence.

"Those are the best," he said, pushing a couple onto her plate; one of them burst, and spread, like a joke egg.

"This one got burnt. I wasn't concentrating enough." Actually both the eggs he gave himself were burnt, not through lack of concentration, but because he had been so fascinated by the gold to deeper-golden, and finally the burning ruffs.

"Mmmm!" Rhoda was chewing on the frizzled bacon.

A brittle rind stuck out of her little pointed mouth. She helped it in with a finger: not altogether clean, he noticed. He couldn't criticize his sister because his own nails were on the grubby side.

Hunger they had in common, and a childhood, and probably a respect for the basic acts and values.

So it didn't occur to him to offer her any of the loaf from which he tore off an occasional handful, to mop up the egg smears and congealing fat; she would help herself. He was right: whenever necessary, Rhoda prised out little clawfuls of bread, to screw around the terrain of her plate. In an awful way, and as Maman's true child, she was more delicate than he.

"Lovely!" Rhoda sighed and popped her fingers into her mouth to suck up the last of goodness; on her sharp chin there was a dribble of egg it was impossible for her to know about.

He would have liked to enjoy a fart now that they were finished, but supposed he shouldn't, even though she was his sister.

"When I first heard about you, Hurtle, after I'd come back— God knows why we do—to Australia—except that a cat prefers to die in the gutter it belongs to spiritually—this was after I'd inherited from Mrs Huxtable, the one in Warwick Gardens." Rhoda was weaving her story over some brandy he had remembered in a cupboard. "When I first got back I was living over by the part they call The Gash. Do you know it?" He knew so well he didn't feel he had to answer; it was from there that his "Lantana Lovers" had come to him; he knew it so intimately he could feel the dew from the moonlit bench working into the seat of his pants. "Well, that was where I was living, and it was my friend Mrs Cutbush who told me about you. She reads the newspapers as a compensation."

"Cutbush?"

"Yes. The grocer's wife."

"But you can't know *Cutbush*?"

"Him, too. Why shouldn't I? Though he's not my favourite person. Incidentally, Cutbush once suggested you were an intimate friend. I didn't let on I was your sister. Nor did I believe in the relationship he claimed. He has the kind of fertile imagination in which acquaintanceship grows, tropically, into a friendship."

"But Cutbush!" He was nauseated by the smears of egg and congealing fat still left to mop up from his plate. "Is Mrs Cutbush the friend you mentioned living with?"

"Oh dear, no! Mrs Cutbush, poor thing, is too highly strung: she mightn't be able to endure the extra strain. In any case, I lived only a few years in Gidley Street before moving to these parts."

He was in no way comforted by Rhoda's break with the Cutbush couple. The handfuls of soft-sounding rain flung at the window, and increasing threats from a bellyful of bacon fat, contributed to his great unease.

"As a matter of fact, the Cutbushes moved, too, a short time ago, and opened a shop a few streets away from here," Rhoda continued.

"Why?"

"I suppose they thought this is where life and business are. I never asked them."

He got up to scrape the dishes; while Rhoda continued loving her brandy. She drank it by such neat sips she would probably hoard it half the night: a cheap drunk at least; or was she temperate out of cunning? He would have liked to force open her little mouth and pour half the bottle in, then wait for his sister to illuminate a world he found he didn't know, while living in it. But Rhoda continued sipping her brandy; while he, as he scraped and stacked, could only feel his depression growing. To counteract it, he took a good swig himself, straight out of the bottle. Hadn't she turned down his plan to protect an innocent soul?

The night was full of an evil she didn't seem aware of, and he had failed to exorcise. Sometimes Kathy's breasts developed with the purity and logic of flowers, sometimes they had the wholesome stodginess of suet dumplings, but a wholesomeness which threatened to explode. He could see how rotten they might become, like persimmons lying in long damp grass. Whenever he heard Kathy, it was on the stairs: afterwards, a silence of maidenhair.

Rhoda cut the silence with something like a burp. "Actually, I don't think you realize the influence you have on people. I've heard of several who came to live round here because of 'Hurtle Duffield the painter.'"

"Balls and crap! Balls and crap!" he shouted. He who could not yet influence himself didn't want to hear about his influence on others.

Rhoda lowered her eyes, ignoring words, as Maman and her governesses had taught her. "It's true, though." She smiled. "Lots of normally undemonstrative, unimaginative people like to cluster round a name. I remember I was cutting up the meat for my cats when some of them burst in. 'Is it true that this painter—this Mr Duffield—is your brother?' I replied: 'No. It isn't true.' Because it wasn't!" She sniggered. "Not physically, anyway, and that seems to be the part which matters. I had to drive them out after that. People don't notice the attraction meat has for flies."

"Balls!"

"They're looking for somebody to exalt."

"Or kill."

Rhoda laughed and swallowed. "There was one young girl said to me: 'I'd die if I ever met him.'"

"Rhoda," he said, leaning forward, getting hold of the bottle, taking another swig, "we still have a lot of life to live—why do you dismiss the possibility of our being a help to each other—just because of the stairs?"

"Oh—stairs!" She snickered and helped herself to another tot. "Would it have been fair not to explain you might have a corpse on your hands because of my physical condition?"

He couldn't believe it: she was too tough.

"Rhoda," he said, "it's hard to put—but I'd like to tie the end of my life to the beginning. I think, in that way—rounded—it might be possible to convey what I have to."

He was too fuddled: while her lip protruded like a small shoe-buckle above the Woolworth glass.

"I don't say it couldn't be arranged," Rhoda said. "I could move my few things into that room—that rather small room—what is it? this side of the conservatory. I've taken a fancy to the conservatory. And the cats could move in and out freely—through the conservatory."

"The cats?"

"Yes. My own fifteen. You haven't met them. Street cats are something different: a duty. But one's own cats!"

"All right, Rhoda." Dutifully he bowed his head.

He could feel her hand her laughter running over his hair like birds or mice. He heard: "Hurtle hurtle" out of the throats of early-morning doves.

At least Kathy Volkov would be protected from debauch and himself from destruction by his sister's presence.

When they went out to manœuvre the deal go-cart, the rain had crystallized on the fringes of the araucaria. "Good-night, brother," she said, and a few of the drops fell down in accompaniment to her still clear, while drunken voice.

The brother should have bent down to embrace his sister, or easier conscience, but it was far too far, and would have looked grotesque even in an empty street.

The following morning he woke later than usual, and at once recognized a malaise, less the result of brandy and the undertones of his reunion with Rhoda, than of rain falling, steady and grey. He got up to look at it. His shanks were thin, his veins prominent, his testicles hanging low. A greater cause for gloom was his suspicion, no, the knowledge, that he hadn't written the address for Rhoda, nor heard her promise to move in on a specific day: not even at a vaguely future date.

As his main defence against Kathy Volkov, Rhoda was to have

been quickly installed, if not most suitably in the room next to his own, at least in Miss Gilderthorp's morning-room. She had her hearing and her hump. No woman who had carried a hump through life would surely be able to resist snarling at a man's last attempt to enter an earthly paradise, particularly if that paradise was in any way perverse, as well as under her nose. But circumstances were threatening his plan. What if Rhoda thought better of her promise? Or, equally disastrous though not so drastic, if continued rain made her postpone the move? It sometimes poured for weeks; and Kathy might come bursting in, raincoat running with light and water, hair clinging, her skin a rosy delusion, while actually as cold and firm as freshly caught fish.

Moving across the room, back to the crush of tepid blankets waiting for him in his bed, he knew the real source of his gloom was the probability that Kathy would *not* come before Rhoda was installed. The rain was dousing all his hopes: what child, even the kindest, or most inquisitive, or romantic, or bored, or depraved, would think of visiting a scruffy elderly recluse in a downpour?

He lay half the morning behind his eyelids, a prey to visions of electric flowers flickering with girls' faces, of such banality he grew ashamed. All the time he told himself he only had to catch sight of Kathy from a window and he would be able to reinvest her with the perfection and purity of his original spiritual child.

During the day, as the rain continued falling in heavy, transparent ropes, he mightn't have been invented, except to paint the paintings, the ones he could see, opaque and muddy by the prevailing light and any standards of truth. His paintings deserved to become investments. If that cat hadn't run away he might have tried taming it; or if Rhoda had come, at least they could have exchanged symptoms of their physical crack-up: or quarrelled.

Towards dark he went out. The rain was slanted now: as thin as wire, and tougher than before. Walking the streets, looking for signs of cat life, he was rewarded only by this cutting lash. In the lane where he had come across Rhoda the evening before, he hung around for some time, accompanied by the sound, the slash of rain. He noticed on a ledge a gobbet of horseflesh which had been bled white by its prolonged punishment.

Back in the main street, he felt so morally emotionally creatively bankrupt he almost masturbated through his pocket outside a butcher's. Nobody would have guessed; the passers-by were too busy cosseting their own bedraggled souls to suspect, let alone pounce on, a vice so reprehensible because so solitary. He alone was disgusted with himself.

Next morning it was still raining, but the rain of resignation by now: out of which he received, when he opened the box, two rain-blurred letters.

He almost swallowed them he gasped so deep and fast tearing the damp blotting-paper envelope of the first.

Kathy had written in purple ink, which gave her letter the look of a tattoo:

Dear Mr. Duffield,
    I intended to come and visit you this afternoon after school to see how the cat got on, but started to practise when I came in. I ate a cheese sandwich first, and drank some milk. The day has been so dreadful, it is what my mother calls a Day of Retrebution. It could be, though I don't altogether believe in all that. I only believe in music, and would like to fall in love I think. Well, I had two good hours practice. I am studying the No 1 Concerto (E Flat Major) of Liszt which Mr Khrapovitsky says I should play eventually in the competition. I am having trouble with the Quasi adagio. I think I am too anxious, and my left hand isn't strong enough yet. But I shall be good. I feel it in my veins.
    Well, I might have worked some more because this is what I love, and it is wet tonight, only my friend Angela Agostino came just now and wants me to go with her so I must cut this short. Angela is a silly kid, I don't know why I bother with her, except I know her. She says she has some boys Italians from Temora who are here in a bomb they bought, they want to take us for a ride, but her Father mustn't know, he would kill her. I think boys are silly. When you really look at them they look away.
    Last night I dreamed about you (may I call you Duff? that is how I call you in my mind) it was such a beautiful dream I must tell you about it when we meet, tomorrow or the next I hope.
    Angela is pulling my elbow. I must sign off.
                                        Yours very sincerely
                                        Katherine Volkov

P.S. I send you a hundred kisses, one of them the special kind you seem to like.

Before he read the second note he walked to the top of the house: he hadn't room for more immediately after Katherine Volkov's letter. He continued seeing her name: a grave name engraved, which still only half fitted its owner; while her words came back in gusts, and died out in breathlessness. (What was her dream, though? The dream might undo them. He must prevent her telling it if she remembered to try.)

People have heart attacks walking upstairs, people of a certain age. Not yourself, though. How could you? Kathy's letter, he noticed only now, hadn't a stamp. Then she must have passed and stuck it in the box, and the falling rain had prevented him from hearing the clatter of the brass flap. Her footsteps retreated so coldly through him, he was able to contemplate the second note, which, he knew before opening, was from his sister Rhoda; it was smaller in format, its purpose declared: a note, in fact, in a formed hand.

Expect to be with you Thursday if the weather permits. Have engaged a lad to move my few belongings in his utility truck. He will have to make a second trip for the cats, the transport of which is causing me considerable outlay: packing cases, wire etc. Dear Hurtle, I must admit our reunion was a great joy. But I *warn* you I am *not at all a compatible person.* I am too old—and they tell me I am hard. I have had to be. However, you who are Buddha Himself, I am informed, should understand the soul's condition.

Looking forward to being the sister to my brother. Affectly—R.C.

Rhoda's letter, too, was without a stamp, he noticed somewhat morosely. But he would be happy to receive his sister, with all the disadvantages. In fact, he was resigned enough to wonder whether their relationship wasn't the only logical solution: to sit beside the hearth, spooning up milk puddings, and listening to each other's stomachs. In the creative end, blood couldn't race music, only trickle like tepid milk. He couldn't see the milk-string swinging from his own lip, but visualized it on Rhoda's little, intensely preoccupied mouth.

Yet, on Thursday morning, he flung open the door in anger on the gently muscular, uncommunicative young man who had brought Rhoda's things in his truck. At least it had stopped raining, if nobody had recovered yet.

"I'll give you a hand," he told the carrier in a jolly voice which certainly didn't convince himself.

He had never been good at this sort of thing, and he would soon have lost patience if it hadn't been Rhoda's furniture they were carrying in. His curiosity was appeased by a low-built, no, a sawn-off, sideboard, atrociously carved with harpies and other unnecessary protuberances; a grandmother chair (minus a caster); a wardrobe of the kind found in a child's bedroom, its fly-speckled pale pink ornamented with wreaths of washed-out forget-me-nots; an iron cot acting as bedstead. There were pots and pans besides—a minimum of these—together with the utensils of her obsession, including a chopping board still moist from the evening before. Several pieces of battered luggage, of a Bond Street elegance he had forgotten, were stamped with the initials "A C," from which the gold had almost completely flaked off.

"You can leave the things standing as they are." The carrier showed no sign of noticing his surliness. "No doubt she'll want me to juggle them around." If he had given it a chance, emotion might have made a fool of him. "When does my—when should I expect Miss Courtney herself?"

"Next trip. Now. With the cats," answered the immovable young man.

Rhoda appeared in the early part of the afternoon, thus giving her arrival a moral tone. In his opinion there was no bleaker stretch of the twenty-four hours. Obviously his sister didn't approve of daylight sleep.

She was also in a brisk temper, her lips whiter than he remembered, the stockings wrinkled in distraught veins on her spaghetti legs.

"My God, Hurtle, whatever possessed me!"

She would have liked to curse the carrier handling her crates of glaring cats, if she hadn't, it appeared, fallen a little in love with him.

"Gently, Dick!" she mumbled instead, and actually stroked a beefy arm. "They do hate it! My poor darling! My Possum!"

Her attempts at tenderness were made in a mezzo voice, as opposed to the soprano knife she kept for human intercourse; but it didn't work with the cats. They were carried growling moaning into the little morning-room: the other side of the wire mesh their flat-eared, pale-eyed hatred continued to consume the darkness in which they crouched.

"Shouldn't think they'll ever like it here": any more than he could develop an affection for Rhoda's cats.

"Of course. In time. You get used to anything in time," their owner had decided.

If she had sounded at all exhausted or discouraged, she revived when he paid off the carrier.

She began to shout and command as though she also kept a dog. "Hurtle? Windows, please! All windows and outer doors must be kept shut for the first week. That way the poor things will accustom themselves."

"And we shall die of cat—or each other."

She decided not to hear, and he helped her shut the windows, most of which were pretty stiff.

Rhoda began unfastening the hateful wire for the cats to squeeze out of their prisons. Some of the beasts slunk away in search of a refuge in which to nurse their neuroses; others sat, fairly bland, licking their pads or shaking themselves with frilly motions of the shoulders to restore their outraged fur. One big, one-eyed, one-eared tom eased himself backwards and sprayed the sofa without his mistress appearing to notice.

For the moment she was suffering from anticlimax. She had flopped into her three-castered chair, her nostrils deathly delicate, her body so placed, because of the omnipresent hump, you were reminded of someone prepared to vomit into the basin the steward had arranged beside them on the deck.

Rhoda gasped. "Give us time, dear boy, and we shall all show our gratitude."

It was a great effort for her, he realized, to express any kind of tender emotion. (How fortunate it was for him to have his art!)

Then she recovered her knife-edged soprano and hawked up: "I shall also get you to help me arrange my bits and pieces."

Because he, too, was exhausted and outraged he made off upstairs, and didn't work. He switched on the wireless he had been cunning enough to move from the kitchen before Rhoda's arrival; but the wireless didn't work either, except by fits of politics and agricultural instruction: all the music had been wrung out of the evening air.

Later that night when he went down to share their despondency in the kitchen, she was sharpening a knife over a nausea of horseflesh.

She said: "I've failed in my duty tonight. I've failed my extramural cats. I simply wasn't up to it."

416

"I expect they have their ways and means," he consoled, though he couldn't care. "What did they do before you came?"

"Exactly," she said. "But I've failed."

He had made them a stew, of some subtlety, if she had realized. She dabbled in it listlessly after the cats had been satisfied.

"Purple ink," she murmured, fingering a letter lying on the dresser. "Remember the diaries we kept when we were children, in green and purple inks? Oh no, you didn't: you were a boy. I don't think boys need to colour their lives before they've begun to live them—not the way little girls do, writing novels about themselves in their diaries. One day I might write a proper novel."

"For heaven's sake! What kind?" He put the letter in his pocket, for safety.

"Ho!" She laughed. "You'd be surprised. You might be shocked."

After they had squeezed her few pieces of furniture in amongst Miss Gilderthorp's, she announced she was going to get ready for bed.

He went back once, and found her arranged for death, it looked, rather than sleep: her eyelids so definitely closed; or perhaps she was a person who said prayers, and was angry and deceitful on being discovered.

When, out of pity, he made the formal gesture of kissing, she screeched out: "No! No! I can't bear being touched! Not even by a cat, Hurtle"; though several of the fetid animals were crouched around her on the Indian counterpane.

He went upstairs, and lay for a long time in the dark listening to his eyelids close and open. His sense of emptiness suggested that Kathy Volkov had been exorcised: equally, that creative impotence might at last have come to him.

Morning was all jollity in Chubb's Lane: little stubble-headed boys pummelling and shouting; the heavy sails of wet sheets filling with a breeze; motors ripping and purring individually before settling down into the mass monotone of traffic. He sat on the bed cutting out forms from coloured papers, letting them fall to the floor, to settle freely on the white sheet on his drawing-board. All the discordant forms, the coloured notes of street life, hitherto only arbitrarily related, were moving into plan or focus. All his joy in morning sang as he helped the less resolved cut-outs into position with a finger. He fetched gum. Some of the paper, superficially more frivolous, he was ready to stick. You could always be certain of some shapes: like old familiar furniture, they will become invisible, while remaining necessary. One big square of golden brown belonged to this category. He stuck it. And smoothed it with the flat of his hand. All the little joy-notes of children's voices still eddied delectably unpredictable around it in yellow splinters and arrows, and green, ballooning clover leaves. The big crimson heart-shape, he could be certain of that, like furniture, or at least for the moment: he stuck it carefully in position for life. The doubtful quantities he continued pushing around, helping them settle.

"Hurtle?" That was Rhoda—of course—calling up. "What do we do in the morning I'd like to know?"

"What we bloody well like!" Women like Rhoda never heard what they didn't want to.

He had intended to develop his paean of colour further. He did bring out gouache and dabbled a little; but presently he put on his gown and went down to face his awful duty.

Since the evening before there was a smell of cat everywhere. Rhoda, in a surprisingly clean apron, was an actress playing a part larger than it appeared at first.

He skidded once or twice.

"I've cleaned it up," she told him in a languid voice, "but there are always places which escape one's notice."

She got him a breakfast of grey, leathery liver.

"When I was here before," she said, "I thought I noticed a wireless in the kitchen."

"There was an old wireless. I took it up to my room. I like to listen to music while I work. I'll buy you a transistor, Rhoda." He added: "I'm also thinking of buying you a fur coat," though it hadn't occurred to him till now.

"I don't want a fur coat." She composed her lips over her teeth and at the same time blushed.

"We'll talk about it."

"I was looking forward to that wireless I saw."

She stood scraping off the veins of liver he had left on his plate, and as they fell, four or five of her depressed cats came to life, clawing and spitting.

"As a matter of fact, I never thought you cared for music or understood it," Rhoda said.

"It's very close to painting. I don't 'understand' painting—not all the theories talked about it. That doesn't mean painting isn't my life."

"Yes, but music!" Her voice whined: it seemed to annoy Rhoda that he didn't fit into the category to which she had decided he belonged.

He went back upstairs to his own country.

During the morning she announced she would be going out to fetch the evening's ration of horse. He heard the door bang, the flap on the letter-box clatter, then the squeal of the go-cart trailing behind her. From considering the awfulness of Rhoda's reign, he had clean forgotten to look in the box, till reminded by the sound of its flap. He went swooping down, the panels of his gown flying open on his bare legs, sinewy in their sudden compulsion.

The letter-box was empty, though.

He tried to ignore his disappointment by converting the mission into a reconnaissance of Rhoda's quarters. Cats stared at him: some with an empty insolence; some with suspicion; others were so shrunken by his coming their skulls expressed pure hatred. Two matted monsters were stretched along the mantelpiece. One of these raised his head and yawned while scarcely opening his eyes, then dangled a leg, a pad with a glimmering of claws, from the marble ledge. Nobody actively defended the fortress against his invasion: they ringed it round instead with psychic dragon's teeth and cynical rejection of such a contemptible enemy.

As for the furniture of Rhoda's life: the photographs of Harry and Maman in tarnished Asprey frames; the three-footed chair now propped on a child's alphabet block; and the iron cot with the pseudo-child's form of its owner almost visible under the Indian counterpane; these were the more articulate guardians of Rhoda's spiritual demesne, or opponents of his will to create in his old age children of unprecedented beauty. His incestuous foster mother and crooked sister would hardly have understood a work of art like Kathy Volkov. As for Harry Courtney, he should have been the brutal minotaur concocted by legend; whereas he was, in fact, the gentle bull-man who submits to his women's darts, and even dies of them, out of respect for the rules of the sport. Harry would have understood as much of Kathy as the bull understands the motives behind the poleaxe. But Harry could no more be conjured up from his "telling likeness" than Kathy would materialize out of her first promises.

Going upstairs, the sole of one of his slippers monotonously slapped the bare boards. This pantaloon found himself almost wishing for Rhoda's return.

She did, and at once he resented it: the sound of her little squeaking cart; the dead noises as she dragged the sacks of horse-flesh over the kitchen floor; her own divorced, scratching movements; and the expiring expectations of cats.

He wouldn't go downstairs; he wouldn't hear if she called him: in any case, he had never existed on food.

She called up: "Hurtle? I bought a pie for luncheon."

. . .

She called up: "There's some cheese. You're not sulking, are you?"

They were listening to their thoughts clashing like pebbles in mid-air.

After a while she left him alone.

During the afternoon he suddenly remembered Loebel had threatened to come, at a precise hour, bringing an American client. He got into some clothes. How would he receive Loebel and the client? Ingenuously? Or by sombre stealth?

He didn't have time to practise, for noticing that, in spite of the impending visit and Rhoda's prowling thoughts, his collage had come to life again: he could visualize the crimson heart-form behind an opalescent veil. He was soon busy arranging the gouache in bridal folds; while his own heart, always quick to recognize inevitability in composition, settled back into contentment.

Exactly at four, Loebel came with Propert, the promised American.

"Ah maestro!" From the doorstep the dealer was visibly steaming with flattery, the object of which stood sideways, and let it steam past.

"Faht is ziss? Sommsing hes heppened?" Loebel sniffed, incredulously, jovially.

"An infiltration of cats." It was fortunate Rhoda had left again on business; most afternoons she visited any of the local restaurants sympathetic to her work amongst cats, and carried off what they allowed her: anything too old or too gristly to convince the evening's clientele.

Propert, it seemed, would have accepted Rhoda, along with the cats, as another agreeable detail in a background of eccentricity.

Skidding down the hall, the American laughed and explained: "My godmother kept cats. The whole of her house in Vermont was given over to them—though she was ruled by one in particular: a Russian blue. I remember the combed-out fur from the Persians blowing in the wind. It was a godsend to nesting birds."

None of this had been foreseen. Loebel began to draw his client's attention to paintings in that lowered voice a successful painter's house demanded.

"Zese faht you see are all early lyrical veuorks. Zere is greater *Kraft*—depth—later; but *purity*—ze *lyrical* purity of youss hess its appeal, I sink you vill agree." He lowered his voice still lower. "I heff one early *fah*bulous Duffield—little—very small—if the maestro isn't personally interested in selling any zet you here see."

Propert was sold on cats. "My godmother's Russian blue had a particular yen for sweetbreads. He could detect the smell. He would sulk till she fed him at least the membranes—as an appetizer to the main dish of swordfish steak."

Propert was also incidentally interested in paintings. He smiled rather inanely whenever his attention was caught. He preferred not to comment, but touched the air in front of the object of his interest, very briefly, with one finger. He was of no particular age, but his chubby forms and downy texture reminded of a ripe quince.

Upstairs, Loebel heaved down to business amongst the "important veuorks"; while an opalescent veil persisted, which the dealer perhaps didn't perceive, or if he did, couldn't penetrate.

"What is this, Mr Duffield?" Propert asked.

"A collage I'm playing about with. Haven't finished. It may not develop into anything much." Lying on the floor, it looked as though it wouldn't, not beyond its initial stage of haphazard seductiveness: you couldn't help kicking at it.

Propert, on the other hand, couldn't resist picking it up. He was smiling. They were both smiling; while Loebel remained holding an important work the other side of the veil.

Propert said: "Oh, I like this! Will you let me have it, Mr Hurtle Duffield?"

"No. I'm working on it."

"But when it's finished—after you've gone on from here and done whatever you have to."

"No. I can't think there'll be too many stages. Doesn't interest me enough. From the beginning, it's too indeterminate."

They still liked each other, however. They continued genuinely smiling: and Loebel couldn't interpret what was happening.

"What appeals to me is its tentativeness," Propert was saying. "I'd like to keep it in a state of becoming"—his chubby, quince face was taking an enormous risk—"before the music sets into architecture."

Fortunate Loebel had the window to look out of, into the concrete world: it was he who made the discovery. "Maestro, you heff visitors. Are zey unexpected?"

The latch on the back gate had clicked. You could hear the squeal of Rhoda's little cart as she dragged it into the yard.

"No. I was expecting her about this time."

In the upper room the figures of all three had been transformed into statuary by the unexpectedness of the expected.

Close enough to the window, the chubby Propert had grown uncharacteristically sharp: out of his fixed eyes arrows shot along his line of vision. "An unusually pretty girl. Is she your daughter?"

It was too exhausting: it was too cruel.

"No. My sister."

"You heff such a sister? So small?" Loebel floundered.

A kindly attempt at pity landed like the clumsiest of blows: when lightning struck the third statue into man.

"Yes. I have a sister." He parted the other figures to arrive at the window. "The old—the oldish woman. The little girl isn't— naturally—my sister. She's a friend—less than that—a neighbourhood acquaintance," he heard himself babbling on.

The two visitors had retreated with their shame into the middle of the room, leaving him in full possession of the picture of Kathy and Rhoda together in the yard. He was the one who should have felt ashamed: of Rhoda. In fact he felt nothing of the sort; for Rhoda had been drawn into the circle of Kathy's radiance. Whether two children, or two women, Rhoda and Kathy were equals, it appeared, not to says familiars. Rhoda was recovering her breath after the journey with the laden cart. One of Kathy's arms was loosely linked to Rhoda's as they stood chattering and laughing, aimlessly and breathlessly. He couldn't—in any case he didn't want to—hear what they were telling each other, because their loving smiles suggested they would not have wished him to share in their conversation.

Loebel hid his embarrassment in saying: "Vee are using your valuable time, maestro."

Propert had put on silence for the hunchback sister of a great man. Of the two visitors, he was probably the more shocked: Loebel, as a Jew, would have experienced a wider range of humiliation.

Down in the yard Rhoda and Kathy were straining again, dragging the cart with its tins of refuse on the last lap of its journey to the kitchen. Kathy was doing most of the pulling: she was full of the strength of youth and affection; while Rhoda, too, appeared fulfilled as she jerked dreamily at the cord in token gestures of exertion.

"Vee vill pop!" Loebel's buzz came from the doorway. "It is how long—I did not know—you heff zis relative viz you? In fact, I did not know you heff any relative at all. It goes to show it is so very difficult to completely know."

"No. Yes! I'd be obliged if you'll see yourselves to the door. Yes. I'm a little tired."

Propert was smiling an unhappy smile for the bright collage of their relationship which, in spite of its early promise, had come visibly unstuck.

"Good-bye, Hurtle Duffield. Next time we must discuss the paintings."

His handshake demonstrated all the assurance of middle-aged collegiate manliness: which his smile seemed to deny. Propert's smile was struggling to get out: you were reminded of the membrane on the sweetbreads his godmother in Vermont used to feed to her Russian blue.

When the two visitors had left the house the only sounds were those of muffled voices in the kitchen, tins jostling each other, a grizzling of awakened cats. Apparently Rhoda had no intention of announcing her return or producing her friend. Instead, she had taken the steel and started what became a long sharpening of her knife.

The two voices laughed together intermittently, their laughter strangely similar in tone. Surely Kathy could only be imitating Rhoda?

Lying on the bed, in the ever more deeply burnished light, he must have looked an inanimate lump of grey; though his mind, fidgeting through possibilities, didn't allow him any rest. Would Rhoda's friendship with Kathy lessen the chances of his destruction? Would it, on the other hand, destroy what he hoped to create from Kathy? Rhoda's presence, planned as his comfort and moral defence, could end, like many a sulky fire, by burning down the whole house.

So he continued brooding as the sky smouldered over Chubb's Lane.

In the dusk a door opened and closed below. He knew then that Kathy was coming to him. It could only be Kathy flying up the stairs. The house shuddered. He decided she should find him sick.

"Duff?" she called. "What—lying in the dark! You're not sick, are you?"

She was making it easy to that extent.

"It's not dark." He was too conscious of a last glow of light which her forehead and bare arms were rekindling. "But I *am* sick."

"What's wrong? Eh?" She spoke with a spontaneous warmth, dropping down beside him on the bed, prepared to catch anything infectious.

As for himself, he caught his breath. "Nothing exactly *wrong*— nothing you could put your finger on: old age nudging."

"But you're not what anyone would call old!" She crept farther, insinuating herself like one of those damned cats around Rhoda their patroness.

He would have liked to shout: "Go away!" Instead, he murmured, heaving: "You're cutting off the circulation in my legs. You're heavy, Kathy."

"Don't you like to be comforted when you're sick?"

"Comfort" wasn't acceptable to anyone on fire: too eiderdowny; he couldn't have explained that.

"I expect Miss Courtney 'ull bring you up a bowl of broth, won't she?"

"You didn't tell me—neither of you did—that you knew each other."

"Oh? No. She had the little room that my mother lets. We didn't know she was your sister."

"She isn't."

Kathy had crept closer up. At least the darkness would prevent him watching her skin burn, and the moment when those dangerously inflammable strands at the nape of her neck must catch. If she was still unaware of the fire inside him, she could only be simple, or inhuman.

"What's the matter?" she asked.

His mouth moved, but didn't succeed in articulating.

"Oh!" She sighed. "I'd like to fall in love—with somebody appropriate."

"What's 'appropriate'?"

Her downy mouth was drifting over his; she seemed to have abandoned speech for touch.

"Haven't you your music?" He tried to thrust her off with his thighs; but a law of nature engineered his failure: she settled deeper.

"Yes, my music," she breathed. "Mr Khrapovitsky says I must study harder."

She was digging into his maternal, his creative entrails.

"Old enough to be your grandfather," he muttered against her lips.

But she didn't hear, because fire and sea were roaring through them: if only one could have halted the other.

At least he was, technically, the passive one; he could console himself morally with that: he hadn't attempted.

In the hot dusk Kathy was devouring him, with sticky kisses at first, then, not with words, but a kind of gobbledegook of jerky passion. The surprising part of it was she took their behaviour completely for granted—excepting his passivity.

"Don't you like me?" she asked between mouthfuls.

From amongst the wreckage of what he had aspired to, he didn't. He had hoped to love, not possess her.

"Don't you?" she gasped.

"No, Kathy, I love you." That seemed to satisfy her: now she could accept the dry science of his approach.

Anatomically, she was in every detail what he could have desired —or almost. The shock of discovering her only deficiency made him spill out incontinently and without thought for the consequences.

He became as curiously unafraid as Kathy, and finally, unsurprised. She was by now half snoozing, at the same time exploring his stubble; while he listened to Rhoda pulling her charitable cart across the yard, up the lane, away. Had it occurred to Rhoda at any point that her charity might be needed at home?

"Kathy," he began, swallowing hard, because since she was nothing more than his mistress, whatever he might say must sound embarrassingly trite, "I only wonder how it happened that you learned so much so soon."

"About what?"

"About men."

"Honestly," she said, "I've never ever been with a man. My mother would have had a fit."

Honestly, she was becoming intolerable.

"Boys, though," she mumbled in her drowsiness, "boys won't always leave you alone: you do it to have peace."

Suddenly he was free of her weight, by no effort on his part. He could hear and feel her sitting up in the surrounding darkness, reviving her conscience, or brushing off her lethargy, or both: it intrigued him to realize all the sounds she was making were those of a mature woman.

Kathy seemed to be agitated by the first inroads of guilt. "Oh dear!" she began to mutter, then moan: "I'm late! I'm late for practice. How I hate that—to be late." The darkness was all movement, the windowpane quivering with artificial lights. "Khrapovitsky is right: I must study harder. I was good, though, at the last lesson. Khrap even had to admit it."

He tried to invoke deafness, and did succeed in retreating into himself for a moment; when he was sucked back he heard: ". . . if only I will give all of myself—all my time—to music. So he says."

The fireworks of Liszt were coruscating in and over Chubb's Lane: the cheap bangers, the intoxicated Catherine wheels, the soaring, feathered rockets.

He heard her scratching after the switch. "Don't turn on the light, Kathy."

"Good-night, Duffle," she said, feeling with her lips, giving him a cool wet kiss.

He listened to her blundering down the stairs: his aborted spiritual child.

Incredible to think it was still that night: he was going down, after hearing Rhoda return with her empty cart. He would have liked to give her fairer warning than the sound of his slippers or a cough before opening the kitchen door; though he was wearing a shirt and trousers he was afraid he might look naked. Appeased sensuality helped him temporarily not to mind. He put on a slight swagger, to show he didn't. But Rhoda kept her eyelids lowered. From behind these she was preparing a meal: of cold sliced luncheon sausage, which would taste of nothing, not even sawdust;

some lettuce she had shredded into thin ribbons; hard-boiled eggs, blue as bruises where the white met the yellow. She was brewing tea, but he got out the brandy bottle and had him a good slug, still without Rhoda choosing to notice. One day, he promised himself, he would bring home a plump chicken, and stuff it with truffles, and lace it with *fine champagne*—didn't they accuse him of being rich?—and nurse it gently, gently, on a bed of spitting butter: a meal for an elderly sensualist, and, of course, his sister, or lapsed conscience.

He tried out on his teeth a ribbon or two of knife-flavoured lettuce. "You never thought to mention Kathy Volkov."

Rhoda was sucking on half a naked, withered tomato. How sly, he wondered, were the eyes behind their lowered blinds?

"Why should it have occurred to me? We all lead out own lives," she protested. "Mrs Volkov is my friend. I wasn't aware Kathy was yours. She's a child—and an artist in her own right."

Rhoda, he saw, had developed the mouth of a governess. One drooping shoulder, and all her movements as she rearranged the plate and laid together her knife and fork, were the motions of self-righteousness disguised as humility.

He remembered: "That fur coat we discussed—I must buy it for you. We'll go in the morning," he said too forcefully. "You'll have to be specially fitted." He couldn't help it sounding cold.

Rhoda was looking at her empty plate. "But I don't want it. Expensive presents are in every way an embarrassment. Besides"—she smiled and raised her eyes—"fur coats are one of the traditional bribes women are offered by men."

"Aren't I your brother?"

She didn't answer, but got up, to move virtuously around in the strait asbestos kitchen. She was in a tidying mood; if untidiness hadn't already existed she would have invented it.

He was so exasperated he took another swig of brandy.

"How did you come to meet Mrs Volkov?" He couldn't leave it alone, or disguise his impatience: waiting for her answer he started swinging a leg, youthful, but desperately so.

"How?" She repeated, sweeping invisible crumbs. "We first met— as far as I can remember—when I was living over by The Gash. I think I met her with Mrs Cutbush. Bernice Cutbush is a friend of Mrs Volkov's."

"Cutbush! The grocer? Is Cutbush also Mrs Volkov's friend?" His swinging leg, which had felt comparatively limber, and lithe, and youthful in spite of his irritation, was immediately petrified.

"I can't say Mr Cutbush has ever been Mrs Volkov's friend. That wouldn't be possible."

"How not possible?"

"Not according to her moral code. Mrs Volkov is very strict, though I'm sure—well, I know Mr Cutbush was present on some occasions—it couldn't have been otherwise—in his own house. Mrs Volkov was sorry for Mrs Cutbush. You might say they have disappointments in common. Mrs Volkov's husband ran away; Mr Cutbush stayed at home, but might have run. This, I believe, is why the two women were drawn together. Mrs Volkov would walk over to Gidley Street: she used to be a great walker, and walking's cheaper. Sometimes she'd take Kathy with her."

"Is Mr Cutbush known to Kathy?"

"He could hardly help being. When she grew older she'd sometimes lend a hand in the shop, only Saturdays of course. Of course it was only a sort of joke—an entertainment for the child—though he used to pay her a shilling or two."

"But a man of that character!"

Rhoda gave a short laugh. Her rather prominent teeth glistened. Although she had lived close to life, her affliction had kept her aloof from it. Like a statue, her marble was prone to breakage only. "Kathy could hardly come to harm with a man like Cecil Cutbush. He's a man's man." Again she laughed, quite naturally. "Or boys'."

He just prevented the bottle from toppling.

"Poor Cutbush was almost caught out once: he got off by the skin of his teeth. It was a horrid pimply boy, too."

"What sort of age?"

"Oh, I don't know. Of an age by which vice has had time to develop. Twelve, perhaps—or thirteen. This boy, luckily for Cutbush, was well known as a liar—though Cutbush himself is what you would call a compulsive liar—respected as a man of business, however—and churchwarden. He had to resign from the Council after the scandal."

He could visualize the Cutbush circle: the two women drinking tea, the grocer's tearful wife, and the Scot whose virtue was probably her vice, holland blinds half drawn against a heat they intensified;

it collected round the brown teapot and the cut-glass stand with its enormous floured scones. Miss Courtney the lodger had been allowed in because she was small enough to stimulate the charitable aspirations of her two companions. They put up with the stench of horseflesh which, frankly, used to nauseate Mrs Cutbush almost as much as her husband did. Because he, too, lived in the house, he couldn't very well be kept out, but sat sucking his moustache after his cup of tea. Cecil's shiny serge thighs were what nauseated Bernice most of all. And Kathy? *Kathy will be holding the fort*: Mrs Volkov glowed with the virtue of having produced a child, whether by husband or mere, casual male. The grocer's phlegmy voice confirmed that Kathy was a girl with a head on her shoulders; while the blowflies settled on the turned butter melting out of their scone feast.

Kathy amongst the canisters, under the lowering bacon-flitch, her throat reflecting the kaleidoscopic labels on the tins she popped into paper bags, could still have been immaculate. But for how long? with her boy's bum and starfish breasts: only the pimples were missing; or perhaps they existed subcutaneously, along with the lies, the compulsive lies.

In the circumstances his hands were almost throttling the brandy bottle. "I wonder you can enjoy the company of liars, and buggers, and hysterics, and Scottish prigs."

Rhoda seemed hypnotized by his blenched knuckles. "Aren't they other human beings? Almost everybody carries a hump, not always visible, and not always of the same shape."

"But that child—I wonder how much she understands?" If he could have burned Rhoda open with the blow-lamp he was becoming, he would have done so: to find out what she was keeping locked away from him.

She only said, and that slowly: "*You* should know, Hurtle."

"How—I?"

"You were a child, weren't you? I think, perhaps, in many ways, you are still; otherwise you wouldn't see the truth as you do: too large, and too hectic."

Shortly after, she finished her imaginary tidying and shut herself up with her cats. He went to the back door and chucked out the empty bottle, which exploded somewhere in the dark yard.

At least he had his work, however closely he was threatened by human vice, his sister Rhoda, the approach of old age, and the behaviour of those who only bought his paintings to flog. There were the paintings; but fortunately there was also painting: the physical act which rejuvenated and purified when he and nameless others were at their most corrupt. Of course it was a miserable refuge, too —oh God, yes, when he cared to admit it: he was an old man, turning his back and distorting truth to get at an effect, which he did, he knew, better than anybody else—well, almost anybody. But there were the days when he himself was operated on, half drunk sometimes, shitting himself with agony, when out of the tortures of knife and mind he was suddenly carried, without choice, on the wings of his exhaustion, to the point of intellectual and—dare he begin to say it?—spiritual self-justification.

Anyway, he painted.

During the days which followed Kathy Volkov's necessary but forgettable visit, he drew constantly and furiously. He did many drawings for what he could see was becoming his "Girl at Piano." Out of numerous false starts and the vulgar gloss of a concert grand, the old upright piano grew, the sloping line of the inclined case almost parallel to the straight line of the young girl's back, her thick plait, the candlesticks empty except for the solid drifts of wax and encrustations of verdigris. As he saw it, any light must flow from a suggestion of the girl's face.

So he continued drawing, and rejecting, and compiling. At one stage he drew the boy of sinewy thighs and starfish breasts with Kathy's shadow falling across him. Perhaps the boy's mouth was Kathy's; the ribs were a boy's, as primitive as bacon bones. He destroyed the drawing for having no connection; though in some actual sense it could have been a complement to the wholly feminine girl inclined at the upright piano with its blind candlesticks.

Obsessed all these days, he realized he had forgotten his promise of a fur coat to Rhoda. He decided to pretend he had never made it; or at least he would pretend for the time being. Soon after her arrival he had bought her the promised transistor, which continued tinkling and reverberating amongst her permanently indolent cats even after she had gone out on cat business. Fortunately he was too busy to hear the twangled music except by snatches.

It appeared from these that Rhoda was dedicated to pop. But wasn't Kathy, his spiritual child, a daughter of the neighbourhood?

While preparing a board for the painting he was almost ready to paint, it occurred to him he hadn't seen Kathy for days: it might have been weeks. He coughed slightly on finding himself so unmoved: shocking, no doubt, to some busybody of a moralist born without a visual sense. But he had his drawings; he had conceived this painting in which Kathy was present, not the sweaty schoolgirl of vulgar lapses, touchingly tentative aspirations, and at times brutal, because unconscious, sensuality, but the real Katherine Volkov, almost a woman, of studied ice and burning musical passion, who was daring him to transfer his own passion to the primed board. The face he caught sight of in the glass surprised him: haggard and drained for one who was at the point of running over to excess.

Though he would have liked to wait till the following morning early and work through the hours of daylight, he could no longer restrain himself. He began that afternoon. At times he heard his panting, or groaning, or wheezing (a bronchial old age?) as he thrust against the virgin board. There were the other moments, after the initial terror, when it became so exquisitely easy he could feel the flesh returning to his face; the sweat tasted deliciously salt, which his tongue lapped from a corner of his mouth. In the same way, his possessed girl was beginning to create in spite of herself. The inclining body was both exhilarated by the music escaping out of it, and tormented by what might escape altogether. Avoiding the accusation of technique and emptiness, he must somehow fill the rectangular board with a volume of music. It was their common problem: the girl appeared to writhe, to one side, as she crouched at her piano.

The piano remained a dead expanse. The candlesticks he could build up with a brilliance of verdigris and icicles of wax; but he couldn't so far bring the bloody piano to life. Yes, *bloody*. He drew blood: slashing and gashing; and retreated from the thing he had so foolishly undertaken.

As the light was failing he went down in search of Rhoda his sister, whom he didn't exactly want to find, and who would be out, in any case, dispensing her charitable offal. Her own cats, acclimatized by now, were mostly limbering up for the night; he caught glimpses of them, trying out their claws on privet trunks, their voices on the dusk, or lurking amongst the leathery leaves of the conservatory. He found himself beginning to resent Rhoda's absence, even the exodus of her cats: when he sighted one old matted tom lolling on the mantelpiece against the marble columns of a clock. Immediately the clock pinged, the cat opened his yellow eyes, the claws shot out from their sheath of cracked pad, to fight a duel of understanding.

The intruder could have shouted. At once he went clambering back up to his room snatched at paper tried out the wire entanglement the barbs the coiled springs of the cat: or Cat. He could visualize the great barbed pads coiled glimmering inside the scrims of the piano case.

When Rhoda came in she called out triumphantly: "Hurtle? I bought a cooked chicken!"

His mouth sagged, but he went down to her wretched chicken. Rhoda was breathless and radiant from her labours. At once they began tearing the chicken apart with their equally exhausted, grubby hands: while cats hovered. The king of the mantelpiece got the parson's nose, and almost choked on it.

After wiping the grease from her mouth Rhoda announced: "I'm going to bed. I don't know when I felt so tired."

He might have echoed her remark if it wouldn't have been against his principles.

While she was blundering around the kitchen, clapping the used plates together, Rhoda happened to touch him on the arm. "My dear boy, I'm so happy for you!" he couldn't surely have heard her say; his consummation was such a private matter, it became immoral for Rhoda, who was also his sister, to refer to, let alone feast, on it.

So he escaped as quickly as possible from his *voyeuse*. He stumbled up the stairs, barking one of his shins—lucky not to have fallen on his face—and slept.

In the clear light of morning he scrabbled after clean brushes; he couldn't have wasted time ridding the dirty ones of their crust: he had to paint.

He painted the coiled tiger just visible inside Katherine Volkov's piano. The keys under her fingers were yellow and slightly clawed. The gashes in the woodwork would stay. He painted the long thick plait waiting to lash the music out of its glistening tail.

Finishing at what was still an early hour, he felt sleek, jovial, and generous. Whether she liked it or not, Rhoda would have to submit to his generosity.

At breakfast he began: "Do you know what I'm planning to do

this morning?" He looked out through the kitchen door at the almost amiable cat inhabitants of his yard.

By contrast Rhoda was looking pinched and sour. "It can't be much of a plan if you propose to share it."

He was so full of kindness he wouldn't let her reject him. "We're going to get dressed and take the tram to a fur '*salong*' I investigated some time ago. I'm going to have them fit you out."

Rhoda was standing on her usual little box to lend her height for the washing up. The silence sounded made for breaking as she recklessly stirred the crockery in the sink.

Presently she said faintly: "I wonder whether you know how cruel you are—to expose me to ridicule."

"How more ridiculous in a good coat than looking like something off a dump?" He sounded the soul of bourgeois reason. "You used to be a great one for clothes and dressing up."

"Oh yes!" She sighed. "Then! And 'dressing up' is just what it was!" It might have ended in bitterness if steam from the sink hadn't made her sneeze.

Suddenly she asked in a different voice: "What time should I be ready?"

It was such a volte-face he felt a bit resentful, but mumbled: "Give us time to get into our clothes."

As she flung the water off her hands he recognized her feverish look.

They so seldom went about together, any neighbour seeing them that morning must have been surprised. His stride carried him somewhat ahead. Because it was a cold day he had put on his overcoat. He hid his unemployed hands in the pockets. He couldn't hide Rhoda, though. She was wearing a cloak in green-tinged black serge with a large wooden button fastening it under her pointed chin. He had hit the nail on the head mentioning the dump at breakfast: all her clothes looked come-by-chance, when her size and shape must have forced her to have them made for her.

Who, seeing him with Rhoda, would believe in his success? Didn't believe in it himself: such transparent brilliance only emphasized his deformities.

In desperation he turned round from time to time and called back over the intervening space: "Are you all right? Am I walking too fast?" and finally: "It isn't far now"; as though she didn't know the tram stop.

Rhoda had obviously got it into her head that he was trying to make a fool of her. She composed her mouth and didn't answer as she trotted along after him.

It was the same in the tram: his attempts at adorning a sense of duty with love, all seemed to fall flat. He truly loved Rhoda. Wasn't she his past? The knowledge they shared had a common source.

He cleared his throat of an obstruction. "How do you like the idea of nutria? That's a practical, discreet fur." What came out in a blast ended as too much of a whisper when muted midway.

Rhoda, who never wore a hat, pushed back her greying, straying hair, held up her wedge-shaped chin, and said: "Squirrel is what I've always hankered after. I wanted Mummy to give me squirrel, but she wouldn't."

"Perhaps she was right. Squirrel was a soubrette's fur. Don't think it's in fashion any more. Probably tears very easily, too."

They must have looked and sounded odd, seated side by side on the tram bench, fatally belonging to each other while not owning to it. Most of the passengers were too refined to stare: only the children did, fish-mouthed, in one case picking his nose; the children looked right inside.

Rhoda said: "If I have to go through with this, I want squirrel, Hurtle."

Because she was deforming his intentions he remained silent for a whole section.

Then he said, looking with distaste at the circumspect expressions surrounding them: "It isn't a major issue, though you want to turn it into one." The tram bell seemed to mark the end of a round, with him the loser.

Rhoda was sitting as erect as her body allowed. It was he who could afford to loll, not sloppily, at an elegant angle, as he had sometimes noticed in the glass, having shoes fitted, for instance.

"Who's trying to expose you to ridicule, I'd like to know? Tarting yourself up in squirrel! My idea was to see you warmly, presentably clothed in winter, instead of looking a fright."

"Oh, dry up, Hurtle! I couldn't begin to compete with your vanity and arrogance."

A couple of children began to laugh; while all the hatted ladies had been born deaf, it seemed: they glanced at the view or their engagement books. Only one of them, less controlled, or more honest, was fascinated by his ankles in the left-over pair of Sulka socks, a present from Boo Davenport, he had come across that morning.

He uncrossed his legs and squirmed around on the unyielding bench. He hated the prudent faces of the powdered ladies; he hated them for their discretion towards his hunchbacked sister, and at least one of them for her stupid admiration of what she saw as elegance of form: when he, too, if they had known, was a freak, an artist.

It brought him very close to Rhoda. It made him glance at her, wondering whether she could have been hiding some secret gift inside her deformity all these years; but her expression wouldn't allow him even to guess at its nature.

Arriving at what he had taken to calling the 'fur *salong*,' and which Rhoda had refused to see as their private joke, they were accepting each other, if not as closely united as he wished.

The big Jewess in charge surged towards him with a smile which acknowledged his fame. "You remember," he fairly spat it at her, "I discussed with you a relative who would need special attention."

"Oh yes, Mr Duffield!" The Jewess tilted her head till her moist lips were glistening with light and understanding.

"This is my sister." He stepped aside, unveiling Rhoda.

The woman had been well trained; but it was obviously something of an occasion. The fitter she brought was nervous to the point of neurosis. The manager came as they contemplated Rhoda's hump.

"I thought, perhaps, nutria."

"Squirrel, Hurtle. We agreed on squirrel."

Once this was established, Rhoda settled down as though in the hands of Maman. He wished Maman had been there: even Harry would have managed the situation better; Harry's worldliness would have risen to the choosing of skins.

Both the Courtney children grew noticeably shyer, he knew, in leaving the 'fur *salong*.' Would he pay a deposit? He did—humbly, if they had guessed—in notes: while Rhoda turned her back.

They were received into an almost empty tram for the return journey. As they rode the hills of Sydney, the luxury of seeming privacy and a glow from his recent generosity allowed him to ask: "What about Kathy?"

"Who?"

"Kathy Volkov. Have you seen her?"

Rhoda's nostrils began to get their pinched look: scenting a prelude to bribery, no doubt.

"Oh, I see her. Yes. When I visit her mother," she casually admitted. "I go there fairly often. They're very excited."

"Why should they be—excited?" His voice sounded dislocated; the motion of the tram was churning them round against each other whether they liked it or not.

"Because of the recent developments, of course."

Rhoda was perhaps attempting to tell calmly, unless he had irritated her by not knowing. Had she already told, and he was drunk or thoughtful at the time? or was he already senile? He certainly couldn't remember, and was relieved when the tram pitched her into her narrative.

"Yes. Mr Khrapovitsky retired from the Con," she shouted against the screeching of the tram. "Mrs Khrapovitsky—well connected, it appears—has inherited property in Melbourne. They are moving —down—there. He's keeping Kathy on because she's an exceptional pupil. She'll stay with a relative—Mrs Volkov's cousin."

"When is she leaving?" he shouted back into Rhoda's teeth.

"End of the month."

He quickly calculated, and saw how cruel it was, but only too probable: the sort of thing that does happen.

"Will you be seeing her?" he asked with assumed meekness.

Rhoda wet her lips. "I've been bidden," she began (why the hell did she use "bidden"?) "by Bernice Cutbush—to a little afternoon party. It can only be boring for a child—but poor Mrs Cutbush— and Kathy at times does suggest she's older than she is."

He subsided on the wicked seat he was sharing with Rhoda. They were mostly silent. He tried to nauseate himself by remembering the smell of school tunic on a hot evening; while the poetry of Katherine Volkov constantly headed his misery in other directions.

It was fortunate he had his work. In the following weeks he painted several versions more or less abstract of his "Girl at Piano." There were drawings, too, which poured out on his board, on odd scraps of paper, on the walls of the dunny. He even returned to his conception of the boy-girl, both in drawings and, finally, in paint. The half-veiled face might have been tattooed in purple: or was it an eruption of pimples? Evil-looking by either interpretation; but the evil painting, coming to a head, relieved him to some extent.

In the meantime Rhoda had been for several fittings for the fur coat, which was giving trouble.

"She's so nice," she said, "really—when you get to know her."

"Who is?" He was irritated by Rhoda's sly innocence; he almost put up an arm to prevent her brushing against Katherine Volkov, the actual one he was at present creating in his mind, as opposed to the figment of his original lust.

"The lady at the fur place," Rhoda was explaining. "So understanding. She was in Auschwitz. Has the numbers tattooed on her arm."

"Too flabby."

"You reduce everything to a physical level. How do you suppose anyone survives? How did Mrs Grünblatt, for instance?"

In the end you couldn't talk to Rhoda.

She had taken to smothering herself in powder, which didn't at all improve her nose: the transparent tip kept its same gleam of gristle, while a chalky residue collected round the periphery. Whether Mrs Grünblatt was the sole reason for these attempts at camouflage he couldn't decide: Rhoda was so secretive, yet at the same time naïve.

For instance, she threw in: "Mrs Grünblatt used to be acquainted with a painter—his name, I think, was Groze—or something like it."

"Grosz?" He snorted; if Mrs Grünblatt was of the school of Grosz, he could visualize her mental drawings of Rhoda.

One evening she returned wearing a dab of dry rouge on each cheekbone and an unmistakable thread of lipstick. He restrained himself from telling her she had been to the "little afternoon party" given by Mrs Cutbush for Kathy and Mrs Volkov; nor did Rhoda confess.

As the deadline approached he looked regularly in the letter-box for the tattooed message. He bound one of the boy-girl's ankles, in spite of which the sores continued escaping through the bandage.

By now he might have dispensed entirely with the original Kathy if, on a steamy morning, he hadn't believed he recognized her at a street crossing. Realizing at once that Katherine Volkov, actual or fictitious, was his overwhelming belief, he began scurrying bumping panting retching almost it was such a short green and all his fellow pedestrians equally determined or desperate: while Kathy sailed on, away.

She appeared leggier than before: long, burnished legs. As she ran, and propped, and ran, her eyes, of the same blazing blue, flashed a white warning from their corners; and what had been her starfish breasts were jolted into flesh.

He ran after. Might have been caught in mid-stream by the red. Collided with a vast soft woman the impact made surprisingly hard. It stopped him calling out to Kathy. Fractured the intention at chest level. Almost winded. The woman was a laugher.

He scuttled on freakishly and caught up in a quiet street beside a church under some scorched planes.

"Aren't you Katherine Volkov?" He heard his own stupid giggle.

"Yes—Mr Duffield." She waited with a resigned politeness: he might have been a friend of her mother's.

"So you're leaving," he blathered. "Perhaps we'll see you at Flint Street before you go."

Was his hat set too rakishly? She was looking embarrassed, perhaps sulking, at the pavement, a bundle of sheet music curving under her arm.

She said: "Yes, Mr Duffield," and smiled a rather thin smile.

"You've altered, Kathy. You've grown. I almost didn't recognize you." As silly as that: an old coot embarrassing children with obvious remarks; his hands looked scabby and freckled.

"I'm fourteen in nine days' time."

A whole year.

Then a shower of music burst from under her arm, and he helped her gather up the sheets from the pavement. It saved them further embarrassment.

"I must go now," she said; she had the music to return.

There was no reason why she shouldn't look composed: their meeting had been an accident, not an assignation.

He took a street in an inconvenient direction, while remembering Sid Cupples, an old bloke from his boyhood who knew most of the reasons and answers. Sid had been thrown from a horse, and walked forever after with a bent leg; it gave him a curious wishbone look: frail but resilient.

When he could bear it no longer he didn't ask, but told Rhoda: "The little Volkov must have left by now."

"Oh no." Rhoda was smoothing a grey-white garment with an iron. "She's leaving tomorrow evening. Pity it's the evening. I shan't be able to see her off." The act of ironing always seemed to soothe

Rhoda. "I can't very well abandon the cats again." Kathy, as self-sufficient as a cat, would barely notice. "A long journey for a young girl—on her own—at night." Rhoda's iron felt its way tentatively.

He realized she was ironing a little nightgown of such antiquity she might have worn it as a young girl. It was trimmed with scallops of torn lace, grubby with age, or night journeys.

"Mrs Volkov is going to speak to the guard." She soothed her girl-woman's gown. "She's going to ask him to take Kathy under his wing."

Oh, worse, worse! Some randy old brute easing his serge in between the sheets.

Rhoda was so absorbed in Kathy's abstract journey she didn't notice the details of it. She didn't notice she had singed her gown.

Soon afterwards he got away unobserved. It was most fortunate; because this was the evening Kathy must come—or not.

In fact, she didn't; nor had he expected it, except in fantasies. It was now far too late. She wouldn't, couldn't possibly—unless reckoning on Rhoda asleep. So he lay listening, counted out by the distant clocks, remembering how Kathy had each time come at sunset. This evening's sunset had ratified her defection and his doom.

About dawn he creaked up from his iron rack, intending to work, or at least hoping some creative mechanism might take over. All his brushes were filthy. Must clean them first: honest, sober work, if it hadn't been for his drunken condition, his one and only desire. A mild, Quakerish light failed to cool his fever; though to some extent the fumes from the turps cauterized his nostrils, his skull's burning labyrinth.

She climbed so smoothly, quietly, he didn't hear her till the last stages, then recognized the sound the only possible murderer could make: who glided in with silent, sure, positively fatal steps, while remaining soft, gentle, above all practical, no doubt because of Rhoda downstairs. He must never forget Kathy's divided soul was part Scottish, if also Russian. Her Russian brow was bursting with an obsession, and it must have been the Russian in her who failed to notice his nakedness as she flung herself between his blind breasts, beating her head against the miserable scrabble of grizzled hair.

Himself babbling: "But you didn't come! You didn't come!"

"No!" She blurted crying against him. "I was too frightened! I *am* frightened!"

"What am I to be frightened at?"

"No." She stopped then. "Not you. But everything. Everything that's happening. Going away. My mother's so stubborn she drives me ratty at times, but I'm *used* to her! I know nothing. Not really. Not even in my music. I muck up some of the simplest scales—over and over."

From being angry, she started crying again, and the need to comfort her melted the last of his vanity. He drew her back against himself with such care he could have been negotiating a difficult passage in paint; while at the same time he heard the sounds he was uttering: amorphous, thick-lipped, instinctively tender—cow sounds, he who was nothing of a mother, her erect lover no less, as Kathy was his love, though altered.

Whereas she had been a hot, blubber-mouthed schoolgirl on that other, now unbelievable occasion, bashing up, more or less raping with her lust an old, resisting man, she had become his passive complement. After taking off her incidental dress, she lay so trustfully, so long-legged cool, barely smiling, her breasts asking, as she waited for him to enter her silver-lidded dream. He could have yanked her plait, to express his joy in peals of bells.

O God he loved his Katherine Volkov gliding together through never smoother water.

It was the the electric daylight which finally made her sit up.

Mending the end of her frayed plait, Kathy said: "You must think I look awful."

"How—awful?" Her nipples were the prettiest.

"I've started a spot on the end of my nose. Haven't you noticed?"

When he had squinted he did actually see. "What's in a pimple or two?"

"Oh, it's horrible!" She sighed. "And you can't do anything about it."

It was at its most inflamed and luminous: it wouldn't yet submit to torture; it could only torture.

When she had finished her plait she suffered a fresh outbreak of woe. "What am I going to do?" she moaned. "In Melbourne!"

"We'll write to each other"—he tried to caress her back to him—"darling Kathy." It would never sound professional.

She sat looking at her face in the distant glass, its reflections still too dark to be altogether reliable.

"D'you think," she asked, paddling the end of the plait in her cheek, "I'll ever get a lover?"

He put away his hands. "You have your music." He bared his teeth: not a false one amongst them.

"Yes, my music. I'll become a pianist—if I want to." She was reciting something learned by heart; if she didn't add the word "great," the carriage of her head implied, and the glance at the mirror confirmed, it. "Oh, I must! I *must!*"

Though she had already left him, she might have sat there indefinitely, appalled by future battles between her will and her weaknesses, if they hadn't heard what put an end to any misery of his: the sound of a saucepan crash-bouncing on the kitchen floor.

Kathy said with Scottish calm: "That is Miss Courtney getting herself a bit of breakfast."

"For God's sake, what will you tell her?"

"Nothing. She won't come out." It practically established that Rhoda had procured his destruction.

"But won't you want to say good-bye?"

"We've said it—at the ghastly Cutbush party."

"Was the grocer there?"

"Oh yes! Creepy Cecil!" Because her head was at present inside her dress he could only guess at the expression on her face.

"Who else?" He had to flog himself some more.

"Nobody. Us. Miss Courtney. Oh, there was a friend of Mr Cutbush looked in just as we were leaving."

"Which friend? What was his name?"

Kathy had tugged her dress down; under the influence of early morning she was looking serious, almost religious. She might have submitted to his inquisition if Rhoda hadn't been throwing things about in the kitchen. Rhoda couldn't have slept, and had got up in a bad temper: she was actually screaming at one of her cats.

"What was his name?" he repeated. "The grocer's friend?"

Kathy had come, and was sitting beside him, warm and superior in her dress; but it was the warmth of railway stations: the trains were hooting their woolly, false-maternal assurances.

"It won't be long. Two years at most, Khrapovitsky says. Then I'll be back for the final. So you see, there isn't any need for either of us to be sad. Only two years. And complimentary seats for relatives. You'll come, won't you? as a relative—to hear me play in the competition."

And probably win. Wallowing in Liszt. She had those determined-looking teeth.

"Mr Duffield?"

And little, hard, pushing bubs.

"Yes, Kathy." He kissed at a mouth which had already withdrawn: he kissed the air.

Then she went from him altogether, lowering her practically veiled, her virginal, her dedicated head. If she didn't run, it was because of this dedication, or because she had to pass their Cerberus.

He listened, but Kathy moved so smoothly Rhoda didn't come out. No doubt they had made an agreement; or Rhoda was deaf: this was what he really hoped, though he had never noticed deafness in Rhoda. Anyway, she didn't come out.

He still listened, and when he heard the yard gate, its loose, unmistakable latch, he began a dry whimpering. There was nobody to listen to the great man he was supposed to be: not even Rhoda his sister.

Those years when he stolidly worked—and some of his paintings of this period did look stolid, though only himself and his enemies noticed—Rhoda was his remaining prop. Her presence made itself as strongly felt as Kathy's absence. Unrelentingly, Rhoda chopped up the purple horseflesh to feed all spawned and spawning cats.

Sometimes he wondered, if Kathy were to have a baby, would he be more, or less, distressed to discover he wasn't its father? Of course, she wouldn't have one. *Girls don't have babies nowadays; they're too sophisticated*: that was Rhoda's opinion, how pertinent he couldn't be sure. Babies (clumsy word) blunder out of ignorant wombs; children no longer bear children: old men have them instead, fully clothed, and in the best classical tradition. Nobody, probably not even Kathy, need ever be aware of his spiritual child Katherine Volkov; unless some tittuping archivist picked up a scent on a scholarly ramble and thought to enliven scholarship with muck.

Till then, he had his secret, and his work, and his work was his secret. Throughout this phase of his painting life the colours he used were noticeably clear, which made some of the earlier stuff look oversombre, congested, muddy. He was conscious of wanting to exclude from this new world of transparent lyricism any of the old threats and tensions; yet there was scarcely a canvas where a presence wasn't felt, beyond the frame, armed in some cases with a bludgeon, in others, a bladder. (This was the period when he couldn't resist painting that enormous bladder, inside it the Old Fool

Himself, which so confused and irritated public opinion when first shown.) Most of the paintings of his late, some said "retarded," lyrical phase sold very well, because at one level they were considered "charming." According to another view, they were "too sweet," and those who held it would make a face as though they had a nasty taste in their mouths, before smiling their relief at his "going off." And there was the lady so disgusted she hit the "Old Fool Having Bladder Trouble"; she walloped the canvas with her umbrella and was taken to court by the Misses Ailsa Harkness and Biddy Prickett, in whose gallery the scandal occurred.

This episode and others made him unwilling to exhibit, but he allowed himself to be persuaded, if only to prove he was still alive. One painting he hadn't shown was the "Flowering Rosebush," in which the concept of Katherine Volkov originated. He would never show it. He disliked public ceremonies and was almost never present at them now; their life at Flint Street was too full.

Rhoda complained: "Oh dear! These cats! I sometimes feel guilty, Hurtle, not seeing to things upstairs. You do realize, don't you? I'm strong enough on the level. But doctors have warned me against stairs. Don't want to aggravate my respiratory trouble." She would wheeze and pant in support of the doctors.

"Don't worry. I sometimes do a sweep-out; it's all that's necessary."

Rhoda was at her most abstract, her most conscienceful, over a cup of strong tea. "I'm not one of those in favour of making a Full Declaration—but have nothing to hide—I've nothing to be ashamed of. Anyone interested—or inquisitive—is at liberty any time to ask." She was prepared to be so truthful he wondered whether she wasn't in possession of a secret.

He nursed his own the more closely for that; though he did, once, tentatively inquire: "Has anyone heard—is there, perhaps, news of the little Volkov?"

"Why, of course. Her mother hears regularly. Naturally she writes less regularly to me: only an elderly friend of the family." When the steam from the tea she was drinking allowed her to open her eyes Rhoda added: "I had a letter from Kathy on Wednesday."

He prepared to speak, but hesitated: was Rhoda playing him? "You never told me."

"Didn't I? One never knows. Or one forgets, rather. You live so much to yourself, Hurtle, up there—always painting. Perhaps I thought you wouldn't be interested."

"Did she mention, at least, whether she's making any progress?"

"Oh, not to me. And I wouldn't expect it. She tells me about her underclothes—the trouble she's having with her 'auntie,' who insists on her wearing wool next the skin because of the treacherous Melbourne climate. She has her own normal sets, and the false, woollen ones for the aunt to wash."

"Is Kathy so affluent?"

But Rhoda didn't hear.

"Incidentally," he remembered, "you haven't told me what's happening about the fur coat. When will it be ready?"

"Why, the coat—I brought it home weeks ago!"

"You didn't tell me."

"I must have told."

"Aren't you going to wear it, then?"

"In the heat of summer?"

"I think you might put it on to show me."

For a moment she looked so ferocious emptying the dregs of her tea, he might have been inviting her, not to dress up, but to strip.

Presently she went out, quickly, precisely, in no more than a mild routine anger, and he heard the wardrobe door banged. In the silence which followed he imagined Rhoda's hands, their hooked skin, fumbling with sensuous, virgin fur, and closed his eyes automatically, as if he might thus avoid further visions. Then she must have trodden on a cat.

When she returned she was holding her pointed chin aggressively high. There were patches of natural red on her cheekbones, which looked delirious against her otherwise chalky skin.

"There!" she announced in her largest voice. "You asked for it!"

She gave two or three twirls, punctuated with stamps, in imitation of the mannequins she imagined, or perhaps had seen with Maman. She was, in turn: a little girl; an angry man; the Fairy Carabosse; while always remaining his sister Rhoda. A large fur-covered button growing from her flat bosom had perhaps been given to her to draw attention from the squirrel hump; but it only made her look more grotesque.

"Are you satisfied?" she was asking.

He sank his chin. "It's a fine coat."

"Frankly, I think it makes me look a fright."

"Nobody's ever perfect."

"Oh," she said, "some of us are!"

He would ask from time to time: "Aren't you ever going to wear that coat?"

But it was not yet the weather for it; or she might spoil it; or the cats might tear it. Once he came across her dozing in her chair, wearing the squirrel coat, and an expression of such sublime repose he was afraid to advance any farther. He stood rooted in the brazen light which was pouring in through the conservatory.

Rhoda woke up, however, and said: "I read somewhere—in a magazine—that if you wrap up well in summer it insulates you against the heat." At the same time she was scrubbing the perspiration off her face with a wad of screwed-up handkerchief.

"I'm sorry I ever suggested that bloody coat," he said at last. "You never wear it"; not even when a wind from the Antarctic was blasting them out from under the araucaria.

"There's never an occasion for it."

He couldn't resist answering: "I should have thought you might wear it on your winter visits to the Cutbush *salon*."

Rhoda tittered into the pink tea she was drinking. "Poor Bernice— what a wrong idea you've got!"

Then he leaned across their kitchen table and asked something he had been wanting to ask for a long time. "What is the name of the grocer's friend who came to Kathy Volkov's farewell party?"

"The friend? The farewell party? My God, all that time ago! What do you take me for? I don't believe I ever knew. Or if I did, I don't remember. Why—yes, there was a friend—more of an acquaintance—who looked in. I seem to remember his name was Shuard. Yes, a Mr Shuard."

"Shuard?"

"Yes. They say he's a music critic."

"But that's impossible! How could Shuard be known to Cutbush?"

"Well, he was at one time living in Gidley Street, in a furnished room—between wives. I understand he's had several wives—not that Mr Shuard could be called an immoral man, Mrs Cutbush says; he only lets the wrong ones choose him."

"But why should they invite Shuard to Kathy Volkov's party?"

"What could be more thoughtful? And he wasn't invited—he was only asked to look in—because, Mrs Cutbush felt, it might be an advantage for Kathy to know a music critic."

"To start so early! And with Shuard!"

"How—so early? And with Shuard? He's such a well-travelled man. And witty raconteur."

Yes! Warming himself in Berlin between little girls.

"I don't understand you, Hurtle. Some of your remarks are so peculiar." She was looking into the bottom of her cup as though reading a fortune.

He got himself out of the way: he felt so sick.

That winter he did fall ill, with pneumonia. Rhoda sent for a strong fellow, the carrier who moved her things in the beginning, to bring down one of the beds from upstairs and set it up in the living-room: "So that I can attend to my brother."

She made him lie there on his own bed surrounded by geographical features he would have to learn more accurately. Rhoda brought him thin, greasy soups which he drank with forced gratitude. She produced a Spode-looking chamber pot, and would carry it out slip slop to empty; for some time he was too weak to crawl as far as his sanctuary the dunny.

He asked her: "Do you remember St Yves de Trégor?"

"Never 'eard of 'im."

"The place in Brittany where we stayed with Harry and Freda Courtney. There was a full pisspot under the bed."

She blushed. "No—I don't remember."

"Don't you? I remember everything."

"You! You're peculiar!"

"It isn't peculiar. It's natural. If you've lived it."

"Oh, I've lived it enough! But some of it you like to forget. Surely that's more normal?"

He couldn't argue with her.

At one stage he asked her to bring him drawing paper: he wanted to compose a letter to Kathy; though he didn't tell Rhoda that. He wrote secretly:

My dearest Kathy,
    I am

There he stopped, because that, finally, was as much as he knew. In any case, he had never been good with words. It would have been more natural if he could have painted a picture. He did in fact make a drawing to send instead; but that, too, he destroyed: a confession of such tenderness might have shocked the wrong person should she have picked it up, perhaps even the one who should have received it.

How dispose of the destroyed drawing, the crumpled failure of a letter? He didn't trust the furniture in a room which didn't belong to him. In the meantime, the scraps of paper were always present, as tangible as twisted iron, moving around inside his bed. Eat them by small crumbs? He might have choked. So his guilt remained precariously hidden in the bed.

At the beginning of his illness Rhoda, in spite of her respiratory condition, had insisted on making up the bed, or tugging at the rumpled clothes from the sides. Now he obviously couldn't let her.

"But you haven't the strength!" she gasped.

Who had, remained to be proved. "I can't let you," he hissed. "Rhoda!" He was sweating cold like a boy who must hide the stains of shame.

Finally he planned a journey, out of the house, across the yard, as far as the incinerator. It was on a day of drizzle; he couldn't wait: Rhoda would be away from home collecting catmeat. The rain was falling softly enough; but traps were set all the way across the yard: shards of glittering blue slate; jags of bottle; puddles of water deceptively dimpled; the soaking curtains of *Bignonia venusta* hanging from the dunny ballooned out and clung to his gown, the pockets of which were crammed with guilty paper.

Watched by a crouching piebald cat, he was slowly advancing on felt feet from one stationary position to the next: when Rhoda tore round the corner of the house. Must have been in the conservatory; she usually stood her Wellingtons there.

Rhoda tore. "I caught you out!" she shrieked. "You! When all we do is for your own good!"

At least he had reached the incinerator. In opening up, the lid showered him with flakes of charred rust. Too much to hope the match would kindle.

He could imagine Rhoda's white look as she tore across the yard.

Matches breaking. He got a thin little flame going on a shaving of paper, which ought to have blazed up—it was positively incendiary—if his papery hands hadn't fumbled, and the lid of the incinerator crashed shut.

Rhoda was using language she never used: "You bloody fool! You mad devil of an old *bugger*!"

While the gentle rain taunted them both, she was dragging at his waist, at his dressing-gown cord—slipping; she was away out at last on the acorn at the end of the cord.

Although he was laughing he was desperate to return to the incinerator; while she wouldn't let him.

"What are we to do with you?" she screamed. "Put you in a strait-jacket?"

"The Gestapo should know!" His shout came out as a whisper; for rain in finest webs was gumming up his lips.

It was so deadly important that he should burn the incriminating evidence: when the incinerator began to roar; and he was led easily enough back into the house.

Rhoda had exhausted herself.

He put his hand on her wet hump, as he had never done before, and it was solid. "Poor Rhoda, I know you are my rock, but I'm so happy to have recovered my independence." Since the burning of the papers he was not so much physically weak as light with joy.

Rhoda subsided. "Independence—whatever that means. I've just been with Mrs Volkov, who woke up this morning and found her speech was blurred. It gave her such a fright she wants to send for Kathy. If she does, Kathy's career may be ruined—and perhaps others."

Rhoda was so hysterical, melodramatic, he decided she ought to be left to recover. Because Mrs Volkov had never emerged from her name and her abstract virtues to become a person, her blurred speech could only remain a matter for his conventional concern, in spite of their secret relationship.

It was the sudden thought of a blighted hand which paralyzed him as he floundered into bed. So he lay wondering whether he believed in God the Merciful as well as God the Vivisector; he wondered whether he believed in God as he lay massaging his right hand.

The following summer there was a drought in which he flourished physically, though it did nothing to improve the yellow wastes of his spirit. In all his paintings of that summer the faceless forms floated in search of a reason. Gravitating towards a promise of metamorphosis, his embryos did add up to something if the eye could see; the trouble was: most eyes could not.

When, for instance, he took two or three of his canvases over to the Tank Stream Gallery, the directors descended on him, all smiles, but sideways glances at the paintings, and hints, and murmurs, and jolliness, and grunts: Ailsa Harkness the steel eagle, and her partner Biddy Prickett; there was more of the red ferret in Biddy.

He stood fanning himself with his Panama hat, still elegant, but stained, in the tussore suit which never showed its age because it had always been that colour. The timeless is never dated: then why was this pair of ignorant, self-opinionated women shilly-shallying over the paintings?

Miss Harkness smiled, and glanced, and said: "Are you *well*? You *look* well. You must take care of yourself, you know."

Miss Prickett was without lashes, or else they were too pink to see. "Why don't you take a trip, Hurtle? There's no use pretending you aren't disgustingly rich." In spite of Biddy Prickett, he could feel the smirk settle on his face. "Or marry some luscious girl. If you haven't already gone and done it. You were always such an old pretender." Biddy's laugh was meant to jolly you along, but had an utter mirthlessness.

Ailsa Harkness was grasping a painting as though it needed breaking open. "So these are the newest. Lovely! There are at least three Americans waiting for you to fill in their cheques. I'd say they'll be more than excited to find you've started a fresh phase."

Fresh phase: or the end? He could never pass judgement on his work, except in his depths, the way to which is so tortuous.

When he got in, Rhoda was out, and a letter had come. He began at once fumbling to read: lucky he still had his eyesight.

Dear Mr Duffield . . .

Mustn't lose heart. He couldn't. It was for the moment the major part of him.

How dreadful of me not to write when I promised. But nor did you! It is just that whenever I start a letter in my head I know how insipid I am going to look. When you think of all the time I am made to spend at ghastly school I ought to be more literate.

I am studying day and night now for the state heats of the Concerto Contest. (I shall perform here because, they say, I am residing in Victoria.) I am studying the Piano Concerto in E flat Major of Liszt, which I find more and more of a challenge! I have made some progress, Khrap thinks, though my left hand is still a little weak. O God I've got to be good! I wonder if I was a Roman

Catholic would that make it any easier? Or Christian Science? Unfortunately I am only me, and nothing or no one will ever change that.

I study so hard I seldom see my friends, of whom I have many by now in Melbourne. Sometimes I take time off to go to the house of my best friend Meredith Thurston. She is my age. Her mother died when she was six, and her father is a physiologist, very brilliant though great fun. Last Sunday Gerry took us to Davy's Bay. We sat on the sand licking ice-creams without our shoes, it was blissful. On her sixteenth birthday Gerry allowed Meredith to choose a dress at Foy and Gibson's, and because it was almost my birthday too he gave me the same opportunity. No expense spared! I chose the most fabulous white gown which I shall keep to wear (with alterations) on the platform at my famous "debut"!

Don't think I am not grateful enough to Gerry for his kindness, and any girl would be flattered, he is such a handsome man still, only going a bit round the middle, but I feel his gesture was more than anything charitable, he sees me in much the same position as Merry who has lost her mother, myself with a father who ran away.

Another if smaller reason why I must succeed in what I am doing—to be out of reach of charity!

Well, I shall see you this winter if all goes well, I know it will, in Sydney, because I shall win the State, I shall play in Sydney, I shall win the final, the Commonwealth!

Yours most sincerely
Katherine Volkov

Oh dear this looks as insipid as I knew it would, and you will think me of no account. I wonder why you intimidate me? Gerry Thurston doesn't, and he too is a brilliant man. Love and kisses and the best kiss of all.

Kathy.

The Quasi Adagio is still giving me trouble. I can't always bring it out clear enough, then at other times it becomes so very easily and naturally pure.

K.

He had reached the upper floor by this. He sat down on the edge of the bed, wetting his lips; they had dried right out. He was palpitating. The stairs combined with the letter had made his heart his blood chug. A breeze, clattering through the old lopsided blind, to some extent helped reconstitute the bits of him which had come unstuck.

Presently he reached for paper and let his hand loose. It was a vague but soothing preamble, not yet himself really, but his hand. till his head began to follow. The line flowed out of his head, down through the arteries, through his fingers. He began drawing at last.

Rhoda must have come in and noticed his hat; she called up. "Are you there, Hurtle? Are you all right?" She didn't mention Kathy's letter: must have come while she was out; he was glad it was his secret.

"Hurtle?"

He got up, suddenly enraged; he stamped out on the landing, and would have shouted if his throat hadn't been so dry: "For God's sake, can't you leave me alone?" He found himself baring his teeth.

Rhoda shouted back: "All right! Keep your hair on! I only wondered."

"Why the hell can't you leave me alone?" he rattled huskily back.

"I wondered whether you'd had a stroke. That's all. That's what Mrs Volkov had, if we'd care to admit it. Only a very little one. She says God was kind."

If she hadn't slammed the kitchen door Rhoda would have heard him laugh: before he went back to his drawing. Mrs Volkov could bloody well have died of her stroke for all he cared. His hand had to reconnect with his intention before they re-entered the maze together; but it came about with merciful ease. He was again drawing purposefully. He visualized Katherine Volkov carried away by the strong swirl of music, over her mother's dead body.

Out of these drawings he finally painted "The Lopsided Blind" and "Spiral." He worked on them alternately because each originated in Kathy's letter, and though different in their moral climate and aesthetic treatment, they also complemented each other. In the painting of the looped, tatty old venetian, the girl's face was visible in the corner the blind revealed. Her incised shells of eyes contained kernels of vision not yet germinated. Most of the body, except for the rather square hands, was cut off at the windowsill. The girl's face was as rapacious and tragic as a young sun-blinded eagle sensing nourishment in an interplay of colour it couldn't see. He aimed his barrage at this one corner not obscured by the dusty blind or oppressed by the sun-blistered sash.

The second painting appeared less clearly defined, though on second thought, and examination, the architecture of the spiral was unequivocal. The girl-figure was not at the mercy of this whirlwind of music or fatality. Her feet were firmly placed; the ambiguous, half-veiled expression of the face ultimately revealed conscious will, whether also sensibility he bitterly wondered during a series of wet afternoons, remembering Kathy as a vulgar little schoolgirl-tart. How her mac would have smelled of rubber; her sodden plait, with its stringy pink ribbon, would have tasted of rain.

But again, on the first day of sun and redemption, he saw the painting as originally conceived, or as close as you can ever get. If he had never achieved what he was aiming at, he strewed such bloody gobbets of himself along the way, those similarly involved had recognized their own half-realized intentions; the ignorant gushers and sceptics didn't matter.

This winter it was Rhoda who went down with pneumonia. Lying in the iron cot, she looked not unlike the little pink-haired girl who had tried to smother him in a disgusting kiss smelling of talcum powder and hot flannel. His resistance then made him genuinely humble now.

"Rhoda—what can I do for you?"

"Nothing." She didn't even open her eyes.

Anything positive that had ever existed between them was entombed in one word and her small, suddenly marble features.

He couldn't stop looking at her.

Out of his memories of May Noble he cooked dishes for her: fish, of the most delicate, transparent flesh, with oysters nestling round the fillets; breasts of chicken suave with cream and mushrooms. Once he bought a bunch of violets and laid them on the tray, on the corner of an admittedly grey cloth.

But Rhoda said: "Can't you leave me alone? Food nauseates me. It's the drugs that Doctor prescribes, I suppose," always speaking with her eyes closed; at least it eased out her frown.

"Shall I fetch another doctor?"

"No." The oracle began to stir. "What use is a doctor? Everything depends on yourself. Didn't you know?"

His humility was wearing thin. "What about Mrs Volkov? And God's kindness? Which let her off with a *little* stroke!" He allowed himself to indulge in a laugh.

Rhoda snorted through her marble nostrils. "Mrs Volkov is a very simple woman—though she did have Kathy. Parents and children, I think, are only accidentally related."

After that he took the tray out. He took the violets and threw them into the garbage bin.

Rhoda would cough: sometimes her phlegm was marked with threads of blood.

Suspecting he had noticed, she said: "I shall be up in a fortnight." She opened her eyes. "To hear Kathy play in the final at the Town Hall."

"But we don't know that she'll reach the final."

"Oh, but you don't keep up! You're always painting. She won her state. I heard it on my little transistor. She played the Liszt—exquisitely." Rhoda spoke with Maman's voice, apparently unaware of it, and closed her eyes again.

She was up before the fortnight, feeling her way about in a pair of quilted slippers, and coughing drier. Not long after, although the weather was viciously inclined, she started, more slowly, dragging the go-cart down the closer streets, loaded with offal for neglected cats. In a mackintosh cape she looked like a tent hastily erected in wet and darkness.

One evening he saw an opportunity. "Surely Kathy's concert will be an occasion to try out the coat? After an illness, too. In winter."

Rhoda began slinging the dishes around. "If it will give you any satisfaction, Hurtle, to watch other people recognize your generosity."

He must get it out quick, but his tongue was swollen. "Not at all. I shan't be there."

"Not at Kathy's concert?"

He shook his head. "Not to wallow in Liszt. And Tchaikovsky. And Rachmaninov. By a pack of students. For another pack."

"I'm not surprised, Hurtle. You were always an intellectual snob. *I* can't help loving *all* lovely music."

She was too virtuous to argue with.

Instead he nursed his hatred of Kathy Volkov for her failure to tell him of her success, while bitterly accusing his own self-absorbed nature which prevented him reading newspapers. He would make sure not to miss the announcement of the final, so that he could study Rhoda's, probably secret, preparations for the night: to catch her not wearing the fur coat, or better still, wearing it. The hurt he would inflict on himself by not watching Katherine Volkov walk out across the platform, raked by applause from students, relatives, and elderly men, was not his least luxurious thought.

So he read the *Herald*, sometimes twice, in case his mind, diverted by some other detail, related to his own work, for instance, had missed half-a-dozen lines crammed slyly into a corner.

Actually he needn't have bothered: it was enough to watch Rhoda, who looked more and more as though on the point of joining a Church. She grew silenter, her eyes larger; her normally delicate features were still further refined by a transparency and tautening of the skin, till she was all eyes, forehead, obsessed mouth. What if Rhoda, too, were in love with Kathy? He started by thinking of them practising some unvisualized but diabolical perversion, though it tortured him worse to suspect Kathy and Rhoda of meeting on a spiritual level he should never have considered either of them able to attain.

Finally, there were all the signs of physical preparation: wardrobe doors opening and closing; handles rattling; smells of naphthalene and face powder; unexplained sorties at unorthodox hours.

He lost control of himself on hearing her arrive back late for cats yet again. "Great shivoos, I expect, in the Cutbush *salong* to celebrate the return of their star."

"I don't believe either Cutbush has set eyes on Kathy since her return. In fact, her own mother hardly sees her: she's so busy preparing for her concert. Mr Khrapovitsky, who came up from Melbourne to be with her, has rented a studio so that she can work under the best possible conditions."

While Kathy rehearsed for her concert, Rhoda was preparing for the night's ritual of purple flesh. After taking off her coat and menacing her hair she began tuning up the knife which time had almost sharpened away.

"Oh dear, how late I am!" she complained in her most fretful, little-girl's voice. "If you only knew what goes on!" As though he didn't know too well. "You imagine parties, when it's sheer drudging. And nerves. Not only Kathy, poor Mrs Volkov wonders whether she'll be able to face the night. That's why I went this afternoon. To sit with her."

Rhoda's voice kept slithering along the steel with which she was sharpening her scimitar.

"There was one party," she admitted, "if you could call it that."
This was where he sat forward, if not literally.

"Because it wasn't prearranged. Mrs Cutbush was keeping Mrs Volkov company. When Kathy came in from a session with Khrapovitsky. It was already fairly late, and I personally would have preferred to come home to bed. But poor Mrs Volkov made a few dropped scones. Mrs Volkov is famous for her dropped scones. And Kathy, who was tired, revived. That's how the party began."

"All on a few dropped scones."

"Well—Mrs Volkov never touches alcohol. And Kathy is still only a child. But Mrs Cutbush had very kindly brought along a bottle of gin, knowing there might be callers in the next few days. Mrs Cutbush has had experience in directions where Mrs Volkov has never been."

"And were there any callers? To help Mother Cutbush mop up the gin?"

"Well—there was Mr Khrapovitsky, naturally: he's Kathy's teacher, and it's unpleasant for a young girl to walk back alone through the streets at night. And there was that Shuard—the music critic."

"Not prearranged?"

"I think they thought," Rhoda paused, "it might be politic. I heard Khrapovitsky explaining to Mrs Volkov that personal contact is all important."

She was cutting into the meat by now.

"Don't tell me Cutbush wasn't there!"

"No. I think he's lost interest. He's not what you'd call musical. The only other person was Kathy's boy friend Clif—he spells it with one 'f', so Kathy told me."

"What do you mean by 'boy friend'?"

"Frankly, I don't know. But that's the term for it." She was cutting the meat into long ribbons, then across, to make careful squares. "Anyway, Clif is no longer a boy. He's a very brilliant physiologist, they say."

"What—another one?"

Rhoda wasn't listening: she was too busy with the horseflesh, or what she had dreamed, or was thinking out. "Beautiful and gifted women—Kathy is gifted, and will certainly be beautiful—dazzle men as the moon—the planets dazzle them. That isn't to say their men mean much more to them than the men on earth do to the stars they're goggling at. Why should they? Somebody like Kathy has a destiny—a path you don't expect her to diverge from. You can't expect more than their art from artists. If you did, you might forget about the art, and die of shame for what they've shown you of mankind."

Rhoda was so deep in concentration, or trance, he was able to escape into the yard. He couldn't have gone upstairs to the paintings from which she had divorced him. Outside, the night was a tangle of vines and stars. Cold, too: it made the water in him swell. After warding off a cat innocent enough to believe it might merge its entity with his, he began to piss on what he recognized, from the orchestration, as the heap of empty tins.

On the night of the concert he sat waiting in the kitchen through which she would pass, as it was easier to reach the bus via Chubb's Lane. He began his watch unnecessarily early, it might have seemed, but that way there would be no chance of her eluding him. Rhoda would be too afraid she might miss even a competitor in whom she had no interest; she would start far earlier than she need. He could sense from a smell of gunpowder in the air that the occasion as a whole was the experience of her life. Murders were not out of the question, or suicides, on the night of Rhoda's Kathy's triumph.

So he sat and waited.

When she didn't come, but continued dropping hairbrushes, shoes, scratching at the handles of her chest of drawers, he began to call raucously: "Rhoda? You'll be late! Don't you realize? Late! Late!" His voice bounced back.

His nerves were in specially fine tune. He farted once. He rattled the keys and money in his pockets as he disliked hearing others do. And nearly missed Rhoda.

Either because it was a formal occasion, or because she had decided to avoid him, she was going out through the front door. He hadn't heard her leave her room or cross the living-room carpet, and only jumped up when she almost brought down the hatstand in the hall.

He ran, bursting in to catch her, calling, his voice teetering as the bamboo hatstand righted itself: "Weren't you going to say goodbye?" Much too loud.

She, on the other hand, spoke too softly. "I didn't want to distress you by letting you see me leave for the concert." He couldn't tell whether she had meant it.

She had frizzed up her hair into the shape of an urn, choked at the neck by what looked like a gold ribbon off a chocolate box. She had powdered herself almost to death; only the patches of dry rouge on the cheekbones and the unhealed scar of a mouth reminded too vividly of life. She was wearing the squirrel coat, too, the collar buttoned up to her gills. Was she straining after extra height?

Then he remembered he was carrying the bunch of violets. As on the occasion during her illness, when he had bought her one and laid it on the tray of rejected food, he was now offering the bunch of Parma violets; nor had he forgotten the pin.

Rhoda clawed at them, mumbling, and pinned them clumsily to her collar: they made her look more livid.

She had achieved none of the height she had aspired to, and for a moment he feared that, in wanting to express herself in some way, she might be going to kiss his hand. He was almost crying for them. Whatever else they had botched in life, they might have had this child whom they both loved, and who was probably suffering somewhere in a crumpled, department-store dress, crouching over a silent keyboard.

Rhoda said: "You should make yourself a cup of cocoa."

"*Cocoa!* I'll be all right—listening on the wireless, in the studio. Oh God, yes! None of the coughing and the faces."

She lowered her head and began sidling out, as though departure through the front door made this obligatory. Again their love for Kathy might have melted him if he hadn't remembered that Kathy and Rhoda were probably conspiring to finish him off.

So he called: "Enjoy yourself!" and laughed.

He thought he heard Rhoda laughing back, but the noise made by the flap on the letter-box prevented him knowing for certain.

That good tweed overcoat (English) which never wore out, only discoloured, had holes in the corners of the pocket linings through which he used to stick his thumbs. Tonight the holes tore worse; he not only felt, he could hear them tear as he raced along Chubb's Lane, up Dolgelly, up Jones, up Lavernock Streets. Impossible at this hour to cajole a taxi anywhere inside the labyrinth.

So, on reaching the bright lights, he hung himself out breathless from the kerb, to command or seduce by what remained of his authority and "charm."

He arrived slamming and scrambling, not late, but close enough to it. He hadn't reserved a seat: they found him one almost too easily. As he flopped, the victim of his clothes, he was at once engulfed: the strings were tuning, knuckles tightening knuckles; the woodwind croaked mustily. He wouldn't look yet, but it was most unlikely that Rhoda and her claque would be breathing down his streaming neck.

They began to wade through the Paganini-Rachmaninovs, Tchaikovsky and Tchaikovsky. A girl in what her mother would have described as "sea green" chiffon wafted daringly into "Ocean Thou Mighty Monster." A young man, the paler for his black, sank his teeth in Boris and couldn't get them out again, chin stuck alarmingly, your own chin straining with his; because by now every agony was yours.

While the basso bowed his frustrated head under the massive, the decent-hearted applause, an elderly lady sitting at a tangent shouted at her companion: "That is Mr Hurtle Duffield. The one in the check coat. I can recognize him from his photos in the papers."

The friend looked as though she had been taken in: through the subsiding applause he could hear her sucking her teeth. "He's a different colour to what I would 'uv expected. And sort of—unsuccessful-looking."

He looked away.

He realized the interval had come. He hadn't bought a programme, not from stinginess, but because he hadn't wanted to know too much: to know when Katherine Volkov could be expected to walk through the sombre field of musicians might have become too acute a torment. And now that danger zone, the interval, in which Rhoda might parade herself, cynically, accusingly, flanked no doubt by members of the Volkov-Cutbush set. At least in the motley of students, many of them still little girls and in fancy dress, she wouldn't look such a glaring exotic. He was the freak: he couldn't narrow himself in his chair to hide enough of his freakishness.

His bladder was forcing him out. He stood peeing in the row of anonymous men: the relief of a good fart, and the anonymity of it.

"Didn't know you were interested in music, Duffield."

458

A shorter, pursier, superficially younger, too glossy, aggressively dapper male.

"Shuard," Shuard explained.

Possibly for ethical reasons, the critic seemed determined to make no further reference to music. They talked about their friend Mrs Davenport; neither of them had seen her for years, but as they depended on her now, she shone like lacquer in their conversation; memory treated her with an exaggerated kindness.

After getting down from the step which edged the urinal, Shuard began to do up his flies, cocking a leg in the manner favoured by short, pursy men: his thighs, not to mention what lolled between them, revealed themselves to the imagination the more obscenely for being clothed.

Going out the frosted door, Shuard pulled at his companion's arm, dragging his shoulder to a lower level, before whispering: "What price the little Volkov?"

The throaty intimacy of it might have gummed them together for-ever if the critic hadn't started to amble off still easing his fat crutch. Spiritually Shuard belonged to the age of private supper rooms and button boots.

In the second half, renewed orgies of the Paganini-Rachmani-novs: the hired dinner jackets, the dream-dresses run up by Mother's love and the old treadle-it-yourself, embraced their sticky ecstasies.

Snooze a little.

Then something pushed him; it was not a hand: it was Katherine Volkov walking half drugged, half horrified, as he had never seen her, through the field of black-and-white musicians, the menacing crop of their instruments ready to be harvested by anyone who dared pretend to sufficient skill.

He wanted to break his nightmare by calling out: "No, Kathy—don't—wait—I'll save you!" though what had he to offer in-stead?

She came on. At one point she was forced to turn sideways, be-cause the path was too narrow and her dress too wide. (The El-derly Physiologist's birthday present?) A loutish Second Violin leered up out of meaty lips. (Was the Second Physiologist, Clif One-f, leering also, more thinly because assuaged, somewhere in the audience?)

Kathy continued advancing because, it seemed, she couldn't think of an alternative. Anyway, by now her fate wouldn't have let her escape. He was brought so close to her he might have seen the golden down along her long strong arms and the line of her jaw: but knew it by heart. He knew the long legs propping inside the sculpture of the frozen dress.

He closed his eyes for a second.

When he opened them she had sat down and was having the conventional trouble with the stool: she and the mahogany knobs she was twisting contended against each other. She won, though. She was breathing rather too fast. She sat clasping her hands, it could have been in not-too-hopeful prayer. Mrs Volkov, recovered from the stroke which had barely stroked her, only blurred her speech, must have moulded the golden plait into the golden crown. He could see where some of the more tender hairs at the nape of the neck were still resisting.

Suddenly Katherine Volkov bowed her head. Although she had closed her eyes, it was she, not the vegetable conductor, who was in control. Because she willed it, from her quivering shoulders to the toe of her arrogant shoe, they were carried away on the wave of violins. And Katherine Volkov was parting the music with her long strong arms. Her entranced eyes were at times as fixed as electric light-bulbs, as she mounted, and mounted, the flood, at times closed, while she flowed with the stream of overscented dreamed-up music: or curled, an archetypal figure he could no longer recognize, in the troughs between certain waves.

Once she dashed her hand against her skirt, with impatience, it seemed, then clawed at the thigh beneath the tulle. Some of the elderly-relative members of the audience glanced at one another: they could have been shocked by too unrestrained a display of "artistic temperament" in a hitherto normal, young Australian girl.

Others sat, moist-eyed, to watch this creature they could feel drawing away from them. Himself dry: never drier. He was grinding from buttock to razor-edged buttock. As he ground his teeth together he wondered whether anybody could hear.

Katherine Volkov had raised her head to compete with the "pure" bits of the Quasi Adagio. Her wobbling chin reminded him of that weakness in her left hand. Poor little Kathy: tears almost dropping from the blue eyes, for the lovely music, for the orgasm she can't have experienced with the elderly Melbourne physiologist, the music critic Shuard, the grocer-perv Cutbush, or Clif One-f. (He wasn't going to include Himself.)

After what seemed like several hours of jealousy, remorse, suppliant love, hectic passion, to say nothing of coughing, programme dropping, and a halitosis to the left, he watched Katherine Volkov emerge, her serene shoulders, the majestic mother-plaited crown, rising above a vulgar situation. She gave one last shudder: of thankfulness. She had arrived in more than safety: she was received into the world of light. Realization nearly jerked her head off her neck.

They were all clapping and clap clapping vindicated fulfilled drenched by their part in this voyage to Cythera at the end of which they had positively laid eyes on the goddess.

Yet Katharine Volkov might eventually disappoint. Although she was showing them the palms of her hands, and her smile conveyed joy, youth, health, all of which they approved, her attitude was hardly grateful enough. While she was going through the repertoire of gestures the audience expected and wanted, she was holding something back from them: he could tell she had discovered in herself that extra sense which is the source of all creative strength. Anyone unable to recognize nobility might have condemned her as proud, as she stood bowing in her department-store dress and disintegrating hair-do. When the crown actually fell, she caught the plait, easily, laughingly—hadn't she survived ordeal by music?— and casually waved her hair at them while turning to leave the platform.

Still too drunk to feel consciously displeased at anything about her, the audience roared.

He got up and started clambering out, past stubborn knees, trailing his overcoat across the laps of resentful strangers. Here and there he trod on the spongy insteps of seemingly dropsical women, who didn't scream, but moaned in harmony with his own painfully throbbing silence.

What mattered was to escape the trauma of Kathy's performance, and more particularly this new Kathy, herself escaping in the direction she had chosen.

Once he thought he caught sight of Rhoda peering from under powdered lids.

Because he had to forestall Rhoda he continued trampling pushing through the human walls obstructing him. Night and the neon-lit streets promised relief, until he found that every taxi had flitted from them. In the end he walked over half the way home, his anxiety subsiding as he imagined Rhoda at sea in worse difficulties: keeping her nose above the tide, rejected by already overloaded buses. He would be sitting high and dry at Flint Street long before she could possibly make it.

He was crossing the hall when she sprang out of her room at him: each might have been surprising a thief.

"Why—Hurtle—how very unexpected!"

"I took a stroll." As he exhaled he explained that he had felt the need for air.

"Walking at night can be agreeable, if one is in a happy frame of mind."

She had had time to change into the old grey gown, and a flannel nightie gathered at the neck like a Christmas cracker. She was holding a comb which had belonged to Maman, and as the tension eased she resumed combing at the dusty-looking wisps of her hair, the powder and rouge gone from her cheeks, absorbed, no doubt, by the evening's emotions.

"Did you enjoy your concert?" he asked.

She closed her eyes and composed her mouth in a girlish smirk. "It was altogether divine."

It was a word he had never heard her use: probably picked it up from Kathy.

Rhoda opened her eyes; looking at him with the utmost seriousness, she dared him to contradict her. "Kathy played magnificently, as of course you'll know from listening to the wireless."

He grunted, taking off his coat, while Rhoda continued combing her hair: if she wasn't careful there wouldn't be any of it left.

Irritated by the action of the comb, the dull hair, and the unexpected turn of events, he sharpened his tongue on her. "I'm surprised you got back so early—perhaps by levitation."

"Mr Cutbush very kindly gave me a lift each way in their car— Mrs Volkov and myself."

"And Kathy? And Khrapovitsky? And Shuard? And Clifff? All squeezed in, thigh to thigh! Kathy"—he laughed—"sitting in somebody's fat lap?"

She ignored the tone of this. "What the young people do is their own business. Mr Shuard, I believe, went off to write his review."

It was time he turned round: he had been arranging his coat far too long on the bamboo stand. Because the knobs were too large, he couldn't hang the coat by its loop but had to drape it: which gave the back an obvious hump.

"And what were the results?" He wheezed it at her: when he almost never wheezed.

"You mean to say you didn't listen in for the results?" Rhoda's scorn rose between them; she looked as though she might be going to hit him with Maman's old ivory comb. "They always announce the results on the wireless."

"No. I'd gone out." He felt so genuinely tired he no longer expected his voice to convince; there was nothing he could do about it, though.

"It's extraordinary," she said, "what a self-centred man you are. Of course you have a right to be, but it's still extraordinary—on some occasions."

Although she was withdrawing, it was he who had been dismissed, not by his sister Rhoda whom he had engaged as a conscience, but by Maman; and again, as Rhoda reached the door, it was Maman with a vengeance, translated into terms of Rhoda through an inherited comb, smiling with discoloured, conspiratorial, at the same time vindictive teeth.

"What did you think of the young lady who sang the Weber? Didn't you find her dress a little *outré*? In the higher bits we were waiting for her to burst out." Comb poised, Rhoda was not only listening, she was also watching for his reply.

"No," he said. "It didn't worry me—the dress. In fact, I scarcely noticed."

He was too tired: or too fascinated by that comb; he couldn't make the effort to disguise his blunder. He saw how he might paint the comb, with the drift of dead hair in its teeth: he was already groping his way towards placing it as a formal link between their present and their past.

Rhoda's eyes, surprisingly, filled with a brilliant tenderness. "You're fagged out. You should take a hot bath, Hurtle. Make yourself a cup of cocoa." He was relieved she was compassionate enough not to offer to make the stuff for him.

She had gone, but called back a warning: "That thing—the geyser —will blow up in your face one day if you don't have something done about it."

He couldn't care: the geyser was one of the minor volcanoes in his life.

Next morning he didn't go down, though Rhoda, he sensed, was anxious that he should.

"No," he called in answer to her question.

"Would you at least like the paper?"

No, he wouldn't: whether Kathy had won or not. That she *had* won he knew; Rhoda's voice would otherwise have conveyed failure. As far as he was concerned, Kathy's success had exorcised her.

The whole morning he could feel Rhoda brooding over his indifference, except when she was gone with her cart to fetch the evening's supply of horse. About lunchtime he went down to her. He felt delightfully comfortably sloppy in his loose old gown. And cocky. How dreadfully boyish old men could become; but he understood what made them so: it was the unimportant victories.

Rhoda had arranged the still apparently untouched morning paper like an antimacassar over the back of his chair.

He clapped his hands together in jolly explosion and asked: "When does the little Volkov propose to leave us?" So hearty pompous: he could see himself as he acted it.

Rhoda hesitated: she was wearing the apron which normally proclaimed her authority, establishing her as cook, as opposed to mere mistress of the house. "You did know, then—that Kathy won."

Squeezing off a corner of cheese, he ignored the accusation. "What are her plans? Has she decided where to study?"

Rhoda's decision to abandon subterfuge had the effect of a blind going up too quickly. "Mr Khrapovitsky favours Vienna." A name was mentioned, which conveyed nothing. "She's leaving in the spring —*our* spring."

"Our spring" in Maman's accent gave Kathy's departure a high glaze.

"Good luck to her," he said.

He could feel the cheese already turning his stomach sour, and belched in an attempt to rid himself of some of his gloom. Rhoda didn't hear: she had her own loss to bear. She brought him a slice of fried bread, left over from breakfast, with a limp rasher of bacon on it: he pushed away the lot.

If the image of the yellow comb which had flared up in his imagination died away almost at once, it was perhaps something to do with his being physically run down, or mentally depressed, or because his work as a painter was finished: not that he hadn't plenty still to say; he'd only lost the desire to say it. He wondered whom he had been addressing all these years. No artist can endure devoted misinterpretation indefinitely, any more than he can survive in a vacuum of public contempt; or was he the self-centred monster Rhoda accused him of being? God knew, he had multiplied, if not through his loins; he was no frivolous masturbator tossing his seed onto wasteland. He had sympathized with the passionate illusions of several women, and could hardly be held responsible for their impulse to destroy themselves through what they misunderstood as love; until finally: had he himself been destroyed by a little egotistical girl whom he valued above his vocation? On an occasion of desultory doodling, the cowled phallus wore Kathy's face. In the end he bought a bottle of mixed vitamins from the chemist to save the fuss of consulting doctors.

"Hurtle," Rhoda began, "I'm going to ask a favour of you. Kathy Volkov is leaving for Vienna in under a fortnight. She would like to pay you a visit, but is too shy to suggest it."

Was the spring already upon them? From Rhoda's first intimations he had visualized it as an abstraction in distance, not their actual turbulent fortnight of searing westerlies and brown blossom.

"Kathy shy? I hadn't noticed it in the past."

"She's growing up now."

"I should have said she sprang out of her mother fully grown."

"You're so brutal at times. And what you have against Kathy I'll never understand. Not her loving nature, surely? Her beauty? Her brilliance? I know parents sometimes grow to resent their children if they're in any way transcendent—as much as if they were ugly or stunted. What so many of them really look for is a healthy, normal, biddable child who will flatter their complacency like a glass. But Kathy will never be that. And you, Hurtle, are not a parent."

He was hardly in a position to modify her statement, and having made it, Rhoda was preparing to leave him; when she remembered: "What am I to tell her?"

He felt limp; he mumbled, rubber-tongued: "Kathy will come if and when she wants."

465

When she didn't materialize, his subservience forced him to ask: "What did you tell her?"

"Nothing. You gave me nothing to tell."

He hated Rhoda, the reflection of his complacency: when Rhoda, the reality, not Katherine Volkov, the figment, was what he had been given to love. He did, of course, love her, because she was his sister: or he would learn to, under the dictatorship of the past.

He must, at least, inquire: "When is it Kathy leaves?"

Rhoda answered: "The day after tomorrow," and went on arranging a litter of kittens on the teats of a recumbent mother. She might have been screwing them on, but it appeared logical, the way she did it.

It was a Sunday morning, and he stood sizing a couple of canvases recently bought. The soothing servility of the occupation, the broad, effortless strokes, the colourlessness on colourlessness, was helping paint out his mind. He was enjoying himself in a purely negative way: which made it no less delectable, possibly less destructible. As he worked, the Sunday air was treating his skin with lanoline, distant bells lulling the less manageable emotions, one or two shavings of harmless cloud curled in a bland sky, the big snow-green breasts of a viburnum across the street nuzzled by the iron noses of a fence. He remembered seeing—was it "The Pretty Baa Lambs"? Was it the Tate? The Ashmolean? On a Sunday. Maman in white, for spring, and because she fancied herself in white. *By Ford Madox Brown*: he read it out. *No*, she corrected, *it's Patou*.

He was enjoying a laugh at his childish thoughts, drifting like cotton-woolly baa-lamb clouds, or inflating into green-tinted parasols of stationary guelder rose, when something started cutting in: a canned evangelical hymn, a thundering blur from several streets away—or actual, closer voices.

Perhaps from growing deaf, like Rhoda, he hadn't at first heard the voices, now an accompaniment to hers down in the kitchen. Rising above the distant hymn, they cut and grated, unpleasantly and unavoidably. He threw away his brush, but stooped to pick it up. His back. He trod size into the boards. Then he was revolving in desperation looking for a hiding place: though he had nothing to hide.

A door was thrown open below.

Rhoda must have stopped laughing the moment before: her voice was so clear and girlish. "Hurtle? Are you there, *dear?*" So unheard of: what was she planning to do to him? "Kathy Volkov has come. She would like to say good-bye. Not if you're busy. Kathy doesn't want to disturb you. She's flying tomorrow to Vienna." It might have been Murwillumbah by train. "*Hurtle?*" Rhoda angrier, less girlish.

He had to answer.

He called back, trying to keep his voice down in case it might sound unnatural. "Tell her to come up. If she wants."

In the meantime he had to occupy himself. He threw the sized canvases against the wall; one of them bounced off something else and showed a black streak across its surface.

Feet were ascending. Could it be Rhoda as well? To spoil his chances on a last, perhaps the very last, occasion. He listened for her wheezing, her little clicketing steps. Instead he heard an outbreak, followed by a quick suppression, of laughter. He failed to separate or to identify the footsteps, except that, as they approached, he realized a man was taking part in the visitation.

Although she didn't "want to disturb," Kathy strode in; the room was shaking. Nor was her appearance what he would have expected; but perhaps he was too old to keep pace with the evolution of appearances. She had let her hair flow free; or more probably, she had brushed it out to give it that electrified look. Though Rhoda had told him Kathy was growing up, she was dressed in a little girl's, an Alice-in-Wonderland style. Well, Kathy was cool and cryptic enough for Alice. Her shiftless shift, almost a pregnancy uniform, now that he came to think, ridiculed his memories of her body.

When this should have been a moment of intimate poignancy, its messages addressed only to him, he suspected he was half the purpose of her visit; in fact, the young man who followed her in became too obviously the other half, or worse: the sole reason for her coming.

Arching her eyebrows, lowering her chin, swallowing—which made a dimple come in spite of her apparently sterner intentions—Kathy casually announced: "I'd like you to meet my boy friend—Clif Harbord—Mr Duffield. Perhaps I ought to say Harbord's a doctor, but not the ordinary kind." Nervousness made her giggle.

She might have intended to create a situation jagged with vulgarity; or her jaws could have taken the wrong direction: they were so busy chewing. Out of loyalty to Dr Harbord?

For Clif, too, was gummed up. He was of the leaner, more sinewy type of male animal, with continuous eyebrows, his handshake an encounter with wire.

"An honour to meet you, Mr Duffield!"

Evidently Clif was one who felt the set forms of human intercourse would never let him down. When he had spoken, he put his hands on his hips, and stood breathing an invigorating air, as he looked around a famous room from under those straight black eyebrows.

"So this is it!"

Kathy, too, was looking, though not at the room. "Clif's interested to see the paintings. Anyway, that's what he says." At any moment she would have to bludgeon somebody; but which would it be? "Of course he doesn't understand *art*. He's a scientist." She glanced an instant at the painter, before her laughter, glugging upward through her throat, got into trouble with her gum; when she had sorted things out, she sighed juicily, and added: "A scientist who wants to understand."

"Lay off the scientists!" Clif complained; and the effort of getting it out, over his pellet of gum, made his lips look even juicer than Kathy's. "There's nothing so esoteric as it looks—or sounds. I understand music, don't I?"

"Okay," Kathy yelped, gulping on her gum. "Music's a science as well as an art. Don't you agree, Mr Duffield?"

Although she had hinted, by a glance, that he might be her ally, he was feeling too remote to reply.

Clif had dropped on the bed, where he lolled around, appreciating art. His approach was somewhat physical. He scratched his chest once or twice, and once grabbed at a handful of his flies. His lean shanks, above the socks, seemed pleased to advertise their bristles.

There was a moment when Clif and Kathy exchanged gum. They got the giggles as they mouthed it into each other, swallowing at the same time borrowed saliva and siphoned laughter. He didn't *see* their embrace, but sensed it from behind his back. The lean and hairy Clif charged Kathy with vitality: or so the scent and

468

violence of chewed gum conveyed; and straining of the rusty bed; and the ends of Kathy's frayed-out, electric hair.

At one point he was forced to turn. He stared so hard he would remember forever these two young human animals wordlessly involved: it was a matter of skin, claws, and the fascinated retina.

He stared so long, Clif looked at his wrist. "Ought to be going, Kathy—keep to the schedule. And Mr Duffield will 'uv had us." Not that he was prepared to consider Mr Duffield as a physical fact: he was concentrated between the shining hair on his own polished shinbone, and Kathy, who wasn't bothering.

Till she burst out loudly: "Okay—yes! We must have bored him by now." She stuck out her tongue, with it a veil of gum through which she sniggered: "We're so horribly *infantile!*"

At once she began pummelling her lover out of the room, denying him any opportunity to say good-bye, because, in her own case, she didn't want to expose herself to that.

So there was a scrimmage on the stairs, a dangerous creaking of matchstick banisters, before Kathy, surprisingly, returned.

She must have got rid of the gum, for her mouth was still and resolute. Her eyes had something of the explosive violence of splintering ice. Her electric hair was floating: if it hadn't been rooted in her scalp, it might have flown.

"You know, don't you, Mr—Hur—*Hurtle*—I didn't mean it to be like this." She bit on the words ballooning inside her blistering lips.

Having reached him, she slid her arms up under his, till the palms of her rigid hands were resting on his shoulder-blades, and he recognized the woman Rhoda had tried to tell him Kathy was becoming. At the same time she thrust herself up against and under him, till they fitted more perfectly than in any sexual holt. In fact, there appeared to be nothing sexual in Kathy's present motives; her eyes alone would have beaten off an attempt.

Instead, he realized, as the eyes swam closer, larger, he was merging with her in an empathy such as can only be acknowledged at the moment and discarded afterwards as an impossible illusion.

"Did you hear me play at the concert?" she asked with a moodiness, or diffidence, in a voice which suggested catarrh.

He confessed to being at the concert.

"I was awful—*awful!*" She rested her head against his cheek; but even though she had closed her eyes and dropped her defences, he knew he shouldn't offer a caress: collaborators can only be sceptical lovers.

"They gave you the prize." Now it was the way parents comfort little girls: when she wasn't one any longer.

"Khrapovitsky told me I was technically atrocious. He won't forgive me. I know it wasn't what I wanted—what I *should* have done —but felt it was what they expected. Otherwise, how could I have ever escaped—begun to live?" Kathy Volkov was still the little girl, trickling warm against his shoulder.

Then she opened her splintered eyes.

"That's all!" she shouted with such force it racked his shoulder-blades. "When I come back I'll play for you and show you!" Her conviction bit into his cheek with a fury of actual teeth; only they weren't lovers: they were the dedicated collaborators. "I'll play!"

Then the physical part of Kathy disentangled itself from their pact and he heard her going down the stairs.

Again an old man, he hoped he hadn't smelled musty to a young girl, who for her part had smelled too eager, and of chewing gum. From the window he watched her cross the yard, entwining an arm with one of Dr Harbord's: the two arms might have been wire; and in spite of Kathy's confidences, he would have liked to take a pair of pliers, and snip the arms off at the shoulder, and watch the blood spurting from the wire snakes after they had tinkled on the asphalt. His spirit was not yet strong enough to forgive the flesh.

When the gate was closed between them, and he could no longer see her, he went and twisted the wireless on, and an edifying music came out, because it was Sunday.

Rhoda didn't comment on Kathy's final departure, but he knew she had gone, from a photograph in a newspaper: of "Katherine Volkov the young Australian pianist leaving to further her studies in Vienna." The airport had worked disastrously on the Kathy he wished to remember. A gale along the tarmac had inflated her unbound hair till there was far too much of it tugging at its moorings around her face. This was peculiarly expressionless considering the grin she had put on for the cameras, or perhaps to hide her true feelings behind the glare from her smile and the contorted planes of her cheeks. She was carrying a souvenir koala and a presentation bunch of carnations from which a couple of ribbons were suspended. Attached to one of these was a fleshy (middle-aged) official of the ABC, practised in joviality and the appropriate gestures, while a tall, coarse-boned woman, who could only have been the Scot her mother, cautiously fingered the tail of the second ribbon, which they must have ordered her to hold. Mrs Volkov was cast in a hat and clothes which in combination with herself reminded of a work of iron sculpture. She might have looked a gloomy person if it hadn't been for the smile; or no, it wasn't a smile: it was the mark of the "little stroke" reported by Rhoda, which had ruffled Mrs Volkov's lips, casting these, too, in iron.

At least the Cutbush clique—with Shuard?—and of course Clif Harbord, had been thwarted at the gate, so that after the traveller had detached herself from the avuncular official and her mother, and entered the steel capsule waiting to fly her away, the purity of line, almost *his* creation, must have been restored to her face, under the influence of those allied states of mind: sleep, flight, and music.

He didn't hear from Kathy, but hadn't expected to; it was as though they were agreed that a further attempt at correspondence could only be as ineffectual as the others.

He grew accustomed to remember events not by works finished, but whether they had taken place before or after Kathy left. If he remembered other relationships in his life, considerable ones like Nance Lightfoot, for instance, or Hero Pavloussi, it was with irritation, shame, and disgust, that they should have fallen so far short of his masterpiece Katherine Volkov: a flawed masterpiece certainly, but one in which the artist most nearly conveyed his desires and faith, however frustrated and imperfect these might be.

Then there was also Rhoda; but Rhoda was scarcely a relationship, let alone a creation: his "sister" was a growth he had learned to live with.

Rhoda remarked: "I've often wondered, Hurtle, why you continue keeping me under the same roof. I'm willing to leave, you know. You only have to say the word. I realize I'm aesthetically offensive, and that my cats are squalid and smelly. So please tell me, won't you? Mrs Volkov is willing to have me back, any time I like, to keep her company. She's lonely now that Kathy has gone."

He was surprised to surprise a sweetness, even a temptation, in Rhoda's voice. Though her eyes were daring him, boring in, they had a beautiful lucidity he didn't always achieve in his painting.

"Why," he said, dry as toast, "why you should begin, at this stage, to imagine things, I don't know. This is your home, isn't it?"

"I don't want to appeal to your sense of duty, my dear."

Her rather prominent teeth were involved with the toast she had just burned under the gas-griller. (He really must get one of those pop-up electric contraptions.)

"Aren't we," he mumbled on the black toast, "what is left of a family?"

Rhoda smiled a faintly yellow smile. "I think you're an artist, aren't you?"

"But not the monster you'd like to make me out."

"What I meant was *sans famille*." Here was his brute-sister trying to prise out of his hands the painted toy he wanted to hang on to.

Rhoda went on masticating her toast. For some reason she was wearing on the collar of her everyday dress a cameo brooch which had been their mother's—no, it had belonged to Maman. The brooch made him more than ever determined not to submit to the operation Rhoda suggested.

He was relieved she didn't bring the matter up again.

In the years after Kathy left, he was persuaded to allow two exhibitions of his more recent paintings: one with the girls at the Tank Stream Galleries, the other at Loebel's marble palace. The exhibitions were decorously received, the paintings vulgarly snapped up. He wouldn't have told anyone details of the sales, only the press got hold of half the story.

In 1964 Hurtle Duffield refused a knighthood, partly because he wasn't the man they believed they were honouring, and partly because he wouldn't have dared confess to Rhoda that he had accepted the thing.

So they continued living and blundering and working and chopping up the purple horseflesh in Flint Street.

He decided that, before he died, he must paint a picture which would refute all controversies, even convert his sister's scepticism.

Rhoda said: "I think I'm beginning to understand your painting, Hurtle, after these last two exhibitions. The horrors are less horrible if you've created them yourself. Is that it?"

She was looking at him, waiting for him, then lowering her eyes because she had been taught discretion as a girl.

"No," he said, and it cannoned off the coarse white kitchen plate.

"I'm trying"—already he realized how stupid it would sound—"I'm *still* trying to arrive at the truth."

"Then perhaps I don't understand after all. The truth can look so dishonest."

"Exactly!" He ricocheted, when he should have shot her straight to the floor. "That's why we're at loggerheads." He was beating the stupid plate with his spoon. "It's not dishonest! It's not! If it were only a question of paint—but is it dishonest to pour out one's life-blood?"

He felt in himself a terrible void, which he identified at once with the absence of his daughter Kathy; yet, if she had been present, he knew he wouldn't necessarily be able to invoke her intuitive genius in his defence. More likely, the carnal, brutal, thoughtless (or calculating) Kathy would blow bubblegum in his face and confirm Rhoda's opinion of him.

Rhoda said: "Do you remember the tutor you had who committed suicide? And you painted it on the wall?"

"Whatever made you think of that?"

"I've often wondered about it. It was so bewildering at the time. I'd always seen Mr Shewcroft as unkempt and repulsive, but as soon as he's killed himself I began to think of him as handsome and brave, though Miss Gibbons tried to convince me his suicide was a dishonest act. But whatever made you do something so horrible and unnecessary as that painting?"

"I was only a child of course, but I think I was trying to find some formal order behind a moment of chaos and unreason. Otherwise it would have been too horrible and terrifying."

"Don't tell me you're a mystic! At least I can honestly say I believe in nothing. I need never be afraid."

"Of what?"

"That the conjuring trick won't come off. That my 'god' may let me down."

He found himself crushing the empty shell of the egg he had just eaten.

"I really do pity you, my dear," Rhoda pursued, "if you should believe in a 'god.' Whatever I suffered in my childhood and youth from being ugly and deformed, at least it gave me this other strength: to recognize the order, and peace and beauty in nothingness."

"I believe," he said, "in art." He would have liked to elaborate, but was only strong enough to add: "I have my painting."

"Your painting. And yourself. But those, too, are 'gods' which could fail you."

This, perhaps the worst truth of all, he had never been able to face except in theory. Had he brought Rhoda into his house to help him to?

"Ah yes—failing powers!" He laughed. "I hope I may be struck blind." He jibbed at using the word "dead."

Rhoda laughed, too. "We shall be a fine pair!"

In the silence which followed he scented a dishonest terror in her. As for himself: he felt curiously calmed by Rhoda's weakness. If critical opinion ever decided before his death that he was worthless as a painter, he might discover in his fingertips some unsuspected gift for expressing himself; he might even calm Rhoda's fears.

He must watch himself, however. He entered a phase of attrition by apprehension, as a result of which his cunning hand was forced to increased displays of virtuosity. Perhaps Rhoda didn't notice. Certainly none of the buyers did. Flattery flowed as never before. Americans would pay grotesque sums for paintings he sometimes secretly admitted to be amongst his worst.

On one occasion Rhoda remarked, after a painting had been crated up: "That was one I couldn't believe in, Hurtle."

"I'm surprised you believe in any of my paintings. Doesn't it go against your 'faith'? Undermine the strength you were trying to explain to me recently?" As he went upstairs he hoped his reply had been savage enough.

Some of his paintings and drawings of this period would not be seen in his lifetime unless dragged into the open by force. Certainly Rhoda would never see them. They were the fruit of his actual life, as opposed to the one in which he painted pictures for Americans to buy, and where the dealers jollied him along. His actual life, or secret work, was magnificent, if terrifying. It was lived almost exclusively at night while Rhoda was lying in her salvaged cot. As he roamed through the overflowing house the flora and fauna of his past were released, sometimes also the suppurating flesh and green-tinged offal. He appropriated all of it: the corpses with the goddesses, pressed flowers and furry, wet-nosed animals, not least the glove which fitted tightest and neatest, of smoothest kid.

The landings creaked. Once during a storm he heard an urn fall from a parapet. Only after years he was getting to know the house, by its smooth grain as well as its splinters: not forgetting the crash of its disintegrating ornamental urns. If only he could have reached the derelict conservatory; but Rhoda always lay between, turning in her iron cot. So he never succeeded wholly in reliving the poetry Katherine Volkov had danced for him, and which they alone knew how to interpret.

He would return upstairs: to draw; sometimes to paint, because the artificial light furthered his real illusions. Sometimes he would wake up in the crisscrossed yellow morning, and find on the floor beside his bed drawings on which his mind wouldn't comment. There was one drawing in which all the women he had ever loved were joined by umbilical cords to the navel of the same enormous child. One cord, which had withered apart, shuddered like lightning where the break occurred; yet it was the broken cord which seemed to be charging the great tumorous, sprawling child with infernal or miraculous life.

Though they were horrible and frightening, the secret drawings and occasional paintings of this period were what sustained his spirit; even when he couldn't always grasp the significance, he could bask in his own artistry: that monstrous child, for instance, with the broken umbilical cord. Superficially the cord was reminiscent of a dry string of bryony waving from an English hedge. It was only when he began to consider its deeper implications that his body would tingle painfully as though from an electric shock. Was he the child who still had to expect birth? And what of death? Sometimes he stood shivering as he waited on the river bank, until his little psychopomp appeared, dressed in the silver tunic, hair streaming with light and music. She would never approach closer than to show him she was beckoning; after which, he was content to follow.

By daylight he was still outwardly the cold-eyed elderly gentleman, known or anonymous, for whom other people—Rhoda excepted—put on their sickliest smiles. He no longer cared for functions in the drawing-rooms of predatory new-rich women, or the intellectual pillories, but liked to meander through familiar streets, nowadays exchanging a Victorian conformity of blistered brown for Sicilian splendours in cassata pink and pistachio green. He would potter up to the thoroughfare, with its piles of lentils and haricot beans, its second-hand vegetables wilting for the poor, and fish mummified for all those who weren't wise to it. The smell of the streets made him feel alive: warm pockets of female flesh; lamp-posts where dogs had pissed; fumes of buses going places.

He liked to take a bus himself, away from Rhoda, on missions of importance: insurance; or winter socks. In the big pneumatic buses, manners from the age of trams continued to reveal themselves: old men with raised veins on the backs of their hands still felt the need to apologize; elderly women would suddenly attempt to coquet, as though their beige or black might impress itself on minds soaked in garishness.

That winter, on a morning when he was riding down to the Quay, reducing his ticket to crumbs in a somewhat small-beer fit of *joie de vivre* while mopping up his fellow passengers with his blotting-paper stare, he noticed a person across from him in the corner, her head nodding, nodding, as she gazed out the window, at the street, or beyond it.

In a fairly empty bus he had chosen a gangway seat, not caring to rub pockets or knees with this gaunt woman, whose formal airs and iron hat he began to enjoy from a distance, while she nodded and smiled at the winter sunshine the other side of the window.

They were approaching Wentworth Avenue when he was sur-prised to see the woman turn, and hear her address him out of her intractable smile: "Excuse me, sir, but I recognize you—naturally—from the papers—and know about you besides—through our con-nections."

Here she coughed. She looked embarrassed, in spite of her mili-tant Scots; or perhaps the smile wasn't all that it ought to be: as though making excuses for it, she was holding her hand in front of her mouth.

He didn't help her, but waited: it was more important that she should declare herself in her true colours; and out of the essential grey and black it was Mrs Volkov who gradually emerged.

"My little gairl will be coming home this winter—this season—to perform with the symphony orchestras. It will be a great joy to her mother—and to all music lovers—though she'll only be with us a wee while on account of her engagements overseas." Her Scots had be-come as piercing as a dagger; then she licked her smile and said: "No doubt Miss Courtney will keep you posted."

Like hell she would.

The bus rolled, and rollicked them on, past some dying trees set in concrete.

"I wonder which works she's chosen?" he found himself asking his busboard acquaintance, or monolith-relative.

"I've no idea, I'm sure!" Mrs Volkov recoiled from this unexpected assault on her discretion. "It wouldn't occur to me to inquire. Kathy might jump on me. I've learned to mind my own business, Mr Duffield."

If only the mother had known how she intimidated him: it was as if she had caught him fucking with Kathy in the hall under Maman's buhl table. He only prayed Kathy wouldn't dish out the Liszt, that she would choose something worthy of their not-so-secret collaboration: the whole bus must be aware of that.

At Foy's, Mrs Volkov descended, still smiling her inevitable smile. Perhaps to uphold her views on discretion, she hadn't said good-bye; though what was the point in becoming further involved with someone whose deeper reactions would always be reported to her by their common informer?

He forgot why he had come to the city. He roamed instead around the Quay and up Lower George, without seeing the merchandise in the windows he was peering into. On a morning so obviously joyous he should have felt less depressed, looked less cadaverous. Everyone else had an air of bounced rubber. What would happen, he wondered, if he fell in the street and failed to bounce back into the vertical position of walking automata? If he continued lying on the pavement, how would those professionally charitable amateurs and trained ambulance men be able to identify him? (Remember for next time to write—no, to print, a card with name and address, to outwit unconsciousness.)

When he got in, Rhoda barely acknowledged his return: she went on shredding lettuce, shelling the bruise-coloured eggs for their lunch; but he could tell she sensed something had happened. She began humming in her slightly cracked, girl's voice a tune he couldn't identify, or not at first; then he woke up to the full viciousness of her behaviour: it was one of the juicier tunes from Liszt's First Piano Concerto.

He decided not to be drawn; nor would he depend on Rhoda for any of the information Mrs Volkov naïvely presumed she would pass on. This time he would read the papers.

Probably it was what Rhoda feared would happen. As they sat

eating the nasty salad, she passed the cruet without his asking. He ignored the cruet, in which the vinegar alone was kept replenished, and which must have started life on some boarding-house table or in a railway refreshment room. Each time she ate one of her own salads, Rhoda seemed to be doing penance for something: for the crinkled jade hearts, exquisitely perfumed with tarragon and lemon, unctuous with oil, which Maman liked to prepare herself, white hands formally poised, in an illumination of sapphires.

"What's the matter?" Rhoda mumbled, as he watched a ribbon of darkened lettuce suspended from her shoebuckle mouth.

That night he dreamed he was the centre of a strangely prearranged accident: he walked out into the street, as though obeying a signal, and lay down in front of one of the trams they had done away with. The brown tram galloped bucking and screaming towards him, bells ringing, sides encrusted with human heads. Additional evidence of prearrangement was provided by Rhoda: she was standing on the kerb, in her squirrel coat, waiting to step off when the tram wheels should tear into his legs.

It happened as planned: the blood gushed; yet he remained unfeeling, as though made of marzipan specially moulded for the occasion. His head began to sprout long-necked crimson flowers, if only the onlookers could have seen.

Kneeling beside him, Rhoda was saying: Mrs Cutbush—oh dear no, Mrs Volkov is giving a little party for Katherine her daughter after the concert in the Town Hall, and would like you to be of the company.

Rhoda was choosing words with particular care, and wearing rings Maman must have sold to be able to bribe Julian Boileau.

In the teeth of so much formality and splendour, all he could answer was: You've torn your good coat, Rhoda—your squirrel coat. You must do up the place with a safety pin. And what is this?

There was a kind of twisted string hanging out from where the coat opened in front.

That's unnecessary! Rhoda snapped. A sort of tie-string. I can't think why Mrs Grünblatt gave it to me. As for tearing, speak for yourself!

She was right. He was wearing a yellow, rubberized overall of the type worn by men who work with acid, or those who test fire extinguishers; how he had acquired it he couldn't remember, probably from one of the shop windows on Lower George. In any case, his travesty had been slashed to ribbons by the tram.

How can I go, Rhoda, in this?

It doesn't matter. Everybody will be recognizable.

What sort of a party?

A service. Mrs Cutbush has baked a batch of fairy cakes, and the celebrants will masturbate in turn on the corpse.

But whose corpse?

The corpse of Katherine Volkov, who escaped in time, before any of us had possessed her.

Are you joking, Rhoda?

But perhaps she wasn't. She was too serious for that: white acrylic tears were squeezing out of her rat's eyes, down her withered cheeks, painting them with a beauty he hadn't noticed before, though of the stalactite order.

He tried unsuccessfully to put out his hand. What are we doing here? he asked.

It is not yet to know, she mumbled through the mouth of Mrs Volkov; then, painfully making the effort to correct her bungled speech: Not not possibly.

His inability to put out a hand, and increasing absence of mind in Rhoda, trussed and knotted him so tightly it put an end to this DREAM.

"What on earth is the matter with you? Are you sick?" She was screeching up at him, through the sallow daylight, from the hall.

"Oh no, dear, a dream! Oh dear!" he mumbled coughing laughing spluttering back.

"What?" From deep down in the house she was laughing too, while at the same time angry. "I thought you were sick. I never heard such a rumpus."

"A dream!"

Because it was Rhoda she didn't ask about the dream: she closed the kitchen door, and soon after he smelled the smell of burning fat.

He began to read the papers, watching for an announcement of the Volkov concert. In the meantime dealers were bringing him clients anxious to buy his paintings; but he seldom opened to them. He would look down on the crowns of their heads, but couldn't make the effort to go downstairs and let them in. After a while the heads would retreat. The dealers would send him letters which he recognized by instinct, and didn't read because of the polite anger they must contain.

Then one evening Rhoda remarked: "Mrs Volkov has given me a couple of complimentary tickets for the concert on Wednesday night. One is for myself, the other, she insists, is for you. She says she met you on a bus. I told her I thought you disliked listening to music in public, and in any case you probably wouldn't fancy sitting with me."

"But the concert—has She already arrived?"

In the state of shock and alarm in which Rhoda's announcement left him, he couldn't bring himself to use the Name. He would feel less vulnerable if She remained an abstraction.

"It's all over the papers—which you never bother to read. Didn't you at least see the photo taken at the party, with Lady ffolliott Morgan helping Her cut the cake?" Nor could Rhoda bear to use the Name.

He shook his head, like the old shaven goat he must look.

"It was a party given by the Committee in honour of Her arrival. Why a cake, I can't think. As if it were a wedding—or a birthday. Her birthday's in summer, I seem to remember. I remember Mrs Volkov telling me she'd turned twenty-five."

He had never stood so close to death. If he could face this, surely then, he might look at the press photograph?

"Where is it?" he asked. "The paper? I'd like to see."

Rhoda was watching him. "I'm afraid you can't. I threw it out with the potato peelings. At least, I'm pretty sure I did."

He was pretty sure that, if he looked when she went out, he would find a cutting under Rhoda's handkerchief sachet. He mustn't be tempted, though: too dangerous—not Rhoda's catching him, but his first glimpse of the Face.

"Have you seen Her in the flesh?"

"Oh no—too busy, what with the receptions, and the press, and rehearsal with the orchestra. Mrs Volkov is a wreck from sitting waiting for a few moments with her own daughter. Their best and almost only time is when she takes in the breakfast tray."

So much irrelevant chatter helped him partly recover his toppled balance.

During the day which separated them from the concert he was conscious that he hadn't given Rhoda an answer to her offer of the ticket. He would have liked to think he wouldn't accept, but knew he would, and that Rhoda took it for granted; otherwise she would have pressed for a definite answer.

"What is Kathy going to play?" He was quite pleased with the sound of his planned indifference, at one of those moments when he and Rhoda were crossing like strangers in the yard.

Rhoda, surprisingly, rattled off: "Mozart's K. 271" as though she had been brought up on it; she spoiled things, though, by tripping just afterwards on the hem of her dressing-gown which had come unstitched some months before.

He warned as gently, as genuinely as he could: "You'll fall down and hurt yourself if you insist on wearing that old gown."

Rhoda clawed at the back door and tore it open.

When he got inside she was blowing her nose in the scullery. "What is it?" he asked, still gentle, perhaps horribly so.

For she answered: "I thought I'd managed to escape pity while we were still children."

"Don't you know—you who read the papers," he couldn't resist, "we're living in the age of 'compassion, tenderness, and warmth'?"

In spite of it, they were most considerate towards each other all that afternoon.

He confessed: "I'd like to come with you to the concert," but he said it so low he could see she hadn't heard.

Or hadn't she wanted to hear?

The night of the concert was filled with a cutting wind, which added a rattling of window sashes to that of furniture handles as they got themselves ready. His stomach was threatened by the boiled haddock they had eaten in a hurry. What if he farted out loud during a subdued passage? Or if, on condescending to embrace, She should smell the haddock juices the pores of his cheeks were exuding? He unearthed a bottle of left-over eau de Cologne, a present from some woman who had expected to get a painting cheap, and soused his breast-pocket handkerchief with the stuff. The tonic smell encouraged him: he sprinkled more of the eau de Cologne down the front of his monogrammed shirt, another present from another woman. Perhaps if She smelled the smell She would be reminded of invalids, and treat him kindly. So he dashed eau de Cologne at his armpits.

When he went down Rhoda wasn't ready, though he caught sight of her moving about her room dressed in the squirrel coat. This time she hadn't tarted up her hair: it was hanging round her face, giving her the appearance of a grizzled monkey.

Armed with his masculine authority, he marched into Rhoda's camp and said: "Next time I sell a painting we must restore the conservatory."

"Oh," she murmured, "should we recognize it afterwards? Wouldn't it lose its charm?"

As he kicked at the displaced tiles and fragments of glass he was glad they shared this obsession for the conservatory in which Katherine Volkov had performed her dance.

But Rhoda had begun swearing: she said "damn" several times quickly, like a woman imitating Harry Courtney.

"What is it?" he asked, returning. "You've torn your good coat?"

She had: by catching the pocket on a knob; a triangular piece of skin was hanging loose.

"You must mend it!" he panted.

"There isn't *time!*" Her rodent voice had asserted itself.

"Do it up with a safety pin."

The idea seemed to appeal to her: or anyway, she followed his advice.

Although the damage had been patched up, he was disturbed by remembering the torn coat in his recent dream. Was he to be cut down, then, by K. 271? The operation promised to be less bland than that of the tram ploughing into his marzipan flesh: music can draw actual blood.

Foreboding must have been at large in Rhoda, too: she started gasping; she grabbed his hand with her monkey's paw. "I'm so frightened!" she whimpered when they were trampling out, pulling the front door shut.

They began to negotiate the never quite familiar labyrinth, looking for non-existent taxis, the wind slashing at them.

"Have you been using scent?" Rhoda shrieked against the wind.

"A drop of eau de Cologne."

"The same. I can't bear scent. It affects my sinuses."

She tried to produce some soggy sounds, but the wind was from the wrong quarter, and by the time they found a taxi, and were enclosed in its airlessness, she had discovered other fears.

"Mrs Volkov has developed a bladder complaint. I do hope she can last till the interval."

Mrs Volkov, he saw immediately, was sitting in the same row several seats away from them. Without the protection of her iron hat, and probably in a state of nerves over her weak bladder and the approaching performance, she looked paler, more monolithic, suggestive of granite veiled in cloud. She was smiling her permanently swivelled smile out of gelatinous lips. It would have fascinated him to calculate how much of herself she had contributed to her daughter, if he hadn't scented a danger on her far side: he noticed what could have been Cutbush the grocer, skin grown loose on his now shrunken fleshiness, clothes baggy over all. Cutbush was seated on the aisle; between himself and Mrs Volkov sat the lady who must be his wife, visible for the moment only as a swirl of greenish-purple hair.

The start of the evening was unpleasant enough to make you wish you hadn't come. And the haddock. And the woodwind tuning up.

Nor could he really believe they would be given what they were promised, not even when the first item, printed clearly in the programme as "Overture to The Magic Flute," did in fact turn out to be *The Magic Flute*. Under the spell of scepticism, he skipped the artist's photograph, unwilling to discover which persona they might expect: whether the Pamina of his tenderest longings, some vindictive Queen of the Night, or worst of all, the Complete Stranger; though from what she had told the radio it would most likely be Little Kathy Volkov from Paddo: "I am so happy to be back—so very happy—in Australia. . . . No. There is no one. I haven't any thought of marriage. Not for the moment. Music is my life. . . . I have so much to learn. . . . Oh yes, truthfully (*giggle*) . . . Australia is so wonderful. So *warm*—except when it blows stone cold on you (*giggle giggle*), but I love it. . . . Well, yes, it is short, but I have other engagements. . . . Yes, London next, then New York. . . . But I adore Australia. . . . No. No thought for the moment. Of course, in time. It's only natural. . . . I'd love to have a baby by an Australian" (*Rhoda reported Mrs Volkov had been most provoked by that bit; perhaps understandably, because it hadn't been for want of trying on the part of Paddo's Little Kathy*) . . . "I adore the sunshine . . . the gumtrees (*Had she seen one?*) . . . the ABC for giving me such a wonderful start in my musical career. . . . So you see, my heart can belong only to Australia. . . ."

Little did they know Her Heart Belonged to Daddy, and that she was capable of breaking into a tap routine, a chewed pink bow going flop flop at the end of her floppy plait, in front of the desolated piano.

He shuddered to find somebody walking over his grave.

The orchestra was playing a work by a contemporary. Imprisoned between walls of Mozart, the subscribers were prevented from stampeding out. He wished he could have supported the despised composer, but his hands had been made feeble by the collapse of faith in his ability to sway himself, let alone others. The scattered applause sounded like an old venetian blind stirred by a feeble breeze.

The trial was imminent. The conductor, a Dutchman, was disappearing, his buttocks too casual for the circumstances, to drag the prisoner from her mahogany cell.

At once it became obvious that precautionary measures were unnecessary: she made her entrance with an eagerness almost too pronounced. Where Kathy had once edged tortuously through the field of musicians, Volkov arrived at the front of the podium with steely, though graceful skill. Very briefly her fingertips touched those of the conductor, who hadn't after all led her out: he had been led. She seemed all matt white, of skin, and black, of watered taffeta, an explosion of diamonds on one shoulder. She was wearing her hair in a dangerously heavy, though expert coil, resting in the nape of her proud neck.

She wheeled so smoothly, that and her faultless white back reminded of the Königliche Reitschule; so far in her *haute école* she hadn't put a hoof wrong.

But as soon as she was seated he recognized the concealed panic which rose in him daily at first touch of the whip. He could almost hear her knuckles cracking as she kneaded them; he could hear her stiff, watered skirt seething with black nerves.

Not for long: she was required to intrude indecently soon; but the violins inclined towards her, in courtship, and the too suave (elderly) Dutch conductor. Then they were all united in the noble charges and intensified caracollings of the music: he, too, when at last able to free his throat his locked hands hypnotized by the point of a black silken elbow the throat pulsating white the white the whitest turbulence of bosom as this nameless artist humbly lowered her eyelids at what she had seen reflected in the mirror of perfection.

There were, on the other hand, the moments, the unaccompanied ones, when the unnecessary orchestra of husbands and housewives and raw boys and tired spinsters sat clasping their instruments, while his mistress Katherine Volkov played to delight her lover in a room empty except for themselves; or when his darling Kathy called in her brood, and the golden chicken-notes, in danger of scattering too far, scuttled fluttering for protection under the flounce of her swelling black.

Oh God he was in love with music. He raised his head to it: his Adam's apple must have stuck out inordinately. He wouldn't have dared look at Rhoda, whom he had forgotten anyway. He did glance once at Mrs Volkov, who might have been having her child again, there in the Town Hall.

He wondered what part the Russian had played in the making of Katusha, beyond planting his seed in a granite crevice. Perhaps a soul had sensed the rebirth of its own tormented glories, and defected. He had a vision of the recalcitrant creator standing in the middle of a gibber plain tufted with saltbush, dangling a grimy calico bagful of uncut opals. The crumpet-coloured, crumpet-textured face didn't reveal: but here was Katya in the Andantino polishing the crude stones into an opalescence of music.

He recognized the milky lustre, the spirts of black fire as theirs: dark tragedies hinted at resolved themselves in limpid strength. The tragedy was Mrs Volkov's. And Rhoda's, from the look of her: she was rocking on her little dried-up-peanut buttocks; though her eyes were closed, her smile exposed her shockingly.

An ambulance clanging down George Street entered through closed doors and reopened a dream he had been hoping healed.

Along the rows the intellectual public servants and unassimilated Europeans were sitting tensed by the Andantino. Lady ffolliott Morgan in pink ostrich curvette and enough jewellery to stock a shop (perhaps it did) promised to lay her chin on her navel. The ladies from the right suburbs loved to doze, but only to the right accompaniment. (That *Schönberg*, that *Webern*! Oh, Sir *Charles*! *No*, Sir Charles!) For the time being at least, the waves on which they were rising and falling wouldn't suck them down into some horrid abyss, or so they believed; they were riding safe in their own opalescent radiance.

The Finale almost woke them up: too brisk. The Volkova might have liked to shed her sleeves, but settled down to business. In the middle she looked up, as though remembering her neglected lover, and began to cosset him back, into the curves of her white flesh, and more intricate spirals of pink shells, only to cast him up again, at the fussy business of life which she couldn't ignore: after all, she took such pleasure in it.

There she was, standing in front of the piano. The public servants, the awakened ladies, the displaced Europeans, all were clapping. And clapping. While the artist kissed the tips of her fingers. She shook a firm hand with the conductor, a limper one with the leader; she nursed the cellophane bundle of flowers as though they were the baby she wanted to have by an Australian. No practical situation would ever find her at a loss. If she had appeared possessed only a few moments before, the spirit had withdrawn from her. There remained the swathe of watered silk, the explosion of diamonds: also perhaps a trace of diffidence towards the one by whom she had been consummated and her achievement made possible.

Seeing it, he rejoiced in the vision of pure joy they had shared, both then, and tonight. It seemed as though the heart were a cupboard one simply had to open: innocence hides nothing; and perfection bears looking at.

So he sat sunken, misted up, and because he was less than innocent, wondering how he could hide his shame; while Rhoda had started a dry cough, and was rattling a dented *bonbonnière* with half-a-dozen lozenges in it, one of which she began to devour, then almost at once another, apparently having no faith in the first.

"Why"—beating her flat chest—"does music always make me—*cough*?"

The audience was going out for the interval. Eyes suggested theirs had been the subtlest experience, though in some cases the unsavoury-looking pair of eccentrics in their midst spoiled the pleasures of self-congratulation; to rub up against anything so deplorable might have haunted them forever after.

The Mozart still inside him would have curdled if Rhoda hadn't twitched round suddenly and hissed in liquorice gusts: "I didn't tell you, but Mrs Volkov expects us to look in at the artists' room. She expects *you*, that is. Naturally the poor woman is out of her water."

"What a relief—for everybody!" He laughed heartlessly, and kept it up.

"Out of her depths, I mean." Rhoda blushed and frowned. "What I mean to say is," she battered away, "it's rather a burden for Mrs

Volkov, and she'd like some friend of a different level to help her out."

The prospect hardly appealed; but he saw that he was commandeered. "I thought of slipping away. Don't feel like any more," he was muttering pitifully while keeping the top of Rhoda's head in sight.

A more studiously charitable crowd parted to allow a hunchback to pass, and they entered the mahogany canyon at the end of which was the artists' room. A guard in mufti hovered round the open door. Inside, Katherine Volkov, looking pale, stood glancing out spasmodically through a cluster of admirers.

Seated in a far corner, smiling her stroked smile, the mother mumbled and beckoned. The new arrivals were admitted.

While haunting the outskirts of the carpet, he thought he recognized the one-f-ed physiologist inside the tomcat cheeks which come with regular steak and bed. Plastered against him was a young woman of delicate bones and enormous pregnancy possessive enough to be a wife. Ignored by the object of their visit, the couple was staring in sulky admiration at the signs of her achievement.

Lady ffolliott Morgan and a trio of satellites were congratulating Katherine Volkov on her dress.

"By a little person in Vienna. I shan't tell you her name, because she's nameless." The Volkova remained silent a moment while admiring the fall of her own watered skirt. "Of course, I *influenced* her!"

The ladies all laughed in appreciation.

Accepting that her time was up, Lady ffolliott Morgan looked wistful as she asked: "We shall see you on Sunday?" It was tentative, but hopeful.

"I have it tattooed on my mind—a quarter to one, punctually."

The ladies laughed again because she made it sound so amusing.

The Dutchman dug a forefinger into her shoulder where the skin took over from the taffeta. "Vee vill even so make sure: I vill bring you." Then he went off to conduct the Brahms.

At last Kathy was free to rub cheeks. "Clifff! And this is Trish? When is it expected? Isn't that beaut! I'm so happy for you." She glittered the more for her descent into suburbia.

"And darling Miss Courtney!" She descended lower still to embrace this quaint dwarf.

Her back bent, the Volkova might have been helping pull the go-cart full of stinking offal for cats. On straightening up, she drew a deep breath—the room was smelling of tuberoses enough to deaden a corpse—and gave Rhoda her healthiest smile. "I'm terribly grateful to you. Mum does depend on your support."

Mrs Volkov nodded and prepared words which wouldn't form.

Kathy all the while was flickering her eyelids in the right direction, just about to—she'd have to say something soon surely to God.

He couldn't help trying to carve into the tended skin, through the technical smiles, to the vision they had created together; but instead of helping him revive it, she was growing hobbledehoy; she clasped her hands in a tight ball at her waist: there was nowhere about that severe dress in which to hide them.

What made the situation more embarrassing, Rhoda seemed to understand it; she whispered loudly: "Hurtle was tremendously impressed." (Her dolt brother.) "We must go now," she whispered louder still. "They make such demands on you."

As he followed Rhoda out of the room Kathy blundered after them, and was apparently speaking to him. "Thank you for coming to hear me play." Her face was pursed up in a gross vegetable shape; she was so hesitant she almost tottered. "I do appreciate it," she managed to blurt before planting on his cheek a kiss which immediately bounced off: it was so clumsily done.

Ignoring Mrs Volkov, a grey blur waving vaguely from her mahogany corner, he ran snorting down the now deserted corridor to catch up with Rhoda. He hoped she hadn't seen anything of what had just happened between Kathy and himself: the two geniuses.

Rhoda almost certainly hadn't, because of an encounter which was putting her on her mettle. Without any difficulty, alas, he recognized Shuard.

Shuard didn't age like other people: always only a little plumper than the time before, the steel wool only a shade more silvery, the whole man so smooth and preserved, no doubt at the expense of the several wives on whom he had battened. He was aided and abetted, of course, by the banality of his mind: nothing like an empty head for keeping the wrinkles at bay.

Rhoda was playing up to the man, who bent down in a caricature of gallantry.

"Didn't you enjoy it, Mr Shuard?" She had launched into her

best imitation of Maman. "Such a charming—an *exquisite* performance!"

Because he couldn't reach down as far as her elbow, Shuard tapped her on the shoulder, which made it look less gallant than he might have intended, but more in keeping with his patronizing nature. "Stylish, yes. But not Mozart. Not yet. Perhaps if she works at it. And Kathy is a determined young lady."

Rhoda made the laughing sounds, half protest, half agreement, Maman would have made in the circumstances, but drier because of her own little wizened throat. She wasn't exactly betraying Kathy, only obeying a convention.

"You understand?" Shuard gargled from behind his perfectly false teeth.

"Oh, work—yes—I agree—so necessary—and rewarding!" Rhoda gurgled.

Shuard was standing so firmly on his own ground he looked in no particular direction while greeting Duffield. His handshake felt warm and cushioned. Whatever else, the man was an adept.

You glanced back irresistibly to watch the enemy's continued progress down the corridor: the intolerable saunter, shortening a leg every few paces, as in the lavatory when buttoning up his flies, here in the corridor still easing his fat crutch. And Katherine Volkov appearing at the door of the artists' room with her moistest smile: she must have livened it up in the meantime. She had put on a pair of long black gloves, which made her arms look more experienced, her hands more predatory, as Shuard, the slippery bugger, whirled her round, their mouths attaching themselves with the sure suction of roused sea-anemones.

To one side, in the hall, Brahms was beating his chest while the waves broke around him. Rhoda had already done such duty by music she mightn't have heard if an attendant hadn't approached and silently hushed her clatter.

She continued to whisper while performing an elaborate tiptoe across the tiles. "Mr. Shuard enjoys living, whatever one may think of his way of life." She giggled in what sounded like sympathy.

"But isn't he a critic? What's he doing ambling off during a concert? Or perhaps he knows enough already."

Rhoda looked over her shoulder. "Between ourselves, I believe the paper sacked him. Now he's just enjoying himself—living off his last wife's bribe-money."

Their footsteps teetered away, while the souped-up Brahms surged in browner, more turgid waves.

Rhoda whispered: "He's really a very kind man. He's promised to deliver Mrs Volkov home. Then, I'm told, he's taking Kathy to supper at the house of some Viennese—of the musical world. I don't believe musicians ever want to leave that world; they certainly never admit outsiders, though sometimes they may pretend to."

They went out into the darkness. Rhoda started clawing up at his arm: she who had so recently and lightly betrayed Kathy in chit-chat with Shuard, after the convention of the class she believed she had repudiated, was looking for protection from a crueller truth, he presently realized.

"There was a man staring at me during the concert," she told him. "At first I thought it was because I'm the sister of a famous man. Then I came to the conclusion, from the way he couldn't stop eyeing me, he was admiring my fur coat. Squirrel isn't too common now."

"He must have been on your good side—the side away from the safety pin."

The wind had started to cut again.

"Did you notice," he asked, "Shuard is full of false teeth?"

"Is he? Most people are. On the whole I think false are more presentable than our own discoloured, crooked ones. Yours and mine, anyway. Kathy's teeth are splendid, but she's in the flower of her womanhood, and we're a couple of old crocks hanging on to what we've got—out of stinginess and pride."

It was an unimportant hour of night, too late for one crowd, too early for another: it made the giggling more personal, and turned glances into guided missiles.

Katherine Volkov's successful tour was over quicker by the calendar than his private suffering would have shown. On account of her engagements in other parts of the world, it was actually very brief: after the orchestral concerts in Sydney, there were those in Melbourne—with the First Physiologist thrown in—then the return to Sydney and her farewell recital.

He refused to go to the recital, and knew Rhoda was relieved because she would be able to live it in her own way. She could go round afterwards, uninhibited by his presence, and rub cheeks, and be snubbed along with the whole Cutbush gang; while the chosen sycophants, the ffolliott Morgan set and Shuard, wearing their invisible rose-petal masks and gold-leaf leotards, waited to carry off the artist, not to debauch her, but to learn from her. After the recital, none of the tumult of Brahms to deaden departure, only single, lingering notes aimed with deadly accuracy.

Since Kathy had finally exorcised herself, this time he needn't even listen in.

The weather had turned warm enough for Rhoda to dispense with her fur coat. In any case, it was hardly wearable by now: the safety pin too visible in the unmended tear; signs of horseflesh gumming up the maltreated squirrel. In the absence of the coat she proposed to present herself in a lilac creation, or more accurately, confection. Somehow the material was too rough, its nutty basis too liberally treated with fondant for anybody as delicate as Rhoda (he wouldn't label her as "subtle"). Draped over the hump, there was a little pleated, frosted cape, and down the front a lovingly worked, out-of-proportion corsage of orchids in pink gauze. She looked awful, particularly the patches of rouge, and the strings where her calves should have been; but she was determined her camouflage should make her feel beautiful.

"Where did you get the new dress?" it was his duty to ask.

"Mrs Volkov made it for me. She always has. For any important occasion." She stood ruffling up the spray of artificial orchids. "Less since her attack. But recently it's done her nerves good to occupy herself."

He had heard Mrs Volkov was known to the neighbourhood for her dressmaking; she had brought up Kathy on the proceeds from it, augmented by the money she earned from child-minding, washing up, and letting her spare room. If he couldn't remember any other dresses, Rhoda's important occasions had probably occurred before she came to live with him.

"I'm glad you like this," she told herself with prim pleasure; her kiss—for the occasion—felt as dry as chalk.

When she came home he could see that a headache or something was raging in his lilac clown.

"How was it?" he asked.

He was positively languid from feeling free of Kathy at last; while Rhoda's chalky brows were as pleated as her cape.

She seemed unwilling to goad her sensibility further by discussing the recital, but screwed up the pleats in her forehead tighter still, and answered from behind closed lids: "Her Scriabin was exceptional. Even Mr Shuard had to admit it."

"Scriabin? Don't think I've ever heard a note of him. Tell me about the Scriabin."

But she wouldn't. Her clown's face shuddered and cracked under its chalky silt.

"And did they carry her off to the fleshpots afterwards? To round off her Scriabin?"

"Oh no. Mrs Volkov is too unwell. It's the thought of parting. Kathy is off early in the morning."

Then she was as good as gone, he realized. She had gone out of his life without a murmur from either of them. Of course it wouldn't have occurred to Kathy, and since she had killed by her vulgarity and vice anything he had created in her, there was nothing left for him to regret. He would learn to live with nothing, as his deformed sister advocated.

But Rhoda, he saw, had begun to cry: it was trickling down through the remnants of her powder.

"For God's sake," he shouted, "what's the matter with you?"

"Nothing," she sobbed. "Everything," she corrected herself with increasing sogginess. "This dress, for instance!" She dashed the back of her open claw against her friend's handiwork.

Shortly after, she went to bed, no doubt deciding she might lose more sympathy than she would gain by prolonged sniffles; while he sat on with his guilt for company: for withholding his affection. Probably he had given her the squirrel coat in its place, and to pay him out, Rhoda had caught the disease from which he suffered. By the time they were both riddled with it, when each had become the same exotic fungus, would it greatly matter who possessed whom?

Anyway, Kathy was gone, trailing rococo clouds and the worst screamers of radio advertisement. Her slogans streamed across the air: "My boomerang will always come back. . . . Even if I'm sort of married to Mozart and Beethoven, I'll find the time to love all you bloomin' Australians. . . ."

For days afterwards he was back and forth between the upper floor and the incinerator, destroying a whole pile of drawings. (Nothing of any value, however: it was his latter-day trash, his senility going up in smoke.) He hacked less effectually at several masonite boards. He could feel Rhoda listening; he could feel her watching, unable to do anything about the smoke which was rising through the slits in the scaly incinerator. He burned letters, too, remembering a tussle which had taken place during another holocaust.

Now it was Rhoda who brought him the letter when it came. She carried it impersonally on her flat palm, as Edith might have offered it on a salver with the Courtney monogram. Rhoda didn't comment, perhaps because she didn't recognize what was certainly a changed writing: large and dashing.

The envelope was tough, because expensive; he waited till Rhoda had gone before starting the struggle with it.

My dear friend . . .

(Not the expected suburban clanger "Dear Mr Duffield," though a stiff translation from the German was no more appropriate.)

. . . our trouble is you intimidate me still. I'm as nervous as a little girl wondering whether she will find the words to express herself, or a thought in her head worth expressing. And that is how I was changed into a lump of suet as you were leaving the concert, why I started stupidly kissing when I hadn't meant to, only it is what they do on such occasions—people of Hal Shuard's kind!

I had planned to embrace you with my eyes, in gratitude. Or would that have given a wrong impression—too much like a prostitute's invitation? Oh, I am that too, I know! I must experience all there is to experience. I'm a glutton of the senses. I shall end up fat, perhaps bloated, probably destroyed, but I hope that on the way I shall contribute something of value. That is possible, even out of the worst. I am too pliable, not only physically. I say the things they want to hear, because it's easy after what has been hellishly difficult. After trying to praise great men in their own accents, adulation from the nongs (for what they think they love but don't really) is like mutual seduction under a warm shower. Then I promise them I'll come back someday and play them Chopin and Gershwin and the lot, and that their Little Kathy from Paddo will always love them. If I were a polio victim as well, I'd be seven times more their idol, but I hope they will never get the chance to take advantage of me to that extent.

I didn't mean to bitch when I started. This was to have been a letter about *us*, full of the things we haven't said. I realize the dangers I may run into, but because I was brought up close to the gutter I'll take the risk.

If I've learned anything of importance, it was you who taught me, and I thank you for it. Yes, I know there was Khrapovitsky whipping me along to perfect my technique—important certainly —but I've come across several machines put together by Khrap alone—impressive except that they were never anything more than machines. It was you who taught me how to see, to be, to know instinctively. When I used to come to your house in Flint Street, melting with excitement and terror, wondering whether I would dare go through with it again, or whether I would turn to wood, or dough, or say something so stupid and tactless you would chuck me out into the street, it wasn't simply thought of the delicious kisses and all the other lovely play which forced the courage into me. It was the paintings I used to look at sideways whenever I got a chance. I wouldn't have let on, because I was afraid you might have been amused, and made me talk about them, and been even more amused when I couldn't discuss them at your level. But I was drinking them in through the pores of my skin. There was an occasion when I even dared touch one or two of the paintings as I left, because I had to know what they felt like, and however close and exciting it had been to embrace with our bodies, it was a more truly consummating love-shock to touch those stony surfaces and suddenly glide with my straying fingers into what seemed like endless still water.

Of course my approach and reactions were childish, personal, egotistical—let's face it, aren't we appalling egotists?—but I think this was how I began to feel I could reach the truth, if I filtered these sensations through my true self, however limited that area might be. And that is how I have always gone about it, my darling—I can't call you "lover," although I suppose, *technically*, that is what you have been—or "dirty seducer"! if I hadn't wanted, *had to be seduced*—still I prefer to think of you as the father of anything praiseworthy that will ever come out of me.

We are approaching London, everywhere a dirty yellow, just before dark. Although it is summer below, it is icy in the air. I am shivering. My lovely sables ought to keep me warm and safe, I paid for them myself. It's so important to feel materially safe when you are the bastard of a runaway Russian seaman and my sainted Scottish mother. But I'm always cold and frightened in the beginning. And now we're coming down. I am so afraid. I have never been here before. I might never have performed anywhere.

It will be flat, pallid, airless, till I can rise about it—if I am ever again given the strength. Pray for me if you know how.

Love—K.

Because he didn't know where to direct his prayers, and would never have the courage to answer her letter, he began priming a board on which, probably tomorrow, he would start to paint, when his idea had descended out of the clouds, into the more practical extensions of space.

❄ 9 ❄

He had set out on some mission to the city, but got off the bus at the Cathedral, and for no very clear reason was making for the State Gallery. Sick-witted ever since the bus began jolting his head apart. The women wouldn't let him open a window; the draught might have blown their hair about. Ought to have exploited his gloom: felt numb ever since my daughter my little girlie left to further her overseas career; if it mightn't have sounded as though he had committed a murder instead of creating life. Anyway, he disliked people who tell their life stories in buses. Anyway, they always left the murders out, because nobody would have believed.

At least his thoughts made him laugh while walking under the Moreton Bay figs in the heat of the day. He might have gone up in the furnace if the trees and his own cold limbs hadn't prevented it: curiously cold for such a shadowless hour, in which only those of wide-open face strolled laughing and talking exchanging their unexceptionable ideas streaming with sweat and fellowship up the Gallery steps some of them down into the little unrefreshment pavilion.

He was the black stroke in the landscape, though they didn't recognize it.

Probably this was the reason he had left the bus: he had felt the need for recognition, and the most puritanical artist is unable to resist loving himself a little in the mirrors offered by his own paintings.

Cynicism revived him as he went up the steps to the Gallery. There was no actual cause for gloom. He felt as physically fit as the other man always appears, as he looks smiling at you, or at what he believes he sees. At least the attendants recognized, and could hardly fail to behave with kindness towards an old, three-legged, milky-eyed, stump-toothed dog which had hung around the place so long. The soppy expressions on the attendant faces made him feel he ought to wag his tail.

Nobody else at that hour could possibly know him, and he was glad of it now, stalking through the courts past the schoolgirls, earnest or giggly; young men in shorts showing their all; nondescript middle-aged sexless couples; that skinny old biddy and her scabby-handed relic of a husband. It was the humility of the old couple, looking as though they were about to apologize for something, which made him shoot into a side court. Why should old people wear humble expressions when probably they had copped the lot? He swore nothing would ever make him look humble, not if he was brought to the gutter.

So far he had managed to behave very discreetly walking past other men's works, carefully avoiding the room in which he would most likely come across his own. Storing up the pleasure, or eking out his impatience. None of these parties of smudged schoolgirls, skintight young men, or the almost allegorical pair of Ancients would notice how his heart was bumping, any more than identify his face. He must be looking greedy, though. He not exactly ran, but tripped a step or two, before he thought to restrain himself. And found none of his. Nothing yet. Not one.

Supposing they had done away with him holus-bolus into the basement? Supposing he had died and not yet ascended? His material limbs returned coldly, and he slowly walked over what was only parquet.

Honeysett, the Extrovert-in-Chief, was approaching: chubbier than ever. "Thought you'd caught us out, did you? Thought we'd given you away?" Honeysett laughed so loud the place might have belonged to him.

He took you by the elbow; he was behaving, not as though you were the attendants' pathetic, scruffy dog, but an elderly, brittle, humourless child.

"There's some of you—I hope it'll please—amongst the Recent Acquisitions."

They were again in the entrance hall, where the two Ancients turned their backs.

There was no need to draw his attention to what must have been the whole of his "Rocks" series (including that painful fleshy one), his "Electric City," his "Marriage of Light": in fact, Olivia Davenport's collection.

"Is Nance—is Olivia *dead*?" In challenging Honeysett to tell him what he didn't wish to hear, he could feel the spit jump out of his own mouth.

Honeysett received it without flinching. "Not dead. She's living in Rome."

The plaque confirmed that the paintings were a gift, not a bequest: by "Mrs Olivia Hollingrake."

Honeysett partly explained: "She's gone back to her maiden name. Don't ask me why."

"I wouldn't dream of it."

Honeysett was the last person who'd know. He'd like to ask Boo herself one or two questions. Have to think of them, though.

He stuck his nose almost on the surface of "Electric City." "Have they been mucking about with it?"

"Not that I'm aware." Honeysett at last sounded cold.

"Something has happened in the top left corner." Or had he been a too impulsive, ignorant young man? "Wonder why she gave them away?"

"She didn't tell us. It was done through solicitors."

"Can't have cared for them. I always suspected Boo. Anyone who starts telling you about their deep understanding of your work is a bit suspect."

He wished Honeysett would leave him: he wanted to do things to the paintings which might have looked immodest to an extrovert outsider.

Honeysett seemed to take the hint in spite of his extrovert temperament: he was moving mumbling smiling towards some mission of official urgency.

It was good to be alone with the paintings.

Already on the bus he had wanted to touch something he had achieved in paint. Now he could run his fingers over the surfaces: saliva running, he realized, out of his mouth; he tried to snap it up, but it wouldn't be caught. Didn't matter. In the almost deserted gallery.

Some of the colours were blinding him: "Marriage of Light," for instance.

"A major work!" He looked round to share his discovery, but of course Honeysett had gone.

498

Nobody there now.

He began to touch the jagged "Rocks." And the more painful fleshier ones. Nance Lightwood? Lightburn? by any name, her spirit rose out of the glazed past, together with a whiff of body.

He looked round again to catch a possible intruder: schoolgirls are never able to disguise what they know; they have to giggle.

But nobody was there. Only himself. Filling with mucus and tears. He was so grateful for any vision of himself which wasn't that of the old mangy dog. The murderer was more acceptable. Almost.

Of course—he remembered now why he had set out, not to wallow, but to buy the heart. Rhoda saying: *Poor Ruffles my beloved my only affectionate cat Hurtle is sick not a tooth in his head but likes to mumble on something tasty not if you don't want to but would you when you go out look and buy us a nice heart sheep's if I cut it up fine I think Ruffles might fancy it.*

So it was Ruffles, not himself. So he had come out with Rhoda's horrible plastic bag; nobody could deny Rhoda his sister brought out the best in him.

On leaving the Gallery he would have forgotten the bag if the attendant, his smile grown extra sentimental for the blue plastic lace, hadn't handed it to him. He took it and went out. Something ominous seemed to be preparing, against the railings, amongst the columns, at the entrance. The pair of Ancients turned and began approaching: the skinny woman in her best crow's black a little in advance; the scaly man shambling after in nubbly pepper-and-salt synthetic tweed. Behind them sheets of light were quivering.

All three of the figures at the entrance suddenly became paralysed.

Till the woman began, after wetting her dried-out-leather lips: "Don't you recognize me—Hurt? HURTLE?" On the second attempt it came hurtling out.

He stood holding Rhoda's blue plastic bag against his belly: to protect himself from the knife-thrust.

"I'm your sister—don't you know? I'm Lena. The eldest."

He held Rhoda's bag, a plastic shield, against Lena's accusations.

"We come up from Tralga for a week or two. It's been easier since the kids was married. This is my husband, Hurtle—Ernie Cobbold."

Ernie Cobbold held out his hand, scabbed by the stones, the frosts, the wire fences of Tralga: the palm felt of hardened tar.

"None of the kids with us," Lena persisted in her thin, recollected, girl's voice. "We got four kids. Thirteen grandchildren by now." She lowered her head: she was wearing a red hat with her black; she licked her beige lips and smiled. "We're expectin' the first of the *great*-grandchildren."

She hung her head as though it were too heavy; nor could her husband help in the situation: he was no more than the monolith who had got her with their sculpture of stone children.

The plastic bag dangling empty against your belly, you tried to count up the paintings, to show Lena what you had got, but couldn't do it quickly enough. And probably forget a couple.

"We looked at your paintings. Yairs." Lena remembered to smile kindly.

Ernie Cobbold probably hadn't seen them at all. His eyes were too puzzled: rims red and sagging; they needed stitching.

Lena said: "Of course we seen about you, Hurtle, in the papers. Oh yairs! But didn't wanter interfere. Our dear Mumma, she read about you—talked about you. She said she'd stick to the agreement. Never to interfere. Pa died years ago, Mumma only recently."

He said: "Oh?" Must remember why he had brought Rhoda's bag.

"Yes," said Lena, "don't you remember—don't you see the likeness, Hurt? As I remember, we was so alike as kiddies."

"Wa—were we?" The blue plastic bag shuddered. "Better write to my solicitors." He pushed past Ernie Cobbold: you could almost smell the scourings; in Lena's case, it was watery homemade plum jam.

His heart was rent: when he had to keep himself whole for some further, still undisclosed, purpose; painting could be the least of it, though at heart it was all.

Revived by the paintings he had seen and touched, he was able to make quite an athletic getaway. He cut down Cathedral Street, then into William, to be with life. He was enjoying the kind of walk only good health and a temporary absence of responsibility can ensure. If his clothes and skin were melting together, that was because the day was blazing higher. At least his sweat was cold.

He had disliked Lena as a kid. How can you be expected to love someone just because you have blood in common? If he had been tempted to let himself get bogged down in her emotion on the Gallery steps, it was from the sudden shock of finding the past transformed from a conveniently vague abstraction into a persistent, tearful old woman. It was a very definite shock; he might succumb even now.

But it wasn't skinny Lena, or Mumma who stuck to the agreement, or the Adam's apple in Pa's throat, which made him want to give way; there could be something else he was beginning to remember. To want. Really nothing to cry about. Something probably nobody had, if they stopped to think, and that was why most of them took the trouble not to: emptiness of mind is less disturbing than the soul's absence.

"Your change, sir—*please*. And Mr Sitsky has your parcel." It was the pink-rinsed hair-do talking at him as if he were deaf, clinking with a coin, too, on the marble.

Use had carved the butcher's chopping block to look like a work of art. In all the refrigerated shop, with its staff who bossed you in your own interest, the wooden block was his one comfort.

He had half a mind to catch a bus in William Street, or hail a taxi; but hesitated: hadn't they walked all the way to Sunningdale, him and Mumma in the old days, Mumma always with a baby in her? Besides, he felt so fit. Must have looked it too: several women pretended they weren't taking an interest, you could tell by their mouths, always tell when you were being undressed for a quick one before hubby stuck his key in the lock. He couldn't let himself think when or how he had last enjoyed a fuck. He was above it.

In London she had played, not their K. 271, but the D Minor. And Brussels. And Paris. Mum Volkov, inexorably, kept Rhoda "posted."

The night Ruffles was supposed to be sick unto death, Rhoda remembered something deadly funny: *I really oughtn't to tell you, because it's—well, shall we say—humorous. The reason Mrs Volkov wanted you to have the complimentary ticket for Kathy's concert is that, when she saw you in the bus, she recognized a lost soul. She's slightly psychic, you know.* Not too psychic when she opened her legs to that legendary Russian.

On entering the suburb to which they all belonged, he spat down into the part of it which some of the locals refer to as Shitters' Lane. The dust-coloured houses were congesting along the irregular skyline, the air condensing on his eyelashes. He wiped them with the last of the good silk Sulkas Mrs Olivia Hollingrake had presented.

It would be a thankful homecoming. Shed Rhoda's infernal bag, which had no possible connection with any part of him, but which he had accepted without question. Perhaps because he liked to make little inessential purchases, especially from grocers': *champignons au beurre* okra medium natural artichoke hearts (or were bottoms a better buy?).

On Saturday afternoons she used to serve behind the counter for a shilling or two.

This was where he began falling down falling falling. It was nothing to fall and reach the pavement.

They began running spilling out so many too many people around him.

I might suffocate, he wanted to shout up at them, but found he couldn't, or push them back, he couldn't, he was bound, his strength wasn't strong enough to burst the iron.

Then the big starling-woman flapping out of the window from behind the tins of Campbell's Soup the Old Fashioned Hop Scotch.

"Are you all right?"

His tongue was stuck.

"Arr Cec CEC the gentleman SICK ring the ambulance Cec *Cecurrlll*?"

A draught of cold sawdust. The starling hovered didn't watch to touch him wasn't her kind of worm.

"Howdyer do it? Never rung for an ambulance in me life."

Knew the slack-looking man. Knew his apron.

"How do *I* know? Oh Lord! Dial Triple O and see what happens."

Angry. Not a starling after all. A gull growing out of her purplegreen-black.

UTBUS in gold as you floating out.

When he returned they were all at it an irregular fence around him he was getting accustomed to it growing on the pavement.

"She says it's old Duffield the artist. She knows him well. Friend of Mr Cutbush."

"You don't say!"

The gull-starling flapped and screeched still not touching not prepared to be deceived by any pseudosewage.

"Someone must fetch his sister. Cec?"

"Is it a coronry?"

"No, it's a seizure."

"Isn't it the same?"

"Give the poor bloke a chance. You're treading on 'is 'and."

"Oh Lord, Cec! It's his sister's blue plastic bag. I recognized it. Rhoda Courtney's."

"They say they're very close—Miss Courtney and Mr Duffield."

"Is she married?"

"Who—'Miss'? Don't ask *me!*"

"Poor little thing—don't it make yer flesh creep!"

" 'Ere, you ladies are gunner trample the man."

"It's a coronry."

"No. I told yer, didn't I? It's a stroke."

"What about the doctors?"

"We rung for the ambulance. It'll take 'im to the Casualty."

"Sister Mary Veronica, she's in charge. She's Mrs O'Hara's cousin."

"They put Jock in the Recovery Ward. That means you're gunner die. 'Is mother don't know."

"You *ladies!*"

Knew their shoes down to the last crack the least bunion.

The slack man returning you recognized the Utbus apron put a cushion under your head. Strong though hairless wrists. By now withered thighs kneeling. Queens probably better nurses they have to try harder. And this was this was—CUTBUSH. Couldn't apologize.

"What is it?"

"It's a stroke."

"Tt-tt!"

All steps twittered then rooted at his crossroads was becoming.

"Mrs Cutbush recognized 'is sister's blue bag."

"*Aahheuggh!* What is ut?"

"Must 'uv rolled outer the bag."

"It's only a heart."

"A sheep's heart!"

"Must 'uv bought it for the cat."

"A heart's nice stuffed for tea."

"Couldn't come at it! Look at the veins!"

"Don't kick it, Mrs Mac!"

"Nasty thing! Looks so dead!"

"It's Mr Duffield's property."

Not his. He wasn't dead. The colours vibrating. Too vivid. The extra indigo sky above cassata houses the drab human drabs. Noises too tambourines great bong gongs of brass never got the clap ever and o-boes good word the bells bells bells.

Hang on to the last and first secret the indi go.

"The ambulance is here, Mrs Cutbush." As they shuffled him out on a tambourine.

In something too neat for a bed.

"He's been unconscious for two days. He's my brother. He's had a stroke."

"Arr!"

The noise vibrating disintegrating distributed itself in pins and needles throughout his body.

Rhoda's voice a little drill. "I've never owned a floor-polisher. How often do you have to renew the wax?"

"When it looks dirty, dear."

Must burst the too clean curtains all around him.

A woman or sister a same white did just this.

"Why, Miss Courtney, didn't you notice? He's recovered consciousness."

Rhoda's face ought to look less looking more frightened.

"He is. Isn't he? Yes, sister."

Too many sisters Rhoda Lena the nameless starch.

"You must talk to him from time to time, Miss Courtney. You never know how much gets through to them."

Rhoda's gar gargoyle looking petrified down. "Yes, sister."

Sister went. Rhoda perched. Where is lean old bloody Lena?

"Do you hear me, Hurtle? Ruffles died. I didn't even cry. I think you reach a point where you're beyond crying. And all my cats have always been dirty, selfish, cruel, lazy. Don't know why I ever kept them. Except you've got to have something. And men were never interested."

Rhoda didn't believe he in any way worked not certainly by ear-work. Didn't believe other sisters. Only herself.

"Oh dear! Do you think the others in the ward will have heard the rubbish I started talking? You forget these are only curtains."

Not not this pale painfully vibrating ice encasing two of them he hear he couldn't help couldn't fend Rhoda's eyes her eye picks her hiss pissing testing temperature of ice reducing to melt.

"I was only ever interested in men. Not their minds—their minds are mostly putrid—but their bodies. Their lovely strong straddling legs. Their backs. Whatever else they know—whatever feeds their vanity—they can't know about their own backs."

Rhoda had the indergestion by whispers. Got the hiccups.

"I'm only—*hpp*—*tiring* you, Hurtle."

Didn't believe it anything about him her cat her buried brother she was Rhoda only only why she had come clean.

"There's nothing I can—nothing I was ever able to do for you."

God's sake another crying sister. A hiccupping handkerchief.

"This is Dr Westmacott, Miss Courtney. Miss Courtney is Mr Duffield's *sister*."

"Distinguished brother."

"Smy brother. Never think of him as anything—*hpp*."

Professionally kind man with all sisters floating out backward through zese why wires trapeze or tram tram trampoline slippering with new wax.

When he could walk, or shufflle, say a few words, if not compose a sentence, or not more than to refuse the mauve blancmange, they said he might go home. Rhoda came. She didn't bring a taxi; regardless of expense she engaged a hire car. He wondered what the patients watching from the balconies would think. He would have liked to look less conspicuous; but that was not possible: he couldn't answer for his right side. For that matter, his whole tingling body was only nominally his.

"The tinkling," he complained.

"The what?" Rhoda tried to smile what she understood as a sweet smile.

He was too busy shuffling to the car in the way the therapists had tried to teach him. He had never been good at "learning" things: he had functioned intermittently by painful vibrations followed by illumination. But now that he vibrated all the time, the light wouldn't switch on.

"Why the hire?"

"Well, it's a big occasion, isn't it? And you have the money. Miss Harkness told me you've got pots of it. So we decided to spend some of it on you." Rhoda was sitting as upright as she knew how, her legs dangling. "Doesn't a car like this make you feel 'diplomatic'?"

Rhoda and him the dips!

She had meant it as a joke, and thought he was enjoying it, whereas he was searching for a lost word.

"Few . . . near . . . real," he said at last. "My own funereal!"

It was going to be very difficult for them both: not only because of words; there was noise, too. He couldn't protect his ears, except with his left hand, and often he couldn't be bothered. It might be better to get it over quickly: to die of the explosions of glass and clashing of cymbals.

"Isn't it very noisy?" What might have been a protest wasn't really: they had told him he should develop the habit of conversing; and the nice little girls would have been pleased to think he was trying.

"Not particularly," Rhoda said. "In fact, this is rather a quiet bit. Don't you remember Centennial Park? And there's a golf course over there. You're probably still a bit sensitive to noise."

He was at the molten core of it. Himself the noise perpetually disintegrating.

He would have liked to cry; but his handkerchief was on the wrong side. Wouldn't ask bloody Rhoda. Cursed with a dwarf. She, cursed with *him*. When there were comfortable upholstered normal people walking throwing bread to ducks in parks.

And Rhoda said: "I hope you're not going to be unkind, Hurtle, because all that anybody wants is your recovery and happiness."

He wondered whether their thoughts and remarks were inflicting themselves on the hire-car driver's blackheaded neck.

Rhoda had got one of her her her *minions* to carry down a bed and set it up in the living-room—as though she were prepurring to nurse you into a state of dependence. When it was from just that sort of thing that he had to run away. Was already beginning.

"But how can I look after you?" she moaned.

Rhoda!

"The stairs are what. Sister and Miss Therap told me exercise." He was already beginning to drag himself up, kneel whenever, there was all evening: to escape from Rhoda. "Just the job."

It was of the utmost importance that he return into himself: find out what was left.

"Nobody stops the cats' meat." He was too exhausted, but attempted to explain. "Take away—I don't *steal* your knife." He was kaput at three stairs below the up landing. "Eh? Rhoda?" It went ricocheting down, unlike anything he had ever used. It was the new, incalculable self.

"But what am I to do? Up and down stairs! Who will take care of you?"

"Don Lethbridge," he remembered and gasped.

The door shuddered open on the dust of his cold closed belonging room. He burrowed like a screw into an old instinctive screwhole. At its kindest the smell was sawdust, at its blackest burning rubber.

Don Lethbridge was his luckiest bet yet.

Rhoda said: "He's willing to come. He'll come morning and evening. But the times will vary depending on the classes he has to attend. He can help you learn to wash and dress yourself. And things of that nature."

Rhoda blushed, but not enough: her flesh remained a pale veil barely covering her thoughts as she visualized necessities of the body. Imagine how he would lay on the fine gauze of paint for Rhoda the bride surrounded by her straddling strong-backed men. Safe, safe enough. He wouldn't paint. Except in blacks, in Chinese.

"What else?" he asked.

"There was the question of payment. We discussed that."

Good old Rhoda wouldn't guess at Ron Cuppaidge's real role. Weren't sure yourself, only that something vast was painfully vaguely forming.

"I told him that of course you were going to pay him for his help. A student can always find uses for a little extra money."

"Heaps of money."

Because without this Cup Lethbridge he couldn't hope to to entertain? a secret existence so necessary to the *un*-reason.

"Well, I didn't want to raise the poor fellow's hopes too high, because you know you *are mean*, Hurtle."

He wanted to try out a laugh, and dared. "Mean as old bacon yourself."

However his laughter sounded, Rhoda appeared to enjoy it: she laughed back. They were enjoying it together. He felt better.

Rhoda, remembering, got her prim serious look. "Actually he said he'd be only too glad to do it for nothing—if he might look at the paintings when he comes."

Were Rhoda and the young man conspired?

"What did you?"

"I said it was a matter I wasn't in a position to decide. You would have to talk it over together. I had no idea how you'd react. You're such a peculiar man."

"But not mean. Generous when—when necessary."

She went down the stairs in gigantic clopping salt-boxes sighing for her respiratory system and things peculiar. Herself included, he imagined.

"No stinge!" his lopsided voice roared after her.

Then sinking back he began sweetly deeply sleeping because of what had been arranged. And woke up trying to see what he had dreamed about. He never dreamed now, though. His dreams had been withered in one stroke. Even if his thoughts were beginning again. Would somebody new hold open the right door?

"Sir? Mr Duffield?"

The lad at the door had yellow lank hair, and by that light a look of something else. Of of a spotty downy archangel. On Hero's island. Only there they were black, on blue sky.

"Miss Courtney told me to come up."

What to ask him to do? Hadn't thought enough about it yet.

"What was it?" His own voice sounded pitiful. "Have to remember," he said at last. "Only beginning to find my way about." Not through a new mind, through the wreckage of an old one. "A vandal broke in!" He tried another of his new laughs.

But his servitor wasn't as tough as Rhoda. Or hadn't lived with deformity. Lethbridge looked away. Blotches of embarrassment came in his cheeks nourished in milk bars and on greasy twists of limp chips. Long yellow hair, visible pelvis and saucered buttocks were a mod re reen—renaissance!

"Miss Courtney says I'm to help you wash and dress." Though of indeterminate sex, the creature sounded determined enough.

If it had been Kathy's gunpowdery arms. But warmth was of the past.

"Washing and dressing? That's the least of it!" Somebody else's cough came out of him. "The body can get a bit smelly, I suppose—in waiting. Yes, feet. Feet, Cuppaidge!"

The relieved buttercup of a lad went quickly out, down, to conspire—all always conspiring—with Rhoda.

What was it had made you ashamed? While he was gone, you dared look in the glass, saw the lip pulled down into a flap or stilled clapper anyway lopsided.

Looked away.

But this is what you have to to ac *cèpe: a kind of delicious French toadstool, darling, which Maman is sure you'll adore when you're accustomed to it.* Learn to use the withered arm. Dried mushrooms you soak in water, use the water, the mushroom itself has served its purpose: throw it away.

The don brought in an old enamel basin could remember seeing somewhere rust-pitted in the yard rain spitting from long forgotten. He peeled the slippers off you the stiff socks.

"Pongifaction might set in." This was a joke for the servitor. Who didn't respondle. The Don was no Sancho. Hands seriously flowing through yellow soap. The dangling light from hair.

One foot was dead. Both all all were this vibrating pain dividing and multiplying. Forever, it seemed.

The lad knelt and flowed around the dead fungus as though life depended on him. Never had it with a boy. Could have been another funny joke the lolloping Lifebuoy appendicles and winking arsehole. Or: *un délice gastronomique pour Maman.* Non-poisonous toadstools.

Complain. "The good foot tickles, Don."

A corner of the body left didn't mean anything more than a tickle. The body wouldn't renasce. Nor the mind. The spirit an only hope. It flickered a little above the warm soapulent water.

It didn't flicker it stabbed him to watch his servitor's curved backbone the hanging light of unconscious flossy hair. To recognize the vulnerable indestructibility of a fellow spirit.

Don Lethbridge wasn't to be caught looking at the paintings, but you could tell he was worming his way into them by odd means of perception.

"Look!" It was cruel, but unavoidable at some point. "Here is some filthy money to spur." Spurn? Forgot how it finished.

Out from under the pillow he fished the notes to dangle for the archangel-servitor. Who took it like some young neophyte prostitute disgusted-greedy.

They didn't speak to each other much. Everything was implied and disguised. Their bodies came resentfully gratefully in contact. Their minds touched gingerly amazed. The disciple blushed amongst his down and pimples.

"What are you aiming, Cuppaidge"—must learn to remember ends of sentences however painful the found object—"to a chiev . . . in paint? Your peculiar goal."

The lily was spinning on her moorings she was so embarrassed.

At last Don Lethbridge grew reckless. "Well, I suppose I'm sort of trying to realize a feeling or a thought or emotion in pictorial terms sort of."

"You? Balls!" He couldn't make them round enough. "Don't tell me!" So shaken the vibrations must have burst through. "You! The first and only!"

Laughter and visible needles weren't going to scuppaidge the don. He was shining with his own vision. Which you recognized as the twin.

"See you in the morning, sir. Give you a hand with the washing and dressing. And anything else."

All the wrong subjects kept coming to the surface in your relationship with this sally willow.

"All right, Don."

"Not if I drive you up the wall!" Now it was the twin's turn to laugh.

"Please. I'm only going to try to remember . . . what I want you."

Don Lethbridge took up the freckled basin which was beginning to dominate the room the way objects will. He carried it out. Didn't even say good-bye. You don't when almost all is implied.

Try to remember why you sent for this second jailer. Not that anyone escapes ever. Not with the door wide open. Not very far.

"Where are you going, Hurtle?"

"Exercising."

"Oh dear! I ought to be going with you."

Supposing he dropped dead, stroked again, in Oxford Street, Rhoda's conscience would never forgive her for her brother's murder; on the other hand, she had looked after too many cats: she was too tired, though she no longer fed the neighbourhood.

"Exercise is all very well, but don't overdo it."

Two or three times he had gone to the class organized for fellow victims. They had wanted him to bowl a hoop. Too many mirrors. Two many grunting cunts and elderbellied stockbrokers. His own grotesque contributions corresponded too clearly to their gyrations.

"I won't! I won't! I insis! Snot my meteor."

All his stars had shot unaccompanied on an often unexpected, but well defined, fiery curve. He wasn't for constellations, unless the constellation were was were fragments of his own daring.

"I'll recover—if you let me—in my own way. In the streets," he added.

That was dishonest. He didn't believe it for a moment. Only that the streets were rivers of life. And to bathe in the waters of . . . could could.

So he advanced with the hopscotch shufflle and corner technique along the river banks grasping railings with his good hand whenever he failed to make HOME.

There was never any rest in this game he had begun, no it had been begun *for* him, his half-shrivelled body pursuing the course it had been started on, his mind more hesitant because too green and tender, shooting in all directions from old cut-back wood, feeling for recognizable holds, and suspicious of its own growth. He was reduced to this. When he had always got there by jumping out into darkness flying flying then landing on what his presence made believable and solid. After the first spitting, and gnashing of teeth, they had believed in what he showed them. Would show them again, too. Ready for the jump. If the spirit would only move in him. But the spirit plopped and slucked like hot lazy mud.

Oh God it was the colour of the sky he must try to remember. He hadn't seen it before or since. "Extra indigo" was the code word he had used while lying parcelled on the pavement. This same place.

In his vertigo he propped himself up on the shop window. What if it happened again of course it couldn't most unlikely it was only emotion from being in the same place and remembering the code word for the colour.

She ran out all jiggle joggle still a sexy bloody woman wanting to air her feelings on him.

She began to speak out of flaking lips, addressing someone supposedly deaf or moronic: "Oh, Mr Duffield, I'm so very glad to see you've made such progress. You know me, don't you? I'm Mrs Cutbush."

She, too, was looking uneasily at the pavement. At the Place. Afraid it might happen again.

"It's wonderful to think!" she harped.

The gull had by now almost devoured the starling in her hair. Must tear the guts out of that poor creep her husband.

"Haven't seen Miss Courtney. Is she, I hope, well? I expect she misses Miss Katherine Volkov." The gull seemed to swoop, squawk. "There's no one in our little circle who doesn't believe *they* have the only right to Kathy."

This Mrs Cotbus, who had probably saved his life, wanted to destroy something even more important in him. Mustn't let her smudge the indelible writing.

Lucky he had the window to lean on; instead of relying on conversation he read out an answer of sorts: "*Fonds d'artichauts, citrique, eau, sel. Laver avant* cooking. ARTICHOKE BOTTOMS." Tactless word in Cutbush circumstances; but she drove him to it.

She looked along the street, away from him. "The unusual lines aren't what you'd call popular," she said.

To console, he told her: "Keep at it, and they will be."

"Cecil's too artistic for a man—for a business—a *business* man." Her throat swelling turned a confession into an accusation: she couldn't forgive poor old Cec his unusual line in *cuissons*. "That's our whole trouble," she said.

Probably a good woman, and the grocer, who had saved your life by Triple O, good also, if "artistic." Two goods could obviously make a bad marriage.

Just then Cecil Cutbush himself steamed out from behind glass, trying to be a grocer, and church warden, and the Progress Association, and ex-councillor all rolled into one. "Well, Mr Duffield, you're looking a picture! A living picture!" Still a personage, he laughed for his appropriate remark; but at once the queen in him began to queer things: realizing the personage had crushed the wrong, the stroked hand, Cec was reduced to sensitivity. "So sorry—so clumsy."

And Mrs Cutbush was disgusted, less by the clumsiness and sensitivity than the interruption. She would have liked to stay, perving undisturbed on a great man to whom she had given suck that day on the pavement, almost sucked up into her womb as her own baby and lover-husband.

Unluckier for the grocer's wife when Mrs O'Hara came clacking hard towards her wanting the sago and split peas.

The noise, the people's inquiring faces, were becoming diabolical. Mrs O'Hara had a hairy raspberry on one nostril. But worst, the needles at work, in the dead flesh as well as the live. Your mind was just about popping out: the lid wouldn't hold it if you didn't didn't.

Stagger on. Or BACK. Sisters are colder.

But the grocer insisted: "I'll walk some of the way, Mr Duffield"; although he was wearing his apron and pencil.

Cutbush could have been waiting all his life to make a declaration of love. First he looked over a shoulder to be sure his wife had taken Mrs O'Hara inside. At least he had learned one lesson: he didn't attempt to touch; their affair was going to be "spiritual."

As you shambled endlessly in the direction of Flint, the grocer tiptoed in company. He was still a large man, if no longer upholstered, and his plush vanished. Age, it seemed, had made Cutbush fluid: he moved like plastic with half its volume of liquid inside. Coming at them from the sea, the wind agitated his wide trousers: they were flapping like flags, or a skirt.

For his great unburdening, the grocer was beginning to choose the unsaleable delicacies among words: exotic stock which had gone dusty rusty on his frustrated shelves, oozing oils from Palermo, rancid juices from the Côte Basque. He licked his lips.

"Mr Duffield"—he selected the name, and held it up—"I have never had an opportunity to tell you how much it has meant to us— to US—our comparatively small, but no less *avid* minority—to have you living in our midst." His nostrils enjoyed it the more for smelling slightly off. "Our confraternity may be underprivileged, and despised by some, but no one can deny that we appreciate the Higher Things. To walk past your home is, for us, a deeply moving experience. Flint Street has become a place of pilgrimage."

Oh Lord oh lard lard if you could only reach Flint your own pilgrim seize the cold pure rose by her thorns before being larded up in homogrocerdom.

"You remember the night we inadvertently met at The Gash? When the moon came up? I was severely troubled at the time, by conflicts between my home life and my—temperament. I often wondered afterwards whether the distinguished, anonymous—and handsome—stranger had noticed any signs of stress. Then, several years later, a malicious individual I happen to be connected with, explained a certain painting to me. I was horrified—which is what Malice had been hoping for—till suddenly I realized that, unbeknownst to myself, I had been consummated, so to speak!"

Oh Lard! The grocer's whispers were thunderous, his words working like sheet lightning.

"It was more than that. It was like as if, after attending regular service for years in a not very eyesthetical church, the same surroundings was illuminated by a—*religion!*"

O Lord save us it was the grocer who was going to have the next stroke. Scuttle scuffle away to Rhoda the cold rose a sister.

"Of course I never told anybody that we'd sort of given birth. I never pointed out to the wife that barren ground can sometimes be what the seed needs. I suppose I'm what people would call a coward." The grocer didn't attempt to hide the drops which were beginning to ooze. "I've often thought Judas must have been of a homo-sex-ual persuasion."

Poor bugger didn't seem to know the thing had caught on. Anyway, now that all was said, the unsavoury disciple flapped to a standstill. Murk couldn't obscure Luv: the big dope was shining with it.

"Forgive me, Mr Duffield, if any indiscretion on my part has embarrassed you. I wouldn't want—never ever—to be an embarrassment to the one I—I—I—" He couldn't make it.

Piteous what they lay on your altar, itself a rickety affair, so much shoved out of sight, from bottles of cheap port to unconfessed putrefying sins.

"Grateful for our interesting conversay, Mr Utbus. Mustn't be late for my lunch. My sister . . . my . . . my Rosa . . . will be hungry."

If you knew how, you could use words to get out of anything unpleasant, or important, which was why social intercourse had been invented.

Rhoda said: "Where have you been? I'd begun to worry. You knew I was planning something hot for luncheon."

"Yes, Rhoda." The exercise, or intercourse, made the words feel almost normal on his tongue. Had to edge into his chair, though, accommodate his dead side. That done, he said, and again it felt smooth: "I've been intercoursing. I had a nice talk with your friends Mr and Mrs Cutbush."

Rhoda appeared upset. "What about?" The cubes of fibrous chuck almost shot out of the casserole; the lengths of half-cooked carrot might have bounced if she hadn't been prudent. "What about, Hurtle?" Naming him made her sound angrier.

"About business. And religion. And sex."

Rhoda went a thinned-out white. "I hope you haven't been overdoing it," she said. "I shall be the one to blame, because I'm responsible for you."

On the contrary, he felt so strangely normal, perhaps thanks to poor old Cec Cutbush his lover. The lip subtle, almost supple enough, it could begin to pour at any moment. If he had had a sister Rosa of creamy pork flesh enormous Karl Druschki bubs he might have committed comfortable incest and painted a pagan goddess instead of looking for a god—a *God*—in every heap of rusty tins amongst the worm-eaten furniture out the window in the dunny of brown blowies and unfinished inscriptions.

Ah, he saw! He knew what he must tell Archangel Lethbridge the art student and footwasher. He didn't throw his fork, but let it fall in the soupy mess in front of him. The fork clanged against the plate.

"What is it?" Mumbling through the blue-grey gristle, Rhoda frowned furiously.

"Eureka!"

"I—*what*?" She hadn't received a classical education.

He got away, laughing at what he had found and what he must do.

Rhoda was livid. No Frau Druschki, more like one of those Japanese pellets which need a tumbler of water to flower. In other days, he might have explored the variations on Rhoda's paper rosette opening into an underwater rose. He couldn't now. There was no time for trifles.

While the torments of the body persisted, mind was no longer the irreparable mosaic, thought began fitting into thought, there were less shattering bursts of frustration: he might almost have hit on the secret of the maze. Even so, it would probably never become too easy. Nor would the dead arm, the dragging leg, give up their electric life although officially written off. He developed a technique of presenting himself sideways when acquaintances couldn't be avoided. Human turnips frightened him at times, themselves obviously frightened by the company of what they considered half a vegetable. (How electrified they would have become if he could have introduced them to half the shocks in that so-believed vegetable arm.) Rhoda frightened him most. She understood him so little after all, he began to wonder whether he understood Rhoda, whether he might catch sight of a different person standing naked in the ruins of the conservatory. And the gentle Don, particularly when you caught him looking too discreetly at the paintings:

what was he seeing? Was he falling into the same trap as Cutbush?

But none of these characters, whether fictitious or actual, would matter in the end: they would scatter like tarot cards during the long moment of the Second Fall. This was his great fear: that he should find himself parcelled again on the pavement before he had dared light the fireworks still inside him.

So he started preparing: stretching out his "good" arm through the never-ending electric rain. He must perfect his speech, too, that nobody should misinterpret his spoken intentions. So he sat darting his lizard's tongue. He caressed his lip perpetually, to correct a smile which would never have expressed his joys, and only leered boozily at disaster. If he was drunk, it was a deep, secret intoxication.

On a certain evening while a black wind from the Antarctic was threatening not only the last of the ornamental urns on the parapet, but the whole, cracked, reeling house, he was preparing to launch his rehearsed speech; when Don Lethbridge showed signs of forestalling.

"Mr Duffield, I don't see why you need me any more. There's nothing any more that I can do for you." He began picking at the boards with the point of his long Turkish-Italianate shoe. "And I need the time. More than the money. Frankly, I can't go on coming."

It brought on a cold sweat. It broke up the rehearsed speech into one of the old jig-saw puzzles.

"But this is . . . un sus pected . . . Col . . . ridiculelse. When I've only begun to need you. Never told you. I wasn't capable. The point . . . now . . . *is.*"

"Okay, go easy, man—sir—Mr Duffield."

The disciple squatted beside the chair in his crackled patent leather shoes. First time you had asked for anybody's pity, and the request was granted. (Perhaps prayer would pay.)

The boy continued squatting, in a patent leather martyrdom, kneecaps threatening to slit the strained cloth of his pants. "Okay, what is it?"

Composure came more easily in such kind circumstances.

"Well." A silver chain of anxiety still swinging, you saw, from your slob's mouth. "My handkerchief is lost."

Don Lethbridge reached up with his hand and swept the slobbery cobweb away. (Must remember Lethbridge is the other word for goodness.)

"Well." Never felt so frank and purposeful, not to say businesslike: *cunning.* "You will buy me . . . Don . . . Don . . . several boards of . . . of hardboard." The number, the proportions, had to be worked out again since agitation had made him forget the carefully calculated mental sum.

"But they're huge!"

"They have to be."

"What if they won't get in through the doors?"

Don Lethbridge, the simple saint, could bring about your destruction.

"They must! Ease them in! Bring somebody . . . enough . . . to help. I'll . . . I'll . . . *pay!*"

"Orright! Don't do yer block! What else?"

"Then you must prime the boards. Won't you, Don? I . . . will . . . show you . . . exactly. Haven't the strength for priming. *For painting only.* Take me my whole lifetime perhaps. Don? I am painting . . . *in my mind* . . . all the time. Now I have to teach my arm."

"And I reckon you'll teach it, dear!" Shooting upright, the Archangel had come over so girlish: annunciation made this Virgin spin on the balls of her Italianate feet, her floss of hair full of the glad news. "You can depend on me—now that I know."

The carriers forced the boards through the doorways, after long manoeuvring at unorthodox angles, more passionately up the stairs, under flakes of plaster, and once a whole fist of it. The stairs were reeking of cursing men with dewy armpits.

Rhoda came out below. "What is it? What's happening?" she called up. "We can't live at such close quarters and still have secrets."

Like hell you couldn't.

Rhoda was holding a handkerchief over her nose for fear of succumbing to drunkenness; while the men writhed struggling and thrusting upward with the boards.

Finally Rhoda screamed: "What a bloody shambles, Hurtle! And all for what? To die of it? You're mad, mad!" She slammed the door and shut herself in the kitchen.

The carriers were heaving inside their singlets. He didn't mind what he paid them. They went down glancing chastely at the scads of notes they were holding.

On his next visits Don Lethbridge primed the boards. Under further instruction he built a platform: something from which to attack the outer reaches of space. Ascent and descent were equally hellish, by way of solid enough steps, with a rail for the hand to haul on. The body protested, while the will drove; but none of the agonies would be proportionate to the rewards.

The importance of his mundane occupation had given the virgin don an Adam's apple. Now and then he offered pieces of masculine advice. "Steady on, mate! Don't wanter break yer neck before you get there."

He was right. Mustn't dither. You could have been stroked with Parkinson's disease as well.

"Leave me, will you . . . please. Don? D'you understand? Thank you."

You had to throw overboard everything known good loving trusted which might interfere with the wretched trembling act of faith.

When the Archangel had left him he sat with his hands between his thighs, his live hand holding his dead (or was it vice versa? he'd soon find out) this one hand pressed against his limp jack his aching balls.

Finally he stood up. To mount. There was no alternative: his paints laid out on the table clamped to the rostrum. He drove, he dragged himself. And began with little niggles in the non-colours he still only visualized for his purpose. This would be a black painting, with only the merest entrance into a light which was dead white: all that he had experienced under the dead pressure of despair.

So he was painting again, however painfully. Before he could contemplate his vision of indigo, he had to paint out the death which had stroked him. Some at least of the brush strokes, he recognized, were alive. His painfully electric arm performed extraordinary miracles; though not often enough. The white core had begun to glow, but there were the flat dead stretches leading to it.

Disregarding her afflictions, Rhoda had climbed the stairs: she was banging on the door. "Aren't you coming, Hurtle? I've made us a nice fricassee of rabbit. People eat to live, you know. And they eat together because it's sociable." When he didn't answer she shouted: "Then you *are* mad!" She had got drunk on the smell of strong men the day the boards were delivered, and her drunkenness had lasted.

"Oh—*God!* Go, fool!"

He dragged himself down from his rostrum. But she didn't expect him to open the door, and he didn't: he was too full of his own failure; he sat and belched out a lot of superfluous air, listening in between to Rhoda clumping down the stairs trailing the rose- peony-camellia-flesh she couldn't offer. All her men were dead to her: poor Rose, as withered as his once fluent arm, and its arrogantly hopeful substitute.

At least she hadn't watched the marionette jerking on his little wooden stage, failing in his act of faith. Don Lethbridge would have to know. He only came now when sent for. He would have to be fetched to manipulate the board. And slosh out the non-painting.

Don said: "Yes, it's a bit black. It's a bit dead." Here was the beloved disciple as detached as the most brutal critic. "Mmmhh. Interesting in a calligraphic way." Then, as coolly as he had inflicted them, he set about healing the wounds. "The white's beginning something, Mr Duffield. It's sort of leading out somewhere."

O God of mercy and straitjackets.

"Will you take off my shoes, Don? Just tonight? I haven't the strength."

When the pains from his affliction weren't scourging him into trying to paint works he was still incapable of realizing, they were thrilling him with half-glimpsed visions, of an intensity only comparable with his experience on the pavement at the moment he was forced to surrender his will. However he tried to persuade himself, his present compulsive, not to say convulsive, behaviour wasn't dependent on willpower as he had known it: by which he had been driven in the past, and by which he had bound others. He would never be able to rely on the little flickers and jerks generated by his dynamo to re-create what he perceived. He waited for the grace by which hints of it seeped out through his fingers, not of what he actually saw, but of what he was living, and knew: green-sickness of privet blossom; mildew-blue of its formal fruit; the blacker-green despair the araucaria had soaked up from the surrounding earth. Occasionally, when his arm failed him, he would slosh the unreceptive board with a stroke which, more often meaningless, sometimes pointed straight at the heart of the matter. At such moments he tremblingly believed he might eventually suggest—why not?—the soul itself: for which the most sceptical carcasses of human flesh longed in secret.

Standing in the lower reaches, the Archangel trumpeted up, but muted: "I think I'm beginning to see, Mr Duffield. It's—it's"—you weren't sure, it could have been—"beaut!" A solemn vindication.

Oh but at the same time you were so much scrabbled garbage waiting to be tossed into the pit.

"Will you help me down, Don? I'm tired."

He was also the respected character whom age and illness had transformed into a national monument. Deputations arrived: by arrangement, it could have been. In any case, Miss Courtney the unfortunate sister had on her best dress to open the door. She conducted them to the plinth on which the tribute was laid.

Honeysett came, with Sir Kevin and three guilty Trustees, dressed anonymously in business black. Evidently Honeysett had been chosen to play the official interpreter: it was he who spoke, to their accompaniment of grunts, restless eyebrows, and whimsical or frightened smiles.

A dark day outside and a roomful of listening furniture brought him quickly to the reason for their visit. "Sir Kevin—and the Trustees—feel you'll be doing the Gallery an honour by allowing us to hold a Retrospective of your work." The interpreter's eyes had the glazed look of someone who may not have memorized the written word; so he laughed, and it deflated him. "I don't expect you'll object, Hurt."

The grunts and murmurs of the others weren't so sure.

At his most jolly-extrovert, Honeysett began to stroke the dead knee across from him, but the shock of realizing what he was doing transferred him sharply to the live. His mistake made him laugh his heartiest; while Sir Kevin hung his nose, and the other Trustees were possibly trying to remember what they had heard about Art from their wives, in between being a barrister, a manufacturer of refrigerators, and a former night-soil contractor.

"We're planning for next year." Sir Kevin vibrated with seriousness.

"Time to call in stuff from overseas." Honeysett was shouting as though you were deaf, when Rhoda was the deaf one.

What did they expect you to say? "Well, it's an honour—yes—certainly." He heard himself: humble-mumble, mock-surprised—nauseating. "It's an honour for the paintings—independently. It's so long ago—there doesn't seem to be—much connection." *That was a lie*; but if they embalm you, they must expect a mummy.

They left him in his chair, in the sealed room used only as a waiting-room: or tomb.

In the hall they were making conversation with Miss Courtney. Somebody was a busybody.

"Oh yes," she was telling. "He's painting all the time. . . . No, I don't know. But he's very absorbed in it. . . . It's wonderful, isn't it? Because painting has been his whole life. So you can't say he isn't very much alive—can you?" She giggled: silly old Rhoda asking for reassurance.

He obliterated them after that, not by cultivated deafness, but with the swirling onrush of half-visualized images and raw ideas.

He continued painting, or agonizing. And exercising. They told him he was looking fine. In time he forgot to contradict.

When they began preparing for his exhibition Honeysett came to him at Flint Street. Rhoda had no right to let him upstairs, but she did. Because her brother hadn't died after all, because she felt safe again, she indulged in her old spitefulness.

Honeysett's invasion almost blasted you off the perch. "You must come in, Hurt—to the Gallery—any time you like—discuss the hanging—let us have your views." Always a masculine man, he lost his voice on a high, tentative, feminine note. "So this is what you're working on, eh? The new paintings!"

You were so indecently exposed on the scaffold you could imagine your own buttocks trembling white old into the intruder's face hear the little *pfft pfft* of fright smell the smell of puffballs unearthed.

Turn round and/or fall.

"Get out, Gil! Why do you persecute me? Why did Rhoda? She's the devil's!" Always in moments of distress the words clotted round the root of his tongue.

"Okay, Hurt. Don't upset yourself. Okay. It was a mistake. We'll let you know when everything's ready."

Honeysett began to retreat, his great sponges already on the stairs: a pneumatic bull threatening matchwood; while you continued gasping throbbing for what you had experienced for what you now understood of the indignity of rape.

Couldn't paint any more but clamber down off the squeaking scaffold it mightn't hold together long enough nothing would if the termites got to work.

On the other hand, there were mornings when the mere physical pains throbbed higher, to break into life, or live paint. He dabbed and scratched frantically. He reached out and drew his brush across the hard surface in a broad blaze of conviction, and watched the few last drops of fulfilment spurt and trickle and set forever. He was learning to paint; but as he tottered on the crude block, groping for some more persuasive way in which to declare his beliefs, it seemed that he might never master the razor-edge where simplicity unites with subtlety.

In between perching—in the dressing-table glass he had once caught sight of what was half a vulture half an old buckled umbrella rustily clawing a trembling paintbrush—he practised at improving his physical condition. Nowadays he trailed only slightly, unless he happened to come across someone he hadn't expected, or when the great buses began to topple screaming ballooning down on him. Then he recognized at once, in the eyes of strangers closest to him, his own fear disguised as pity. They were glad of this excuse to pity, because it made them feel virtuous again; and wouldn't this demi-corpse, standing between themselves and death, act as proxy for them?

"May we help you," asked their sweet smiles, "to cross the street?"

"No, thank you," he answered severely, because his own half-buttoned smile might have frightened them. "There's no need."

Then he walked with what he hoped was a hardly noticeable shuffle between the waters Jehovah was holding back. He must face not only the floods of time and traffic, but the Egyptian army of friends, critics, lovers, admirers, with which the Trustees of the State Gallery were threatening him. He must toughen himself.

They decided that, on the evening before the opening of Duffield's Retrospective Exhibition, the painter himself should be invited to the Gallery: ". . . alone if you prefer it, Hurtle, though of course Miss Courtney also is welcome, and anyone else you care to bring along to a preview." Then, as though Gil Honeysett suspected it might be construed as considerateness, or even sensitivity on his part, he safeguarded himself by adding: "Make the most of it, old horse; it will be your last opportunity to look at the paintings before the mob hacks into them."

"You surely aren't thinking of going out this evening! Oughtn't you to save up your strength for the awful thing ahead of us tomorrow? Hurtle? Whatever can you want to do tonight?" As though Rhoda didn't know; probably she never went so far as to read his letters: she didn't need to.

She had come out, wearing her apron, and was standing in the hall watching. Take Rhoda with him: like hell he would! Themselves alone together amongst the paintings: no gimlet would have bored so deeply. Was he afraid of the sawdust in him? Not all sawdust, but that is what Rhoda would have fetched out; she specialized also in moral flaws and sickness of spirit.

Hearing the flap of the letter-box as he tried not to slam the front door, he wondered if he had remembered to lock the doors which mattered. Too tired already, he couldn't contemplate turning back, climbing stairs. In any case, what were locks to Rhoda?

It was drizzling very slightly: in the street the lamps were shedding long, oily blurs of light. He looked back, and Rhoda was standing, in actual flesh, at one of the lower windows. From street level it looked as though her pointed chin was piercing the sill. Her receded eyes reflected the same blur of night and rain in which he had been plunged. Or was it something less impersonal? He remembered her saying: *I don't believe artists know half the time what they're creating. Oh yes, all the tralala, the technique—that's another matter. But like ordinary people who get out of bed, wash their faces, comb their hair, cut the tops off their boiled eggs, they don't act, they're instruments which are played on, or vessels which are filled—in many cases only with longing.* Was it this? Or had he dreamed, or imagined, or heard it from another quarter?

He hurried off as fast as he had learned, away from the house his sister had taken over and populated with his dwarfing thoughts.

The State Gallery, at which he arrived by secretly commissioned taxi, was an illuminated block of stone: no blurs here, or half-remembered night thoughts. Two or three of the attendants had been persuaded to stay behind for the unorthodox occasion; it was their turn to put on the hangdog look of sentimental subservience, while he straddled the entrance in what they must have recognized as show-all shorts. (Rhoda would have admired his legs!)

It was all the more irritating when Honeysett rushed forward: he couldn't get there quickly enough, to take an arm, no matter which, as though dealing with an old, breakable man; and the old man himself noticed his good black suit was looking shiny, and his wide trousers were flapping as deviously as the grocer's skirt.

"Here's the catalogue, Hurtle. Hope you like it."

"Thank you, Gil-bert." Out of politeness, he attempted the full name, but it split; all their words, like their gestures, were wooden.

He daren't look at the catalogue except to notice the carved-out DUFFIELD. Oh God, there was no avoiding it now: he was going to be held responsible.

As they walked across the blaze of parquet he heard himself start a rigmarole: couldn't be blamed in the circumstances. "The lettering, Gil—whatever possessed you to let them print the name in red? Red's too—too aggressive. It's coming at you on a motorbike. And the spacing makes the whole thing look out of proportion."

"Too late. It's done now." The extrovert patience of it made the speaker sound too vulnerable.

"It's tragic nothing ever comes out perfect." Well, Gil had asked for it.

They had almost crossed the desert: the plodding director and the silly old babbling coot. At least that was how it could seem in the game of appearances, and rejecting half the evidence: all these paintings along the walls, the windows to your actual, *willed* life, your every iridescent tremor and transparent thought.

As Gil Honeysett led from room to room it was some consolation to be able to touch the surfaces of paint and take refuge from the immodesty of words.

Only Honeysett, in his innocence, wouldn't leave it at that. "Aren't you *pleased*, Hurtle?" Determined to draw you out when you weren't going to be drawn.

"Yes. It's splendid." It was, too, as a concrete achievement. "Yes. I'm happy about it." When a flow of saliva started, and you had to swallow. "A bit of a give-away, though." He cackled, and hoped it sounded dry.

"How a give-away?"

"To see your life hung out—your whole life of dirty washing."

"How can you avoid it? Not if you're an artist of any account."

"Oh no, you can't help it. Anyway, the important part isn't here. Not what matters."

They were both growing uneasy.

With deliberately ugly gestures, Gil had begun to ease his pants.

"You mean those paintings you're working on?" Guilty over what he shouldn't have seen.

"Not what I'm working on. What I shall begin. When it has been worked out in me."

Poor Gil was looking terribly embarrassed. Shouldn't be surprised if he was wearing corsets under that suit too tight and too flash for his age.

They lingered a while in the paradise gardens, watching the display of fireworks and listening to their own thoughts.

Then Honeysett kindly offered: "I'll drive you home, Hurt, if you like. You ought to get some sleep, to face the fashionable rabble tomorrow."

"Yes, please."

As they wound through the dark, corkscrew streets he remembered to remind: "Drop me before the corner, Gil. I'd rather finish it on foot. My sister's very inquisitive, and would like nothing better than to find out where I've been."

Honeysett laughed: he was one of those who would always sound a big boy.

The night of what she had referred to as the Awful Thing, there was no avoiding Rhoda. Mrs Volkov, who would be there, as familiar, or relative, had run up a dress for her in rose silk. Some of its seams had escaped its creator's machine in places, but the colour of the silk assured a certain festive panache, and the folds seemed to breathe a scent of musky potpourried rose. Rhoda herself was burning with a fever of gaiety. She had tried to smother it under a blanket of white powder, but its hectic fire had broken out along the ridges of her cheeks.

In this context, her arthritic knuckles were more obtrusive than usually. "Are they painful?" he asked, and just prevented himself from putting out his fingers to explore; they had the same quality as carved horn.

"No." She composed her lips over her teeth. "Mrs Cutbush is thrilled. She always knew you were kind and thoughtful."

"After all, the bloody Cutbush couple picked me up off—off the pavement. And everybody has a Cutbush or two in their collection."

Tonight he and Rhoda, together, were slinging the dishes around in the sink. One of them broke one dish. He threw it in the bin.

Rhoda said: "Mrs Cutbush has read that 'everybody' will be at the Gallery for the opening of the Retrospective. She's read they're going to serve champagne."

Although it was a mild winter, they put on their coats, Rhoda's bald squirrel, and his old yellow tweed, for protection.

"We should have bought you a new fur coat."

"At the end of our lives?" She dropped the remark like a cannon-ball, when it should have sounded no more than air escaping from a balloon.

The Department had sent a long black car, which made it something like the occasion when she had brought him back from the hospital.

"I told them I didn't want it: not to be in their debt any more than is necessary."

"*I* wanted it," Rhoda said.

So he was in her hands, as far as you can be in human ones. He rather enjoyed it. With his live hand he held the dead one against his stomach. The motion of the car made him feel almost randy. They might have been driving to a rorty party instead of to a slaughter.

"With one thing and another, I've neglected my cats, Hurtle—but what could I do?"

Neglect or not, she smelled of horseflesh, and he wondered what the company would think. Probably most would have had a snifter beforehand; he and Rhoda were both comfortably brandified.

Once or twice he risked burping in the obsequious departmental car. Hardly ever drunk, except on paint. And Pa, that bottle-o, drunk once on misery.

Rhoda said: "How happy Father and Maman would have been."

"You didn't see my father."

"No."

"Or mother?"

"Of course I did. Mrs Duffield. I remember her wedding ring. It was the broadest I had ever seen."

"Did you know my grandfather died of a stroke on the Parramatta Road?"

"No. I didn't know, Hurtle." Rhoda was leaning forward, dangling her legs from the sumptuous seat, chafing her arthritic knuckles. "What if I did?" she began shouting. "And some get over it!"

"Yes. If they're allowed."

"Yesss," she hissed, bowing her head.

By the time they arrived the brandy was glittering in them again. Rhoda said: "I couldn't calculate when I last went to a reception. But I feel as slithery as a snake."

"Did you brush up your epigrams?"

Bundling out of the car, they enjoyed a little giggle for each other's wit. A pity the driver was only able to assess their bodies; so intent on dragging them out, he ignored their finely tempered minds.

"I never felt better—not, anyway—not since it happened."

But Rhoda was looking frightened again as they mounted the steps, either because she could hear herself wheeze, or because of the leg he was dragging after them, or perhaps on account of their common and unjustified daring.

Almost nobody had arrived.

Honeysett brayed: "Welcome, Miss Courtney, to the Auspicious Occasion!" and almost clapped her on the back. Restraining himself in time, he still couldn't avoid at least touching its unclassified substance.

Rhoda seemed more frightened than ever, not necessarily by Honeysett's near assault—she might even have enjoyed that—but because the late arrival of the guests made it inevitable that she should be noticed looking at her brother's paintings.

"Good God," she complained, "what an awful lot of them there are! And how rich you must be, Hurtle, to have sold so many enormous paintings. I wonder who you'll leave it to."

Grateful to Miss Courtney for ignoring his gaffe, Honeysett brayed worse than ever.

At the same time a young woman, cool as a lettuce, but with rather bulbous calves, came up and said: "All these for you, Mr Duffield." She gave him a fistful of telegrams. She also offered to take their coats, and seemed not a little curious to see what might be hidden underneath.

He delayed opening the telegrams, partly out of perversity, more because it would force him into declaring his hand on a night when it was unusually weak.

"Aren't you going to see who they're from?" Not that Rhoda was interested: since her birth as a rose out of a balding squirrel, she had stood prinking her petals, moistening her no longer drought-stricken lips. "I can't remember ever receiving a telegram," she murmured as though it were one of her virtues.

He decided to open one or two of the envelopes, but coldly. First he had to lay down the whole wad on a ledge. Alone in her deformity most of her life, Rhoda must have been planning this, though she hid her ploy under a vague grandeur and the rosy dress. Everybody watching was wondering whether to offer help. Rhoda at least joined him in warding them off with a stiff silence.

When he had steadied with his dead hand, and with his live one, torn out a lump of envelope, he read:

All praise to the delicious monster—Boo Hollingrake.

"That's from Olivia Davenport," he told Rhoda. "You remember Boo?"

"Oh dear, will she be here? I never liked her."

"But you and she were bosoms as girls."

"I didn't like her. She only liked me because I made her laugh."

He couldn't remember ever making Olivia laugh; for that matter he couldn't remember Olivia Davenport: her jewels, her dresses, her parties, perhaps. Slightly more, he remembered Boo Hollingrake: under the *Monstera deliciosa*, and in the William Street post office.

Distraction drove him into opening another of the telegrams:

Courage for tonight love and thoughts—Volkov.

"Why should she send a wire?" Her "thoughts" made him furious. "Isn't she going to be with us? Besides, I hardly know the woman."

"Who?" asked Rhoda, from a cloud since accepting a cigarette offered by Mr Honeysett.

"Mrs Volkov."

"She sent it out of kindness, I expect. And because she admires you."

But he didn't care to be admired by one who had recognized a "lost soul."

"It's"—he was panting—"it's a waste of money." He was conscious that even the good side of his face was going. "Since when have you begun to smoke?"

"Since now."

"But it doesn't—it isn't like you!"

The way she held the cigarette it was something offensive but inevitable: a cat's turd, for instance, discovered in the corner of her room.

"I think I thought it might be bad for me," she said and laughed.

Ostensibly because his little sister was playing up he didn't open any more of the telegrams; while actually he was too intent on frisking Mrs Volkov's image for her motives.

As they sauntered through the glaring rooms, Rhoda breathed: "All of Hurtle's naked women!" Her languor was for Honeysett, who enjoyed the unlikeliness of the situation; but Gil, like Mrs Volkov, was kind.

Remember those pale lips in the bus trying to draw you into what could only be an ectoplasmic relationship.

Irritation drove him to shake out the telegram again: it was a cable—no, a rocket, he realized, launched from New York.

Glad he had fallen behind the others, he was still gladder he hadn't opened the rest of the sheaf. What if Hero? What if Nance—*Colthirst*? oh God, senility was the worst threat of all, and here were the ghosts threatening him with it, the polterghosts standing him on end.

But why VOLKOV? Unless to show him she was his equal. It was what he had wanted for his spiritual child, his Kathy: other names could only be adoptive. She was not his equal, however; her *love and thoughts* stroked him with the tails of Maman's sables. He was their little boy, whose head they were shoving inside the wardrobe, to drug him with scents, to protect themselves from his third eye.

At the first opportunity he detached Rhoda from Honeysett. "It wasn't Mrs Volkov. It was Kathy. In New York," he whispered.

Rhoda must have been expecting it. "Why not? I believe the child was very fond of you. And you were too self-absorbed to notice." His accuser had never looked so ravaged, still holding her cigarette on high, though no longer parallel with the parquet.

Suddenly he realized the floors were buckling and groaning as the wheels of the enemy chariots began to grind across them.

"Boy! We're for it!" Honeysett ran forward bellowing, jingling his money, as though to dive head first into waves there was no question of stopping.

The Trustees had been at pains to harness society with intellect.

There was, in addition, a rabble of nonentities wished on them by the painter, with such ill humour one could only suppose he regretted his own sense of duty. Naturally the sister had to come, and in any case, everybody would want to have a look at the sister; but some of the others lowered the tone: they smelled of failure or modesty.

So, whatever the organizers had intended, the elements of their rout were varied: some arrived, their fashion the blowsier for formal dinners, trailing, along with their stoles and the fringes of their conversation, scents of the liqueurs and cigars from which they had been rudely dragged; others more ascetic, in day clothes, discovered traces of the delicacies they had swallowed in a hurry: aspic from chicken's breasts, oil dribbled from dolmas, the last exquisite grain of caviare stuffing a hollow tooth; while a humble few were round-eyed still from their strong cuppa and beans on toast. Almost all had fortified themselves in some way at some earlier stage of the evening, and were now controlling a resentful scepticism arising out of gas and heartburn. One or two were possessed by a devil of excitement: they hoped for an experience; which nice people and professional intellectuals were for once united in condemning as ignorant and tasteless.

"Are we going to come clean? Do you—*honestly*—believe he's any good?"

"They buy him overseas."

"Oh yes, ill-advised Americans. The press never stops telling us. But I can't believe in the great myth. I haven't the faith expected of me."

"No, Elspeth. Faith isn't expected of university graduates."

"All the worst bitches are dogs! I wonder, darling, why I adore you?"

They looked back over their furs or ritual black, to determine on what ground their words had fallen, but failed disappointingly to identify it.

"D'you think that's him?"

"Too young."

"Too old."

"I can recognize him from the pictures in the papers."

"Too shaky. He's had a stroke—not Parkinson's disease."

Listening to them trample across the parquet, he was reminded of a visit with Harry Courtney: a prehistoric landscape, in which sheep were mounting a ramp, pressing inside the woolshed, pattering over the slatted floor, automatically scattering their pellets.

The present mob might have trampled Rhoda underfoot if it hadn't suddenly realized she was something beyond its experience; so it propped, and divided: to avoid an object which looked strange and could have proved dangerous. While continuing to patter in their changed directions, the human sheep bleated their distress, or in milder, woolier cases, sympathy, or self-pity.

"Certainly quaint. To say the least. Poor little thing!" Foetuses stirred uneasily in the alcohol of memory: it wasn't as bad as this, but might have been, if it had lived.

"Never went much on culture. Ten dollars, too. You expect more for ten dollars."

"Look at all the lovely paintings."

"Where's the champagne?"

"Too soon. And it won't be—you realize that, don't you?"

"Champagne's what I paid for."

"You expect too much, Clyde. You'll get the bubbles at least."

"Whatever else you accuse us of, you can't say we aren't a *sound* society. Don't look now—that's the painter over my left shoulder. And the sister."

"The sister's his worst distortion yet. I wonder what they talk about."

"Technique."

"You've got it on the brain."

"I want to look at the paintings."

"You don't come to look at paintings. If you're all that keen, you come back one morning when there's nobody here."

"Isn't it lovely? Lovely! A lovely party."

"This is the biggest con man Australia has produced."

"At this rate we'll never get round. Look, there's Margery!"

"I propose to take the paintings in chronological order."

"If you're going to be a stodge podge. This isn't professional night."

"You can't call him an amateur; he fetches too much."

"I just want to look at the paintings. They do things to me. I don't know what. But they do."

"Can't wait."

"Darling, there are too many people."

"One has to admit old Hurtle's a wizard."

"Most of this raggle-taggle wouldn't."

"Oh yes—I think they'd agree he's a wizard. They might argue whether he's great."

"Aren't you destroying one of your own stable, Bid?"

"Whether he's mine or anybody else's, I can't help being honest. Nonetheless, I adore Hurtle."

"With your dried-up peanut of a tasteful spinster's mind."

"Mrs Macready has an early one. She says the early ones are the ones."

"If you want to be insulting."

"They're an investment."

"Every Sunday at St Stephen's."

"If you want to show me the worst in you, you're going about it the right way."

"They'll catch him over his income tax."

"Mrs Macready's going to sell the early one."

"If you want me to tell you why you're a misfit, Patrick, it's because you hate everybody."

"Mrs Macready says London and New York are off him. He was never what he's cracked up to be. But there's still a market for him in Australia."

"Because I can't love peanuts, Biddy, it doesn't mean I don't love."

"I'm going home. You've upset me too much. You've made me feel ill."

Oh oh.

"Where's the *pissoir*?"

"Somewhere in the underworld."

"It's the champagne, buddy."

"She's a Jewess."

"What do I think of them? It's as if I haven't been seeing till now —and now I'm blinded."

When all but the wooliest had thrown off their sheepskins, the forms most of them revealed were heraldic in their ferocity. Even those who spoke in his defence screeched with tongues of thin metal; their armoured claws might have sacrificed his liver to their convictions. He found himself moving sideways: a technique he had adopted after his return from the dead, and thought he no longer needed; but on the present occasion there was no escaping, except along walls of paintings, which might at any moment pronounce a more vindictive sentence than that of the judges themselves.

"Look—a bat, wouldn't you say? Practically embracing one of his own excremental daubs!"

"Oh, come! It's the crush. You couldn't fit in a praying mantis."

"I do believe Hurtle Duffield's got the wind up. Never thought I'd witness that. Cold fish!"

"Vicious bastard!"

"I think he's divine. I'd adore to sleep with him."

"You must be the only one who didn't."

"I've never slept with an old man."

"And little girls."

"That's the propaganda. I was told by Arch Parfitt—and he ought to know—that Hurtle Duffield switched to boys."

"All his life. There's an old queen, a Paddo grocer, his bosom friend."

"But it's all so gimmicky—one conjuring trick after another. Painting is pure today. This is an austere age. Illusions don't belong in it—not his kind anyway."

"I'd part with ten years of my life to have painted that 'Pythoness at Tripod.' "

"And hanged yourself afterwards out of remorse. Anybody but Hurtle Duffield would have."

"Look at those saltcellars he's given her! The saltcellars alone are genius."

"I'm going, Dick. D'you hear? I've gotter go. Something funny about those oysters. If I don't go I'm gunner spew on the spot."

"Oh, Mr Duffield, what a wonderful evening for you—and so soul-satisfying for the rest of us. Will you sign my souvenir catalogue, please? Oh, not if it—not if it—in any way . . . If he hadn't looked so peculiar, Mildred, I'd say the man meant to be rude."

"He's sick."

"You don't suppose he thinks I'd sell the autograph? Mrs Macready did. But that was a whole handwritten letter. She sold it to an American."

"He's sick, I tell you. He's a sick man."

"The paintings are sick."

"I'd like to speak to him, but of course I never shall. There are so many things I'd like to ask him to explain."

"Don't ask a painter, don't ask anybody to explain. All you'll ever know is what you find out for yourself by butting your head *through* the wall."

"I like to believe in revelations. And these paintings are, for me, almost revelations. That is why I could go down on my knees, and beg, *beg* him for one little word which might remove the last scale from my eyes. Because I'm sure he has the answer. I'm sure it's here in the paintings. If I could only see."

" 'Numen' is the word I've been trying to remember all the evening. Not apropos. I'll probably die a sceptic."

O numinous occasion sighted in distorting mirrors of variable treachery! Now that the trap was closing on him, what he longed for was a room of reasonable proportions furnished with a table and chair. The thought of himself perched on a chopping block, reaching up with his functional arm, became so ludicrous he almost toppled. But steadied himself on one of the paintings. By coincidence or design, it was one of that series of furniture he had painted after Hero's death, soon after the Second War, at a time when he felt his creative life must be leaving him; yet the tables and chairs now appeared the most honest works he had ever conceived, and probably for that reason the most nearly numinous.

Which didn't mean he could stop himself attempting to reach higher, from his chopping block or scaffold, towards total achievement or extinction.

He fished out his handkerchief to mop up his sweat.

"A glass of champagne, Mr Duffield?"

"Is it good?" A blunt question, it sounded unintentionally severe.

"Oh yes, it's good!" The young waiter, his rather innocent skin freshly scrubbed, his smile too ready, lowered his eyes: on such a night the counterfeit made the true look fake.

When the waiter had left him, he sank his chin and guzzled the insipid gaseous wine. It didn't make him feel what is known as "better," only unhappy in a different way, as he wandered a little through "his" exhibition, holding the empty glass as though it were some other object.

Here and there they filled the glass, not the original waiter, though it could have been: they were all alike in their confident, though transient modernity.

Good Gil Honeysett, that bloody extrovert, came and held him by the elbow and said: "Everybody's asking to meet you, but I staved them off, just in case you mightn't want it."

"What do you take me for? A nut?"

Gil didn't answer, but smiled around in other directions out of his decent, sweaty face.

You were standing, you realized, beside a small dais spread with a square of Axminster carpet.

"That carpet, Gil—it's about the most hideous I've ever seen."

"Yes, it is, it's hideous."

"And the chair—it reeks of public service."

Brought out of a board room probably, it stood displaying its chafed leather, waiting to fulfil some possibly reprehensible function.

Suddenly Gil Honeysett tickled the ominous ramrod of a microphone very lightly. "Later on, the Prime Minister wants to say a few words, Hurt. We'd be happy if you'd reply—making it as brief as you like."

Play for time, play for safety, play for silence, the only state in which truth breeds.

"Okay, Duffield?"

"Mm."

Gil was so radiant in the innocent conviction that human nature is predictable. If you had been younger, if you had been in a position to indulge in the more extravagant licence of creativity, you might have done a face, mouth but no eyes, swathed in the fleshy veils of the human arse.

"In the meantime, here's an old friend of yours." Again the Extrovert-in-Chief sounded so extraordinarily convinced. "I'll leave you to it."

A person was definitely evolving out of the aimless struggle of art lovers: a man if it hadn't been for the aggressively mannish clothes, a woman except for a certain priestly air. The straight black hair had abandoned all pretences, unless its black black. What really let the creature down was the mouth, overflowing with anachronistic crimson, and the jewels, of an importance which refused to be renounced.

"Hurtle," she began at a distance, while telling her enormous pearls as though they had been humble little beads, "I don't want to appear vindictive—forcing my wreckage on you. I should hate to be guilty of that, but I do honestly believe age can be a source of inspiration."

She probably realized he didn't share her view, for when she reached him, with the determination of the old and crippled, and her fire of rubies, she laughed a discoloured laugh. "I see you can't, or don't want to, recognize. 'Hollingrake' is the name."

"Why—Boo—of course—Boo Davenport." She was forcing him to obey the social convention she would have liked him to think she had abandoned.

"Hollingrake," she corrected.

She kept turning her head as though looking for others who might applaud. Or was it for someone she still had to meet?

"I heard you'd gone back to 'Hollingrake,' though nobody explained why."

It must have been what she expected. "Well"—she lowered her blancoed chin—"I never managed to throw off the 'Hollingrake.' Since we last met—at some ghastly party, wasn't it?—I remarried. Sebastian was the least demanding of my husbands. He was so considerate I found it intensely mortifying. I should have divorced him if he hadn't saved me that worst mortification. He died. Now I've reneged. I'm a confirmed bachelor."

The thought struck him that his own bachelorhood might have crossed her mind, and that her joke was an accusation in disguise. He hoped one of the slaves might fill the empty glass each of them continued holding; but nobody came; and he was to experience worse than Olivia's dirty crack.

Surprisingly she said, though in such a loud voice her remark couldn't be intercepted: "At least nobody can accuse you, Hurtle, of being a virgin soul. Not with all these paintings to contradict them." Then, after a quick look over her shoulder, she added in a seismic whisper: "I've wanted, off and on, to talk to you about the paintings."

He twitched at the idea: and Olivia had the feverish look of those who can never resist discussing religion.

Fortunately, at that moment, their glasses were filled, and they stood pretending to sip, while gulping, the mock champagne.

"I've even culled a vocabulary," Olivia Hollingrake confessed between gasps and a near sneeze, "on nights when I couldn't sleep —by which we might communicate."

"No," he protested into the flat dregs of resentment.

"Oh, but why not?"

"Because," he said, and it seemed to be coming out from the dead side of his face, the buckram half he no longer bothered hiding from her, "I'm just beginning. I'm only learning."

Now it was his turn to look over his shoulder; so many hated him for the sins they believed he had already committed against them, would they be able to endure this supreme flouting of their reason?

He only slowly realized Olivia had taken him by the wrist. He rather enjoyed, from inside his own painfully prickling carapace, her soft, cushiony palm protected by its mail of jewels. She must have caught him staring at one cabochon knuckle in particular, because she lovingly murmured, swallowing the sounds almost at once: "That one is pigeon's blood. An Indian prince—I forget which —gave it to Mummy." But that was only incidental; she had arrived at the next stage in the unfolding of her plan.

"I want you to take me to your sister. I'd like to congratulate her for the part she's played in your success. Rhoda was so sweet." Olivia laughed. "How she must have suffered—she, too!"

It was the more indefensible in that Rhoda and her cronies were gathered within hailing distance, against a period of his work which particularly exposed his frailty: his love for Kathy.

Rhoda couldn't have helped noticing the straits he was in; in fact, she made it clear that she knew. The rose clown was laughing up at her companions, at Cec and Bernice Cutbush, at the transparent Mrs Volkov, and Don Lethbridge in his slackest woolliest blackest sweater and skinniest blackest pants. Rhoda, in her determination to ignore an outside situation, was doing everything but handsprings to amuse her circle. Her little pointed teeth were working overtime in smiles.

Olivia Hollingrake kept looking in the opposite direction. "I remember," she said, possibly hoping to avert the present at the last moment. "I remember getting the fright of my life when I discovered Rhoda still only reached my navel, while I kept on shooting up. It made me feel abnormal. But Rhoda was so understanding. I'd invite her in while I was having my bath. And she'd sit stirring the water—telling me about the brother I had a crush on."

The elderly archness of it shrivelled the senses which would have liked to drag him under, amongst the drowned mangoes and floating ferns, while Rhoda—indeed—stirred the water.

"Rhoda doesn't know—Rhoda knew nothing!" He dragged his hand out of the crustaceous grasp. "Never!"

"She used to write down *everything* in a diary."

If Rhoda and Olivia were allowed to get together—but each

seemed determined it shouldn't happen, anyhow tonight.

"With drawings," Olivia continued, but vaguely, while looking in the opposite direction.

"Drawings? I'm pretty sure Rhoda never drew a thing. Tell me, Olivia?"

But Boo Hollingrake was smiling the smile she had caught from her mother. "There's the Prime Minister. I must go and have a few words with Sam. I have a message for him from a cardinal. You know I'm living in Rome? For purely aesthetic reasons," she explained. "It's never too late to be converted to other forms of beauty."

She set off on her next mission as quickly as her bones and the crush permitted; and he would have joined Rhoda, to dissect the relationship Olivia claimed had existed, to discover whether, in spite of her professed dislike, Rhoda had been in fact Olivia's confidante and spy; only the crowd wouldn't let him. Not only solid bodies but tumbling spillikins of voices were against his arriving; for as the latter fell into their disorderly spillikin heap, it was impossible to ignore the game: against his will, of course, he continued detaching the more detachable straw-remarks.

"They say all this is nothing to what he's still got stashed away in the house. There are nightmares of perversion, really bad, mad things, which he won't allow anyone to see, and which even he can't bring himself to look at."

"But somebody must have seen them. Otherwise, how do you know?"

"Somebody told me in confidence. Actually, it was Biddy Prickett."

"Then probably Biddy's been shown all these delectable obscenities."

"Probably she has. She and Ailsa handled his stuff for years."

"Let's go and look for Bid."

"I couldn't help overhearing—but Miss Prickett's gone off in a huff. Somebody insulted her."

"Oh, nonsense, Max. A waiter spilled a glass of champagne down her cleavage."

"Would one glass break the drought? She seemed to be crying."

"She was insulted by someone."

"Biddy was insulted."

"Hurtle insulted Biddy. I know from a very reliable source she aspired to be his mistress. That's the root of the matter. Of Biddy's whole trouble."

"The root? Oh, sorry!"

"Oh Max!"

He was by now so close to the reason for his setting out, he could no longer see Rhoda herself. She was hidden somewhere inside the heap of spillikin voices, behind the frieze of normal human bodies, or masked Furies, none of whom would rest while there was a murder to avenge. None of the masks deceived: they were too obviously jolly, too jolly drunk, and not on false champers.

While he was struggling, a particularly cynical waiter, himself a little drunk, offered in a shout: "Let me freshen you up, Mr Duffield, with a drop of this nice sparkling Moselle," and waved the bottle above the sea of greedy heads.

A woman leaned over, one arm restraining her runaway breasts, the other raised to strike. "I want to touch you, Hurtle Duffield," she called through her cut-out, scarlet-varnished, papier-mâché mouth.

She did touch, too, and withdrew her hand as though it had been shocked by electricity. It should have been: the parts of his stroked body were tingling relentlessly.

Cecil Cutbush was waving, whether to draw attention to himself in his role of Bosom Friend, or simply to encourage the drowning. The closer you came, the heavier the swell of voices, the stronger the undertow. Don Lethbridge, up to the chin, looked anxious: never learned to swim perhaps.

"I find it hard to believe in—what shall we call them?—the pornographic series of drawings or whatever—which everyone talks about, but nobody has seen."

"I entirely agree with you, Sir Jack!"

"And even less, the latest crazy myth."

"Oh, what? Do tell us, Sir Jack."

"The God paintings."

"The what?"

"The God paintings."

"What exactly do you mean, sir?"

"Is Duffield painting God?"

"Painting himself, more like it."

"How rich! Now that *will* be obscene! At this stage. If only he'd painted himself while he was still only a god."

"I consider it frivolous to make such remarks, or pass judgement, before we've examined all the facts."

"Oh, entirely! I do agree with you, Sir Jack."

"I don't, because by then the cove'll be dead. He won't be answerable for the blasphemous muck he leaves behind. And which some of them will feel it their duty to 'understand.' I hate the phonies of this world."

"But these new paintings—whether they exist or not—somebody must have thought they did."

"Oh, I do think it's exciting to be living now—what with space and everything."

"Let's ask Benny Loebel. Benny? Benno! What about the God paintings?"

Loebel closed his eyes and smiled an appropriately mystic smile. "I do not know faht you expect to hear." He wasn't born a Viennese for nothing.

"Silly old shyster! Have you SEEN?"

"I wonder who ever thought it up. God is dead, anyway. Anyway—thank God—in Australia."

"Only hypothetically, Marcus."

"I'm on your side, Sir Jack—at least, I think I am. Even though Marcus will probably kill me for it, I do hope the God paintings exist. The whole idea's rather beaut."

"I hope for your sake they do, my dear. You're at your most spectacular when most enthusiastic. Particularly in pink."

By practising a kind of sidestroke, by half closing his eyes against the spray of words, by straining his neck muscles and kicking out with his good leg, he had almost reached the haven of a still corner under the lee of columnar cliffs where friendly hands were waiting to haul him to comparative safety. Cecil Cutbush was the first to help, his grip clammier than you would have liked, too damp-spongy, too awful by half; and the irony: that the Cutbush-Volkov set, Rhoda's friends, should be yours. Rhoda his pseudo-sister, still no more than a rosy blur to the right, could turn out to be only a papier-mâché rock when put to the test, but Cec and Bernice Cutbush had appointed themselves his personal lifesavers.

The Cutbush couple appeared in favour of physical methods of resuscitation. Bernice was all for massaging the biceps and kidneys; for two pins, Cec would have given the mouth-to-mouth a go: his face approached so close, the daring little dash of rouge was the only dry in his largely liquid pores.

"How are you keeping, on this—this epic night, Mr Duffield?"

Because your smile felt more than ever lopsided, and an answer might have meant a painful struggle, you rewarded Cecil by squeezing his elbow, and at once his face put out flags.

Bernice saw. "You must take care of yourself—remember your health, Mr Duffield," she warned, and frowned. "Keep a hold of your emotions—even when thoughtful friends encourage you to let go. We wouldn't want to see you take another fit—would we?"

Mrs Cutbush, also, longed to be touched, but he was too cruel, or too prudent, to oblige.

Of all people, it was Shuard the music critic who saved him from his saviours. (Shuard shouldn't have been invited; but why had anybody been invited?)

Shuard whispered: "Some evening I'd like to celebrate in camera —among friends—your great success. Ask in a few girls. There are so many variations now that they're letting in the Asians to study. And old Cec Cutbush, needless to say. Wouldn't be complete, would it?—without Cecil's act."

"I've no idea."

But Cec had. At mention of his act, jet began encrusting the bosom of his business suit: he was all smirk in the shadow of his ostrich feathers.

"Incidentally, Hurtle," Shuard attempted an even more confidential tone, which remained as audible as brass, "I received a letter by this evening's mail—an *air* letter—from the little lady"—(actually digging you in the ribs)—"from Kathy Volkov!"

Peugh! Shuard's breath stinking of stale underclothes.

"There's a message in it she wants me to deliver. She wants me to tell—"

"No. No! Not now! Some other time." Not Shuard undressing their relationship.

"She said," the man insisted, " 'Tell my dear old mate, my darling old rooster—' "

"No! I don't believe. I don't want to—know. Never!" His pure soul, his spiritual child.

At least the incident gave the mother her cue. Mrs Volkov, so pale, so shy, so unworldly as to be the ghost of a woman—a wonder the Russian ever got it in—sidled up in an impersonation of somebody who had suffered a stroke. Certainly she'd had one herself, but so slight, or so overcome, she could only count as a cryptovictim.

Looking to one side of him, Mrs Volkov said: "I've never thanked you, Mr Duffield, for the part you played—in—in *moulding* my little gairl."

Mrs Volkov had probably never shown a blush: she was too anaemic; but now something was happening to her: she all but gave off pale vapours, together with the innocent perfume from some kind of health soap.

"*Moulded?*" He shouldn't have: but what else?

And now the abnormal word, from hanging out of Mrs Volkov's mouth, was protruding from his also, contoured like a film-star's breast.

As soon as he could manage his lips again, he assured the mother: "I think Kathy was born with a pretty good idea of the shape she must take."

"I don't know, I'm sure," Mrs Volkov murmured. "I received no education, but came here at sixteen, from Carnoustie. And keep to myself." Then she actually did blush, a brilliant satiny rose, as she realized for the first time, it seemed: "My daughter is my only extravagance."

They laughed so easily and happily together, acknowledging the ailment they had in common; he only had to go and spoil it by remembering what he was looking for.

"Where is Rhoda?"

Mrs Volkov appeared alarmed; her answer was in an intake of breath. "Miss Courtney—she's here, of course, Mr Duffield—at your elbow."

So he turned, and there was his sister, as Mrs Volkov had predicted.

Rhoda lowered her eyelids, and drew in her teeth, which he suspected had been glistening and laughing the moment before in some piece of by-play with Don Lethbridge. (Don was certainly her spy, as she was probably Olivia's.)

"I've been looking for you, Rhoda."

She grew increasingly sullen. "I don't know why you should. With everybody courting you." One of the seams of the rose dress, so devotedly machined by Mrs Volkov, had burst right open.

"Don't you know I depend on you?" Draw her out.

"Are you ill then?" The drifts of powder still clinging to her face made it look more anxious.

What he saw reassured him; though with Rhoda you could never be absolutely sure. "I wanted to ask whether you had noticed Mrs—Mrs Davenport," he tried, and watched.

Rhoda hesitated. Though outwardly still—she might have been carved out of grey pumice—her mind, he saw, was skipping on ahead.

"Olivia Hollingrake," he explained, to help them both in a difficult situation.

Immediately Rhoda's eyelashes, such as they were, began to sift the guileful possibilities with which her mind had been playing.

"Oh Boo!" It was accompanied by what was intended, no doubt, as a radiant expression. "Yes, I've noticed Boo several times this evening. What a magnificent figure! How wonderfully preserved!"

"Olivia? About all Olivia's been able to preserve are the Hollingrake jewels."

But Rhoda didn't seem to hear. "That dress—it might have screamed on anyone else—a gold dress. I wasn't close enough to examine it in detail, but from a distance you had the impression of pure, beaten gold. Imagine! And so few women can afford to display a naked back." She had faltered at no point in saying her piece.

"Olivia? A gold dress? To me she looked more than anything like a scruffy old Italian priest stuck with ill-gotten carbuncles."

Rhoda sighed. "Perhaps I tend to see Olly"—(no one in his memory had referred to Olivia as "Olly")—"in a golden light. Don't you remember how the light at Sunningdale was always golden—always morning?"

He did; but the light was beside the point.

"Why didn't you approach this vision of gold and nakedness?"

"Oh, I wouldn't dare!" She laughed, and contemplated her burst seam with detached interest rather than concern.

"She said she loved you very dearly. That you had shared secrets and jokes, which you recorded in a diary. I wonder which secrets and jokes you shared with *Olly*."

"I destroyed the diaries while I was still a girl."

"Then nobody will tell. And the bath water's gone down the hole."

Rhoda flinched only very slightly inside her trance. "What astonishes me, Hurtle, is that you should need to ask. With an exceptional memory like yours. I've never envied you a bit of it."

So Rhoda, too, was putting on the mask: wasn't there one they called "Megaera"?

"Oh, memory—memory's too full in the end. If you could tear it up—like a bloody diary."

Rhoda dropped her mask: she was the tattered moppet smelling of a cheap face-powder she had put on to spite Maman; spiritually, but only spiritually, she was floating in Maman's borrowed shoes.

"Then you *are* sick!" Her pronouncement sounded hopeful, if not joyful.

"Is that what you want?"

"You can do things for people when they're sick. Or old."

Was it—dreadful thought—what they had *both* always been longing for? To be united, in one senile mind, mumbling over a basin of groats.

"Not if I'm struck dead!" he shouted.

Rhoda gave him such a frightened look, she could only be superstitious, in their rational Australian society.

"I have something to finish," he added with less passion, and tried to find consolation in his wrist watch.

But the minutiae of their surroundings were crowding back on him: the white shaft from an overhead lamp turning a painted surface into a sea of molten glass words proliferating *I can't see what it's meant to be a man is it a woman a very gnarled one a tree then I expect it's whatever you want it to be* like most things gold threads in a brocade coat the jujube colours of the seemingly victorious young the few pale pink hairs tenaciously resigned in a very old neck something something particularly horrendous the Prime Minister's speech and after.

Speech is surely more brutal than paint because it tends to dictate rather than state.

Here in this foetus, for instance, in a fringe of beard, not in jackboots certainly, elastic sides, who has stood the Archangel up. This foetus thing is dictating to the Faithful Disciple what he must tell the magic wand and black box.

"Surely, though, if you're so close to—to the 'master'—the painter —Mr Hurtle Duffield—you must have seen these paintings everybody's so interested to hear about? These so-called 'God paintings.'"

"I don't know. It's none of my business."

544

"But haven't you any—any sense of historic importance? You're his associate, aren't you?"

"His what?"

"Well—let's put it another way—aren't you a fellow painter?"

"No! I'm not a painter. I'm a student. I'm not a painter. And may never be—a painter."

"Ah, modesty! I hope you mean what you say, Don, because if you don't, that would make it less—refreshing. *Ha-ha-ha!*"

Mumble mumble gurgle gurgle.

"Then what are you, if you're not a painter. A male nurse?"

"I haven't had any training."

(Isn't he divine? So moving. This is what's so exciting about being alive today—to be able to *participate* through television.)

"What is your official function, I mean—Don?"

"A what?"

"I mean—what do you do for—for your friend Hurtle?"

(Heugh-heugh! He's a real winkler!)

"Oh. I helped to wash and dress him when he came back from hospital. Miss Courtney's an invalid."

"Miss Courtney?"

"His sister."

"Courtney?"

"Yes."

"Hmm. So you *washed* him."

"Yes. Only for a little. Because he learned to manage. Well, I still wash his feet now and again. He can't reach so far. Not when he's tired."

(Divine, isn't he? This is what I call really *warm*. How did we exist before the telly?)

"But you can't tell me—Don—so intimate and all—and you not a male nurse—an aspiring *painter*—you can't tell me Hurtle hasn't let fall a hint or two—while you were so nobly washing his feet—or given you a *peep*—come off it, mate—at the so-called 'GOD paintings'!"

All the sawn-out mouths of the masks within hearing distance were working flat out. The telly young man had it sewn up. (Going to give him an award.) So the lacquered mouths clacked, some of them salivating Moselle; one lady was using her lover's back as a ladder to climb to higher things.

"Don?"

"No."

"But you can't tell me they don't exist. When everybody knows they do."

"No."

"Well, in that case, we'll have to terminate our interesting relationship, and disappoint our viewers. Shan't we?"

"You can't talk about what's too big. The paintings are too big."

"Ah? What do you mean by 'too big'? What are their dimensions, Don?"

"Mr Kircaldy, you've got me wiped! My father's only a carpenter. I know. But I know there's a point you can't sort of talk beyond. You can only do. Or *be*, sort of. And that is what Mr Duffield. The painter. I can't talk. I can only. Why can't you let us all alone to *do*? Otherwise there'll be nothing—no thing—*done*. There'll only be people squatting in front of the box, hoping somebody they thought too big for them will turn out as little as themselves. Then they'll be happy. Watching him pull himself off at a camera."

What might have grown into a worse scandal than the possible existence of the "God paintings" was fortunately strangled at birth by the crowd which, normally, would have nursed it. Their instinct for something really of this minute began to prick those who specialized in the ephemeral, with the result that the whole of the amorphous monster was moved to suspect, murmur, groan, shuffle, and finally shove. The lady who was climbing her lover brought her ladder crashing to the floor.

"The Prime Minister."

"Is he here? I read he was in Pakistan."

"Somebody will speak. Got to thank the painter for conning us a good seventy years."

"But the Prime Minister—I saw Sam a moment ago. Talking to Gil Honeysett."

"Oh, beaut! Don't you adore Sam? He's one of the few men who can make a paunch look chic."

"Never get another vote from me. Not since he smirched our image overseas."

"I'm not interested in images. Men aren't images. I'd adore to sleep with Sammy-lamb. He looks so utterly tenderized."

"Thanks to his missus. She mightn't let him out, though."

"Where are we going?"

"The main court. Looks like it, anyway. That's where we're being swept. That's where all the gear was."

"Should have got there early—got us a good pozzy. Never be in the picture now."

"Nobody else ever is. The Brundritts must tip the cameras."

As the monstrous black sea receded, boiling, sucked through archways, frothing round columns and buttresses, along static cliffs, a few pools were left behind: to trickle, according to some law of water, in the same direction as the original flood.

Smiling her most transparent, her most watery smile, Mrs Volkov started to tiptoe on long feet; then, when it decently could, her shadowy form tripped ever so lightly towards the mass from which, unwisely, she had allowed herself to become detached. "Oh dear," her voice blew back in faint droplets, "I do hope—never meant—not that kind of person." She was last heard resigning herself to what she only perversely dreaded. "And Kathy said the Prime Minister did her a very great kindness."

As for the Cutbush couple, they burst out from the sense of duty which had been damming their true desires, and poured away as hard as they could pour, without looking back to explain their natural conduct; while Don Lethbridge followed swiftly, rearranging the clothes the telly had tried to strip from him. The sighs made by his Italianate shoes lingered across the emptied floors.

This left Rhoda. "Shall I come with you, Hurtle? Would it, I mean"—she had to cough it up—"help if I stood beside you?"

When it was he who must help Rhoda, if he couldn't immediately see how: certainly not let her stand beside him on the dais.

She must have realized very quickly how awful her proposition looked, for she allowed herself, that is to say, her brutally irregular lump of pumice, to be dragged in what seemed the unavoidable direction, almost colliding with Gil Honeysett as he rose dripping out of the black collective wave.

"Hi, fella—Hurtle! Where 'uv yer bin? We're waiting for yer. Or all but. Are yer ready?"

"Yes, Gil. But my bladder isn't."

"Oh Christ!" Gil Honeysett's schedule made no allowances for an old man's waterworks. "I suppose you'll have to do it. Won't you? Give you five minutes at most. After that, there'll be hell to pay with the ABC."

All along that side of the deserted gallery the pictures had revived: the Duffields. There was scarcely time to glance at them: never look enough at your own paintings.

Though whipped along by Honeysett's warning, he might have paused to indulge, if the perspective of archways and parquet hadn't been flooded with a vision: of a figure, small certainly, but in its formal, golden grace instinctually true to archetype. He was walking giddily, as he hadn't for years, but without illusions or expectations; his great joy was in recognizing his psychopomp, so very opportunely descended with "love and thoughts" to give him courage. As they advanced towards each other, her golden, boy's figure melted into all the tones of rose. She bowed her head, as though to hide the face which might give her away too soon. So they hurried, she coolly, he feverishly: not that he would have dreamed of touching this embodiment of a spirit. He would speak to her, in few, though significant words: let her know he had received and understood the messages.

So he called out: "Have you come to show me the way?" In other circumstances he might have embarrassed himself: too loud, too brazen; it was all the fault of the Trustees' inferior wine.

Instead, he had embarrassed the psychopomp. "The way? To where?" A voice unexpectedly tuneless, cracked, panicky.

"Why," he shouted louder, laughing, "to the Infernal River!" as his psychopomp became an anonymous wrinkled soubrette hurrying in her pink from the LADIES.

"Sorry," he mumbled, "the loo is what I'm looking for."

And she scurried faster: to catch the Prime Minister's speech, and the famous painter's reply.

Of course he knew too well the gloomy latrine where he had often taken refuge from personages and situations; but now, as though his hermetic guide, his Kathy Mystagogue, had sent her proxy to liberate him, he turned in the opposite direction.

The entrance hall was deserted, except by the postcards, and a couple of well-lit attendants scoffing a plateful of sandwiches. He went out. The unlikely building was groaning with the legend it couldn't contain. The audience had begun to applaud the delay, then to thump and stamp; or were they trying to force the creative spirit into its coffin? Jumping on the lid for luck before nailing it down, so that nothing of what was inside would escape them—ever.

He went down the steps, one side of him dragging the other half behind. His body was exhausted, but his mind darted prickling around him as he staggered laboriously over the grass, and stood pissing, propped against the fortified trunk of a Moreton Bay fig. It was a lovely relief. The evening might have remained one of predominantly watery impressions: of water shifting over knives; if he hadn't eased his head back, and at once the stars began to ricochet off the branches in a galaxy of resumed activity.

So he shambled on, over the fallen fruit. He succeeded in hailing a taxi somewhere near the Cathedral, and was whirled home, into that silence where he had spent half a lifetime begetting, and giving birth.

10

They were sitting at breakfast in the asbestos compartment which served as kitchen, the usual hugger-mugger of unwashed crockery and battered aluminium waiting at the sink. It was agreeable to prolong breakfast; though neither of them had ever admitted to enjoying its luxury, unless through irritation: which is another luxury. He particularly mistrusted indulgence in the wetter emotions from having to protect the gift still burning inside him. But at breakfast, while their habits were of the slackly instinctive, not yet of the obsessive kind, he did feel drawn to his sister Rhoda. He was not certain how she felt about it; but her more relaxed behaviour suggested she was in agreement with the essentials of their relationship, if not its details. Rhoda was at her most relaxed, her most catlike, surrounded by her complacent cats, as she read the morning papers, particularly the advertisements, and deaths.

It was like that the morning after the opening of Duffield's Retrospective. He was wearing the nondescript dressing-gown which had outlasted the years, and would jolly well have to see him out in spite of its patina of food spots and paint smears, and general scumble of forgotten origins. It was so comfortable, and would have been a comfort, if you could afford to let yourself be seduced by comfort.

Rhoda, on the other hand, must have thrown away the old dark gown he remembered. Recently she had come out in a net-and-lace garment, which only Mrs Volkov could have created, in dusty pink. Probably it was its off-colour which made Rhoda's gown look old from the beginning; but she was an old woman, after all, and in the pink confection the impression she gave was unfortunate: she reminded him of stale Turkish delight rolled in grey icing sugar.

(What on earth had possessed her to doll herself up like this? Or was it Maman, reaching out from those last rooms in Battersea?)

The morning after the opening Rhoda sat reading the news. The deeper she got into the sheets the worse she always messed them up; and that morning she must have ordered all the papers: to read deliberately under his nose what they were saying about him.

Rhoda's ankle clicked: still pretty neat; the veins, swollen in what passed for calves, hadn't affected the ankle. "It seems to have been a success," she revealed.

"That is what they *say*. It isn't necessarily what they *mean*."

"Oh, I shan't pretend it was an *unqualified* success."

"Not if I know the *Telegraph*."

Her ankle went click click as she shucked the newspapers. "The Prime Minister appears to have made an extremely witty speech."

"Didn't you hear it, then, last night when you were there?"

"No. They were very kind. Mr Honeysett found me and took me up on the dais. I sat in a leather chair. While the speech was made. But I didn't hear it. Everybody looked interested to see the painter's sister. We were photographed for television. They wanted me to speak. But I couldn't. Not even when they asked me questions. Because I wasn't sure what you would have wanted me to answer, Hurtle."

"Poor Rhoda, you must have suffered."

"No. I've learned not to suffer."

She had got herself into training, no doubt, dragging that converted go-cart round the neighbourhood. Though health and age had forced her to give away the go-cart, the habit of endurance had stuck.

"I understand the film will be shown tonight. Bernice Cutbush has invited me to go and view it on their set." Rhoda couldn't resist picking up scraps of the vernacular. "You, too, if you feel like it."

"No, thank you! Watch a funeral without a corpse?"

Rhoda laughed and said: "Don't tell me you're becoming cynical," trailing a sheet of the *Herald* through the bacon fat in front of her. "In any case, I stood in for the corpse."

He got up and began the climb to his room. He could have wept for Rhoda, whom he heard putting down the paper by what sounded like handfuls of galvanized iron. Through the hall, even on the stairs, there was a smell of what she referred to as "cat pooh"; whereas what he wanted to convey was already rising above the animal—and human—bowel stenches: not that he hadn't often been inspired by a successful stool, in surroundings of weatherboard and whitewash, under the *Bignonia venusta.*

He went upstairs. Where Rhoda's martyrdom had been the dais, stared at by human eyes and the camera, his was the block, made for his secret purpose and to his own specifications by Ron Cuppaidge the art student.

Now that he was so far improved in health he could dispense with the attendant Archangel's help in mounting the block, but needed, and probably would always need, someone to prime, and manoeuvre into place, the enormous blank boards.

Himself a blank at times, the live hand clamped by his knees, he would sit teetering on the edge of the bed, dreading the desert he had to cross. Experience never lessened the prospect of tortures, the possibility of failures, even death if the spirit refused to accompany him. Just as you can twist the tail of human love once too often, perhaps the creative spirit couldn't be flogged into climbing that additional inch. In which case: O God, have mercy on us. (He would look round, afraid somebody might be tapping his thoughts.)

On the morning after the big shivoo at the State Gallery, he, not Duffield the painter, was stranded in such a condition: his throat had never felt so parched; all the tributaries of his body had dried up; films were forming over his eyes; his mind, worse than passive, pricked in every direction like a pack of unthreaded needles scattering amongst the barren forms of furniture.

Downstairs, Rhoda had begun to bash away at the accumulated pans. How enviable are those to whom it is given to express themselves by scouring a saucepan: their art so contained, finite, yet lustrous. He would even have envied Rhoda the disgusting little cart she used to drag round the streets, with its gobbets of purple flesh and amorphous offal from restaurant bins. This morning he would almost have exchanged the dead weight, the gross deformity of his non-art, for Rhoda's hump.

Once he got as far as the landing and called out, though diffidently: "Rhoda? Can I be of any help with all that stuff you've got piled up?" Then a little louder: "Rhoda?"

But she didn't hear; and at once he was glad: not that it relieved his emptiness to know he could keep his shame a secret.

As he continued shuffling, sitting, getting up to look inside drawers, rummaging through junk, turning over derelict drawings, almost everyone was enviable: free to read newspapers, open letters, answer doorbells, waste their lives yarning on the telephone—happy human beings who hadn't preserved themselves for a final statement of faith they probably wouldn't be capable of making. Most of them would die in bed, not in desert places.

Rhoda, with her nose for failings, had smelled a rat some way back. "If you no longer read the papers, you'll cut yourself off from life."

"I have more important things to think about."

"Well—in some ways—I expect it does no harm not to realize what a bonanza you're missing out on."

They were able to join in laughing at that one.

When Rhoda said: "And this big dishful of letters—aren't you ever going to open them?"

"No. Who would be writing to us? Nobody we want to hear from. And rates and income tax—we can recognize those easily enough."

"Yes, but there might be just that letter—that moment more delicious than any you've experienced yet—from somebody more *fatale*—more rejuvenating."

She wasn't going to tempt him. He swept up the lot and carried them out to the incinerator.

No. Not the lot. There was one: an air letter from the United States.

But it was a time-waster, from a woman asking him to discuss his paintings in connection with an essay she was writing for an intellectual magazine. At the end there was a touch which appealed to him: "P.S. After reading this over I feel I should add: I'm not half as dry as I sound."

Rhoda asked at a later date: "That American letter, Hurtle—was it from Kathy?"

"Kathy and I don't need to write each other letters."

"Oh, but they're nice! She writes such charming, affectionate letters to her mother."

"This was a letter from some American bluestocking."

Rhoda asked in her driest voice: "Did you—in your broad-minded days—ever try on a bluestocking?" Immediately she burst into shrieks for her own wit, and he went out so as not to listen to them.

Was he as ludicrous as her outbreak of forced vulgarity seemed to imply? Achievement didn't help reduce absurdity. Perhaps Rhoda was the only one who recognized this, and now, at the end, he recognized himself in the glass she was holding up to him; to the others, he remained reason for admiration, for hate, for shy worship, or plain honest indifference.

If he could have chosen, if, rather, he had developed the habit of prayer, he would have prayed to shed his needled flesh, and for his psychopomp to guide him, across the river, into an endlessness of pure being from which memory couldn't look back.

But how bloody dishonest! As if he could ever wish to renounce his memories of the flesh even when renounced by its pleasures: the human body, unbroken by its own will, leaping and bucking to unseat, but rapturously, the longed-for, the chosen, though finally abstract rider; yellow light licking as voluptuously as tongues; green shade dribbled like saliva on nakedness; all the stickinesses: honey, sap, semen, sweat melting into sweat; the velvets of roseflesh threatened by teeth; exhausted, ugly, human furniture, bulging with an accumulation of experience acquired in years or by a stroke of lightning.

The morning after the Grand Inquisition into the nature of his heresies, it was the furniture by which he began to rehabilitate himself. In and out of the upper rooms. Groping the no longer barren forms. Clutching when he misjudged his step. Smooth mahogany rocks, split open in places by time, in others by human vagary, disgust, or desperation. Arabesques of cobweb, mildew bloom coming to organic life: lichens in their own right. Dust offering paths only taken before by fly or spider; over one unbroken expanse a rat must have dragged its tail.

Of all geographic features, the great crater of a bath was by far the most tactile: higher up, the extinct geyser, with its spattering of verdigris and scattering of dead matches. The same bath, brown-stained, the bottom scarred where the enamel had worn off: they had intended to replace it and do the bathroom up; but he didn't use it all that much, and Rhoda, unwilling to risk the stairs, owned a child's hip-bath shoved out of sight in the conservatory.

On this significant morning it was not the bathroom which moved him so much as a feeling of floating back through a blur of sensory experience: of warm water bubbling into tender crevices; of rough towels; of the first, shamefully realized, deliriously seeping orgasm.

Returning to the front room, making his way from object to object, still opening and closing drawers, he was trying to relate what he saw to what he knew. The desert was beginning to flower: not that he had any illusions about its flowering. The sensory gardens of the past were no substitute for what he had to do in the present. He would not be allowed to find permanent rest on a bed of shivery-grass, only enjoy it a moment or two, as lyrical sensation and silvery image, before the wrestling match.

As he climbed up once more onto the scaffold, arranging on the little adjustable table the Archangel had made according to instructions, the tortured tubes, the prepared brushes, the peanut-butter glasses filled with clear, shuddering water (never cared for peanut butter except for the uses to which you can put the glasses), he renounced the temporary delights—or those which couldn't be squeezed out in proliferating colour, and compressed into a vision which, by its compression, would convey the whole.

So he was beginning again. In his altered technique. With what Rhoda and he referred to as his "good" hand, but which perhaps only he knew was about as crook as you could come by: if the violence of blood throbbing and prickling in his still functional veins hadn't seemed to add a vibrancy to what he needed to convey. As he niggled and stickled with brush after brush, none of which was the right one. While all the whirligigs of memory, aureoles and chandeliers, dandelions and tadpoles, pulsed and revolved. He almost lost his balance once, trying to coerce the crimson arteries, or life-bearing rivers, across the vast steppes of his still only partly cultivated hardboard. He would build at one point a city fortified against assault by art lovers, music critics, besotted grocers, psychic seamstresses, vivisectors, and any others possessed by doubtful intentions: a citadel to protect those whose love was of such an identical nature it became interchangeable. (Send a p. c. with details of hermaphroditic pudenda so that his psychopomp could precede him through whatever Hades of Tchaikovsky or Rachmaninov holding it in her hand as a passport to truth and Mozart.)

When Don Lethbridge came (why? had Rhoda sent for him?) the light was long past its best.

"Going for the colour again, aren't you?"

This was not criticism, nor—more odious—encouragement. Each realized it was communication pure and simple, which required no answer. And after Don had helped him down from the block, words might have stumbled. Important to conserve strength: it was going to be a long trudge to the Elysian Fields.

In spite of the continued whispering overheard through walls and from distances, he worked for weeks on this same painting. It wasn't by any means his last testament, but might grow eventually into what he saw as his compendium of life. Sometimes memory fed him; more often, intuition: insights of such intensity he felt he should have been able to relate them to actual experience; but in this he failed mostly. For instance: the blood horses wallowing in sea shallows at dawn, milky water filling the satin troughs between belly and thighs as they shimmy on their lovely backs, before lunging to their feet, to shake their barrels, all feathered with light and motion, flinging into the used sea the beads of water from their stringy manes. Where had he seen these bathers? He must convey something of the horses, not themselves, their spirit. In the same way the girl in the crushed pink hat and cotton frock strumming out of an old banjo all the remembered songs: fingers, nails blunted by the strumming, sanded texture of the arms, tremors of the breasts inside the gritty dress. As the girl entered the trees, her skin brindled by light and shade, the old banjo made a papery thump thump trailing behind her through the tussocks. Because, of course, this was a self-indulgent work, not what he intended or what he was intended to paint once he had mastered himself, he was also this girl with whom he might or might not have slept. Lying under the paperbarks, he identified the shammy-leather skin, the goose-pimples growing in it, the sand tasted on interchangeable mouths. Now it was himself alone watching the great pantechnicon driving for what reason through the shallows. And the essence of smoky cat slipping through long grass at dusk looking for a kill, at the same time to curl her tail around some something in the name of love. Everything private perfect reduced to a kill if not by time the super-cat by the khaki klan of killers. Tear off a hand or leg it doesn't belong to you anyway forever and blood is made to bleed. Like letters. *My dear Cat.* He composed letters just as he painted pictures in his mind, and lost them before he could get them down. Everything comes back, though, like the homing pigeons pensioned men keep in their yards. Stalagmites of white droppings, lacy scribbles in pigeon shit, a coral scratching over worm-eaten boards. *My husband my God took me by the windpipe and shook it to buggery after the spaghetti on toast.* From where did he know the horses, the shammy-skinned singer, the pigeon-loft held together by the rusty ends of kero tins? He didn't know. But he knew. Where and when doesn't in the end matter.

Though some of it was actually near actual. Himself the near stroked one encapsulated in a spatial bus with Mrs Volkov the stroked and stroking pseudomother because of course Kathy hadn't been born she had sprung like himself. Even so Mrs Volkov and Himself co-creators were blowing bubbles at each other which didn't contain the words. Whoever pricked the empty bubbles first, it was Mrs Volkov who got down at Foy's, her grey worsted and long groping shoes.

Often the martyred tubes of paint would retaliate by toppling off the adjustable table; once a peanut-butter glass fell, splintering splashing its content of muddy water.

The Archangel appeared before he had been summoned; or perhaps Rhoda had sent for him according to some conspiracy.

Best ignore.

Don ignored: always the soul of stillness.

So it was you who had to ask when the silence could no longer be left to ping: "D'you make anything of it?"

Almost at once Don replied: "Sure."

Oh God, nothing easy is ever anything but crap. If crap is easy. Not always, nowadays.

But try him out. "What, then, Don?"

"Well, just about everything—hasn't it?"

"What d'you mean by everything?"

"Well—the whole of life."

Good Christ, better give up! "What do you know about life?"

"I dunno. You just *know*."

How jealous can you become of the truth when unborn children know? Only the permutations are fresh—or so you like to kid yourself.

"Is it finished, Mr Duffield?"

"Yes, it's finished. You who know so much ought to know that. It's finished. Help me down, Don. Normally I don't need." YOU never needed: your body did when the flow was interrupted. "I'll want you to stand the board over there. So I can look at it. It's not what I set out to paint. I didn't get there—I can see that already. But I'll want to look—on and off—see how I might've done better. I can't stay painting the same painting forever, can I?"

Pity Don had seen. Pity you hadn't a big enough blanket to cover up the whole mess. Or uncover at night. It was good: "The Whole of Life." That is, it wasn't too bad. (Nobody need know how rich you are till you're dead. If they did they might whack into you and love you, which could be more disastrous, creatively, than their hate.)

Sign it tomorrow. Or leave them guessing.

"Thank you, Don. I'm grateful. I'd also like to mention I'm remembering you in my will."

Poor Don, blushing amongst the down and pimples, the remark was in such bad taste: his father a carpenter, his mother a waitress at The Slap Up, himself dedicated to art and Duffield.

"I'll come, Mr Duffield, any time Miss Courtney sends for me."

"Why Miss Courtney? Who's my master I'd like to know? My sister's no connection."

Don Lethbridge smiled back, perhaps even murmured something, and went away.

When she sent for them to come and stuff him in his coffin, that was where Rhoda would take over: wind up the Punch-and-Judy show with her own little song-and-dance act.

That winter, as they sat in the grey asbestos kitchen, amongst the broken eggshells she hadn't yet gathered up, the picked-at bacon rinds, the pots of Gentlemen's Relish and Cooper's Oxford Marmalade—no substitutes, Harry Courtney always insisted—he had never felt closer to Rhoda. At breakfast at least, half the rules mightn't have been written.

He was at peace, almost.

He might ask: "Did you forget to turn the gas off, Rhoda?" and she would answer, fairly gentle: "No. I'm pretty sure I turned it off. Well, perhaps there's a trickle—only a slight one."

"That's the way people get gassed."

"I don't think so, Hurtle. Not if they've developed the fresh-air habit and left the window open."

Here Rhoda made a show of inhaling the mixture of gas and chilly air; the window was certainly open, on a pale, moted sunlight and the smell of what passed for earth between Flint Street and Chubb's Lane: a compost of rubble, flower-pot shards, rusty tins, tamped tightly together, and dew-cold.

Rhoda's theory finally made her cough. "As a matter of fact," she said when she had recovered, "a gas man once told me: when they're called to investigate a case of gassing, more often than not it's been deliberate."

"Yes, but there are also the old people we read about."

"Oh, of course there are the *old* people. That's different. But we aren't as old as *all that.* And still have our minds with us."

Rhoda was wrong more often than not, but here he was inclined to agree with her. "No. We're not quite senile."

They both laughed.

Although he no longer bothered with the papers, Rhoda made a point of reading bits aloud: murders, rapes, adulteries; each of them, he suspected, rather enjoyed the experience.

She developed also the less agreeable habit of reading aloud from the Deaths column.

"Hold hard!" he protested at last. "Who wants to read about death?"

"It's real, isn't it? It concerns us, doesn't it? And what about the murders? You like listening to the murders, Hurtle. They stimulate you."

"Murders don't concern us personally."

Nance? But Rhoda his sister, drifting round London in her *broderie anglaise,* with Maman and that "stepfather," wouldn't have heard about it.

"Take the names of the dead"—Rhoda couldn't tear herself away from the last page—"haven't they a kind of poetry? Even the most grotesque are an attempt at it. And on the practical level, you might come across someone you have to do something about—send a wreath—or write to the family."

He admired her for her knowledge of procedure, which men didn't have to worry about: they left it to wives who had learned it from mothers.

He hadn't had a wife who knew, only mistresses troubled by the state of their souls; till here was Rhoda.

Rhoda said, on a morning of cold floating greenish blurs of light and vines, of birds' wings opening and closing in frail but convinced sounds of ascent: "Do you remember Mary Challands?"

"No." He was more interested in the parallels between light and sound. "Who is Mary Challands?"

"She was one of the girls who used to come to Sunningdale. I shared her governess later on, after the Hollingrakes gave up theirs, after Boo went to Tasmania to recover from Andrew Thingummy's death."

"No. Apart from Boo, they were just a mob of girls. I can't sort out one from the other."

"Mary was pale and thin. Compared with most of us, distinguished-looking. She was said to be anaemic. They expected her to die young. She was forced to do—oh, the most *disgusting* things! She had to drink blood!"

"What made you think of her now?"

"I've just read she's died."

How Rhoda persisted: as if she were trying to test him; when there was this morning of increasing light, full of the frilly sounds of birds; when there was this painting upstairs which the Archangel had named "The Whole of Life"; when she had seen entire walls at the Retrospective covered with affirmations. But Rhoda had no eyes for paintings. If he had fathered a child, if somebody had offered him a godson, if he had adopted—say, Don Cuppaidge—he might have evoked life for Rhoda and diminished Mary Challands' triumph.

All the while Rhoda was carrying on: "Jolly lucky I remembered her married name. Otherwise they'd wonder why I hadn't sent a wreath."

"Would they—whoever they are?"

"Oh yes. I don't doubt she would have mentioned me in conversation with her husband. Here he is in the Column: 'beloved wife of Leicester Mildmay.' I'm sure Mary would have referred to someone as—as different as I. And when you're living with a person everything comes out in time because you've got to find something to say."

"Hmmm."

"Mary became a Roman Catholic—surely you remember that? Converted while still a young girl."

"It seems to have done her good. Or else it was all that blood she drank. To be dying only now."

Years earlier, he might have painted Mary Challands Mildmay. He could see her corpse so clearly: the bones of her transparent feet, the skin of a pale fish-saint—possibly skate.

"Oh yes, you can laugh, Hurtle—you, a sceptic!"

"But I thought you were the sceptic?"

"Oh yes—I am and I'm not. Fancy—poor Mary Challands!" Rhoda kept her nose on the Deaths, practically guzzling the page in her desire to do what she had been taught: the Right Thing.

He would have liked to comfort his sister with some kind of faith, but had never gone over to one. He sat staring at his paint-stained hands.

Rhoda was determined to carry on: "He was in insurance, I believe—a bachelor with a fine collection of old silver. They married later in life. Mary told me, while we were still in correspondence, he 'left her alone,' and they were very happy together."

"Oh God, Rhoda, then it *was* the blood and the Roman Catholicism which sustained her! It wasn't life!"

"I don't know."

Some of the empty eggshells had bounced off like ping-pong balls. Rhoda bent to scoop them up. She bumped her nose on the edge of the kitchen table.

Because he felt to blame, he began protesting: "I don't want to criticize the dead."

"Nobody's criticizing anybody. Everybody's free to hold their own opinions." The bump had made her eyes water.

He went out after that: to loose the warm stool he had been nursing inside him as a comfort, to let it uncoil into the Pit, under the *Bignonia venusta*.

Who was winning? He still hadn't finished the inscription on the dunny wall. Most likely it would finish him.

When he had girded himself again, he decided to go very quickly upstairs to have no more truck with Rhoda, but she waylaid him in the hall.

"Last night I had to go out in connection with finding a home for a cat. On the way back I looked in at Mrs Volkov's, and as I was leaving she gave me this letter for you."

"Why on earth should Mrs Volkov write me a letter. What's it about?"

"She didn't offer to tell, and I was too discreet to ask." Rhoda gathered her gown around her and retired into the asbestos kitchen.

He was tempted to leave the letter lying on the bracket of the bamboo hatstand where she had let it fall. Most letters are suspect because they make demands: most suspect a letter from Mrs Volkov, whom he had never considered as a writer of letters. It could only be a huge demand, though nothing material, he imagined: which made it more disturbing.

He took the letter, however, and went upstairs. The faint hope that a person like Mrs Volkov, with her reputation for peculiar powers, might reveal something of the substance of her letter

through the envelope, made him fumble at it through his pins and
needles, unusually painful that morning. On the half-landing he
tripped with his "dead" foot over the hem of his gown. He heard
the tear only distantly.

On reaching the top-front he was conscious of a stream of ice-
green light pouring through the araucaria, with the waters of the
bay in the distance a glistening pale sunlit white.

He opened the letter. Mrs Volkov had written in a laboured—
more, in an anguished hand:

> Dear Mr Hurtle Duffield,
>
> I will tell you at the start that I am *making no demands of you*
> in this letter I was driven to write. I do not expect you to more
> than glance through it if you have not already thrown it away. If
> you have it will not inconvenience you.
>
> I must apologize for that we was only poor folk from Dundee,
> my Father died at sea with the trawlers, Mother dead before
> that. As a child I went to Carnoustie to my Auntie, to help with
> the guests. It was a poor town by other standards, but there were
> the summer visitors who came to the Links. When I was not at
> the dishes or otherwise cleaning or mending I would go down and
> paint the used golf balls. Uncle was a hard man. He was caddy
> master. He was an elder of the Kirk though I do not think a Be-
> liever, with him it was a Duty. Because I could not discover my
> right Duty I was mostly at odds with Uncle. I dreamed of God's
> Love and an understanding of His Purposes. I did once for a
> moment understand if I cannot properly explain. There was some
> pine trees awful lean it was the sandy soil above the sea I had
> gone for a walk along the Links because something or everything
> had forced me out. There was a wasp nest hanging from a bough.
> I got stung not by putting up my hand my hand was put. I was
> shocked white, it felt. Although dizzy I should say I remained
> standing on my feet. It was like red hot needles entering at first
> very painful then I did not notice any more, only sea and sky as
> one, and me like a rinsed plate. I have often remember this, and
> was never struck to the ground, not in the cruellest moments.
> I cannot tell you more, but you are an artist Mr Duffield and will
> guess.
>
> So I came to Sydney to the other Uncle who shortly passed on.
> I was not afraid Mr Duffield. This is where I had been directed,
> and to have my little girl in sinful joy with a stranger who gave
> me no love or affection only this wonderful human child. I make

no excuses for Kathy who does not need them. She is as you will appreciate a work of art. I do not "understand" music, I do not "understand" painting, except through what has happened in my life.

I have discussed this with our common friend Mr Cecil Cutbush who agrees he has understood the same through what he calls his "Infirmity" (which I am told is also known as the "Third Sex"). Some years past I suffered a mild stroke, and you recently a worse. As Mr Cutbush remarked who has more Education, we was all perhaps *stroked by God*. This is what I sensed in the bus, of the two of us at least. And Mr Cutbush has his own ways. Poor Mrs C. it is her lot to bear her unlikely marriage. Then there is Miss Courtney I would never mention any of this matter to her, she is a lady, and me a "Sewing Woman" the mother of Katherine Volkov.

I have ventured to run on Mr Duffield because I believe the afflicted to be united in the same purpose, and you of course as an artist and the worst afflicted through your art can see farther than us who are mere human diseased.

Yours in respectful apology
Christiana McBeath

My dear friend Miss Courtney I do not love less for not including among us, and who must have suffered most inhumanly, but Miss Courtney is of the earth she is *strong* and would carry us all on her back—or so I would say—to the end.

He put Mrs Volkov's letter as far away from him as he could, not because it was muddled, illiterate, gratuitous, distasteful, but because it was too pertinent: he understood not only with his mind, but through his fingers, both the live and the bunch of dead twigs, Christiana McBeath's horribly illuminating argument.

To fortify himself against the truth he hunched his shoulders, but not high enough: he was protruding. And still had to face the board his server had stood ready for him.

As he approached, loitering, this fresh emptiness promised to be the vastest desert he had ever set out to cross: not the faintest mirage to offer illusory solace; and to share the inevitable agonies, the limping army into which Christiana McBeath had conscripted him.

So he began soberly enough, in sombre colours. For these later paintings, themselves an exploration, he made no exploratory drawings—there was no longer time, nor had he the hand for drawings—and here, at least, the direction in which he had to go was already pricked out in him.

Somewhere in the lowest depths of mind or board, he had a sudden irrelevant, half-formed vision of a tucked-up mongrel dog, beggarly tail scraping the ground between its legs. Blot it out. Never felt the least bit doggy, except when clamped to the operating table. Never asked for charity, even at his lowest: though you can't avoid accepting it at times. Why should he beg now? Not when about to enter a hinterland of infinite prospects. He only dreaded the prolonged physical exertion. There was also the nightmare he hadn't dreamed, but might have: his fall, backwards, through the railing, off the block.

Even that at last was made impossible on this morning of clearest light and indelible sensations. An immensity of space had given him his visual freedom, or more: he was being painted with, and through, and on. While conscious of his articulated crab's claw going through its usual jerky motions, the strokes themselves on the primed surface often surprised by being unlike what he would have expected, or intended, certainly never during the blaze of his controlled technique, not even since physical limitations had reduced him to niggling round the edges of totality. Watching these daringly loose strokes of paint, which might have looked haphazard if they hadn't been compelled, he experienced a curious sense of grace.

It was midday and Rhoda had called from below she had something ready for lunch.

He recognized a twinge of guilty satisfaction to think that Mrs Volkov hadn't admitted Rhoda to their company; though if she were the woman's "dear friend" how could she have failed to reveal herself to Rhoda in her other role of Christiana McBeath? Unless Rhoda hadn't wished it, as the letter might have been implying in the end. You reveal yourself to strangers: himself to that printer on the ferry, and to an unknown grocer met by moonlight. To which strangers had Rhoda revealed her love, and for whom? To be honest: he had failed to love Rhoda. Pity is another matter: his "Pythoness at Tripod" had expressed a brilliant, objective pity for an injured, cryptic soul and a body only malice could have created. But pity is half-hearted love.

Rhoda was still calling. "Hurtle, are you not coming? . . . It's something hot, and *always* as if to spite me whenever it's a hot lunch you go out of your way not to come. It's a soufflé if you'd like to know."

He didn't believe Rhoda could have thought of a soufflé, let alone made one.

Then he realized he hadn't answered, so he went out on the landing and shouted: "I'm not coming." He only breathed: "I don't dare leave off."

Rhoda didn't slam the kitchen door.

He worked all that afternoon except when exhaustion drove him to a brief spell on the rucked-up bed; otherwise he might have toppled off the block. He lay, but was unable to close his eyes: the lids could have been propped open with pointed toothpicks, and the grit under them was terrible.

He worked till the light began to waver.

When Rhoda called again: "Hurtle, our dinner is waiting." The way she stressed it she seemed to attach particular importance to their eating it together.

It was a most unorthodox hour: she should have been chopping up the horse for her surviving cats.

"I can't come. Not tonight."

Rhoda was perfectly silent, which emphasized the mewing of a kitchenful of cats.

Then she began to shout and curse as best she could. "I'm not interested *personally*. The bally food can waste itself. Not that it will. Nothing's wasted. The worms will eat it, if no one else."

During how many days, not continuously, but a week probably, he had been working on what he no longer considered a painting. Occasionally he went downstairs, and they sat in silence over food, of what nauseating kind he couldn't remember afterwards: he was indifferent to it; except on one occasion, when he had found behind the mountain of unwashed pots the ruin of a castle, or a collapsed bathing cap, or—Rhoda's soufflé. He quickly drowned his anguish and the thing itself in a torrent of aluminium.

He would hear sounds outside his door: he realized it was Rhoda listening for whether he had died; when the scratching and snuffling stopped, she must have decided he was not yet ripe for the Deaths column. (How would she record their relationship? *Adored brother? Beloved foster—? Son of Jim of Alfreda of Harry of Bessie?* It was too involved to think about.)

He shouldn't in any case think along such frivolous lines. He was working. His flighty mind must concentrate. Yet that, too, was beside the point since he was being worked on. Cunningly, they were piling it up, detaching the difficulties one after another. (Spillikins again, he was ominously reminded.) They were all at work strewing and construing. Cec Cutbush was giggling audibly as they struggled towards the summit. Wherever their common sweat fell, the desert didn't flower, but thorns sprang up in celebration of their victory. If flowering occurred, it was in the gelatinous light throughout the upper realm of—how would the Archangel name this one when he appeared for its summation?

Tired, though.

If the hand could reach the last inch; but you would never convey in paint: in words perhaps, or phrased in music—modelled in clay—dough—in any other medium. (Your own sheer drudgery is always utter shit.)

But there were the occasions when, confronted with the board, his vision would leap out at him and he was liberated afresh.

There was this day he sensed his psychopomp standing beside him. At once he began scrabbling according to direction on his rickety palette-table. He was mixing the never-yet-attainable blue.

He pursed his lips to repeat the syllables which were being dictated: N–D–G–O. A thrumming of this stiff tongue. The gaps—nobody recognize. She insisted they would, apparently unaware of the precarious state of his faith.

Whether it was she or he who knew better, he took his broadest, though frankly feeble brush and patted the blue on: brush was leaving its hairs behind, he noticed. All his life he had been reaching towards this vertiginous blue without truly visualizing, till lying on the pavement he was dazzled not so much by a colour as a long-standing secret relationship.

Now he was again acknowledging with all the strength of his live hand the otherwise unnameable I–N–D–I–G–O.

Only reach higher. Could. And will.

Then lifting by the hairs of his scalp to brush the brush-hairs bludge on the blessed blue.

Before the tobbling scrawl deadwood splitting splintering the prickled stars plunge a presumptuous body crashing. Dumped.

Light follows dark not usually bound by the iron feather which stroked.

566